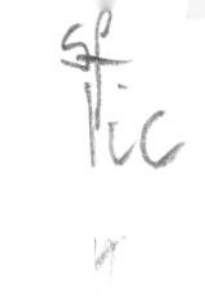

In Her Name: Redemption

Empire, Confederation, and Final Battle

By
Michael R. Hicks

This is a work of fiction. All of the characters and events portrayed in this novel are products of the author's imagination or are used fictitiously.

ISBN: 9780615208534
IN HER NAME: REDEMPTION

For Jan.
Your love saved me.

What Readers Are Saying

Drawn straight from some of the reader reviews of *In Her Name: Redemption (formerly known as In Her Name Omnibus Edition)*:

"Just finished this omnibus and had a great time. This book was well written with engaging characters, well paced story line and a plot that held my interest. I don't usually review the books I read, but I'm making an exception for this one. I highly recommend In Her Name and I've come back looking for other books by this same author."

"I'm going to keep this short and to the point. This is one of the best classic sci-fi books I have ever read, and you could feel the bond between the characters. It was an amazing series that I would recommend to any sci-fi nerd that hasn't read it yet."

"I bought this for my husband's kindle and didn't see him for several days. He couldn't put it down."

"The writing and story is great and even if you don't really like the genre, you should still try it out, this series is written so well that at times when things happened in the book to the main character or his friends, that I felt the emotions that go with it, fear, sadness or joy."

"I was hooked from the start of the first book. The character development and plot line was well done. I could not but it down! I am now on to the prequels and expect to be entranced some more. Thanks, Michael Hicks!!"

"I just simply could not stop reading. I fully intend to read it again, after I read the prequels."

"This author has risen to the top of my list and I look forward to reading the prequel to this series as well as anything else written by this author."

"These are honestly the best new Sci-Fi books I have found in the last 2 years and Michael Hicks has found his niche as a great writer. Buy the entire series, you will enjoy them all."

"I got sucked into Michael Hicks' world with Season of the Harvest. It was so compelling that I looked up the rest of his books and saw In Her Name. Hmmm, I thought. Could be OK. Could suck. Weird title. What I found blew me away."

"You hear the phrase 'un-put-downable' a lot, and I for one ofter wonder what exactly that means, well, I've found out now. Hicks writes beautifully, believably, and has created something really special here. Am very much looking forward to the next installment."

"In Her Name: Omnibus is THE best Science Fiction book I have read in a long time. Glad I got the Omnibus edition that contains the the whole story. Reminds me of Robert Heinlein, it's that good."

"Of the 183 books I purchased from Amazon last year this is one of one two books I have read twice."

"This was a terrific page turner and a nice departure from the typical SciFi/Fantasy plots."

"A wonderful universe is created by this author, one that is very complicated, but not confusing; vast but not rambling; magnificent but never overdone. It is an intelligent and thoroughly enjoyable read that intricately weaves sci-fi and sci-fantasy with great characters, mystery, adventure, romance and violence and is an anthropological journey of discovery into an alien race that takes you from hating their mindless killing to admiring their culture and their wanting them to win against all odds."

"I don't want to waste any of your time so I will get straight to the point. I loved this book. From the moment I began reading the first chapter I was hooked."

Discover Other Books By Michael R. Hicks

The *In Her Name* Series

First Contact
Legend Of The Sword
Dead Soul
Empire
Confederation
Final Battle
From Chaos Born

Trilogy Collections

In Her Name: Redemption
In Her Name: The Last War

Thrillers

Season Of The Harvest

Visit *AuthorMichaelHicks.com* for the latest updates!

EMPIRE

ONE

The blast caught Solon Gard, an exhausted captain of New Constantinople's beleaguered Territorial Army, completely by surprise. He had not known that the enemy had sited a heavy gun to the north of his decimated unit's last redoubt, a thick-walled house of a style made popular in recent years. Like most other houses in the planet's capitol city, this one was now little more than a gutted wreck.

But the Kreelan gun's introductory salvo was also its last: a human heavy weapons team destroyed it with a lucky shot before the Territorial Army soldiers were silenced by a barrage of inhumanly accurate plasma rifle fire.

The battle had become a vicious stalemate.

A woman's voice suddenly cut through the fog in Solon's head as he fought his way out from under the smoking rubble left by the cannon hit. He found himself looking up at the helmeted face of his wife, Camilla. Her eyes were hidden behind the mirrored faceplate of the battered combat helmet she wore.

"Solon, are you hurt?"

"No," he groaned, shaking his head, "I'm all right."

She helped him up, her petite form struggling with her husband's greater bulk: two armored mannequins embracing in an awkward dance.

Solon glanced around. "Where's Armand?"

"Dead," she said in a brittle voice. She wiped the dust from her husband's helmet, wishing she could touch his hair, his face, instead of the cold, scarred metal. She gestured to the pile of debris that Solon had been buried in. The wall had exploded inward a few feet from where he and Armand had been. The muddy light of day, flickering blood-red from the smoke that hung over the city, revealed an armored glove that jutted from under a plastisteel girder. Armand. He had been a friend of their family for many years and was the godfather of their only son. Now... now he was simply gone, like so many others.

Solon reached down and gently touched the armored hand of his best friend. "Silly fool," he whispered hoarsely. "You should have gone to the shelter with the others, like I told you. You could never fight, even when we were children." Armand had never had any military training, but after his wife and daughter were killed in the abattoir their city had become, he had come looking for Solon, to fight and die by his side. And so he had.

"It's only the two of us," Camilla told him wearily, "and Enrique and Snowden." Behind her was a pile of bodies in a dark corner, looking like a monstrous spider in the long shadows that flickered over them. The survivors had not had the time or strength to array them properly. Their goal had simply been to get them out of the way. Honor to the dead came a distant second to the desperation to stay among the living. "I think Jennings's squad across the street may be gone, too."

"Lord of All," Solon murmured, still trying to get his bearings and come to grips with the extent of their disaster. With only the four of them left, particularly if Jennings's squad had been wiped out, the Kreelans had but to breathe hard and the last human defensive line would be broken.

"It can always get worse," a different female voice told him drily.

Solon turned to see Snowden raise her hand unenthusiastically. Platinum hair was plastered to her skull in a greasy matte of sweat and blood, a legacy of the flying glass that had peeled away half her scalp during an earlier attack. She looked at him with eyes too exhausted for sleep, and did not make any move to get up from where she was sitting. Her left leg was broken above the knee, the protruding bone covered by a field dressing and hasty splint that Camilla had put together.

Enrique peered at them from the corner where he and Camilla had set up their only remaining heavy weapon, a pulse gun that took two to operate. Its snout poked through a convenient hole in the wall. From there, Enrique could see over most of their platoon's assigned sector of responsibility, or what was left of it. In the dreary orange light that made ghosts of the swirling smoke over the dying city, Enrique watched the dark figures of the enemy come closer, threading their way through the piles of shattered rubble that had once been New Constantinople's premier shopkeeper's district. He watched as their sandaled feet trod over the crumpled spires of the Izmir All-Faith Temple, the most beautiful building on the planet until a couple of weeks ago. Since the Kreelans arrived, nearly twenty million people and thirty Navy ships had died, and nothing made by human hands had gone untouched.

But beyond the searching muzzle of Enrique's gun, the advancing Kreelans passed many of their sisters who had died as the battle here had ebbed and flowed. Their burned and twisted bodies were stacked like cordwood at the approaches to the humans' crumbling defense perimeter, often enmeshed with the humans who had killed them. Enemies in life, they were bound together in death with bayonets and claws in passionate, if gruesome, embraces.

Still, they came. They always came.

Solon caught himself trying to rub his forehead through his battered helmet. *Lord, am I tired*, he thought. Their company was part of the battalion that had been among the last of the reserves to be activated for the city's final stand, and the Territorial Army commander had brought them into action three days before. Three days. It had been a lifetime.

"One-hundred and sixty-two people, dead," he whispered to himself, thinking of the soldiers he had lost in the last few days. But they had lasted longer than most. Nearly every company of the first defensive ring had been wiped out to the last man and woman in less than twenty-four hours. Solon and his company were part of the fourth and final ring around the last of the defense shelters in this sector of the city. If the Kreelans got through...

"Hey, boss," Enrique called quietly. "I hate to interrupt, but they're getting a bit close over here. You want me to light 'em up?"

"I'll do the honors," Camilla told Solon, patting him on the helmet. "You need to get yourself back together."

"No arguments here," he answered wearily, propping himself against the remains of the wall. "I'll keep on eye on this side."

Camilla quickly took her place next to the gunner. "I'm glad you didn't wait much longer to let us know we had company, Enrique," she chided after carefully peering out at the enemy. "They're so close I can see their fangs." She checked the charge on the pulse gun's power pack. A fresh one would last for about thirty seconds of continuous firing, an appetite that made having both a gunner and a loader to service the hungry weapon a necessity.

"Yeah," Enrique smiled, his lips curling around the remains of an unlit cigarette butt he held clenched between his dirt-covered lips. He had tossed his helmet away the first thing, preferring to wear only a black bandanna around his forehead. His grime stained hands tightened on the gun's controls and his eyes sighted on the line of advancing Kreelans. "Looks like they think we're all finished, since we haven't shot back at 'em for a while." He snickered, then snugged his shoulder in tight to the shoulder stock of the gun. "Surprise..."

Solon was hunched down next to a blown-out window, looking for signs of the Kreelans trying to flank them, when he noticed the shattered portrait of a man and woman on the floor next to him. He picked up the crushed holo image of the young man and his bride and wondered who they might have been. Saying a silent prayer for their souls, he carefully set the picture out of his way. Somehow, the image seemed sacred, a tiny reminder of the precariousness of human existence, of good times past, and perhaps, hopes for the future. These two, who undoubtedly lay dead somewhere in this wasteland, would never know that their own lives were more fragile and finite than the plastic that still struggled to protect their images.

He turned as he heard the coughing roar of Enrique's pulse gun as it tore into the alien skirmish line. He listened as the gunner moderated his bursts, conserving the weapon's power while choosing his targets. Solon was glad Enrique had lived this long. He was as good a soldier as could be found in the Territorial Army. They had all been good soldiers, and would make the Kreelans pay dearly for taking the last four lives that Solon had left to offer as an interest payment toward humanity's survival.

As he looked through the dust and smoke, the thermal imager in Solon's visor gave him an enhanced view of the devastation around him, the computer turning the sunset into a scene of a scarlet Hell. He prayed that his seven-year-old son, Reza, remained safe in the nearby bunker. He had lost count of the number of times he had prayed for his boy, but it did not matter. He prayed again, and would go on praying, because it was the only thing he could do. Reza and the other children of their defense district had been taken to the local shelter, a deep underground bunker that could withstand all but a direct orbital bombardment, or so they hoped. Solon only wished that he had been able to see his little boy again before he died. "I love you, son," he whispered to the burning night.

Behind him, Camilla hurriedly stripped off the expended power pack from the pulse gun and clipped on another. She had come to do it so well that Enrique barely missed a beat in his firing.

Solon saw movement in a nearby building that was occupied by one of the other platoons: a hand waving at him from a darkened doorway. He raised his own hand in a quick salute, not daring to risk his head or arm for a more dashing salutation.

He made one more careful sweep of the street with his enhanced vision. Although he had spent his life in service to the Confederation as a shipbuilder, not as a hardened Marine or sailor, Solon knew that he needed to be extra careful in everything he did now. His body was past its physical limit, and the need for sleep was dragging all of them toward mistakes that could lead them to their deaths. Vigilance was survival.

As he finished his visual check, he relaxed slightly. All was as he had seen it before. Nothing moved. Nothing changed but the direction of the smoke's drift, and the smell of burning wood and flesh that went with it. He felt more than heard the hits the other side of his little fortress was taking from Kreelan light guns, and was relieved to hear Enrique's pulse gun yammer back at them like an enraged dog.

He glanced back toward the building occupied by the other platoon just as a massive barrage of Kreelan weapons fire erupted on the far side. He watched in horror as the structure began to crumble under the onslaught. The human defenders, sensing the futility of holding on, came boiling out into the street, heading for Solon's position, only to be cut down in a brutal crossfire from further down the lane.

The firing tapered off, and Solon saw shadows rapidly flowing toward the other platoon's survivors: Kreelan warriors silently advancing, swords drawn. They killed with energy weapons when they had to, but preferred more personal means of combat.

"Oh my God," Solon whispered, knowing that his own final stand would soon be upon him: they were surrounded now, cut off. His throat constricted and his stomach threatened to heave up the handful of tasteless ration cake he had eaten earlier in the day. He flipped up the visor for a moment to look at the scene with his own eyes, then flipped it back down to penetrate the smoky darkness.

Suddenly, a lone figure darted across the street, plunging suicidally into the raging battle. Under the figure's arm swung what could have been an oversized doll, but Solon knew that it was not. The little arms clung to the neck of the madly running soldier and the rag doll's little legs kicked at empty air. With a sinking sensation, Solon realized who it was.

"Reza!" he shouted, his heart hammering with fear and joy, wondering how in the Lord's name the boy had gotten here.

With a crack of thunder, the soldier's luck ran out as a crimson lance struck him, spinning him around like a top. He collapsed into the rubble, shielding the boy's body with his own.

Solon roared in the protective fury only a parent can know, his voice thundering above the clamoring of the guns. Camilla turned just in time to see him leap through the blasted wall into the carnage raging beyond.

"Solon!" she screamed, struggling up from her position next to the hammering pulse gun.

"No!" Enrique yelled at her, grabbing for her arm. He was too late to stop her as she bolted from the pit. "Dammit!" he hissed, struggling to change the empty and useless magazine himself. He pried the heavy canister off the gun's breech section with blind, groping hands while his bloodshot eyes tracked the rapidly approaching shadows of the enemy.

Solon suddenly staggered back over the shattered wall. His breath came in long heaves as if he had just finished running a marathon, and his armor was pitted and smoking from half a dozen glancing hits. In his arms was a small bundle of rags. Camilla nearly fainted at the sight of Reza's face, his skin black with soot and streaked with tears of fright.

"Mama," the boy cried, reaching for her.

"Oh, baby," she said softly, taking him in her arms and rocking him. "What are you doing here?" Camilla asked.

Solon collapsed next to her, wrapping his arms around his wife and child.

"What happened to the bunker?" Snowden shouted in between bursts from her rifle as she tried to kill the Kreelans who escaped Enrique's non-stop firing.

"The same thing that's going to happen to us if you guys don't start shooting!" Enrique screamed hoarsely, finally slamming a new – and the last – magazine into his pulse gun. "The Blues are all over the place out here!"

Reluctantly letting go of his wife and son, Solon grabbed up his rifle and thrust its muzzle through a hole in the wall. Gritting his teeth in rage and a newfound determination to survive, to protect his wife and son, he opened fire on the wraiths that moved through the darkness.

Camilla, after a last hug, set Reza down next to Snowden. "Take care of him," she begged before taking up her station next to Enrique.

Snowden nodded and held Reza tightly as the thunder of gunfire surrounded them.

* * *

The sky was black as pitch, black as death, as the priestess walked alone over the arena this world had become. Her sandaled feet touched the ground but left no sound, no footprint. She looked up toward where the stars should be, yearning for the great moon that shone over the Homeworld. But the only sight to be had was the glowing red smears of the fires that were reflected by the wafting smoke and dust.

As she made her way across the field of carnage, she touched the bodies of the fallen children to honor them as they had honored their Empress. They had sacrificed their lives to show their love for Her. She grieved for them all, that they had died this day, never again to feel the flame that drove them to battle, the thrill of sword and claw, never again to serve the Empress through their flesh. Now they basked in the quiet sunset of the Afterlife, someday perhaps to join the ranks of the Ancient Ones, the warriors of the spirit.

She moved on toward her destination. It had once been a human dwelling, but now was a mound of ashen rubble. It squatted impetuously in the wasteland created by weapons the Kreela disdained to use. The humans had never realized that the destruction of their worlds was caused by their own predilection for such weaponry, to which the Kreela sometimes had to respond in kind. The warriors of the Empress sought battles of the mind, body, and spirit, of sword and claw, and not of brute destruction.

Watching the battles rage here for several cycles of the sun across the sky, she had become increasingly curious about these particular humans who fought so well, and at last had decided that perhaps they were worthy of her personal attention. She bade the young warriors to rest, to wait for her return, before setting out on her own journey of discovery.

She paused when she reached the back of the crumbled structure that hid the humans she sought. She listened for their heartbeats, smelled their pungent body odor, and felt for their strange alien spirit with her mind. After a moment she had an image of them, of where they sat and stood within.

Silent as the dead around her, she moved to a chosen point along the wall. Her breathing and heart stilled, she concealed everything about herself that made her presence real. Unless one of the humans looked directly at her, she would be utterly invisible.

Then she stepped through the wall, her flesh and armor melding with the essence of the barrier as she passed through without so much as a whisper.

* * *

"Is that all you remember, honey?" Camilla asked Reza softly, brushing his unruly hair back with her hand, which was temporarily freed from the armored skin she had been wearing for the past several days.

"Yes, Mama," he replied. The fear had mostly left him, now that he was with them again, and that they thought he had done the right thing. "All I remember was lots of smoke. Then someone started to scream. People ran, hurting each other, because they were afraid. Someone, Madame Barnault, I think, led me out, but I lost her after we got outside. I remembered where Papa said you would be, so I came here to find you. I almost made it, except the Kreelans were everywhere. That's when Kerry–"

"That's enough, son," Solon said gently, not wanting to force the boy to describe the death of the soldier, who had been another friend of their family. "It's all right, now. You're here and safe, and that's all that counts." He exchanged a quick glance with Camilla. *Safe* was hardly the word to use, he knew, even though the Kreelans had apparently given up for the day. Reza would now have to suffer whatever fate was in store for the rest of them. Solon could not justify risking someone else's life for the boy's benefit. One had already died for him.

"Reza," Camilla told him, "I want you to stay with Snowden and help her find more ammunition for us." She leaned close to his ear and whispered, "And I want you to watch out for her and protect her. She's hurt and needs a big boy like you to care for her."

Reza nodded vigorously, glancing in Snowden's direction, the horrors of the past few hours fading. He had a mission now, some responsibility that helped to displace his fear. "I will, Mama," he said quietly so that Snowden would not hear.

Later, as his father and mother rested under Enrique's watchful eyes, Snowden kept an eye on Reza as he busied himself with hunting for the things she had told him to look for.

Peering through the darkness, his father having told him that they could not use a light for fear of bringing the Kreelans, Reza spied what Snowden had told him would be a great prize in the game they were playing. A bright metal clip protruded from under a stairway crawlspace, its surface reflecting the occasional flash of artillery fire that showed through the mangled roof. He saw that it was attached to a big, gray cylinder: a pulse gun magazine. Grinning with excitement, he scampered forward to retrieve it. He had heard Enrique say that they didn't have any more of the magazines, and the big gun wouldn't work.

He reached down to pick it up, but found that it was much heavier than he had imagined. He pulled and heaved, but the magazine would not move. He started sweeping the dirt away from around it, to try and dig it out. His hand brushed against something, something smooth and warm, totally different from the rubbery pocked coating of the magazine that was supposed to make it less slippery.

Curious, he reached out to feel what it was. He did not need a light to tell him that he was touching someone's leg, and they had their foot resting on the magazine. Looking up into the darkness above him, he could see only a shadow.

"Who are you?" he asked quietly, curious as to how and why someone would have come into the house without letting his father know about it. "Are you one of Papa's soldiers?"

Silence.

A flare burst far down the street, slowly settling toward the ground. In its flickering glow, Reza saw clearly the monstrous shape above him, saw the eyes that glared down from the dark-skinned face and the glistening ivory fangs that emerged from the mouth in a silent snarl.

Reza stumbled back, screaming at the nightmarish shape, all thoughts of the precious magazine vanished from his mind. He scrambled backward on all fours like a terrified crab, screaming. "Mama! Papa!"

"Reza, what is it?" Solon asked, picking the boy up from the debris-strewn floor as he burst from the hallway. "What's wrong?"

"One of them's in here! By the stairs! There, Papa!" Reza pointed, but the monster had disappeared. "It was right there!" he cried, stabbing at the air with his trembling finger.

Solon peered through the darkness, but could see nothing. "Reza, there's no way anyone could be back there. That's the one place where they can't get in, because it's a solid wall, no doors or windows, no holes."

"Papa, one of them's in here!" Reza wailed, his terrified eyes still fixed on where he knew the monster had been.

Solon hesitated. He knew how tired and confused Reza must be, how much they all were, and he knew he had to humor the boy.

"I'll take a look," Snowden volunteered. In the time since the last wave of Kreelans had attacked, Camilla had finally had time to splint her leg properly and block the nerves. Walking on it would probably do permanent damage, but Snowden had figured that it was better to be alive and mostly functional than just plain dead. She snatched up her helmet and put it on. The shattered interior of the house, enhanced into precise detail by the visor, came into focus. "He's probably just wired over what happened at the bunker," she said. Camilla nodded, but Snowden could tell that she was nervous. "Don't worry, Camilla," Snowden reassured her, hefting her rifle. "I'll take care of him." Then, turning to the boy, she said, "Can you show me, Reza?"

Reza did not want to go anywhere near the stairs or the back rooms again. But everyone was looking at him, and he would not act like a baby in front of them. After all, he was seven years old now. "All right," he said, his voice shaking.

Solon set him down, and then looked at Snowden. "Just be careful, okay?"

"No problem, boss," she replied easily. Her outward confidence wasn't foolish arrogance: even as exhausted as she was, she was still the best sharpshooter in the entire company. "C'mon, Reza." Taking the boy's hand, her other arm cradling the rifle, she led him down the dark hallway toward the back of the house.

Once into the hallway, she became increasingly edgy with every crunch of plaster under her boots, only one of which she could feel, the other having been deadened to stifle the pain. The hairs on the back of her neck were standing at stiff attention, but she could not figure out why. *There's nothing here*, she told herself firmly.

She finally decided that it must be because Reza's grip had tightened with every step. It was a gauge of the little boy's fear. But her own senses registered nothing at all.

Reza moved forward, about half a step ahead of her, one hand clinging to hers, the other probing ahead of him through the murk. He knew he had seen the alien warrior. But as his fear grew, so did his self-doubt. *Maybe I was wrong*, he thought.

Behind them came a scraping sound like a knife against a sharpening stone. Snowden whirled around, pushing Reza to the ground behind her with one hand while the other brought the rifle to bear.

"Hell!" she hissed. A fiber optic connector that had been part of the house's control system dangled from the ceiling, the cable scraping against the wall. She shook her head, blowing out her breath. *Don't be so tense*, she told herself. *Take it easy*. "Reza," she said, turning around, "I think we better head back to the others. There's nothing–"

She stopped in mid-sentence as she saw a clawed fist emerge from the wall in front of her, the alien flesh and sinew momentarily merging with stone and steel in a pulsating mass of swirling colors. The hand closed around Snowden's neck with a chilling *snick*. The alien warrior's hand was so large that her talons overlapped Snowden's spine. Gasping in horror, Snowden was forced backward as the Kreelan made her way through the wall and into the dark hallway.

Snowden's mouth gaped open, but no words came. There was only a muted stuttering that was building toward an uncontrollable ululation of terror. She dropped her rifle, the tiny gap between her body and the alien making it as useless as a medieval pike in a dense thicket. Desperately, she groped for the pistol strapped to her lower thigh, her other hand vainly trying to break the Kreelan's grip on her neck.

His mind reeling from the horror in front of him, Reza backpedaled away, his mouth open in a scream for help that he would never remember making. He watched helplessly as the warrior's sword, free from the wall's impossible embrace, pierced Snowden's breastplate. It burst from her back with a thin metallic screech and a jet of blood. Snowden's body twitched like a grotesque marionette, her legs dancing in the confusion of signals coursing through her severed spine, her arms battering weakly at the enemy's face. The pistol had fallen to the floor, its safety still on.

Satisfied that the human was beaten, the Kreelan let go of Snowden's neck. As the young woman's body fell to the floor, the alien warrior pulled the sword free, the blade dragging at Snowden's insides with its serrated upper edge. She was dead before her helmeted head hit the floor.

Reza bolted for the main room, his scream of terror reverberating from the walls and battered ceiling.

"Reza!" Solon cried as his son burst into the room to fall at his father's feet. "Where's Snowden?"

"Solon," Camilla whispered, slowly rising to her feet as she saw the dark shape silently move from the hallway. A burst from down the street lit the thing's face with a hellish glow, leaving no doubt as to its origin.

The Kreelan stopped just beyond the hallway. Watching. Waiting.

Enrique reacted first. Instinctively he brought up his rifle, aiming it at the alien's chest.

"Bitch!" he cried, his finger convulsing on the trigger.

Solon saw her arm move like a scythe in the eerie display of his helmet visor. The movement was accompanied by a strange whistling noise, like a storm wind howling against a windowpane.

Enrique suddenly grunted. Solon saw the gunner's eyes register disbelief, then nothing at all as they rolled up into his head. His body sagged backward and the gun discharged once into the ceiling before clattering to the floor at his side. Solon saw a huge wet horizontal gash in Enrique's chest armor that was wide enough to put both fists in, as if someone had split him open with an ax.

Camilla reached for her rifle, propped against the wall behind her.

"No," Solon said softly. "Don't move."

She stopped.

Reza lay face down on the floor, his body pointing like an arrow toward where his father now stood frozen. He blinked away the tears in his eyes, his entire body trembling with fear. He felt something sharp under his right hand, and without thinking he closed his fingers around it: a knife. He clung to it desperately, for he had no weapon of his own. A brief glance told him that it was his father's. He knew that his father always carried two, but must have somehow lost this one in the rubble during the fighting. Reza held it tightly to his chest.

"Why doesn't she attack?" Camilla whispered, terribly tempted to reach for her pistol or rifle. The sight of Enrique's gutted body stayed her hand. And then there was Snowden. Undoubtedly, she lay dead somewhere deeper in the house.

"I don't know, but..." Solon hesitated. He suddenly had an idea. "I'm going to try something."

Before Camilla could say a word, he drew the long-bladed knife he carried in his web gear. It was an inferior weapon to the Kreelan's sword, but it was all he had, and he didn't know where his regular combat knife had disappeared to. Then he slowly moved his free hand to the clasps that held his web gear to his armor. With two quick yanks, the webbing that held his grenades, pistol and extra weapon power packs clattered to the floor.

"So far, so good," he muttered. Sweat poured from his brow down the inside of his helmet. "Now you do it," he ordered his wife. "Draw your knife and drop the rest of your gear."

"What about Reza?" she asked, her eyes fixed on the alien as she repeated what Solon had done, her own equipment rattling to the floor around her feet a moment later. "Solon, we've got to get him out of here."

Crouching down slowly under the Kreelan's watchful, almost benevolent gaze, Solon reached down to where his son lay.

"Reza," he whispered, the external helmet speaker making his voice sound tinny, far away, "stand up, very slowly, and look at me."

Reza did as he was told, his body shaking with fright.

"Listen carefully, son," he said, tearing his eyes away from the Kreelan to look at his son for what he knew would be the last time. He fought against the tears that welled up in his eyes. "You must do exactly what I tell you, without question, without being too afraid. You're a young man, now, and your mother and I need you to help us."

"Yes, Papa," Reza whispered shakily as he stared into his father's dirty helmet visor. But instead of his father's face, Reza saw only the dull reflection of the apparition standing behind him, only a few paces away.

Holding his son by both quivering shoulders, Solon went on, "Not far from here, there used to be a really big schoolhouse, the university. Do you remember?"

Reza nodded. His father had taken him there many times to show him the great library there. It had always been one of his favorite places.

"Our people have built a big, strong fortress there," Solon continued. "That's where I need you to go. Tell them your mother and I need help, and they'll send soldiers for us." He pulled Reza to him. "We love you, son," he whispered. Then he let him go. "Go on, son. Get out of here and don't look back."

"But Papa..." Reza started to object, crying now.

"Go on!" Camilla said softly, but with unmistakable firmness. Her own body shook in silent anguish that she could not even hold her son one last time. Fate had held that last card from her hand, an alien Queen of Spades standing between her and her child. "Go on," she urged again, somehow sensing the Kreelan's growing impatience, "before it's too late."

"I love you," Reza whispered as stumbled toward a hole in the wall, a doorway to the Hell that lay beyond.

"I love you, too, baby," Camilla choked.

As her only son crawled through the hole to the street beyond, Camilla turned her attention back to the waiting Kreelan. "All right, you bitch," she sneered, her upper lip curled like a wolf's, exposing the teeth that had once illuminated a smile that had been a young man's enchantment, the man who later became her husband. But there was no trace of that smile now. "It's time for you to die." The blade of her knife glinted in the fiery glow that lit the horizon of the burning city.

Together, husband and wife moved toward their enemy.

* * *

Reza stumbled and fell to the ground when the blast lit up the night behind him. The knoll of debris that had been his parents' stronghold vanished in a fiery ball of flame and splinters, with smoke mushrooming up into the night sky like the glowing pillar of a funeral pyre.

"Mama!" he screamed. "Papa!"

But only the flames answered, crackling as they consumed the building's remains with a boundless hunger.

Reza lay there, watching his world burn away to ashes. A final tear coursed its way down his face in a lonely journey, its wet track reflecting the brilliant flames. Alone now, fearful of the terrors that stalked the night, he curled up beneath a tangle of timbers and bricks, watching the flames dance to music only the fire itself could hear.

"Goodbye, Mama and Papa," he whispered before succumbing to the wracking sobs that had been standing by like friends in mourning.

* * *

Not far away, another lone figure stood watching those same flames through alien eyes. The priestess's heart raced with the energy that surged through her body, her blood singing the chorus of battle that had been the heart and spirit of her people for countless generations.

The two humans had fought well, she granted, feeling a twinge of what might have been sorrow at their deaths. It was so rare that she found opponents worthy of her mettle. The humans would never know it, but they had come closer to killing her than any others had come in many cycles. Had she not heard the *click* made by the grenade, set off by the mortally stricken male while the female held her attention, she might have joined them in the fire that now devoured their frail bodies. Some of her hair, her precious raven hair, had been scorched by the blast as she leaped through the wall to safety.

What a pity, she thought, *that animals with such instincts did not possess souls.* Such creatures could certainly be taught how to make themselves more than moving targets for her to toy with, but her heart ached to give something more to her Empress.

Standing there, nauseated by the acrid stench of the burning plasticrete around her, she heaved a mournful sigh before turning back toward where the young ones lay resting. Her time here was terribly short, but a single moon cycle of the Homeworld, and she had yet much to see, much on which she would report to the Empress.

She had just started back when she heard a peculiar sound, an unsteady pulse under the current of the winds that carried the embers of the fire. It came at once from one direction, then from another as the fickle winds sought new paths over the dying city. She closed her eyes and reached out with her mind, her spirit flowing from her body to become one with the scorched earth and smoldering sky, using senses that went well beyond any her body could provide.

The child.

She hesitated, tempted simply to let it go, to die on its own while she returned to the young warriors who awaited her. But she found herself overcome with curiosity, for she had only seen their children in death. Never had she seen a live one. She debated for a moment what she should do, but in the end her curiosity demanded satisfaction. To blunt the pup's whimpering misery with death would be an indulgent, if unchallenging, act.

* * *

Reza blinked. Had he fallen asleep? He rubbed his eyes with grimy fists. His cheeks were caked with a mortar of tears and masonry dust. He glanced around, unable to see much in the dim glow that filtered into his hideout. Not really wanting to, but unable to help himself, he looked toward where his parents had died.

He sucked in his breath in surprise. A shadow blocked the entrance to his tiny hideaway. With arms and legs that felt weak as stalks of thin grass, he crawled forward a bit to see better.

"Mama?" he whispered cautiously, his young mind hoping that perhaps all had not been lost. "Papa?" he said a little louder, his voice barely rising above the wind that had begun to howl outside.

The figure stood immobile, but for one thing. Extending one arm, the fingers slowly, rhythmically curled back one by one in a gesture he had long been taught meant *come, come to me*.

His teeth chattering with fear and anticipation, he gripped his father's knife, his fingers barely long enough to close around the handle. He crawled forward toward the gesturing apparition, still unsure if it was a man or woman, or perhaps something else. He was terrified, but he had to know.

Coming to the last barrier of fallen timbers that formed the doorway to his hideaway, Reza gathered his courage. He fixed his eyes on the shadow hand that continued to call him, mesmerizing him with the thought that help had arrived and that his parents might yet be saved. Placing his empty hand on the bottom-most timber, the other clutching the knife by his side, he poked his head out the hole.

The shape seemed to shimmer and change in the light. It moved with such speed that Reza's eyes only registered a dark streak before an iron hand clamped around his neck and plucked him from the hole with a force that nearly snapped his spine. He cried out in pain and fear, never noticing the warm flood that coursed down his legs as his bladder emptied.

His cries and struggling ended when he found the cat-like eyes of the Kreelan warrior a mere hand's breadth from his own. Her lips parted to reveal the ivory fangs that adorned the upper and lower jaws.

For a moment, the two simply stared at one other, Reza's feet dangling nearly a meter from the ground as the Kreelan held him. Her grip, strong enough to pop his head like a grape with a gentle squeeze, was restrained to a force that barely allowed him to breathe. His pulse hammered in his ears as his heart fought to push blood through the constricted carotid arteries to his brain. Spots began to appear in his vision, as if he were looking at the Kreelan through a curtain of shimmering stars.

Then the alien closed her mouth, hiding away the terrible fangs. Her lips formed a proud, forceful line on her face, and Reza felt the hand around his tiny neck begin to contract with a strength that seemed to him as powerful as anything in the Universe.

As his lungs strained for their last breath through his constricted windpipe, a voice in his brain began to shout something. The words were repeated again and again, like a maniacal litany, the rhythm surging through his darkening brain. As his body's oxygen reserves dwindled and his vision dimmed, he finally understood.

The knife!

With a strength born of desperation, he thrust the knife straight at the Kreelan's face.

Suddenly she released him, and he fell to the ground. His feet crashed into the brick rubble over which he had been suspended, his legs crumpling like flimsy paper rods. Stunned, he fought to get air back into his lungs, his chest heaving rapidly. His vision returned at an agonizingly slow pace through the fireworks dancing on his retinas. He groped about, desperately trying to get away from the alien warrior.

His hand smacked into something, and he knew instantly what it was. He had felt it before. It was the Kreelan's leg. He looked up in time to see her kneel next to him, her mountainous form overshadowing the world in his frightened eyes. He tried to push himself away, to roll down into the flat part of the street where he might be able to run, but a massive clawed hand grasped him by the shoulder, the tips of her talons just pricking his skin.

His pounding fear giving way to resignation, he turned to face her. He did not want to watch as she killed him, but he had to see her. Whether out of curiosity or to face down the shame of being a coward, he did not know. Reluctantly, his eyes sought hers.

The knife, he saw, even in his tiny hand, had done its work. A vertical gash ran from a point halfway up the brow above the Kreelan's left eye down to the point of her graceful cheekbone. The blade had somehow missed the eye itself, although it was awash in the blood that oozed from the wound. The weapon had fallen from Reza's hand after doing its damage, and he held out little hope of recovering it. Besides, he thought as he waited for the final blow, what was the point?

He sat still as she reached toward him with her other hand. He flinched as one of the talons touched the skin of his forehead, just above his eye. But he did not look away, nor did he cry out. He had faced enough fear during this one night to last a lifetime, and when death came, he thought he might welcome it.

Slowly, she drew a thin line of blood that mimicked the wound he had given her. Her talon cut deep, right to the bone, as it glided down his face. Just missing his left eye, it lingered at last on his cheek.

He blinked, trying to clear the blood away as it dribbled over his eyebrow and into his eye. The flesh around the wound throbbed with the beating of his heart, but that was all. He was sure she was going to skin him alive, and he knew that her claws were as sharp as carving knives.

Instead, the Kreelan's hand drew back, and her other hand released his shoulder. She looked at him pensively, lightly tapping the talon smeared with his blood against her dark lips, her eyes narrowed slightly in thought.

His heart skipped a beat as she abruptly reached forward toward his hair. He felt a small pull on his scalp and instinctively reached to where he had felt the tug, expecting to feel the wet stickiness of more blood. But there was none. He looked up in surprise as the Kreelan held out a lock of his normally golden brown hair, now a filthy black from the dirt and smoke. With obvious care, she put it into a small pouch that was affixed to the black belt at her waist.

A prize, Reza thought, his mouth dropping open in wonder, a faint spark of hope sizzling in his breast. Was she about to let him live?

In answer to his unvoiced question, the huge warrior stood up. She made no sound, not even a tiny whisper, as her body uncoiled to its towering height. She glanced down to the ground at her feet and, leaning down, scooped up his father's knife. Turning the blade over in her hand, she made a low *humph* and put it in her belt. She looked at Reza one last time, acting as if the bleeding wound on her face was nothing, and bowed her head to him.

He blinked.

And she was gone.

Two

Five Years Later, On The Planet Hallmark

A plume of dust rising into the dry air warned of the approaching vehicle, a bulbous van that could hold over a dozen passengers. Like a fat beetle on some unfathomable insectoid quest, it crept across the arid land, threading its way through the pyramids of rocks strewn across the landscape that marked the labor and toil of tens of thousands of young hands. The vehicle's paint, reassuringly bright at a distance, faded to a chipped, diseased gray as it drew closer. The rattling cough and billowing blue smoke from its poorly maintained engine announced the unwelcome noontime visit to those who hadn't already been watching its approach.

The vehicle wheezed to a stop, its four oversized wheels sending skyward a last cloud of bitter dust. On the side of the van, in letters that had once been a bright cheery blue, was stenciled "House 48."

A side door slid open with a tired shriek of metal, and eight frightened children stepped out into the harsh sunlight. Aged from five to fourteen, the newcomers – war orphans all – looked with disbelieving eyes at the bleak and arid plain that was to be their home until the day they left the orphanage. These were the fields of the planet Hallmark, the home of nearly a hundred Confederation Emergency Orphanages, and here the children would begin their service to the state that now provided for them. Each of the orphanage complexes housed a thousand or more children who had lost their families. And each and every child would spend his or her youth pulling rocks from the soil to help make more room for grain to grow, grain that fed Confederation troops and helped the planet's corrupt administrators grow rich on illegal trading and price fixing.

The van suddenly groaned and shuddered as the driver's door was thrown open, and a tree stump of a leg probed downward until it found the firmness of the ground. As the man – at least his chromosome structure made him a man – put his full weight on the resilient earth, the vehicle's springs gave an audible sigh of relief. On the florid face, shaded by a gaudy aqua baseball cap, was a humorless smile exposing teeth that were as rotten as the soul within. His name was Francis Early Muldoon, and he was the overseer of House 48's field labor teams.

He wasted no time, barking harsh orders to the children and gesturing with his arms. Sausage-like fingers pointed out the various labor teams. In singles and twos they began to trudge toward their assigned groups, staying close together like longtime friends, though they were yet strangers to one another.

All had been assigned but a pretty teenage girl, the oldest of the group at fourteen years, who was left to stand alone. She watched, uncertain, as the giant thing that masqueraded as a man turned his attention to her, his smile transforming into a leer.

* * *

Some meters away, a group of tired, sweat- and dirt-stained children, having paused from their labor of wrenching the sharp-edged rocks from the unyielding soil, watched the newcomers with grim interest. Standing at the front was a lean, brown-haired boy now twelve years old, holding the work-smoothed wooden handle of a pickax in his callused right hand. His jade green eyes had been following the van since it had appeared on the horizon, and now he felt his grip involuntarily tighten around the pick's handle as Muldoon turned his attention to the girl.

"Is he going to hurt her, Reza?" a young girl beside him asked in a hushed voice, her wide eyes fixed on the overseer and his latest object of interest.

"No," Reza growled as he watched Muldoon step closer to the new girl. Reza could not hear what was being said between the two, but he could well imagine. In exchange for food and protection from some of the older children who were as dangerous as rabid wolves, Muldoon usually got whatever piece of flesh – male and female alike – that his diseased cravings called for. Reza could remember many days when the van was parked near one of the little stone pyramids, rocking chaotically from the hideous sexual ballet playing within, and he well knew that participation was not strictly voluntary. But trying to tell the orphanage administration, whose bureaucratic heart had no room for the mindless prattling of youngsters with over-active imaginations, had led to more than one untimely death under "mysterious circumstances." The children had gotten the message: they were on their own against Muldoon.

But this girl, new to Muldoon's little operation, resolutely refused him. She met his groping advances with scratching nails and a hail of curses in a language Reza did not understand.

"You little bitch!" Reza heard Muldoon shout as she raked the nails of one hand across his face, drawing several streaks of blood. Reza's heart turned cold as the overseer struck the girl in the face with a meaty fist, knocking her to the ground. The man reached down for her, grabbed her blouse and pulled her toward him, ripping the vibrant yellow fabric that had struck Reza as being so pretty, so out of place here. Muldoon's hands grabbed for her budding breasts, now showing through the torn blouse. She tried to roll away, but he pinned her with his bulk, crushing her beneath him as his hands worked greedily at her clothing.

Reza had seen enough. He hefted his pickax and ran to where the girl lay writhing under Muldoon's gelatinous body. The other members of his work team followed him instantly, without question. Reza was their guardian, the only one who had cared about any of them, and their loyalty to him was absolute.

* * *

Muldoon was enjoying himself. He had wrapped his arms around the girl's chest, and now his hands were firmly clamped to her breasts as she struggled beneath him. Her face was pressed into the hard ground, the breath crushed from her by his one hundred and fifty kilos. He brutally squeezed her tender flesh, his fingertips pressing against her ribs just as his throbbing penis bulged against her buttocks. Only once before had he taken one of the children in the open, outside the van; he was normally very conscientious about that kind of thing. He firmly believed that sex was a private matter. But there were exceptions to every rule.

And this one was definitely an exception, he thought as his hands groped downward and began to work on unfastening her pants, his untrimmed fingernails cutting into her smooth skin.

The ground beside his face suddenly exploded, with dirt flying into his face. Crying out in surprise and pain, he struggled to free a hand to wipe at his stinging eyes. His vision cleared enough for him to see the gleaming metal sprouting from the earth not five centimeters from his sweating nose. As he watched, the metal spike levered itself out of the ground and rose above his head. He followed its trail until his eyes were drawn to the silhouetted form standing over him.

"Let her go, Muldoon," Reza ordered quietly. He held the pickax easily in his hands, hands that were stronger than those of most adults after the years of hard field work he had endured. Its splintered metal end was poised directly above Muldoon's head. "God knows, I should split your skull open just on principle, but the stench would probably be more than I could bear."

"Mind your own business, you little bastard," Muldoon hissed, his face twisting into the one that he saved for scaring the little children when they did something that really pissed him off. His hands bit even further into the girl's chest and belly, eliciting a groan of pain.

"This is your last warning, Muldoon," Reza said, raising the pickax to strike. He figured that he would almost certainly go to juvenile prison for killing this beast that almost looked like a man, but how much worse could prison be over this place? Besides, for all the suffering this bastard had caused, it would be worth it.

"You'd never get away with it, you little fuck," Muldoon warned. "You've got too many witnesses. You'd spend the rest of your worthless life in prison, if they didn't just fry your ass first."

Reza laughed. "Look around you, Muldoon. Do you think anybody here is going to be sorry if I ram this thing into your rat brain? And arranging an 'accident' would be pretty easy, you know. You don't drive so well sometimes. It would be a real shame if you hit one of the rock piles and flipped over or something. Maybe even the fuel tank would light off." Reza smiled a death's head smile. "Let her go," he said one last time, his voice hard as the stones they pulled from the ground.

"Kill him, Reza," one child said fiercely. Muldoon had been the monster of his nightmares until Reza had taken him in. "Kill him. Please."

Several others joined in until it was a chant. Reza knew that in a moment he wouldn't need the pickaxe to take care of Muldoon: the children would work themselves into such a frenzy that they would fall on him like hyenas and rip him to pieces with their bare hands. *And maybe that wouldn't be such a bad thing*, he thought.

But Muldoon saw it, too. He was many things, but he was no fool. He had heard stories of children murdering their overseers, and he had no intention of letting it happen to him. It was one of the reasons he sought to keep them terrorized, so he could keep them under rigid control.

With a grunt of effort, Muldoon rolled himself off of the girl. Eyeing Reza with unconcealed contempt, he got to his feet. The girl lay motionless between them like a beautiful garden that had been trampled, corrupted.

For a moment, the only sound above the dry breeze that constantly swept this arid land was the wheezing of Muldoon's overtaxed lungs as they fought to support a body that was at least three times Reza's own weight.

Muldoon's eyes flitted from Reza to the girl, then to the others who stood watching him, silent now. Muldoon considered his options, and decided that he would have to yield. This time.

"Listen, boy," he growled, his voice barely audible as he leaned toward Reza, "I'm going to get you one of these days. Maybe not today. Maybe not tomorrow. But I'll get you." He nodded to the girl, curled now into a fetal position on the ground. "And then I'll get your little slut, here, too." He hawked and spat on her, a gesture of defiance, of promise.

He turned away and headed back toward the van, conscious of the two dozen sets of eyes boring into his back. Once safe inside the vehicle, having slammed the driver's door shut, he leaned his head out the window. "You'd better have this section of the field cleared by sundown, boy, or your ass is gonna be in a sling with the headmaster!" As if noticing the other children for the first time, he bellowed, "What are you gawking at, you little shits? Get back to work!" Then he started up the van, gunned the engine, and drove off in a swirl of dust and choking exhaust.

"Go on, guys," Reza urged the others. "Get back to work. We don't need him back again today."

Heads down, the group began to break up as the children reluctantly made their way back to their work groups.

Reza was about to turn his attention to the girl Muldoon had been mauling when he suddenly found himself facing a child whose drawn face could have been mistaken for hundreds, thousands of others throughout the orphanage houses that dotted Hallmark.

"You should have killed him," she said quietly. Then she was gone, trailing after her two teammates as they trudged back to their designated spot. Like lifeless rag dolls, they collapsed onto their hands and knees and got back to work.

Reza turned his attention to the girl, who still lay on the ground, weeping. Three of the biggest boys from his own team stood around her like guards, waiting for his orders.

"It's all right," he told them. "You guys get back to work, but keep your eyes open. I'll take care of her." Kneeling next to the girl, Reza said softly, "How bad are you hurt?"

Almost unwillingly, she turned over, and Reza helped her to sit up. His face flushed with anger at the sight of the scratches and bruises that were already rising against her porcelain skin. She said nothing, but shook her head. Since hardly anything was left of her pretty blouse, Reza took off his shirt and offered it to her, careful not to touch her. She had already been touched enough for one day.

"Here," he said gently, "put this on."

She looked at him with her dark eyes, brown like a doe's, but with the spirit of a leopard's. There were tears there, but Reza saw no weakness.

"*Merci*," she said, wincing in pain as she reached for the shirt. He caught a quick glimpse of her exposed breasts and quickly averted his gaze, blushing with embarrassment at seeing that part of her body and anger at the mottled bruises he saw there. He turned his back to her as she stripped off the torn blouse and put on his shirt.

"Sorry it's so dirty," he said about the shirt, suddenly ashamed that he did not have something clean to offer her. "It probably doesn't smell too good, either."

"It is fine," she said, her voice quivering only slightly. "Thank you. You're very kind." He felt a light touch on his shoulder. "You may turn around, now."

He found himself looking at a girl whose skin was a flawless ivory that he knew from long experience would have a hard time under Hallmark's brutal sun. Her aristocratic face was framed by auburn hair that fell well below her shoulders, untrimmed bangs blowing across her eyes. Reza felt his throat tighten for no reason he could explain, other than that he thought she was the most beautiful girl he had ever seen.

"I'm Reza," he said, fighting through the sudden rasp that had invaded his voice, "Reza Gard." He held out his hand to her.

Smiling tentatively, she took it, and Reza was relieved to note that her grip was strong. This one, he could tell from long experience, was tough. A survivor.

"I am Nicole," she said, her voice carrying a thick accent that Reza had never heard before, "Nicole Carré."

* * *

Wearing a blouse loaned from a sympathetic girl, Nicole sat next to Reza that evening at the mess table that Reza and his group had staked out as their own. Many of the boys and girls here, Nicole noted with disbelief, had formed alliances to protect one individual or group from another, almost like a system of fiefdoms, replete with feudal lords. Those who did not belong to one of the gangs sat alone or in very small groups at the fringe tables, their eyes alert for intruders. Sadly, from what Nicole had seen today, she thought that the loners would not stand a chance without mutual protection. Truly, she thought, there was safety in numbers.

What she found even more surprising was that the groups were not necessarily led by the oldest or strongest. Reza clearly led the group she now found herself in, although there were at least four others here – not including herself – who were older or stronger.

"Everybody," Reza said to the dozen or so sitting at their table, "I want to introduce Nicole Carré, the latest addition to House 48 and the one who put those neat scratches on Muldoon's ugly face." Reza had found out through the grapevine about the questioning Muldoon had been put through by the chief administrator about the scratches, scratches that would leave scars, Reza had noted with glee. But, as usual, Muldoon had explained it all away. Not all the administrators were bad and not all of them were idiots, Reza knew; it just seemed like the ones who were in positions to influence things were. It was just tragic fate that the children had to pay the price.

A little cheer went up from the group at the thought that someone had struck a real blow against Muldoon and lived to tell about it, and it was accompanied by a chorus of spoons banging on the metal table in celebration.

"Story time! Story time!" called out a young girl, maybe six, with lanky blond hair and a large purple birthmark across her chin. The others joined in, chanting "Story time! Story time!" while looking expectantly at Nicole.

"What is this?" she asked Reza, unsure of what was happening. She wanted to trust this boy and his friends, but her once bright and loving world had become dark and dangerous with the coming of the Kreelans, and had not improved with her arrival on Hallmark.

"It's just a little tradition we have," he said easily, gesturing for the others to quiet down. "Whenever someone new comes, we like to have them tell us how they came to be here, what rotten luck landed them on Hallmark." He noted her discomfort and shook his head. "It's totally up to you. It's just... it helps people sometimes to talk about it. But if you don't want to, it's okay."

She looked at him a moment, unable to believe that a boy his age could have such bearing and strength. The children around him were tired and unhappy about their fate, yes, but they were hopeful, even proud, and obviously stuck together because they cared for one another. It was a sharp contrast to many of the other faces she saw about her: frightened, angry or hateful, dead. She had not realized before how lucky she had been to fall into this group.

"There is not much to it, really," she said at last, embarrassed at the rapt attention the others were giving her and saddened at having to recount her recent past, "but I will tell it to you, if that is what you wish."

She paused for a moment, her mind caught on the realization that she had never really related to anyone what had happened. No one had ever asked or seemed to care, outside of establishing the simple fact that her parents were dead. The adults saw Nicole as just one more burden to be tended by the state until she was old enough to take care of herself or serve in the government or the military. The looks and rote lines of compassion she had received from the endless bureaucratic chain had once been sincere, she thought. But after hearing the same stories and seeing the same young faces thousands of times over, the orphans had become a commodity of war, and the compassion the administrators might once have felt had long since given way to weariness.

Yet here, in this group of children, total strangers with only tragedy to bind them together, she found an audience for her grief, and it was almost too much to bear.

"I come from La Seyne," she began, her eyes fixed on the table before her, "one of the provincial capitals of Ariane. It is a pretty place," she said, briefly glancing up at the others and giving them a quick, shy smile, as if they would hold the claim of her homeworld's beauty against her. But their attention was rapt, their minds already far away from Hallmark, imagining to themselves what such a place might be like, a place that to them was equivalent to the paradise of the gods. "The Kreelans have never successfully attacked it, though they have tried several times.

"Papa is..." she bit her lip, "...*was* a master shipfitter, and he decided that we should have a vacation away from home this year, to get away from the yards for a while. He told Mama that we should go to Earth. He wanted us to see Paris, a place he always talked about – he had grown up there – but we had never seen it, Mama and I having been born on La Seyne. He never stopped talking about the wonderful tower, *La Tour Eiffel* that had been built before the days of artificial gravity and load lifters. He spoke of the lights at night, of the buildings that dated back to the times of great kings and queens. And so we boarded a starliner for Earth. There were three other ships in our little convoy, two merchantmen and a light cruiser."

Reza saw her eyes mist over, her gaze somewhere far away. God, he thought, how many times have I had to see this? And how many more times before I can leave this godforsaken place? Under the table, he sought out one of her hands and took it in his. She held it tightly.

She nodded as her mind sifted through the images of times she wished she could forget. "We were only two days out from La Seyne when the convoy was attacked. I do not know how many enemy ships there were, or exactly what happened. I suppose it does not matter. Our ship, the *Il de France*, was badly hit soon after the alarms sounded, and Papa went aft to the engineering spaces to try and help them." Her lower lip trembled as a tear streaked down her face. "We never saw him after that."

She paused a moment, her eyes closed as she remembered her father's parting hug to her and her mother before he ran down the companionway with the frightened young petty officer. "The ship kept getting hit like it was being pounded with a great hammer. Either the bridge was destroyed, or perhaps the speaker system was damaged, because the order to abandon ship never came, even though we knew for sure that the hull had been breached in many places. Mama, who herself had never been on a ship before, did not seem scared at all, like she had been through it all many times in her head as she worked in the kitchen at home, making Papa's supper. When the normal lights went out and the emergency lights came on, she said only, 'We are leaving,' and took me by the hand to where one of the lifeboats was still docked." A sob caught her breath, but she forced herself to get on with it. "But the boat was already filled, except for one seat. But the aisle down the middle was clear. 'Look, Mama,' I told her, 'there is plenty of room for us.'

"But I did not know that these boats had no artificial gravity, and that anyone not in a seat might be killed during the launch. I did not hear the warning the boat was giving in Standard. There was so much noise coming from our dying ship, and Mama spoke only French. She made me take the seat and she knelt in the aisle, praying, when the door closed. I... I blacked out after that. And when I woke up, she... she..."

Nicole collapsed in wracking sobs, the guilt and loss that had been eating away at her heart finally exposed. But a part – be it ever so tiny – of the burden had been lifted from her shoulders. She felt the comforting touch of caring hands as the others extended their sympathy, and Reza wrapped his arm around her shoulder, drawing her to him.

"It's all right," he said softly. "It wasn't your fault–"

"But the warning," she gasped angrily. "I knew Standard! I should have listened! I could have saved her!"

"And where would that have left your mom?" asked Tamil, an acne-scarred girl with hair cropped close to her skull. "Back on the ship to get spaced when the hull gave way?"

"I would have stayed with her!" Nicole shouted defiantly. "At least we all would have been together."

Tamil shook her head. "She wouldn't have let you, girl, and you know it." While she was not very old when her own mother had died, Tamil remembered her mother well, and how she had saved her daughter's life at the cost of her own. "She would have knocked you over the head and strapped you into that last seat to save you, if it came down to it. She loved you. She wouldn't have let you die."

That remark was met with nods and murmurs of agreement from the others.

Nicole suddenly understood that a consensus had been reached, and the look of sympathy in their eyes was joined by something akin to forgiveness. It was a tacit understanding that Fate was to blame. There was nothing she could have done to avert the tragedy that had taken her family away. More than that, they had accepted her. She was one of them now, if she wanted to be. Thinking back to what Muldoon had done, she gave thanks to God for her good fortune.

"Listen," Reza told her, "the pain... never really goes away. But you learn to deal with it." His voice was nearly lost in the background banter and clatter of nearly a thousand spoons scraping the remnants of the evening meal from the trays of House 48, her new home. "You have to, if you want to get out of this lousy place in one piece. If you don't, people like Muldoon and some of the kids here will use you and throw you away like a toilet wipe. And you've got friends now to help."

"Besides," said a short, stocky red-haired girl two seats down from Reza, "you're a short timer. What are you, fourteen, or so?" Nicole nodded. "Jesus, Nicole, you've got less than a year here until you're fifteen and you can apply for one of the academies. You look like you're pretty sharp and in good shape. They'll probably take you. If you don't," she shrugged, "you'll just have to wait it out until you're seventeen."

"Fifteen," she lamented. "It is forever." The thought of spending the next six months here until her fifteenth birthday was appalling, but having to wait until she was seventeen was simply unbearable. Strangely, applying to one of the academies was a thought that had never occurred to her in her former life. La Seyne was very traditional, clinging to many of the ancient Western traditions brought by its early settlers. Most of the women born there spent their lives caring for their husbands and raising their children, any thoughts of becoming a "professional" being scorned as sacrilegiously self-serving. But, to get out of here in six months instead of two and a half years, she was more than willing to abandon tradition.

"It's a lot less than I've had to spend on this rock," Reza said darkly, his pre-pubescent voice carrying the resignation of the damned. His eyes blazed so fiercely that they burned her with shame for thinking that the paltry time she would have to spend here was unendurable. Reza had been here for some time before she had arrived, and would still be here after she had gone.

"Please," she choked, suddenly flushing with empathy for him, for all of them, "forgive me. I did not mean it that way." She reached out and gently stroked his cheek with her hand. "*Mon Dieu*," she whispered, "how horrible."

Reza shrugged, his face dropping its melancholy veil. "It could be worse," he said. "At least it's not like for some of the really little kids who came here without even remembering or knowing their parents, like little Darrow over there." A tiny black boy a few seats down nodded heartily and gave her an enchanting smile. "At least we knew our parents and can remember them."

Nicole nodded thoughtfully as Reza turned his attention back to the others.

"Does anybody else have anything?" He looked around the table like a chairman of the board or councilman, his eyes intense pools of jade. "Okay, that's it, then, except to remind you that we're on alert for Muldoon and his slugs. Nobody goes anywhere alone, so stay with your blockmates. Jam your doors when you go to sleep and don't open them again until your team leader – Thad, Henson, or Charles – comes to pick you up in the morning. Little kids, if you hear the fire alarm, don't leave your room unless you recognize one of our voices outside and we give you the right signal on the door. Muldoon pulled that trick last year and nailed a girl from Screamer's bunch. He's going to be gunning for us for a while this time, and there won't be another load of newbies for him to go after for another two weeks, so watch out and stick together."

With a murmur of acknowledgments, the children quickly got up from the table. Moving in formation with almost military precision, they dumped their trays in the waiting bins and followed their team leaders to the bunkhouse, leaving only Reza and Nicole behind.

"Should we not go with them?" she asked, wondering if the two of them would be safe, alone.

"No," he told her, gesturing for her to follow as he got up from the table and headed toward the tray bin. "We're not going back with them tonight. They'll be all right, but I think it's too dangerous for us to go back to the bunkhouse until tomorrow, at least."

"But," Nicole stammered, "where will we sleep?"

"Trust me," Reza told her. "I have a place Muldoon can't get into very easily."

He led her outside, following a path that led them through the various buildings that made up the House 48 complex. It comprised the bunkhouse itself, which was really a collection of dormitories; the school, which was only occupied during the winter, when even Muldoon could not bear to herd the children into the fields; the tiny medical clinic; and the administration building. The last, ironically, was also the largest, as it also housed House 48's shelter, visible from the outside by the universal red and black striped blast portal that was kept lit at all times. The exact same buildings could be found at any of the other Houses dotting Hallmark's surface. All of them were pre-fabricated, tough, cheap and easy to build and maintain. They were true modern architectural wonders, and all ugly as sin.

Up ahead, Nicole could make out a squat structure at the end of the path, the last of House 48's buildings that didn't seem to fit in with the others. Light showed through the slender windows, evenly distributed around the circumference of the octagonal building, reaching from about waist-high nearly to the roof over the second story.

"My home away from home," Reza announced, gesturing toward the revolving door. It looked almost like an airlock, and was intended to keep the dust of the fields out of the building.

"What is it?" Nicole asked as Reza ushered her through the door, the cylinder swishing closed behind them.

"It's the House 48 Library," he answered.

Nicole was about to laugh until she realized that Reza was completely serious. As they emerged through the door and into the light of the interior, she saw the look of unabashed wonder on his face. Her smile slipped as she thought of how many times he must have come through that door, and yet his expression was as if this was the very first.

"Reza," she asked, following after him into what must have been the lobby, "what is so important here?" She looked around at the meager collection of holo displays and the disk racks. "These devices are very nearly antique!"

Reza favored her with a quizzical look, as if her question had revealed a stratum of incredible, if easily forgivable, ignorance. "This," he said disdainfully, pointing to the disk racks and study carrels arrayed around the lobby, "is junk: old periodicals, some of the new literature, and other stuff. I stopped bothering with that a long time ago." He led her around the front desk as if he owned the place, which she suspected he might, in a way. Then he punched in an access code to a locked door. She noted that there appeared to be no one else here, a thought that was not entirely comforting. "This," he explained quietly, "is why this place is important."

Pushing open the door, they found themselves in a darkened room, but there was still enough light for Nicole to see angular shapes that radiated away into the darkness. Reza closed and locked the door behind them. Only then did he switch on a light.

"Oh," Nicole gasped. In the gentle light that flooded the room, she saw row after row of books, real books, with pages and bindings. Some were made of the micro plastic that had found its way into favor over the years, but most were made of genuine paper, the exposed edges yellowed with age, their covers and bindings carefully protected with a glistening epoxy sealant.

"Besides being real antiques," Reza told her, "and having some monetary value for anyone who can waste the transport mass charge to haul them around, they can be a real brain saver in this place." He picked up a volume, seemingly at random – although he knew by heart the place of every book in the room – and held it up for her to see. *Hamlet*, the book's binding said, followed by some strange symbols and then the author's name: Shakespeare.

She took the book from him, careful not to drop it. It was terribly old, and one of the few such books she had ever seen. Every major publisher had long since done away with physical books. Electronic media were so much cheaper and more efficient.

But it was not the same, as her own father, a devoted book reader himself, had often told her. Watching the action on a holo screen left too little to the imagination, he had said once, holding one of his own precious volumes up as if it were on an imaginary pedestal. The screen fed the mind, but its calories were empty ones, bereft of the stuff on which thought depended. She had thought him quite comical at the time, her own young life having evolved around the holo images that invaded their home daily. But perhaps, as was most often the case, his words had more than just a kernel of truth in them.

"You asked why this place is so important to me," Reza said, watching as she turned the pages, his ears thrilling to the sound. "I'll tell you why. When you come in from the fields, you eat, you sleep, and then you get up to go to the fields again. Over and over, for as long as you have until you can leave here.

"And every day that you let yourself do just that, just the stuff you have to do to get by, even when you're so tired you can't see straight, you die just a little bit. Not much, not so much that you notice that day, or even the next, but just a little. Your mind starts eroding, and you start forgetting about anything that you used to think was interesting or important, whether anyone else thought it was or not. Pretty soon, all the useless crap that we do here becomes more and more important to you, as if it really had some meaning." He spat out the last few words, disgust evident on his face and in his voice. "After a while, you start finding yourself in conversations about how many kilos of rocks people dug up. There's even an official contest. Did you know that? People talk about how many blisters so-and-so got, and who had sex with whom, what kind of stunt Muldoon pulled today, on and on and on. Remember the porridge you liked so much?" Nicole grimaced, the tasteless paste still coagulating in her stomach. "That's what your brain starts turning into around here. Mush.

"And the worst part is that they start not to care about anything or anyone, even themselves. Why should they, when the most important thing they did today is clear a few more meters for some farming combine that doesn't even give us a percentage of the grain they grow?"

Nicole's mouth fell open at that.

"That's right," Reza told her, his eyes burning with anger. "All of our food is imported from Peraclion, because the grain there has a higher bulk than stuff grown here, for whatever reason, and so it's more expensive to ship long distances. So all our stuff goes out-system, and Peraclion feeds us... after a few kickbacks get paid off to some of the admins here.

"So," he shrugged, "here we all sit, droning our lives away until we're old enough to either enlist directly or apply for an academy assignment. We're slave labor for the farming combines that need the land cleared but are too cheap to send machines to do it."

His expression turned grim. "But the worst part for most of the kids here is that, regardless of how bright they were when they came, they fail the entrance exams because they haven't gotten the right schooling, or can't even figure out what *abstract* means, let alone come up with an abstract thought." His face twisted in an ironic smile. "No fighter jocks coming out of that group."

Reza had no way of knowing at the time, but his last remark struck Nicole to the core. She loved the thought of flying, and had always secretly dreamed of piloting one of the tiny, darting fighter ships she saw in the movies. And in that instant, she knew what she wanted to do with her life, now that the old one was gone, washed away.

"And what of you, Reza?" she asked, her thoughts returning from her own hoped-for future. "Your mind has not turned to mush, I take it?"

"No," he told her, his expression softening as he lovingly ran his fingers along the spine of a book, "not yet, anyway. Thanks to this place."

"I still do not understand, *mon ami*." She still could not see what Reza was driving at.

"When you come in here and pick up one of these," he gestured at *Hamlet*, "or even watch one of the crappy holos out in the main room, you're not just an orphaned kid marooned on a dustbowl planet anymore, with no more rights than any slave might have. It's a way out of here. You're a hero, or a villain, or anything else you could imagine, and a lot of things you probably can't. Every time you turn a page you can go somewhere, even someplace that's never been. But anywhere you go is somewhere far away from here. And the best part about it, the part that keeps me alive and sane, is that the words in the books leave a lot of blanks that your mind has to fill in. It makes your mind work without you forcing it to, and you get better and better at it without killing yourself like you have to sometimes in the fields."

Nicole considered his words for a moment, her mind conjuring up images of some of the children she had seen around her since arriving at House 48. So many of them, it now seemed to her, had just been blank, without expression, without animation. Had they not been breathing, one might have thought them dead. And, perhaps, in a way they were.

"But Reza," she asked, suddenly finding a hole in his escape theory, "how do you find the time? Or the energy?"

"I make it," he said grimly. "I come here every night after dinner, no matter how tired I am, no matter if there's mud from the rain or snow in the winter. And on the one day off we have after our six workdays, I spend all day here." He shrugged. "What else am I going to do? I'd like to just spend that time sleeping like most of the others. I hate being tired all the time, but it's too important. I'm not going to let myself turn into a vegetable in this place. When I'm fifteen," he vowed, "I'm going to pass the academy entrance exams. I'm going to make it into OCS and be a Marine."

"And then," Nicole said, finishing the thought, "you will seek revenge." He nodded, but turned his eyes away from her. He did not want her to see the hate that burned so fiercely there for the enemy that had stolen his parents, his life, from him to leave him marooned here.

"Reza?" a voice called from the desk area. "Are you in there?"

Nicole was surprised at the immediate change in Reza's expression as a smile lit up his face like a beacon.

"Hi, Wiley!" he called, quickly unlocking the door and letting it swing open. "Hey, I've got someone I want you to meet."

A face poked through the door, and for a moment Nicole was sure it was an enormous apple, left too long to dry, its sun-worn skin crinkled into innumerable peaks and valleys as it aged. The wrinkled face was topped by an unruly mop of gray hair that must have been cut with scissors by the man himself. Peering out from the apple-face was a pair of ice blue eyes that once might have been the object of interest and desire for many a woman, but now were clouded with an expression that left some degree of doubt as to the owner's intelligence.

Those eyes swept from Reza to Nicole, and a mischievous smile crept across the man's face. "You got yourself a lady-friend," he exclaimed, his voice one of neutral innocence, rather than with the lecherous undertones that Reza would have expected from almost anyone else. "Showing her your collection, are you?"

"Yeah, Wiley," Reza nodded, turning to Nicole. "This is Nicole Carré, one of the newbies who came in this morning, and the newest member of our group. Nicole," he gestured toward the old man, "meet William Hickock, Colonel, Confederation Marine Corps, Retired. He's been my mentor and protector since I came to Hallmark," Reza explained. "And in case you were wondering, these are all his books. He brought them with him when he first came here."

Nicole's eyes widened. A collection like this must be worth a fortune.

The old man stuck out his hand, nodding his head toward Reza. "Nice to meet you!" he said with a disarming grin. "All my friends just call me Wiley."

Nicole could not help but smile as she took the man's hand, noting the restrained strength of his grip. "*Enchanté, monsieur*," she said, bowing her head slightly.

As she looked back up at Wiley, she knew that something was not quite right, but she was not sure what it might be. There was something in his voice, or the way he carried himself, slouching slightly as if in acquiescence, that seemed out of character for a former Marine colonel.

Then she noticed the scar that crept away from the man's forehead and into his scalp like a lumpy, pink centipede, and she realized that his last battle – for that surely was where the scar was from – must have very nearly killed him. As it was, it left him less a man than he used to be, with some tiny part of his brain destroyed. She immediately pitied him, but she did not let it show on her face.

But Wiley, slightly brain damaged though he was, was nonetheless quite astute. "Yeah, missy," he told her, his voice wistful as he traced his finger along the scar as it wandered halfway across his skull, "I lost a few marbles, I guess. Lost this, too," he said, rapping on his right leg, the metal prosthesis echoing hollowly.

"But hey, that there's old news," he said, brightening suddenly as if someone had just turned an invisible toy wind-up crank on his back. "What are you all up to?"

"We're watching out for Muldoon again," Reza told him seriously, his voice reflecting as much concern as if a Kreelan attack had been underway. "He really took a fancy to Nicole."

Wiley's face changed for just a moment, so quickly that Nicole might have missed it had she not been looking right at him. A glow of anger flared in his eyes, the kind of chilled anger that came from living a life where death was always just a moment away, a life that was far too short for sorting out the complexities of human evil. She was sure that, had Muldoon been within arm's reach of the old man, he would have killed him in that blink of an eye.

Then it was gone.

"Well isn't that the damnedest thing," Wiley whispered, shaking his head. "I just wish he'd leave you kids alone."

"That's the main reason we're here, Wiley," Reza said, looking sadly at Nicole. Reza had read – memorized, more like it – the biography of Colonel Hickock, and he knew that the tragedy of the man's intellectual demise was little short of monumental. "I was wondering if we might be able to stay with you for a couple days or so."

"Why, sure, Reza!" the old man exclaimed, delighted. "You know you're always welcome. I like company, you know." He gestured with his still-strong hands for them to come with him. "Come on, come on, let's get you settled in downstairs."

They followed him out the door, Reza locking it behind them. They went through the lobby and down some stairs into the building's basement, the bare plasticrete walls echoing their footsteps.

Opening a door that had MAINTENANCE stenciled on it in neat block letters, Wiley showed them into the room beyond. "It ain't much," he said, ushering them in, "but it's home."

Nicole found herself in what looked like an apartment, replete with a tiny kitchen, a separate bedroom, bathroom, and a fluffy, comfortable-looking sofa that took up nearly half of the living room. On the walls, themselves painted a light pastel blue, were holos of ships and people in uniform, even a few actual photographs, all presented in what Nicole guessed were expensive frames. While various other knickknacks could be found throughout the room, everything was neat and orderly, every visible surface clean of dust or the slightest trace of dirt. It was immaculate, but homey, without any of the fastidiousness that was nearly pathological with some people.

Looking at the sofa, she suddenly realized how tired she was. She had forgotten how long she had been awake, and was trying hard not to think of the ordeal she had faced earlier in the day with Muldoon.

"C'mon, honey," Wiley said gently, taking her by the arm. Even with his damaged brain, he could see when someone was exhausted. "Let's get you to bed."

Reza unfolded the sofa into a bed that nearly took up the whole room, quickly spreading out the sheets and blanket wrapped within. Nicole could see that it was an operation he had gone through many times before, and was glad for his quick handling of the matter.

She fell more than lay down on the old mattress, the clean, crisp smell of the sheets penetrating her brain, the downy blanket soft in her hands. Burying her face in the pillow, she closed her eyes.

Reza watched her fall away into sleep, and hoped that her dreams would not be troubled by the events of the day or the trials he was sure would yet come. He found that he liked this girl very much, and vowed to never let her come to harm, regardless of the cost.

THREE

Hallmark's hot summer gave way to fall without any noticeable change. The fall was still warm – hot, on many days – with rain that fell regularly and predictably across huge sections of the planet's three continents. It was an ideal location to grow grain, but offered little else of any strategic value.

And so it was no surprise that Hallmark had turned into a major grain producer, supplying nearly twenty percent of the quota for the sector, enough to feed forty combat regiments and all the ships and logistical support necessary to keep them in action. Much of the initial clearing had been done by machines. But the rock clearers were taken elsewhere after someone had come up with the idea of putting orphans there to build on the initial clearing efforts. Hallmark was safe from attack, they had said, since it had no military installations that might appeal to the Kreelans, who seemed to be far more interested in contesting well-defended worlds.

On the other hand, Reza had often thought, that philosophy had left Hallmark utterly defenseless. But that's the way things had been for the last twenty or more years, and clearing the rocks from the land had become the traditional – and enforced – role of the orphans there.

"Busy hands are happy hands," Reza grunted as he heaved at a rock that must have weighed nearly fifty kilos, trying to pry it from the clutches of the hard earth beneath the loose topsoil. The rains had made the ground a bit less reluctant to give up its rocky treasures, but it was still backbreaking work that had to be done. For only after the rocks were removed and the tilling machines came through, adding nutrients as they did their normal work, would the field resemble something akin to arable land. Now there was only the indigenous steppe grass that blew in the wind, its razor-thin edges a constant hazard to exposed skin.

"What?" Nicole managed through her clenched teeth as she pushed against the rock's other side. She seemed to be doing little more than digging a hole in the ground with her feet as she pushed against the unyielding stone. But at last it started to give way.

"Nothing," Reza sighed as the rock finally came out like a pulled tooth, flopping over onto the ground with a solid thump. "Just philosophizing."

"About what?"

"*Je ne sais pas.*" He smiled at her reaction to his intentionally atrocious accent.

His talent with French had surprised even Nicole, who carried a trace of the linguistic chauvinism that had characterized her forebears. In the months the two had spent together, however, Nicole knew that he spoke it well enough to almost be mistaken for a native. *Well*, she thought to herself with an inner smile, *almost*. She was terribly proud of him.

She grimaced theatrically, wiping her forehead clean of sweat with her bandanna in a sweeping gesture. "You need beaten, *mon ami*," she chided, using a colloquialism she had picked up from Wiley. She sat down against the rock to take a break. "Your instructor has not been so deficient as to allow the language of kings to be so horribly mutilated."

Reza favored her with an impish grin as he looked around at the nearby groups of laboring children, then at the sun. "I think it's time to have lunch," he announced, clapping his hands and rubbing them together as if a truly tasty meal awaited them. He stood up, cupping his hands to his mouth, and shouted, "BREAK!" to several figures off to their right. He repeated it to the left, and the other eleven members of his field team gratefully sat down for their noon meal break. It was the only one they were allowed during their twelve to sixteen hour workday.

Nicole got out the meatloaf sandwiches she made for them that morning. The meatloaf was a spread from a can. Reza had observed drily that it had probably not come from any sort of animal, so probably was not any sort of meat, nor had it ever been part of any kind of loaf. But that was their feast for today. She set the sandwiches out on a white embroidered cloth she always brought with her for the occasion. It was something she had managed to make in her free time, virtually all of which she spent in the library with Reza and Wiley. Making their lunch had been her idea, and the extra work it took made her feel good, and it had since become a kind of tradition. It was a tiny thing that bound them a bit more closely together, staving off a little of the ugliness that filled their lives. Again reaching into her pack, she pulled out two battered metal cups and poured water for the two of them. Then she settled down to wait as Reza went about his noontime ritual.

She watched as he walked toward one pair of his team. He talked with them for a moment as they ate, making sure they were all right, then moved on to the next. He had always made it a point to take care of his people first, something he once told her he had learned from Wiley. On days when there were problems – and there were plenty of those, even on a job as mundane as this – he often did not get to rest or eat at all. The librarian, Mary Acherlein, whom Nicole had instantly liked, once told her that Reza had been a team leader for over a year before Nicole had arrived, despite his young age and Muldoon's best efforts to the contrary. Of course, Muldoon did not try overly hard to get in Reza's way: his team consistently outperformed the others in House 48's field clearing totals, and that made Muldoon look good.

If that was possible, she thought sourly, thankful that the ponderous bulk of a man had left her alone, aside from an occasional visual appraisal that left her skin crawling with the memory of that loathsome first day when she had been trapped under his throbbing mass. She shuddered, pushing away the memory.

Watching as Reza started back toward her, most of his own eating time gone, she could not help but wonder if someday they might not become something more than friends. It was a pleasant thought, a dream that she kept quietly to herself. But for now, she treated him much like a brother who just happened to be very mature for a boy so young. He was still prone to mischief and the other emotional conundrums that plagued children his age, perhaps even more so now that he had someone to express them to, but there was no denying that he was already a young man, and she found herself very attracted to him. *Someday*, she thought.

"Well?" she prompted, handing him a sandwich.

He peered between the thick slabs of bread – one thing they had plenty of – and made a face. "Gross," he said, a grin touching his lips. Nicole batted him in the shoulder. "Everybody's okay. No more than the usual, except for Minkman. Said he had a broken finger on his left hand."

"What did you do?"

Reza laughed. "I told him to use his right hand and not to worry about it." Nicole frowned, sometimes not quite sure if he was joking or not. "Okay, okay. I splinted it for him, too. If he wants more than that before he can get to the infirmary tonight, he has to go to Muldoon, which he did not want to do. I can't imagine why."

"*Bon*," she said. "Now, sit down and eat."

"*Oui, madame*," he said, this time with a perfect La Seyne accent. He plopped down across from her, somehow not getting dirt all over the picnic cloth. Taking a long swallow of water from his cup, he began to devour the first of three sandwiches and an anemic apple that served as dessert. The first day Nicole had offered to pack his lunch for him she had only made one sandwich, and Reza had been more anxious than usual to get back from the fields, this time to the dining hall instead of the library. He had never said a word about it, but she had felt awful when she saw how hungry he was that evening. She had not repeated that mistake since.

She stole a glance at him as he was looking off into the distance at something, the left side of his face turned toward her. Despite the scar that marred his skin, the keepsake left by the Kreelan warrior who had killed his parents, he was a handsome boy. He wasn't gorgeous or glamorous as some children promised to be upon their entry into puberty, but his face and his body radiated his inner strength and spirit. His skin was a golden color, not all of it from the tan from his years of work in the fields. Nor was it quite the olive color often associated with descendants of Terran Mediterranean races, nor was it European. He was all of those, yet none of them. The same was true of his hair. Almost chocolate brown, bleached somewhat by the sun, it was thick and lush, almost oriental in its texture. Haphazardly cut close to his skull when she had first met him, she had taken it upon herself to give him a proper haircut. Now it tapered evenly in the back to his neckline, with his ears and forehead neatly exposed in what she jokingly referred to as House 48's *haute couture* hairstyle.

"You'll be leaving soon," he said quietly.

"What?" she asked, unsure if she had heard him correctly.

"Wiley got your acceptance papers this morning from Lakenheath Training Center," he told her, his eyes focused on the ground. "You maxed out on almost all those tests you took a few months ago. Made you look like kind of a hot shot, I guess. There'll be a ship coming to pick you up on your birthday next week." He smiled, still not looking at her. "You've reached 'free fifteen.'" He finally looked up. His eyes were a confused mixture of relief that she had been accepted and sorrow that she would be leaving him, probably forever. "I... I wanted to tell you as soon as I found out this morning, but..." He trailed off. "I couldn't," he finally whispered. "I didn't want to say it, that you're really going to be leaving. But I couldn't put it off any longer." He offered her a sad smile. "Congratulations, trainee fighter pilot Carré."

Nicole was speechless for a moment, her mouth working, but no words came out. The time had passed so quickly, her brain sputtered. It was too soon. It was impossible.

"Reza..." she managed. And then, like a dam bursting, she began to cry. She wrapped her arms around Reza and held him tight, overcome with joy that her future was not completely bleak, that she had something to look forward to. "Oh, Reza," she exclaimed, her French accent nearly obliterating the Standard words, "this is so wonderful! We can leave this rotten place! And in only a few days! We..."

"I can't leave, remember?" Reza reminded her softly, fighting to hold back tears of his own as he held her. He had lost so many friends to time and circumstance that he thought he would be hardened to this, ready for it when it came, when it was time for her to leave. But he wasn't. He could never be ready for the things he felt now, inside himself. He knew she had to go, knew that it was the only thing for her. But it hurt so much to think of what things were going to be like without her.

In that moment he knew the truth about his feelings. He loved her. He knew he was only a barely pubescent boy with emerging hormones, but he knew in his heart that it was true.

Her voice faded away as the realization forced itself upon her like Muldoon's groping hands.

"*Mon cher,*" she whispered, the joyful tears suddenly becoming bitter and empty. "Oh, Reza, what will you do?"

He tried to smile, failed. "The same as I always do," he choked, shrugging. "I'll make do somehow. I'm just happy that you made it, Nicole," he told her. "As much as it's going to hurt to see you go, I'm so glad for you."

They held each other for a while longer, trying to forestall the bittersweet future that vowed to separate them, brother and sister in a family bound together not by blood, but by trust and love.

Finally, without saying another word, they rose unsteadily to their feet and got back to work.

* * *

Muldoon let the field glasses he had been holding to his eyes slap against his chest, the once bright finish of the instrument long since corroded by hours of being held in his sweaty palms.

He spent a goodly portion of his day watching Gard and his crew from an unobtrusive distance. He especially enjoyed watching the French girl. *Yes*, he thought, licking the sticky sweat from his lips, *especially her*. After the confrontation that very first day, Muldoon had been forced by Reza's tactics to leave them more or less alone. He had taken out his frustrations on his usual victims, although he had never thought of them as such. To Muldoon they were only young children who should have liked him, but did not for some inexplicable reason. But the lust in him for the little wench from La Seyne refused to die. If anything, it grew the more he tried to satisfy his urgings in other ways.

Muldoon had received word through his grapevine that Nicole would be leaving soon, and the diabolical device that served as his brain was churning through possibilities, looking for options, an opening.

Yeah, he thought to himself, feeling his crotch begin to throb, *I'd like to explore an opening, right between the little bitch's legs*. And he would not mind sticking it to her little boy benefactor, either, he thought as his teeth ground together in frustration. Just before he choked the life out of the little bastard.

He turned to get back in the van, his mind still churning, looking for a scenario that would work. He was not worried about the house administrators, or even the Navy ship coming to get the girl. It was the kids themselves, plus the joker that was the old man. Muldoon had always thought him a senile idiot, at least until he had tried to push the old Marine around, threatening him after Wiley had witnessed one of Muldoon's little indiscretions. The ground had never hit Muldoon that hard or fast. When he came to, the old man was sweeping the floor nearby as if nothing had happened. He was a wild card, and one thing Muldoon despised was unpredictability.

His mind began to bubble with frustration. He was usually so good at making plans quickly, and he kicked one broken-arched foot at the steppe grass, watching the dust trail away like smoke.

Like smoke.

And then it came to him. "Oh, that's just rich," he told himself, chuckling softly as he swung his bulk into the driver's seat. "Brother Muldoon," he said, "you certainly do have a way."

He started the engine and drove off, heading for the compound to make the arrangements for the French girl's coming of age.

* * *

Reza frowned. "That Muldoon," he muttered under his breath. "What an idiot."

It was the day before Nicole was to leave. The two of them, plus four others from Reza's team, had been assigned a ridiculously small quadrangle to clear. But it was not the area's size or shape that puzzled Reza, but the location: on all four sides there were quads of wheat that were almost ready to be harvested. Genetically modified over decades from original Earth stock, Hallmark's grain grew taller than Reza could reach with his arms extended over his head and produced four times as much grain per hectare. Normally that didn't matter to him. But now, standing inside this quad, it was impossible to see anything past the wall of gently waving stalks, and it made Reza nervous.

"What difference does it make, *mon ami*?" Nicole asked, reluctantly putting her gloves on. "Rocks are rocks, *non*?"

"Sure," he replied, "but you don't normally bother clearing little patches like this just before the harvest. It's easier to wait until the wheat's been taken out so you can get the rocks through to the road." He remembered how Muldoon had come to pick them up that morning in one of the huge combines, a first in Reza's time on-planet. Neither the large buses that were their normal transport when working far from the house, nor Muldoon's van could penetrate the wheat to get them to the barren quad where they now stood. They had to walk in from the road. And it wasn't his full team, just the six of them.

She touched his shoulder. "Perhaps we should get to work, Reza," she told him quietly, a tentative smile on her lips. "I think perhaps you have other things on your mind that make a little thing seem very big."

Reza looked at her. "Yeah, you're probably right," he sighed. Her leaving was indeed a big thing on his mind, and it did seem to make everything else – the bad things – worse. But a part of his mind still wondered why Muldoon had put them here. It was different, out of his normal routine, and that made Reza worry.

* * *

The morning passed without incident. Reza was working hard on digging out a particularly recalcitrant rock, simultaneously considering the feasibility of a lunch break, when he heard Nicole call to him from where she was digging a meter or so away.

"Reza," she asked, pointing to the north, "what is that?"

He looked up, and his heart tripped in his chest. There was smoke. Lots of it. And close.

"Oh, damn," he hissed, tossing down his pickaxe. His eyes swept the horizon around them, his stomach sinking like a lead weight over a deep ocean trench. Smoke billowed out of all the adjoining quads, as if nearly a combined hectare's worth of wheat had simply decided to ignite.

And he knew that was simply not possible.

"Goddammit!" he cursed. "Drop everything and get over here, now!" he ordered the others, his eyes judging the flames while the touch of the air against his skin helped him gauge the wind. He knew that wheat that was ready for harvest would not normally catch fire too easily, but once it really caught – especially if there was a wind to drive it – it would burn as well as kerosene.

The others joined him and Nicole at a full run. Their eyes were wide with fear. Every child who had worked in the fields for very long knew the danger of fire. Whipped along by the winds, it killed or maimed hundreds of orphans across the planet every year. Those who died were generally the lucky ones, for the house clinics were ill-prepared to deal with major burns, and off-planet medical transport for orphans was hardly considered a priority by the bureaucracies that controlled the planet's operation. The fires, a constant hazard throughout the year, were started by everything from lighting strikes to spontaneous combustion; any of a dozen causes. Not least of which was arson.

Reza called up an image in his mind of the field they were in, a process made difficult because he had not worked this area for nearly two years. Since then, it had been bursting with wheat, and the orphans had nothing to do with that; that was the Hallmark Farm Combine's business.

"There should be a road about a klick south of here," he remembered, the image of the arrow-straight track coming to him from a map of the area he had studied with Wiley a long time back. He looked in the direction he thought the road should be, and was relieved to see that smoke had not yet begun to boil toward the sky.

"We're going to have to move fast," he said, "or the wind'll help the fire kill us. Come on!"

He led them in the direction of the road at a restrained jog so the younger kids could keep up. Moving through the tall wheat was tricky as it was, the stalks grasping at clothes and skin, fouling their legs when it was stepped on. The others followed Reza without complaint or argument, with Nicole bringing up the rear. Reza pushed the pace as fast as he dared, his biggest fear hearing the crackling of a blazing fire but not being able to see where it was coming from. Should they lose their sense of direction, they could find themselves trapped in the middle of an inferno with no escape.

Nicole, last in the line of fleeing refugees, kept looking behind them. Her eyes reflected the licking tongues of the flames now just visible over the tops of the wheat stalks, coming closer under the driving influence of the wind.

The child in front of her – a new girl, Nicole did not know her name – stumbled and fell to her hands and knees. Nicole helped her struggle to her feet, urging her onward. "*Allez! Allez!*" she cried, pushing the girl forward.

"We're almost there!" Reza called from the front. He had spent enough time in and around the fields to have learned how to navigate with a sort of dead reckoning, using the sun's position and his pace count to keep him on track. "Only about fifty meters left!"

A few moments later, he breathed a sigh of relief as he saw the regular outline of the road through the last layers of wheat. He stood to one side and passed the others of his team on through first, giving Nicole a quick hug as she emerged from the trampled trail behind them.

The road would not necessarily protect them from the fire, Reza knew. But at least they could move in a direction opposite to the one that the fire was taking, keeping out of its way.

"Oh," Nicole gasped, her chest heaving with adrenaline and the effort of running what had seemed like such a long way, "*Zut alors*. I did not think–"

"Reza!" someone shrieked. "Look ou–"

The voice was suddenly cut off with a sound Reza knew all too well: the *smack* of a powerful hand striking a child's face.

Darting through the wheat to the road's edge, Reza just had time to see the other children fleeing down the road past Muldoon's van. The field master and three of his goons, his teenage hatchet men, stood in two-man cordons off to either side of where Reza stood, blocking the road. They had let the other children pass, even the one who had tried to warn Reza, because they were not of interest.

For that, at least, Reza was thankful. Without wasting another second, he disappeared back into the wheat, grabbing Nicole's hand.

"Follow me!" he hissed, dragging her along behind him.

"What is it?" she gasped.

"Muldoon," Reza replied, his breath a controlled heaving of his chest as he fought a new path through the wheat. He was desperate to avoid their pursuers, whose footsteps he could hear somewhere behind them, crashing through the stalks. "He brought some friends with him this time."

Nicole quickened her pace.

Muldoon watched as the two older boys, whom the other kids called Scurvy and Dodger, chased Reza and Nicole through the field. Climbing atop a specially fortified portion of the van's roof, Muldoon was high enough that he could see the bending and weaving of the stalks as his remote hunters closed on their quarry. The older boys were able to make better time through the wheat, especially with the trail the Gard kid left behind him. A smile of certainty crept across Muldoon's face. Gard wasn't going to get away this time, and neither was the girl. It had been easy to track their progress to the road. Now he would track them as his human hounds chased them down.

He glanced down at the other boy waiting below, whom he had dubbed Big John in honor of a certain very important part of the boy's anatomy. Muldoon had given him his own special touch over ten years ago, and the boy had been unflinchingly loyal ever since.

Big John mutely smiled back.

Reza wove through the wheat in an intricate pattern that he had learned from other kids when playing in the fields. That was in the days before Wiley had convinced him to spend that time in the library, earning himself a ticket off of Hallmark that few of the other kids would ever receive.

While it appeared to Muldoon that Scurvy and Dodger were gaining, Reza was keeping them at about the same distance, but at a cost. He and Nicole, already flushed from fleeing the fire – which still boomed and crackled around them – were getting tired. The weaving that confused their pursuers also meant that Reza and Nicole had to take at two or three steps to Scurvy and Dodger's one or two, the time being made up by the older boys hunting around for their path after missing one of Reza's sharp turns. Worse, Reza now had no idea where they were.

"Reza," Nicole gasped behind him, "we cannot run forever!"

"Don't stop!" he ordered grimly. His legs and lungs were burning as hot as the flames that consumed the wheat around them. Some of the smoke was now settling toward the ground, causing him to gag. "Keep going!"

Without warning they burst into an open quad. Reza, his legs accustomed to trampling through the wheat stalks, lost his footing and fell to the ground, skinning his palms and knees.

"Damn!" he cursed, grabbing Nicole's hands as she helped him up.

They were only thirty meters or so across the quad – less than a quarter of the way – when their pursuers appeared behind them.

"Give it up, maggot!" Scurvy cried. His acne scarred face was flushed with the exertion of running. "Game's over."

"Save it, Gard," Dodger chimed in. His lopsided eyes, one placed nearly two centimeters higher than the other, were bright with anticipation, and his brutishly large hands flexed at his sides. "You're good in the wheat, man, but you're dead meat in the open." He smiled, showing perfect vid-star teeth that were completely out of place in his lumpy face.

Reza slowed at the boy's words, then stopped.

"Reza!" Nicole cried, "What are you doing?"

"He's right," Reza told her as he caught his breath. "Those two bastards are quick. They'll catch us before we get to the wheat on the other side."

"Then what do we do?" Nicole whispered. Her eyes were fixed on the two approaching boys who now merely sauntered, apparently sure that she and Reza could not get away.

Reza smiled thinly, the fear in his eyes overshadowed by determination. "I'll have to use my secret weapon," he replied cryptically.

She watched as he reached into the little cloth bag that he always kept at his belt. Knowing what was in it – a few polished stones that she thought were pretty, some scraps of paper with names of books written on them, and a strip of leather that Reza sometimes did a parody of jumping rope with – did not make her feel any better. But her trust in him, especially now, was implicit.

Unhurriedly, he withdrew the leather strip and one of the stones, a spherical piece of quartz that he had meticulously ground and polished with the tools in Wiley's little handyman shop in the admin building's basement.

"Stand behind me," he said quietly, and Nicole gladly moved herself a few paces back, putting Reza between herself and the two advancing boys, who were now about twenty meters away.

"What's that supposed to be?" Scurvy demanded mockingly. "A wimp-sized whip?"

"Maybe he's gonna hang himself," Dodger said, laughing. "Too bad there's no tree, or we could give him a hand."

Reza paid them no attention as he placed the stone carefully in the center of the leather strap, which Nicole now saw formed a perfect pouch for the sparkling rock. He let it dangle to his side, his right wrist beginning to flex, judging the weight and response of the sling and its ammunition.

He looked up to see Scurvy and Dodger still approaching at a leisurely pace, confident in their victory. Reza's mouth was compressed in a thin line of concentration, his eye calculating the distance and speed with the accuracy of a computerized laser range finder.

"Reza," Nicole said quietly.

"Shhh," he responded softly, his mind now focused on Scurvy. In precisely measured movements, he began to rock the sling. As it built up momentum, he brought it up into an orbit above his head, the sling now a brown blur as it whirled around like a propeller blade.

Reza had become an expert in the sling's use under Wiley's tutelage, and sometimes used it to focus himself when his mind seemed listless, or just to have fun. He and the old man would have contests, setting up old food cans at various distances and then trying to see who could knock the most down the fastest. Wiley won most of the time, but Reza never pushed too hard just to win. To him, it was the camaraderie that counted, the togetherness, not who bested whom. Wiley was, in fact if not in blood, his father, and had been since the first day Reza came to this world. It was Wiley who met him at the spaceport, Muldoon having fallen ill that day, and the old man had taken the boy under his wing as if Reza was his only begotten son. It was one of the few twists of fate that had gone in Reza's favor, and he had given thanks for Wiley's patronage every day since then.

But it was now, here in a vacant quad in the middle of a burning wheat field, that the games of the past were about to show their dividends.

Scurvy and Dodger had taken notice of the whirling leather, but they had no idea what it was or what it could do. Wiley had never shown his little toy to any of the other children, and Reza had carried on the tradition.

Until now.

"Maybe he thinks he's just gonna take off," Dodger joked.

Scurvy smiled as his hand reached into the rear left pocket of his jumper, extracting a knife that Reza easily recognized, even at this distance. Illegal on most worlds because of the harder-than-diamond metallurgy that made them the galaxy's best edged weapons, the Kreelan blade now in Scurvy's hands was undoubtedly a gift bestowed on him by Muldoon. The boy's arrogant smile grew larger as he turned the knife in his hand, the blade winking with the reflected light of the sun.

With a last mental calculation, one end of the sling slipped from Reza's fingers, releasing the stone in a straight line tangent to the whirling circle over Reza's head. The buzzing of the sling sighed to a stop as it fell, empty, to Reza's side.

Scurvy had time to blink once before the stone, about the size of a large marble but much heavier, hit him precisely between the eyes. The impact staved in his forehead and drove a splinter of bone into his brain. His sightless eyes fluttered upward as his body collapsed to the ground, twitched once, and then lay still.

There was utter, complete silence in the quad. Even the crackling of the fire seemed muted.

"Son of a bitch," Dodger whispered, looking at his fallen companion. He looked at the little white rock that now lay on the ground near Scurvy's head, partly covered with his blood.

The humming of the sling began again as Reza readied his next salvo.

But Dodger was not as dull-witted as Reza had hoped. Fortunately forgetting the knife still clutched in Scurvy's dead hand, he burst into an all-out charge at Reza, his legs eating up the distance between them as Reza readied for another shot.

"Run, Nicole!" he cried.

"But, Reza–"

"Run, dammit!" he shouted as he loosed his second shot at less than ten meters range.

Nicole watched as Dodger earned his nickname, his torso performing an uncanny twist as Reza released the sling. Had Reza not aimed at the boy's center of mass rather than his head, the rock would have missed completely. As it was, it hit Dodger in the left shoulder with a hearty thump. It was enough to splinter the bone in his shoulder joint, making him stagger with pain, but it only slowed him down for a moment.

Nicole turned and fled.

Reza did not waste time trying to finesse another shot with the sling. He reached down and picked up the nearest rock and hurled it at Dodger, hitting him in the stomach and doing no damage other than making the boy even angrier. Then he turned to follow Nicole across the quad and into the wheat.

"You're dead, you little bastard!" Dodger shrieked as he held his injured shoulder, the bone splinter grinding painfully as he raced after his quarry.

* * *

Nicole was terrified. She had lost Reza, and now was lost herself. Running blindly through the wheat, her nose clotted with the smoke that swirled through the fields, she had no idea which way to go. She just ran.

Stopping for a moment to catch her breath, she wondered if she should call out to Reza. But no, she decided angrily, that would alert Dodger to her presence, and Reza might even be dead.

"I never should have left you," she cursed herself, angrily wiping away the tears of guilt that sprang to her eyes. Memories of her mother, dead because Nicole had not thought to warn her of a lethal danger, rose unbidden. Perhaps, she thought miserably, she and Reza could have beaten Dodger. She knew she should have stayed with him...

"*Merde!*" she cried quietly, pulling at her hair in self-recrimination. She had to find a way out of this, she had to find Reza. Looking at the sun, now past its zenith, she tried to guess which way to go. Picking a direction, hoping it was the right way, she headed toward where she thought the road to the orphanage might be.

Such was her surprise when, after only a few tens of meters, she burst from the wheat onto the road that led to the orphanage. Falling to her knees, she sobbed in relief, at the same time wondering what had happened to Reza, knowing that she had to find help.

"Well, I'll be," she heard a familiar voice coo from nearby. "Look what we have here."

She looked up just in time to see Muldoon's obesity blot out the sun, his shadow falling across her face like a burial shroud.

* * *

Reza's time was almost up. His legs were ready to give out, and he could hear Dodger's labored breathing close behind him. No number of maze tricks was going to save him now.

"Got you, you little freak!" Dodger cried as he latched onto the collar of Reza's shirt.

Reza tried to struggle out of it, but it was too late. He collapsed to the ground, quickly rolling onto his back to free his hands for his last great act of defiance.

Dodger straddled him, pinning him to the ground. Balling up his good fist, he said, "You're gonna pay, you little fuck," before he slammed it into Reza's face.

Reza did his best to ward off the piston-blows that rained down with unerring precision, but no war was ever won through defense alone. Leaving his face completely open to attack, Reza shot his own fist upward while Dodger was cocking his arm for another blow, managing to land a glancing hit to the older boy's injured shoulder.

Dodger let out a cry of agony, and Reza bucked his body upward and to the side like a wrestler fighting a pin, squirming from between Dodger's legs. Reza plunged away into a curtain of smoke as Dodger tried to get back on his feet.

Through the slits left him by the swelling around his battered eyes, Reza suddenly became aware that he had led himself into a trap. Flames danced all around him and his skin prickled with the heat. His nose, accustomed now to the acrid smell of smoke, could no longer screen it from his lungs, and he began to gag and cough.

"Where are you, you little son of a bitch?" he heard Dodger call from somewhere off to his left. "Come on out!"

He can't see me, Reza told himself. The smoke was a much better screen than was the wheat itself. *Now, if only I can get myself out of here*, he worried. Carefully avoiding the ravenous flames and Dodger's angry searching, Reza managed to work his way out of the fiery trap.

Behind him, lost in the smoke, he heard Dodger's voice calling, calling...

* * *

Nicole lay spread-eagled on her back inside the closed van. Muldoon's silent assistant had stuffed a rag in her mouth and bound her hands and feet to the cargo tie-downs with heavy tape. She quivered in fear, her eyes locked on the rolls of blubber emerging from Muldoon's uniform as he fought with the overstressed velcro down its front. The van was filled with the mingled scent of his body odor and the breath mints he always chewed before taking one of his pleasure rides. The smell alone made her want to gag.

The boy who had taped her to the floor had only smiled at her, no matter how much she had struggled. He had not hit her or threatened her, but treated her like she was amiss for not wanting to participate willingly, as if sure that she would chastise herself later for being so silly. He kneeled in the back of the vehicle, near her head, his eyes gleaming knowingly, as if she were about to learn a very important secret, a very special one.

"Ah," Muldoon gasped as the uniform suddenly flew open down to his crotch, releasing his manhood from its fleshy confines. "I've been waiting for you for a long time, honey," he said in quick gasps as he waddled forward on his knees, taking up station between her legs. His hands groped under her blouse, and he sighed as he squeezed her breasts. "They've grown since last time," he said over the muffled screaming that made its way through the sock stuffed in her mouth. "Did you know that?"

His hands, shaking from the adrenaline rushing through his system, worked their way down, down over her belly, then grabbed roughly between her legs, his fingers probing through her panties.

Nicole closed her eyes and fought against the wave of nausea that would kill her with the gag in her mouth. But she knew that suffocating on her own vomit would be better than succumbing to what this man had in mind. She squirmed as his fingers grabbed the elastic waistband of the flimsy panties the orphanage issued, his dirty, untrimmed fingernails scraping her tender pubis as he began to pull them down, to tear them off.

"You'll like it," he soothed. "I know I wi–"

The last word was cut off by the sudden grating of the van's cargo door as it slammed open, letting the bright glare of the sun shine into the darkened interior and momentarily blinding its occupants.

"What the hell?" Muldoon roared, whirling around like a rutting walrus facing off against a competitor, his erect penis pointing like an accusing finger toward the man who stood in the doorway.

It was Wiley. But in Muldoon's state of hormonal confusion, he did not notice the eyes that burned from under the knitted brow or the expression that had once belonged to a fierce warrior, a man who had killed – and, in a way, died – for God and country. He wasn't looking at Wiley. He was staring into the face of a colonel of the Confederation Marine Corps.

"Close that door and get out of here, you senile old fart!" Muldoon screamed, his face turning a beet red as he reached for the door. His hand faltered when he caught a glimpse of something metallic in the old Marine's hand.

Without saying a word, Colonel Hickock pumped two rounds from the pistol into Muldoon's skull. The tiny flechettes minced the big man's brain as they ricocheted within the bony structure, lacking enough velocity to make a clean exit out the back.

A third red eye gracing his forehead – the only evidence of injury and proof of the colonel's marksmanship – Muldoon somersaulted out of the van like an obscene high diver, his twitching body flopping to the dirt like a two hundred kilo bag of fertilizer.

"Come on out, son," Hickock said in a low growl that Nicole would not have recognized without seeing the man's lips move in time to the words.

Big John, his face sad now, crawled out of the van as he was told, neither his face nor his body reflecting any sign of defiance or resistance. And when the colonel turned away toward Nicole, sure that the boy was not a threat, Big John walked into the wheat field toward where the hungry fires burned. With his lover and benefactor dead, his own twisted and defiled soul had no more desire to live. Unseen and unheard, he cast himself into the flames.

"Wiley!"

The old man turned to see Reza huffing up the road from where he had emerged from the blazing fields, his face mottled with bruises and caked with blood.

"Where's Nicole?" he gasped, running up to the van, "Muldoon, he–" Then he caught sight of the mound of flesh lying motionless on the ground and the gun in Wiley's hand. "Oh, Jesus."

"Better help your girl, son," the old man said slowly, shaking his head as if something was in his ear. "And take this," he handed Reza the gun. "I won't be able to keep track of it much longer. The other kids," he went on groggily, "they came and told me what happened, and..."

The man who was Colonel Hickock never finished what he set out to say.

Taking the gun, Reza watched with soul-deep sorrow as the man's eyes suddenly transformed to reflect the good-natured innocence of Wiley the janitor. All traces of Colonel Hickock that had been there just a moment before disappeared like mist under a hot sun.

"Where's Nicole?" Wiley asked, cocking his head and looking around as if he had just come on the scene.

"Oh, God," Reza gasped, leaping into the van, terrified of what he might find. "Nicole!"

Relieved to find that she still had most of her clothes on, Reza carefully pried away the tape that covered her mouth, pulling the roll of gauze bandage out of her throat. Then he freed her hands and feet.

"Reza," she choked, hugging him so hard he heard one of his ribs crack. "Reza, I was afraid...I thought you had died."

He kissed her, and then held her even tighter, rocking her back and forth. He never wanted to let her go.

"You know what they say about bad pennies," he whispered, not willing to let on just how close he had come to losing it out there, how close he had come to losing her. "They just keep turning up."

"If Wiley had not shown up," she shuddered, "Muldoon would have–"

"Shh," Reza whispered in her ear. "Don't think about that." He looked down at Muldoon's bloated corpse. "It's over now. For good."

"Come on, kids," Wiley said quietly, his child-like eyes watching the smoke as the wind shifted back toward them, the dark curls billowing into the sky. Even in his senile state, he was no fool. There were no firefighters on Hallmark. The fires would be left to burn themselves out, and anyone caught in them would be dead or horribly maimed. "I think we'd better be getting back."

Reza helped Nicole out of the van, careful to keep her clear of Muldoon's stiffening body. She paused to give it a single look, just to make sure he was really and truly dead. Satisfied, she let Reza lead her away.

Arms around each other's waists, the three of them made their way back to Wiley's battered utility truck. They were a tiny family with no home, but with enough love to make life worth living on any world.

FOUR

Mon cher Reza,

Things are going so fast here. I have been here only ten months, and already I have begun the real flight training, my head now filled with tactics and maneuvers that we will only now begin to apply. I made my first flight yesterday – with an instructor, of course – and might be able to solo in another twenty flight hours.

I cannot tell you how exciting it is to fly! To be so free, strapped to such a powerful machine (*oui*, even the tiny trainers they use here!) is like nothing I have ever imagined. I have spent many hours in the simulators, but they do not do justice to the real thing. My only regret is that you are not here to share in my happiness. I know you would love it.

As you suspected, I have many 'suitors,' as you call them, but I have not the time for them. To study and learn to fly and fight is all I allow myself to be interested in, for I am determined to be the best pilot in my class. Perhaps later I will consider such things, but we have gone through too much getting me here, *non*? I will not throw that away for anything, ever.

I must go now, my brother. The Officer of the Deck is shouting for lights out, and I am so very tired. The days sometimes are so long here that it reminds me of working the fields! I will write again as soon as I can, probably next week after a class exercise that is coming up.

Please, Reza, take care of yourself and give my love to Wiley. I have leave coming up for next month and hope to find a transport to Hallmark so I may visit. I will let you know. Please – write when you can. Sometimes it is all that keeps me going.

All my love,
Nicole

Reza read the letter several times, as he always did, before he folded the paper and put it in his breast pocket. Mary, the librarian, was hardly liberal when it came to printing out hard copies of personal mail (paper – even synthetic – was very expensive), but she made an exception for Reza. He did not even bother to read Nicole's letters on the vid-screen when they first arrived, but printed them out straight away. Holding the paper in his hand when he read her words made her seem a bit closer, more real. They had agreed to write this way, rather than send personal vids. Most of the other kids thought he was crazy and ridiculously old-fashioned, but somehow it made Nicole seem more real to him. His hand strayed to the small silver crucifix around his neck, his most prized possession that he never let out of his sight. It was her gift to him on the tear-filled day when she left for Lakenheath, nearly a year ago now.

He looked out the window to watch the kids file by on the way to their noonday meal, and he wondered if Nicole would even recognize this place when she came to visit on her first leave. *When she came home*, he told himself. For that is what he had finally decided Hallmark was: home.

Muldoon's death had sparked a high-level Confederation investigation of the orphanage system and the Hallmark Farming Combine, and had resulted in nothing short of a miraculous change in the lives of the orphans. The field work, a back-breaking tradition for more than twenty years, was abolished as cruel child labor. The chief administrators of the orphanage system – not just at House 48, but all across the planet – were interviewed, cross-examined, and dismissed if they could not answer the commission's questions satisfactorily. Many of them now found themselves in prison at the sort of hard labor that the children had endured.

The farm combine itself received a tremendous fine for its part in the exploitation of the children, and more than a few of its senior managers also wound up in Confederation prisons.

All this was no surprise to Reza after he had first seen the makeup of the commission: thirty-five Navy and Marine Corps officers, with a handful of civilians from the General Counsel. Though he had been retired for quite some time, the name of Colonel William Hickock still carried a lot of weight. The Marine Corps took care of its own.

Now the orphans enjoyed three solid meals a day (although the food wasn't much better than it used to be, Reza lamented), went to school full time, and did not have to go to the fields anymore except to play baseball.

Reza had to shake his head at that, remembering how Wiley had taught them how to play the ancient Earth game in one of the open, dusty quads. The children, their minds focused on futile toil for so long, ate up what Wiley showed them. Soon there were baseball games going on all over the complex every day after school using bats, balls, and mitts that the older kids put together in the machine shops that were part of the physical plant and power generator station.

The game had spread like wildfire, and kids had been sent from almost every other house to see how it was played. There was even talk of forming a league with equipment donated by the Marine Corps. Reza was terrible when he came up to bat, but he could pitch better than anyone else in his house, and was looking forward to meeting the kids from other houses.

It would be a first for all of them.

Yes, Reza thought, *things certainly have changed*. He now spent time in the library not only because he wanted to, but because Mary had appointed him chief assistant librarian. He attended school, alternating half days and full days, depending on the courses that were being taught by the new instructors who had been brought in. He spent the rest of his time before dinner working the desk and helping the other kids who had begun to mob the little building, so much so that the administration was thinking about expanding it. Preparing school papers, reading tutorials, or just for fun, Reza had never seen so many kids here before. They had never had time under the old regime, and Reza often wondered why the combine had financed the library in the first place, it had been so little used.

Fate certainly could be fickle, he told himself wonderingly as he watched the animation on the faces of the other children, where before one could only see exhausted eyes and blank expressions.

"We're human again," he said quietly to himself, unconsciously patting Nicole's letter in his pocket

Getting up from his desk in Mary's office, Reza headed out to answer the bell at the front desk, thinking that his remaining time on Hallmark wasn't going to be so bad after all.

* * *

Thirty million kilometers away, deep in the blackness beyond the orbit of Hallmark around its yellow star, a gravity well appeared at a point without a name or special significance, warping the void around it into a vortex of space and time. As the well deepened toward infinity, it created a fleeting, transient event horizon, and matter was instantaneously injected through the tiny rift in the fabric of the universe.

A solitary Kreelan warship, an enormous battlecruiser that dwarfed any vessel ever built by Man, emerged from hyperspace. Her sublight drive activated, and she turned her raked prow onto a trajectory toward the nearby planet. Her sensors reached out before her like ethereal hounds sniffing out their quarry, searching for the planetary defense network orbiting the human world.

On what humans would have called the ship's bridge, a warrior priestess sat in the throne-like chair from which she commanded the great vessel and its crew. She tapped her ebony talons in a gesture of anticipation that had been one of her trademarks for many cycles of the Empress Moon, the sharp rapier tips eroding even the resilient metal of the chair's arm. She had left her mark in many ships of the Fleet in the hundred and more cycles of service she had rendered unto her Empress. But this ship, the *Tarikh-Da,* had always been her favorite. It was the greatest warship the Empire had ever built.

She had been greatly honored when the Empress had chosen her for this mission, for it was the first of its kind in the war against the humans. For all the cycles since the Empire had made contact with them, the ships of the Empress had come to the enemy's planets to do battle. They came to destroy these lesser beings in feats of combat to honor their ruler and expunge the plague of yet another species not worthy of Her spirit.

But this was to be different. There would be killing, yes, but only the older ones. The pups, the young, these were to be spared. They were to be taken back to the Empire.

She glanced at the tactical display, noting with satisfaction that hers was the only ship within parsecs of this *human enclave*. Not that it would have mattered, she thought. The Empire's flagship could annihilate a fleet of lesser vessels, but had never been unleashed upon the humans; it would have offered the Children of the Empress no challenge, no honor.

"Their defenses have activated," the weapons officer reported. "Orbital batteries are reorienting toward our approach vector." A pause as she studied her instruments. "There are no planetary emplacements."

Which they already knew, the priestess thought to herself. She nodded toward her subordinate, pleased with her diligence. Prudence required that they be sure. Humans would never have made such good opponents had they been perfectly predictable.

"Very well," she replied. "You may deal with them at your leisure, Mar'ya-Nagil." She did not have to add that the ship's main batteries were to remain silent; the huge guns would not only destroy any satellite defenses, but the planet's surface below, as well. "Report to me when the defenses are destroyed."

"Yes, Tesh-Dar," the young warrior replied, proud that the priestess was again in command of her vessel, the ship on which she had spent most of her own life. She turned to her task as if the Empress herself had given the command.

Tesh-Dar, high priestess of the Desh-Ka, watched the golden planet grow larger in the huge three-dimensional display before her. One hand softly drummed on the command chair, while the other reflectively probed the scar that stretched down across her left eye.

* * *

Reza was putting books back on the shelves when the raid sirens began to wail. He looked up, wondering at the sound. Drill sirens erupted frequently enough, their goat-like bleating the butt of many jokes among adults and children alike.

But this was no drill. The low, mournful growl of the raid siren boomed from a rickety tower atop the main admin building, then rose to a screeching pitch that set the windows shuddering before dropping back again.

A chill slithered its way up Reza's spine and froze him in place for a moment. His gaze met with several others nearby, all of them welded to their seats or the floor where they stood as the siren began to climb toward a deafening crescendo once again.

Then pandemonium erupted. Children and adults broke free of their momentary paralysis and began to flee. They poured from the library stacks like forest animals driven before a blazing fire, tossing about whatever they were holding like plastic confetti.

"Reza!"

He heard his name called above the commotion as people pushed through the exits and into the street beyond. The children headed for the shelter while the adults ran for the Territorial Army armory to draw their weapons.

"Reza! Where are you?"

He looked stupidly at the armload of books he was still carrying, suddenly realizing that picking up *Canton's Sonnets: A Jubilee Collection* probably was not terribly important at the moment, if for no other reason than the collection was filled with uniquely ghastly verse.

"Here, Mary!" he called, carefully putting the books down on a shelf before running to the banister that overlooked the first floor atrium.

"Reza, make sure there isn't anyone left up there, will you?" she asked, her face flushed with excitement and anxiety. "Hurry, dear, we've got to get to the shelter!" The younger children were gathered around her like ducklings to their mother, their faces registering the fear of the adults who were now running headlong to their defense posts.

Reza called back, "Go ahead and get started. I'll meet you there!"

Mary looked toward the door, then back at Reza, indecision checking her. Reza was mature for his age, but she was not sure if she should leave a boy not quite fourteen years old to his own devices in an emergency like this.

"Go on, Mary," he called quickly, deciding the matter for her. "I'll be all right."

Mary finally nodded and began herding the preschoolers and the dozen or so numbed teens out of the lobby and into the street, forming them into a line that she aimed at the huge shelter blast door a block away. A stream of bodies was already pouring into it.

"Be careful!" she cautioned him.

He waved, then turned to begin his task. Starting at the end of the second floor that was bounded by a wall and no adjoining rooms, he worked his way through the stacks, noting with amazement the number of books, disks, and other things that had wound up on the floor. It was as if an army of gremlins had declared war on his tiny domain, flinging to the floor everything they could get their tiny invisible hands on.

"God, what a mess," he murmured to himself as he continued to weave up and down the aisles, his eyes darting all around him to make sure there wasn't anyone hiding behind a cart or under a desk.

Having finished clearing the upstairs, he paused a moment to take a quick look at the sky through the windows. Everything looked normal to him: the same pale blue sky, a few scudding clouds, and the ever present fiery ball that was Hallmark's sun.

He turned away just in time to avoid being blinded by a flash that erupted from sunward and threw his shadow deep into the library's atrium.

Reacting instinctively, he dove for the nearest cover he could find, a study carrel next to the teen non-fiction section, and waited for a blast wave to come rolling across the fields from whatever had caused the explosion. A dozen seconds later came but a single thunderclap, then several more explosions that sounded like huge fireworks.

"Orbital bombardment," he muttered, daring to open one eye to peek toward the window. But nothing was visible on this side of the building.

He got up and quickly continued his sweep of the library, finishing up in the basement.

"Wiley?" he called, opening the door to his surrogate father's apartment. "Wiley? Are you here?" Quickly checking all the rooms, Reza satisfied himself that the old Marine was not there.

"Probably in the shelter," he told himself as he headed back out into the hall and bounded up the stairs into the lobby. His own feelings about the shelter were clear: while they had undoubtedly saved many lives, he still had nightmares about the one he was in on New Constantinople that had been breached. It had been a death trap, and he did not think he would be able to willingly lock himself into such a giant sarcophagus again.

As he came around the last row of books and past the desk, he caught sight through one of the tall thin windows of a black cloud rising in the direction of the spaceport. He skidded to a stop. Leaning forward, his quickened breath fogged the glass as he looked outside.

That's what the flash and explosions were, he thought grimly. A single salvo from the attacking force had obliterated the spaceport and any interceptors it could have launched, had there been any. The two defenseless grain transports there had been reduced to molten heaps of slag. Their internal explosions had sent debris, including thousands of tons of wheat from their holds, into the air to fall onto the parched fields, which were now burning out of control.

He turned his attention to House 48 itself. The complex looked dead. Nothing outside moved except the Confederation flag, which fluttered in the light breeze with all the vigor of an unenthused geriatric. The street and walkways were deserted, people having hastened somewhere else before the inevitable landing began.

Perhaps the drills will pay off, Reza thought hopefully as he watched the sky. Maybe everyone managed to get to their posts and could protect this rock from whatever the Kreelans had to throw against them, at least until the Navy could bring in some real Marines to help.

But then white streaks appeared in the sky, trailing behind tiny pinpoints that bobbed erratically as they descended: the condensation trails of incoming assault boats. Reza hissed a curse at them, wishing them to fall from the sky like rocks and crush themselves against the unyielding soil of the fields, spattering their death-dealing passengers into lifeless jelly.

He stood there, counting them as they wound their way down, some arcing far away over the horizon toward the other houses and the few actual settlements Hallmark could boast. His hopes withered as he counted more and more, finally dying out completely as he reached fifty. And still more trails swarmed from the sky.

"Oh, God," he moaned. Hallmark's tiny Territorial Army – more than half of them untrained teenage orphans – could field a little over two thousand soldiers across the entire planet. But even if they had all reached their positions, and Reza doubted they had, it would not be enough. Not nearly enough.

The crackle of light weapon fire startled him. He looked to his right just in time to see a group of six camouflaged human figures diving for cover behind one of the thick stone fences in the House 48 complex.

A line of enemy warriors suddenly appeared out of the waving stalks of wheat at the end of town, coming in behind the humans crouched by the wall. Not being professional soldiers or killers from birth as were their opponents, the squad of defenders did not realize that they were being flanked. For the Kreelans, they were nothing more than a target of opportunity.

"No!" Reza shouted, banging his fists on the glass in a futile attempt to warn the defenders as the Kreelans filtered through an old gap in the wall that had never been repaired, their ebony armor glinting with Death's promise. "Look behind you!" He watched helplessly as the encirclement began to close like a hangman's noose, and he wished desperately for some way to warn them.

But it was too late. The Kreelans swept down upon the unsuspecting amateur soldiers like vultures converging on a dying man, too weak and confused to defend himself from their frenzied slashing and tearing. Reza watched the gleam of the blades as they hacked and pierced their victims, the Kreelans disdaining the use of energy weapons in any fight at close quarters.

He thought he saw a soldier reach out a bloody arm toward him, his face contorted in a plea for help, for mercy. In that instant, he was sure that the face was his father's.

Reza closed his eyes as the blade fell.

* * *

Wiley was lying on his back under the old truck, tinkering with one of the servos that acted as a brake motor on the left rear wheel when he heard the thunder of the attack on the spaceport.

"What the devil?" he cried, banging his head hard on the old hauler's frame as he tried to sit up. Gasping in pain, he flopped back down on the dolly, his hands clutching his temples as his head threatened to burst with pain. "Lord of the Universe," he muttered, blinking his eyes.

But the eyes were no longer those of Wiley the janitor. They were hard and commanding, as the body and mind once had been. When the sound of the two grounded transports blowing apart reached his ears a moment later, he reacted as if a different man had inherited the old body. Without hesitation, he pulled himself completely under the truck in case the ceiling of the garage collapsed.

When it was clear that he was in no immediate danger, he moved out from under the truck with a grace and speed extraordinary for a man his age, moving his artificial leg with the finesse of a dancer. After hitting the switch that opened the garage's rust-streaked articulated door, he jumped into the truck's cab and started backing out through the still-opening door into the blinding sunlight beyond.

He raced down the rough track that connected the garage complex with House 48's main buildings a few kilometers away, keeping his eyes on the sky. He ground his teeth when he saw the telltale streaks appear that heralded a landing with boats only, no decoys. He muttered a curse, knowing that the Kreelans must have been completely confident of an easy victory to leave such targets open to anti-air defenses, had any existed.

But this was Hallmark, not Ballantyne, or Sevastopol', or Earth. The keen military mind that had temporarily retaken its proper place in the battered skull knew that Hallmark was about as easy a target as an invader could wish for. The Kreelans always preferred more heavily defended planets, but it was no excuse for leaving a world like this one so lightly defended. With the orbital satellites gone, there was nothing standing between the invaders and the children but Hallmark's joke of a Territorial Army. They didn't stand a chance.

With a white-knuckled grip on the steering wheel, Colonel William Hickock raced toward House 48 as the first exchanges of ground fire began.

* * *

"Mary, the door has to be closed!" the man said, his voice flushed with fear as his finger hovered over the oversized red button. It was the emergency control for the massive vault's blast doors and glowed like a flickering coal.

"But Reza hasn't come back from the library!" she protested hotly, prepared to come to blows with the man if his finger moved any closer to the door controls.

"Look behind you, woman," the man demanded, pointing over Mary's shoulder with his other hand. "There's nearly a thousand people in here, the Blues are popping rounds off out there, and you want me to keep this damned thing open?"

"What's going on?" a steely voice suddenly demanded.

They turned back to the doorway to see Wiley striding across the hash-marked frame of the meter-thick blast door.

"Why isn't this door closed, Parsons?" he growled. Wiley leaned past the open-mouthed Parsons to hit the button himself. The enormous door immediately began to cycle closed.

"But Wiley," Mary blurted, suddenly realizing that the man before her wasn't the one who normally wore this body, "Reza's still out there!"

The old colonel's eyes narrowed. "Where?"

"In the library," she said. "I asked him to make sure everyone else got out. He said he–"

Wiley did not wait for her to finish. In one smooth motion he snatched the flechette rifle from Parsons and disappeared back out the door as it closed.

"Hey!" Parsons shouted indignantly after him. "That's mine!"

But he did not try to pursue the old man as the door thrummed into its lock, the huge bolts driving home to seal them in, and the enemy out.

They hoped.

* * *

Reza found himself frozen at the window, watching the enemy's advance. The landing boats had set down in a rough circle around the house complex, and the warriors they had been carrying were now emerging from out of the wheat like black-clad wraiths, their armor bristling with weapons. He couldn't hear any more firing, and figured that the last of the defenders had been mopped up. It had been a massacre.

That was why Reza had decided not to make a run for the shelter. There was no point. Assuming he was not cut down on the way there, he would certainly be trapped in a tomb that the Kreelans could open without too much difficulty. The shelter's vault should hold them off for a while, but not nearly long enough for human reinforcements to arrive.

Only one thing really puzzled him: why hadn't the Kreelans used their ships' guns to blast the vault like they did the freighters at the spaceport? Why go to the trouble of making a landing at all?

He was startled by the sound of small arms fire from right outside the library, followed by someone crashing through the front door, knocking the smoothly turning cylinder off its bearings.

Dropping without a sound to the floor under the heavy desk he had dragged near the upstairs windows, he waited for the inevitable.

"Reza!" he heard a voice unexpectedly shout from below. "Are you here, boy?"

Reza thought the voice sounded vaguely familiar, but he could not quite place it. Not knowing that the Kreelans had never been known to use such tricks to lure humans into a trap, like a timid snake he slowly slithered toward the banister to take a cautious look.

"Son?" the voice shouted again.

"Wiley?" Reza asked incredulously as he saw the old man crouching near the front door. "Is that you?"

"Lord of All, son!" he shouted. He gestured sharply for Reza to come to him. "Get your butt down here! We've got to get out of this place–"

A Kreelan warrior suddenly leaped through the damaged entryway, rolling with catlike agility to her feet.

In the blink of an eye, Wiley's finger convulsed on the trigger of his flechette rifle, hitting the Kreelan's torso armor with half a dozen rounds that killed her instantly. The impact flung her body against the wall. Her mouth still open in a silent snarl, she slumped to the floor, her talons twitching at the tips of her armored fingers.

With a pirouette that Reza thought should have been impossible for a man with one stiff, artificial leg, Wiley turned and fired another volley into the warrior's partner, whose shoulder armor had caught on the lip of the canted entry cylinder door and prevented her from raising her own weapon. Her head vanished in a plume of bloody spray and gore.

"Come on, boy," the colonel beckoned, "while we still have time."

Reza wasted no time in bounding down the stairs to the lower level, hurling himself into the old man's waiting arms.

"What... what happened?" he asked, looking up at the bloody smear on Wiley's forehead where he had knocked his head against the frame of the old truck. "I almost didn't recognize your voice."

The colonel's face broke into an ironic grin. "Seems God chose to give me back my marbles for one last game," he said, holding Reza to him with one arm while the other held the flechette rifle pointed at the entranceway. "Listen," Wiley said, "I don't know how long I'll be any good to you, son. This thing," he tapped his temple, "can short out at any time, assuming the Blues don't get us first." He reached down to grab the strangely contoured rifle the first Kreelan warrior had been carrying. "Take this," he said, passing the flechette rifle to Reza, keeping the alien weapon for himself. "All you have to do is point and shoot. Just don't hold the trigger down too long or you'll be out of ammo before you know it."

"Wiley," Reza whispered as they crouched down near the Kreelan's body, "what are we going to do? There are Kreelans all over the place. I saw them from the upstairs windows. I suppose the people in the shelter will be safe for a while, but–"

"Baloney," the old man spat. "Those shelters are the damned most foolish things anybody ever dreamed up. All they do is trap people in one place and make it easy for the Blues. It'd be better to give every kid a rifle and bayonet and teach them how to use it as they grow." He looked pointedly at Reza. "But who's going to give a planet full of orphans their own weapons?"

He suddenly closed his eyes and rubbed his forehead with an age-spotted hand.

Reza saw that hand shaking as a tear rolled down the old colonel's face.

"I'm starting to lose it, boy," he muttered, his mouth drawn in a thin, determined line. "Wiley the Clown is knocking on the door–"

A muffled boom that set the windows rattling and dust sprinkling from the ceiling stole away the end of his sentence. The two of them stared at each other in the silence that followed, wondering what the noise had been.

"Maybe the Navy..." Reza began, but a gesture from Wiley cut him off.

"The squids aren't going to hit a friendly site from orbit," he whispered hoarsely. "They'd send in Marines. Every ship bigger than a corvette carries at least a company."

Then they heard the spitting of Kreelan light arms fire and someone screaming, but while the scream was only from a single terror, it had many, many voices.

"Oh, my God," Wiley said, closing his eyes. "They breached the shelter."

Reza thought of Mary worrying about him, whether he would be all right by himself until he could get to the safety of the shelter. And now all of them – a thousand or more children and adults – were being massacred. Reza started to shake.

"Boy," Wiley said quickly, afraid that both he and Reza would lose their will and their wits if he waited but a moment longer, "it's now or never. You're going to have to make a run for it on your own." Reza opened his mouth to protest, but Wiley hushed him with a finger across his lips. "I can't go with you, son. I'm too old and too slow, and my brain's going to turn to mush again here pretty soon. I can feel it."

He took something out of his coat pocket, the one over his heart, the only one on his janitor uniform that had a button on it. It was an envelope, plain except for the Confederation Marine Corps seal at the closure.

"I wrote this the same night I wrote the one for Nicole," Wiley told him. "I knew you wouldn't need it for a few years, but when you have a noggin like mine, you do what you can when you can. Here," he said, pushing it into the boy's hands. "Read it."

Reza opened it to find a single sheet of paper inside. But the paper was by no means ordinary. In addition to the embossed Marine Corps emblem that showed through the paper when held up to the light, it carried the symbols of two Confederation Medals of Honor, the Confederation's highest award for valor in the face of the enemy. During the course of the war, only fifteen men and women had ever won two such honors; the Medal of Honor was almost always given posthumously. Colonel William Hickock had been one of those fifteen, and the only one who still lived. The words that were scrawled on the page were few and to the point:

To Whom It May Concern:

Being of sound mind and body as I write this, I submit that the young man bearing this document, Reza Sarandon Gard, be considered for acceptance into the military academy of his choice upon reaching the Confederation legal age of decision, that being fifteen years from his stated date of birth.

The Confederation Services will find no finer pupil for the military arts and the leadership on which the Confederation depends for its continued survival.

(Signed,)
William T. Hickock
COL, CMC (Ret.)

"Wiley," he began, "I don't know what to say..."

"It's the least I can do," the old man said quietly. "If it's what you want, that'll give you a little muscle to get past some of the stuck-up boneheads screening people for the academies." He looked around, as if he had suddenly forgotten something "But that's for another time," he said as he stuffed the envelope and its precious contents into a pocket in Reza's shirt. "You've got to get out of here, son." He looked hard at Reza, then pointed to the flechette rifle in the boy's hands. "Think you can handle that thing?"

"Yes, sir," Reza replied in a voice that sounded small and alone. "But–"

"No *buts*, boy," Wiley said gently, but firmly, leaving no room for argument. "This is it. For real. I'll try to create a diversion for you." He nodded toward where the screams from the breached shelter still rose and fell like pennants in a gale. "Besides," he went on quietly, his voice echoing memories from another life that Wiley the janitor had never known, "I want to die the man I used to be. Not as some senile broom pusher." His eyes pierced Reza. "You understand that, don't you?"

Reza nodded, biting back the tears he felt coming, remembering how he and his real father had parted a lifetime ago. *It's happening all over again*, he thought wretchedly. "Yes, sir," he choked.

"Do whatever you can to stay alive, son," Wiley told him softly. "If anybody can make it out of this, you can." He embraced Reza tightly.

"I love you," Reza said, holding on to his adopted father for the last time.

"I love you, too, son," Wiley said, stroking the boy's hair, fighting back his own tears.

Reluctantly, Wiley let go. Then he rose in a crouch, holding his artificial leg behind him like a kangaroo's tail for balance. "Good luck, Marine," he said.

This was how he wanted it, Reza told himself. He only wished it could be some other way. "You too, colonel," Reza said, snapping his arm up in a sharp salute.

The old man saluted him in return before making his way to the front door. After pulling the second Kreelan warrior's body into the lobby and clearing the exit, he squeezed through to disappear into the street beyond.

Feeling as if he were trapped in a holographic nightmare, Reza turned and made his way to the emergency escape at the rear of the library. Peering through the adjacent window, he saw that the area behind the library was clear, at least as far as he could see. The closest wheat fields were about two hundred meters away. Maybe a minute of hard running, he guessed. *Only a minute. Plenty of time to die.*

Holding the flechette rifle close to his side, he pushed open the door and headed outside, the door's emergency alarm blaring uselessly behind him.

* * *

Wiley crouched near the rock wall, not too far from the first group of soldiers that Reza had seen being wiped out by the attacking Kreelans. He had exchanged the alien weapon for a pulse rifle and a spare magazine from one of the dead soldiers. The pulse rifle was a bit heavier than the flechette guns, but had more firepower in its crimson energy bolts than a flechette could ever hope to boast. Unfortunately, their higher cost made them a low volume commodity on all but the best-equipped worlds.

He snaked forward along the wall, trying to get a glimpse of what was happening at the shelter. The firing had stopped, as had most of the screaming.

"What are you bitches up to?" he wondered aloud as he peered through a hole in the wall toward the admin building.

Kreelan warriors were clustered about the entrance to the vault, standing in two lines that extended from the vault's entryway where the great door had been blasted from its hinges, to where a vehicle resembling a flatbed trailer hovered in the center of the street. The warriors were passing objects from one to another, moving them from the vault to the carrier.

Bodies, Wiley thought. They're taking the bodies away.

The lone wail that suddenly pierced the air made his blood run cold. He watched as a child, five or six years old, emerged from the vault and was passed along the chain of warriors like a bucket in a fire brigade to where the other bodies were being stacked on the carrier. There, a Kreelan in a white robe – a type of alien that Wiley had never seen or heard tell about – did something to the child, who suddenly was still.

His eyes surveyed the carrier closely, and he noticed two things: there were no adults, only children, and the children apparently were not dead, just sleeping. Drugged or stunned.

The old man's mind reeled. There had never been a confirmed report of prisoners being taken in the war against the Empire. Sometimes, for reasons never understood, the Kreelans would leave survivors. But never had they taken prisoners.

Yet, here they were, making off with a few hundred children from this house alone. If they were doing the same at the other houses, they would be leaving with tens of thousands of children.

"I've got to get out a message, a warning," he whispered to himself.

But a presence behind him, a feeling that he was no longer alone, removed that concern from his mind forever.

He whirled in time to see a huge enemy warrior standing behind him, her form lost in the sun's glare, sword raised above her head. His old arm tried to bring the rifle around, his teeth bared in a snarl that matched the Kreelan's, but he wasn't fast enough. The warrior plunged her sword through his unarmored chest, burying the weapon's tip in the ground beneath Wiley's back.

His hand convulsed on the trigger of his rifle as he saluted Death's coming, sending nearly a full magazine blasting into the rock wall around them. And as the blood stopped surging through his arteries and his body lay still, he made a remarkable observation through his still-open eyes as the warrior knelt down to collect a lock of his hair: the Kreelan carried a scar over her left eye that was identical to Reza's.

* * *

Pushing his way through the chafing wheat, Reza heard the hammering of a rifle and stopped in his tracks. He knew that it must be Wiley, and that the old Marine would never have fired off a full magazine like that unless he was in dire trouble.

He hesitated, wondering if he should go back, desperately wanting to. He knew that Marines did not leave their own behind, and Wiley was one of his own. He felt the envelope with Wiley's letter burning in his breast pocket, and his indecision made him feel unworthy of it.

But he knew it would be too late. If Wiley were in trouble, there would be no helping him. And that was the way the old Marine had wanted to die, Reza reflected somberly. He silently hoped that he had taken out a dozen of the aliens with him.

Damn them all to Hell, he cursed.

Completely alone now, he continued on through the wheat, not knowing where he was going, no longer caring.

* * *

He had been walking for nearly half an hour when he heard the aerospace vehicle's screaming engines. He threw himself into the dirt just as its dark shape passed directly overhead.

"I think I've had it," he murmured, clutching at the flechette rifle as he lay still. He could hear the ship somewhere nearby, no doubt dropping off a hunting party. *Maybe more than one*, he thought glumly as he heard the ship move off to his left and hover again.

Then the ship left, its engines a muted roar against the wind, and Reza decided it was time to move. He got into a crouch and quietly made his way forward. Pushing aside some wheat stalks, he found himself face-to-face with a Kreelan warrior.

Death was literally staring him in the face.

With a cry of surprise, the Kreelan suddenly flew backward through the wheat, her body carried by the volley of flechettes fired from Reza's rifle. The reflexive spasm by his right index finger on the weapon's trigger had been the narrow margin between his life and her death.

Shaking like a leaf from the adrenaline surge, he quickly forged onward through the wheat, his heart hammering in his ears as his mind relived the brief battle a thousand times in the blink of an eye. He looked about wildly for more warriors, but with visibility of less than a meter, it would be another chance encounter, with the odds stacked well against him. Fate would not favor him a second time.

Unexpectedly, he burst onto an open quad. While he desperately wanted to cross over the clear ground instead of struggling through the wheat, he knew that to be seen was to be killed.

But the sounds of pursuit that suddenly arose above the wind and the whispers of the stalks as they caressed one another made his decision. There was no going back the way he had come. He pounded across the field at a full run, glancing back over his shoulder for signs of the enemy. The sound of his footsteps and his labored breathing thundered in his ears, as if his senses became more sensitive the further he went across the quad.

"No!" Reza shouted as the Kreelan ship suddenly shot overhead to hover directly above him. He raised the rifle and fired, but the flechettes merely ricocheted harmlessly, not even scratching the vessel's hull. He stumbled, dropping the rifle, then began again to run toward the safety of the wheat, which beckoned to him from the far side of the quad.

I might make it, he thought hopefully, as his legs pumped and his chest heaved. He bolted the last few meters to the waiting wall of golden wheat.

A Kreelan warrior, crouching unseen, suddenly rose up in front of him. The weapon she held looked incredibly huge. She squeezed the trigger.

For a moment Reza went blind and his ears rang from the buzz of a thousand angry wasps. But then he suddenly felt as if something soft and warm had embraced him, driving the air out of his lungs and the strength from his limbs. He crashed through the first few rows of wheat to land, unconscious, at the warrior's feet.

* * *

"These animals have all met the standards you set forth, priestess," the young warrior declared, her head lowered to honor her superior.

Tesh-Dar ran her eyes across the hundreds of human children arrayed like so much cordwood near the base of the shuttle, their bodies stunned and then drugged into a stasis sleep for the long journey ahead. Knowing – and caring – little about human physiological development, Tesh-Dar had set height as the main criterion for selection, as it was a convenient reference, easily measured. Any child taller than about one and a half meters was not acceptable. And therefore would die.

"Carry on, child," she ordered, returning her subordinate's salute and watching as they went about loading the human pups for transport to the great ship waiting in orbit. Across the planet, thousands of other human young were being collected for transport back home. Back to the Empire.

The sound of an approaching scout flyer drew her attention as it settled into a hover nearby. The clawed landing gear hummed from recesses in its belly and locked as it settled to the dusty patch of ground that served as their main landing zone.

Several warriors descended from the gangway before it had finished opening, bearing two bodies between them. The first, a small human, was deposited unceremoniously at the edge of the enormous pile of humans that would be left behind to die when Tesh-Dar's party took their leave of this world. Hundreds of them lay there, many long since crushed to death by the inert weight of those on top. Few, except for the adults who had been killed out of hand, bore any blast or penetration wounds. After being stunned and measured, they were simply discarded like trash.

The second body, Tesh-Dar saw, was that of a warrior, her chest armor riddled with the tiny holes made by the humans' flechette weapons.

Curious, nodding toward the dead warrior, Tesh-Dar asked, "What happened to her?"

The lead warrior, an elder as old as Tesh-Dar but far less accomplished, replied, "A young human killed her as he fled through the vegetation." She flicked a glance at the tiny human body, her cobalt blue face passionless. "Kumar-Etana was not fast enough, it would seem." She turned back to Tesh-Dar. "We stunned the animal, but it was not within your parameters, priestess."

Tesh-Dar nodded for the warriors to continue their duties, her mind idly pondering the likelihood of such a situation. She had noted the size of the human when they threw it onto the open grave, and it was far too small to have been trained as a warrior. Yet, it had killed Kumar-Etana, who had never been noted for sloth in combat, in what Tesh-Dar had implicitly understood to be a fair match.

Curious, Tesh-Dar allowed herself to be drawn to the mountain of dying humanity. Pitiful cries rose from the heaps of flesh as the effects of the stun wore off, for those humans who would not be leaving with her were not given the stasis drug.

Prodding one or two of the bodies with her sandal, she stepped to where her warriors had left the small human who had killed Kumar-Etana. It lay face-down, its frail form wrapped in clothing that was torn and battered. She hooked one powerful foot under the animal's left side and lifted, flipping the body over onto its back.

"The scar," she gasped as she saw the creature's face. Kneeling next to the human, she touched the scar over its left eye, wondering if it was possible for another human to have such a mark.

But, no, she decided, after studying the pup's face. The hair was darker perhaps than it had been that night, and the scar had lengthened as the skin stretched with growth. But on this creature she could clearly see the face of the pup she had nearly killed those few cycles ago. The one whose scar she shared.

Her mind probed into the human's spirit, examining the ethereal thing that lived within the shell of flesh as she might an insect pinned to a tree. It did not sing as did her spirit, but there was no denying that it was the same human.

"Much have you grown, little one," she said to the still form, fingering the human knife that still rested in her waist belt, a treasured curio she valued for the memories it brought to her. "And, perhaps, much may you yet learn."

Effortlessly, she picked Reza up in her arms and carried him to the healers who were preparing the other human children for transport. "This one shall go, as well," she ordered, setting him down next to a little African girl whose skin was as black as Tesh-Dar's armor. "Ensure that he survives."

"As you command, priestess," the healer replied as she continued her tasks. Tesh-Dar watched as the boy was drugged into stasis for his voyage to the Empire. As the healer worked, stripping everything from the pale body down to the skin before injecting the necessary potions, Tesh-Dar saw her remove a tiny object from around the boy's neck, tossing it toward the pile of human debris that would be left behind.

Effortlessly, the priestess snatched it from the air and held it up to the yellow light of the planet's sun. Its shape and manufacture intrigued her. It must have been of great importance, she thought, for the young animal to be wearing it around its neck.

"Curious," she murmured, glancing at the child, who was now being wrapped in amoebic tissue as if he were being rolled into the tight embrace of a pulsating, living rug. It would keep him alive for the long voyage ahead.

With a final nod to the healer, Tesh-Dar put the small cross of shiny metal into the pouch in which she collected her trophies before heading toward the shuttle's landing ramp to await the time of their departure.

* * *

The sun had not yet set when the Kreelans lifted from Hallmark with their human cargo. Once back aboard the battlecruiser *Tarikh-Da*, Tesh-Dar resumed her place on the bridge and began the final stage of their visit into human space.

The human survivors – those who were conscious – left behind on Hallmark rejoiced as the last of the Kreelan shuttles left for orbit. But their revelry was to be short-lived.

Seventy-seven black spheres, each about five meters across, were dispatched at precisely timed intervals from special bays arrayed along the *Tarikh-Da's* flanks. One after another, sometimes in pairs, they flitted away like melancholy balloons, seeking their orbital nodes with unerring accuracy to form a shell around Hallmark.

The last was launched from the battlecruiser only moments before the ship broke orbit for its jump point. As the *Tarikh-Da* sped away, a signal from the ship initiated the detonation sequence of the seventy-seven orbital weapons. In moments, Hallmark's atmosphere was transformed into a cloud of churning plasma, and the planet's surface temperature soared to that of molten lead.

Four hours later, when the lone Kreelan warship jumped into hyperspace, Hallmark had been scoured clean of all signs of life.

* * *

Nicole's flight bag was so full that she had to sit on it to get it to close. She had found half a dozen books for Reza and some chocolates for Wiley, and somehow had stuffed them all into the bag, along with her clothes.

Having won the battle with the flight bag, she appraised herself in the mirror. Trim and dashing in her dress black Navy uniform, her epaulettes carried the single thin stripe of cadet ensign, and her boots shone like mirrors. Even though the trip itself would take nearly a week – a third of her leave – she wanted to look her best for them from the start. For her friends. For her family. She got along well with the other cadets (even the upperclassmen) and the instructors, but Reza and Wiley were her only family.

She had half an hour to catch the shuttle that would take her to the orbiting freighter and on to the first leg of her trip to Hallmark. Hefting her bag, she had just started down the hallway toward the elevators when a voice caught her from behind.

"Carré!"

She turned to find three of her friends rushing toward her. They all looked as if they had just lost a close relative.

"*Oui, mes amis?*" she asked as an unpleasant tingle ran up her spine.

"Nicole," Seana, her roommate asked quietly, "have you heard?"

"Heard what?" Nicole asked, her throat constricting with foreboding. The three of them looked at one another in a manner Nicole had seen often enough. It was the unspoken vote as to who would break the bad news.

"What is it?" Nicole demanded.

Seana looked at her two companions and knew she was the one who had to do this. She was Nicole's roommate and the best friend Nicole had here. But this was a duty she did not want to perform. Nicole always talked about the orphan boy on Hallmark, referring to him as her brother (although Seana knew that Nicole was deeply in love with him), and doted on the old man – a Marine hero, she had said – who was her surrogate father. Sometimes all the talking about the boy annoyed Seana, who could not wait to get away from her own four brothers. But she could not deny the obvious love the girl felt for the boy and the old Marine, and she had come to find that listening to Nicole made her think more about how much she missed her own family.

And now this.

"Nicole," Seana said, taking a step closer to her friend and gently putting a hand on her shoulder. "A report came in across the op's desk. A week ago, something happened... on Hallmark." She paused, unsure as to how to continue, her mouth working as if she were chewing something unpalatable, indigestible.

"Dammit, Seana," Nicole lashed out, her heart thundering with dread, "what is it?"

"The Kreelans attacked Hallmark, Nicole," Seana said softly, ready to break down in tears herself. Then she went on with the brutal truth, knowing that Nicole would not tolerate any of the candy coating so many others needed to take with their dose of tragedy. "They used something – some kind of new weapon, or so the rumor goes – that burned away the planet's entire atmosphere. The surface..." She shook her head. "There was nothing left." Her voice had fallen to a whisper as she watched the blood drain from Nicole's face.

José finished it for her. "There were no survivors, and no record of what happened during the attack, except some debris from the orbital defense network. That's the only reason they're sure it was an attack instead of some bizarre natural disaster or something."

"That's enough, José," Seana told him. "I think she gets the picture."

Nicole did not hear her. The flight bag that she had been clutching so tightly in eager anticipation of her departure fell to the floor with an empty thud, the precious books and chocolates now dead weight without destination or purpose. The image of Hallmark boiled into her mind, the planet's atmosphere burning away, incinerating the surface as it blew off into space. Tens of thousands of human bodies swirled in its wake.

"*Non*," Nicole murmured, shaking her head slowly as first Reza's, and then Wiley's face swam out of the maelstrom, the flesh burning away until there was nothing left but a charred husk, the jaws locked open in an unending scream of agony. "*Mon Dieu, pourquoi?*" she whispered, her hands pressed tightly to her eyes to shut out the living nightmare. The only family left to her had been torn away like a tender sapling in a brutal whirlwind, spinning away into darkness. "Why? Oh, God, why?"

But God had no answer. He stood silently by as she collapsed into her friends' waiting arms.

Five

Reza awoke with a blinding headache, waves of pain pounding inside his head in a symphony of agony. He was not sure how long he had been floating on the edge of consciousness, but bit by bit he came to the conclusion that he was still in one piece, alive.

He tried to open his eyes, but his eyelids were solidly gummed shut. With a seemingly Herculean effort, he managed to pop them open with a sickeningly loud crackle. Mercifully, the light in this place, wherever he was, was turned down low, the features around him lost in shadow, blurry. He felt some sort of bedding underneath him, hairy and thick like an animal hide, its faint musky odor reminding him of the real leather coat he had seen Mary Acherlein sometimes wear to the library before she went out on a date.

As his hands probed his surroundings, he incidentally discovered that he was completely naked. Any other time he might have tried to be modest. Right now, however, he was still in too much pain, and the memories of the attack on Hallmark filled him with dread.

He sensed movement to his right. Much to his regret, he tried to turn his head. The resulting typhoon of pain threatened to render him unconscious again, but after a moment it began to subside. He stifled a groan and tried to keep himself from recoiling as the Kreelan who had been silently sitting next to him applied a cool, moist cloth to his forehead.

"Who are you?" he murmured at the blurred shadow with blue skin, the sound of his voice reverberating painfully in his skull. His forehead tingled from whatever the cloth had been soaked in. The Kreelan held it there for a few moments, watching him with the inscrutable expression of a reptile.

She reached to her side to pick up a wide-brim cup holding a foul smelling concoction. She lifted his head with one hand, careful not to scratch his skin with her talon-like nails, and put the cup to his lips. He vainly tried to turn his head away. The smell of the cup's contents forced him to the brink of vomiting.

"Drink." The alien's command, spoken in Standard with the husky voice of one used to being obeyed, caught Reza completely by surprise. He involuntarily gaped at her, never having heard of a Kreelan speaking in a human language, and she used the opportunity to toss the oily liquid down his throat. That left him with no choice but to swallow it quickly or drown. He decided to swallow, as his benefactress looked in no mood to try and resuscitate him.

"Ugh!" he croaked, trying with all his might to keep from throwing up. The alien pinned him with one silver-nailed hand and forced him to drink the dregs that remained in the cup. "Oh, God," he gasped, "what is that?"

Not surprisingly, she did not respond. Instead, she gave him a cup of water to chase down the offensive brew. After he had drunk it all, she released him, taking the cloth and wiping his face and neck free of the liquid that had spilled from his lips. She threw the cloth into a small earthen bowl and returned her gaze to Reza.

"What is your name?" she asked in eerily accented Standard, her white fangs glistening as she spoke.

Reza saw that her skin was as smooth and sleek as the handmade porcelain he had seen in a spaceport shop once, with lips that were a very deep red and lustrous as satin in the soft light. Her silver-flecked cat's eyes, perfectly spaced above a sleek nose that probably was much more adept at its job than his, were clear and bright, taking in everything in an instant. The talons on the ends of her fingers were short and silver, and stood in marked contrast to the gold-trimmed ebony neckband with its hanging pendants that was a trademark feature of every Kreelan ever observed by humanity. Had she not been the enemy, she might have been considered beautiful.

"Reza," he said, choking back the pain in his head. "Reza Gard."

She gave a quiet huff at the information. "This," she held up the cup that had held the horrible liquid, "will relieve your pain and allow you to begin soon."

"Begin what?" he asked. He looked around again. "Where am I? And who are you?"

His warden narrowed her eyes. Then she reached forward with one hand and flicked a single finger against Reza's still-throbbing skull. He gasped at the pain.

"Animals do not ask questions," she growled. But after a moment she went on – whether in answer to Reza's questions or as part of a prepared speech, he did not know – in near perfect Standard, spoken slowly as if Reza were a complete imbecile. "I am Esah-Zhurah." She considered him silently for a moment. "You, and those like you, were chosen by the Empress to come among Her Children, that you may be shown the Way, so that She may know if animals such as you have a soul."

For a moment, Reza was simply shocked, but then her words gave rise to anger. "Of course I have a soul, you–"

She flicked his head again, harder this time, and Reza let out a yelp of pain.

"That," she hissed, "you will have ample time to demonstrate, human."

She suddenly stood up. "You will rest now," she ordered. "When I return, you will be ready to begin. We have much to do." With that, she disappeared down a dim hallway, her black armor and braided jet hair melding into the shadows.

Shaken and confused, Reza wondered what new Hell he had fallen into, and if anyone else from Hallmark was still alive.

* * *

In the days that followed, Reza found himself clothed in animal skins and introduced to the "apartment" (he had no idea what else to call it) that was to be his world for the foreseeable future. There were no windows, nor could he open the door he thought might lead to the outside world, whatever it was. There was a single main chamber in which he himself slept, as well as an atrium (with walls too tall to climb) containing an open pit fireplace that served as a kitchen. The second door in the apartment led to the Kreelan girl's room. Both doors were kept firmly locked.

Air vents, much too small for his growing body to negotiate, were arrayed about the apartment and kept the air from getting stale, although it was always either too hot or too cold. This did not bother his keeper, and he decided not to let it bother him, either. He had lived through much worse in the fields, and even the Kreelan girl was more socially palatable than Muldoon had been.

Each day began with the same ritual, a portion of roasted meat brought to his bedside by the Kreelan (she apparently did not trust him in the kitchen) and however much water he chose to drink. She did not eat with him, but watched silently, as if she were observing a rodent in a psychology experiment, taking notes in her head. The only time he asked her if there was anything else to eat – vegetables or fruit, perhaps – she had grabbed his meat from him and disposed of it somewhere, refusing to feed him for the next two days.

He did not make that mistake again.

Once the morning meal was over, she sat him down in the atrium and began to teach him their language and a seemingly endless series of obscure customs and protocols, grilling him mercilessly on what he had been taught as they stopped for the mid-day ration of meat and water. The language came to him quickly, but many of the other things she tried to teach him – so much of it based on a hierarchical symbology of Kreelan history that was often totally beyond him – were difficult to understand at all, let alone absorb and remember. But he tried, and quickly he learned.

During these inquisitions, her reactions to his answers varied from thoughtful contemplation to severe beatings that left him with bleeding welts and horrendous bruises that did not go down for days. He had learned to accept them quietly, as protest or complaint only seemed to make the treatment more severe, and he did not feel quite strong enough to challenge her. Yet. Survival was paramount, but his pride ensured that he looked her in the eye, even if he had to pry them open from the swelling to do so.

When the endless hours of study were over, she returned him to his room where she directed him to exercise. She did not care what he did, as long as he expended energy doing it. He did pushups, sit-ups, and chin-ups from the rafters in the ceiling, or just jumped up and down on the pad of skins that was his bed. He did this for as long as he had to, for to stop before she ordered was to invite anything from a scolding to a beating, generally depending on how well he had done during the preceding learning period.

After that, she made him wash himself from the cold water that dribbled from an open pipe in one wall of his room that provided water for drinking, washing, and sanitation. This was also when he discovered that modesty was something the Kreelans apparently did not believe in. After the first few times he had to stand naked under the frigid water and Esah-Zhurah's equally frigid stare, he stopped feeling embarrassed. His haste to get dressed was more to get warm and dry than to conceal his nakedness from her alien eyes.

Then there was the evening meal, consisting of yet more meat and water, after which he was allowed to collapse into an exhausted sleep.

He was able to keep this up for what he thought must have been several months before he realized that he was becoming ill, and he was fairly sure of its cause: malnutrition. He knew that his body could not survive on meat alone. While it was adapting as well as it could after the trauma of the voyage to wherever he was now, given enough time his present diet was as lethal to him as poison. He knew of rickets and other diseases caused by malnutrition, and knew that if he was to live for much longer, he needed more than just the stringy red meat served to him three times a day from an unclean plate.

The only problem would be to convince his keeper of these facts. With him being a mere animal in her eyes, that wasn't going to be easy. Reza had to act.

When the girl came in one morning with his hunk of meat and water, she found Reza already awake and clothed, standing near his bedding. She usually had to rouse him from his exhausted stupor with a rap on the head or leg, whichever happened to be protruding from the skins, and actually showed surprise that he was awake.

"So, my animal is eager this morning, is it?" she commented as she plopped the meat down on his bed and stood back to watch him eat. Reza did not glance at the meat.

"My name is Reza," he said firmly in Standard, an offense that itself warranted a beating, for he was only to speak in what she called the Language of Her Children, or not at all, "and I'm not your pet animal." He gestured at the smoldering meat. "My body needs more than just meat to survive. If you want me to keep playing your stupid little games, you're going to have to give me some fruit and vegetables and let me out of this hole to get more sunlight."

For a moment, she simply stood there, utterly stunned. Her eyes went wide and her fists clenched and unclenched at her sides.

When she finally reacted, Reza was ready for her. Another resolution he had made in the night while he contemplated his failing health was that he was going to make her earn the right to beat him, because if he waited much longer, he might not have the strength to defend himself at all.

She hissed an alien curse between her teeth and stepped toward him, her right hand reaching behind her to the short whip clipped to her back armor, the instrument she used to deliver the worst of the beatings she meted out.

Predicting her move, Reza rushed her the moment she was committed to working the whip's catch. Her surprise was such that she simply stood there as he launched himself into the air over the short expanse between them, bowling her over onto the floor where they struggled in a desperate embrace.

Reza held her from behind, pinning her arms so that she could not lash out at him with her claws, but he was unable to hold her for long. She was larger than he was, taller and stronger, and several times she bashed his head by flinging her own back and forth.

Realizing the precariousness of his failing grip, he let go and rolled away, barely avoiding her talons as they gouged the floor centimeters from his spine.

The two got to their feet, and Reza noticed that the whip lay on the floor near his bedding, practically at Esah-Zhurah's feet. But she had no need of it. Her claws were all she needed to kill him.

"Well, come on then!" he shouted, adrenaline surging through his body. He knew that if he died now, at least he would die fighting, which was better than many could ever hope for in this war.

Esah-Zhurah moved toward him slowly, her eyes fixed on his and her fangs bared in rage. Her nails were spread in a calculated pattern that would do the most damage should they make contact with her prey. The small room gave little opportunity for maneuver, and Reza saw his options evaporating with every cautious step she took.

But then he saw with slow-motion clarity her mistake, the mistake he needed. She stepped onto the hide rug, the edge of which lay at Reza's feet. Suddenly dropping to the floor, he grabbed the rug's edge and yanked it up and back with all his strength, snapping it like a magician pulling the tablecloth from under a full setting of priceless china.

Esah-Zhurah gave a startled yelp as she flipped backward, her arms flailing in a futile attempt to balance her fall. Her head made a sickening thump as it hit the stone floor, hard.

She lay dazed, moaning, and Reza snatched up the whip. Rolling her over and leaping onto her back, he wrapped it tightly around her neck above the neckband. He held the whip's ends in his hands and planted one knee in her back, putting his full weight behind it. As her senses returned, she began to struggle, weakly at first, and then with growing strength at the realization that she had been fooled. But Reza tightened his grip, forcing her to the brink of unconsciousness before she stopped struggling.

She lay there gasping, her hands reaching feebly for the black leather whip. Her eyes bulged, and saliva ran from her gaping mouth.

"Stu...pid animal," she rasped, straining against the dark clouds of unconsciousness that loomed over her.

Reza leaned close to her ear. "Listen to me," he said, his own breath coming in heaves from holding her at bay, his arms beginning to burn furiously from the exertion, "I want to live. But I'm not going to live as an animal in whatever experiment you're running here. I am something more. I need more to survive: more food, more light, more freedom, and you're going to give them to me." He tugged savagely on the whip, eliciting a gag from Esah-Zhurah. "And you're not going to beat me anymore. If you don't want to see me as your equal, that's fine. I know I am, and that's enough for now. But if you want to go on treating me like an animal, then just nod your head and I'll kill you now and take my chances." He paused a moment, catching his breath. "What's it going to be?"

She hissed and strained against him, and then finally gave up. She laid both hands on the floor, palms down.

"*Kazh*," she said softly, bitterness evident in her voice. "Stop."

"All right," Reza said warily. He let go of the whip with one hand, then uncoiled it quickly from her neck before she could get hold of it. "I think I'll keep this for now, if you don't mind," he told her, quickly backing away and making ready for a renewed assault, "as a reminder of the bargain you just made."

She made no move to strike out at him. Instead, she lay gasping for a few moments before finally rising to her feet, turning toward him as she did so. He could see that she was still dazed from hitting the floor, but she surprised him with what she did next. He thought for a moment that she was collapsing. Instead, she knelt to the floor, bowed her head to him, and crossed her left arm over her breast in an alien salute. Then she stood up, without lifting her gaze, and unsteadily made her way out of the room.

A few moments later he heard the thick door to her room open and then close behind her. Then all was quiet.

Reza collapsed on his bedding, too physically and emotionally drained to enjoy any thrill of victory he might have felt.

Damn, he thought, *how the hell am I going to make it here?* He had no friends, no allies, no one but himself. "I don't even know what planet I'm on," he whispered quietly as he rubbed his arms, the muscles aching and sore from fighting the girl. His entire body ached and shivered, and it dawned on him that he was starving.

"Breakfast," he sighed with morose resignation, "hurrah." He looked around on the floor of his room for the morning's meat, but could not find the plate. He frowned. He did not remember Esah-Zhurah taking it back when she staggered from the room.

Puzzled, he wandered into the atrium where the morning's fire smoldered in the open pit. There, balanced carefully on the pit's stone rim, was a clean bowl of what could only be some type of weird fruit. There were at least two kinds, one that looked something like a purple squash, the other of a bright orange color but no particular shape, as if it had formed in variable gravity without any genetic code governing how it should turn out. There were also a few strange cakes, off-white with darker flecks of brown, which perhaps had been made from some sort of alien grain.

Next to the bowl was a large metal mug that he had never seen before, containing something that, on closer inspection, smelled of alcohol. He tasted it carefully, and found that it had the bitter taste of what Wiley had called "ale," something he occasionally served Reza and Nicole from out of the back closet of his library apartment.

Reza took a long swallow of the ale and with his other hand reached for the fruit, curious as to how it might taste. He could only assume that Esah-Zhurah had taken his body chemistry into account. If she had not and the food was poisonous to humans, he might well be about to eat his very last meal.

He was half finished with his small bounty (he found that the orange fruit had a sour taste that he hoped meant it was high in vitamin C) when he heard her voice close behind him.

"Is it what you need?" she asked, her voice brittle. She stood in the doorway of her room, clutching at the frame. She obviously had not yet recovered from her encounter with the floor. She did not look him in the eye.

He looked around and stood up to face her. There were long black streaks down her face, as if she had rubbed charcoal from under her eyes down to her neck. *Kreelan tears*? he wondered.

"Yes," he replied quietly. He was shocked that she was treating him with such respect. "Thank you."

"*'In'she tul'a* are the words in the New Tongue, human," she told him, still looking down at the floor. "There is more food in there," she gestured to a previously empty cabinet under the hearth.

Reza nodded, wondering when the fruit and bread had been put there. Could she have somehow been expecting this?

"You will rest now," she said. Her voice was subdued, but there was no mistaking that it was still a command. "We will continue tomorrow."

With that, she turned and disappeared back into her room and was quiet for the rest of the day.

Reza did as he was told, but only after finishing off a second bowl of the fruit and dry tasteless cakes. His mouth salivated uncontrollably as he gobbled down the precious food, praying that his stomach could take it all.

When he returned to his room, he stretched out on the bristly hide and settled down to a contented, restful sleep, his first in he did not know how many weeks.

* * *

"*...karakh-te na tempo Ta'ila-Gorakh.*" Reza heaved in a breath, his lungs empty from reciting the first eleven commandments of the *Se'eln*, the orthodoxy that governed the equivalent of Kreelan public behavior and etiquette.

"You learn well the words, human," Esah-Zhurah commented. "But do you understand the meaning?"

Reza shrugged. It was one of the few uniquely human expressions that his ever-present companion had never punished him for. "Some," he told her in what she had told him was the New Tongue. He spoke without any accent, and could have passed for a native if he had been a female with blue skin. "I understand that status is shown by the pendants hanging from the collar, the length of the hair, the depth of the ridge above the eyes. I understand that one's place in life – the Way, as you call it – is measured in some kind of steps from the Empress's throne, but I have no frame of reference for that."

She nodded for him to continue.

"I understand that warriors always salute their superiors, but warriors who are seven steps below another are to bow their head in passing or kneel when they are stopped, together." He paused. "I believe that much is correct. As for the other things, I do not yet understand them."

Reza waited as she considered his answer. This had been going on for months now, endless hours of instruction in the Kreelan language and their customs, a veritable treasure trove for any of the xenospecialists Reza had read about in his other life before coming here. He thought of all those researchers who would literally have given their lives for the opportunity he had now. But it was an "opportunity" that had been thrust onto Reza's unwilling shoulders.

After their pact made over the issue of food, Esah-Zhurah began to treat him more like a sentient being, his defiance apparently having aroused a degree of grudging respect from her. The beatings became less frequent and severe, both because Reza gave her less reason to beat him and because she chose not to. He only tried to stave off the most damaging blows, and did not try to retaliate against her; he knew she no longer underestimated him and would never afford him an opportunity again as she had the first time.

All in all, they lived an endurable if uncomfortable coexistence. Reza was determined to live as long and as best he could, while Esah-Zhurah was burdened with an agenda she kept quietly to herself.

He folded his arms over his chest and looked at her. She sat there like a coiled snake, silently appraising him with her silver-flecked eyes, absently running a talon up and down her right thigh and cutting a shallow groove in the rough leather armor.

"We are through with this," she said suddenly. "Tomorrow will be different."

"How so?" Reza asked, curious and somewhat afraid. "Different" could mean too many things.

Her mouth curled around her fangs into what Reza thought might have been something like a smile. It was chilling.

"Patience, animal," she said, intentionally barbing him with the reference she knew he despised. "You shall see soon enough."

SIX

Reza was jolted out of his sleep by a sharp rap on the bottom of his foot. Peering from beneath the warmth of his bed of skins, he saw Esah-Zhurah standing beside him, a short black baton inlaid with a complex silver design in her hand. He blinked his eyes a few times, trying to clear his head. She hit his foot again, harder this time, his nerves sending a sharp report of pain to his brain.

"Ow!" he exclaimed, drawing his foot away from her and under the comparative safety of the skins. "What is that?" he asked about the baton, never having seen it before. He spoke only in the Kreelan New Tongue now, only rarely having to resort to Standard.

She looked at him, head cocked to one side. "You tell me," she said, holding it up for him to see more clearly. About as long as her forearm and the thickness of Reza's thumb, the baton was a gleaming black shaft crowned by silver castings and a series of runes in silver that must have been incredibly ornate when new. But now only the ghostly impressions of the strange runes (they were obviously Kreelan, but did not match the character set he was learning to read) glimmered in the polished metal, untold years and hands having taken their toll.

"A Sign of Authority?" Reza guessed. It was the only thing he could think it might be. A Sign of Authority, Esah-Zhurah had once explained, was like a public symbol of an elder who had delegated both responsibility and authority to a subordinate. With such a symbol, the populace at large would have to treat the bearer with the same regard as they would the elder. The bearer had great power, but also carried the liability that went with it. Esah-Zhurah had made it abundantly clear to Reza in many lessons that personal responsibility was not taken lightly in the Kreelan culture. It was literally a matter of life and death, and he wondered if he would finally have the opportunity to see it in action.

"Very good, human," she said. "Get dressed now. We will be going outside this day."

His excitement matched only by his apprehension, Reza hurried to dress, lacing his skins on over his naked body. Pausing to relieve himself, he felt her hands working at the back of his neck.

"What–?" he exclaimed.

"Be still," she ordered as she removed his old leather collar and replaced it with a new one. Larger, thicker and made of cold metal, at least he no longer felt that he was being slowly choked to death. "You grow quickly," she commented, clipping a leash to the collar and giving it a quick yank to make sure it was connected properly.

"Why the leash?" he asked as he finished getting dressed.

"You are my responsibility," she told him, holding up the leash for him to see. It was made of a tight, dark metal chain, with a studded leather thong at the far end that was looped around her wrist. "You are unfit to walk among Her Children without proper supervision. It will help remind you of your place."

He was tempted to react to her taunt, but her expression and body stance – he could read her alien nuances now, sometimes – made him give in to caution. He elected to let the comment pass.

She led him to the door and stopped, turning around to face him. "You must listen, and do exactly as I say," she commanded. "You will not speak. You will not look directly into the eyes of another, especially those with special markings here." She pointed to the center of the collar that hung just below her throat.

Reza nodded, his stomach knotting in excitement. Whatever lay beyond these walls, he was eager to see it. He had been imprisoned here for far too long.

She opened the door and led him out. Much to his surprise, the door led to a long corridor lit by triangular windows set high in the arch that formed the corridor's ceiling. The light that filtered through was warm and bright, with the slight magenta hue to which he had become accustomed from the light flowing down into the atrium where the fire was kept. Reza could smell a faint odor that reminded him of an old stone house he had once known on New Constantinople: it was the smell of age and time, the smell of quiet strength. The walls, though, were smooth and seamless, without visible signs of having been hewn or carved.

As Esah-Zhurah led him toward the door at the end of the corridor, Reza could see that there were many other doors like the one they had left behind. But they were not evenly distributed along the hallway as they would have been in most human-designed buildings. Some were very closely spaced, while many meters separated others. And the doors themselves, apparently of some type of dark wood, seemed different from one another, not so much in dimension but in the pattern and tone of the wood, as if the doors themselves were of vastly different ages. All of them appeared unique, as if each had been made by hand.

Reza listened, but could hear no sound other than their footsteps and the occasional clinking noise of the chain that bound him. He watched the girl walking smoothly before him, and noticed that she had put the baton in a sheath that was part of her left arm's leather armor, the wand's silver head protruding near her shoulder. He also saw that she wore a weapon today, something he had never seen her do before. It was a long knife, almost a short sword, with an elaborately carved bone handle and, judging from the shape of the leather scabbard hanging from her waist, a blade that was as elegantly shaped as it was deadly.

Reza was amazed that so much of what he had seen appeared to be, by and large, handmade. The quality of the workmanship was incredible, he admitted, but where were the mass-produced items that virtually every human took for granted? Where was the technology? Computers, appliances, everything up to starships and even terraformed planets were trademarks of man's industrialization. The Kreelans obviously had the technology to reach out to the stars and wage war on a galactic scale, but it was certainly absent from this place. Of the little he had seen so far, they seemed to be living on a level close to that of lost colonies that had lost contact with the Confederation for decades, and survived with only the most rudimentary technology.

He was under no illusion, however, that this race was not capable of every technological trick imaginable, carved bone knife handles or not. They had mastered interstellar flight and the myriad intricacies of related engineering, and had shown equal brilliance and innovation in every other sphere in which they and humanity had come in contact.

Except for communication and diplomacy, he thought grimly.

They reached what he took to be the main entrance, a large two-sided door that conformed to the shape of the arched walls.

Esah-Zhurah stopped, and again turned to him, her eyes narrowed. "Remember what you have learned, human," she told him gravely, "for failure outside this door will not bring the pain of the lash. It will bring death."

"I understand," Reza told her firmly, reciting in his head the commandments she had taught him, cramming them into his consciousness until they came to him automatically, without thinking.

She opened the door and led him outside. The first thing he noticed was the air. It was fresh and clean, with a slight breeze and the mingling smells of alien vegetation and some mysterious fauna. He involuntarily took huge gulps of it through his nose, his system becoming inebriated on the flavors. His head cleared and his senses sharpened after a few breaths, and he felt his energy level soar.

He stood behind Esah-Zhurah on a stone terrace at what he mentally designated the building's front, and looked down the steps before him into a large area that looked like a garden. It was not of the food-growing kind, but had a variety of stunningly beautiful trees and flowers – none of which he had ever set eyes on before, of course – in a definite, though alien, pattern, the whole of it scrupulously maintained.

Further out, he saw several circular fields bounded by thin, closely spaced pillars of rough black stone with shapes, indistinguishable at this distance, carved into the tops.

Arenas, he thought absently. *They look like some kind of arena or training ground.* He remembered seeing holos of horses and other animals being trained in similar rings, and he instinctively knew that he would come to know the sand in those arenas very well, if he lived that long.

Beyond the fields lay a forest of emerald green and amber trees that rose many meters into the air. The tremendous golden spires of what could only be a city pierced the sky beyond, and his heart raced at the thought of going there.

A slight tug on his chain reminded him that he had been gawking. The girl was obviously eager to get on with whatever errand she had in mind for them.

As they walked down the steps of what had been Reza's home on this world, he saw that there were other, smaller buildings clustered near the one from which they had just emerged. A tremble ran through him as he recognized many similarities between the layout of this place and the House 48 complex.

He wanted to ask Esah-Zhurah so many questions, but bit his tongue. He did not want to spoil this, especially if there was any chance of escaping, although he held only slim hopes for that option. Alone, on a world inhabited by the enemy, where could he run? When he was locked up in the apartment, he had fantasized about somehow getting away from Esah-Zhurah and escaping back to humanity. But being outside and seeing the world around him put an end to that. He knew he was on an alien-occupied planet, perhaps even their homeworld. And a lone human boy simply was not going to get away unnoticed in a society of blue-skinned aliens, and females, at that: no human had ever seen a Kreelan male, and no amount of hypothesizing had been able to explain why.

As Esah-Zhurah led him down the smoothed earthen path that cut through the trees toward the city, he thought it odd that there were no other Kreelans about. While he had never heard any sounds from other tenants in the building where he had been held, surely there must have been someone else somewhere. Certainly they would not have dedicated an entire complex such as this solely for his benefit.

Or would they? What did he know of the Kreelan thought process? While he realized that he was now undoubtedly the human expert on Kreelan psychology (since no other human had ever been able to communicate with the Kreelans and live to tell about it), he still knew next to nothing about what lay behind their feline eyes and inscrutable faces.

But the further he walked into the shadows of the forest, the more convinced he became that his curiosity about the existence of other denizens was being rewarded. While he had never been in a real forest, he could tell that something here was not entirely natural, not quite right.

Suddenly he realized why.

They were here. He could not see or even hear them, but he was certain that there were Kreelans nearby. As he walked steadily behind the girl he became aware of at least ten sets of eyes following him from various points in the forest. He was not sure if the others were following them or just happened to be there as they passed, but the eyes watched. He was sure there must have been even more, deeper in the brush, moving like whispers, but he could not be sure. And he did not really want to find out.

A chill running up his spine, he picked up his pace, moving closer behind Esah-Zhurah.

On through the forest they went, and eventually they left the prying eyes behind. Reza occasionally heard an animal grunting off in the woods, or the screech of some unknown beast of tiny proportions lurking high in the trees. He did not notice any creatures flying through the air, but by now the dense forest canopy obscured much of the sky itself, and such creatures would have been beyond his view.

After a while, he caught sight of the city spires again through the tops of the trees. They were very near now, or seemed to be, and he was caught between the excitement of seeing something no other human had seen before and the anxiety of knowing that he probably would never have the opportunity to tell another of his kind what he was witnessing.

"What is the name of this place?" he whispered.

"This is Keel-A'ar," she told him. "It is the place of the First Empress's birth."

He wanted to ask her more questions, but he could tell from her tone that she was not inclined to explain the history of the place now, although he knew that she would later, if he asked.

The trees suddenly thinned away until he found himself standing on the crest of a hill overlooking the city. The spires were tremendous, rising from stout bases to soar hundreds of meters into the air, thinning to nearly invisible points in the sky. Each was translucent, each a different color than the others, shimmering in the sunlight. Among the great spires were huge domes of gold and crystal, with streets and boulevards running like sinuous rivers between the buildings. The city's layout held no apparent pattern, yet it seemed in perfect harmony, each structure complimenting the next. On the city's far side ran a river, whose last bend took it directly through the city, and the Kreelan engineers had made the river an integral part of the overall design, buildings and bridges gracefully spanning the water.

"It's beautiful," he breathed, his eyes drinking in the city's magnificence.

Esah-Zhurah, in what he thought an uncharacteristically thoughtful gesture, let him gaze about for another minute before ushering him onward.

Walking for over an hour without seeming to get any closer to the surrounding wall, Reza began to appreciate just how large the city was. He could now see Kreelans moving through a huge gate in the wall. He imagined there must be several such gates around the city, but this was the only one he could see. Most of the Kreelans wore armor, while some wore robes of various colors: white, deep purple, cyan, and others that he did not even have a name for. Some carried satchels of various sizes and types, while others carried nothing that he could see and had their hands folded inside the billowing sleeves of their robes. None but the warriors had ever been seen by humans in a century of warfare.

At last, in what he guessed was three or four Standard hours of fast walking from the tree line, they reached the great gate. It was embedded in the city wall, which stood at least twelve meters high and must have been at least five meters thick. He could not understand how it had been built, as there were no visible seams or cracks, not even the scratches and other slight damage that must come with time. It was smooth as a polished stone, its mottled gray exterior, like the scales of a sleek reptile, stretching off to his right and left until they curved away from sight.

There were many Kreelans here, and Reza felt distinctly uncomfortable under their unabashed stares. He recognized the *tla'a-kane*, the ritual salute, as the aliens passed one another, crossing their left arm, fist clenched, over their right breast and bowing their head. It was one of the aspects of their etiquette that he found baffling.

An older Kreelan would salute a much younger one, even younger than Esah-Zhurah, and nearly every passerby might salute a particular individual of indeterminate age and social standing, regardless of whether they wore armor or the flowing robes. Their nearly instantaneous grasp of all the factors that made up an individual's standing within the caste system that determined their rank from the Empress on down astounded him the more he watched. It was only with the greatest of effort that he held his eyes downcast, for his curiosity to look at everything was overpowering.

But no matter where he looked, of all the people they passed or could see at any distance, all he saw were females. Reza had read that humans had never encountered any males, and it was a subject of endless speculation among xenobiologists. Kreelan females did not have any particularly exotic sexual traits, and were in fact quite similar to human females, which strongly suggested that there should also be a male of the species. Otherwise, how could they reproduce?

So where are the males? Reza wondered as he surreptitiously glanced around. *There certainly aren't any here.*

The palatial structures became ever taller the closer they moved toward the city's center, as if they were ascending a mountain made by Kreelan hands. All had intricate carvings and runes adorning their superstructures, written in a dialect of their language that he couldn't read, but that didn't keep him from trying.

Lost as he was in gawking at the world around him, he nearly ran into Esah-Zhurah when she stopped. She had been watching him and the citizens that passed by, most of whom were exhibiting more than a casual curiosity in the human, and had decided that a reminder was in order.

"Remember," she whispered, taking him by the neck with her free hand and whispering into his ear. Her mouth was so close that he felt one of her upper fangs brush against his skin, sending a chill down his spine. Her hand gave a firm squeeze around his neck to emphasize the single word. She looked him in the eye for a moment, and then turned to lead him further into her world.

Except for an occasional glance at the spires that towered above them, Reza now kept his field of vision limited to the ground, with only an occasional peek to see where they were going and what was happening around them. He noticed with growing concern that an increasing number of the city's inhabitants were stopping to stare at him. A few very young ones had even begun to trail along, as if they had never even seen an image of a human, let alone a real one. As he walked he began to feel the feathery pressure of small hands reaching out to touch him as if he were an animal in a petting zoo.

Many of the older ones, the full adults, stopped and stared for a moment, sometimes speaking quietly to one another before moving on. Others simply gawked, continuing to do so until Reza and Esah-Zhurah had disappeared from their sight. But none made a move to interfere or harass him or his young keeper, and they passed their way into the heart of the city unmolested.

The population seemed to rapidly increase in density as they moved inward, and soon they were passing through a very large but orderly throng moving about a gigantic central plaza. The plaza had several levels, and was bounded by four of the largest spires in the city. Despite having four corners, it was hardly a rectangle: the plaza flowed from one spire to the next in elegant curves. Everywhere, it seemed, the Kreelans had forsaken the angularity and symmetry so treasured by humans.

The bottom level was an enormous garden park that stretched several kilometers across, and at its center was a huge obelisk that towered to nearly a third the height of the surrounding spires. It had a crystal at its peak that looked like an enormous sapphire of deep blue that blazed in the sun. Reza could see a number of people strolling about or sitting on the intermittent grassy areas near the base of the obelisk. It was orderly, peaceful.

The edge of each higher level was set further back from the center than the one below, so that all of them were open to the magenta-tinged sky above, and every level was well adorned with trees and bright flowering plants. Reza could not see anything that looked like shops or businesses along the periphery; rather, it seemed like the entire plaza had been constructed simply because it formed an attractive and peaceful core for the populace, a gathering place for their people.

They wound their way down a curving avenue of inlaid stone into what looked like a marketplace. There seemed to be hundreds, perhaps thousands, of vendors selling their wares from stores set into the buildings or from small wheeled carts scattered about the square (which, of course, was in the shape of anything but a square). Many of the items that were being offered were completely unfathomable, but others were readily identifiable. Food, much of which did not appear very appetizing, was in great abundance here, and in a much wider selection than he had experienced in his meager diet. Weapons of various intriguing shapes and functions – knives, swords, and others that he could only guess at – were the subject of discussion and what he assumed to be bargaining.

But again, even here, he saw no real evidence of a high level of technology. There were no vid-screens or their equivalent, no appliances of any type, nothing even so innocuous as a hand-held computer. Even among the weapons, there were no projectile or energy weapons, only weapons that would have been recognizable on Earth during the Middle Ages. Everything he saw here was probably the same as it must have been centuries, or even millennia, before.

And as he looked at the people around him, he saw Kreelans that seemed to come from different places, groups, or maybe professions (if they had any other than slaughtering humans). But no matter the details of their outward appearance, they still broke down into two general groups: those with robes and those with armor. He did not see a single warrior type vending, the Kreelans in robes of several colors fulfilling that task. Nor did he see any robed ones with weapons.

As he passed the shops and stalls on his way to wherever the girl was taking him, he also noticed that there was not really any buying going on. He never saw any kind of money (so far as he could tell) exchanged, even when the would-be buyer walked off with the goods. Nor did he see anything like credit discs that were the standard in the Confederation, and he could not understand the process at work here. A Kreelan would walk up to a vendor, apparently choose whatever they wanted, chat with the vendor a moment and then walk away with the goods, the vendor turning to whomever was next in line.

While the buying process was a mystery, the order in which people were served was not: it was clearly defined by the rank protocols. What he took to be lowly individuals, usually girls about his keeper's age, but often older, sometimes stood a considerable time while others stepped up in front of them to do business. But he saw no sign of frustration or anxiety on the part of those who had to wait, only seemingly endless patience.

His observations were interrupted when he felt Esah-Zhurah's hand suddenly clamp down on the back of his neck. She forced his head down so far that his chin practically touched his chest, the cartilage in his neck popping in protest.

Out of the comer of his eye, he caught sight of a warrior's black talons. He remembered Esah-Zhurah's repeated warnings to avert his eyes, but his curiosity nearly overpowered his sense of self-preservation. The warrior's claws were jet black and shiny, like razor sharp obsidian, and were considerably longer and more lethal looking than Esah-Zhurah's. The owner's hand, arm, and lower body – that was all he could see – were all tremendously developed and obviously much more powerful than all the other warriors he had glimpsed. Her leather armor bulged with muscle, giving the impression of a champion bodybuilder and athlete.

But they moved on, the great warrior passing into the throng behind them.

Finally, they arrived at their destination. It was, at least compared to some of the other places they had passed, a nondescript aperture into a building adorned with the usual indecipherable runes.

Before mounting the steps, Esah-Zhurah stopped and hailed a much younger warrior, apparently chosen at random from among a group of similar minors. The young girl, maybe all of six human years old, saluted and bowed her head.

"See that the animal remains here," Esah-Zhurah commanded, handing the young girl his leash.

"Yes, Esah-Zhurah," the tiny warrior replied, bowing her head again.

Reza was not sure which was more shocking: that she would leave him under the care of such a young girl, or that they all seemed to know each other's names.

"Stay here," she told him, pointing at the ground where he stood. Without another glance, she turned and went up the steps, disappearing into the arched doorway.

As he watched her go, he idly noticed that this was one of the few buildings he had seen that had real windows. Many of the others just had what looked like slits randomly disposed about their exterior, shutters opened to the side.

He looked at the girl holding his leash. She seemed terribly young, but her face radiated a sense of authority and determination that few human children would ever boast, even as adults. She stood at a kind of attention, her cat's eyes never straying from him, her hand securely locked in the loop of the leather thong at the end of his leash.

"What is your name?" he asked her quietly, hoping his voice would not carry to the passing adults and arouse their attention any further than did the simple fact of his being there.

She glared at him, and he instantly realized his mistake. There was some key or trick to their names that Esah-Zhurah had not described, some way they immediately recognized one another, and to ask this girl her name must have been an insult.

He sighed in frustration and turned away from the glowering blue-skinned imp.

After a few minutes, Reza saw that more of the children, as well as adults, had taken time out from their alien day to get a closer look at him. None made threatening gestures – at least from what he could tell; they all seemed threatening enough as it was – but the circle about him was rapidly growing in size and diminishing in distance.

His fear of being torn to pieces by an alien mob brought home the importance of his relationship with Esah-Zhurah. While he could hardly consider her an ally, much less a friend, she was the only link he had to life. Without her, he stood no chance at all of survival on this world, among these people, and he frantically wished she would come out of the building and lead him away from the overly inquisitive group forming around him.

At last, she emerged with a black tube about the length of her forearm clutched firmly in one hand. Taking the leash from the young girl, she started off again, Reza in tow. Flowing with the increasingly thick crowd of people, he occasionally bumped against warriors whose shoulders were above his head.

"What is that?" he asked Esah-Zhurah quietly, discretely pointing at the tube she carried.

"It is the priestess's correspondence," she answered. "It is a task certain of us undertake for her each day." She looked askance at him. "Consider yourself honored, human."

Reza raised his eyebrows in surprise. He had never been on a planet or known anyone who communicated by hard copy means, "the post" always having had an electronic connotation. But letters written by hand were akin to the books he had so treasured, and he began to believe that maybe the Kreelans were not complete savages after all.

"We will go to the bath," she told him as she led him around a tight knot of warriors arguing heatedly over something that he could not quite make out. "What is your saying?" She thought a moment. "*Nature calls?* Yes?"

"Yes," he replied earnestly. Although he had not had anything to drink for hours, he suddenly felt like his bladder was going to explode. Of course, he had been so preoccupied with gawking at the city that he hadn't noticed until Esah-Zhurah mentioned it.

She led him to a doorway along a street that looked no more or less unusual than the others cutting through the metropolis. Through the doorway was a large softly lit anteroom. Kreelans in dark blue robes, barely contrasting with their skin, were in attendance, and Reza was shocked to see that everyone else – Esah-Zhurah included – was stripping off their clothing.

She turned to him, naked now except for her neckband and the ubiquitous baton, and snagged his skins with one of her claws. "Off," she commanded tersely, wrinkling her nose in a sign of disgust. She gestured toward the robed attendant who already was holding Esah-Zhurah's armor.

Reluctantly following Esah-Zhurah's command, he stripped and gave his motley skins to the attendant, who took them as unwillingly as he parted with them before carrying everything away through another door.

Reza heard a growl behind him. Turning around, he found himself toe to toe with a warrior, her taut breasts – the left one carrying a terrible scar running from the left armpit to her stomach – a hair's breadth from his nose, so tall was she. Even though they were aliens, they still had more basic things in common with human females than not, and he felt his face flush with embarrassment. He also noted that Esah-Zhurah was observing his predicament with keen interest.

The other Kreelans in the anteroom stopped what they were doing and stared, as well. Most probably had never seen a human other than himself (or had only seen one long enough to kill him or her, he thought), and by their reaction they certainly had never seen a naked human, least of all a very young male. Most of their eyes were focused below his waist.

Determined to show some courage, he raised his gaze from the warrior's chest to her eyes and held her stare. From somewhere behind him, drops of water splashed, and he began to count them to mark what probably would be the last few moments of his life. He reached a count of eleven before he heard Esah-Zhurah's voice behind him.

"Enough, animal," she said, tugging him by his leash away from the still-staring warrior. "Combat is not permitted in the bath."

Without another word, she led him through another archway and past the staring patrons in the anteroom. They went down a corridor lined with some kind of mosaic scenes of swirling rune-like shapes before entering the next room.

Reza stopped in his tracks, just inside the archway. *This is too much*, he thought. It was a public bath, all right, as in bathroom. As in bodily functions. He sighed heavily and followed along behind Esah-Zhurah, who had stopped when she noticed the resistance on the end of the leash. His stomach churned.

This is really disgusting, he thought. He had never liked the open bathrooms of House 48. But at least there, even in an open bay bathroom, everyone had to endure the same level of public humiliation, and so it generally was not that big of a deal. And, if nothing else, everyone in the room had been human. And of the same sex.

After a moment's pause he followed after Esah-Zhurah, who took her place on a strangely shaped throne of dark green. He took the seat next to her and tried to keep his mind on what he was supposed to be doing, rather than what was going on around him.

Esah-Zhurah finally stood up (he had already finished, such was his eagerness to get out of this place) and took him through the next archway, where a cleansing waterfall cascaded over them from the ceiling. The water itself smelled different, as if something – a detergent or antibiotic agent, perhaps – had been added, but he noticed nothing different about the taste as it poured over his head. The water ran down through sculpted drains in the sides of the chamber to disappear below.

After passing through a short tunnel past the waterfall, they found themselves in a large chamber that was, in fact, a soaking bath. Esah-Zhurah led him into the water, its scalding heat making him hiss with pleasure as it crept up his body. She propped her back against the side of the large pool, and he stayed close to her; even her despotic company was welcome over the hostile faces that peered from the water like sea monsters wreathed in a steamy mist. He kept inching closer to her, until their shoulders and arms touched under the water.

After he was sure she was not going to push him away, Reza closed his eyes, shutting out the alien faces around him. He forced himself to relax, letting the water's heat penetrate his body. After a few minutes, and hoping he wasn't going to breach any codes of etiquette, he took himself all the way under the water, rinsing out his rapidly lengthening hair and washing the accumulated sweat from his face. He felt his pores opening up from the water's heat, and he sighed with the unexpected pleasure of actually having a real bath, a *hot* bath, for a change. Up to this point he had only the freezing water from the spigot in his room and a crude metal basin with which to wash. Blowing like a broaching whale as he returned to the surface, he met Esah-Zhurah's eyes with a smile. He figured she would not understand its significance, but it felt good to have something, anything, to smile about.

Esah-Zhurah gave him a perplexed look, but nothing more severe.

When they were finished, she led him out the other side of the pool to a large area open to the sky. There they settled onto comfortable mats among the many other bath-goers who were drying off in the warm sun.

* * *

Reza did not realize he had drifted off to sleep until Esah-Zhurah poked him with a claw.

"We go now," she said. They stood up, completely dry, and headed off down yet another corridor to the anteroom to retrieve their clothes. Reza noticed that his had been cleaned and smelled almost pleasant now.

As they headed through the main entryway, an incoming group of Kreelans made to enter, neither party seeing the other until it was too late. The ensuing confusion resulted in some unexpected jostling. But no one took offense, and Reza and Esah-Zhurah rejoined the throng of Kreelans moving through the boulevard.

Near the edge of the plaza, they happened to pass a group of older warriors in the undulating crowd. Reza, now used to the drill, lowered his head and averted his eyes, while Esah-Zhurah performed the ritual greeting.

But something went wrong. One of the warriors barked a question at Esah-Zhurah in a dialect Reza didn't understand. Surprised, Esah-Zhurah started to respond, eyes still lowered. But she stopped in mid-phrase, looking at her left arm.

The baton, the Sign of Authority, was missing.

Esah-Zhurah's hands flew across her armor in search of it, as if she might have accidentally misplaced it when dressing at the bath. Then she shot a questioning look at Reza, as if he might have had it. Her eyes were frantic.

"Reza," she gasped. It was one of the only times she had ever called him by name. "Reza, where is the Sign of Authority? What has happened to it?" Reza could see she was petrified.

It must have been at the bath, he thought. It must have fallen out when we ran into that group of warriors when we were leaving.

He was just opening his mouth to tell her this when the questioning warrior, quite formidable in appearance, spoke to Esah-Zhurah in a harsh tone using the same dialect she had before.

Esah-Zhurah was silent, her head hanging low in what Reza understood with a chill to be total, utter defeat. Without the baton, she had no authority and therefore had no right to claim him as her own. In this society, rank and authority were everything, and she had little of the first and none of the second in the eyes of the accusing warrior. The end result would be that the challenger could kill them both, or – even worse in Reza's mind – take him as her own, for purposes he did not care to contemplate.

His fears grew deeper as the warrior momentarily turned her attention from Esah-Zhurah to himself. From her belt hung what could only be ears. Human ears. There were least twenty pairs strung on a cord. He felt a hot flame of rage flare in his heart, a worthy companion to the chill of fear that ran down his spine.

The warrior turned from Reza and spoke briefly to her comrades, and they murmured a response. He couldn't understand the words, but he didn't need to: he and Esah-Zhurah were in deep trouble.

The warrior took one step closer to Esah-Zhurah and – without any warning at all – flattened her to the ground with a brutal open-handed blow to the side of her head, the rapier claws gashing the girl's scalp to the bone above her right ear.

Reza watched, wide eyed, as Esah-Zhurah yelped once and then crumpled into a dazed heap on the ground, dark blood pulsing from her wounded head. The warrior viciously kicked her over onto her stomach and then reached for a knife. Leaning down, the warrior grabbed Esah-Zhurah's hair and used it to lift up her head, exposing her throat to the knife the warrior held in her other hand.

Reza moved without thinking. He rushed the warrior from behind, kicking out at her with both legs in a flying leap. She grunted in surprise and went tumbling over

Esah-Zhurah's prone form, nearly impaling herself with her own knife. But she recovered quickly, rolling deftly to her feet.

The other warriors and passersby gasped in astonishment, and a crowd instantly began to gather around the mismatched combatants. Their guttural comments merged into a buzz of curiosity as they formed a ring that marked the onset of what in their culture was an everyday occurrence: ritual combat. The only difference was that this would be to the death.

The warrior bared her fangs and roared a challenge at Reza. He backed up, trying to draw her away from Esah-Zhurah, who lay terrifyingly still. Reza thought frantically about his biggest problem: he had no weapon. Even if the advancing warrior had nothing but her talons, he stood no chance against her. Unless...

Acting quickly, Reza tore at the thin ragged animal skin that served as his shirt, coming away with a strip of thin leather that was almost twice the length of his arm. Then he quickly searched the ground for the other vital ingredient he needed: a simple rock. On the well-swept boulevards they had been on, he didn't hold out much hope, but for once Fate favored him: a small piece of chipped cobblestone lay only a few paces away.

Praying that the warrior's arrogance would give him a few more seconds, he dashed over and picked it up. Placing it carefully in the makeshift sling, he began his windup, wondering if the brittle leather would hold the sharp-edged projectile long enough before the sling came apart. The air filled with the whirring sound as he whipped it around his head, faster and faster.

The warrior stopped, regarding him with what he took to be bemused curiosity. Then she let out a harrowing bellow that was echoed by the other warriors surrounding them.

Ignoring the noise, Reza whirled the sling even faster, waiting for the right moment.

Now! he thought, releasing the stone just as the warrior stepped into the sling's line of fire. The cobblestone shard flew straight and true, its jagged edges mincing the Kreelan's right eye. Her scream filled the void left by the suddenly silent onlookers. Dropping the knife, she fell to the ground, clutching her injured face and wailing in agony.

Reza wasted no time. His lips pulled back in a snarl of rage, he dropped the tattered leather strip and grabbed up the fallen knife. Leaping onto the warrior's back, he entwined his left arm in her hair and levered her head back, exposing her throat to the blade clenched in his other hand, just as she had done to Esah-Zhurah.

The Kreelan went very still, as if she were expecting this and wasn't going to struggle.

Reza hesitated, his resolve suddenly cracking. What was he supposed to do? he wondered. He knew the woman's life was his for the taking, and he had no doubt that, were their positions reversed, she would have no compunction about killing him. Esah-Zhurah had not spoken of how such things were handled, perhaps in the firm belief that if Reza ever found himself in such a situation, either she would be able to get him out of it or he would simply be killed.

And yet, here he was.

This, he thought ironically, is what in a more lucid moment Wiley had once called a "command decision." There was no one from whom he could ask advice or consent. The burden of success or failure was on his shoulders and his alone.

The Kreelan, trembling beneath him from a kind of pain Reza hoped never to have to endure himself, waited with a patience grown through a lifetime of conditioning. Around them, the crowd of observers was deathly quiet, waiting for the contest to be resolved.

Remembering the sets of human ears hanging from the warrior's waist, he suddenly knew the course for his vengeance. Taking a handful of the woman's braided hair, he cut it off with the knife.

She screamed in agony, from a torrent of incomprehensible pain that Reza someday would come to understand himself. Esah-Zhurah had told him that a Kreelan's hair was her strength, her bond to the Empress, and he knew that it was as precious to them as it had been to Samson in the Old Testament of Earth. He didn't understand all of what Esah-Zhurah had told him, but it was enough that the Kreelans believed in the importance of their hair. And he had just deprived this warrior of a goodly portion of hers.

He left her, stepping away to where Esah-Zhurah lay bleeding. He carefully turned her over to look at her wounds. The four ugly gashes across her skull were deep, and there was a tremendous amount of blood in her hair and on the street.

"Oh, God," he whispered in Standard, wondering if she could be bleeding to death, or if her skull had been fractured. He had no idea what to do.

Her eyes fluttered open. She tried to focus on him and opened her mouth to speak, but no words came out before she passed out again.

The stricken warrior had stopped screaming. Now she glared at him, the blood and fluid from her devastated eye seeping down her face like a smashed egg. He watched her carefully, waiting for the next attack, the one he would not be able to stop.

Her face finally locking into a frigid mask of utter hatred, the warrior got to her feet faster than Reza would have thought possible. Her claws flexed like the talons of a predatory bird as she began to move toward him.

He moved between her and Esah-Zhurah, clutching the warrior's own knife in his hand as he made ready for a last desperate stand, his hopes of survival all but extinct.

A shadow suddenly fell over him and a huge hand with obsidian claws clutched his shoulder from behind, pushing him back down beside Esah-Zhurah with the irresistible strength of a mountain. He went perfectly still as a voice behind him, oddly familiar, spoke to the advancing warrior in the same dialect that Reza could not understand, but in a tone of unquestionable authority.

The warrior stopped. She listened intently to whomever was standing behind Reza. His opponent said nothing. She glared at him one final time and then, much to his surprise, she bowed to him, her arm across her chest. She reached around to her back and tossed him the scabbard for the knife he still held.

And then she slit her throat with her own claws.

Reza watched in horrified fascination as blood gushed from the ghastly wound and air whistled from her severed windpipe like someone blowing over the top of a bottle. The warrior stood at rigid attention until, as the flow of blood slowed to a trickle, her good eye rolled up into her head and she fell to the street, dead.

Reza vomited, but nothing came up. He simply knelt in the street, wracked with dry heaves. When he was finished, he felt the great hand on his shoulder again. Turning his face up, he looked at the woman standing over him, and his heart froze at what he saw.

Silhouetted against the slowly setting sun, standing at least a head taller than the tallest of the other warriors and with a frame whose strength could have matched any two or three of their kind, was the most powerful Kreelan he had ever seen. A great gnarled staff that Reza doubted he could have even carried was held easily in one hand. Her breast armor, a glistening black that seemed to have an infinite depth, boasted an intricate series of crystal blue runes inlaid into the metal that sparkled like diamonds in the sun. From her neckband hung several rows of silver, gold, and crystalline pendants, and the neckband itself had a cobalt blue rune at its center, a feature whose importance was evident by its uniqueness.

She was a priestess, he knew. This much, Esah-Zhurah had taught him.

Her eyes blazed at him from beneath the ridge of bone or horn that made up her eyebrows. The ridge over her left eye and the skin of her cheek had been cut, leaving an ugly scar...

...that was the mirror image of his own.

"No," he whispered hoarsely in the New Tongue, as the nightmare image from his childhood became the warrior priestess now standing over him. "It cannot be."

"And yet, so it is, little one," Tesh-Dar replied, speaking in the New Tongue so he could understand. Her eyes darted to his hand, the knife shaking in his quivering grip. "Do not raise your hand against me," she warned, "for I will not be so charitable as the time we first met."

Her words sank into Reza's skull, and he realized the ridiculous futility of even attempting to attack her. The scar that marred her proud face was the result of a fluke that she had taken with good humor. To try and repeat the feat would be nothing less than suicide.

Reluctantly, he held the knife out to her, handle first.

"No," she told him, her voice echoing her satisfaction that the young animal was not going to act foolishly. "It is yours, a prize of your first contest. Your resourcefulness and spirit have saved you yet again, child."

Turning her attention to Esah-Zhurah, she knelt down to examine the girl's injuries, delicately probing the gashes with her talons. Esah-Zhurah twitched, but she did not regain consciousness.

Tesh-Dar stood up, satisfied. After a moment of reflection, she leaned over and took hold of the thong on Reza's leash, and Reza wondered how he had not tripped over it during the fight. She put it around her wrist and spoke to Reza, gesturing toward Esah-Zhurah with the staff in her other hand. "Carry her," she ordered.

Reza knelt down and picked Esah-Zhurah up in a fireman's carry, the blood from the wound on her head occasionally dripping down his back. Staggering under the load, he followed after the priestess as she strode down the street, occasionally tugging on his leash. The crowd respectfully parted in front of them, leaving eddies of conversation behind as they made their way out of the plaza and toward a different gate in the city wall.

They stopped just outside the gate at a corral that housed strange dinosaur-like creatures that Reza hadn't seen before. An attendant wearing a rough leather robe brought one of the animals, already saddled and bridled, to the priestess, who smoothly mounted the snorting beast. Then she turned it about, neatly plucking Esah-Zhurah from Reza's shoulders and laying her down across the animal's back, just in front of the saddle. Esah-Zhurah's head and feet dangled limply toward the ground on either side.

Tesh-Dar regarded Reza for a moment, wondering if she should let him ride with her. It was a long way to their destination.

"I will run," he told her without being prompted, his spirits buoyed by a sense of determination, even if he were to regret it later: he had no idea how far they had to go. He had already walked for hours that morning, but he was not about to ride with the creature that had killed his parents. His day for vengeance would come, he vowed to himself. Perhaps not this day, nor the next, but it would come. Until then, he would not give her the pleasure of seeing weakness in him.

"As you wish, little one," she said, wondering with some interest if he was up to the trek. If he were not, his carcass would feed the animals that roamed the forest. She had saved his life twice now. She would not do so a third time.

Or so she believed as she prompted her mount to a fast walk, Reza trailing along behind her like a hound following its master.

Seven

Reza sat alone under the shelter in the corral, watching the rain fall. He had no idea where he was, yesterday's journey ending well after dark. Nor did he know how far they had traveled, although it had been far enough that he could barely move his legs, they were so sore.

Upon their arrival last night, Kreelan girls had appeared to help the priestess with Esah-Zhurah. They carried her off into the dark, the priestess following them after dismounting her animal, entrusting it to yet another of the young warriors. Almost as an afterthought she had ordered that something be done with Reza, and some of the girls brought him into this stall and chained him up in what he had come to think of as the dinosaur pen.

He had already gauged his chances of breaking his chains and given up any thoughts of escape as hopeless. He was not too worried about water, as the troughs for the animals were full (although rather foul smelling). But food would soon become a problem. As would the vermin that had infested his scalp, he thought in frustration as he forced himself not to scratch the incessant itches that now plagued his head.

He watched as the strange animals – *magtheps*, they were called – nibbled at the coarse grain that had been dumped in their food troughs. Somewhat larger than a Terran horse, they had shaggy dark brown hair with black tiger stripes. Two powerful hind legs could propel the beasts at an impressive run, as he had observed from his rather unique vantage point the evening before, and each hind foot carried a set of talons that seemed obligatory for every species on this accursed planet. The front legs, diminutive in size, seemed well adapted for holding onto the fruit or leaves these creatures might have eaten in the wild. But despite their athletic build, their heads were nothing but homely, having short, droopy ears and incredibly large eyes set close over what looked like a beak with lips, and two wide nostrils on either side.

The beasts seemed almost to regard him as one of their own – something for which he was very thankful, considering their size and strength – and were nothing but gentle and reserved in their disposition toward him.

Sighing as he scratched one of the curious beasts behind an ear, he turned toward the morning sky and wondered what lay beyond it, in the depths of space. He fantasized that a human fleet was even now on its way here...

Then he sighed with resignation. There would be no Confederation Marines coming to his rescue. No Navy battlewagons were coming to save young Reza Gard from his blue-skinned alien captors. He was alone and would have to fend for himself. As it so often seemed he had.

He looked at the knife, the trophy from the warrior he had defeated. Only this morning, when there had been plenty of time to look at it, had he discovered that it was human-made: a Marine combat knife. Itself a grim reminder of his plight, it was the only physical link he had left to his own people. Everything else he had ever had, even the little silver cross that had been a gift from Nicole, had been taken from him. The knife's edge, while not as advanced as Kreelan blades, was nonetheless a testimony to human craftsmanship. It was razor sharp, exquisitely tailored for the act of killing another living being.

And that is what he had to look forward to, he knew. This race lived and died by a code of conduct based on the glorification of mortal combat, and he had to adapt to that code and make it work for him if he wanted to survive.

* * *

He awoke the next morning to the familiar smell of cooked meat, and opened his eyes to see a plate, a real china plate, sitting centimeters from his nose. It was loaded with properly cooked meat, fresh fruit, and the wheat cakes he had come to detest but forced himself to eat anyway. Esah-Zhurah, sitting next to him and watching him with her feline eyes, held a cup of ale for him.

Reza saw that the wounds on her face were all but healed.

"That is impossible," he breathed. He reached out a hand to touch her face, to make sure it was real. "How can your wounds be healed already?"

"Our healers make short work of such trifles," she said blandly, pushing his questing hand away.

Reza shook his head. Such a feat was well beyond anything he had ever read about for human medicine.

"How do you feel?" he asked, curious about her condition.

"Well enough," she said, bowing her head to him slightly in acknowledgment.

She looked into his eyes, her own glinting in the morning sun. "You must have fought well, human," she said, "for the priestess to take such an interest in you."

"What do you mean?" he asked, grabbing one of the tangy fruits and biting into it eagerly to satisfy his loudly-complaining stomach.

"Tesh-Dar, the priestess of this *kazha*, this school of the Way, has adopted you into the ranks of her pupils." She paused. "It is something for which there is no precedent. You should be very honored."

Reza glared at her. "How can I honor the one who killed my parents, who helped destroy my homeworld, who attacked yet another world to bring me here?" He broke a piece from the cake he held in his hands, half of it crumbling in his angry grip. "Maybe if I had not been so terrified," he muttered bitterly, "I could have rammed my father's knife into her brain instead of just cutting her face."

Esah-Zhurah leaned forward, her eyes wide. "You made the scar over her eye?" she whispered in awe.

Reza nodded, opting to stuff more food in his mouth rather than say anything more, trying to avoid those painful memories.

Esah-Zhurah silently pondered this newest revelation as Reza ate. When he was finished, she asked another question. "Why did you not let the warrior kill me?"

Reza stifled a bitter laugh. "If I would have let her kill you, where would that have left me?" he asked. "Alone on this world, without a single friend or ally, I cannot even blend in with your people in some vain hope of camouflaging myself, for my skin is not blue, nor do I have talons or fangs." He gestured at her chest. "Nor am I female."

"There is more to your actions," she said, her eyes noting the small nuances in his body language that she had been studying for so long.

He sighed at her probing of his motivations, but did not think it worthwhile to try and avoid answering her. "I do not consider you a friend," he said, looking her in the eye, "but you have kept me alive, for whatever reason. And for that, perhaps I am in your debt, and maybe by taking care of you I might increase my own chances of staying alive," he looked away, "until I can return home."

"That, human," she said slowly, "you shall never do." She swept her arm about her. "This is your home, now, for however long you may live. You shall never venture far from this place, and certainly shall never leave this world."

"Then what am I doing here?" he asked angrily, his hopes of a future fading to a dim, lifeless gray. His finger traced the edge of the china plate, now empty, that carried the words *C.S.S. Arizona* stenciled around the edge, and had the old battleship's crest emblazoned in the center. The *Arizona* had been destroyed in a horrendous fleet engagement near Kyrie the day Reza had been born. There had been countless fleet battles during the war, but that one had made it into the school history books. The irony was not lost on him.

"From this day on," she said, "you are to learn of the Way, as if you were to become one of us."

Reza opened his mouth in protest, but she silenced him with her own words, having anticipated his response. "You need not worry about serving the Empress, human," she said derisively. "We do not ask your allegiance to the Way, for you are not of it. You are here to satisfy Her curiosity, to see if animals such as yourself have a soul." Her voice left little doubt as to her own beliefs. In her mind, Reza was as much a spiritual being as the snorting magtheps in the stalls behind them.

"You do not believe I am your equal, do you?" he said. It was more a statement than a question as his mind grappled with the implications of what she was saying.

"No," she responded curtly. "I do not."

Reza smiled at her, baring his teeth as he had seen her do sometimes. "You will," he said, "even if I have to prove it to you." He leaned closer to her, his eyes burning fiercely. "In fact, I will prove that I am better than you. All you need is the courage to give me the chance."

The girl grunted, unimpressed. "That," she said, "the priestess has already granted." Her mouth crinkled in a Kreelan grin. "You will have ample opportunity to demonstrate your superiority, animal."

She gathered up the plate and cup in one hand and took Reza's leash in the other as she stood up, signaling an end to the conversation.

"Come," she ordered, leading him out of the barn. "You smell like the animal you are." Her nose wrinkled in disgust. "It is time for you to learn civilized ways."

* * *

Reza spent most of the morning trying to wash in the freezing water of a nearby stream under Esah-Zhurah's steady gaze. Modesty had long ceased to be a factor in their relationship, whatever it might otherwise be called. Esah-Zhurah gave him some kind of soap that he put in his hair to kill off the mites that had attacked his scalp, but the stuff burned his skin so badly that he almost would have rather left the tiny parasites in peace. When he finished, he stumbled out of the water, looking for the skins he had washed earlier and hung up to dry in some nearby bushes.

They were gone.

"Where are my clothes?" he asked her, shivering with cold, the breeze against his wet skin making him even colder than he had been in the water.

"You will need them no more," she replied cryptically. She stepped close to him and ran a hand over his chest, marveling at the blue cast of his skin. "Why do you change color?"

"Because I am freezing!" he answered testily, rubbing his hands over his arms to get his circulation going again. "No blood is reaching my skin," he explained through his chattering teeth. "That is what changes the color." He was less than amused by the inopportune disappearance of his clothes, but he forced himself to have patience. His keeper often worked in mysterious ways.

She *humphed* to herself and led him naked from the stream. He had never had anything on his feet since coming to this world, and now it seemed that the rest of him would go naked, as well.

"Damn," he cursed under his breath, too low for Esah-Zhurah to hear.

After a short brisk walk they found themselves at the entry to one of the many buildings of the kazha, a school that was as large as most human universities, ensconced here in the forest.

As Esah-Zhurah opened the arched door and ushered his naked, shivering body inside, he saw that it was an armory. Weapons ranging from short stilettos to pulse rifles and many others that he had never seen before were arrayed in orderly rows in racks on the walls flanking the well-lit main corridor. She led him down to the second archway on the left, and Reza temporarily forgot the cold that had been wracking his body. He saw nearly a dozen figures robed in black, fitting armor to several young female warriors, each of whom was clad only in the thin black gauzy material he had seen under his keeper's armor.

But this armor was not the same as that worn by the Kreelans in the city, Reza saw. It had no adornments of any type, no scrollwork or runes. It was completely utilitarian, and the robed Kreelans, the armorers, fitted each piece with exacting skill and precision. This armor was going to be used for its intended purpose, and their honor was at stake in its fitting.

Two of the girls were finished at the same time. After bowing to the armorers, they brushed past Reza with a hiss and bared fangs.

Esah-Zhurah bowed and then spoke briefly and rapidly with the senior armorer, gesturing toward Reza. The woman disappeared from the room.

"Stand here," Esah-Zhurah ordered, ushering Reza toward where four other armorers waited. Hands clasped inside the fabric of their robes, they eyed him – particularly his maleness – curiously.

"What–"

"Silence," Esah-Zhurah said sharply. "You will answer any questions they may put to you, but you will not ask any and interrupt their work. They must concentrate, or your armor may be less than perfect." She paused. "That would be an unfortunate situation in the arena."

While Reza worried about the ominous reference to the arena, one of the armorers unclipped his leash with her clawless hands, a trait Reza had not noticed before. Others began measuring his arms and legs with what looked like nothing more impressive than an ancient-style fabric tape measure that some human tailors still preferred to use.

After interminable measuring, one of them disappeared into another room, emerging an amazingly short time later with one of the black undergarments for Reza while the others continued their tasks.

"My thanks," he said fervently. He was grateful to finally have something to put on over his freezing skin.

They then measured him again, after which they began to test fit various pieces of leatherite armor, taking away the ones that were not perfect for reworking and refitting.

After several hours, Reza stood in a full complement of matte black leatherite, including sandals with wraps that came nearly to his knee. They had very tough soles and were without a doubt the most comfortable footwear he had ever worn. It was ironic that here, among the enemy of his race, his clothing and footwear was custom made; in House 48 he could never have even dreamed of such a luxury.

He flexed his hands in the black gauntlets that fit as if they were a second skin, feeling natural despite the metal claws that had been added to the fingers to even the odds against his naturally-endowed counterparts. Standing in this armor made him feel like he might have a chance of survival after all.

The armorers finally stepped away, except for two who bore the breast and backplates that shielded the wearer's vital torso area. Reza had fully expected to have two conic projections on the breastplate, such was the pervasiveness of the female form. He was amazed to see that, like everything else, the armorers had crafted plates just for him. They fit his chest perfectly.

Finished at last, the girl saluted the armorers, and Reza bowed his head to them, omitting the crossing of the arm. It was a ritual mandated by the many commandments they followed, but since he was not of "the Way," it did not apply to him. Yet he still wanted to show his respect.

The armorers, apparently somewhat less apprehensive or bigoted toward the alien among them than were the warriors, returned his gesture with no discernible malice.

"Come," Esah-Zhurah beckoned, leading him away by the arm. The leash had been left behind in the fitting room. Their trust in him to obey – and his understanding of that trust – was now implicit.

Once outside, she guided him to a secluded patch of grass in the midst of a stand of trees. They sat down, cross-legged, facing one other.

"Tomorrow," she told him, "you will begin a new life. All that has gone before, all that you have known and believed must be pushed aside, purged from your mind, if you wish to survive. There will be little margin for error, and no allowance made for weakness. You asked for the chance to prove yourself; so shall you have it.

"From now on," she explained, "you will learn to live and fight as we do, as have the warriors for the last twenty-seven thousand generations who have passed through the gates of all the kazhas such as this one. You are about the size and strength of those entering the intermediate combat training that is taught here. Thus you will be handicapped, for you have not had the training given the young ones, and you will be given no allowances for this shortcoming. Do you understand?"

"Yes," he said, wondering just what kind of nightmare he had fallen into.

Satisfied, Esah-Zhurah continued. "You will be taught in the ways of the Desh-Ka, the order of the priestess who brought you here. And I," she said with audible resignation, "am to be your *tresh*, your… partner."

"My partner?" he asked incredulously.

Esah-Zhurah shrugged. "There is no better description of it that you would understand, human," she said contemptuously. "The bonds of the tresh are much deeper than mere partnership or your concept of *friendship*. It is beyond your understanding. Besides," she added, "I doubt you will survive long enough for it to become an issue."

"We shall see," he said coldly.

Esah-Zhurah went on as if he had remained silent. "You no longer have a leash, yet you must be with me always, and I with you, unless I tell you otherwise. This is not because you are human; it is simply the way of the tresh. We will eat, learn, fight, and live together."

I am so looking forward to it, he thought sarcastically.

"For at the end of every cycle," she went on, "all of the tresh take part in The Challenge, a competition among the peers that begins the process of our adult ranking in the Way. Those who do well, rank highly. Those who do not… sometimes do not survive. Those tresh who die leave their partner standing alone, for tresh are bound for life to one another, come what may."

That thought hit Reza like a slap to his face. "So," he asked tentatively, "what would happen to you should I die?"

"I would be left alone," she said bitterly, "as I have been since my real tresh died two cycles ago."

"And what would become of me should you die?" he asked quietly. "What is to prevent one of the peers from taking any opportunity to kill me outright?"

"My death would be consistent with the Way: you would be left to fend for yourself, alone. It is an unenviable existence for any tresh, but especially for you, human.

"As for the peers trying to kill you, it is very unlikely unless they become careless or overzealous in the arena. The priestess demonstrated the good will to bring you here, and has given you armor from her stores, food and drink from her commissary." She gave him a hard look. "You do not understand the honor that she has accorded you, human, but perhaps you will learn. I do not believe she would look kindly upon anyone who killed you without just cause. Your life rests under her authority now, and it is much more powerful than any power I shall ever boast. Why she has intervened in your life is something she will reveal at a time of her own choosing, if she chooses to at all."

She leaned closer to him. "But beware," she warned, "for while her benevolence has kept you alive, it may just as easily get you killed. Death comes easily in the Way of my people. From my studies, I do not believe you will find life pleasant here. You will suffer extraordinary physical pain and exhausting hardships with little to hope for but to take yet another breath."

She leaned back. "Our training begins each day at dawn and ends at dusk. You will be subjected to tests of the body and the mind, and the price for failure will be pain or, worse, humiliation before the peers. And, like all things among the tresh, your partner will suffer with you until your learning is complete or one of you dies. I will suffer pain gladly," she said, "but do not humiliate me, human. Ever."

Reza could not believe how much today differed from yesterday. Then, he had been something between a slave and an animal, and now he was to learn how they lived, had been given a chance to survive. He did not care about the girl's warning of hardship and pain. He welcomed it. He had hope, tenuous though it might be, that he might someday, somehow, get back to humanity again.

But he was nagged by a persistent thought: would he still be human?

"If you teach me well," he told her, "I will not fail you, or myself."

Her eyes gleamed at the challenge in his voice. "Then let the new day come forth," she said, her fangs reflecting the red glow of sunset.

* * *

Reza lay awake, unable to sleep. His mind drifted from one thought to another as he pondered the coming dawn. He had asked Esah-Zhurah to explain more about what would happen, but the details she would not say.

He rolled over in his hide blanket to look at her, asleep nearby. What humiliation must she be enduring, he wondered, to be the tresh of a human, an animal? How must she feel, having to sleep outdoors in the forest rather than in the shelter of the dormitory buildings because Reza was unclean, and she was bound to him?

He glanced up at the stars. Somewhere out there were people he had known, going about their daily business. Maybe one of them paused now and again to think about the child with dark brown hair named Reza Gard, the one who loved to read for endless hours, the one who entertained the little children reading stories about princes and princesses from ancient times. Perhaps, Reza thought, Wiley Hickock's face suddenly surfacing in his mind, there was a Marine Corps recruiter somewhere asking if anyone knew the whereabouts of one Reza Gard, whose pre-draft requirements had come up. Maybe one of the billion specks of light in the cloudless sky was a human ship, a battleship, about to rake an enemy vessel with its fiery broadside. Or perhaps it was Nicole in her fighter, tight on the tail of a Kreelan destroyer.

He listened to Esah-Zhurah's deep, steady breathing next to him, and wondered what Wiley would do if he were here. That thought brought about a wave of guilt. Was Reza collaborating with the enemy simply by wanting to stay alive? And what would people think – if he ever did return to human space – when they discovered that he slept with the enemy, ate with the enemy, and had learned to think and speak like the enemy? Would he not become the enemy himself?

He tried to force the thoughts from his mind. He would become an alien to survive while he lived among them, but he would not let go his roots. The Kreelans had taken away everything else that he had known, but he would not give them his soul, a soul they did not even believe he possessed.

He looked at her again. Now that he thought about being her partner, he rapidly came to the conclusion that he could have done a lot worse. She seemed tough, but not as brutal as some of them appeared, and she was obviously extremely intelligent. She had treated him fairly well, considering her origins. He found that he did not want to disappoint her, did not want her to be humiliated. He wanted very much to survive the things that lay ahead, but he wanted to do it with dignity and honor, something that these people did not believe he had.

Her eyes suddenly flew open, startling him. He had been looking straight into her face.

"Reza," she spoke quietly, "you must sleep now. Tomorrow will come of its own accord. You must be rested. Sleep."

He stared into her silver eyes, lit by the enormous moon – the Empress Moon, he reminded himself – that shone high above. Of all the things about her and her kind, it was the eyes that captivated him. He held them for a moment longer, mesmerized by their beauty. His mind warred with itself, guilty for feeling such thoughts, but unable to deny them.

Finally putting off that particular battle for another time, he nodded to her, and she closed her eyes.

After a few minutes, his own eyes closed as he fell into an uneasy sleep.

* * *

Reza awoke as the Kreelan sun cast its first rays over the valley. Surprised that he had arisen before his keeper – his tresh, now, he reminded himself – he took the opportunity to enjoy a brief moment of this alien planet's natural wonder as the sky sparkled in vivid hues of crimson and yellow. But the transition lasted only a moment before the odd magenta shade of the daytime sky began to claim its territory from the dawn.

He put on his armor and was preparing their usual morning meal – dried meat for her and some fruit for himself – when at last Esah-Zhurah began to stir.

"Good morning," he said.

She only looked at him as she stretched and began to put on her armor.

Reza shrugged. *She's never been a morning person*, he thought. He handed her the strips of stiff dry meat he had cut off the hunk in her pack. She accepted them without comment and began to tear them up with her canines before swallowing the pieces almost whole. That was unusual; she normally chewed her food carefully and took her time.

"Is something bothering you?" he asked.

"Yes," she answered without hesitation.

"Well," he prompted after she remained silent, "what is it?"

She sighed. "There will be a ceremony today," she said, "the most important one a tresh will ever attend. For you, it probably will also be the most difficult. And if you fail to perform it, I will be forced to kill you." She paused briefly. "And myself."

Reza sat down, suddenly serious, suddenly angry. "Why did you not tell me of this before?"

"I was forbidden," she told him. "In any case, it does not matter. What is important is that you must take what you would call an oath," she told him slowly. "Not to declare your honor to the Empress," she said, "but as a sign of your responsibilities as a tresh. Even for you, an animal, the priestess believes this important. And you must do it freely, and with conviction. You must consider this carefully, human." She glanced at the rising sun, calculating the time. "When the sun is there," she gestured with her arm to a point where the sun would just be fully over the tree line, "it will be time."

"And if I refuse?" he asked.

"If you refuse, you will die. And after you have breathed your last, then so shall I. It is your choice."

He unsteadily rose to his feet and began to pace, occasionally glancing at the sun as if to slow its inevitable rise into the sky. He did not have long. If he died, here and now, he thought, who would know of it, and who would care? Certainly not these people, to whom he was a mere beast. But neither would humanity, he told to himself. To them he was almost certainly dead and gone, a memory at best, a forgotten burden on society at worst, never having had the chance to make a small mark on the universe. Perhaps Nicole would think of him from time to time, but only in the past tense, as another casualty of the war, an element of the past in her own tragic life.

Reza wanted so much to go on living. He would not sell his soul for an extra minute of life, but he was willing to suffer for it. He had been suffering for his next breath for most of his life, and if he had to declare himself willing to submit to their rules of life in order to live, he would. That was not a question of loyalty; it did not make him a traitor in his mind.

And even his loyalty, he decided at long last, was not really to his race. It was to certain people, the people he had known and loved, even if they only lived on in his memory. Wiley, Mary, and the few others he had called friends, all from Hallmark, all probably dead. All except Nicole, the girl he had loved, and still loved. But the rest of human society, he knew from bitter experience, had treated him little better than the Kreelans had, and in some cases, worse. To them he owed nothing.

"You must not accept if you cannot pledge yourself sincerely, human," Esah-Zhurah counseled. "By accepting, you accept all that is the Way: the physical, mental, and spiritual things that bind my people together. You must, in effect, become one with us, if you can. If you feel incapable of this, it would be better to die now as the alien you are, rather than inflict dishonor on yourself and on me. If you are not sincere, the priestess will know. She can see what is in your heart."

"And if I did make it through all of this, would your people accept me?" he asked sharply. "Will I ever be anything but an animal to you and the peers? Or will I endure all that you inflict on me, only to be killed at the end of this grand experiment?"

Esah-Zhurah stood and walked over to him. She grasped his arms in her hands and leaned very close. "Should such a thing ever come to pass," she said quietly, "should you survive all that is to come, and the Empress judge you worthy of the Way, you will receive one of these," she touched her collar with a silver talon. "This signifies your entry into Her family, and endows you with more than what you would call citizenship. It is your badge of honor, the signal of the Empress's blessing. Any who would not accord you every tribute due your standing would be shamed in Her eyes, something that is intolerable to all among Her Children. For this," she tapped the collar again, "is not easily earned, is not given to all who are born into this life." She ran her nail along the several rows of pendants hanging from the collar. "But first, human," she said, "you must prove that you have a soul, that your blood sings the melody of the Way."

"I do not understand what you mean," he said, confused. "How can my blood sing?"

"That is what we have yet to discover," she replied cryptically.

Reza pursed his lips, his concentration easing as the inevitable conclusion presented itself. "I agree," he said simply, bowing his head to her. There was no other choice.

"Very well," she said, her voice echoing barely concealed doubt, whether at his intention of fulfilling his part of the bargain or at the likelihood of his survival, he did not know. She looked quickly at the steadily rising sun. "I must teach you the words of the ceremony. We do not have much time."

Under the gathering dawn, Reza began to learn the declaration of his acceptance of an alien way of life.

* * *

When it was time, Esah-Zhurah took him to one of the arenas where several hundred other young warriors were gathered. Many were arrayed around the edges of the circular field. These Kreelans all had neckbands. Those gathering within the arena itself were without, and several senior warriors were putting them into orderly rows.

"You will be on your own for this, human," Esah-Zhurah told him. He nodded that he understood, and she gestured for him to enter the arena.

He walked forward through the dark sand to where the others were gathering and made toward one of the warriors arranging the neophytes for their proclamation of faith. She took him roughly by the arm and escorted him to a point of the hexagon that had been marked in the sand that was well away from the other neophytes. The warrior then resumed her place at the front of the group that now numbered about two hundred. She turned to the assemblage.

"*Ka'a mekh!*" she bellowed, and the young warriors knelt as one, crossing their left arms over their breasts in salute and lowering their heads in submission. Reza knelt, but did not salute; in their eyes, he was not yet worthy. The warrior turned around, her back to the neophytes, and knelt herself.

Then the priestess, Tesh-Dar, appeared from among the warriors surrounding the arena. She strode to a position well in front of the kneeling throng before her, the early morning sun gleaming from her ceremonial armor, her long braided hair swaying to her gait. She stood before them, feet planted shoulder width apart, head held high, and she began to recite the preamble to the rite of passage.

"Oh, Empress, Mother of our spirit, before you kneel those who would seek the Way–"

"–to become one with their ancestors," Reza heard himself murmur in time with the others, "to become one with their peers, to become one with all who shall come after."

"Those who kneel this day seek the privilege of The Challenge–"

"–to learn to fight and die in the flesh, that the spirit of Thy Children may grow ever stronger, that our blood may sing to Thee."

"Bound shall they be from this day forward–"

"–to the honor of the collar, the symbol of our bond with Thee, the badge of our honor–"

"–to be worn unto Death," the priestess finished.

One of the elder warriors stood and ordered the young neophytes to stand. Once they had done so, she led the priestess through the rows on what appeared to be a rank inspection.

When Tesh-Dar reached him, he bowed his head as the others had done, averting his eyes from her gaze. She stood there for a moment, perhaps a bit longer than she had in front of the others, before she moved on.

Finally, she returned to the front of the formation and spoke a few words to the accompanying warrior. She, in turn, ordered the neophytes to kneel again, and the priestess departed without another word. Then, with a final order, they all stood once more, and the Kreelans surrounding the arena let out a horrendous roar of approval.

Reza stood quietly, unable to dispel a feeling of despair that had deepened with every word. No matter what Esah-Zhurah had said, what he had taken was still an oath of fealty to the Empress, for to follow the Way – whatever that truly meant – was to follow her.

"You did well," Esah-Zhurah said as she came to his side. "Your words were clear among the voices of the peers, which speaks well of your commitment."

"For all the good it may do me," he replied somberly.

"Come," she said, taking him by the arm, apparently uplifted by his depressed mood, "we have much to do this day. It is time to begin your training." She guided him toward one of the smaller arenas where a number of other neophytes had gathered, eyeing the two of them with great curiosity. "It shall be a day you will long remember."

Reza shot her a sideways glance. "I have no doubt."

* * *

He lay that night in an aching heap in his bedding of soft skins. Esah-Zhurah had told him that the first step to the Way was to build a sound body, but what he had endured in the arena that day had been brutal.

After the ceremony and until the sun set and the huge gong at the kazha's center rang to sound day's end, the tresh ran, jumped, sparred, and wrestled with one another. The routine was broken three times by the appearance of three different senior disciples, who instructed them on different weapons and techniques that they put into practice immediately.

Reza, not having had the benefit of any such training when he was younger, had been hit and battered by the blunt ends and edges of the training weapons so many times that his body felt like one enormous bruise. His lip had been split open, he had a deep gash above his right ear, and his legs had been pounded so much he could barely walk. Esah-Zhurah had to help him hobble back to their little camp in the woods where a healer tended to his wounds. But even after she had finished, his body remained an ocean of pain.

But he had never cried out, nor had he complained. No matter how many times his legs were tripped from under him, no matter how hard the other tresh – particularly Esah-Zhurah – struck him, he staggered back to his feet so he could take some more.

He rolled over to face the fire that burned brightly in their little camp near the stables, biting back the urge to groan at the throbbing pain. He watched Esah-

Zhurah as she unbraided her hair, meticulously combing it out with her talons once it was free.

Reza idly considered the condition of his own hair as a diversion from his aching body. Now shoulder length and dark brown, it was festooned with knots and mats, for he had nothing to comb it with. On impulse, and despite the gnawing pain, he decided just to cut off most of his hair with his knife. He had always liked his hair cut short, and it would be much easier to care for.

He sat up, hissing through his teeth at the pain of simply moving. He tossed aside his hides, letting in the evening chill. The black gauzy material that formed his undergarments was incredibly comfortable, but was not a very effective insulator against the cold. He probed with his fingers through the thickening thatch of hair over his skull, trying to get an idea of where to start. In the end, he simply grabbed a handful at random and reached for his knife with his other hand.

The blade was just biting through the first strands when he was tackled from behind, Esah-Zhurah wrenching the knife from his hand.

"No!" she cried, flattening him against the ground.

"*What the hell?*" he sputtered in Standard. "What is wrong?" he demanded in the New Tongue, struggling against her weight.

She rolled him over on his back, flashing the knife in front of his eyes. "Never do that!" she exclaimed. "Why would you do such a thing?"

"What?" he asked, utterly confused. "Cut my hair? It is matted and snarled, and I prefer it short. I–"

With a growl of frustration she plunged the knife's blade into the ground, burying it nearly up to its handle.

"You must never cut your hair," she told him. "It is one of your most sacred possessions. Have I not told you this, fool? The only ones who follow the Way and have short hair are those who have been disgraced and been denied suicide. It is the worst punishment among our people. If you follow the Way, you must let your hair grow, for it is the only mark of longevity for my race. Except for those like the ancient mistress of the armory, our bodies do not age in the same fashion as do yours. Our skin does not decay, nor do our muscles weaken until we are very near death. By the hair and by this," she tapped her collar, "are you judged by the peers."

Reza sat back, confounded. "Well, if I have to grow it, I will need something to comb it with."

"You use these," she said in frustration, as if Reza were a slow-witted child, holding up her hands and wiggling her fingers. "Have you not seen me use them for this purpose?" The firelight shone on her silver claws as they danced to and fro. Then she pointed at his gauntlets with their imitation talons. "Here," she said, grabbing them, "I will show you." She made Reza put them on. Then she sat up behind him and began to comb his hair with her own claws, skillfully ferreting out and eliminating the snarls with only a rare painful pull.

"Now," she said after she had done most of the difficult work, "you try."

He put on the gauntlets and began to work their claws through his hair, but was so clumsy she felt compelled to grab his hands before they had gone more than an inch past his hairline.

"Be careful," she warned. "You will cut yourself badly. You must do it like this." Her hands guided his through the gradually aligning strands, and she soon left him to do it himself.

He only scratched himself once or twice by the time he had combed everything out to his satisfaction. When he was done, it felt much better, although the hair that hung over his eyes remained a problem. He tried to brush it back, but it stolidly refused, instead sticking out at all angles as if he were carrying a hefty charge of static electricity.

Esah-Zhurah leaned over his shoulder to get a look at his face, and she burst out in what he thought must be laughter. Brief though it was, she had never made that sound before.

"Are you laughing?" he asked skeptically, watching her face closely. "Do you think I look...*funny* with my hair like this?"

"Perhaps that is what you would call it," she answered. "I do not think it is quite the same for my people. But yes," she said, considering the question, "you do look *funny*."

Without warning she reached toward his face and grabbed the hair in front of his eyes. She cut it off cleanly with one of her claws in the time it took him to blink.

"This, you do not need," she informed him. "Only that which flows down your back." She regarded him for a moment, then nodded in approval. "Your hair is yet too short to braid. That will come later." She ran a hand through his hair, her touch sending a pleasant tingle down his spine. "You must groom well every day. Your hair is thick, but will foul easily." Then she turned her attention to the lock she still held in her hand. "May I keep this?" she asked.

"If it means something to you," he told her, "you are welcome to it."

She bowed her head to him and carefully placed the hair in a pouch that hung on her waistband, nearly identical to the one the priestess – and all the other warriors, he realized – carried.

"We should sleep, now," she told him. She banked the fire and returned to her bedding.

Reza followed suit, stifling a groan from his protesting muscles.

"Tomorrow shall soon be upon us," she murmured as she lay down.

He did not need further prompting. He buried himself under the thick skins, and was asleep as soon as he closed his eyes.

* * *

The days became weeks, then months, and Reza's body grew toward the man he might one day become, if he lived long enough. He had already outgrown three sets of armor, and the seams on the newest were stretching at the shoulders.

Esah-Zhurah, too, was gradually changing as the shadows slowly lengthened toward winter in the planet's extended seasonal cycle. Her body was filling out and becoming more powerful, her arms and legs rippling with lean muscle. She moved with the grace of a dancer, and he did his best to emulate her, learning how to move quickly and quietly. Her black hair grew ever longer. The beads attached to the ends now reached her waist, and the protuberances that were her eyebrows had formed into a graceful arch over her eyes.

After the furious hours of their normal training, the two often walked or ran long leagues under the ceaseless sun and cool, fresh air, and Reza felt himself growing stronger day by day. They silently challenged one other in undeclared races through the forest or up a hill, and while she often won, the margin was an increasingly small one.

As time went on, he and the other tresh began to build on the foundation that had come with the endless exercises and mock combats. Reza discovered with some surprise that they had something akin to team sports, with hardwood poles serving as swords, and he played them just as aggressively as his blue-skinned companions. While he often spent the nights nursing welts and bruises, increasingly he was able to compete on their terms, and his Kreelan counterparts were beginning to show him some degree of respect.

However, as Reza one day discovered, there was more to be found at the kazha than endless hours of fighting practice and nights filled with pain.

Late one evening, he and Esah-Zhurah were in the armorers' chambers having their weapons and armor checked. While the duty armorer and her apprentices were busy with Esah-Zhurah, Reza happened to notice a lone armorer sitting alone at a small stone table in an adjoining room. She was quite old, judging from the length of her hair and the slight palsy that caused her neck to twitch. She bent close to her work, her eyes perhaps having grown weak from countless years (he still had no idea how long Kreelans could live) of such painstaking labor. A lamp hung close to the table's surface, and he caught sight of what appeared to be a brush of some kind in her hand. His curiosity mounted as he watched her make a stroke on whatever was serving as her canvas, dipping the brush in a small container, then continuing to paint.

Without conscious thought, he wandered over to where the old woman worked, curious as to what she was doing. Lying on the table was the metal that would become a warrior's ceremonial breastplate, and on it she had traced a design whose origins and meaning were beyond him, one of the runes in what he knew was the Old Tongue, but which he could not read. But the beauty and intricacy of the woman's craftsmanship were universal. It was an ice-blue rune, arcing its way across the metal surface like an ancient scimitar, the colors used in its creation precise to render an effect that was almost three-dimensional, each shade and hue regulated and blended to perfection.

He stood quietly behind her as she slowly filled in a segment that would be the design's center, fascinated by the steadiness of her ancient hand.

"If your hands hold the interest of your eyes, little one," she said in a soft voice, startling him, "yours is it to try." She looked up at him, her eyes milky with cataracts, so old perhaps that the healers could do no more for her. Or perhaps she did not want their help.

Reza, dumbfounded, nodded stiffly. The woman rose from her stool, her joints creaking loudly, and gestured for him to sit. She handed him the brush and proceeded to guide his hand along the trace of the rune with one hand, while supporting herself on his shoulder with the other. When she judged that the brush needed more dye, she guided his hand toward the appropriate vial. There were dozens of them, Reza saw, as well as a seemingly endless variety of hues the old woman had created by mixing other colors, placed with exacting care on the palette next to his elbow.

Time was lost to him for the rest of that evening. He had forgotten everything except the glowing design that was assuming its final form under his hand, with the old woman's help.

At last, it was done. He had finished the last quarter of it by himself, with only occasional prompts from the woman. His hand was cramping from holding the brush, but he felt oddly triumphant. He had helped create something of beauty, and had not had to fight or be beaten to do it.

"Good is your work, little one," she said as he held the breastplate up to the light for her inspection, her tired eyes still somehow able to see. "The priestess shall be pleased."

"The... priestess?" Reza stuttered.

"Of course, young tresh," she said, her nearly toothless mouth curling into a kindly smile. "Did you not notice its size?"

"No..." he said, shaking his head. But it was immediately obvious, now that she had pointed out the fact. The plate was nearly twice the size of his, if not larger. "No, I did not."

"More observant should you be, then," she advised. "Short is a warrior's life, otherwise."

"Of course..." Reza paused, looking at her helplessly. *Her name*, he thought. *I should be able to figure out her name. But how?*

"Pan'ne-Sharakh," she said, as if reading his mind. "Her Children know each other by blood, human," she said cryptically. "But it is also written here," her fingers pointed in sequence to five of the many pendants that hung from her collar, "in the shape of the stars that are brightest in the sky when the Empress Moon is directly above. Look at the sky this night, and you will know the ones of which I speak. Their names your tresh shall teach you. They are the key."

"Thank you, Pan'ne-Sharakh," he said gratefully, bowing his head. "Thank you for your kindness."

"I serve Her in my own way, little one," she answered softly, patting his shoulder gently before turning back to her work.

He turned to leave, and found Esah-Zhurah standing in the doorway. He realized with a shock that she must have been standing there for hours.

She brushed past him to greet the old woman, bowing with reverence, and spoke quietly with her for a moment. Then Pan'ne-Sharakh slowly shuffled from the room, her back bowed with age.

"She seems to feel you have a talent for such work," Esah-Zhurah told him, obviously surprised. "You shall develop that skill in addition to your others, but not in their stead. Should you have the time," she added dubiously. She gestured impatiently toward the exit. "Let us go."

He followed her back to their little camp, looking at the stars in the sky.

And there they were, as the old woman had said they would be: the five bright points of light that would frame the Empress Moon when it hung directly overhead, the key to the names of Her Children.

Eight

The sword flashed down in a savage arc, the sun's glow blazing from the metal as if the weapon itself was made of light.

Reza pitched himself to the right, dodging the blade, then kicked out with his left foot, his thigh like a massive piston that drove the air from Nyana-M'kher's lungs and flung her to the ground. The few seconds of surprise his parry had given him was all he needed. Smoothly drawing the black shrekka from its holder on his left shoulder, he hurled the hand-held buzz saw and watched with satisfaction as it buried itself in the ground five centimeters from Nyana-M'kher's head, showering her with sand from the arena's floor.

"Enough!" called the arena's umpire, a stocky warrior by the name of Syr-Kesh. A gesture of her hand made Reza's victory official.

Reza collapsed on his knees into the sand next to Nyana-M'kher, who was also trying to get her breath back. She struggled to her knees, and the two of them bowed their heads to Syr-Kesh, Nyana-M'kher saluting as she did so. Then they both knelt there for the brief time that was allowed for meditation after one combat and before the next, a mental cool-down that the Kreelans considered an essential part of their routine.

Reza closed his eyes as his mind made the rounds of his body, sounding it out for damage and weakness, evaluating and relaxing each muscle in turn. Their combat had taken an unusually long time – nearly ten minutes, so evenly matched had they been – and his shoulders and legs ached fiercely from the duel. It had been the third one today for both of them, and this one had been Reza's only win. He had lost the first match to a senior tresh in a spectacularly one-sided – and decidedly brief – engagement, and the other to a very young tresh who felled him with a lightning-swift cut to the legs that would have crippled him for life had the sword carried any edge.

In these moments, when he turned inward like this, he was amazed at how much control he was gaining over his body and his mind. With a handful of exceptions, notably in his mid-back and feet, he could flex each muscle individually, leaving those around it totally relaxed. His breathing and heart rate, too, were gradually coming under better control, and he found that he could hold his breath for nearly three minutes before he felt compelled to take a breath. Even then, he could force himself to breathe normally and keep his heart rate at a steady cadence, rather than take huge gulps of air as his heart raced to get oxygen back into his system and to his brain.

His fighting skills, while hardly impressive by Kreelan standards, had improved to the point where he was no longer the punching bag he had been when he had arrived. While he returned with Esah-Zhurah to their tiny camp each night bruised and often beaten, those who faced him in the arena treated him with respect for his cunning and tenacity, if not for his neophyte fighting skills. The days of underestimating the human, the human many of them had been convinced would simply wither away and die in those early days, were over. Reza had quickly come to understand the soul-deep importance of combat to the Kreelans, and had devoted himself to its study. He observed and mimicked the others, especially Esah-Zhurah, and invented his own tactics. He went over moves in his mind, awake and asleep, before putting them to the test in his waking hours.

And after the combat was finished for the day and they had eaten, Esah-Zhurah would lecture him for hours on the ways of her people, on the Way itself. Gradually, he came to understand that the Way was not just an ideology, a set of abstract concepts meant to structure their lives such as the laws of humankind sought to do, but it was also a physical thing. While he did not yet understand just how it worked, the Way was intertwined with their racial bloodline: when Esah-Zhurah described her people as the Children of the Empress, it was – literally – true. There was some physiological thread that bound them together in much the same way that ants or bees of a particular colony identified themselves and their functions as part of a much larger whole. But how this worked, he did not yet understand. Nor, surprisingly, did Esah-Zhurah.

"It simply is," she had told him once. "Her will is as fundamental to us and as evident as is the air we breathe. I do not hear Her voice in my mind; I am not a telepath. But I sense in my blood that which She seeks for us, and I know my place in Her design."

Reza had pondered those words many times since, with a vague sense of loneliness, and perhaps even jealousy, clouding his heart. For he did not know Her will, and he feared his own destiny within the strands of the web the Empress wove for Her people.

"Time," Syr-Kesh called, and Reza's reflection disappeared like sea mist blown clear by the morning wind. He bowed his head once more to Syr-Kesh before getting to his feet, walking to where Esah-Zhurah stood waiting for him near the entry to the arena. Behind him, several tresh frantically raked the sand smooth for the next contest.

"You did well, my tresh," Esah-Zhurah said as he approached, and he bowed his head to her in respect. "Much better than I expected, especially without the sword on which you have so heavily depended to this time." Reza ignored the barb, a ritual habit of hers that never failed to annoy him, but about which he could do nothing. A part of him hated her deeply, but another part, what he often hoped was the most human part, wanted her respect, wanted her to be proud of him. "But these practice sessions are as nothing compared to the Challenge you will face in four days. Your opponents here do not show all of their skill or their strength, they do not waste their energies here, as do you, but save them for the time when they will need them most."

"What does it matter?" he asked angrily. "I can only do my best. If I am beaten in the first match of the first Challenge, then so be it." He shrugged out of his armor, letting Esah-Zhurah open his black shirt to apply one of the writhing living bandages to the creased welt on his shoulder. Nyana-M'kher had brought her sword down on the joint between his shoulder armor and the metal backplate, pinching a hand's breadth of Reza's flesh into a puckering tear that had proved incredibly painful for the rest of the extended combat. "But one day," he said, more to himself than to her, "I will stand in the final arena with the winning sword in my hands."

"That," Esah-Zhurah said as she massaged the oozing mottled mass of the bandage into the wound on Reza's shoulder, her voice tinged with sarcasm that sounded all too human, "is a day I wish not to miss."

Reza flinched as she pressed at the wound. A shudder of revulsion swept through him as he felt the amoebic mass of tissue begin to merge with his flesh, mysteriously healing it. It would leave a sculpted scar in its wake, a trophy of his tiny victory. He knew that whatever the thing was, however it and the things like it were made – or bred – it was infinitely beyond any comparable human technique he could imagine. The scope of wounds and injuries, even diseases that it could treat was apparently limitless. But having another living thing pressed into his flesh, and knowing that it would become a part of him, a perfect symbiosis, left him yearning for the cold touch and electric hum of the instruments and analyzers, the smells of ozone and alcohol, of the little clinic of House 48.

The pain made him think of the last, and worst, time Esah-Zhurah had punished him for anything. The only thing among the countless subjects they discussed that she adamantly refused to reveal to him was if there were any males in their society, and if so, where they were. On this one subject he could get nothing out of her other than, "You shall know when the time comes, if it comes," and the subject would be considered closed.

The one time Reza had tried to push her on it, the last time he had asked about it, she had turned on him like a lioness defending her cubs. She had beaten him so severely that he missed nearly three days of training, spending most of that time in the care of the healers as they reset the five ribs and one arm that Esah-Zhurah had broken in the course of his punishment. The healing process had been nearly as bad as the beating itself, especially when they held him down and forced his mouth open, pouring a wet mass of the undulating healing gel down his throat. It slid across his tongue like a wet oyster before pumping itself into his airway and then his lungs. In the moment before it stilled the pain of the jagged edges of the ribs tearing into his lungs and made breathing easier for him, he thought he would go mad at the thing churning within his body. Esah-Zhurah had chastised him afterward for being a coward, shaming her before the healers with his squeals of revulsion. Her words had burned themselves into his heart and mind as he lay in the infirmary for the next three days with her sitting next to him, back turned, silent. If she had heard him call her name, or felt his tentative touch, or sensed the silent tears he shed, she did not show it. Only when the elder healer had cleared him as being well and he had risen from the bed of skins had she addressed him, and then as if nothing had happened.

"There," she said, closing his shirt. She helped him get his torso armor back on, the bandage throbbing uncomfortably. "Come. You have completed your three obligatory matches for this day, and I have something for you."

"What?" Reza asked, his mind alert to the mischievous undertone in her voice.

"Patience," she said, her eyes laughing at him. "You shall see."

He followed her, and was surprised when she led him to the stable where the magtheps honked and snorted as they stomped about their enclosure. Reza's nose quickly filled with their musky smell, a smell he had become quite accustomed to in his first few days here, when he had to sleep with the animals, chained to a post.

"What is this about?" he asked her.

"Tomorrow we begin our free time before the Challenge," she told him. "From sunrise tomorrow to sunset the second day after that, we may do as we please."

"So?"

She turned to him. "I wish to take you somewhere," she told him, "and, unless you wish to run to the mountains," she gestured to the distant peaks on the northern horizon, "you will need to learn to ride."

Reza's heart suddenly began to beat faster. "You will teach me this?" he asked, his voice betraying his hopefulness. How long had he been here, he wondered. A Standard year, perhaps? Two? And this would be the first time he would ride one of these fascinating animals, rather than running along behind them like a dog.

Esah-Zhurah smiled, mimicking a human, her lips parting to reveal her ivory incisors. "I will provide you an animal," she said. "The rest will be up to you." She paused a moment, watching Reza's face turn from hopeful excitement to wary reservation. "It should be interesting to see one animal ride another."

"Where is it?" he asked, forcing himself to be calm, forever wondering why he continued to hope for some kind of real respect from her, or even a little genuine warmth. *Without doubt*, he told himself cynically, *you are the galaxy's greatest optimist.*

"Come," she said, beckoning him to follow. She led him around the enclosure, stopping in the low-ceilinged tack room at the far side of the stable where she retrieved a riding harness and a light saddle, which she gave to Reza.

When he followed her around to the far side, he found himself standing at the gate to a large, individual enclosure that he had not seen before.

"This is the animal," she told him, pointing into the enclosure.

A single beast stood there, a young bull that was larger than any magthep Reza had ever seen. The animal stood alone, except for the scrub rats that darted across the enclosure, searching for food. Its eyes were fixed on Esah-Zhurah and himself, and Reza could see that the animal was uneasy at their presence by the way it perked its floppy ears and nervously shifted its weight from foot to foot. The talons, grown too long on this soft ground without a trim, raised small clouds of dust from the parched soil. Its hide was dirty and unkempt, and Reza could easily make out the whitish tracks of scars that crisscrossed the massive animal's back and withers.

"This animal has been mistreated," he remarked coldly.

Esah-Zhurah snorted. "That is not so," she protested. "It simply refuses to be tamed. The scars you see were left by riders when thrown from its back. It has never been beaten as punishment."

A clear advantage over my social status, Reza told himself sourly. "If no one can ride it," he asked, "why is it kept in the stables? Why not let it run free or kill it for meat?"

"Because," she said, "there are those who find such challenges entertaining."

"And those," he finished for her, "who are entertained by watching someone as they are thrown and then trampled."

"Here," she said, pointedly ignoring his comment as she gave him the bridle, the leather saddle already in his other hand.

He was about to mention the fact that she had not bothered to show him how to attach the saddle and bridle, but decided against it. Both of them were relatively simple devices that he had already seen on other animals, and he was sure he could figure them out. The major problem, he thought, was going to be getting close enough to the snorting magthep to put them on. And, until that was accomplished, he did not have to consider the prospect of being thrown. He only had to worry about being trampled and then shredded to pieces by the hooked talons on the animal's feet.

As he pondered his first move, a glint of green near his sandal caught his attention, and he saw with surprise that he was standing in a patch of *yezhe'e* plants, which he knew magtheps liked. Looking at the beast's enclosure, he saw that he was standing on the edge of a green border that marked the magthep's reach beyond the wooden bars, everything closer to the fence having already been plucked from the ground and eaten.

Gathering the saddle and bridle in one hand, he leaned down and pulled as many shoots as he could hold. Reza noted with satisfaction that the prospective food had not eluded the magthep's wary eye. With cautious steps and flared nostrils, it moved slowly toward him.

Reza motioned for Esah-Zhurah to open the gate. Once inside, she closed it behind him, the squeak of the wood jangling his nerves. He let out his breath quietly, forcing himself to relax as the beast came closer, its large almond-shaped eyes and their yellow irises fixed on him. He decided to leave the riding gear behind for the moment, setting the bridle and saddle down slowly so as not to startle the animal. If he could not gain its trust, he would not need them. Then he took off his gauntlets with their gleaming talons and hooked them onto his belt, hoping the touch of his bare hands might be more reassuring than the lethal weapons his fingers became when encased in the armored gloves.

Now armed only with the tempting plants, he began to slowly walk toward the magthep, calling to it quietly. "Easy, boy," he said in Standard low enough that he knew Esah-Zhurah would not hear, and thus take offense. "Take it easy."

Esah-Zhurah watched as Reza began to play out whatever strategy he had decided upon, and was not surprised when other tresh began to take an interest in the proceedings. They came to cling to the fence like iron filings to a magnet, eager to see the outcome of the human's fourth combat of the day. For a moment, a streak of an unfamiliar emotion passed over her heart like a wisp of cloud before the sun: guilt. She had not told him that the scars on the animal's back had been left not by simple riders thrown by an unruly beast, but by the best trainers in the kazha who had all tried – and failed miserably – to train the magthep, to make it a riding animal. One of them had even been killed after the animal had become enraged, tearing the helpless fallen rider to pieces. But even after that, no one had suggested that the animal be killed. It was a challenge to be conquered, a mountain to be climbed, and those were the things on which her species thrived. But the others who sought to try their hand knew the animal's history. Reza did not.

It did not matter, she told herself firmly. The animal – Reza – would not, could not long survive in her world, among her people. His death would come soon. If not today under the magthep's feet, then a few days hence during the Challenge, when there were few rules and death was an unfortunate, if infrequent, consequence. And if not then, her mind went on as she watched him come under the animal's nervous shadow, there was always the Challenge of the next cycle, and the cycle after that...

Reza and the magthep had come as close as either dared for the moment, each eyeing the other warily, alert for any sudden or suspicious movement. Reza could see that the bull was a very young adult, its tiger-striped fur thick and lush under the coating of dust and grime, the hair around its wet muzzle still dark, with no sign of gray. But its size was nothing short of extraordinary, its powerful shoulders well over his head. The beast's nostrils flared at his scent, but he saw the animal's attention inexorably drawn toward the plants he held in his hand, their scent a powerful distraction. Carefully, slowly, Reza took one of the shoots in his free hand and extended it toward the magthep, palm up and open to avoid losing his fingers should the beast try to snatch it away.

But the animal would have none of it. Snorting furiously, it backpedaled several paces, then whirled in a circle, prancing on its taloned feet as the smaller arms on its shoulders made random clutching motions, as if instinctively grasping for the plants he held.

"Take it easy, boy," Reza murmured, standing absolutely still. *Be patient*, he told himself. *Take your time*. "It's all right. I won't hurt you." He continued to hold his arm out, the light breeze carrying the scent of the plants to the magthep. Again, it came closer.

Closer. Craning its neck so far that Reza could hear its vertebrae popping, the magthep stepped forward just close enough for its prehensile upper lip to tug the shoot out of Reza's hand. Instantly, the plant was sucked into the animal's mouth. It backed away again, but not as far as the first time, and not quite as fast, while it enjoyed its treat.

Slowly, Reza took another shoot in his hand, holding it out to the animal. Again, the ritual was repeated, the beast slowly coming forward to take the offering. And again. And again.

By the time the shoots in his hand were gone, the magthep no longer backed away, but stood towering over Reza, patiently waiting for its next treat as Reza spoke to it quietly, calming it with the sound of his voice. After the animal had swallowed the last of the plants, Reza held out his empty hand. The magthep leaned down, smelling the scent of the plants, and began to lick Reza's hand, then tried to grasp it with its questing lip. As it did so, Reza slowly raised his other hand to the animal's muzzle, and then slightly higher, stroking the front of its head very gently.

"Good boy," he whispered softly as he moved his hand around the beast's head, scratching lightly, trying to show that he meant it no harm. Taking it very slowly, he began to run his hands through the animal's fur, scratching and petting it, letting it get used to him. He moved his hands over its head, neck, and shoulders as high as he could reach, then across its flank and back toward the tail, always maintaining eye contact with the animal as it turned to watch him, careful not to make any sudden moves.

Sometimes the magthep would get unnerved and dart away from him, but it always came back. It was not accustomed to such attention, and it seemed to be intrigued by Reza's smell, something it had never been exposed to before, and the taste of his skin.

The salt, Reza thought to himself. Esah-Zhurah had explained to him once about how precious salt had been in the ancient times. Reza remembered how he used to sweat in the fields, and how the white salt crusts would form in his boots around the ankles and in the wrinkles of the clothes pressed tight to his skin. Here, when the days were hot, he would sweat so much in his leatherite armor that parts of it would turn gray and then white with salt from his sweat before the armorers insisted on remaking it.

He let the magthep lick his hands with its coarse black tongue as much as it liked, pulling his hand away only when the beast became overzealous and reached out for him with its grinding teeth. Then he began to pet and scratch the magthep again.

His shoulders burning from holding them high enough to scratch or touch the animal everywhere he could, Reza made his way back once more to the magthep's front and then down the opposite flank, choosing not to try and cross around the animal's rear and the powerful legs. Then he started all over again.

"There," he murmured, unconsciously switching back to the Kreelan tongue as he finished the third and last go around. He was filthy from the dust and dirt that had spilled from the beast's coat, and his hands were dark brown with oil and grime. But when he looked up into the animal's face, he saw that he had accomplished something. The ears seemed to be poised in a posture of attentiveness, rather than fear, and the animal's eyes seemed to look at him with curiosity rather than mistrust. "Well," he said to the magthep, "what now?"

For lack of any better ideas, Reza walked back to where he had left the saddle and bridle, and was pleased to hear the magthep's quiet footsteps close behind him. It was so close, in fact, that its head was poised almost directly over Reza, the massive skull blocking the hot sun like an umbrella. Looking at the bridle, Reza considered his chances for any further success. He had never ridden any animal, let alone one of these alien creatures, and had no idea how it might behave if he tried to control it. He felt that the magthep no longer really distrusted him, but he knew that could change very quickly if he did the wrong thing at the wrong time. The scars on the animal's back attested to its willingness and ability to rid itself of unwanted cargo, and Reza did not want to push things too fast. But how fast was that, exactly? How long should it take to turn one of these things into a riding animal? An hour? A day? A whole cycle? He just did not know.

Looking away from the animal for a moment, he saw that the fence behind him was lined with his would-be peers, three or four deep, as they watched one animal try to tame another. He saw Esah-Zhurah, her face caught in something between a grin and a sneer. She knew how badly he wanted to get away from the kazha for even a little while, to see something other than the hundreds of blue, hostile faces that greeted him each day as he learned how to fight and kill. And bringing this magthep to heel was the only way he could do it, the only way he could escape this great cage for a day or so. He felt a wave of anger boil up as he swept his eyes over his unwanted spectators, and channeled it into determination. He reached down for the bridle.

The magthep suddenly snorted and began to back away, and Reza stopped. He straightened up, the bridle still on the ground.

So, he thought with resignation, *it seems we will have to do this the hard way*. He knew that the beast had probably been tricked more than once into wearing the bridle, and would not fall for it again. He stepped toward the beast, palms out. It did not back away, but stood to sniff at his hands, then lick them tentatively, attuned for any trace of the hated bridle. Reza scratched the magthep's ears, and once again, it seemed to accept him.

Moving again down the beast's flank, Reza started to lean against its side, patting it, stroking it, then pulling on its hair, lightly at first, then harder in hopes of sensitizing the magthep to his presence. He found a particularly good spot to scratch, and the magthep elongated and twisted its neck in pleasure, its upper lip reaching out to flip at the air.

Holding on tightly to thick hanks of the animal's fur, Reza suddenly leaped up. Twisting his right leg over the animal's back, he planted himself in the wide, shallow valley between its shoulders and hips. His hands curled around the longer hair further up on the animal's neck with a grip that bled his knuckles white, anticipating the pounding he was going to get when the animal reacted.

Esah-Zhurah held her breath as Reza mounted the animal. Around her, the other tresh gasped, waiting for the beast's savage twisting and bucking that would send the human flying.

But nothing happened.

Reza watched, wide-eyed with surprise, as the beast's head slowly turned toward him on its graceful neck. It blinked its eyes twice as if to say, "Oh, it's only you." Then it turned away and began to amble toward the shelter that housed its water trough, Reza clinging to its back like a confused tickbird.

"In Her name," Esah-Zhurah heard someone beside her whisper, an oath that was repeated many times up and down the rows of onlookers.

"How is it possible?" someone else asked, and she felt a tug at her arm. "Esah-Zhurah," asked Amar-Khan, the most senior among the tresh of the kazha, "what trickery is this? Is it so that one animal may speak to another? How can the human do this, when our best riders and trainers have failed?"

"I..." Esah-Zhurah began, her gaze torn between the tresh's angry eyes and the sight of Reza, scratching the magthep's shoulders with both hands, seemingly oblivious to any danger of being thrown. "I do not know. I do not understand their Way."

Amar-Khan let go her arm, baring her fangs in a grimace. "Their Way," she hissed. "You give animals a great deal of credit, Esah-Zhurah. Perhaps you, too, would speak with the magtheps?"

Esah-Zhurah felt a surge of fire in her blood, and the rational thoughts of her mind boiled away as her hand sought the handle of her knife.

"Enough!"

The tresh parted before Tesh-Dar, who came to stand beside Esah-Zhurah, dismissing Amar-Khan with her eyes.

"Offense was given, Esah-Zhurah," the priestess said quietly, "but I bid you pay it no heed. Neither Amar-Khan, nor the others – myself included – understand the life you have accepted as Her will, and you will encounter such ill-conceived notions from time to time. Your blood sings to Her, but your mind must control the fire in your veins."

"Yes, my priestess," Esah-Zhurah said, grateful for the older warrior's understanding. She sheathed her weapon, feeling a chill run through her body as the fire faded from her veins.

"He again surprises me," Tesh-Dar murmured thoughtfully, stroking the scar over her left eye as she watched Reza begin to communicate his wishes to the magthep in an as-yet uncoordinated signaling of hand and foot. "Already the beast acknowledges his commands," she said. "And without a bridle, without a saddle." She paused for a moment, cocking her head, as if listening. "He speaks to it."

"I hear nothing, my priestess," Esah-Zhurah told her. She could see Reza's mouth moving slightly, but they were many strides away, far beyond Esah-Zhurah's hearing. "What does he say?"

"I do not know," Tesh-Dar replied, shrugging. "It is in the human tongue so many of them use." She sensed Esah-Zhurah bristle at the knowledge. It was one thing about which she had been adamant: Reza was to speak only the language of the Empress. To speak any human language was to summon fast and furious punishment. "Allow him this one day to speak as he would," Tesh-Dar suggested, commanded, sensing Esah-Zhurah's reaction. "If he can tame such a beast with this," she tapped her foot at the base of a mound of yezhe'e plants, "and alien words and thoughts, then he has earned such a privilege. Our own ways fared not nearly as well."

They both looked up at the sound of the rhythmic pounding of clawed feet in time to see Reza bring the magthep to within a meter or so of the fence and stop. The beast flared its nostrils and bared its flat, grinding teeth at the Kreelans. The young human warrior sat erect on the dirty back of his mount, his hands resting on his thighs, arms shaking from the exhaustion of his intensive acquaintance with the animal. But his eyes did not waver as he looked over the crowd. His gaze lingered on Esah-Zhurah, making sure that she saw and understood the contempt in his own eyes before he sought out the priestess's gaze. He bowed his head to her.

"This," he said proudly, "is *Goliath*."

Nine

After a hasty breakfast of barely cooked meat and a handful of small fruits, Reza and Esah-Zhurah joined the hundreds of other tresh who were making their way from the kazha to wherever they had chosen to spend their free time. Some would go to the city, many to the forests and mountains, and still others to places Reza did not yet even know of. Only the priestess and some of the more senior warriors would remain behind.

The weather that morning was magnificent, the sunrise breaking over the mountains to fill the valley below with the promise of a warm day under a clear magenta sky. The cool air was crisp and filled with a cornucopia of scents that Reza had come to subconsciously accept as the smell of home.

As he rode beside Esah-Zhurah, towering above her on Goliath's back, he found that he could hardly wait to get away from the suffocating closeness of the peers. They treated him with more respect than they had when he had first come among them, but he was still the lowest form of life on this planet, lower even than the simpleminded animals raised for meat. Ironically, it was Esah-Zhurah who had consistently proven the most difficult to sway, her arrogance virtually undiluted from the day he had first awakened to her scowling face.

Yet, he was increasingly unsure if her behavior was entirely sincere. Sometimes he awoke to find her staring at him, her eyes flickering in the glow of the low fire they kept to ward off the night's chill. The look on her face was always thoughtful, contemplative, rather than the perpetual sneer he was used to seeing during the day. But always, as soon as she realized he was watching her, a cloud passed over her eyes, and she would roll over, turning her back to him.

The way he had seen her interact with the tresh also made him wonder. As the months had come and gone, she had become less and less tolerant of the other tresh making derisive comments about Reza or bending the rules in the arena just far enough to try and do him serious injury, something he had thus far managed to avoid. For just a moment he would think – or at least wistfully hope – that she was acting on his behalf. But the hope died as soon as he saw the look of conceit on her face or heard the arrogant tone in her voice, and the anger and loneliness that were his heart and soul would pierce him like a white-hot knife. Hot and cold, hard and soft, she was at once one thing and yet another, gently applying a bandage to a wound one minute, brutally punishing him the next.

"What are you thinking?" She asked, eyeing him closely. "I have learned that expression you now wear, that tells of your mind contemplating alien thoughts."

Her thigh brushed his as they rode side by side, and he felt a sudden rush of heat to his face. He reflexively guided Goliath on a slightly divergent path.

"I was thinking about you," he said.

"Oh? And what great thoughts are these, human?"

"I was wondering," he said, "if you really care as little for me as you would like me to think? Is all of your conceit and arrogance genuine, or just a façade to conceal your true feelings?"

He suddenly found himself talking to empty space. He turned around to find the girl and her magthep stopped, her hands clutching the bridle tightly, her face as still as the eye of a hurricane.

Touché, he thought.

She was quiet for a long moment, her expression completely unreadable to Reza, who had never before seen her like this. Had she been a human, he thought, she might have been about to cry.

"I applaud your powers of deduction, human," she told him quietly. "But what I feel, and for whom, is not the business of an animal whose existence is measured in terms of the charity the Empress has chosen to bestow upon you. Never will there come a day when you shall be privy to the workings of my heart and mind."

With a less than gentle kick, she started her magthep walking again.

Reza bowed his head to her, bringing Goliath alongside her mount, reining his beast in slightly to match the smaller animal's slower pace. He claimed the round as a tactical defeat against himself, but a strategic victory of sorts. Despite her emotional screen of anger and, perhaps, embarrassment, he knew that he had touched on a nerve, and could not resist one final thrust. "Among my people," he said, "there is a saying: *Never say never*."

"My eternal thanks for the wisdom of your people," she replied acidly, kicking her magthep in the ribs and pulling away from Reza and Goliath at a gallop. "Follow if you can, animal!" she shouted.

Reza took up the chase, disappearing into the cloud of dust behind her as the two of them raced away from the thinning caravan of tresh, heading toward the distant mountains.

* * *

The sun had just passed its zenith by the time they departed the great plain on which the city and most of the forests stood, and began to move into the range of mountains that lay beyond. Reza had never imagined he would find such color or beauty here. When viewed from the kazha, the mountains always seemed shrouded in darkness, their details lost in the distance and an ever-present crown of water-laden clouds that obscured the jagged peaks for all but a few precious minutes of nearly every day. But the deep purple granite around him sparkled and shimmered as the rock's tiny facets reflected the sunlight like millions of tiny diamonds. The ancient canyon walls, severed and shifted by eons of irresistible pressure from beneath the planet's crust, revealed bright mineral veins that wound their way through the host rock like glittering rivers. The ground that passed beneath the magtheps' feet was virgin soil, for all Reza could see, the hard earth revealing no signs of any previous traveler's passage.

As they rose higher through the canyons toward wherever Esah-Zhurah was leading him, Reza saw tiny oases of startling violet flowers whose petals waved in the air, beckoning to the insects that hovered and flitted near the ground, that they might bring life-giving pollen to the flowers.

Still higher, the violet flowers gradually became a seamless background to the other species that began to appear. Reza saw everything from tiny lichens clinging tenaciously to rocks, to enormous ferns that towered above the two riders on their animals, their house-sized fronds waving ponderously in the light breeze that swept up the mountainside.

"How much further is it?" Reza asked, his eyes wide with wonder at the sights that surrounded him.

"Not far," Esah-Zhurah called back as she maneuvered her magthep through a particularly dense stand of vines and ferns. Behind them, Goliath plowed straight through the plants, his muzzle snatching occasional mouthfuls as he went, a bad habit that Reza had not yet figured out how to cure.

"Here!" she called at last, reining her beast to a stop and smoothly dismounting onto a carpet of iridescent orange moss that had appeared like a welcome mat.

Reza nudged Goliath to a stop as he gawked around him. They were on a ledge, halfway up one of the mountains of the range that ringed the plain. Through the ferns and moss-covered boulders he could just make out the shimmering spires of the city far in the distance, and the forest in which lay their kazha. To the other side, a mountain lay very close by, like a wall that rose straight up as far as he could see, disappearing into the clouds that danced in the winds. Everywhere the purple granite had disappeared, replaced by the vibrant greens and oranges of the plants and mosses that were dominant here.

"It is beautiful," he whispered in awe.

"You have not yet seen beauty," Esah-Zhurah said quietly. "Come. Gather your things, for we have not yet reached our destination."

The two of them stripped the magtheps of their riding gear and released them to wander and eat as they pleased.

"Will they run away?" Reza asked as he let Goliath go.

Esah-Zhurah looked at him. "Why do you ask? Are you afraid of walking back?"

Reza frowned, not enthused at the idea. But watching Goliath devour the nearby plants eased his mind. Unless something frightened him, he would stay here where there was plenty of food.

They left the saddles in a convenient enclave of dry rock and forgot about the feasting animals. Hefting the packs of supplies that Esah-Zhurah had made up for them, they began to climb higher up the mountain face, scaling their way along a natural stairway in a huge crevice that split the mountainside like a mischievous, toothy grin.

They had climbed only a few minutes before they came to a tunnel that disappeared into the mountain. Esah-Zhurah waited for Reza to join her before she stepped off into the near darkness of the tunnel, feeling her way along, her talons lightly scraping the tunnel walls. Reza was fascinated by the echoing sounds of their footsteps and the smell that is peculiar to ancient stone places that have never seen the full light of day. But after a few paces his ears pricked at something new: the rushing sound of water.

"Esah-Zhurah..." he said tentatively, a trace of fear in his voice as his mind conjured up an image of the two of them being swept down the mountainside by a sudden torrent of water erupting from the mountain's bowels.

"We are nearly there," came her voice from the darkness, and Reza felt her hand take hold of his forearm to lead him along; she could still see clearly in the dark, while he could barely see a shifting shadow where she might – or might not – be.

The rushing sound grew into a roar, and Reza was opening his mouth to speak again when suddenly, as if dawn had broken within the tunnel, light began to return.

He found himself standing on a ledge overlooking paradise.

"*My God*," he whispered, his eyes lost to the wondrous sight before him. Esah-Zhurah overlooked his comment in his old tongue, forgiving him as she herself embraced the scene.

They stood overlooking what had once been an ancient volcano. It was a tremendous crater whose walls rose nearly vertically to a height of hundreds of meters to the clouds that swept along the crest. Mosses and lichens covered the walls like tapestries of fire, their reds and yellows swirling like the surface of a gas giant. Leafy green plants also flourished, clinging insistently to the ledges protruding from the sides like tiny green outposts in the midst of a desert of rampant color. And on the far side from where the two of them stood was a waterfall that roared its existence, born from the tap of a stream far above them to fall into a crystal pool that lay at the bottom of the ancient caldera, forming a beautiful grotto. The surface shone like the shimmering mirror of some great telescope, the falling water leaving behind a gentle mist that floated in the air as if by magic.

"Come," Esah-Zhurah said, tugging on Reza's arm. Had he looked down at just that moment, he would have seen the trace of a smile on her face as she saw the wonder on his, but it passed swiftly, as if stolen by the steadily setting sun.

He wordlessly followed her toward an enclave whose overhang kept the rock within dry.

"This," Esah-Zhurah said as she set down her things, startling a small lizard that disappeared into the vegetation, shrieking, "shall be our home until we return to the kazha, and the Challenge."

* * *

Reza awoke the next morning to the sound of a group of lizards, perched somewhere high above, trumpeting their territorial claims to one another like a brass ensemble gone mad. The sun had not yet risen high enough to reach the bottom of the caldera, but it would: on this day, unlike most, the clouds that normally concealed the grotto's inhabitants from the piercing rays of the sun, leaving it instead in a soft glow of filtered light, had parted. Already some of the more adventurous – and boisterous – inhabitants had gathered to await the arrival of the warmth that would come from above.

He was reluctant to shed the musky skins that had protected him from the slight chill of the night, but his stomach was insistent. Dinner had been light the previous evening, as neither he nor Esah-Zhurah had wanted to spoil the sunset and twilight with cooking chores, and both of them had gone to bed early, lulled to sleep by the steady roar of the waterfall.

Reza listened to the tumultuous sound of the water and thought that it would be nice to see if he could manage a swim later on in the pool below. Reluctantly, he tossed aside the covers and began the ritual stretching the tresh were taught early on to perform, readying his body for whatever lay ahead during the day.

"Late do you rise, my tresh," Esah-Zhurah called from a few meters away where she was cooking him something to eat. It was a seemingly incongruous task that she took upon herself, despite his protestations.

Perhaps, he thought cynically, she only does it so she can burn the meat.

"And soundly do you sleep. The lizards," she pointed to a place high on the far side of the grotto, "have long been calling to you."

"Perhaps," he said, starting to pull on his black pajamas, as he had come to think of them, "they were simply keeping me informed about what you have been doing while I slept."

Esah-Zhurah looked at him, then at the lizards, a look of considered suspicion on her face. "Is such a thing possible?" she asked him finally.

Reza shrugged, trying to keep his face straight. "It is something for you to think about, is it not? You believe I talk to magtheps. Why not lizards, as well?" He sat down next to her at the fire, quietly enjoying her mental squirming as she tried to figure out if he really could talk to the animals.

Finally, she looked at him sharply. "I do not believe you can speak with the beasts," she said. Then she paused, unsure. "Can you?"

Finally, he could stand it no more, and he burst out laughing at the serious expression she bore. "No," he admitted as he saw her face cloud over with anger for laughing at her, "I cannot. Please," he told her, bringing his laughter to a swift end, "forgive me. I did not mean to make you feel a fool."

In reply, she only scowled at him before turning away, thrusting his meat deeper into the coals where it sizzled and popped, then finally caught fire.

"Here," she said, thrusting the stick that held the flaming meat into his face. "Eat."

Dodging the flames, he took the stick like the baton in a relay race, snatching it quickly from her hand before she dropped it or impaled him with it, and then blew out the torch that was his breakfast.

"Thank you," he said quietly. "Esah-Zhurah," he said after a moment. She paid him no attention, focusing herself on paring strips from the raw hunk of meat that was her own morning meal. He reached out and gently touched her arm. She did not pull away. "Please forgive me," he said quietly. "I meant you no harm. It was only meant as humor, a joke, nothing more."

"Do not do it again," she said after a moment of silent consideration, her eyes still focused on her food as her talons tore it to shreds. "I do not like it." Reza nodded, letting her go. "I forgive you," she added softly.

Reza sat back, stunned, his mind seeking a precedent for this development. There was none.

After a few moments he asked, "What would you like to do today?" He was unsure if the free time before the Challenge brought with it some kind of unannounced itinerary.

"Today I would bask in the sun, as do your lizard friends," she said. "To lay upon that rock," she pointed to a peninsula of moss-covered stone that jutted into the pool, "and become one with the earth is my sole desire for this day."

"A more noble ambition there has never been," he said, tearing the meat with his teeth.

It was not long before the sun's trace began to work its way down into the grotto. The chorus of the lizards – dozens of them now – grew louder as the sunlight dropped deeper into the caldera. He and Esah-Zhurah were finally compelled to put their hands over their ears as the animal shrieks reached a shattering crescendo. But then, as the light reached the bottom and struck the pool, almost at once the trumpeting and chirruping ceased, the animals now mollified by the sun's warmth.

"In Her name," Esah-Zhurah breathed, "such a noise they make!"

As she made her way down to the pool, Reza went and opened his pack, rummaging around near the bottom for what he sought, his hands curling around a thin-skinned case that was roughly as big around as his chest, but not nearly so thick. Pulling open the top flap, he looked to make sure that everything inside was as he had put it. The old armorer, Pan'ne-Sharakh, had given him his own palette of dyes and brushes, and he had eagerly taken up dye-setting – painting – as his escape from the brutal life he had been forced to lead. He used whatever metal he could scavenge for canvas, usually damaged backplates that the armorers deemed unworthy of salvage. He hammered them as flat as he could and put them to use for his own designs. The images he had made did not have the texture of real paintings, being dyes on metal, but his interpretation of the Kreelan art lent them a depth and perspective that made the images almost three dimensional, surreal. He did not consider himself to be a modern incarnation of Monet or Da Vinci; he was content to be himself. It was the only thing he had that, for a few moments of each of his hellish days, allowed his soul to go free.

Turning around, the satchel in hand, he saw that he would not have to search far for a subject. Against the backdrop of a misty rainbow born of the waterfall, Esah-Zhurah lay nude on the chaise of stone that protruded into the pool, her blue face to the sun, her braids hanging toward the pool below like ebony streams. Her eyes were closed; she was probably already asleep. One hand was draped over her torso, lightly cupping her left breast, and the other lay at her side.

Reza's heart suddenly thundered in his ears as he looked at her. The hot pulse sent a jolt up his spine as he suddenly found himself smitten with the beauty of this alien girl, this young woman, who was at once his ally and his enemy, his savior and would-be killer, all rolled into one. In that blink of an eye, he wanted to reach out and touch her, to hold her against him. He wanted to feel her warm lips on his, remembering how it felt when Nicole had kissed him goodbye when she left Hallmark. He could remember that kiss like it was yesterday. But he could barely remember what she looked like now.

He tore his gaze away. He knew his body was on the edge, or even through, the age of puberty and all its attendant changes, and resolved to blame this treacherous feeling on the hormonal pranks of his growing body. Still, he could not deny the heat that blazed in his core at the thought of how closely he and this alien girl lived together, despite how far apart they would forever remain.

As if in sympathy, thin gray clouds drifted over the caldera, muting the dazzling sunshine reflecting from the pool below and softening the light to an even glow.

Blinking his eyes clear, he quietly arrayed his arsenal of colors and began to paint.

* * *

The morning stretched into afternoon, and at last Esah-Zhurah stirred from her long nap, stretching like a cat. Reza, his hands and upper body tired from his tender labors over the canvas of metal, surveyed his handiwork as he began to put his things away. Looking at the traces he had made, the first shadings now setting into the blackened metal, he smiled. It would be the best work he had ever done, he thought, the best by far.

"Do you paint your friends, the lizards?" Esah-Zhurah called to him.

Reza looked up to see her lying on her side, watching him, one hand lazily stirring the water lapping at the rock. A thin sheen of mist covered her nude body from head to toe, making her glisten like an unearthly siren beneath the waterfall's rainbow.

"It is my time to do with as I please," he told her, knowing that she did not really approve of his undertaking of the old armorer's craft. "And if it is a lizard that I paint," he went on, sealing the etching into the satchel, "it is a lizard that speaks in Her tongue."

"How amusing," she replied sarcastically as Reza made his way down to the water's edge and began to take off his clothes. "What do you intend to do?"

"I..." He could not think of the word, and resorted to one of his few acceptable uses of Standard, to explain what words or phrases he did not know in her language. "I wish to go... *swimming*." He carefully folded his black underclothes, putting them on top of the pile of metal and leatherite that was his second skin before stepping gingerly into the water, expecting it to be freezing. Much to his delight, it was warm against his skin, a wonderful feeling after having bathed so many times in the ice-cold stream that ran near the kazha, barred as he and Esah-Zhurah were from the normal bath facilities because of his being human. "This is wonderful," he sighed as he moved into deeper water, wading in past his waist.

"Be careful," Esah-Zhurah said suddenly, kneeling over the edge of the rock and watching Reza with wide eyes.

"Why?" he asked, suddenly wary. His eyes darted to and fro, searching the crystalline water. "Is there some beast in here that I should know about?"

"No," she said firmly. "But do not go in above your head."

"Why not?" he asked, puzzled at her concern. "What happens if I do?"

She snorted. "You will drown, fool. This even a magthep knows."

Reza laughed at her and then leaped backwards, disappearing in a huge splash that drenched Esah-Zhurah.

"Reza!" she cried, jumping to her feet in a panic. She crawled as close as she dared to the edge of the rock and peered into the water, desperately searching for his body.

She did not see the shadow directly below her. As Reza's head broke the surface, she shrieked, drawing back in surprise as he spouted water on her like a cherubic fountain.

"What," he asked, trying desperately to hold back his laughter at her reaction, "are you so afraid of?"

"I do not like the water," she said angrily. "And you should not be so quick to disobey me when I warn you of something."

"You cannot do this – swim – can you?" he asked, treading water next to the rock.

"No," she admitted quietly. "Very few of my people can do this." She told him the Kreelan word for *swimming*, one that she had never used with him before. "It is not considered a high priority for the learning period of youth."

Reza swam up to her and clung to the rock with one hand, sweeping the other through his soaking hair. "Let me teach you," he asked hopefully.

She looked at him and saw nothing but sincerity in his eyes, but there had always been something about water that troubled her, and sometimes she had dreams. They were nightmares about cold black water that closed in around her, filling her lungs as Death closed its icy fist around her heart, leaving her soul trapped in a lifeless body that would be forever spinning, spinning beyond the reach of Her light, Her love.

"No, my tresh," she told him, turning away so he would not see the fear on her face. "I know you mean well, but I do not wish to."

"Is there–"

"I do not wish to," she said again, facing him now, her eyes hard.

Reza nodded. "Very well," he said, his heart sinking like a stone. He had so much wanted for her to say yes.

Pushing her from his thoughts as he kicked away from the rock on which she stood, he turned and began to explore the wondrous pool. He probed through the shallow water, imagining himself as one of the ancient mariners about whom he had read once upon a time, the men and women who had explored the great seas of Earth.

Esah-Zhurah watched him swim and dive like the aquatic creatures she had occasionally seen in the river that flowed through the city, faintly envious of this ability of his. He appeared to be enjoying himself tremendously, blowing water into the air and then taking a breath before diving back down again to observe some unfathomable sight at the bottom of the pool.

Something that I will never see, she lamented quietly to herself, unconsciously drawing away from the water's edge and the waves kicked up by Reza's frolicking. She saw him wave to her as he swam under the waterfall, and she managed a halfhearted gesture in return, still uneasy at being able to see only his head above the water. And then even that disappeared as he dove under once more.

Perhaps for the first time since he had been brought to the Empire, Reza felt completely free. Alone in this tiny world of water, where even his tresh feared to come, his heart seemed to unfold. The horrendous load on his mind and soul that sometimes threatened to crush his sanity lightened, fading away to nothing in the warm embrace of the grotto pool. He watched with fascinated eyes the grotto's creatures – none of them overtly threatening – as they swam, crawled, or scuttled about the pool. Brightly colored fish stared at him with wide black eyes from their tiny holes among the rock clusters that dotted the pool's bottom, and tiny crab-like things tussled amongst themselves on the bottom, raising a tiny cloud of sand as they dragged one another in a miniature tug of war.

Beneath the waterfall itself, Reza found a darker world. Having taken a deep breath after waving to Esah-Zhurah, he descended into the maelstrom of the waterfall. He emerged on the other side, the light fading and swirling in time with the roiling water behind him. He was about to leave when he spotted what looked like an underwater tunnel in the rock behind the waterfall. Without thinking, he dived into it to find himself swirling down a subterranean passageway that ended in total darkness.

* * *

Esah-Zhurah clicked her nails on the rock in growing apprehension as time passed and still Reza did not reappear.

"Reza?" she called, finally giving in to the mounting tension that was constricting her chest like a metal band. "Reza!" she shouted again, standing on the rock so she could better see out over the pool.

Nothing. There was no sign of him, only the darting shadows of the grotto's fish as they went about their business. She had been thinking of asking Reza to try and catch some for their dinner, but that thought vanished as her concern grew. It had been too long.

Gingerly, she made her way into the water, venturing in up to her waist, then up to her breasts, the muscles in her belly clenched tightly with fear as she made her way deeper into this unfamiliar, and potentially deadly, environment. "Reza," she whispered hoarsely, "where are you?"

* * *

Spots were dancing before Reza's eyes, bright stars in the blackness of the tunnel he had ventured into. His lungs burning for want of oxygen, he groped in the darkness with his hands, seeking a way out of the trap he had gotten himself into. He cursed himself for following the tunnel until the light was gone. *I've got to find a way out*, he thought frantically. He waved his hands across the water-worn rock ever faster in hopes of finding his way back.

Suddenly, his left hand found an empty place, and he quickly followed it to find smooth rock leading upward through the darkness. He kicked hard, driving himself through the water in a desperate race for air, his muscles tingling with the pricks of invisible needles and his lungs threatening to explode with pain.

He suddenly burst from the water into blessed air. He stayed where he was for a moment, treading water while sucking in deep breaths of the cool damp air that caressed his face. He thought he might have gone temporarily blind, for when the dazzles cleared from his eyes, he could see nothing at all. But after a moment he did see something in his peripheral vision, a dim reddish glow that had no particular shape and did not move, but hung suspended in space above the water to his right. Swimming slowly toward it, his foot struck a submerged ledge and he let out a startled cry of pain.

More carefully, he moved closer to the glowing thing. The bottom of what he now took to be some kind of cavern rose higher until it finally broached the water's surface like a boat landing, and Reza found himself standing on dry rock in a low chamber.

Putting his hand out, he touched the red glowing thing that was brighter now as his eyes became accustomed to the darkness. His hand touched something soft and spongy, yet resilient enough that nothing stuck to his fingers when he pulled them away. The thing pulsed more brightly for a moment, then returned to its earlier state. *It must be some kind of plant*, Reza thought, unconsciously rubbing his hand on his naked thigh, vaguely repelled by the way the thing had felt to his touch.

Putting his hands to the walls, he moved about the chamber until he came to a large fissure that led upward, toward where he heard the waterfall's roar more clearly. Carefully placing his hands and feet, he climbed into the fissure, plenty wide for his lean body, and began working his way upward.

He had only gone a few meters when light began to trickle down the shaft, growing steadily stronger as did the sound of rushing water. Suddenly he found himself standing in another cavern, much larger than the first tiny vestibule: it was like an open balcony that lay directly behind the waterfall, a vertical crack in the caldera's face forming a window from which Reza could see the water cascade past as it fell to the pool below.

"Incredible," he whispered, awed by the miraculous luck that had brought him here. The cavern itself was completely dry except for some spray that coated the edge near the waterfall. He walked over and put his hand out to intercept the falling water, bringing a handful to his mouth and drinking.

"Reza!" he heard a voice call, barely audible over the crashing of the waterfall. "Where are you?"

"Esah-Zhurah!" he shouted, peering through the waterfall to try and catch a glimpse of her, but he could see nothing past the shimmering blue and green wall of water. "Up here!"

"Reza!" he heard again. The concern in her voice was unmistakable, and he quickly decided to return to her, eager to tell her of his discovery.

"I am coming!" he shouted, hoping that she would be able to hear him.

* * *

Daring to go no further into the water, Esah-Zhurah stood breast-deep, calling repeatedly to Reza. Once, she thought she heard his voice, but after that there had been only silence.

Finally, overcome by a sense of anguish that she would never dare admit to any but the priestess or the Empress herself, she turned and began to trudge back to the shore, convinced Reza was dead.

Such then, was her surprise when he burst from the surface near the waterfall.

"Esah-Zhurah!" he cried excitedly after he drew in a single deep breath to replenish his lungs. The return trip had been much easier than had been the way in, and he had reached the grotto pool long before his lungs had begun to burn. "I found a way behind the waterfall! You will not believe it!"

Her heart hammering with relief, she waded back into the water and took him by the arms as he swam toward her.

"Never do that again," she scolded him, trying to conceal her relief with an angry façade. "Never! I forbid it."

"But," Reza stammered, totally confused and ignorant of the thought that she might actually have been concerned for his welfare, "it is incredible. You must see it." He pointed to the waterfall. "Up there, there is a cave that–"

"It matters not," she said sharply, cutting him off. "The priestess would be angry with me if I let you perish during the free time before your first Challenge. You will not disobey me again." Her eyes carried the look that Reza had come to understand well: punishment was close at hand. And both of them knew she was his physical superior.

For now, Reza thought coldly. His spirits wilted like flowers put to the torch, and he lowered his gaze. He swiped angrily at the water with one hand, sending a flurry of droplets out into the pool.

"Yes, Esah-Zhurah," he murmured, trying to contain his anger and disappointment.

"If you would like," she went on, satisfied that he understood that she was serious, "you may try and capture some of the swimming things; I think I can prepare them in a way you would find acceptable. The ones with red stripes and yellow tails are good to eat, as are the violet sponge plants. The others are poisonous to us, and probably to you, also." She looked at the fading light in the caldera as the afternoon drifted toward evening. "You must hurry, for they hide in the rocks at night."

Nodding, but saying nothing, Reza swirled past her on his way out of the pool, stomping onto the beach to retrieve his knife. He returned to the water, but did not look at her. His knife held tightly in his hand, he swam through the water, hunting alone.

* * *

Esah-Zhurah lay against the side of the rock enclave that served as their camp within the caldera. She silently observed Reza as he stared off toward the waterfall, which now was backlit by thousands of tiny iridescent flora that made the water glow topaz in the absolute darkness within the grotto.

After their dinner, of which Reza had eaten surprisingly little, he had quietly excused himself and taken up a seat on the far side of the enclave from her, and said nothing since. It was a stark contrast to most of the nights they spent together, when Reza would ask one of his ever more complex questions about Her people and the Way. They were questions that were becoming increasingly difficult to answer and challenged Esah-Zhurah's own understanding of her culture. Sometimes they would spend hours this way after their training day had ended, stopping only when Reza's seemingly insatiable curiosity at last was put to rest, or Esah-Zhurah forced him to go to sleep, postponing the session's completion until the following evening. It was a ritual she had come to secretly enjoy, so different was it from the normally quiet and contemplative lives of the initiate tresh. And since Reza had begun to speak the Empress's tongue well, he constantly asked questions, wanting to know more, to learn.

But tonight he had been silent as the stone around them, and it concerned her for a reason she could not quite identify.

As if anticipating her question, he suddenly turned to her, the low fire dancing in his green eyes.

"Would you tell me just one thing?" he asked softly above the murmur of the waterfall.

"If I am able," she said carefully, kneeling closer to the fire, and to him.

"When I step into the arena, to face my first Challenge," he said evenly, "do you hope I will die?"

The question caught her completely by surprise. She opened her mouth, but no words came forth, for she truly did not know at that moment how she might answer him truthfully. She snapped her mouth shut, her face twisting into a mask of concentration.

Is that what I wish? she asked herself. *Do I honestly hope that he will die, this creature with whom I have spent so long, this animal with whom I have lived and suffered, to whom I have betrothed myself as a tresh?* Despite all the things she had ever imagined or been taught, she had come to feel a sense of pride in Reza, a pride that was more than one should feel for teaching an animal tricks, as the handlers were sometimes wont to do. She knew that he must hate her, must despise her entire race, and she often sought to use that as a weapon against him, to break him down, to make him fail.

But he had only become more determined, rising unfailingly to every test she put before him. His success or failure was, at that stage, immaterial; he consistently made the attempt, and that is what counted, all that mattered. Gradually, his perseverance had paid off. Many of the peers were discreetly jealous of her tresh, if that was possible. She herself had become possessed of a strange fondness for him, despite the revulsion she felt toward his species, despite the continued irrepressible urge to force him to her will, to show her own superiority, a superiority that she knew was fading as he grew stronger, quicker. *If only his blood would sing*, she often cried to herself. If only his spirit – if he possessed one – would show itself, all could be... different, in a way she was afraid to fully imagine.

If only his blood would sing...

Turning back to meet his glowing eyes, she knew in her heart that he must someday die, that he would – no, that he must – never leave the Homeworld alive. But she could not find it in herself to wish it upon him.

"Reza..." she said, trying to find a way of saying what she felt without exposing the weakness she had developed toward him. "The oath you took when you were brought into the kazha, the oath by which you bound yourself as a tresh, I also have taken, though long before you came to me. It is an oath taken only once in life, but it lasts for as long as the heart beats, as long as two work together as one, as tresh. The one to whom I was bound, cycles ago, died in a... training accident, you might call it. But my obligations to her honor were passed on to you when I was called upon to become your tresh. Your teacher. And in that capacity, I can be nothing but pleased, for you have learned well, animal – human – or no." She looked away toward the water, struggling to admit what she had to say. "There will come a day, my tresh, when your blood will soak the sands of the arena," she told him, her claws digging silently into the rock as she willed the words forward, as if her throat was suddenly too small to contain them. "But I shall not rejoice in it."

She could see relief wash over Reza's face. She was surprised how well she could interpret his body language, not because she could understand that of the humans, but because the language of his body had become Kreelan.

"Esah-Zhurah..." he said. Then he stopped, not sure how to continue.

She watched as he struggled with himself for a moment, until the strange strength that dwelt within him surfaced, washing away the creases of doubt on his face.

"There is much for which I feel compelled to hate you, to hate your kind," he explained, his eyes drawn to the fire as if in search of the meaning of his fate. "For the deaths of my parents, at the hands of the priestess herself. For the destruction of the world of my birth, and the many lives that perished there. For the destruction of the planet from which I was taken, a world I often hated, but which I had come to call home. And for all of the death that has been wrought upon my people, on a scale I will never be able to understand, and will never truly be able to feel in my heart." He looked up at her, his face betraying an open vulnerability that shocked her as strongly as if she had been doused with freezing water. "For all this, I cannot find it in me to truly hate you, my tresh, my teacher. There are many among my kind who would condemn me to death as a traitor for those words, but they are nonetheless true, and to deny them, or leave them unspoken, would be to lie to myself." He looked back to the fire, helplessly. "There was a time, not so long ago," he whispered, "when I wanted to beat you, to destroy you, to make you feel pain a thousand times what I felt every time you beat me. But..." he shrugged. "But I found, after a while, that I wanted your respect, your trust, more than anything else." He fell silent for a moment. "The greatest fear I have," he went on, "is that I will fail you, will bring shame upon you. And that... you will shun me."

Esah-Zhurah did not know what to say. Never had she thought such a time as this would come, when this human, so full of fight and anger, would reveal such a thing to her, something that could be exploited as a terrible weakness.

But that was the point, she told herself. He had laid himself open to her, in hopes that she would not turn his words against him, that he could trust her. And, in a decision that shocked the part of her mind that carried the xenophobic character of her race, a race that had exterminated over a dozen sentient species in past millennia, she committed herself to guarding his trust.

"I will not abandon you," she said simply, openly. "Whatever the Way brings us, we shall share in it together."

* * *

Later, after they had banked the fire and lay down for the night, Reza remained awake. His mind was consumed by thoughts that swirled and circled like wolves around a stricken deer, darting just to the edge of focus before they faded into the shadowy darkness once more. The more he watched them, the more they seemed to carry the faces of people he had once known, some of them of a kind his people called "friends," a relationship that did not exist among the society that had kidnapped him.

One of the wolf faces, an old man with the eyes of a young warrior, especially troubled him. The eyes did not accuse, but Reza could not help but feel that he had somehow betrayed the being that lay behind the mask that lunged and retreated within his mind.

Wiley, he suddenly thought, wincing at the foreign sound of the name even as he breathed it in his mind, *am I a traitor?*

"*Do whatever you can to stay alive, son*," the old colonel had said that day so long ago, "*If anybody can make it, you can...*"

Wiley, Reza cried to himself, *must I become one of them to make it? Do I have any choice?* For just a moment, he bitterly resented the old man's leaving him, going off to die himself as Reza was taken by the cruel fate that had pursued him since the fall of New Constantinople.

But the moment blinked away into nothingness, just as the wolfish thought-face blurred into oblivion. Wiley had been wise enough to know when it was time to die, and had done so with the dignity of soldiers throughout history who had made one last, hopeless stand against the invaders of their homeland. And, aside from the admission letter he had given Reza for the academy, the old man had left Reza with the only other gift he could give: a chance at life. And Reza knew then that if he chose to trust this alien girl, to allow himself that vital weakness before her, Wiley would understand.

Slowly, the beasts in his brain retreated into the darkness, only their glittering eyes remaining, flickering in the glow of the fire.

He blinked, but the glowing eyes remained. Suddenly, he realized that he was seeing the silvery glint of Esah-Zhurah's talons. Her hands lay on the skins near her face, the ebbing firelight making them twinkle like stars against the satiny glow of her deep blue skin as she slept. Reza felt another sudden twinge of guilt at the thought of how much he had come to need her, to rely on her. Worse, he found that he was beginning to like her.

What might things be like, he thought, should she someday come to lead her people? Would her association with him have any effect, make any difference in how they viewed humanity? It was difficult for a boy, struggling simply to remain human, let alone to become a man, to comprehend the fact that he was an ambassador, of sorts, to these people. While this particular course of his life had not been chosen willingly, he was nonetheless determined to make the best impression he could, to do whatever he could to help the people of his own blood. Who could tell, he asked himself, if the girl who lay asleep an arm's length away might not someday sit on the throne that commanded the Empire? The thought settled onto his brain like an insistent ache, an itch that insisted it be scratched.

"Esah-Zhurah," he said quietly, hating to disturb her, but unable to put off the question until morning.

Her eyes flickered open and she looked around, confused. "What is wrong?" she asked, one hand instinctively reaching for the knife that lay nearby.

"Nothing is wrong," he told her, ashamed now for awaking her. But the question in his brain pounded against his skull. "Nothing. It is just that... I have to ask you something. I am sorry, but I did not think it could wait until morning."

Ah, she thought, *he is back to his normal inquisitive self. Good.* Even after the revelations earlier in the evening, he had still remained uncharacteristically quiet, and this urgent need for information reassured her that all was yet well. She knew that he would have to discipline himself against the urgency of his curiosity, but this was not yet something she thought fitting to punish or dissuade; in fact, it was a vice she found enjoyable. "What is it," she asked, "that cannot wait for the light of the sun?"

For a moment, Reza was almost afraid to answer, suddenly realizing that she had taught him virtually nothing about the succession rites, that his question might put him on perilously thin ice culturally: matters regarding the Empress were not to be addressed lightly. It was something they'd never talked about before.

"I was wondering," he began, swallowing as he forged ahead, "how... the Empress is chosen. I mean, could you someday become Empress?"

Esah-Zhurah's expression clouded, became unreadable. Reza feared that he had made a major blunder.

"No, Reza," she told him after a moment. She spoke not with anger, but with sadness. "Of all the things I may accomplish in my life, I may never become Empress." She paused. "Never."

"Why?" he asked, rolling onto his side, propping his head up with his arm to look at her.

"It is because of what happened long ago," she began, "in a time when our Empire was of one world, when warriors – male and female – answered the call of their blood." She rolled over on her back, her eyes focusing on the far distant stars. "Mine is a very old race, Reza, far older than your own. We live now in the time of the First Empire, which began over one hundred thousand of your Standard years in the past. But the earliest records of our civilization go back much, much further, perhaps as far as five hundred thousand of your years. And it is in the twilight ages between those times that the legend of the First Empress was born, in the days when the Old Tongue was widely spoken and unbridled warfare was rife across the land.

"Before the First Empire was founded," she explained, "the legends say that rival city-states vied for dominance, for power. We rose to the pinnacle of civilization time and again during the course of many generations, only to be plunged into renewed dark ages by frenzied, uncontrollable warfare. Many times, leaders banded their nations together with strength and cunning to lead us out of darkness, but when they fell the land was plunged into chaos once more.

"But there came a day," she said, her voice filled with awe, "when a child was born in the city of Keela'ar, born to a great queen and her consort. The child, whose hair was white as the snow atop the mountains and had rare red talons, was named Keel-Tath.

"Keel-Tath's parents, as was the custom in those days, entrusted their daughter's training to one of the warrior priestesses of the Desh-Ka, and in time she took the reins of her mother's domain into her own hands.

"Cycles passed, and time saw her expand her domain across the face of the known world. And before her hair had grown long past her waist, she stood before her entire race as Empress: the leader of all, the first to unite our world.

"In the cycles after the Unification," Esah-Zhurah went on after a moment of silent reflection, "Tara-Khan, a male warrior who was the greatest of his kind, perhaps the greatest who has ever lived, won her heart. He had slain her enemies upon the field of battle just as he now warmed her bed with his love. In time, she was with child, a child who would be born with white hair, who would someday become her successor upon the throne. The two were happy, so say the legends, and the Empire prospered in Her good graces.

"But there came a warrior who sought to usurp the power of the Empress, a warrior whose name has long since been stricken from the Books of Time in the darkest of disgrace. For he was Tara-Khan's tresh, and he betrayed his brother of the Way. As the Empress lay in her chambers, giving birth to her child, the usurper lured Tara-Khan away from her side, telling him of a plot within the palace to kill the Empress and her child. The usurper led Tara-Khan into a trap, where the betrayers and his followers fell upon him. Many did Tara-Khan slay, but he did not count on the treachery of his companion; the usurper's blade pierced Tara-Khan's back, and so did he fall.

"When the deed was done, the usurper and his mistress, the high priestess of one of the ancient orders, now long forgotten in the depths of its disgrace, led more of their followers to the Empress's chambers, killing all present save the Empress and Her child. 'Give me the child,' the usurper demanded of the Empress, 'and I shall spare its life, and thus shall Your daughter live as mine own.' For the great priestess was barren, and longed for what the Empress had, but she could not; and for his twisted love for this woman did the usurper demand the Empress's child.

"'And what of Tara-Khan?' demanded Keel-Tath as the evil ones surrounded Her. 'His body feeds the wo'olahr of the forest, as yours shall feed my desires,' the usurper spat in reply as he moved to force himself upon her in a grotesque consummation of his lust and greed."

Reza's skin crawled at the thought, his long-forgotten memories of Muldoon's diseased cravings suddenly surfacing in his mind.

"But he was never to touch her," Esah-Zhurah continued. "Her heart broken at the death of Tara-Khan, Her blood burning in blind rage, She invoked the Curse that has vexed us to this day. The conspirators did Keel-Tath curse, calling upon the powers that lay deep within Her, powers that could change the very shape of our nature.

"First was cursed the usurper who had betrayed Tara-Khan and threatened to defile Her. Such was the power of his lust, Keel-Tath told him, that lust is all that would remain. And not just for him, but for all his kind. And in moments the warrior began to writhe in agony as his body withered to half its once-proud size, his head shrinking to house a brain that knew only of mating, and could never be home to another treacherous thought. But then she decreed that the urge would be satisfied only once, whereupon he would die in horrible agony. The legends say that on the day following her judgment, there were no more male warriors to be found in the world, only shells that were nothing more than breeding machines that could function but a single time. Only her imperial guards were spared this fate."

Reza shuddered at the thought. Even a boy such as he knew that legends were often no more than empty fairy tales, no more real than the Tooth Fairy. But Esah-Zhurah told the tale as if it had happened only yesterday, not millennia – *a hundred millennia* – before.

"Then," Esah-Zhurah went on softly, and Reza had to strain to hear her above the waterfall, "she cast judgment upon the usurper's mistress. Her punishment was equally terrible. Keel-Tath decreed that the woman and all who shared her bloodline would have what they so desired: to be able to bear children. The usurper's mistress would be fertile and forever intertwined with the usurper and those like him, now a mere animal in search of a female in heat. Her punishment was that she must breed every cycle of what we now call the Empress Moon, or she would die in terrible pain. She must embrace her lover once, then watch him die in agony. And so she would never forget that she had been barren, one daughter of every two would be infertile, and born with silver claws as witness. The claws such as are upon mine own hands."

She turned to face Reza, silently wondering what this alien, this outsider, could think at the misfortune of her race.

Shocked, Reza understood. She was barren, disgraced by a nameless woman who died millennia ago, and only those who could bear children could sit upon the throne of the Kreelan Empire.

"And what of the clawless ones?" Reza asked quietly, not wanting to dwell on Esah-Zhurah's tragic fate. "Did they play a role in this?"

Esah-Zhurah shook her head in the Kreelan way. "After Keel-Tath had delivered the curse upon the usurper and his mistress," Esah-Zhurah went on, "She summoned the priestesses of the other orders and bade them to kneel before her. Handing the first her knife, the knife that had belonged to her mother, she commanded the eldest priestess to deliver up the talons of her hands, the very badges of warriorhood, as a sign of loyalty. And the priestess did this, cutting her talons from her fingers, one by one, and dropping the bloody claws into the urn the Empress held forward to receive them. The knife was passed from priestess to priestess and the ritual repeated. After the last had tossed her proud talons into the urn, Keel-Tath cast a spell upon them, that the children of their bloodlines would be born without talons, and would be known forever as those most loyal to Her will."

"What happened to her?" Reza asked softly. "To Keel-Tath?"

"The legends say that she was stricken with grief at the death of her lover. That very day She gave up her child to the high priestess of the Desh-Ka, for her to bring up the child and teach her the Way as tradition demanded. And then Keel-Tath plunged a knife into her own heart, destroying the life in her body. Such was her sorrow, that her spirit did not seek a place among the Ancient Ones; instead, she sought out the Darkness to dwell in grief for all the days of Time."

Reza thought for a moment that the terrible tale was finished. But he could tell from her expression that there was something else, a final tragedy on that horrible day so long ago. And then he knew what it was.

"Tara-Khan was not really dead, was he?" he asked.

Esah-Zhurah's eyes focused on him, her eyes gleaming as they reflected the fire's flames. "And thus do you surprise me once again, Reza," she told him before continuing her tale. "He made his way back to the palace, more dead than alive, driven by his love for Keel-Tath. But when he arrived, he found her slain by her own hand, and the infant Empress in the hands of the Desh-Ka, its young spirit crying in grief and incomprehension. He lay down beside his lover, and with his last breath did he vow to protect Her evermore from those who might travel beyond this world to seek Her power in the name of evil. And thus did he die. After that, no one knows exactly what happened to Her. Legend has it that Her body disappeared, Tara-Khan's body and the imperial guard with it. No one knows where they may have gone.

"Over time," she said, drawing her tale to a close, "the bloodlines were said to merge, and now those of the black claws and those with none must mate every cycle, or death will take them. Of the children, those who bear these," she held her silver claws to the light, "are only spectators to the continuance of our people, forever barred from the throne by sterility. And tradition demands that the Empress must be possessed of white hair, a direct descendant of Keel-Tath."

Reza didn't believe in what sounded like magic in the legends, but with a race this ancient, who could know? Regardless, he felt sick. Despite the horrors he had suffered at the hands of these people, despite the untold suffering of humanity before their attacking fleets, he pitied them. With his entire heart, he pitied them. Such a wonderful and proud race, violent though it might be, doomed to such a horrible fate.

"Esah-Zhurah," he stuttered, wanting to offer something, but not really knowing what to say. "I am... sorry. For all of you."

She looked at him closely for a moment, and he thought for just an instant he saw punishment looming in her eyes. But it vanished with the shifting of the dying flames, and her beautiful cat's eyes softened again.

"Save your sorrows for your own people," she told him. "The Children of the Empress need not your pity." With that, she turned away from him, drawing her skins tightly around her as she fought to ward off the chill of the night and the visions of Keel-Tath's legacy to her people.

And as sleep stole upon her, she thought of something that never would have occurred to her, never in all her life, had not Reza asked his question this night.

What would it be like, she thought to herself as she drifted away into the land of dreams, *to become Empress, the Ruler of Eternity?*

* * *

Reza's eyes snapped open. His heart was tripping like a hammer, and he found himself breathing rapidly, as if he had been running for leagues. He looked around cautiously, but could see only the ethereal glow of the moss that lined the bottom of the grotto, twinkling in the mist from the waterfall. Other than that and the light from the stars, it was completely dark. The night was yet full.

Had he been dreaming, he wondered? After a brief inspection of his body's condition, he decided that no, a dream was not the cause of his unease. He had awakened from the combat reflex that was slowly but surely becoming an integral part of him, his senses having warned him through his subconscious that something was wrong. But he did not yet know what.

Esah-Zhurah continued to sleep peacefully, her body turned away toward the grotto beyond the shelter of the alcove. He found it difficult to believe that whatever had awakened him had failed to do the same to her, but he was even more skeptical that the hairs standing on the back of his neck were a mistake.

His eyes darted about their limited field of vision as his nose and ears searched for clues as to what was troubling him. He lay perfectly still, searching. He had learned long before that to move before isolating a hidden threat was often a fatal mistake. One did not have to be a veteran of the Challenge to know that.

There. The cry struck him like a blow. It was the sound of the magtheps outside the entrance to the grotto, screaming in fright.

"Goliath!" he said, throwing aside his blankets and getting to his feet. He had no idea what was out there, but his instincts – even bred as they were from a different order of evolution – were crying out in alarm. He bolted toward the rocky trail that led to the opening to the side of the mountain where the magtheps had been grazing.

"Reza!" Esah-Zhurah called, grabbing his arm. "Wait!"

"But–"

"Listen."

And then he heard it, a basso growl that ripped across every nerve in his body like a twisted, clawed hand. He had never heard such a frightful sound before, but he knew it was close. Too close. Even in the darkness, he could tell that Esah-Zhurah's skin had paled. Her hand was gripping his arm so hard she had drawn blood. She was terribly frightened.

"What is it?" he breathed.

"Genoth," she whispered hoarsely, her body beginning to tremble.

Reza looked at her, the word meaning nothing to him. "What does that mean?"

"It is terribly dangerous, Reza," she said, drawing herself closer to him, dropping her voice even further. "It is a... a dragon, a great carnivorous beast."

Reza looked up toward where the magtheps' cries had echoed through the portal, but could see nothing. The sounds had faded without any squeals of pain.

"Goliath and your animal must have fled down the mountain," he said, relieved that they might be safe.

The growl came again, louder this time, and Reza realized with sudden dread that the sound had begun to echo. *It was in the caldera.*

"It is in here," he whispered, stepping carefully beyond the alcove's overhang, scanning the walls around them.

"Reza, do not–" Esah-Zhurah's voice caught in her throat as she saw the shadow atop the far side of the grotto, a great dark blob of matter that seemed to consume the stars in the sky. "There," she whispered, pointing to where the beast sat, perched atop the grotto's rim.

Of all the ways to die, this was the one that Esah-Zhurah feared most of all: to be eaten by another creature that was ignorant of all things but hunger and primal instincts.

The creature remained dormant for a while, and the two young warriors waited through minutes that seemed like ages, waiting to see what it would do. Hoping beyond hope that it would turn and leave them alone, they knew with the certainty of those condemned that it would not; that it would, at long last, begin its fateful descent.

Reza's mind was working frantically. Somehow, there had to be something they could do, something better than an offering of token resistance that would not even serve to annoy the beast as it gobbled them up. He had never seen what one of these creatures looked like, but from the silhouette on the grotto's rim he could tell that it was huge, and Esah-Zhurah's fear was an indicator of how fierce it must be. He cursed himself silently, tearing his eyes from the beast to search the grotto, thankful that the sound and mist from the waterfall seemed to have protected them from detection thus far.

They were trapped, he thought desperately, trapped in a tomb of beauty, but a tomb nonetheless. If only–

The waterfall...

–there was somewhere–

The waterfall...

–they could hide.

"The waterfall," he murmured, his eyes fixed on it now. And then he knew. "Of course," he said. "The cave!"

"What?" Esah-Zhurah asked, barely able to shift her attention from the mesmerizing form of the beast as it sat, waiting. Watching.

"We have to get to the water," he told her.

"Why?" she asked, pulling on his arm as he tried to creep forward.

"Do you not see?" he asked, roughly pulling her to him, his face so close to hers that their noses touched. "We will be safe in the cave behind the waterfall!"

"No," she said, trying to pull away from him, her fears doubled now at the prospect of having to swim in the dark water. She would rather face the genoth, a fear and enemy her heart and mind could cope with, not like the shadowy darkness of the water, which perhaps was the water of her nightmares. "I cannot. I–" A roar that shook the entire grotto drowned out her words. The black shape that was the beast shifted and became smaller, then disappeared against the darkness of the side of the caldera.

"It is coming down the wall!" Reza hissed, knowing now that it had spotted them. "Come on!"

Pulling Esah-Zhurah behind him, he half led, half dragged her toward the edge of the pool, stumbling and tripping over the rocks that were only shadows upon shadows. Guided more by the sound of the falling water than the dim glow of the moss illuminating the pool, he suddenly felt the cool water lapping around his feet, and he surged forward.

"No!" Esah-Zhurah cried, pulling her arm away, turning to run back toward the shore.

Reza cursed in frustration. His eyes caught a glimpse of a dark form slithering down the wall as his ears picked up a faint *click-click-click* as it came for them.

He grabbed her by the shoulders and whirled her around to face him. "Esah-Zhurah," he said quietly, holding her with all his might against her struggling, hoping that she would not decide to impale him with her claws, "you must trust me.

Please." She broke his grip and raised her hands toward him, ready to strike. "I trusted you this night," he said hastily. "Now it is time for you to do the same."

She paused, his words echoing in her mind, echoing with the sound of truth, of wisdom. Then her eyes caught sight of the genoth as it casually scaled the grotto's wall toward the bottom. Toward them. Her eyes wide with fear, she nodded assent, and Reza quickly turned and began to splash further out into the water, holding her hand like a child's.

"Here," he told her, turning to hold her with one arm crossing over her breast and up to the opposite shoulder. "Just relax and let me do the swimming," he said.

Panic-stricken as he pulled her backward into the water, Esah-Zhurah grabbed at Reza's arm, cutting him badly, as she tried to get away.

"Trust me!" he shouted, grimacing in pain as her talons again raked his forearm. "Be still!"

With a monumental effort, she did as she was told, and let Reza propel them through the water with powerful kicks of his legs, his free arm guiding them toward the sound of the waterfall.

Reza had lost sight of the genoth, but it did not matter. Either they would make it to safety, or they would not. Of the many gray areas life presented, this was not one: they would survive or they would die. The pain in his arm left by Esah-Zhurah's talons boosted more adrenaline into his circulatory system as he swam. He picked up his pace, surging through the water.

"Do you see it?" he cried above the waterfall's roar. "Where is it?"

"It is nearly to the water!" she shouted back, her talons again pressing into his flesh as she watched the beast – a huge animal, larger than any she knew to be on record since times long past – scale the last few meters of rock and lichens to reach the pool. Without missing a step, it slid its dark form into the water, the phosphorescent wake of its reptilian body arrowing directly toward them. "It is in here!" she screamed, struggling to escape, still with her hand clamped firmly to Reza's arm.

"Hold your breath!" Reza shouted, turning her around to face him. "Do you hear me? Hold it!" He caught sight of the animal bearing down on them. It was so close now that he could smell its alien musk through the cloud of dark water that hung about them like a cloak. He heaved in one last breath before plunging beneath the surface, dragging Esah-Zhurah with him into the blackness.

Esah-Zhurah was beyond fear as she clutched Reza's arm, her mind pulsing with terror of the thing that must even now surely be right behind them, ready to lash out with its tremendous jaws at their frantically kicking feet. While she was terrified beyond her wildest imagination, she found herself trying to match the urgent rhythm of Reza's strokes with her own powerful legs, letting him guide them deeper into the maw of the dark cave.

Her head suddenly crashed against an unseen rock, and she let out a cry, more of surprise than pain. But the effect would have been the same. She involuntarily inhaled some water, and she began to drown.

Reza felt her sudden panic and the spasms of her body as water began to fill her lungs. With one final, desperate kick of his legs, his hand made contact the smooth surface of the stone floor. In a motion born of terrible need, he launched himself and his choking companion into the life-giving air of the lower cavern.

Esah-Zhurah began to writhe, still conscious but unable to get the water out of her lungs. Pulling his own shaking body from the water, he hauled her away from the water's edge and into the crevice that lay above.

"Hang on," he panted. "I have you."

He had acted none too soon. A huge geyser exploded from the underwater tunnel as the genoth thrust its head through the too-narrow canal in a last ditch effort to retrieve its coveted meal. The water doused the two of them, but there was no sign of the creature, its colossal head too large, its neck too short, for the tunnel. They were safe.

Turning his attention back to Esah-Zhurah, vainly trying to shake off his own terror, he quickly turned her on her stomach and pressed against her naked back, hoping to expel some of the water that had found its way down her throat. She struggled weakly, then began to gag as water came gushing out her mouth.

"Reza," she managed before she vomited into the water, her shaking body steadied only by his bloodied arms.

"Hush," he said, holding her tightly to him, his eyes desperately probing the darkness for some sign of their nemesis, wondering if even now its head hung above them in the cavern, poised like a cobra ready to strike. "We must get to the next level," he told her. "I do not think it can come through the tunnel, but..."

In the dark, Esah-Zhurah nodded weakly as her hand sought to wipe the foulness from her lips and chin.

Reza wrapped an arm around her waist and helped her to stand. "Can you make it?" he asked.

"Yes," she told him, although her body was trembling like a leaf before the wind. She put her arm around his shoulder, careful to keep her talons from his tender skin, and together they made their way up the narrow fissure to the balcony that overlooked the grotto.

Behind them, the black waters stirred once more, the act of a behemoth denied. Then all was still.

* * *

Reza watched the swirling barrier of the waterfall as it gradually grew lighter, more vibrant. The sun was finally rising. He suddenly remembered his father asking him once what he thought might be on the other side of a waterfall. And now, seemingly a lifetime after his father's death, he knew the answer: sanctuary. Life.

He closed his eyes, acutely aware of Esah-Zhurah's warmth as she slept beside him. Her face was buried in the hollow of his neck, one of her hands covering the deep cuts in his arm as if in apology. It had been almost impossible to get any rest, as the cave was terribly cold and the night beyond the waterfall was filled with the genoth's frenzied grunting and squealing as it cursed their escape in its own language.

Neither of them had been wearing any clothes, a habit of sleep long since established, and had taken flight only with what nature had endowed them and the collars about their necks. A fortunate coincidence for swimming, Reza had thought, but a terrible burden as the cold rock leeched the heat from their bodies. He had taken to standing near the lip of the cave's mouth, listening to the genoth as it rampaged in the water below. A curious chattering sound drew him back into the cave, fearful of some new menace. But it was only the sound of Esah-Zhurah's teeth clicking together from cold, as she lay inert on the cave's floor. Her body was spent and her mind numbed from facing so many private fears in so short a time.

Giving up on the genoth as an immediate threat, he lay down next to her. Gently, so as not to wake her from the exhausted, frightened sleep into which she had fallen, he put his arms around her, cradling her against what warmth his body could provide as he waited for the dawn.

Now, hours later, the genoth was quiet, having grown tired of its fruitless search. But Reza knew it had not yet departed, for the animals of the grotto had sung not a single note. The lizards that only yesterday had clung to the grotto's walls and heralded the coming of morning were ominously silent. Only when they sang again would Reza believe it safe to walk beyond the safety of the water that fell beyond the cave's mouth.

His body was settling into sleep again, the filtered sunlight warm against his face, when the infant light of morning was beset by a shadow that eclipsed the water cascading past. It did not take much imagination for Reza to know that it was the creature's head, a triangular killing machine whose maw could easily swallow his body whole. It hung suspended, perched somewhere on one of the rock outcroppings that lined the waterfall's passage, swaying like a hangman's noose.

Without warning the creature vomited a huge pile of reeking debris from its mouth, voiding its stomach into the pure waters of the waterfall with such force that some of it blasted through the perilously thin barrier of falling water to spatter inside the cave. The stench of the creature's expectoration was almost unbearable as it flooded through the chamber. Esah-Zhurah stirred beside him, and he carefully put a restraining hand over her mouth, lest she suddenly come awake and cry out.

The genoth retched again, sending out another torrent of indigestible material, some of which clattered about the cave. Some debris that bore more than a passing resemblance to crushed and shattered bone fragments tumbled hollowly about before coming to rest. It was then that Reza knew the animal was not sick. It was simply purging itself of those items that its digestive system could not accommodate.

Esah-Zhurah lay frozen against him, her eyes wide with horror. She waited for the terrible beast to peer beyond the curtain of water at which its tongue now lapped, a giant pink worm piercing the veil of the waterfall.

But it did not. With one final heave, the thing's shadow disappeared as it scaled the walls of the caldera to find a better hunting ground.

Their attention turned to what the genoth had left behind, and Reza nearly vomited himself at what he saw. Strewn about the cave by the genoth's explosive heaves were parts of what had once been at least one young Kreelan warrior. Reza could clearly see the metallic glint of the remains of a collar and some of its pendants. There was torn and twisted chest armor. Unidentifiable hunks of partially digested bone were scattered among the dreadful refuse, along with the remains of the warrior's claws and fingertips. He heard Esah-Zhurah suck in her breath as she recognized the remains.

"Chesh-Tar," she murmured, having determined the nature of the collar's design from the pitiful fragments. Unsteadily, she got to her knees and saluted her dead fellow warrior. "Great is my grief," he heard her whisper. "May you be one with the spirits of the Way, Chesh-Tar."

Reza did not know what to say. It seemed so incongruous, that a member of a species that was founded on war, on killing, could show the grief that he beheld on Esah-Zhurah's face.

"I am sorry," he said. It was all he could think of to say.

Esah-Zhurah nodded, as much at Reza's sincerity as at the meaning of his words. "No longer may she serve the Empress in this life," she said quietly. "That is my sorrow, human." She turned tired eyes upon him. "She was a very skilled hunter," she said quietly, moving closer to better see the remains that lay before them like a carnal banquet. She wanted to take the collar in her hands, but she knew it would have been unwise – and horribly painful – to walk through the stomach acid the genoth had vented. Luckily, the falling water created a natural draft that pulled the rancid air out of the cave. Otherwise, she would have been overcome with uncontrollable retching even now. "This must be an extraordinarily cunning beast to have outwitted her."

"What do we do?" he asked, pointed at the pile of chewed and melted debris.

"We leave it," she replied. "There is nothing we can do, now. The priestess will send a party to attend to her last rites."

Reza only nodded, then turned away from the oozing mass that had once been a young woman. Kreelan or not, Chesh-Tar had suffered a fate he would not have wished upon anyone. Together, he and Esah-Zhurah huddled together for warmth that was spiritual as much as physical as they waited for the fullness of the new day, fearful that the creature might be lurking further up the caldera's wall in the growing light.

Soon, much to their relief, the animals of the grotto began to emerge. At last Reza heard the sound he most wanted to hear: the boisterous warbling of the grotto lizards.

TEN

Twelve Years Later

Cold was the wind that howled in Reza's face, and he struggled to more tightly bind the furs that protected his head. He peered ahead over Goliath's powerful shoulders as he gripped the reins in his gloved hands, his body moving in time with the beast's undulating gait as he plodded through the deep snow. Through the tiny slit in the fur wrappings protecting his face, Reza could see little more than glaring whiteness and the occasional gray shadow of a withered tree. Although the dim light from the sun penetrated the white shroud that clung to the earth, the line where land and sky met was all but obscured.

Beside him, Esah-Zhurah rode her magthep, an unnamed cow much smaller than Goliath's aging bulk. Despite their hardiness, even the Kreelans eschewed the cold of deep winter, when the kazha conducted its training in the few indoor facilities dedicated to the purpose.

But there were times when the tresh were sent forth on missions, and this was one of them. The priestess had dispatched the two of them to the city to retrieve her correspondence, a similar errand that had brought him under Tesh-Dar's influence some dozen human years earlier. Their errand was certainly not the first of its type for Reza, but it was certainly the first time he had become genuinely concerned for their safety, and with every passing moment his sense of worry deepened.

They had reached the city and conducted their business there without incident, leaving the black tube that contained the priestess's outgoing correspondence and picking up its counterpart to return to her. After a quick meal in a public hall, where the two of them had perched comfortably next to a huge pit of glowing coals, they had begun their journey back.

The first part of their return trek had been entirely uneventful, with nothing more than a light snowfall and playful breezes. But soon the winds had become threatening, and even the magtheps – as well-protected against winter's perils as they were – had begun complaining. They shook their heads to throw off the heavy coating of ice from their eyes and ears, all the while muttering to each other in their own way. The horizon had closed in around them, finally disappearing in a total whiteout of heavy snow.

Above all else, Reza knew it was taking them much too long to return from the city. He had spent enough time on this world without any chronometer save the sun,

Empress Moon, and stars to know that they had been traveling half again as long as they had that morning to reach the city.

"Esah-Zhurah," he shouted through the furs and the wind, "I think we are lost."

"Nonsense, Reza," she told him. "We are on course," she said, holding up a circular device about the size of her palm with a pointer in the center: a compass. "We are only delayed by the winds and snow."

"Then why have we not seen any markers for the last few leagues?" he asked, referring to the tall stone cairns that lined the roads that spread outward from the city like spokes on a wheel, serving to guide travelers in conditions just such as this. "There is nothing out here but us, and I do not recognize any of this."

Esah-Zhurah ignored him. It annoyed her that he, the tresh who had in some ways become the envy of many of her peers, appeared to be losing his courage and his faith in her. But her pride would not allow her to admit that the seeds of doubt had sprouted in her own mind, as well. The lack of familiar landmarks – the peninsular forest, the three rock outcroppings that lined the road to the kazha like lonely sentinels, the stone pyramid markers – was troubling.

But I have followed the compass unerringly, she told herself. Again she checked that the needle was precisely in the position it was supposed to be. It showed three points left of north, pointing directly toward the kazha from the city's center. "We are going the right way," she said again with finality, spurring her magthep into a faster gait in a demonstration of her resolve. "If you do not accept it," she told him, "you may choose your own direction."

Reza sighed, saying nothing. He did not want to antagonize her needlessly, especially since he was not quite sure of their situation. The compass had been pointing in the right direction. But the conditions they were in were unusual, even for this time of year. Prodding Goliath to move on after his tresh, he tried to silence the alarms in his mind.

Time passed, hours measured by Goliath's bounding stride, and with each step Reza's concern grew. The winds were blowing furiously, and the snow had become a curtain of shrieking whiteness that cut visibility to less than two full strides of Goliath's powerful legs. At last, he could hold himself back no longer.

"Stop!" he shouted suddenly to the shadowy form ahead, his voice strangely muted by the whipping snow around them.

"What is it?" Esah-Zhurah called back, reining in her magthep. Reza heard anticipation in her voice, as if she expected him to be pointing to the kazha, about to tell her he saw something he recognized.

"Esah-Zhurah," he said, moving close to overcome the howling wind, "you must face it: we are lost. Night will fall soon, and we must find a place to make camp or we will freeze to death."

"For the last time, Reza, I say we are going in the correct direction," she said, her voice tight. Her own fears had been eating at her like a maggot feasting on rotting flesh, and Reza's words only served to fuel the parasitic beast. But her pride concealed the extent of the rot, providing her a false shield of self-righteousness.

Inside, she wanted to protect him, to do what was right. But the prideful froth that beat against her brain, the fact that he might be right, was too much for her still-xenophobic mind to grapple with. "It is just that the winds and snow–"

"We are lost!" he suddenly shouted, grabbing her by the shoulders and spinning her around in the saddle to face him, finally losing control over his anger and fear.

It was a mistake. Using his own leverage against him, she reflexively rammed her right elbow into the side of his head. He was unprepared for an attack, and he toppled from the saddle as if struck with a lance. He landed on his back, the fall cushioned slightly by the layer of snow on the ground, but not enough to prevent the wind from being knocked out of him.

Esah-Zhurah watched with hooded eyes as he struggled to his knees, gasping for breath. "I am sorry, Reza," she said, anger ruling her mind, a cheap substitute for reason. "If you do not wish to accompany me, I will not keep you."

She prodded her magthep with her feet, sending the cow galloping away into the curtain of white.

"No, wait!" he croaked, forcing air through his still protesting lungs. He staggered to his feet, only to fall again, his head whirling from her unexpected blow. He crawled to Goliath's side, the claws of his gauntlets grappling with the saddle as he struggled to his feet. "Esah-Zhurah! Wait!" he cried again, finally clearheaded enough to lunge into his mount's saddle.

But it was too late. He watched helplessly as she sped into the wall of snow, swiftly disappearing from sight.

* * *

Esah-Zhurah did not how long she had been going at a full gallop. Her anger at Reza, a demon that had struck with the suddenness of lightning, had been so all-consuming that she had completely lost track of time. But from the magthep's labored breathing, she knew that it was time to let it rest. Forcing herself to relax somewhat, she eased it to a slow trot, then a walk.

She looked yet again at the compass, but she was not entirely consoled by what it told her. As much as she hated to admit it to herself, Reza had been right about one thing: even as bad as this weather had been, they certainly should have reached the kazha – or at least one of the outer ring roads – by now.

Stopping her magthep for a moment, ignoring its hungry mewling, she peered intently into the snowy world around her. She looked for landmarks, but there was nothing. Not a single feature stood out. Not a rock, not a tree, nothing. She found that in itself curious and disquieting. There was not a single lump or disturbance in the ground within the confines of her limited visibility; the ground under the snow seemed to be as smooth and flat as a pane of glass. She looked again at the compass. The needle still pointed insistently three points left of north, exactly as it should. It had not deviated since they started from the city.

As she fumbled with the flap of the compass pouch, she suddenly stopped as those four words echoed in her head. *It had not deviated...*

With a feeling of sickening certainty, she took a close look at the compass, already knowing what she would find. Indeed, the needle still pointed as it always had – no matter which way the device was turned. Holding it close to her face, peering through the driving snow, she saw that the tiny air bubble under the glass face was locked in position, the liquid inside the compass frozen solid.

Baring her fangs and roaring with anger at her own stupidity, she smashed her fist into the fragile face of the device. She hurled what was left of it into the snow with all her strength, watching it disappear as it sailed into the bleak whiteness that had encircled her.

And only then did the magnitude of her predicament become apparent. Having abandoned Reza, she may well have forfeited her own life. Her people ventured into the Homeworld's winter harshness in pairs at least, for one terribly vital reason: one body alone, even in the emergency shelters they always carried, could not produce enough heat to overcome the freezing temperatures of the night. The magtheps were insulated well enough that they could burrow into the snow to shield themselves from the wind, and thus survive. But without Reza's body heat to combine with her own, she would almost certainly die of exposure.

Worse than the thought of death, however, was how she had tainted her honor before Reza with her pride and arrogant self-confidence. She had breached the trust he had vested in her that day in the grotto, now a lifetime ago, yet only yesterday. So much had they shared in the cycles that had passed, and only now did she understand the depth to which their relationship had grown. She accepted that he was not an animal, but a being worthy of her trust and the mercy of the Empress. Of all the things in her life of which she could be proud, he was the first and foremost. Death she could accept. But dying without a chance to redeem herself to Reza – that she could not.

She saw that the snow was beginning to fill her magthep's tracks, slowly obliterating them and marking the time before she might have to lay down to sleep one last time and await Death's cold embrace.

"Reza," she cried, reining the magthep around to head back in the direction from which they had come, "what a fool I have been!"

There was no answer, save the mocking howl of the wind.

* * *

Awkwardly, sometimes stumbling where the snow deepened unexpectedly, Goliath loped along the trail of giant bird-like footprints left by Esah-Zhurah's mount. He was guided as much by his own instincts as by the half-blinded human on his back. Reza knew that normally Goliath could keep up this pace for hours without becoming overly tired, but the deepening snow was slowing him down. Slowly but surely, the great beast was tiring.

But even with Goliath, it would be impossible to catch Esah-Zhurah unless she had at some point slowed to an easy walk. Following her magthep's spoor was becoming more difficult by the minute. The blowing whiteness around him had turned a dull, lifeless gray as the invisible sun began to set, and it would soon give way to the icy depths of night, beset by temperatures that would freeze exposed flesh in a matter of seconds. The wind that drove the snow over the tracks he desperately sought to follow also was attacking his body, impaling him with tiny needles of cold that lanced at his nerves before they disappeared from his sense of touch altogether. Already, he had lost most of the feeling in his toes; a residual tingling was all that remained. If he could not find Esah-Zhurah soon he would suffer from frostbite, his flesh perhaps permanently damaged if he could not reach a healer in time. If he did not find her at all, they both would die.

He was running out of time. Each newfound footprint was shallower than the one before it, covered by the massive snowfall that had reduced Reza's world to a few paces of his own legs. Goliath's stride was almost that long when he was moving quickly, and if Esah-Zhurah made a sharp turn somewhere up ahead as she followed her faulty compass, Reza could easily miss it and lose the trail even before the snow covered it completely.

Cursing under his breath to any god that might be listening, even the Empress, Reza urged Goliath on, driving him as fast as he dared.

* * *

Esah-Zhurah had slowed her mount to a dull plod as she squinted in the dying light to see the spoor her magthep had left coming the other way. She had not realized before how far she had come since leaving Reza behind, but backtracking was leaving her with little hope of finding him. The tracks were all but gone, mere dents in the featureless gray landscape, and the blinding whiteness of the snowy cloak around her was quickly giving way to the deadly darkness of night. If she did not find him soon...

She carefully guided the magthep along the fading trail, but her skill could not forestall the inevitable. The last visible track behind her now, she saw only falling snow, a dark gray curtain ahead of her in the rapidly fading light. The trail was gone.

"Reza," she murmured, "what am I to do?"

* * *

"Well," Reza said to himself, batting his arms against his torso to keep his blood flowing into his numbing fingers, "the hunt is over." After passing an indentation he took to be a footprint, he had found himself surrounded by snow, snow, and more snow, without any further sign of the other magthep's trail. Even Goliath had lost the scent of the other beast, and stood snorting into the freezing air. With a morbid curiosity befitting a cynical embalmer, Reza wondered how it would feel to freeze to death. The accounts he remembered from his fading memory of things human described it as feeling terribly cold, then warm, and at last falling asleep, never to reawaken. "That is not so bad," he sighed. There were plenty of worse ways to die, he knew. But this was fundamentally wrong to him in a way that he was at a loss to explain.

He stared into the snow, where the horizon should have been, but he was not looking at what his eyes were seeing. He was listening to a voice that spoke deep within him. It did not use words, or even images, like in a dream. It was more a feeling that pulsed from his core, a flame that had been kindled in his soul as he slept one night, perhaps. He did not know exactly when it had first come to him, or what it might have been, but he accepted it now as an ally. It was not simply the voice of his will to survive. It was like a living thing within him, an alter ego that played the role of guardian angel by giving him the strength he needed to live. Alien or human, it did not matter. It was with him.

Esah-Zhurah was somewhere close by, the voice seemed to say. And Reza believed. He knew it was true. It must be.

As he drew on that source of inner strength, a rush of adrenaline suddenly surged into his system. Taking the furs from his face, he cupped his hands to his mouth.

"Esah-Zhurah!" he shouted as loud as he could, his diaphragm ramming air into his throat like a turbine, stretching the last syllable until his lungs had no more to give.

Without the tiniest trace of an echo, the wall of snow around him consumed her name.

Closing his eyes, he listened.

* * *

Esah-Zhurah was just about to dismount and set up the shelter when she heard something above the howling of the falling snow. It sounded like a faintly audible note that might have been a voice coming from her left. It grew for a moment into a steady tone that suddenly ended.

"Reza?" she whispered. "Reza!" she shouted, "Where are you?"

Nothing.

"I did not imagine it," she said aloud, sitting ramrod straight in her saddle, as if her body could act as an antenna to gain some additional clarity should the note be repeated.

Beneath her, the magthep threw its head from side to side, growing restless for no reason Esah-Zhurah could fathom. It mewled quietly, stomping its feet, waiting for Esah-Zhurah to make up her mind.

There! The sound came again, and she was sure it was her name being called, and was not simply a wishful hallucination.

"Reza!" she shouted with all her strength. "Over here!"

Her heart thundering with relief, she wheeled her magthep around and began to gallop in the direction of his voice, thanking the Empress that Reza somehow had found her, and that perhaps all would yet be well.

* * *

He was about to call out to her again when he heard a thunderous boom. Goliath suddenly sprawled forward, catapulting Reza over the beast's twisting neck. Reza's arms and legs flailed like a doll's as he spun through the air, his mouth gaping open in horrified surprise.

In the moment he was airborne, surprise gave way to terror as he saw a jagged black chasm yawning beneath him where only snow had been before. Freezing water lapped hungrily at the serrated edges of the broken ice, and welcomed Reza with a frigid embrace that stole the scream from his lips as he plunged into the river.

* * *

The sound hit her like a shot from a rifle, echoing through the air and reverberating through the ground at her feet.

"What is that?" she whispered, peering in the direction from which she had heard Reza's voice.

She could see nothing. Her ears, however, had no difficulty in picking out sounds she recognized instantly: a magthep's terrified squeals mixed with the sound of splashing water.

The river! she realized. We have been traveling along the river. And Reza and Goliath must have fallen through...

"No!" she cried, kicking her magthep in the ribs and sending the beast racing as fast as she could toward the frenzied thrashings. "Reza, hang on!" she shouted into the wind. "Hang on!"

Suddenly, as if someone had whipped a curtain aside, Esah-Zhurah found herself plunging toward the gaping black fissure in the ice where Goliath had broken through. The great magthep was now pawing and kicking desperately at the edge, his tiny forearms grappling pitifully at the icy wall that rose nearly a meter above him.

As she watched, more ice tumbled down into the black waters. The layer that had covered the river was treacherously thin and hollow between the surface of the water and the bottom of the ice. The magthep screamed in terror, his rear legs and tail thrashing as he sought to escape.

"Reza!" she shouted over the magthep's braying. Her eyes scanned the water, hoping to spot him alive among the drifting chunks of ice, or – better by far – somewhere near the edge, out of danger. She would have taken her magthep closer, but she was already dangerously near the snaking web of cracks that spiraled outward from where Goliath lay struggling.

Leaping from her mount, she moved as close as she dared to the crumbling edge. "Reza!" she called again, her voice cracking with the effort.

"Esah-Zhurah," came a hoarse cry, barely more than a whisper it seemed, from somewhere in the water, "here."

Desperately, Esah-Zhurah searched the water for him, edging ever closer as she sought to pierce the undulating shroud of darkening snow.

Without warning, there was another tremendous boom from the ice, and her magthep plunged into the frigid water. Esah-Zhurah was flung clear by a huge chunk of ice that catapulted her into the air like a springboard. Rolling to her feet in the snow, she turned to find Goliath finally struggling to safety, having at last gotten a grip with his rear feet on stable ice. The beast shook himself mightily, flinging away the water that had not yet frozen to his fur. Retreating a short way from the fissure, he turned to bray at his companion cow, now struggling for its life. Lacking Goliath's enormous strength, the smaller animal was doomed.

"Call again!" Esah-Zhurah shouted, "I cannot see you!"

"Here," came the voice, weaker this time.

Her eyes were drawn to two black streaks across a large chunk of ice. They suddenly resolved into Reza's arms, the claws of his gauntlets thrust into the ice. Just before the snow obliterated the scene, she saw his head lolling just above the water.

"I see you!" she shouted. "*Do not let go!* Do you hear me?" she cried. "Hang on!"

She turned to Goliath, the problem of how to retrieve Reza without killing herself consuming her thoughts. Since the day in the grotto, she had learned from Reza how to swim, but she had never tried anything like this, nor had she ever been in water this cold.

"You are going to have to help me, Goliath," she said, grabbing some rope from where it was lashed to the saddle. She shook the ice and snow from it, the fibers crackling as she began to unwind the sturdy hemp. She tied one end through one of the stirrups on Reza's saddle, then dropped the rest to the ground. Bracing herself against the cold, she ripped off her metal chest armor. She would have taken off the rest, but there was no time.

She took up the rope and stood on the thinnest ice that would still support her weight. She knew now that her destiny had arrived. This was the source of her dark dreams, the nightmares that had plagued her since she was young. This was the dark water that would steal her breath away, that would still her heart, that would take her life. She might have laughed at the sudden memory of her fear of the waters of the grotto that night, as Reza struggled valiantly to convince her that lying in a genoth's belly was indeed worse than diving beneath a waterfall. "Have faith," she told herself softly, gritting her teeth. "Be strong."

Gripping the free end of the rope in one hand, she ran toward the water, praying that her body would be able to stand the shock. She leaped into the air just as the ice gave way beneath her and dived head first into the water, arms outstretched, with the rope trailing away behind her like a harpoon's lanyard.

Her thoughts and her breath were ripped away as she hit the water, the cold stabbing into her body like an icy sword. She was sure her heart stopped for just an instant. But then, almost reluctantly, it began to beat again, counting down the few minutes she had before the cold would claim her. She began to swim toward the small berg to which Reza had anchored himself. From land, it seemed like it could only be a dozen meters. But now, in the freezing water, every stroke seemed like a league. She could feel the cold sucking the life from her, the water a much more insidious opponent than the air above. Her heart thundered as it tried to keep warm blood flowing from her weakening core to the straining muscles in her legs and arms.

Without warning, she felt herself jerked up short. Only after a moment of confused turning in the water did she realize what had happened: the rope was not long enough! Hesitating for a precious moment, she finally let it go and kicked away, leaving it behind to sink into the darkness. She had been depending on Goliath's brute strength to get them out, but now she was on her own.

She turned her head just in time to see Reza slip beneath the surface. His hand trailed limply behind him like a periscope until that, too, vanished beneath the roiling water.

"No!" she screamed, kicking madly toward where he had gone down. Frantically, she swam to where she had last seen him clinging to the ice. She dived below the surface and swam in a circle for as long as she could, finally coming up for a gasp of air. She could see nothing, feel nothing in the murk below. How was she to find him in the black water? Which direction was the current flowing? She dived back down, searching with her hands. But all that her numbed nerves reported was the deathly cold water. She swam back to the surface again, her hopes for finding him dying with the light of the sun.

"Please," she prayed to her Empress through her violently chattering teeth, "please let me find him. Do not let it end this way. Please."

Then there came an odd tingling sensation, as if a frail *grensha* moth were fluttering along her nerves, and Esah-Zhurah suddenly felt a comforting warmth spreading through her chest. She knew she must be falling over the edge into hypothermia as her body lost its core heat. But somewhere within her, a flicker of knowing flared into a low blaze, and she saw Reza in her mind, saw his limp body, trapped against an outcropping of ice somewhere below her.

Gathering air in her lungs until she thought they might burst, she thrust herself down a final time, her body following a set of directions her mind did not understand, but dared not ignore. She swam beneath the ice, entering a world of complete darkness, where not even the brightest light could shine through, had there been any such light remaining in the world above. She knew that if she did not find him now, both of them would be dead, food for the swimming things that teemed in the river during the spring season after the spawning.

Her fingers touched something. Desperately, she latched onto it, for there was nothing else to sustain the hope that dwindled with the last of the oxygen in her burning lungs. She grappled with the unseen thing, and finally was rewarded as Reza's lifeless form came free from the inverted ridge of ice where he had been trapped by the slow but irresistible current.

Perhaps infinity was a concept best not dwelt upon by a young warrior still untested in battle, but Esah-Zhurah thought she came to understand it well as she struggled through the water toward the surface. Distance and time merged into numbing agony and fear as she fought for every stroke against the current that had helped her find him, but that now threatened to doom her to the same fate. She clamped her arm harder around Reza's chest to keep his armored body from sinking like leaden ballast. She turned to look at his shadowy outline, wondering if he could even still be alive.

No matter, she told herself. She was determined not to leave him behind. Not ever.

The flame that had burned so brightly within her, the power that had somehow shown her where to find him, was flickering like a candle flame surrounded with mist. Her heart was beginning to slow as her body temperature fell, and the numbness in her limbs was overshadowed only by the intense burning in her cramping muscles as their strength swiftly ebbed.

A hideous apparition suddenly flew at her face from the darkness, teeth bared behind savagely drawn lips, ebony eyes bulging from its unearthly face. Claws appeared, reaching for her...

Esah-Zhurah almost screamed into the frigid water at the sight, but her panicked brain understood – barely in time – that it was only the corpse of her magthep. Its struggles against the water now over, its ragged shell was bound for the ocean that lay far beyond the great wastelands.

Just then, her head shot through the water into the frigid air above, and Esah-Zhurah gasped at the shock of it, the taste of life in her mouth. She fought to get Reza's head above the water, even though she knew he was not breathing, and had not been for she did not know how long. She tugged and pulled with her legs and free arm, propelling herself toward the craggy outlines of the ice rim.

But it was not enough. Just at that moment, her struggling legs failed.

As her head went under for the last time, her free hand touched something, and instinctively she grabbed hold of it.

The rope!

Biting her tongue, the pain forcing one last surge of adrenaline into her arteries, she managed one more kick, pushing her head above the water.

Managing to loop the rope around her free wrist, she screamed a last command to the faithful beast above before the water jealously pulled her back. "Goliath, *drakh-te ka!* Pull!"

Nothing happened. As she began to sink, her legs having given their last, she sucked in one final breath before her head went under

Her arm was nearly pulled from its socket as the slack in the rope suddenly vanished. Obeying the command that Reza had once taught him as a useful trick, Goliath hauled them out with his mammoth strength, running headlong away from the fissure. Esah-Zhurah clung desperately to Reza as the two of them swept through the water like porpoises, leaving a rooster tail of icy water showering behind them.

Ahead of them loomed a wall of ice, the edge of the collapsed ice dome through which Reza had fallen. The top of the ice was nearly a meter above the surface of the water, and Esah-Zhurah visualized the two of them being smashed senseless against it as Goliath pulled them blindly onward.

She opened her mouth to tell Goliath to stop, to slow them down before they hit. But a monstrous roar drowned out her voice as the entire ice dome around them collapsed into the water. They were now surging toward a part of the fissure that was in the shape of a V, spearheaded by the rope that had sawed through the thinner ice under Goliath's power. A tidal wave crashed over them, and then they were smashing through sheets and blocks of jagged ice. Frantically rolling to one side, she tried to use Reza's armor as a shield for her own body as they scraped and bucked over the razor-edged floes. Had her arm not been entwined with the rope, she would have lost her grip and fallen back into the water.

Then they were free, their bodies plowing through the snow as Goliath pulled them at a full gallop. Esah-Zhurah let him go for a while until she thought it might be safe to stop.

"Goliath," she called wearily, hoping the animal would hear her through the still howling wind. She had visions of herself and Reza, frozen to death, twirling on a rope behind the animal until it, too, finally died of exposure. "*Kazh!* Stop!"

The rope went slack.

Esah-Zhurah wanted to lay there in the snow and rest for a long while, but she knew that to do so would have brought Death calling. Reza lay next to her, his body still. She had to act quickly. She gained her feet, staggering like a drunkard, and was met by Goliath's steamy muzzle. Petting the beast with dead hands, she worked her way to the saddle and grappled with the lashings that held the shelter, slashing the frozen bindings free with her talons. It fell into the snow. The small brown roll, about the diameter and length of her thigh, immediately began to grow, quickly assuming a hemispherical shape that was nearly as big around as Goliath was long. A tube extruded itself from one end as the whole thing changed color from a leathery brown to a heat absorbing black. As an afterthought, Esah-Zhurah pulled the saddle from Goliath's back, leaving him free to seek his own shelter.

She pulled Reza into the tube, the shelter's sphincter-like entrance dilating open to accept them as if they were crawling back into the womb, then closing behind them. Groping wearily in the darkness of the vestibule with her numbed fingers, Esah-Zhurah cut away Reza's frozen armor, the ice shattering as she peeled it away like the hardened chrysalis of some exotic species of insect. She tore at his clothes, quickly throwing everything to one side in a frozen heap. Then she dragged him into the main part of the shelter and turned him on his stomach. Doing what he had once shown her, she straddled his back and began forcing the water from his lungs with her hands, pushing down with all her weight on his back.

Beneath her, she could hear the sickening gurgle of water as it gushed from his mouth onto the floor of the shelter. Push, release, push, release, until the water fell to a trickle, then stopped. Then she hurriedly turned him over. She bent down, putting her ear to Reza's naked breast, listening for a heartbeat through the pounding of her own that reverberated in her ears. For eight beats of her heart, there was nothing. Then, she heard a faint *lub... dub* through his flesh.

The sound energized her with the power of hope. She bent over him, praying that she could remember the things he had taught her when she was learning to swim. "*Mouth-to-mouth resuscitation*," he had called it in his native tongue. She had laughed at him at the time, finding the thought of doing such a thing to another Kreelan – let alone a human – repugnant.

But the humor of that day was now replaced by desperation as she took his head in her hands. With one hand cupping his head and the other clamping his nose, she put her numbed mouth over his and began to force air into his waterlogged lungs.

She took another breath, then blew again. Her body shook from sheer exhaustion and cold, and her heart beat so fast that she knew it must soon burst. But she refused to give up.

Suddenly, he began coughing. He spouted water everywhere as his lungs received a signal from his dazed brain that they were to begin functioning again, and they sought to clear out the last of the offending fluid. Esah-Zhurah shuddered, praying her thanks to the Empress.

After a few minutes, his breathing became ragged but steady. Undoing her own armor and shedding her clothing, she held him close, wrapping her quaking arms around him. Beneath them, the shelter absorbed the icy pool of water from Reza's lungs. It left behind only a soft, dry bed that already had begun to warm them, reflecting their flickering body heat inward.

Cradling his frigid body to give it what little warmth her own had to offer, she spiraled into a dark, dreamless abyss.

* * *

Tesh-Dar stood at the great window in her quarters, watching as the muted light of day faded into the cold clutches of deep winter's night. She did not need a thermometer to tell her that the temperature was plummeting, and that any organism directly exposed to the night's ministrations would not long survive.

"All of the tresh are accounted for, save Esah-Zhurah and the animal," her First reported quietly. The task they had been given had been a simple but vital one, carried out by generations of tresh for eons as a service to the priestesses of the kazhas. The journey to the city and back, even in deep snow, should have taken only three-fourths of the day's light. But dusk was now upon them, and the young pair still had not returned. "Perhaps," she went on in the silence left by Tesh-Dar, "the human did something..."

The priestess waved her hand impatiently, dismissing the First's veiled accusation. "Had he wished to do something in that vein," she said, "surely he would have done so before this day. No," she said, turning away from the window, "it is not that. Perhaps they remained in the city through good judgment. I do not know."

"If there is nothing else, my priestess, I shall retire for the night," the First said, saluting before she turned to leave. "If the weather allows, I will send out search parties tomorrow to find them."

"No," Tesh-Dar told her. "If they are alive, they must find their own way. If they have perished, there is no need to risk the lives of others to find frozen corpses. Many lives has the winter claimed in this way, and I will not willingly add to its toll."

"Then it is in Her hands," the other woman observed. "Sleep well, my priestess," she said, softly closing the door behind her.

Turning again to the window, a grimace kissed Tesh-Dar's lips at the First's parting words, for no sleep would she find this night.

Closing her eyes and straining to hear and see with senses far beyond what her body boasted, Tesh-Dar began to wander through the endless cold of the night, searching for her missing children.

* * *

Reza was not sure if he was awake or simply in some kind of strange dream. The world was cloaked in velvety darkness, and his skin tingled in a strange, yet familiar way. After a moment, he realized it was the sensation left by the healing gel as it worked its strange miracles. He lay against something warm and smooth, his face pressed against a firm pillow. His nose relayed a gentle smell he recognized as the alien musk to which he had become so accustomed, the smell of Kreelan skin. Esah-Zhurah's skin.

"Esah... Zhurah?" he rasped, his tongue a flaccid lump of flesh in his parched mouth.

"Yes," came her voice from somewhere in the darkness, accompanied by the cool touch of her hand on his forehead, gently brushing his hair back. "I am here, Reza." When she had awakened from the nightmare that had finally come to pass, she had found Reza lying next to her, shivering and burning up with fever. The shelter had done as best it could to save the frostbitten flesh, automatically coating Reza's skin with healing gel, but there was nothing it could do for whatever raged within his body. Esah-Zhurah had despaired for his survival as she did what little she could to keep his temperature down, comforting him in the few lucid moments the fever had allowed.

"Are you... all right?" he asked.

"Yes," she told him, her heart swelling at his concern for her. He tried to move, but Esah-Zhurah held him back. "Be still, my tresh," she commanded softly, her hands holding him firmly in place against her side, his head cradled between her breasts. She put her hand against his forehead again, reassuring herself that it was only warm, and not hot. "Your body is yet weak."

"Where is Goliath?" he asked.

She smiled. Reza was forever concerned with his animal friend. "Goliath lies buried next to us in the snow, keeping warm in the way of his kind. He, too, is well; complaining of hunger, but alive."

"How long..." he asked. "How long have we been here?"

"The sun has risen and set twice since I awakened, and now it is night," she told him. "I do not know how long I was unconscious before that." She felt Reza's eyes close, the brushing of his eyelashes a pleasant tickle against the skin of her breast. Thinking he had returned to the quiet of sleep, she said no more.

But he was not asleep, only thinking. "Esah-Zhurah," Reza said, breaking the silence, "why are you still here?"

"What do you mean?" she asked, puzzled.

"The storm has long since passed, has it not?" Outside, the only thing to be heard was the muted sound of Goliath's breathing and an occasional groan as the beast voiced its hunger.

"It is so," she answered cautiously, unsure where his thoughts would lead.

"I was as good as dead, drowned in the river," Reza went on, his voice a gentle but unrelenting probe, exploring her motivations. "You could have left me behind.

You could have taken the shelter and Goliath and tried to make it on your own. Why did you not?"

She shifted uncomfortably beside him. "I shamed my honor with my arrogance by abandoning you," she said, her voice low and measured, each syllable a self-punishment exacted by her conscience. "I could not abandon you again. You are strange, and not of our Way, but you... are special to me, in a way I do not fully understand." She paused. "I could not bear the thought of losing you."

His hand found hers. There was no need for words. She held him tightly, feeling the warm wetness of his tears upon her breast. In her heart there was a quiet jubilation that they were both alive, and that this day they were something more than they had ever been before.

As their bodies melded together in the deepening cold, she found herself murmuring softly in a prayer to the Empress, asking if perhaps this human – just this one – might indeed have a soul and a place among Her Children.

* * *

When Reza again awoke, it was to a sensation of rampant thirst the likes of which he had never known. Esah-Zhurah had done her best to give him what fluids she could against the fever that had taken him, and had drained all of the shelter's normal liquid supplies. But it had not made up for what he had lost, and the debt the fever had left in its wake had finally caught up to him. The inside of his mouth felt like it was sewn together from sun-baked leather.

"Water," he croaked.

"Here," she said, holding a small clump of packed snow to his lips.

He opened his mouth eagerly, but found the icy snow, taken from a small pile Esah-Zhurah had brought in for the purpose, to be like acid in his mouth. It burned in his throat as it grudgingly metamorphosed into its liquid form. Even so, his thirst was so overpowering that he began to suck on it greedily, and was rewarded with a fit of coughing as water found its way into his trachea, choking him.

Esah-Zhurah held him steady as his coughing subsided into ragged breathing. He was still terribly weak.

"Wait," she told him, gently rolling him onto his back.

He heard her scoop up some snow from wherever she had it sequestered behind him, and then she was silent for a while.

"What are you doing?" he asked, staring into the darkness.

Then he felt one of her hands reach down to cradle the back of his head, lifting it up, while the other gripped his lower jaw and gently forced it open. With shocked surprise he felt her lips press against his, and then cool water was spilling into his mouth from hers. For a moment, he did nothing, disbelieving that she was actually doing such a thing – the rough equivalent among her kind of a human kissing a dog in the world he had once known – and wondering if he should be thankful or repulsed by her touch.

But then her lips pulled away, and he forced himself to swallow the water she had shared with him, having melted the snow in her mouth with the heat of her body. With a detached, almost shameful sense of curiosity, he found himself analyzing the water for any trace of her own taste that might be there, noting with mixed emotions the lack of anything unpleasant.

"More?" Esah-Zhurah asked. She had discovered that actually carrying out the idea that had struck her had been... pleasant. It was not at all like when she had pressed her frozen mouth to his to force air into his lungs. In fact, it had excited her in a way. She wondered what it must have been like before the reign of the First Empress, when male warriors walked among her race, and there were no clawless ones, no sterile mules like herself. Did they perhaps lie quietly next to one another like this on cold winter nights, speaking only with the beating of their hearts and the touch of their bodies? This was the stuff of legend, of fairy tales, or so many peers thought, and undoubtedly it was so. The ancient tales and songs of those times struck a hollow chord among the Empire's warriors. For they knew that the males of their race were nothing more than instruments for the propagation of their species, and it was hard to imagine they had ever been anything more. Some, like Tesh-Dar, truly believed the ancient legends as historical truth. But many had their doubts. Esah-Zhurah tended to believe that the legends were only stories. But something in her mind, a tiny race memory left in the wake of the long evolution of her people, left her thinking that perhaps the peers, the doubters, were wrong.

Licking the tiny bit of moisture that had spilled on his lips, Reza nodded in the darkness. "Please," he begged, his thirst now completely awakened, a ravenous thing trapped in his parched mouth.

Esah-Zhurah repeated her performance four more times, until her tiny stockpile of snow was gone. She noted with a twinge of alarm that touching Reza this way was beginning to seem more than just pleasant. As she gave him the last of the water, the stream between their joined mouths now spent, she pulled away from him, pausing with her lips a hair's breadth from his, her heart beating like thunder in her ears.

"Thank you," he whispered, his lips brushing hers as he spoke the words, sending a jolt of emotional electricity through her. He reached out, running his fingers across her cheek, through her hair, before drawing her down to him. Like strangers whose destiny was to become fast friends and more, their lips touched in a gentle kiss that left them both breathless. When their lips parted, he only had time to utter her name before she kissed him in her own turn, carefully lowering her body onto his, her breasts pools of heat against his chest.

Reza felt a stiffening at his groin that he had experienced before only in his sleep. It was something he had never experienced in human company. He moaned softly as his erection pressed against the smooth, taut flesh of her belly, and he felt her shiver as his hands moved down her back to stroke her sides, his fingers tracing invisible patterns against her skin.

Esah-Zhurah was nearly lost to a power she had never even dreamt of, something that had not been experienced by a member of her race for thousands of generations: physical love. Her mind sought vainly to understand what her body instinctively knew, and she felt the first stirrings of a part of her that – as a mule –

normally would have remained dormant her entire life. The fire that had begun in her veins when their lips touched had worked its way downward, and the wetness she felt in the furnace that burned between her thighs both exhilarated and terrified her.

"Esah-Zhurah," Reza whispered, reluctantly parting from her kiss, "is this even possible?"

"Yes," she answered huskily, gently running her fingers over Reza's face. "Our bodies... are similar enough to a human female's, but..." She shook her head and began to pull away from him, but he held her back.

"What is it?" he said, holding her face in his hands. "Tell me."

"I must not do this," she rasped. "It is forbidden me to mate, and to do so with one not of the Way..." Her whole body trembled suddenly, as if she had been taken by a wracking sob, and Reza held her tightly against him, ignoring the pain in his body. "We could be punished by death, Reza. Even for this."

The words tore at his heart, but he understood now what was at stake. He would not sacrifice her, or himself, for this desire that threatened to consume them. They had come too far to throw everything away for a single touch that might easily deny them a lifetime together.

"Listen to my words," he told her softly. "There will someday come a time when that will not be so. In this I believe. The day shall come when we may be as one, and until that day dawns, I shall wait for you."

She kissed him again, softly. "I pray to Her that it shall be as you say." She kissed his face, her lips and tongue caressing him with a tenderness he had never imagined possible for her. "You must rest now, my tresh," she said. "Rest, and grow strong again."

Esah-Zhurah pulled him close, her arms wrapped around him, her musky scent strong in his mind. He closed his eyes to the bitterness that welled up in his soul at the unbidden remembrance of terrible things now long past, things that had happened to a human boy who was fast becoming a man among an alien race. Shutting out those images and the guilt they threatened, he focused his thoughts on her hand as it ran through his hair, and the tingling sensation that stirred at the passing of her fingers.

His body swiftly gave in to the need for rest. And as sleep quietly crept upon him, he uttered the question that had been floating in his mind, hidden by the alien code of honor that bound him during his waking hours, but which carried no weight in the world of dreams.

"Do you love me?"

The answer would have pleased him, had he heard the whispered word before he slipped away into the waiting embrace of sleep.

"Yes," came Esah-Zhurah's soft voice. This warrior, who had once pledged her honor to break this human's will, now found her soul bound to his by something her race had not known for millennia. She lay silent, cradling him against the cold of night and the unknowns of the future, wondering if her world would still be the same come the dawn.

* * *

The First strode through the door, snow fluttering from her fur cape as she shook off the cold. "The sentries report that Esah-Zhurah and the human return," she announced. She was obviously amazed that it was possible for them to have survived six days in the wilderness in winter, alone.

"I know," Tesh-Dar told her from where she sat on the floor, legs curled under her, head bowed. She did not tell her subordinate that she had known their whereabouts since Esah-Zhurah had dived into the water after Reza. Her mind's eye had watched her pull him from the water and give him life with the touch of her lips upon his. She had kept watch periodically over the following days as she tended to her own business, wondering if they indeed would survive.

But her wonder had turned to shocked disbelief, as she witnessed from afar the emotional whirlwind that had swept over the two during the following nights. Her hours had been spent in deep meditation since then, with her mind's eye focused on them as they made their way back to the kazha with the coming of the sun and first light this day. "Have their mount taken care of, and bring the two young warriors to me."

"Yes, my priestess."

Time, being a very relative thing to one so old as Tesh-Dar, passed quickly. She opened her eyes to find Esah-Zhurah and her human consort before her on their knees, waiting.

"Greetings, priestess," Esah-Zhurah ventured quietly, unable to gauge her elder's mood. Reza remained silent, his eyes fixed to the smooth stone of the floor.

"You have something for me?" Tesh-Dar asked, as if the two had never been missing at all.

"Yes, priestess," Reza said quietly, holding forth the black tube that held Tesh-Dar's correspondence. Fortunately, it had been strapped to Goliath's saddle, and not to that of Esah-Zhurah's ill-fated mount.

Tesh-Dar leaned forward and took the tube – still cold to the touch – from Reza's hands, noticing that they did not shake, but were firm, confident.

"You have done well, young one," she told him, setting the tube aside. "Go now to the healers and let them tend to your injuries. Then go to the hall to eat. No more do I have for you this day."

"Yes, priestess," Reza told her, bowing his head. He got up from his knees and headed for the door. Esah-Zhurah made to get up to follow him.

"My business with you," Tesh-Dar said ominously, "is not yet complete."

Esah-Zhurah dropped back to her knees, hearing the door open and close quietly behind her as Reza – much as he hated to leave her alone – carried out Tesh-Dar's orders.

"Look at me, child."

Trained from birth to show respect by averting the eyes, it was a difficult thing for her to do. That the priestess had asked this of her drove home the seriousness of whatever matter the elder warrior had on her mind. Warily, Esah-Zhurah met Tesh-Dar's gaze.

"This I will say only once, for I will forgive it of you only this once," the great priestess said. "I cannot prohibit the feelings in your heart for the human. But I now remind you that to show those feelings toward one not of the Way with a touch, a caress," her voice strained as she fought off the shivers of disgust that swept through her at the things she had witnessed, "is forbidden, bestial in Her eyes. No more shall there be, or you will find yourself bound to the Kal'ai-Il, the Stone Place, in punishment." The Kal'ai-Il was an ancient monument to the discipline of the Way, a stone arena where only the most serious wrongs were punished. It had stood for millennia as a symbol of the price to be paid for the Empress's honor by a warrior fallen from grace. "You, like the others in this grand experiment, were chosen for this task because of your strength and spirit, your knowledge of their alien tongue and ways. Do not disgrace yourself in Her eyes again."

Lowering her head nearly to the floor, Esah-Zhurah cringed in shame, her fears realized. No feeling, no thought, no action was beyond the knowledge of the priestess. Esah-Zhurah felt like a tiny grain of sand, infinitesimal, before her gaze. But deep in her heart she felt the forbidden desire burn even brighter, a flame that she could never escape.

"It shall be so, my priestess," she whispered, the words sounding hollow and empty on her lips.

Tesh-Dar nodded, noting the deep turmoil in the child. She frowned, knowing that the coming cycle, Reza's last unless his blood was heard to sing, would be terribly difficult for Esah-Zhurah. Tesh-Dar knew that the child would likely wish to take her own life when the human's came to an end. It was a most unfavorable prospect for such a promising warrior. Worse, Esah-Zhurah was more than just another young warrior to her. Far more. Tesh-Dar would have to watch her carefully. "I will say no more of the matter," she told Esah-Zhurah gently. "Go now in the footsteps of your tresh and rest, for the sunrise shall again call you to the arena to train."

"Yes, my priestess." Saluting, Esah-Zhurah departed.

Tesh-Dar stared after her a moment, wondering at the intensity of the feelings she had sensed in the two of them. Was mere punishment, even shaving one's hair, enough to deter such things?

Then Tesh-Dar thought of the Ancient Ones who had watched over Esah-Zhurah as she had struggled to free Reza from the clutches of the river's icy waters. Never had Tesh-Dar known them to be interested in such affairs. What stake could they possibly claim in the matter of a warrior and her animal tresh? Tesh-Dar did not understand their motivations or what precisely they had done that night, but she had clearly felt their presence, guiding the girl through the water to find the human. She knew from the power of their song that they had not been mere bystanders in what had taken place.

Pondering this thought, Tesh-Dar opened the black tube that had been the catalyst for their tribulations. She began to read the long-delayed correspondence from the Empress, knowing that she must seek an audience with Her to discuss these unforeseen developments.

Eleven

"And there is only the one who remains, priestess of the Desh-Ka?" the Empress asked. The two of them walked side by side in the Imperial Garden. It was a paradise of flora from every one of the Empire's ten thousand worlds. The number and variety of plants were such that, had Tesh-Dar the luxury of time, she could have expended a complete cycle walking about the great greenhouse, strolling for several hours each day, without ever seeing the same tree or blooming flower twice. The aromas that caressed Tesh-Dar's sensitive nose were an endless source of delight. The one time she had dared touch one of the plants – only with the permission of one amongst the army of clawless ones tending to their welfare, of course – her fingers had thrilled to a song of life that was unlike anything she had ever felt before. Primal and pure, it was a feeling she deeply cherished.

But now, walking beside the Empress, even the great garden could not lift her spirits. She felt an acute sense of disappointment at the results of the great experiment that had begun what seemed like only yesterday. But over a dozen years had passed since the raid on the strange human settlement that had been populated almost entirely with their young. Tesh-Dar would have thought that such planets would have been plenty, for that is how their own young were raised. After giving birth at the nurseries, the mothers departed soon after their recovery, leaving the infant children in the care of the Wardresses who would tend to their needs and train them until they were ready to join the kazhas. It was not uncommon for a mother never to see her child again after its birth, and the code of the Way ascribed even the naming of the child to the Wardresses. The only link from generation to generation was the passage of the *Ne'er-Se*, the ritual verse each mother left the Wardresses to teach her child, an oral trace of the females in the mother's bloodline. The males, of course, were not included; they were never even given a name, and those born lived, bred, and died at the nurseries. Thus it was a surprise to Tesh-Dar to learn that the human planet they had raided had been an aberration, a purgatory for the human young who had been forced to live there.

The priestesses of the other kazhas who had participated in the raid had been equally shocked. They should have been walking here with the Empress, as well, save they had no reason to come: in the cycles that had passed since then, all of the human children who had been taken had died on the terrible path that was the Kreelan Way. By disease, overzealous punishment on the part of the tresh, accidents, suicides, and from countless other causes, many never fully understood by the priestesses and the healers. The answer to the Empress's original curiosity had been unavoidable: the humans had no soul. Yes, Tesh-Dar had conceded, some of them rose well to the thrill of battle, the crash of sword upon sword, the sting of the enemy's claw; but still, their blood did not sing. Many times she had seen fire in one or another's eyes as she had traveled through the kazhas spread across the Homeworld and the Settlements, but she had never once heard a single note of the song that united each of Her Children unto the Way. Their voices among the spirits – the Ancient Ones – to which she especially was attuned, had remained silent these many cycles. The plants around her now were more vocal in spiritual song than anything she could detect from the humans, save the occasional insight into their torrid emotions.

Yes, she thought to herself grimly, *they all had died*.

All but one. Reza.

"Yes, my Empress," she replied to her ruler, her twin sister by birth, "there remains only one." In an ironic twist of fate that was so common among her people, Tesh-Dar had been born with silver claws. Her twin sister, whose given name had never been spoken since she assumed the leadership of her people, had been gifted both with black claws and the white hair that tradition demanded of one destined for the throne. Tesh-Dar flexed her claws, black as night now. The color, as well as her tremendous size and strength, had come with the changes wrought during an ancient ceremony performed among the Desh-Ka, the bonding of one soul with another. The one to whom she had bonded herself had long ago died in battle, and Tesh-Dar's heart had ached with emptiness ever since. "The one of my kazha, whose tresh is thy daughter, Esah-Zhurah, yet lives."

"And how," the Empress asked, turning to face her sister, "does it fare?"

"He fares well, my Empress," Tesh-Dar replied, unconsciously substituting the pronoun she herself used for referring to the human. She had long before stopped calling Reza "it." Tesh-Dar would have died before admitting it openly to the peers, but she had become fond of him with a depth that bespoke her respect for the child. Rarely did she miss the chance to watch him fight in the arena, sparring confidently with those of her own race. His first Challenge, fought after he and Esah-Zhurah had returned from the mountains with the fantastic tale of the great genoth, had been less than auspicious, she remembered. The two of them had returned from their free time exhausted and spent from their ordeal, and two days later was the Challenge. Tesh-Dar pictured Reza in the arena that first time, pitted by the draw of the lottery against Chara-Kumah. It was a pairing that Tesh-Dar had considered a fairly even match, at least in terms of size, for the human child.

But the match was hardly even. Chara-Kumah expertly humiliated her opponent, toying with him, drawing him in each time to receive a blow to the legs or shoulders, inflicting pain but little damage. And Reza reacted as if he had never had a moment's training in the use of staff or sword, as if he were still the tiny spirited human pup who had lashed out with his father's knife at a Desh-Ka priestess so long ago. Tesh-Dar had seen the flames in Reza's eyes, and she had found herself hoping beyond all hope that her mind would catch a note – a single peal – of the song she sought to hear. But there was only the grunting and crash of weapon against armor, the cries of pain as exposed flesh was bruised and beaten. Reza lasted for two turns of the timeglass before Chara-Kumah tired of his company. She felled him with a brutal blow to his carelessly exposed legs, then quickly delivered another strike to his head before Tesh-Dar called an end to the affair. Half-carried by Esah-Zhurah, who made her own way to the fourth set of contests before falling to a young swordmistress, Reza staggered from the field, bloodied and beaten.

But he had never allowed himself to suffer such a humiliation again. During the next cycles, he improved tremendously, so much so that Tesh-Dar felt compelled to let him act as a weapons master, a teacher for the neophyte warriors coming into the kazha. His last performance in the arena had been little short of astounding, winning all of his matches to the fifth level, two short of the final match that determined the overall winner of the single-round elimination combats that made up the Challenge. Esah-Zhurah, too, had improved more than Tesh-Dar ever would have been able to believe for one whose collar had been earned as a child on the space-going kazha for those called to serve the Imperial Fleet.

She thought again of Reza. Were his skin different, had he claws and fangs and raven hair, had he been female – one would have believed he was Kreelan. And perhaps, Tesh-Dar thought, he was. In spirit, if not in body. Yet his blood did not sing, and it pained her greatly.

"It is my belief," she said, "that – barring accident – he will survive the rigors of the kazha, my Empress. Well does he fight, and well does he seem to understand the Way, as Thy daughter has taught him."

"Yet," the Empress asked, "his blood does not sing?" Tesh-Dar heard it as a statement, not a question.

"It is so, my Empress," she replied woodenly, for she knew that her words sealed Reza's fate as surely as if she had thrust a knife into his heart.

The Empress looked thoughtfully upon her sister. Tesh-Dar had served Her well, as she had the Empress who had reigned before. And among all the countless warriors who now lived and breathed, Tesh-Dar stood highest among the peers, upon the second step from the throne. Many scars did she carry from innumerable Challenges, and then – after the humans had come – from the battles she had waged against those who were not of the Way, contests fought to the thrill of the Bloodsong that was the will and spirit of their people. To live in Her light, with Her blessing, and to die honorably in Her eyes: these were the things to which all aspired, and no better example existed than the woman who now stood beside Her.

Yet, there was a melancholy about her that the Empress did not understand. About this one thing, this human child whom Tesh-Dar might once have killed simply to sharpen her talons, was the warrior priestess distraught. To the Empress, it was a simple matter: the animal's blood did not sing, therefore it had no more soul than a steppe-beast or winged *gret-kamekh*, and would be killed when it proved of no further interest. But she could feel the blood that coursed through her sister's veins, and knew that her mind was not at ease in the matter.

"Tesh-Dar," she said, lifting her hand to the great warrior's chin, tilting it gently so that their gaze met, "what is it that troubles you so? Surely, if the humans are the soulless creatures we believe them to be, their hearts and blood silent to the ears of the spirit, the life of this one individual, this child, could not mean so much? What trouble is there, to such a warrior as yourself, to taking its life?"

"My Empress," Tesh-Dar said, averting her gaze in deference and embarrassment at what she felt compelled to ask, "I beseech Thee to let him live until the seventh great cycle of his learning is complete. Five cycles has he lived among us, two more remain. I..." she paused, grasping for the words to explain the strange things that ached in her heart. "I have heard whispers from the Ancient Ones," she said at last, "that at once seem clear in my mind, but which have no meaning for me." She looked into the eyes of the one who commanded the lives and aspirations of countless souls, wondering what worth a single human life might hold for Her. "They know of him, Empress," she said slowly. "They do not speak his human given name, as do we at the kazha, but they watch him through our eyes. They watch the human and Esah-Zhurah as if they were one, and they wait. They helped her to save him from death in the Lo'ar River."

The Empress looked away into the garden for a long moment, Her eyes focused on places and times that were remembered now only through crumbling stone tablets and withered parchments. For Her memory was that of all those who had gone before Her, who had worn the simple gold band that now adorned Her neck. Accepting the ornaments of the Empress was to accept the spirit and knowledge of the thousands who had once walked in the Garden, and to know the thoughts and feelings of countless billions. All bowed to Her will. "I, too, have heard these whispers," She said slowly, "and many times have I beseeched them for their meaning. But I cannot believe the answer that I hear."

"Then it is true," Tesh-Dar said softly. "He may be the fulfillment of The Prophecy."

"The thought is a most absurd one," the Empress replied, but Her voice betrayed Her own growing suspicion that She could not rule out the possibility, however faint.

The priestess kneeled, humbled by the Empress's remark, but nonetheless determined in her conviction that it could be true. "Yes, my Empress, but it is a thought I am unable to banish from my mind."

The Empress recalled the words that made up The Prophecy. It had been passed down from generation to generation since the death of Keel-Tath, millennia long past. It gave hope that someday their atonement might be made, but nothing more. None knew if the First Empress had spoken it, for She had gone away into the Darkness, and Her people had to live on as their Way demanded. So long had it been, that even the Ancient Ones had long ago given up any hope of redemption, believing Her Children to be cursed for all Eternity. Until now, perhaps.

And as the Empress thought of where the Way had taken Her people over these many generations, the nearly forgotten words of a passage from The Prophecy came to Her:

Of muted spirit, soulless born,
in suffering prideful made;
mantled in the Way of Light,
trusting but the blade.

Should this one come in hate or love,
it matters not in time;
For he shall find another,
and these two hearts they shall entwine.

The Way of sorrows countless told,
shall in love give life anew;
The Curse once born of faith betray'd,
shall forever be removed.

Shall return Her love and grace,
long lost in dark despair;
Mercy shall She show the host,
born of heathen hair.

Glory shall it be to Her,
in hist'ry's endless pages;
Mother to your hearts and souls,
Mistress of the Ages.

The Empress turned away, looking down the path they had been following, Her eyes tracing the smooth cobblestones. Each stone, like the plants around them, had been brought from a different planet in the Empire. Set into the paths that wound their way through the garden, they formed a galactic mosaic beneath the Empress's feet, the richest mineral collection among the ten thousand suns that were home to Her Children. The Empress knew precisely how many of Her predecessors had walked down this path and had stopped in this very spot, deep in contemplation. Better than anything else, She thought, the stones that She paced each morning of Her life represented the strange thing that was their Way: countless pieces of stone or flesh, it did not matter, for they were all bound to Destiny. It was Destiny, She knew, that eluded even Her vision, just as did the path, turning behind a grove of trees with crimson flowers, a relic of a planet that had long since been turned to dust, the onetime home of an enemy of the Empire.

She could not see the future. But Tesh-Dar's concerns, and the interest of the Ancient Ones, She dared not ignore. If they watched the human child and his tresh, the daughter of Her Own blood, there was good reason. She herself could not hear their voices as clearly as the Desh-Ka priestess who stood beside Her. But she trusted Her blood sister's judgment with all Her ageless soul.

"I grant your wish, priestess," She said to Tesh-Dar. "The human child is yours to do with as you please, unto the seventh – and final – Challenge.

"But if by the eve of that Challenge, when the tresh set upon their time of contemplation, the animal's blood does not sing, its life must be spent upon the arena's sands." She paused, looking at the Homeworld as it hung high overhead, a great blue and crimson orb shining through the windows of the palace garden. "And," She went on, "if by some miracle it should still emerge victorious, Esah-Zhurah is to take its life, and bring its hair to me as a testament to her strength and will."

Twelve

The force of Esah-Zhurah's attack thrummed down Reza's arms as he parried with his own sword, the clash of razor-sharp metal ringing in his ears like a church bell. He dodged to one side and pirouetted, tensing for a thrust against her midsection. But his blow, in turn, was deflected. The two contestants circled each other warily, their breathing coming in controlled heaves, before they crashed together again, continuing the combat that had begun nearly an hour before.

Tesh-Dar watched them from atop the arena's dais, her eyes and ears following the course of the combat in intimate detail. Watching these two had become a ritual for her over the last cycle when other duties did not call her away. She had observed the evolution in their skills since the day Tesh-Dar had informed Esah-Zhurah of the Empress's wishes regarding the human. Her young disciple had been visibly crushed, but had offered no argument as Tesh-Dar had expected. Instead, she had mercilessly driven herself and her human tresh toward technical excellence in the arena and in his knowledge of the Way. Watching them now, Tesh-Dar had no doubt that both of them would be serious contenders in the upcoming Challenge; they would be the ones setting the standards for the rest. And Reza's understanding of the Empire rivaled that of any of the other tresh, and many of the senior warriors, as well.

The priestess had not clearly understood Esah-Zhurah's motivations for some time, but she finally saw that the girl's only hope of saving the human's life was to find a way to make his blood sing, to prove that he had a soul. And for the Children of the Empress, the Bloodsong was never louder than in the rage of battle. Standing here, the girl's melody was clear and pure to Tesh-Dar's spiritual ears. It was a thunderous symphony that was unique in the Universe. But from the human, she felt nothing. Nothing at all. She could see the fire in his eyes, could sense the power of his body and the intellect of his mind, but of his spirit there was no trace.

She glanced at the setting sun, rapidly disappearing behind the mountains and the shining emerald of the Empress Moon as it rose to take its rightful place in the nighttime sky. An end must soon be called to the match, and when it was, the human's fate would be sealed. She felt a great sadness in her heart at what must be done.

Looking at him, she saw a man where once there had only been a boy, a tiny cub she had once held by the neck before he had struck the unexpected blow that had earned him her respect and these years of additional life, only now to perish. She had held such high hopes that she would receive some morsel of proof that he had a soul, for she wished with all her heart to watch him continue to grow, to see what the Way might hold for one such as he.

But it was not to be. As the top of the sun disappeared over the horizon, she called an end to the match, another deadlock. It was the final page in Reza's own Book of Time.

"*Kazh!*" she boomed. She watched with satisfaction as their swords stopped in mid-swing, as if frozen in time. Lowering their weapons, they turned and knelt before her. "Again, children," she told them, "it appears that your only equals are one another. Your final contest before the Challenge is concluded."

Reza bowed his head nearly to the ground, his breathing already easing to its normal deep rhythm. He felt tired but exhilarated, because he knew he was good. *They* were good, together, a force to be reckoned with, possessing combat skills that rivaled those of any of the tresh around them. When he raised his head after rendering the priestess her due, he looked proudly at Esah-Zhurah, but she did not return his gaze.

Instead, she asked, "My priestess, I would speak with you." Tesh-Dar nodded, and then Esah-Zhurah turned to Reza. "Go to our camp and rest," she told him. "I will return shortly."

Reza, understanding the set of her expression, simply nodded without asking what concerned her. It was not at all unusual for her to ask for a private audience with the priestess, and he had come to respect her privacy in such matters when she chose not to tell him what transpired. But something in her eyes made him uneasy, and even in the fading light he thought he could see the trace of mourning marks under her eyes. Bowing again to the priestess, he got to his feet, collected the four shrekkas the two of them had ineffectually hurled at one another, and headed back for their camp.

Esah-Zhurah watched him disappear into the woods in which their tiny home had been nestled since the first day they had come to the priestess. How many nights had they lain there, next to one another under the Empress Moon? Through the calm of the warm season, the chill of winter, the raging storms of spring when even the Stone Place, the Kal'ai-Il, shuddered at the power of nature's fury, they had remained under the stars and the great moon that was their sleep time canopy. She thought of how terribly difficult many of those nights had been since she had first touched Reza on the lips, had tasted the wonderful saltiness of his skin and the sorrowful longing of his tears. Since that wonderful day, that terrible day, she had rearranged their bedding so that they could lie close to one another. Sometimes, when her courage allowed, she extended a hand to touch him, reveling in the pleasure even this merest contact gave her. There were times when the urge to press her lips to his and do other things with him that would be unthinkable to another of her kind was nearly irresistible. Nonetheless, she had not broken her vow to the priestess. To do otherwise would have spelled an end to her honor, and to their lives.

But those were thoughts of the past. It was time to turn her attention to the future, or what little remained. Forcing herself toward the dais, Esah-Zhurah sensed that her Way had suddenly become short, very short indeed.

"What is it, child?" Tesh-Dar asked, already knowing what troubled the young warrior.

Esah-Zhurah knelt at Tesh-Dar's feet, her head lowered to her chest. "Priestess," she began, "must it be this way? Cannot you implore the Empress for more time–"

"For what?" Tesh-Dar snapped, more from her own anguish than any anger at the young woman kneeling before her. "Think, child," she said more gently. "The human has been among us for seven full great cycles now. How much longer must we wait for him to show his inner self, for us to hear his Bloodsong? Do you know?" Esah-Zhurah slowly shook her head. "Nor do I. And do not forget that the Empress already has given him one reprieve. Were it not for that, his bones would have been reduced to ashes two cycles ago." She ran a hand through Esah-Zhurah's hair, thinking how much she had come to think of her as a daughter, though Tesh-Dar had never given birth. The metamorphosis of the ritual that had changed her talons from accursed silver to beautiful ebony and given her the strength of five warriors had done nothing to alter the barrenness of her womb. "It is your destiny, child," she said softly, sensing the trembling of Esah-Zhurah's heart. "And his."

"If he survives the Challenge, or if I must face him in the arena under the code of *Tami'il* – a fight to the death – I... I cannot do it, priestess," Esah-Zhurah said, looking into Tesh-Dar's eyes, pain etched on her face. "I cannot kill him."

"Listen to me well, young one," Tesh-Dar said coldly. "Your soul, as are the souls of all those who are of the Way, is bound to the will of the Empress. Her will is clear in this matter, you can feel it pulse in your veins as well as I. If you cannot do as you are bidden, your hair will be shaved and your soul left in the barren shadows of Eternity." Her eyes softened. "I have heard the cries of those sent to that place, child, the agonies of those fallen from Her grace. It is a fate I bid you to avoid." She paused. "If you face one another in the arena, the human must die. If you both refuse to fight, I will decide the matter myself, and your soul will suffer accordingly." *You do not know the grief that would bring to my heart, my daughter*, Tesh-Dar thought. "And ritual suicide is not an alternative."

"Yes, my priestess," Esah-Zhurah replied woodenly, her body suddenly numb and lifeless. Even the release of suicide had been taken from her, condemning her to live in a lonely, loveless purgatory. "I understand."

Tesh-Dar paused a moment. "Esah-Zhurah," she said softly, noting the black streaks that poured from the child's eyes as her heart cried out its mourning, "I grieve with you. Long have I thought about the coming of this day, and long have I dreaded it, for both of you. Many nights have I lain awake, wondering what could be done, listening for the song of his blood, but there is nothing. Even the Ancient Ones, who once watched the two of you, have gone silent, no longer interested, I fear. They do not hold sway over Her, for She rules even in their ethereal domain, and Her word has been given. Our Way shall be as She wills it."

"Yes, my priestess," Esah-Zhurah intoned, her thoughts now dark swirls of hopelessness.

"Go now, my child, and spend wisely the time that remains," she told her, gesturing for Esah-Zhurah to rise. "Go in Her name."

Esah-Zhurah blindly made her way back to their camp where a fire burned brightly among the forest trees. Her feet trudged along the ancient cobblestones that wove their way about the kazha like a system of great roots, embracing everything. It was a seemingly infinite path that, in the end, led nowhere. As did her Way. She suddenly stopped in her tracks and gripped the handle of her knife. She saw in her mind the image of her plunging it into her chest, feeling the blade part her ribs with its serrated edge, the tip piercing her heart, and the blood in her veins suddenly growing still. It would be the end of life, of suffering against the unknown, of what she knew to be her future. To kill Reza would be to kill a part of herself, a part that she had come to value above all else, save her love for the Empress. And even that...

"Troubled are you," came a husky voice from behind her. Esah-Zhurah whirled around, only to find the ancient Pan'ne-Sharakh, the mistress of the armory, staring at her with her half-blind eyes. She bared her fangs in a friendly greeting, exposing the once magnificent incisors that were now faded yellow with age, worn down so far that she would soon starve, unable to tear her meat properly. Tesh-Dar was old even by Kreelan standards, but Pan'ne-Sharakh was older still: she had been fitting armor to warriors since long before Tesh-Dar was born. There would be much mourning on the day she departed for the Afterlife and her deserved place among the Ancient Ones.

Esah-Zhurah bowed and saluted. "Forgive me, mistress, but you startled me."

"The body is old," Pan'ne-Sharakh said, "but the mind still quick, and the foot light upon the earth, by Her grace and glory. You shall walk with me." Pan'ne-Sharakh held out her hand, and Esah-Zhurah dutifully took it, gently cradling the antediluvian woman's bony fingers in her own armored gauntlet, careful not to let her talons mar the mistress's translucent skin. "Tell me of what troubles you so, my child. For even these old eyes can see the works of sorrow woven upon the tapestry of thy face."

"Mistress... I..." Esah-Zhurah stuttered, not knowing how – or if – she could tell the ancient mistress what she knew, what she felt. But suddenly the words came, slowly at first, but then in a torrent that surprised Esah-Zhurah. It was as if they were not spoken by her own tongue, but by a force that lay within her, beyond her control. She laid bare her heart in a way that would have shamed her into punishment in the Kal'ai-Il had her words become known among the peers or reached the ears of the priestess. But to this quiet ancient who now shuffled slowly beside her, she told everything. Her feelings, her desires, her shames and fears. Everything.

Her words carried them over a path that eventually wound its way to a secluded overlook that took in most of the great plains and the mountains beyond, a place of private meditation frequented by the priestess, although she did not declare it as her own domain. It belonged to Her, the Empress, as did all things that lived or did not live, as far as the eye could see, as far as the stars above, and beyond.

Pan'ne-Sharakh stood silently for a long time, staring into the distance. Her milky eyes, their vision useless a mere meter beyond her face, were still able to peer into a vista of hard-won wisdom that had come with the many cycles of her life and the mystical thing that pulsed in her veins, the spirit of their Way.

"Dearest child," she said, still focused on whatever it was that she saw in her mind, "much have you suffered for this creature, this human, and more are you willing to endure, it would seem. I would caution you against such things, but you are far beyond that, now. Far beyond."

She let out a resigned sigh, and Esah-Zhurah became afraid that she had been foolish to tell the old woman anything. But the look on the mistress's face was nothing if not compassionate. "Long have I walked the Way, my child, and many strange and wonderful things have I seen. But I have never beheld such a wonder as are the two of you, the warrior and her animal tresh. He is still a stranger among us, but his heart and mind have become one with the Way. You have led him that far."

"But his blood does not sing," Esah-Zhurah lamented, wishing she could see something on the horizon other than darkness. Death.

"No," Pan'ne-Sharakh answered, "it does not." She looked up at the young woman beside her. "But still, the Ancient Ones wait. I have heard the priestess speak on the matter, and she believes they are no longer interested in the goings on at our humble kazha. I believe differently."

"How, mistress? What is to be gained by their silence?"

"They wait, child, as if holding their breath, as if a single whispered word would snuff out the candle that flickers here, beneath the Empress Moon. They wait for you." Seeing that Esah-Zhurah did not understand, she went on. "Why, child, does the human's blood not sing?"

"He is not of the Way," Esah-Zhurah replied. "He is not of Her blood."

Pan'ne-Sharakh smiled as if Esah-Zhurah had just explained the answer herself. "That is so, child. He is not of Her blood. And what is there to do about such a thing?"

Esah-Zhurah shrugged in the Kreelan fashion, pained frustration showing on her face. Her patience was wearing thin, mistress or no.

"Do you remember, child, the history of this order, the Desh-Ka, since the times even before the First Empress?"

Esah-Zhurah shook her head. She had been born into and raised in another order, the Ima'il-Kush. Her knowledge of the Desh-Ka, the oldest order known among their people, was far from complete. "No, mistress," she said. "Little is taught of those times, for it is said that the Empire and the Way have always been one, and that what was then, remains as now."

Pan'ne-Sharakh waved her hand in a dismissive gesture. "Long was the Way before even the First Empire, child. But no matter. In those times before Keel-Tath and the Unification, before the curse She later wrought upon our blood, the Desh-

Ka were the greatest of the warrior sects that lived on our world. Many outsiders aspired to come among them, but few – terribly few – were ever chosen." She took Esah-Zhurah's hands in hers. "Once there was a ceremony, long since forgotten in the minds of most, which was the mark of one's acceptance into the Desh-Ka. And even over the thousands of generations since Keel-Tath's birth, every warrior bearing the great rune of this order has also borne a scar," she explained as she ran a callused finger across the palm of Esah-Zhurah's right hand, "that marks their acceptance by one who has gone before them."

"This is the ritual of Drakhash," Esah-Zhurah said, remembering, "the passing of honor from one warrior to another. But what does it have to do with me? I am not of the Desh-Ka, nor is..."

Of course, Esah-Zhurah thought, the truth striking her like a bolt of lightning. It was not just a passing of honor, *but of blood as well.*

Pan'ne-Sharakh nodded as she saw the dawning of understanding on Esah-Zhurah's face. "Now all is clear to you, is it not, my daughter?" she asked.

Esah-Zhurah slowly nodded. Her eyes were wide with surprise, and they opened still wider when Pan'ne-Sharakh brought a sheathed knife from within the folds of her robe.

"This," she said reverently, carefully placing the weapon in the young warrior's hand, "I have saved for many, many great cycles, from when I was almost as young as you are now. It was the first weapon I made for a young warrior of that time, a mere child I could have bounced upon my knee, who one day would become the flesh and blood of the Empress Who now reigns."

Esah-Zhurah's hand trembled as her fingers closed around the weapon, about as long as her forearm, the curved and ornate blade perfectly balanced against the weight of the handle. It seemed to burn her palm, even through the thickness of the armored gauntlet she wore as a second skin.

"After the Ascension," Pan'ne-Sharakh went on, her eyes misting with the memory, "She called me unto Her, and gave me this as a gift, a token of Her love and remembrance. I have kept it safe and hidden from my own extravagances, knowing that there would come a time when it would be needed. And last night, in the dreams possible only for one whose Way is coming to an end, I knew that the time had come, and to what use it must be put." Reluctantly, she took her hands away, her fingers brushing over the ancient metal one last time. "The next step," she said quietly, "is up to you."

* * *

Reza heard Esah-Zhurah coming long before he could see her, especially now that the fire had died down to glittering coals of deep cherry red and amber. He was startled that she was not walking as she usually did, using the nearly silent step that was now his own, but was treading the earth as if afraid of nothing, as if stealth were alien to her. The unease that had been building in him since earlier that evening had reached a feverish peak.

"Esah-Zhurah," he called softly, knowing that she would be able to hear him easily, "what is wrong?"

She knelt down next to him, a shadow in the darkness, and wrapped her arms around him, pulling him close.

"Do you trust me?" she asked, her face close to his. He nodded once. Words were unnecessary. "Then do as I ask this night, and sleep. Rest, that we may leave early tomorrow for our free time. And then I shall explain all. I dare not here."

He suddenly felt her lips pressing hungrily against his, parting to release the warm tongue that set his body aflame. She lingered for but a moment that was itself an eternity in Reza's mind. Then she drew away, leaving him breathless and flushed with a mad desire to hold her, to touch her in ways that came to him with force of instinct, but with the tenderness of the love he felt for her.

"Esah-Zhurah," he rasped, reaching for her, holding her close. She knelt close to him, but did not let him kiss her again. It would have been too much to resist, such was the pounding in her breast and the desire working between her thighs at the thought of what could be, what must be, in the days ahead.

"No, my tresh," she told him, gently but firmly pushing him back down on his skins, running a hand across his forehead before laying down next to him, a painful moat of distance between them. "Patience is a warrior's virtue. There is much about which we must speak, but it must wait until tomorrow."

The word echoed in Reza's mind as he lost himself in the wondrous pools of starlight in her eyes.

Tomorrow.

* * *

Reza sat with his legs crossed, his arms draped over his knees. He stared past the mouth of the great caldera whose edge lay just beyond his feet, his thoughts lost in the sprawling horizon that lay in the distance. The faint rumble of the waterfall was broken only by the whispers of the wind and the rustling of the lush ferns that covered this part of the mountain like a vast forest.

The ride to this place, the grotto that had been their refuge and escape each cycle since coming to the kazha, had been a long, silent one. Reza sat upon old Goliath, with Esah-Zhurah beside him on her mount. Their only contact had been an occasional brush of thigh against thigh, and once he had reached out to take her hand, squeezing it in reassurance. She had refused to tell him what was on her mind until they arrived at their destination. But the mourning marks that streamed from under her eyes, the marks that had been hidden in the darkness of night, did nothing to lift his spirits. After they had arrived at the grotto and set up their camp, she had taken him by the hand and led him here to the overlook, a ledge jutting out into space from which one could see forever.

But to Reza, forever had been reduced to three sundowns hence. For, according to what Esah-Zhurah had just revealed in a halting, agonized voice, he would be dead upon the sands of the arena by the time the sun set upon the day of his seventh Challenge.

"And if I should win?" he asked quietly.

She looked away. "If you win, I am to take your life and your hair to the Empress." Her whole body seemed to tremble. "Reza," she whispered, "easier it would be for me to tear my beating heart from my breast than to spill a drop of your blood this way. I would gladly spend eternity in the Darkness to spare you, but I am forbidden even that. I must wait for death until the Way brings it to my doorstep."

He took her hand in his, and gently turned her face so that he could look into her eyes. "It is Her will, my tresh," he told her, the sincerity in his heart echoed on his face. "If that is what the Way holds for us, then it must be so. I am only grateful that, should I have the honor of winning the Challenge, yours will be the hand that sends me from this life." He stroked her face, smiling with a confidence that came with his acceptance of his own mortality. "It shall be as it must."

She pulled him close and wrapped her arms around his neck, holding him tightly. "When you are ready," she said, her voice muffled as she pressed her face into the hollow of his shoulder, "come to me. There is something we must attend to, something that can wait no longer." Pausing only long enough to kiss him lightly on the cheek, she stood up and began making her way back down the mountain. She did not look back.

After Esah-Zhurah had gone, Reza turned his attention back to the horizon, concentrating not on the future, which had already been written by another's hand, but the past which none could deny him. As if reading a most treasured book, he turned the pages of his life, reviewing the memories held in the storehouse of his mind. He paused on the few remembrances he had managed to keep alive from before he had come to the Empire, saving them as treasured icons of an existence long since past. But even those visions that he had labored to keep fresh seemed to be from another person's life, yellowed and faded with time, the faces now indistinct and the names awkward to his tongue. Yet, they were a part of him, and the feeling the ancient images engendered in his heart warmed and comforted him as the evening breeze swept over the mountain and the sun fell toward the far horizon.

But the humanity left in him was merely a vestige of a human boy who had metamorphosed into a Kreelan warrior, alien to his heritage in nearly every way but the very flesh of which he was made. The imprint of any human society on a prepubescent boy was simply not enough to hold back the cultural onslaught to which Reza had been subjected. And now, reviewing in his mind the few mental tokens that remained of his previous life, he discovered that he could not remember the last time he had really thought of himself as being human, of having descended from the people of Old Earth. Even though the peers called him "human," or "animal," he had come to think of himself as a Kreelan, and that perception of himself had grown ever stronger the closer he had come to Esah-Zhurah. There had been a time when he would have feared the loosening of his grip on what had been human in him, the part of him that was now little more than an afterimage in his mind. But that had passed with his acceptance of the code by which he had lived most of his life; the code by which he would soon die.

He thought for a while about what death would be like. Death, a force that had pursued him relentlessly for most of his young life, would finally get its due. Like an old relative who had dropped by many times to visit, only to miss Reza by a shard of time, it would at last embrace him and welcome him into whatever lay within its dark domain. Reza had never been terrified of death, but had evaded it because he had loved life enough to suffer for it. But now he found death a welcome thing, for then his greatest quest would be over, the search for the answer that was the very reason for his coming here: to discover if he had a soul. Long having forgotten the Christian teachings of his childhood, he now wondered only what the Bloodsong must sound like, the thing that united the Children of the Empress to Her will. But he had never heard it, neither from himself nor the tresh around him. He did not even know what to listen for, or if it was really a "sound" at all. All he had was question upon question, all without answer as long as he lived and breathed. Did he have a soul, or was he merely an animal, as the peers believed? Was he nothing more than animated clay fashioned into human form by Her hands? Would he pass through the portal of Death to something beyond? Or would he simply cease to exist, turning to dust and ash as Esah-Zhurah set his body ablaze in a funeral pyre that was the tradition of Her Children? It seemed that only in death would he discover the truth of what Her Children knew from birth.

As the sky above turned from the pastel magenta of day to the inky darkness of night, he welcomed the stars as they emerged from their celestial slumber, and made a silent wish upon the five stars of Her name.

He wished for a soul, and that all would not end when his body suffered the final blow.

* * *

When Reza returned to the grotto, he found Esah-Zhurah kneeling, her pensive face turned to the fire that burned beside her, the flames licking quietly at the air as if afraid to disturb her thoughts. Slowly, as if breaking herself away from a hypnotist's swaying talisman, she looked up at him, and his heart skipped a beat at the black marks that swept down from her eyes, a window to the pain in her soul.

"Kneel," she said, gesturing to the skins that formed the floor of their makeshift abode.

Reza took his place before her, his knees just touching hers, his hands spread, palms down, on his thighs.

"There is an ancient tradition," she began, "that predates even the First Empire, that was part of our Way before Keel-Tath ascended to the throne, before we became what we are now. It was not a tradition of all our people, but of the Desh-Ka. It was begun from the first day their rune was engraved in the stone of their temple, and which all Desh-Ka have followed throughout the ages. It is the rite of Drakhash, the blood bond.

"In those days, as now, the blood of the tribe was considered most sacred, and to share it with another was both a great honor and a great responsibility, often with terrible consequences during the Reign of Chaos. So legend tells us." She paused, reaching beside her for a knife that lay unsheathed near the fire, a blade that Reza had never seen before, but whose exquisite workmanship was unprecedented to his eyes. "You, Reza, of human birth and blood, have shown the skill and fire that are the marks of our warriors. You, whose blood does not sing, who cannot hear the Bloodsong of Her Children, are as a stranger to our tribe, our people, yet worthy of our respect and trust." Holding the knife between them, the dagger blade pointed at the sky, she said, "Although I am not Desh-Ka by birth, I am a True Daughter of the Empress, born of Her womb, blessed with Her very blood. And thus I may speak without falsehood, for my will is Her will, and it shall be done."

Taking off his gauntlets, as she had her own, she took his hand in hers, clasping it tightly as her other hand kept the dagger aloft, still pointing skyward. "I ask you only this: do you accept Her in your heart of hearts, that you shall follow Her will unto death, that the Way of our people shall be the Way of your heart, of your mind?"

Reza's mind was spinning at the enormity of what his tresh was doing. He knew that the priestess would have categorically forbidden such a thing, yet Esah-Zhurah could not go against the Empress's will. In whatever incomprehensible way these people were bound together, he knew that to be impossible as surely as he could not spread his wings and fly from this mountain to the plains below. But his thoughts were preempted by the words spoken by his heart. "With all my heart, Her will is mine, the Way of Her Children is the Way of my soul. To die for Her honor is to die for Her grace and Her love. So has it been, so shall it forever be."

Esah-Zhurah nodded. Wordlessly, they raised their clasped hands into the air, and she placed the knife between them, the flat of the blade cool as it rested against their palms.

"With this knife, forged long ago for one who would ascend to the throne, wielded by Her in battle, are we now joined." With a slight twist of her knife hand, the blade's razor edge broke the boundary of skin between them, drawing a deep line of blood as she pulled it downward, the weapon slipping from their joined hands like a newborn infant from the womb. Esah-Zhurah set the knife aside, then wrapped her free hand around their joined fist. She felt the warm pulse of her blood, and his, as their wounds sought each other out, mated.

Reza's hand was tingling as if Esah-Zhurah was sending electric currents through it, and as they knelt there, face to face, the sensation began to spread up his arm, then his shoulder. And looking into her eyes, he could see that she felt it, too.

"I must tell you something," she said, her cat's eyes pools of glittering fire, stars in the blackness of mourning that besieged her face. "I feel fear, Reza, such as I have never before felt. I fear losing you, losing your voice... your scent... your touch. In my language, even the Old Tongue that you have not been taught, there are no words to describe these things I feel for you." Slowly, she placed her free hand over his heart. "The only hope of my soul is that the blood now in your veins may sing to Her, that She may know thy voice."

"Esah-Zhurah," he whispered, "I love you." She leaned close to kiss him lightly on the eyes, her fingers in his hair. "Had I my entire life to do over," he told her, "I would change nothing, would suffer anything, that I could be with you."

She kissed him softly on the mouth, and then slowly rose to her feet. He made to rise also, but she gently pushed him back to where he knelt. "Stay," she whispered huskily. "I have learned the tradition of the Old Ways, before the Curse," she told him, her breath warm against his face, "when male and female touched in desire, not desperate need. So it was then, so shall it be now."

The tingling sensation still spreading through his body, she separated her bloodied hand from his. Slowly, she began to undress. She undid the belt that carried her weapons, letting it slide to the ground. Then she began to unfasten her armor, placing it in an orderly stack beside her. Her black undergarment disappeared in the shimmering firelight, then her sandals.

Reza watched, enraptured, as she discarded the last of her clothing. Her blue skin glowed as she stood before him, backlit by the flames. Her muscles were taut in anticipation, and he could see the gleam of wetness between her thighs. He could hear her quickened breathing, the rapid beating of her heart. Her musky scent touched him, teased him, arousing him to the point where he was sure he would explode without her ever touching him.

She knelt down to straddle his body. He reached up to touch her, but she deflected his hands away, neither of them concerned with the blood and pain from their wounded palms, the spiritual consummation of their commitment to one another.

"Do not move," she whispered, running her nails along the side of his face, just touching the skin. "Lie still." Her hands ran down his neck and chest, sending shivers through his body. She began to undo his clothing, slowly exposing his skin to her touch. The armor seemed to simply melt away under her strong hands, and suddenly she was pulling the upper garment over his head and tossing it aside, never taking her eyes off of him. Her hands glided over his skin, sending shivers up his spine as they worked down lower, lower. She undid his waist belt and the lower part of the undergarment, pulling them away. With the agility and grace of a cat she moved away from him to remove his sandals, then returned to her former position, her face only a few centimeters from his.

He leaned forward to kiss her, but she drew away, her lips trembling in restrained urgency.

"No," she whispered. "Not yet." She gripped his shoulders with trembling hands and began to kiss his eyes, his face, carefully avoiding his lips. She continued on to his neck, her fangs lightly scoring the skin.

Reza moaned and closed his eyes, clenching his fists so hard that his knuckles cracked like wet wood on a fire. He had trained so long to heighten his senses, his perception of his surroundings and his own body, that her touch was overwhelming him, burning in his brain as her mouth moved along his body.

Her hands, now running along the inside of his thighs, convulsed slightly. She straightened up with a deep sigh, a shuddering breath. Her eyes were misty, far away. She kissed him hard on the mouth, her incisors nearly cutting into his lower lip. Then she raised herself further and brought his head to her breasts with one hand, the other now supporting her body above him.

"Soon," she gasped.

He took each breast in turn to his mouth, savoring the slightly bitter flavor of her smooth skin with his tongue. His hands caressed her body, moving across her taut belly to her thighs to linger in a cautious exploration of what lay between.

Without warning she pushed him down on their bed of hides. She took hold of his wrists and moved them clear of her body.

"It is time," she whispered. Her breath now came in rapid, shallow heaves. She was at once tormented by need and alight with pleasure. She took his throbbing erection in both hands, drawing an excited gasp of anticipatory pleasure from his lips.

With one last look between them, she slowly impaled herself on him. Both of them cried out at the flame that suddenly surged as their bodies joined. Her nails pierced the flesh of his shoulders, but there was no pain. His mind was in sharp focus, and its point of interest lay nowhere near his shoulders.

Involuntarily he began to move his hips, holding onto hers with his hands, his fingers pressing deeply into the tensed flesh as he drove himself into her.

"No, Reza!" she cried. "Lay still, my love. Lay still."

He managed to regain control of himself, using every bit of willpower he had gained as a warrior to do his lover's bidding. He wrapped his arms around her and held her to him, and they lay entwined, their breath coming rapidly in the night. Her eyes had become unfocused, her oblong pupils dilated wide open, far more than the fire-lit darkness demanded.

He was becoming concerned that something was wrong when he felt the first pulse. Some mysterious mechanism in her body began to stimulate his own, and he felt the same sensation as he had on his tentative thrust, but without moving himself. The pulses, the strokes he felt inside her, came slowly at first, but their tempo built quickly, the intense sense of pleasure obliterating reality.

He cried out as he came inside of her, his body arching upward in blind ecstasy that engulfed him for a few brief seconds that seemed to span eternity. He was lost in waves of sensory overload in an act that had once merely been a part of procreation, but that now meant so much more.

As he regained his senses, he realized that her pumping had not ceased with his own climax, but had grown even more frenzied, her body twitching to the music that boomed inside her. Her eyes were closed now, and her head slumped to his shoulder.

Without warning, she cried out, her voice reverberating off the grotto's dark, invisible walls. He fought her hands to keep her talons from slashing his sides as she thrashed about in the ecstasy that had taken her. Her mouth was open wide, her fangs gleaming white in the fire's glow, and for a moment he was afraid that she would simply plunge them blindly into his throat.

But she did not. The storm left as suddenly as it had come, and her climax left a quiet denouement in its wake. Her mouth closed after a moment more of straining in concert with her body, and then she seemed to relax and laid herself back down on top of him, her whole body shuddering as if she were freezing. Her hands twitched, and he held them in his own, holding them against his sides. Her breathing slowed, and he knew from the rhythm that she must have passed out, gone to sleep. He held her tightly to him, running his hands through her dark braids and across her back. Tears sprang from his eyes as his love for her filled his heart. And for one of the few times in his life, they were tears of joy, not of pain.

After a few moments, he gently rolled her over on her side and lay next to her, lost in her warmth, their union finally broken by his body's flagging bridge. The fire kept him company, and he watched it with the fascination that had captivated his kind for millennia. He lost himself to the flame, until he felt a stirring beside him.

She was looking at him with eyes hooded by the inexorable hold of sleep, but troubled by a terrible sadness. "I grieve for my race, Reza," she whispered. "Most of my people mate. They must to survive. But they do not love. They have never felt this," she stroked his face with her hand, "since the death of Keel-Tath." She pulled him to her and kissed him. "I will carry this with me always, my love, forever as I walk the Way."

"So shall I," he whispered softly. "In Her name, so shall I."

* * *

The Empress dreamed.

It was a dream She had never had before. This might have been less of a curiosity had it been anyone else, but there was something uniquely peculiar about Her dreams. They were not the dreams of the woman who had accepted the simple white robe and band about her neck that were the only adornments allowed the leader of the Empire. At least, not entirely. That woman's dreams were a part of what was now cascading through the sleeping monarch's mind, but only that. A part.

For the rest of Her mind was devoted to the thoughts and dreams of those who had gone before Her, those who had inherited Her body as She had inherited their spirit and wisdom. The woman who lay quietly in her chambers within the Imperial Palace was not simply the flesh that wore the crown of Empire. She was the Empress; She was all who had ever lived since the Unification, save one. Keel-Tath's voice had never come to the Empress of the Flesh, the vessel of the Way, nor to any Empress who had come before Her. The spirit of the First Empress, the most powerful of all, lay forever in darkness. Waiting for Her people to redeem themselves, to prove themselves again worthy of Her love.

And that is why this dream seemed so strange. The knowledge of twenty-seven thousand generations was at Her beck and call, asleep or awake. The visions, the sensations of all those who had worn the very collar that hung loosely from her aging neck were as vivid as the day they were experienced by the Empress of the Flesh in some earlier time, from whence the memory came.

But not this one. All that She was, all the thousands of spirits clustered in Her soul, bound together as one, watched like fascinated spectators in the arena as the vision unfolded in Her mind.

She saw herself kneeling before a young human, a human that She had never seen before but felt She knew as well as Her own blood. And then She saw their clasped hands, Herself and the human, joined together as tightly as the enormous polished stones that made up the wall of the Great City far below the Empress Moon. The words that were spoken She did not hear or understand in the dream, but there was no need. The ceremony was well known to Her, even though Her own hand did not bear such a scar.

There was a silence between them, and then She undressed, at last standing nude before him.

Then came the first touch. The Empress shivered in Her sleep, a moan of surprise and unexpected pleasure escaping Her lips at sensations She had never before felt. Higher and higher She flew, riding the crest of a wave that seemed as vast and powerful as the Empire itself. And when the warm spear She felt within Her erupted in its fury of passion, She cried out in surprised ecstasy.

She suddenly found herself awake, curled on Her side, staring into the wide and terrified eyes of Her First.

"My Empress," the elder warrior gasped, one hand curled around the handle of her sword. She had never seen the Empress awaken in such a state. It had simply never happened before. Ever. "Are you well?" she asked, clearly frightened. Not that the Empress would die, for that was simply not possible but for the vessel that embodied Her spirit. No, she was afraid that the Empress might have been frightened by something. "Empress?"

The Empress lay there for a moment, catching Her breath and waiting for the spasms in Her loins to stop. Never in Her mating years had She known such feelings as this dream had brought upon Her, nor had Her body been thrilled as it had during those few immeasurable moments. But pleasurable though these sensations were, the unknown nature of their cause disturbed Her greatly.

"Empress?" the First inquired again, with increased alarm. So much so that she laid a hand on her monarch to steady Her shaking body.

"I am well," the Empress replied at last, thanking the First for her concern with a shaky caress of the younger woman's hair. "It is past, now." She thought for a moment, the remnants of the dream that seemed to be more than a dream swirling through Her mind, tantalizing Her body with a few more spasms. "Tell me," She asked, Her voice carefully controlled to conceal the quivering of Her chest, "did I speak in my sleep?"

The First bowed. "Yes, Empress."

"What did I say?"

"Only one word, one I did not recognize as being of either of The Tongues," the First replied. No other language besides the Old Tongue and the Tongue of the First Empire had ever been uttered in the palace before this day. "You cried *reza*."

THIRTEEN

The storm clouds that were gathering around the mountain like anxious horsemen intent upon some unimaginable apocalypse were a vision into Reza's soul as he and Esah-Zhurah worked the magtheps down the steep slopes toward the darkening valley below, leaving their beloved grotto behind forever. Since the night they touched, they had scarcely risen from their bed, making love or simply holding one another as the sun rose and then set once more. They had spoken precious little, for there was little to say between them that could or need be expressed by mere words. And there was no time for idle banter, for this time together would be all they would ever have. A caress or a kiss said so much more, and time was valuable to them beyond measure. "Forever" had taken on a very literal meaning for the lovers, for it was now weighed in the trifle of sunsets remaining before Reza was to die.

But the Way was not known for its magnanimity, and their tiny allotment had been cut short by the hand of Nature. The sudden storm that had charged into the mountains would bring heavy rains, rains that would make the tiny mountain streams impassable torrents that would keep the two young warriors from their appointed destiny in the arena. While the thought had come to both of them that it could be used as an excuse to delay, an opportunity to stretch the inevitable just a bit further away, the notion had never been voiced. They were no longer children, and both of them knew their responsibilities as followers of the Way. Reza wore only the collar of a slave, but his soul was no less devoted to the ways of his adopted people. If the Empress willed his death, then it would be so.

He smelled the rain, the peculiar musty smell that bathed the land long before it was touched by water, and knew that they would have to hurry. The almost supernatural senses that his years of training had given him told how long it would be before the first drops would fall; it was a measure of time that could not be expressed in terms of hours or minutes, or angle of the sun, but was nonetheless precise. Esah-Zhurah sensed it, too, and together they picked up the pace, old Goliath lumbering with the gracelessness of age next to Esah-Zhurah's younger and more nimble beast.

Around them the land and sky had grown dark, the bright colors muted to a cold, glaring gray, broken occasionally by the angry brilliance of lightning bolts that struck at the land with the heat of a dozen suns. The echoes of the thunder that shattered the air drowned out the howl of the wind that rose and fell as it chose its fickle path among the canyons and arroyos through which the travelers made their way.

Had the day been clear, perhaps they would have seen or smelled the bloody mass of gnarled steel armor and shredded leatherite that had once been known as Ust-Kekh, now carefully hidden behind one of the lichen-covered rocks jutting from the canyon wall. Or perhaps they would not have simply passed by Ami-Char'rah's severed head, sitting near the side of the trail like a macabre sentinel. Her skull had been an unappetizing tidbit to the otherwise remorseless mind that had been the instrument of her demise.

But the lightning blinded the riders to these dark shapes that now stood silent vigil, and the shifting winds robbed them of the coppery scent of blood that even now dripped from the torn veins of the hapless victims. In the swirling night, they did not see the demonic face in whose eyes their reflections danced in time with the lightning hurled from the angry sky above.

Pan'ne-Sharakh had once told Reza that the day of his birth, as measured in the way of the Kreela, had fallen on the day of the Great Eclipse, when the Empress Moon had shielded the Homeworld from the light of the sun. It was an event that occurred only once every fifteen thousand and fifty-three Earth years, and was considered a day of wondrous promise for those born under its shadow. It was an omen of great battles to be fought, a sign of special love from the Empress. It was the closest thing the Way allowed for what humans might consider being lucky.

But Reza did not feel lucky when a shadow suddenly detached itself from the canyon floor. With startling speed, it grew in size until it blotted out the sky above, towering before them like a dark, angry mountain.

As Reza opened his mouth to shout a warning, his hand grabbing desperately for the battle ax strapped to his saddle, he felt the impact of the mammoth claw against his chest, a horrendous blow that hurled him from Goliath's back. Only his armor – now bent and torn like tissue paper – had saved his life. Reza's ears filled with the sound of crunching bones before his eardrums rang with the monstrous scream of hungry rage that muffled Goliath's squeals of agony. Reza hit the ground hard, but quickly rolled to his feet. And in a flash of lighting he saw it, standing over Goliath's struggling form, a nightmare of fangs, horns, and talons.

He gasped in awe at the thing that had transformed itself from mimicking silent rock into moving, living tissue in but an instant. Its head was larger than Goliath's body, with rows of razor-sharp teeth covered by a scaly lip to conceal them while the creature lay in wait. Horns sprouted from the thing's triangular head, and its blazing yellow eyes were cold and inscrutable. Its body rippled with strength, from the talons on each of its six legs to the needle-like crystalline tip on the end of its whip of a tail.

It stood above Reza like a colossus, an enormous gargoyle that had suddenly come to life. Before he could turn and run, it lunged down at him, its maw gaping wide, its fetid breath enveloping him with the stench of death's promise.

In that instant, as Reza watched death come, the mortally wounded Goliath snapped his powerful jaws shut on the genoth's vulnerable underside, close to its tail. The magthep's teeth were broad and flat, typical of the Homeworld's herbivores. They could not rip and tear as could those of the genoth, but they were powerful enough to grind the tough leaves of the hearty *suranga'a* bush into paste. Goliath's jaws clamped shut like a vise, crushing the unarmored flesh of the genoth's underbelly.

The dragon's teeth snapped together less than an arm's length from Reza's face before its mouth opened in a roar of agony and rage at the insolent magthep's attack. Ignoring Reza, it turned its attention to Goliath, who stubbornly clung like a giant parasite to its underbelly.

Reza whirled and ran to a nearby rock outcropping. Behind him, the genoth made short work of the wounded magthep. With a final squeal, Goliath was silent. Having disposed of its tormentor, the beast turned to reacquire its prey.

It found Esah-Zhurah.

Bearing her fangs in fear and rage, Esah-Zhurah raised her pike toward the creature in what she knew was a hopeless gesture. She had seen Reza get away, but had lost sight of him in the darkness. She desperately maneuvered her terrified magthep around to find him, not thinking of how vulnerable she was while riding her terrified beast. Suddenly, one of the genoth's forelegs lashed out, flinging her out of the saddle. She landed on the canyon's dusty floor with a muffled thud before scrambling to her feet, backing away from the apparition slowly, the pike still in her shaking hands. Her magthep, miraculously uninjured, shrieked in terror and fled into the gathering storm.

The genoth homed in on the young Kreelan woman. The animal had acquired a taste for Kreelan flesh over its many cycles, and it had chosen a most opportune time to come from the great wastelands beyond the mountains, through the ineffective barrier that proved little more than a nuisance to its great armored body. Already had it dined on five of the morsels this season, and now two more had come into its territory. Cautiously, for the tiny creatures were quick and could sometimes inflict pain, the genoth advanced on Esah-Zhurah.

Reza breathed a sigh of fear. He had to help her. *In Her name*, he thought, *what can I do against such a thing?* The ax weighed heavily in his hand as he moved from his cover of rocks, running in a crouch toward the beast's flank as it closed in on Esah-Zhurah, boxing her into a narrow cut in the canyon that was far too steep to climb.

Coming abreast of the beast, just out of its range of vision, Reza readied the ax for a throw. He cocked his arm behind his head and tensed his body to send the heavy weapon on its way in what he knew would be a futile attack at this range against such an opponent. But it was all he had.

Esah-Zhurah's attention was fixed on the beast until she saw the shadow of Reza's form standing to the thing's side, ax at the ready.

"Hurry, my love," she whispered, simultaneously baring her fangs at the thing now towering above her. The creature was maddeningly slow, advancing a step at a time, in no rush to tear her limb from limb, and she was growing impatient. "Throw it," she hissed at her tresh, though he could not hear her. "Throw it now."

Her eyes widened in disbelieving horror as she saw Reza suddenly drop the ax to the ground at his feet. With a startled cry, she looked up to see the beast's slavering jaws descending toward her.

* * *

Tesh-Dar was finishing her letter to the Empress when she sensed it. She was so surprised that she dropped her stylus, ignoring it as it rolled across the parchment, spreading ink over her neat script before clattering noisily to the floor.

"Priestess," Syr-Kesh, who had been awaiting an audience with her, asked, "is something the matter?"

Tesh-Dar merely stared into space, her eyes unfocused, her hands flat upon the writing tablet, utterly still.

Syr-Kesh was about to ask again, concerned that something was seriously wrong with the kazha's most senior warrior, when she felt it, too. It was a tiny warp in the fabric of the Way, a small voice crying out for the first time like a newborn babe. "It is not possible," she whispered, her eyes bulging with disbelief.

The priestess's head slowly traversed so that her eyes fixed the swordmistress like an insect upon a pin. "So have we always believed," she said slowly. "But so it obviously *is* possible." She paused a moment, listening to the spiritual transformation that was taking place, and to which she and all her kind would be witness. She only hoped that it was not too late. The Empress had never before reversed a decision such as She had cast for the human, for there had never been reason to. Reza was still scheduled to die in two days, his blood to be spilled upon the sands of the arena, and Tesh-Dar could not allow that to happen if there was any other way.

She turned to Syr-Kesh. "Fetch my shuttle here," she commanded. "I must seek an audience with the Empress immediately."

As Syr-Kesh fled to carry out her task, Tesh-Dar closed her eyes and searched with the eyes of her soul for the one whose blood had begun to sing.

* * *

Reza stood perfectly still, momentarily entranced by the prickling, burning sensation that was sweeping his body. Quickly, as if it were water spilled from a breached dam, he felt the fire in his blood crescendo into a roaring cascade of power that washed over his mind and flesh in a surge of raw, primal might.

Suddenly, in a flash of insight as illuminating as the lightning that sought to blind him, he knew what to do. Dropping the more cumbersome ax, he reached for the leather sling that was carefully, lovingly attached to his waistband. He quickly undid it and probed his fingers into the small pouch in which he carried the carefully prepared stones that armed the weapon. He found only two, but decided they would be enough. Placing a stone in the wide cup of the sling, he began to whirl it around and around, moving closer to the genoth.

"Here!" he shouted at the thing. "Come to me!"

The genoth whirled around at the sound of his voice, seeing another culinary treat with its glowing, multifaceted eyes. It paused for a moment, calculating the better of the two morsels to devour first. It was just what Reza had been praying for.

The sling circled faster and faster, the stone within gaining more and more energy. Reza's heart pumped in time with the weapon's rhythm as the enemy glared at him with its baleful eyes, perfect targets even in the darkest pitch of night. And suddenly, as if ordered by the Empress Herself, the wind was stilled for just one precious moment, and the tiny missile took flight, propelled with greater force than Reza had ever before mustered behind it.

As with the ancient tale of David and Goliath, the stone hit home. The round projectile blasted the genoth's left eye into pulp, exploding it like an overripe fruit that cascaded down the beast's face. But unlike David's foe, the genoth was not to die under such an attack.

The beast reared up, a shattering shriek of pain echoing down the canyon, humbling even the thunder above. It clawed at its face, at its obliterated eye, roaring in agony and rage.

Esah-Zhurah rushed forward with her pike, her own blood burning with the Bloodsong that was sustenance to her people as surely as the meat they ate each day. She buried it in the genoth's side, the weapon's point piercing the flesh just behind the middle right leg where thinner scales covered the creature's belly. Pausing only to ram it home with all her strength, she retreated, leaving it jammed into the dragon, with half of the pike's shaft buried deep in its flesh.

"Run!" Reza shouted, "Get back!" She needed no prompting from him. She ran as fast as she could, but it was not fast enough. The genoth's good eye caught sight of her, and the beast turned with astonishing speed to trail after its tormentor. Its slow, confident pace had all but vanished.

Its talons lashed out, and Esah-Zhurah was pitched into the air, flying head over heels. She hit the ground with a sickening thud, her metal breast armor screeching along the rocks that studded the canyon floor. Then she lay still.

"No!" Reza cried, running after the monster, now clutching his ax in his right hand. He realized with a sinking certainty that he could not reach her in time. The creature, grunting in its own pain and anger, was nearly on top of her, its jaws widening to crush her body into pulp.

Not realizing the strength that now lay within him, he was still trying to think and react as he always had, quickly, but not fast enough to avert the fate of his lover as the beast's open jaws descended on her.

But he discovered that the Bloodsong was more than a mere voice. It was a portal to things that would have taken Reza many more years – years that he did not have – to understand. His eyes narrowing in concentration, he focused his mind on the ax and projected an image of it buried in the left side of the creature's head. For a split second he felt his body and mind merge in a perfect union, as he were being guided by an unseen hand, and the ax flew with precision and power that he never would have thought possible.

The genoth's scales channeled the razor sharp edge of the heavy weapon as it struck the monster where its head and sinewy neck came together. Blood erupted in a spray as the weapon sliced its way deep into the genoth's flesh, the blade now buried up to the handle.

The creature stumbled forward, stunned, cracking its front teeth on the stone inches from Esah-Zhurah's head.

Reza's fierce battle cry was lost in the genoth's trumpeting of pain. He dashed forward, drawing his sword as the beast whirled about, thrashing with its forelegs in a futile attempt to dislodge the ax whose cutting edge was creeping ever closer to the animal's spinal cord. All thoughts of the prey on which it had been about to feast were forgotten as it fought against a new source of misery.

The genoth's tail whipped to and fro, beating the sand and dirt from the canyon floor in its blind search for a target. Reza paid it no heed, heading straight for the beast's exposed belly as it stood on its hindmost legs, the other four clawing uselessly at the air.

The Kreelan armorers would have been proud of the quality of their workmanship had they seen Reza's sword cleanly cut the left middle claw from its parent leg as he ducked under the genoth's belly. The beast mewled in pain and brought its head down to snap at him, but he whirled away, carried on the rising tide of power that flowed through him, slicing the genoth's belly open in a wide arc. He danced clear of the creature's remaining claws as its bowels spilled out onto the ground in a steaming deluge of viscera and blood.

The genoth whirled, its insides trailing after it like meaty chum from an ancient fishing vessel, and fixed Reza with its remaining eye. Its legs tensed to leap upon the tiny thing that had done it so much injury, and Reza knew that he could not escape. But he felt no fear, and readied his sword in a last act of defiance.

But it was not to be. In a starburst of flesh, the creature's remaining eye exploded as Esah-Zhurah's shrekka struck, sawing its way through the thinnest portion of the beast's skull to embed itself in the genoth's brain.

Relieved of its guidance mechanism, the body fell to the ground with a great thud, shuddering for a moment before its lungs exhaled a final, mortal sigh.

The genoth was dead.

Reza was not sure how much time passed between that moment and when he realized Esah-Zhurah was standing next to him, holding him by the shoulders and repeating his name.

"Reza," she said again, "answer me."

His eyes struggled to focus on her, and it dawned on him that he had been lost to the strange melody that flowed through him, something terribly alien, yet wondrous in its undiluted strength.

"Esah-Zhurah," he rasped, finally lowering the sword. "Are... are you all right?"

Her armor was dented and scored from where she had been tossed by the genoth, and there was a thin trickle of blood down the right side of her face where one of its talons had nicked her. It had been that close.

"Yes," she answered, steadying him now as he began to tremble violently. She took his sword before it dropped from his hand. "My tresh," she said, her eyes full of wonder, "it is within you. Your blood sings."

Numbly, Reza nodded his head. The thundering in his body had abated to a basso thrum. He fell down to his knees, his system reeling. "I have a soul," he whispered, his eyes lost in hers. "I have a soul."

Esah-Zhurah kissed him long and hard, then held him tightly as her own soul rejoiced at what they now knew, at the melody that had suddenly burst forth from her lover. Every soul ever born of Her blood that had not fallen from Her grace had its own voice, but Reza's was different from all of the others in a way that she could not define, but that she accepted as Her blessing in their final hour.

But joy was not the only emotion to be found in the falling rain.

With Esah-Zhurah's supporting arm around his waist, Reza made his way to the formless heap of flesh that was all that was left of his beloved friend.

"Goliath," he breathed as he knelt next to the stricken animal. Taking off his gauntlets, he ran his hands over the fur of the old beast.

"I am sorry, Reza," Esah-Zhurah said softly. "He was a noble creature. I grieve with you for his loss."

Goliath had been much more than a simple beast of burden or a pet. He had been his friend. Reza had often spent long hours talking to him when he was lonely, in the days when even Esah-Zhurah treated him as an animal, in the days when he had no one. No one except Goliath, who had always been there, who would listen to his troubles without complaint, contentedly munching on the plants Reza gave him as a treat. The quiet tears Reza shed for his fallen friend mingled with the rain, watering the earth with his sorrow.

"We must go soon, Reza," Esah-Zhurah said gently.

Reza nodded. "Good-bye, old friend," he whispered.

"There is something we must do first," she told him. Getting to his feet, instinctively replacing his gauntlets, he followed her to where the genoth's head lay stretched upon the rain- and blood-soaked ground. "I hope we are not too late."

"Too late for what?" Reza asked.

Esah-Zhurah did not answer him directly. Instead, she took out the knife that had brought them together, the blade once held by the Empress, and pried at a strange-looking scale above the genoth's blown-out eye. After digging it out of the dead animal's flesh, she held it out to the rain, letting the falling drops cleanse it before handing it to Reza.

"It is an eyestone," she explained. "You cannot see it now, but it should be brightly colored when held up to the light, like a mineral stone. Only this species is known to have them, one over each eye. They are terribly rare, for the beast must be only freshly killed for the colors to remain visible. It does not show while alive, nor after the animal has been dead more than a few moments." She was already moving to the other side to remove the remaining stone. "Long ago, they used to be valued greatly among our people as signs of courage. They are still terribly valuable in such a sense, but the Empress forbade the ritual killing of these beasts long ago, that they may continue to live in honor of the old ways."

"You mean," Reza said, "that the wastelands are filled with them?"

"Yes, according to Her laws. The wastelands are given to the creatures that dwell there. For us, it is a place forbidden. But this one," she gestured at the dead genoth, "trespassed upon our domain, and so is rightly ours to claim." She put the stones in a pouch and then held her face up to the rain for a moment, luxuriating in the cool water. It would quickly become a nuisance on the long trek home on foot.

"Come," she said. "It is time to return home."

Yes, Reza thought. *Destiny awaits.*

Fourteen

E'ira-Kurana was the first to spot them. "There!" she cried, pointing toward the two ragged figures trudging toward the kazha.

Tesh-Dar stepped forward, her eyes narrowed into tight slits against the glare of the sun. The human's Bloodsong had grown in strength as the night had worn on, clearly audible to the senses of her spirit. Only with the greatest of difficulty did she restrain herself from signaling for the two to come to her on the run.

Tesh-Dar's fists were clenched tight in anticipation, the muscles standing out on her arms like bands of steel as the two young warriors passed through the ancient stone gateway. As they made their way through the throng that had gathered to meet them, Tesh-Dar felt at once proud and afraid. Proud that she had taken a weak human who had had nothing to give but his life, and made him into a warrior respectable in all ways save his blood. And afraid that the origin of the song in his heart was not entirely of human origin, and what must happen if this was so.

As the two came near, dropping to their knees to salute her, she knew the truth. All of it. She could smell the human's scent on Esah-Zhurah, and she knew instantly that she had disobeyed Tesh-Dar's orders and touched the human in a way that she found entirely repugnant. And her mind did not have to probe far into the young warrior's soul to discover the rest of it; she did not have to ask Esah-Zhurah to know that there were matching wounds on their hands from the ceremony Esah-Zhurah had performed. For a moment, the priestess was overcome with the temptation to kill them both outright, but she reluctantly stayed her hand. Other things were already afoot, and to kill the two now would not make the situation any brighter.

"Greetings, priestess," Esah-Zhurah ventured.

Tesh-Dar's eyes were hard and her mouth was set in a grim line that reminded Esah-Zhurah of the faces carved in the entryways to many of the buildings in the City. The great priestess was not at all pleased.

"What am I to do, child?" she asked, her voice barely audible above the light breeze. But it was not a solicitation for advice. "Have you cast aside your commitment to the Way, to the Empress?" Her eyes were stony, accusatory. One of her duties was to dispatch justice in the name of the Empress, and it was not one she accepted lightly. Esah-Zhurah was to be given every chance to defend herself, but the evidence against her was already overwhelming. Esah-Zhurah opened her mouth to speak, but Tesh-Dar cut her off with a sharp gesture. "Silence," she hissed, pondering how she would handle the matter. "I would see you in my chambers, now." Both of them got to their feet and turned to go, but Tesh-Dar put a massive hand roughly on Reza's chest. "Not you, human."

Reza bowed his head. "Yes, priestess," he whispered, trembling inside. It appeared that his fate would not be so clean-cut after all, and he was terribly afraid that Esah-Zhurah had sacrificed her own future, as well.

In Tesh-Dar's quarters, Esah-Zhurah kneeled and told the priestess everything. She would not, could not lie.

Before her, Tesh-Dar paced in a seething rage. "I do not understand, child," she was saying, speaking more to herself than the fearful young woman. "You used a sacred ritual of another order – of *my* order! – to give this human that which we hold most dear, the blood of our race. Then you... you mated with him as is written in the legends from the Books of Time? And then you are set upon by a genoth the likes of which has not been found for nearly twenty generations, and the two of you alone are able to slay it?" She shook her head violently, sending her braids whipping around her torso. "Madness this is!"

"Reza carries the eyestones in the pouch I gave him," Esah-Zhurah whispered, any fear she had for incurring Tesh-Dar's wrath drowned in the shame she felt at the priestess's sense that she had been betrayed. But there was no shame in Esah-Zhurah for loving Reza, for doing what she had done. It had all felt... right to her, and had she to do it all again, she would change nothing.

"Have you anything else to add," Tesh-Dar said stonily, "before I pass judgment upon you?"

"Yes, my priestess."

"Speak, then."

Taking a deep breath, Esah-Zhurah told her, "Priestess, his blood not only sings Her glory – be it by my doing or the work of his spirit alone – but he has also invoked the name of the Empress, in his heart. He believes. And..." she heaved a breath, "...never did I deviate from the Way, my priestess, in binding our spirits through the flesh. My blood sang as it mingled with his, and never was there a dissenting note in the chorus that bound us together."

Tesh-Dar silently considered the implications of what the girl had said. If it were true, there was far more to these two than she had ever suspected. But how could it be? Sighing silently in frustration, she told Esah-Zhurah to leave. "You will be summoned when I pass judgment upon you."

"And what of–"

"His fate," Tesh-Dar cut her off angrily, "shall not change for the better with your meddling. Leave me now."

Esah-Zhurah withdrew quietly, leaving Tesh-Dar to fume in a miasma of anger, sadness, and fear. She recalled the sight of Esah-Zhurah's hand, the diagonal cut across the palm, still crusted with blood, a bridge the child had built between her own race and the alien youth. The song from the human's heart as he fought the monster in the valley played through her mind, and she frowned in consternation. She could not make the wrong decision now, for all might depend on it later.

"Oh, child," she exclaimed softly, "what have you done?"

* * *

Reza waited quietly in the priestess's chambers. Kneeling on the floor, head bowed and eyes closed as he waited for the priestess to return, he thought of the rapidly healing scar that marked where he and Esah-Zhurah had exchanged something more than words. He let the pleasant memories of the night occupy his mind while his exhausted body rested.

"You are lax, child."

The voice snapped him awake, and he found the priestess standing near the enormous window that encompassed most of the far wall, looking out toward the mountains of Kui'mar-Gol. "Slayers of the genoth should not become inattentive, even in sleep. Were I of a mind, I could have killed you all too easily."

"Were you of a mind, my priestess, there are few you could not kill," he replied quietly, his eyes on the floor. "Even in my dreams, my strengths could never challenge yours." He noticed that the pouch that had been bound to his waist was missing.

Tesh-Dar instantly sensed his feelings. *How strange*, she thought, *to be able to touch the child's spirit as I can those of my own people. Finally, after all this time.* "It is here," she said, holding the pouch up in one hand without looking at it. She had already surveyed the contents: two eyestones of extraordinary size and color. She held one in her other hand before the window so the light shone directly into it, filling the room with a blaze of cobalt blue that Reza could see reflecting from the floor.

"While alive," she said, almost as if he were not there, "the eyestone warns the genoth of the presence of prey by their heat, and is nearly indistinguishable from the other scales that coat the creature's body.

"But when the genoth dies, if the blood and fragile tissue are destroyed and drained rapidly from the eyestone, it becomes a thing of great beauty, an ornament much sought after, but rarely won in the contest between sword and claw. If not prepared quickly enough, the eyestone becomes opaque as milk, ugly and useless."

She turned to him, slowly twirling the sparkling gem in her fingers. "This one is of the rarest color, human. Only two other sets are known to exist in the Empire. This is the third – and greatest in size." Most eyestones were little more than a finger's breadth in diameter; these were as big as Reza's palm.

She set the prize down carefully, reluctant to part with it, admitting her own vanity at seeing colors the hue of her own skin sparkle and dance with life. She prayed that the stones were a sign from the Empress, symbols of the two young warriors who had come to mean so much to her, despite her anger at their unfathomable actions. Perhaps, as with the eyestones, it was their time to change, to metamorphose into the most precious of jewels, things of value and beauty. Or to die. Esah-Zhurah had said that Reza believed in the Empress, that he had truly accepted the Way. She had to know.

Her cloak whispered as she crossed the floor and knelt in front of Reza. Their eyes met. "It seems a lifetime ago," she said quietly, remembering the day she had first met him as a tiny, terrified boy, "that we once faced each other this way." She took his face in her powerful hands, the tips of her talons meeting at the back of his skull. "I must ask you this, Reza, and on your answer much depends: do you accept Her in your heart, and the Way of our people as your own?"

Reza no longer had to consider the answer to such a question. He met her gaze steadily. "I do, priestess," he said, feeling the pressure from her hands as they pressed gently against his cheeks.

After a moment, she released him. His heart was true. "It is so," she replied, standing up once again, returning to the window.

"This is a difficult day for me, Reza," she said, "as it will be for you, and for your tresh." She paused. "You exchanged blood, an acceptable tradition among certain of our people. But such a thing is only to take place after the final Challenge, and is always decided by the Empress Herself, or the head priestess of the Desh-Ka. It was the greatest gift Esah-Zhurah could give you as one who follows the Way, but it may prove her own undoing. She breached many of our codes to give you what you now possess."

Reza looked up, concern spreading across his face like cracks wending their way across a lake of ice. "My soul," he said quietly.

Tesh-Dar nodded. "Or its voice. Perhaps we will never know. Regardless, by giving you her blood, she imparted unto you her honor, and made you something more than you were before. But the fact of her transgression remains, and it has tainted you in turn," she went on. "I am left with no alternative but to punish you both." She saw Reza's grim expression. "You will both be bound to the Kal'ai-Il for punishment with the *grakh'ta*, the barbed lash. Six strokes for each of you, this day, upon the rise of the Empress Moon."

Reza's relief was enormous. Esah-Zhurah would be spared a humiliating death or the shaving of her hair. The pain of such punishment would be torturous, but it was endurable. He did not have to consider his own chances, however. Six lashes with but a single evening in which to heal would leave him a cripple in the arena for the final Challenge.

It did not matter, he told himself. Whether he died in the first combat or the last was immaterial; at least it would not be Esah-Zhurah who would have to suffer the pain of killing him. She would still have a chance at life, a chance to cleanse her honor. "My thanks for your leniency, priestess," Reza offered humbly.

"I wish... things could be otherwise, Reza," she said softly. Her anger had burned itself away at the thought of him dying in the arena, now to die with the bloody welts of his shame fresh beneath his armor. She knew that the punishment was unforgivably lenient, but there was no force behind the thought that they had done something wrong, as if the wrongness were merely a symbol upon a parchment being consumed by fire. The Ancient Ones were still and quiet. They did not call for blood, as they were wont to do in the rare cases when one of Her children strayed from the Way. Tesh-Dar only knew that they watched still, and their sightless stares into her soul made her wary of her footsteps in this matter. And then, she thought, there was the Empress.

"I thank you priestess," he said, "for everything." He paused, wanting to say something more, even reaching out his hand toward her, a tentative bridge over the rift that had always existed between them. They probably would never speak again, for the punishment would be rendered soon, and the Challenge would begin with the rising of the sun tomorrow, and Reza would be dead soon thereafter. He wanted to tell her that the malice he had felt toward her for what had happened to his parents was gone, that he had forgiven her. She had, he finally admitted to himself, become a surrogate mother to him, and perhaps something more, something beyond his ability to understand.

A quick rapping on the door startled Reza, and he turned to see a tresh enter and kneel. "They have found the genoth's body," she reported, looking askance at Reza. "The tale is true." She paused. "They also found the mutilated bodies of Ust-Kekh and Ami-Char'rah."

The priestess looked at Reza, noting the sad surprise on his face. "We never saw them," he said.

Tesh-Dar thanked her, and the warrior left. She and Reza looked at each other, the moment Reza had been searching for now lost.

"Go now," she told him, "and fetch me Esah-Zhurah, that I may inform her of my judgment."

Reza saluted and left, hoping that at least the final hours before their punishment could be spent quietly together.

Tesh-Dar watched him go. She was saddened that she would never know the words to the feelings she had felt flowing from him.

* * *

Esah-Zhurah was distraught, but not because of her own punishment.

"Priestess," she asked in a determined voice, "is it not possible for one of us to accept the punishment for both?"

"Do not be foolish, child," Tesh-Dar admonished, summarily dismissing the idea. Or trying to. "The punishment of one is suffered by the other. That is the code of the tresh. You have known this. You must withstand six times of the grakh'ta, and so must he, for I can give no fewer, and have not the heart to give more." She stopped her pacing to face Esah-Zhurah, whose own eyes were downcast. "Child, he is to die in the Challenge on the morrow. Is it not better that he be allowed to share in your pain?"

Daring to look Tesh-Dar in the eye, Esah-Zhurah shook her head. "I would rather have him stand a fair chance in combat and die at my hand or yours with the honor he has earned among us, rather than let him be speared like a meat animal, crippled and helpless with injury." Their punishment would be received without the usual support from the healers. If Reza was whipped with the grakh'ta, he would be so badly injured that he would die in the first round of the Challenge, if he lived even that long. "If I were to receive twelve lashes," she pressed, "must he also be punished? Must he, priestess?"

"There is precedent, Esah-Zhurah," Tesh-Dar reluctantly conceded. "It is terribly rare, and has never happened in my lifetime. But..."

"Then it can be done," Esah-Zhurah finished for her. "It is within your power to grant."

"Esah-Zhurah..." Tesh-Dar's voice died, for she did not know what to say. She turned away to look toward the mountains in the distance, hiding the feeling of impending loss that she could no longer conceal, for the mourning marks had already begun their march down her cheeks. Inwardly, she cursed the unforeseen turn the Way had taken. She had held such high hopes for these two, believing that Reza would survive to become something that had never been in all the history of the Empire: one not born of their race, but who might wear the collar in the name of their Empress, with Esah-Zhurah at his side. To see him perish now was a tragedy she mourned with a strength she would never have admitted. "If you must," she said in a despondent voice. "I will let it be so."

Tesh-Dar turned to her, the elder's face unreadable but for the mourning marks that now flowed openly down her face like ebony streams against a twilight sky. "Go now and prepare, child," the priestess told her, "for when the light of the Empress Moon shows in the referent of the Kal'ai-Il, it will be time."

* * *

Reza waited impatiently for Esah-Zhurah to return. Already the Empress Moon was rising above the twilight horizon, and their Way together grew shorter by the minute. He had no illusions about his future: his life would end tonight, save for the stilling of his heart by the sword or shrekka of one of the peers come morning. But he had accepted it as his Way and Her will, and knew that the Bloodsong would carry him from this place to yet another.

He held the knife he had won as a prize in his first combat the day Esah-Zhurah had taken him to the city so many cycles ago, the day that the priestess had taken the two of them under her wing. Carefully, he laid it aside. It was his gift to Esah-Zhurah. It was his most prized possession, and he wanted her to keep it in remembrance of him.

Suddenly he sensed that she was coming, and turned to greet her.

She was not alone. A healer accompanied her through the perimeter of trees that were the only walls to their home-in-exile, the clawless one's robe flowing like water in the light breeze.

"Are you prepared?" Esah-Zhurah asked quietly, kneeling next to him.

Reza nodded, wanting to reach for her and take her into his arms one last time. But the healer hovering nearby gave him pause. "Why is she here?" he asked.

"I asked her to come, my love," Esah-Zhurah said softly, wrapping her arms around Reza's neck. "She is here to take care of you," she whispered in his ear.

He felt a light sting on the side of his neck as Esah-Zhurah pressed a tiny patch against his skin, injecting a tranquilizer the healer had prepared into Reza's carotid artery. His eyes flew wide in surprise and he made to grab for Esah-Zhurah's hands. But it was too late, the drug already rushing through his system, robbing him of control over his voluntary muscles. He fell limply into Esah-Zhurah's waiting arms, asleep, before he could say a word.

"Forgive me," she begged, holding him tightly for what she knew would be the last time. "It was I who brought punishment upon us, and it is I who must answer for it," she told him, knowing that he could no longer hear her. "In exchange for my pain, you will have a fair chance in the arena on the morrow, a chance to win. Perhaps even a chance at life, should it be Her will." She tenderly kissed his sleeping lips. "That is my gift to you, my love. Should I be gone when you awaken, remember that I will always be with you, until the day the voices of our souls shall be one." She placed the Empress's blade, the gift from Pan'ne-Sharakh, in his waist belt. "This is now yours," she said. "Go thy Way in Her name, my love."

Esah-Zhurah kissed him one last time, then gently lay him down upon their bed. Two more healers came from the trees, and Esah-Zhurah watched as they carried Reza away to their chambers to watch over him.

High above, the Empress Moon rose.

* * *

Esah-Zhurah looked up from her meditation as Mara'eh-Si'er, Tesh-Dar's First, approached. The time had come.

"I am ready," Esah-Zhurah told her, standing up and forcing her mind away from Reza to the painful trial ahead. She followed the First toward the Kal'ai-Il, the Empress Moon shining full overhead.

Standing in the center of the kazha, the Kal'ai-Il was an ancient edifice whose worn granite pillars dated back to before the birth of the First Empire, from a time remembered only in legend. Forming a circle, the gray slabs that covered the ground radiated from the central dais to meet two concentric rings of pillars, themselves capped with purple granite blocks weighing hundreds of tons that bridged the tops. Every other pillar of the outer ring, thirty-six in all, supported staircases in the form of flying buttresses; the inner ring, comprising eighteen pillars half the height of those in the outer ring, had simpler stone stairways rising from the circle bounding the massive central dais. It was the largest structure in the kazha, but in all Esah-Zhurah's time here she had never seen it used. She had only walked through it once, at Reza's insistence as he asked her about its purpose in their lives. She had never considered that she would be the first one of the ancient kazha to be punished here since long before she was born.

"In all the kazhas throughout the Empire," she had explained, "there exists one of these. In ancient times, as now, the Kal'ai-Il was where the most severe punishments were carried out. In our early schooling, we are punished lightly, but in a large group. The transgressions of one are suffered for by many, and it is a terrible dishonor to bring shame upon any but yourself. As we grow older, we are placed in smaller and smaller groups, the last being as are you and I, as tresh, before we enter the Way as individuals.

"But," she went on pointedly, "the punishment becomes ever more severe for a given act. What a small child suffers lightly, an adult may well die for. At last, the warrior may find herself shackled in the Kal'ai-Il for offenses that demand public ceremony and atonement." She paused for a moment and looked at Reza, trying hard to make him understand the importance of what she was trying to tell him. "The only worse punishment is to have one's hair shaved and be denied death for a cycle of the Empress Moon, to wander among the peers in shame as one's name is stricken from the Books of Time, to die without honor, without a legacy among the peers, and to live for all eternity in the darkness beyond Her light."

Now, walking behind the First, Esah-Zhurah saw that the tops of the two granite rings were crowded with the peers, who stood two rows deep facing the massive, worn dais, their heads bowed and eyes averted.

Her escort stopped as she reached the two massive pillars of the entrance, sheared midway from the ground like two enormous tusks, broken off in an ancient battle and never repaired.

"Remember," Mara'eh-Si'er said quietly, leaning close to her, "you must pass this portal by the twelfth tone after your punishment has been rendered and you are released from the bindings. It is a test of your spirit above and beyond your atonement. It is a demonstration of your will to live in honor among your peers. If you do not pass this point," she gestured toward the glittering ebony stone marker that was set in the floor of the entrance like a buffer between two different worlds, "the priestess is obligated to kill you, for that is the Way of the Kal'ai-Il." She gestured for Esah-Zhurah to step forward to the ancient dais. Then she turned to join the elder warriors gathered on the inner ring.

Esah-Zhurah walked onward, her pace slow, the odd bit of gravel crunching under her sandals, loud as thunderclaps in her ears over the stillness of the wind and the silence of those around her. She noted with detached curiosity that nothing grew from the cracks in the slabs, some wider than the palm of her hand; the normally fertile ground was lifeless and dull, like mud from a dry lakebed baked into clay by a searing sun. It seemed that even the earth had forsaken those who trod this path.

Before her was the dais, a huge, ponderous structure that reflected the unyielding rigidity of the code under which she and her people were fated to live. The circular platform was overshadowed by a thick stone arch that looked like a natural formation, not something made by Kreelan hands. Two thick chains, their copper sheathing green with age, hung from the arch. Each chain had a metal cuff for the victim's hands.

She could see the priestess waiting for her, Tesh-Dar's black armor glistening in the dual light of evening. The fading sun, just falling below the horizon, was grudgingly giving way to the glow of the Empress Moon, huge now in the sky directly overhead. As she mounted the stairs, one of the tresh lit torches that made the top of the dais into a ring of fire, providing light for the peers to see by.

Having reached the top of the dais, three times Esah-Zhurah's own height, she knelt before Tesh-Dar.

"Remove your clothing," the priestess ordered quietly. Esah-Zhurah did as she was told, taking off her black cloth garment and her sandals, folding them carefully into the prescribed bundle and placing them at the edge of the stairway. Completely naked now except for the collar she wore about her neck, she moved forward to the center of the dais, extending her arms upward.

As if with a will of their own, the chains descended. One of the tresh locked the bronze shackles, the metal rough and pitted with age, around her wrists and fastened them tightly with bolts as big around as Esah-Zhurah's thumb. The young warrior did the same for the shackles on the floor, anchored to the dais by a short piece of chain, attaching them to Esah-Zhurah's ankles; their bent flanges bit into her flesh. The tresh then placed a strip of thick leather in Esah-Zhurah's mouth. It was something for her to bite down on, to help control the pain that was to come. Esah-Zhurah's eyes thanked the girl, for it was a mercy she had performed, not required by the code of punishment.

Then the girl stepped away. Unseen warriors in the bowels of the dais pulled the chains taut, lifting Esah-Zhurah clear of the floor. Her arms were stretched out above her and away from her body, her blue flesh now a glowing crucifix in the flickering light of the torches.

Tesh-Dar stood by silently, eyes closed as she listened to the clatter of the chains, the tired squeaking of the bolts as they were driven home, and then the gentle groaning of the ancient wheels as Esah-Zhurah's body was lifted above the dais. A memory flashed through her mind, a dark and painful one that had rarely surfaced over the years, of her own body being suspended in these very same shackles. It had been many, many cycles before Esah-Zhurah had been born, before the war with the humans had begun. It was strange, she thought, that she could not remember what she had done to earn such a punishment, so deep an effect had it had on her. She vaguely recalled that it was something terribly stupid, something even a magthep would not have concocted. But it would not come to her, and she let it rest.

She ran her eyes along the list of names of those who had taken punishment here, carved into the stone floor of the dais. Some were so old that they were nothing more than shapeless indentations in the stone. But the more recent ones were clearly legible, and she noted that hers was indeed the last before this day. The Kal'ai-Il was generally a silent pillar in their lives, but when it spoke, its words echoed for a long time, indeed.

She gripped the grakh'ta in her right hand as if it were a serpent trying to escape, the seven barbed tendrils that grew from the thick handle, nearly twice as long as she was tall, wrapped around her arm in the customary fashion. It was one of her favorite weapons in battle, but all it brought to her now was a foul and bitter taste at the back of her throat. The lashes she was about to deal out now would be more than she had given in punishment over her entire life, and it sickened her that she had no recourse. Her heart felt wooden, dead.

"All is ready, priestess," the young warrior reported from behind her.

"Strike the first tone," Tesh-Dar ordered, her mind turning to the task at hand, no matter how reluctantly. The tresh saluted, then made her way to the far side of the dais where a huge metal disk hung suspended, its upper edge at the same height as Esah-Zhurah's eyes from where she now hung. The center was well worn, for it sounded once per day as a reminder to the tresh of what lay here. The runes that decorated its surface were in the Old Tongue, a language that had died out in common usage before the First Empress Herself had been succeeded.

Esah-Zhurah watched as the warrior hefted the huge hammer, then cringed as she slammed it into the disk's center. The sound washed over her like a blast of chill air, setting her body vibrating like an insect caught in a spider's web. All around her, the eyes of the tresh lifted to watch the punishment, for it was a lesson for them, as well.

As the sound of the gong began to fade from Esah-Zhurah's ears, she heard a sound behind her like the rustling of leaves in the wind. It grew into a shrieking roar as the priestess flailed the grakh'ta with all her incredible strength.

Esah-Zhurah closed her eyes, waiting for the first strike to fall.

* * *

Reza's eyes flew open. He had been awakened by something, but he could not remember what it was. Looking around to make sure he was not dreaming, he saw the healers clustered about the window that looked out over most of the kazha, their backs stiff under their robes, their hands gripped tightly. Uncharacteristically for healers, who tended to be a garrulous group, they were completely silent.

"What is happening?" he asked, startling them. They had thought he would remain asleep for some time yet. "Why are you..." He suddenly remembered what had happened, what must be happening now.

Crack! A sound like a gunshot echoed across the kazha.

"Esah-Zhurah!" he shouted, struggling against the anesthetic, his body an immobile leaden weight. "Esah-Zhurah, no!"

"No, child," the senior healer, a woman nearly as old as Tesh-Dar, said as she and the other healers gathered to restrain him, "there is nothing to be done. The priestess ordered that you must wait here."

Reza, ignoring her and growling like a trapped animal, continued to struggle against the numbness, trying furiously to regain some control over his deadened body.

"This was a command, child!" the healer hissed, and Reza, shocked by the iron tone of the woman's voice, came back to his senses. There was nothing he could do.

Crack!

"How... many?" Reza choked. "How many must she take?"

They looked at one another, as if taking a silent vote as to whether they should tell him.

"Twelve lashes," the elder replied quietly, her voice brittle. For she knew well the terrible damage that the weapon could wreak on a body, particularly when wielded by the priestess, and she had her own doubts as to the chances of even the most seasoned warrior surviving so many strikes.

"How many remain?" he asked in a small, tortured voice, hoping that he had not come awake with the first lash.

Crack!

"Eight, now," came the reply.

Reza lay back and closed his eyes, tears cascading down his face as he fought to keep from screaming out of helplessness.

* * *

Crack!

Esah-Zhurah's eyes bulged as if they were about to explode from their sockets, so horrific had the pressure within her body become to resist the urge to shriek in agony. Her teeth had ground halfway through the hard leather in her mouth; she would have long since bitten off her tongue had it not been for that small kindness the young tresh had shown her.

Crack!

She groaned finally, but still did not cry out. There was no feeling in her body now, no sensation but stark, blinding pain as she felt the flesh being flayed from her back. Her head hung limply, a stray strand of the whip having stung her on the neck just below where the spine met the skull. Her lungs labored fitfully as the muscles along the front of her rib cage sought to take up the slack of those along her back that had been battered down to the bone. She hung still now, even when the lash struck, for the muscles facing the weapon had lost their strength for so much as a nervous twitch. She heard the whistling behind her and desperately sucked in her breath, clamping down on the leather in her mouth as she anticipated the next blow.

* * *

Crack!

Reza moaned in empathic suffering as he listened to the steady barrage of lashes onto the body of his tresh, his soul mate, and felt her keening Bloodsong. He could only cry silently as the gunshots of the grakh'ta echoed across the kazha.

Crack!

He flinched, then went on with his prayer to the Empress. It was the most emphatic he had ever made in his life, praying to give Esah-Zhurah the strength and courage she needed to survive. He waited for another strike, but it did not come. He was relieved to find that he had miscounted somehow, that the last he had heard had indeed been the twelfth. After a moment, the mournful tone of the gong sounded, informing all who could hear that the ordeal was over.

Almost.

Waiting silently with the healers, now clustered around his bed save one with sharp eyes who watched the dais, Reza counted the beats of his heart as he lay waiting for the next tone. It rang when he had reached fifty.

"Can you see her?" he asked urgently of the healer peering through the window. "Has she moved?"

The healer, a young woman who was also the senior by skill here at the kazha, signed negative. Her eyes were like those of a bird of prey, and she could see the dais clearly except for the floor, which was concealed behind the wall that ran waist high around it. But Esah-Zhurah clearly had not emerged. "She has not."

"Esah-Zhurah," Reza said under his breath with all the force of his soul, "get up. Get up and live."

The third tone sounded.

* * *

Her eyes flickered open at what her body reported as a spurious vibration, but which meant nothing to a mind that bordered on madness. Something told her that it was important, but she could not seem to remember why.

She looked around, swiveling her bloodshot eyes, and found that she was looking at someone's foot, very close up. Her hands lay in front of her, inert, bloody rings where the manacles had been. She was laying in something sticky, but did not know what it was, nor did she really care. She was tired; she wanted to sleep.

She closed her eyes again.

Suddenly, as if from very far away, she got the peculiar sensation that someone was calling her name, wanting her to do something, but she could not hear it clearly through the ringing in her head, the numbness.

The sound, the vibration, came again, and all at once she felt Reza with her. She could hear the song of his blood crying out for her, trying to give her strength.

"Reza..." she muttered thickly with jaws exhausted from biting the now-crushed piece of leather that she managed to spit from her mouth, "cannot... hurts..."

But his Bloodsong would not be still, would not be silent. It was a tiny force to set against the agony assaulting her senses, but its power grew, would not be denied.

With a tortured groan, she rolled over on her stomach, gasping at the effort. Her mind began to clear slightly now that she had a mission for it, and she was thankful that she was not paralyzed with pain. But that would come soon enough after the shock she was experiencing now wore off. She shook her head to clear her vision. She saw that she was pointing the right way, toward the break in the wall that surrounded the dais and the torches that ran along both sides of the stone walk leading to her destination.

She tried to stand, but without the muscles in her back to help lift her body, it was impossible. She slowly scrabbled forward using what leverage her biceps and quivering chest muscles could afford her, pushing weakly with her legs toward the stairs that led down from the dais, leaving a slick trail behind her like a giant, bloody snail.

Tesh-Dar, having finished with the grakh'ta, had moved to stand astride the ebony bar that marked Esah-Zhurah's goal, silently urging her on as the battered young woman met the stairs. Finding it too difficult to pull herself downward, the friction of the stone against the length of her bare body far too great, Esah-Zhurah pushed with her legs until she was parallel with the stairway, then rolled herself down. The priestess ground her teeth together in empathic agony as the young warrior flailed like a rag doll as she plummeted toward the bottom.

* * *

"She has left the dais," the healer reported, "but now lies still." She did not have to say that she did not feel Esah-Zhurah's chances of survival were very high. Her voice reflected a distinct lack of optimism that Reza found infuriating, yet he managed to hold his tongue.

The other healers waited silently. They had little to do, for it was forbidden to give aid to one punished in the Kal'ai-Il. They would make her as comfortable as they could, but that was the extent of the care they could render. The girl's life was entirely in Her hands.

The gong rang yet again, and they looked at each other, hope fading from their eyes. Half of Esah-Zhurah's time had passed, and she had yet far to go.

* * *

She lay there, panting, blinded by the white flashes that flared in her vision. The roll down the stairs had left her unconscious again, and she had no idea how much time remained to her, nor did she care. Her world was pain, only pain.

But the melody of Reza's song in her blood was insistent. Once again rolling onto her stomach, she began to crawl toward the portal, following the glare of the flickering torches. Her hands clawed at the unyielding slabs of rock, her talons fighting for purchase on the ancient stone as she desperately pulled herself forward.

The gong rang again. No good, she thought weakly, no good to crawl like a sand-worm. I have to stand, to walk.

Pulling her legs underneath her as if she were on her knees, bowed over in prayer, she set one foot forward. Then, balancing precariously with her hands on the extended knee, she pushed herself upward with all the strength she could muster. She managed to stand up, and her free foot wavered over the walkway as if blind before it finally found a place that sustained her balance. She made her way forward, swaying to and fro like a drunkard, praying she would not fall. For to fall now was to die.

Fewer and fewer were the torches before her, and she suddenly had a terrible thought: what if she was headed the wrong way?

No matter, she told herself. It would be too late to go back. At least her suffering would be swiftly ended with a blow from the priestess's sword. She nearly paused at the thought, the notion of a quick, painless death suddenly tempting. Her mind dared not contemplate the agony she would endure in the coming hours before she would die of shock and loss of blood.

Another step forward toward the darkness that stood at the portal, and another, and finally her foot touched the ebony bar.

Tesh-Dar caught Esah-Zhurah in her arms as she fell forward, her legs and back finally giving out completely. The final sound of the gong pealed behind her, signaling the end of the punishment. She struggled weakly, fighting Tesh-Dar's grip and moaning unintelligibly.

"You are safe, Esah-Zhurah," the priestess said as she held the girl gently, doing her best to avoid touching the devastated flesh of her back, her own heart a cold shard of steel in her chest. "It is over."

The healers in attendance looked at the young woman and exchanged glances that Tesh-Dar had seen many times before, and her hopes sank at their unvoiced thoughts.

"I will carry her," she told them, and they made no move to interfere.

* * *

Reza could only turn his head when he heard the door to the infirmary burst open; he had feeling through most of his body now, but no control. He watched as Tesh-Dar, followed by a train of healers who Reza knew would not be able to apply their craft, swept through the room carrying Esah-Zhurah's limp form. The sight sent a blade of ice through Reza's heart. He had felt her pain in his blood as she hung upon the Kal'ai-Il, but the sight of her lacerated body was far worse. He struggled upward, fighting against the useless muscles and nerves that stolidly refused his call to duty. But at last he was sitting upright, then was crawling on his knees.

"Is she alive?" he gasped in the direction of the group huddled around the raised dais where her body lay. Staggering to his feet, he caught a glimpse of the bloody mass of tissue that had once been her back, framed by a series of zebra stripes where the white gleam of bone shone through the tattered flesh. "Esah-Zhurah!" he cried, hurling himself forward, reaching for her.

Tesh-Dar materialized suddenly before him, embracing him in an iron grip and turning him away from the sight. "No, Reza," she said. "You can do nothing for her. Let the healers do what they can–"

"Esah-Zhurah!" he cried again, trying to wrench himself free. His anger boiled and madness threatened to take him. All at once he felt it again: the fire in his veins and the melody that hammered inside his skull, a tidal wave of power that he couldn't control, but welcomed now in his grief and rage. "Let... me... go!" He wrenched to one side so quickly and with such force that he broke free of Tesh-Dar's Herculean grip. Before his mind could react, his armored gauntlets were streaking toward the priestess's face, aiming to tear her eyes from their sockets.

But at the last instant, Tesh-Dar's hands rose to break his attack, and with the speed born of the special powers she had inherited from those who had gone before her, she smashed Reza to the ground with a double blow to his shoulders.

"No more, Reza," she commanded, carefully controlling the forces inside her own spirit that clamored for release, to join in combat.

Reza knelt before her, stunned by the blows, the fire burning hotter than before. But before the fire could take him again, he was once again in Tesh-Dar's arms. The elder warrior had sensed the new wave of power surging into the human and had elected to put a stop to it before she could lose control of what lay within herself. She held him so tightly that his armor began to give way, popping and denting with the pressure, and she continued to squeeze until Reza was panting desperately for breath, his arms nearly broken at his sides. At last, she felt the Bloodsong within him abate.

When it had ebbed toward silence, she released the pressure, her arms around him more for support than restraint.

"I am not your enemy," she whispered to him, her own senses awash in the emotions pouring from this young alien, from the young warrior she looked upon in her heart as her adopted son. "I did as she wished, Reza. She begged me for this, to give you a fair chance in the Challenge. Do not disgrace her sacrifice this way."

She released his arms, and Reza wrapped them around her neck. For a long time he clung to her like a child, vainly trying to fight back his tears, as she held him. And on his face and hands, where they had touched Tesh-Dar's armored breast, was Esah-Zhurah's blood. So much blood.

"Forgive me, my priestess," he told her in a trembling voice. "My life, my honor a thousand times over is not worth this."

Tesh-Dar said nothing, but gently rocked him as she might a small child.

Behind them, the healers had done all they could, all they were allowed. They had arrayed the flesh and skin as well as possible and covered the ghastly wounds with sterile blankets, but that was all. They could give her nothing for the pain, put an end to the persistent bleeding, or disinfect the wounds. The chief healer saw the signs of internal injuries, as well, the force of Tesh-Dar's blows having driven the whip's barbs into Esah-Zhurah's lungs. But there was nothing she could do. Ordering her peers to stand away, she signaled to Tesh-Dar that they were finished now, except for the waiting.

"Go to her now, child," Tesh-Dar whispered. "I shall be here should you need me."

Reza nodded against her shoulder, then shakily turned around to look at what had become of his love, to see the price she had paid to give him a few more hours of life. She lay on her stomach, her arms at her sides. Her head was turned to one side on the thick pile of skins that served as both operating table and patient bed. A tiny bead of blood made its way from the corner of her mouth, pooling in the soft fur near her ear. Her beautiful blue skin was horribly pale, almost cyan, except for the brutal bruising that peered from beneath the black velvet bandages the healers had spread across her back, and the ebony streaks of mourning on her face. He knelt next to her and took off his gauntlets, dropping them to the floor. Carefully, afraid that his mere touch would cause her more pain, he ran a hand gently across her face, caressing her cheek.

Her eyes flickered open, and he felt her move.

"Be still," he whispered hoarsely. "Do not move, my love. I am here."

"Do not... leave me," she sighed. Her eyes were glassy with the onset of pain that was burning through the massive shock her body was experiencing.

Reza took her hand in his and squeezed it gently. "Never," he said with a strength that came from the core of his being. He wanted to shout at her, to ask her why she had done this, when his life was forfeit anyway. But he did not have to, because he knew. She loved him, and would have suffered a thousand-fold what she had today for his sake, and nothing more. "I love you," he told her softly, and he kissed her on the cheek.

She gave him a weak smile. "Fight well, my tresh, come the dawn. I will be with thee. And... may thy Way... be long... and glorious." Her grip relaxed as her eyes rolled up into her head, the lids closing over them.

"Esah-Zhurah?" he whispered. Her face was still, and with dread in his eyes he looked at the chief healer. "Is she dead?" he asked woodenly.

She shook her head. "Not... not yet," she told him, averting her eyes, knowing that it would not be long.

"Will she live to the morning?" he asked, his eyes pleading.

"I do not know, Reza," she answered truthfully. Life was a strange thing, and was often incredibly adept at cheating Death. For a time. "There is nothing more we may do."

Tesh-Dar stood close by, shrouded in the storm that tore through her heart. She was well acquainted with the process of death, and already she could sense a change in the melody of Esah-Zhurah's spirit. Very few were as perceptive of such things as was Tesh-Dar, and there was no mistaking it. The child's Bloodsong would soon come to a close, be it in the next moment or a few hours from now. But soon.

For all her life she had welcomed the event and celebrated it for others as she hoped they would someday do for her. It was an occasion for joy, when one passed from the field of honor to the spirit world beyond, where the Ancient Ones dwelled forever in Her light. It was the day for which the warriors of the Empire lived and breathed.

But the tortured lump of flesh that lay dying nearby brought her nothing but anguish, for to die this way was a horrible thing, especially for this child. Esah-Zhurah, born of the Empress herself, had sacrificed her formative years to study this human in the course of Her will, while her own peers sought glory against the alien hordes. And in the end, she had disobeyed a high priestess to lay with him, an act for which Tesh-Dar could have sentenced them both to death, but uncertainty had stayed her hand. The two of them, the whole that they formed together, was something unique in Tesh-Dar's experience, and the strange quiet that had descended over her ancestors in recent times had left her acutely aware of the consequences of the decisions she had to make regarding their welfare.

In the pair of young warriors she had discovered a new force within the Empire, something that before had only existed in legend, when a warrior could feel passion for another, and not all of one's heart was devoted to Her. She had heard Esah-Zhurah speak of love for Reza, but she understood now its true strength. The power that united these two former enemies was beyond Tesh-Dar's ken, and she vainly struggled to understand the force that had driven this young warrior, her pride and joy, to sacrifice herself for the one she had once called "animal," for the one who now lived clothed in the armor and beliefs of Her children, for the one who now knelt, weeping at the child's side. Esah-Zhurah's death would not bring glory to Her name; it would simply be a tragedy, and perhaps not for the two of them alone.

She walked to where Reza knelt and stood close to him, her great hand, still covered with Esah-Zhurah's blood, resting upon his shoulder. "The Challenge comes soon," she said softly. "You must prepare." She did not need to remind him that every combat in which he fought – as many as fifteen – would be to the death. No arena judge would preside, for the only rules governing each battle would be those of survival.

"I cannot leave her," he whispered absently, his hands gently folded around hers.

"Your armor is ruined, your weapons are not ready, nor is your mind," Tesh-Dar went on. "You must do these things or death will find you quickly. Esah-Zhurah paid a dear price to give you this chance to fight the rarest of contests, and the most honored. Do not forfeit her faith in you." She squeezed his shoulder firmly. "I will wait here, her hand in mine, until you return. I cannot hold Death at bay. But should her time come while you are gone, she will not face it alone." *As must most of our people*, she added silently, wondering if someone would be at her own side when her Way came to its end. "Go now, child."

Reza nodded heavily, as if once more he had been inflicted with the strange anesthetic Esah-Zhurah had used upon him, his body a vast numbness to his mind. "Yes, my priestess," he whispered. With a last kiss upon Esah-Zhurah's still lips, he rose and walked stiffly through the doorway, disappearing into the darkness beyond.

* * *

The Empress stood silently over Esah-Zhurah, with Tesh-Dar kneeling at her monarch's side. Not long after Reza had gone to prepare for the coming Challenge, the Empress had appeared. Her arrival was without fanfare, without a Praetorian Guard; She was a part of all Her Children as surely as were the hearts that beat in their breasts, and so was a familiar part of their lives, even to those who had never seen Her in the flesh. She needed no guard, for all the Kreela were Her guardians and protectors.

"I believe that she is The One," the Empress spoke at last.

"My Empress," Tesh-Dar asked, awed by the possibilities invoked by those words, "how is this possible? Her hair is black as night and she was born of the silver claw, barren as myself. How can we know that it is truly... She?"

"I do not know, daughter," the Empress replied. "It is a feeling – a certainty – that refuses to leave me."

"Then what shall be done?" Tesh-Dar still held Esah-Zhurah's motionless hand. The child's heartbeat was becoming erratic, and she would soon – long before dawn broke over the arena – pass from this life. "How may one be sure?"

"If the human is victorious in the Challenge this day, we shall have our answer. He shall bear the burden of proof," She told Tesh-Dar. "For I have realized that this is what the Ancient Ones have been awaiting, priestess of the Desh-Ka."

"Could it truly be?" Tesh-Dar murmured to herself. If what the Empress believed came true, the Curse of the First Empress might someday be undone. Her great spirit had been silent for ages, and Tesh-Dar could not imagine the impact upon the Way were Her voice to join the chorus of all those who had come after Her.

The most powerful Empress who had ever walked the Way, whose spirit had vanished as Her body withered in death, in legend was said to be awaiting a host worthy of Her spirit. And it could be Esah-Zhurah.

Tesh-Dar shook her head. The possibility was simply too staggering. "If this is so, my Empress," she said slowly, "then I shall be to blame for failure. I ordered the child's punishment, and her Bloodsong grows weaker by the hour, by the minute." She looked up to her sister. "She shall die long before the combats of the day even begin."

The Empress frowned. "It shall not be so." Gently placing a hand on Esah-Zhurah's face, She closed her eyes. Her head leaned forward, nearly to Her chest. She spoke no words, no incantations, but Tesh-Dar could sense the power that flowed from Her as one could feel the heat of an open flame. The child shuddered, drew in a sharp breath, and then relaxed into a stronger, steady rhythm. Tesh-Dar could feel the spirit in her grow stronger. "Her spirit will remain with her body until I release it," the Empress said quietly, stroking Esah-Zhurah's face lovingly. The Empress had borne many children from Her Own body, and had forgotten none of them, even the males, who had never even received a name. And this child, above all others, did She hold most dear.

Tesh-Dar's eyes widened. She knew from legend that such things were possible, but no Empress in the last thousand generations had ever done such a thing, commanding a spirit to remain with the body past the time that Death should have its due.

"Are you to stay for the Challenge, Empress?" she asked, her tongue finally returning to the control of her brain.

"It shall be so," She replied. "Long has it been since I have seen the tresh fight, and longer still since combats have been fought to the death. I need to know, to feel the human's strength of spirit and will do so firsthand. If Esah-Zhurah is The One, then he must be completely worthy of her, and able to take the next step." Tesh-Dar looked up. "He must accept the collar of the Way," the Empress said quietly. "He must become one with our people."

FIFTEEN

Morning came, and the horizon shone a brilliant ruby red that would gradually lighten to the pastel magenta of full daylight. The wind was still, and probably would remain so throughout the day, keeping the ripe odors of the magthep pens away from the arenas.

But on this day, even the most malodorous emanations would not have concerned the throng that now gathered in and around the five arenas of the kazha, for today was a special day indeed.

For the first time in many cycles, the tresh would have the opportunity to face an opponent without the intercession of a judge; victory would be measured only by who survived the match. Not all of the combats were to be fought thus, only the ones in which the human was involved. But that alone served to sharpen the competition in the other combats, the other tresh battling for the honor of facing him in the arena. To kill him before the watching eyes of the Empress would be a tremendous honor, and to die by his hands would only be slightly less so. For few of the tresh who had trained with him considered him an animal any longer. He was a formidable warrior in his own right, and had even trained many of the novices.

The Empress stood now on the dais of the central arena. This arena hosted the first and last combats of the Challenge, with the other four arenas coming into play as needed. Thousands of onlookers were gathered, coming from kazhas all over the planet. Even warriors from the Fleet and the Settlements had come to see the spectacle, having received word that a human was about to fight in this, the last Challenge a warrior faced before her spiritual and societal coming of age. And as the mighty gong of the Kal'ai-Il sounded the first tone of the day, thousands watched a lone figure step onto the packed sand of the central arena to face the Empress.

Reza's stride was controlled, precise as he ventured forward toward where the Empress stood upon the elevated stone dais. He stopped before Her and thrust the sword he held in his right hand into the sand before he knelt and bowed his head to Her. He wore not the standard matte black combat armor that had always protected him in the Challenges he had fought before this day, but glistening ceremonial armor, no less functional than its less-enchanting counterpart, that the Kreela wore on special occasions. The cobalt blue rune that signified his kazha glowed from the swirling blackness of his breastplate, and the silver metal talons of his gauntlets, polished to perfection, glittered in the sun's growing light. His hair, drawn into the intricate braids demanded by custom, was entwined about his upper arms like coiled serpents, with enough slack to allow him full movement.

Beside him, the sword towered from the sand like a sharp-edged obelisk, the dark runes inscribed on the broad blade by Pan'ne-Sharakh's ancient hands telling the tale of his life since coming to the Empire, of the love he and Esah-Zhurah shared. Perhaps to give his despairing soul a glimmer of hope, much of the sword's blade still was bare, begging perhaps for the tale of their lives to continue, for more verses to be added to their own Book of Time. The golden hilt blazed like bloody fire from atop its tower of living Kreelan steel.

After checking on Esah-Zhurah one last time, giving her a final kiss as she lay sleeping, Reza had asked the priestess if he might be allowed the honor of fighting in the first combat, foregoing the normal random selections. Tesh-Dar had agreed, and now he waited for the lottery that would call forth his first opponent.

Another tone sounded from the Kal'ai-Il, and Tesh-Dar reached into the massive clay urn at the center of the dais to draw out the first name in the lottery that would begin the single-round elimination combats. Without looking at it, she passed it to the Empress.

"Korai-Nagath," She called in a voice that commanded countless billions of souls across the stars, "enter the arena."

A murmur of disappointment went up through the gathered crowd as the peers discovered they would have to wait for their turn at the human.

In the meantime, a warrior who stood half a head taller than Reza, and whom he had been training in swordcraft over the last cycle, entered the arena. Her pride was evident in her posture and the measured cadence of her stride. It was her third Challenge.

She knelt next to Reza, facing the Empress, and planted her sword and pike – her favorite weapons – in the sand beside her as she saluted her monarch.

The Empress nodded Her head in acknowledgment, then looked upon the assemblage. "As it has been, and so shall it always be, let the Challenge begin."

"In Thy name, let it be so," the throng echoed with its thousands of voices, their fists crashing against the breastplates they had worn nearly since birth.

Reza and Korai-Nagath stood and retrieved their weapons from the sand, then proceeded to opposite ends of the arena and turned to face one another.

"Begin," the Empress commanded.

The two warriors stood for a moment, sizing up one another, trying to match their own strengths against the other's known or suspected weaknesses. Each was heavily armed, in part because the savage battles that were fought on these sands were seldom decided by a single weapon, but also because the weapons first carried into the arena were all that could be used throughout the Challenge. Should a sword or knife break, or a shrekka miss its mark, there would be no replacement. Likewise, except for stanching the flow of blood from one's eyes, there was no medical treatment unless the challenger wished to forfeit the match. And that was one option none of the combatants today would have accepted.

Reza had no choice in the matter.

After only a moment's consideration, Reza hefted his sword and began a wary advance, his quarry doing likewise. She had favored her pike, as he knew she would, and was now moving forward to meet him.

Reza's heart began to thunder in his chest, his blood liquid fire in his veins as the sword became as light as a feather in his hand. The melody that had burst forth while he was fighting the genoth was back now, and he seized upon it quickly before it could overwhelm him. He channeled the energy as he moved forward, and his eyes gleamed with the cold flames that had taken him.

Korai-Nagath suddenly whirled, releasing a shrekka directed at Reza's chest. Rolling to the ground, Reza heard the weapon slice through the air a meter away and restrained the impulse to respond in kind. He had only three of the precious weapons, and once used, they would be gone. Korai-Nagath fought well for her stage of training, but Reza knew that she was fatally outclassed.

He spiraled in closer and closer, and only when he was within range of her pike did she realize her mistake in choosing it rather than the sword that now stood far behind her in the sand like a headstone. The pike, lethal in experienced hands and the right situation, was far too flimsy to parry the slashing attacks of Reza's sword. With nothing left in her hands but an arm's length of useless pole, she charged Reza with a knife in one hand and bared talons upon the other, a cry of passionate fury upon her lips.

The cry ended as Reza's sword pierced her breastplate directly over her heart. The two held each other for a moment in a macabre embrace, the scarlet stained steel of Reza's weapon protruding from her armored back, glistening in the gathering light before he gently laid her upon the sands. Silently, he pulled his weapon from her breast, drawing the flat of the blade across his other arm, a signal of his first kill.

Turning to the Empress, he kneeled. "May this one forever dwell in Thy light, my Empress," he said, energy still surging in his body, his mind so aware of his surroundings now that he could distinguish a dozen different heartbeats among the crowd behind him, "for in Thy name did she follow the Way."

"And so may it always be," thousands of voices echoed around him, completing the ages-old litany.

The first combat had ended.

* * *

The day alternately flashed and crept by. The periods of waiting as others battled their way through the arenas were precariously balanced against the blinding spells of combat that stretched for an eternity, then were gone in the blink of an eye. Each of the tresh fought and rested, fought and rested while others fell to the sand in defeat, or were killed by Reza's hand. As the day went on, the weaker and inexperienced ones were quickly weeded out from among the serious challengers. The pitched battles fought in the five arenas became ever fiercer as those with cunning and endurance slashed and clawed their way toward the final battle.

Despite his acknowledged skill, Reza did not go from combat to combat unscathed. Hour by hour, his body became host to a multitude of injuries.

Individually, they were nothing for him to notice, but over time they began to take their toll. Blood seeped from a dozen wounds hacked through the tough leatherite covering his arms and legs. His beautiful chest armor was horribly dented and scarred, the breastplate a moonscape of bare, pitted metal. A poorly executed fall while avoiding a hissing shrekka had cost him the use of his left hand, the wrist broken. His face, cut and bruised in a snarling hand-to-hand struggle with Lu'ala-Gol, was barely recognizable for the blood and sand smeared across it. One of his eyes remained its natural, nearly violent green, while the other glared at the world as a crimson orb, the blood vessels ruptured during a hard blow to his head.

But the expression he wore was serene. This, he knew, was what he had been born to, no matter that the womb from which he had been born had not been of their race. To tread the Way, to know that She watched over one's soul, to fight for Her glory: this was all that mattered. This was what Esah-Zhurah had suffered so to give him, and he was determined to win, to honor her, as well as the Empress. He could hear the song of Esah-Zhurah's heart, faint though it remained, and it heartened him and gave him strength, for it meant that she was still alive.

But he knew that on this day he would draw his last breath, as would she. His only prayer was that Esah-Zhurah would be waiting for him on the other side of this life, on the bridge that led to the everlasting Way, and that they could spend eternity together.

And then it was again time. He strode into the arena, waiting for the call to begin. Size up the other combatant. Move in close – shrekka! – drop, roll, attack. Parry. Attack once more. Thrust, block, slash. Close in... closer... strike! Move away, regroup.

He fought with the Bloodsong roaring fury and might in his heart, and in his mind were visions of Esah-Zhurah chained to the Kal'ai-Il, suffering for him, dying.

On and on it went, the sound of crashing metal and cries of fury and of pain shattering the air, until the sun began to wane. At last, as twilight crept upon the kazha and hundreds of torches around the center arena were lit, there were only two challengers remaining. Alone now, save for the hushed stares of the thousands watching and waiting for this moment, the two faced each other from opposite sides of the arena.

Blinking the blood out of his right eye, Reza took stock of his final opponent, Rigah-Lu'orh. He had watched her fight during his periods of rest, and had guessed since her second combat that she would be among the final challengers, and so she was. She stood taller by half a head, and was broader in the shoulders. But despite her greater size, she was incredibly nimble. She had performed a number of violent ballets throughout the day that had left two of her opponents dead and the others seriously injured. Her determination was visible even now, her distant eyes burning like tiny coals with the reflected light of the torches. She wanted his head, and wanted it very badly.

Reza wondered as to his opponent's energy reserves, but knew that he would not be able to gauge her strength until they crossed swords. His own body was nearing the end of what even the power pulsing within him could force from it. Even standing still he trembled, and the pain of moving his body with the speed required to survive was becoming intolerable, a constant screeching in his nerves and muscles. The great sword, its razor edge now dented and nicked from hammering and piercing so many breastplates, was like an enormous stone in his hand, his other hand hanging useless at his side, broken now in three places.

The Empress and the priestess stood upon the dais as they had all day, without pause or rest, watching him kill the best of the kazha. Now only this one, Rigah-Lu'orh, remained.

"Are you prepared, human?" the Empress asked, her voice easily carrying the distance across the arena.

Reza kneeled and bowed his head. "Yes, my Empress."

"And you, disciple of the Desh-Ka?" She asked of Rigah-Lu'orh. Of course, she was, kneeling as Reza had, saluting. "Then let it begin."

Reza had not even looked up when the first attack came. He brought his sword up just in time to deflect the whirring shrekka from hitting his face. With sparks trailing after it, the weapon slammed into the stone pillar behind him.

He had one shrekka left, but dared not use it until the right moment. With only one good hand, he would have to leave go his sword to reach the flying weapon, and in that moment he would be terribly vulnerable.

Moving quickly now, the two spiraled in toward one another in a half-walk, half-crouch, weapons held at the ready. Rigah-Lu'orh's cunning was surpassed only by the wiliest genoth, and Reza would not allow himself to underestimate her. Among all those at the kazha, the Challenge had selected her as the best to face him.

Closer they came, until they reached that finite point in time and space where planning gives way to action. In a flash of silver, Rigah-Lu'orh's two short swords slashed at Reza, attacking his upper and lower body at once.

Reza was unable to fend off both weapons, and she scored a flesh wound on his upper thigh. With a roar of anger, he lashed out with the broadsword, cutting a vicious arc through the air where his opponent had just been. Moving in again, she struck quickly at his lower body, slashing his left leg to the bone before darting away again, just ahead of Reza's hissing blade.

The fire in Reza's veins burned so hot that it blinded him. Time and again Rigah-Lu'orh's blades found their mark, his own weapon only occasionally diverting them. Her strategy was one of attrition, not of full commitment. She knew that Reza's sword could cut her in half, armor and all, and so she was careful to stay just out of reach. But she also knew that she was stronger and faster. She had conserved her strength, and knew well how to channel the power of the Bloodsong. Reza possessed the power, but not the knowledge to control it. Now, pouring through his exhausted body and unprepared mind with the fury of lightning, it was quickly – and effectively – killing him.

Reza was staggering backward now, reeling under her assault, his life pouring from his body through a dozen new wounds. Holding the sword up like a shield as she stalked him, he suddenly found himself backed against a stone pillar. There was nowhere left to run.

Dropping the sword from his hand, he reached for the shrekka attached to his shoulder armor. It was his last defense against defeat.

But Rigah-Lu'orh had been waiting. With a fluid motion, she hurled the short sword in her left hand like a dagger.

Reza screamed as the weapon pinned him to the stone like a butterfly on a pin. The blade pierced his right side up to the hilt, the tip burying itself in the ancient stone behind him. His concentration shattered, he dropped the shrekka.

On the dais, the talons of Tesh-Dar's hands cut the stone banister upon which she had been leaning, and her heart leapt to her throat. "No," she whispered to herself.

She did not notice as the Empress glanced her way.

Rigah-Lu'orh regarded Reza as he writhed in pain, twisting around the blade as he reached in vain for the sword on the ground at his feet. Around her, the air was silent except for the thunder of the heartbeats of those gathered to watch. She turned around and saluted the Empress. Receiving a nod in return, the young warrior detached her own remaining shrekka and turned to Reza. He was watching her now, but the look on his face was not one of defeat, but of defiance. With a wail of fury, she cast the shrekka at his heart.

Reza was in a kind of agony he had never experienced before. It was not the agony of physical pain – he could no longer feel the metal burning in his side – but of emotional and psychic overload. The Bloodsong was so strong now, stronger than it had ever been, that he felt about to explode. His eyes were fixed on Rigah-Lu'orh. Even before she reached for the shrekka, he knew what she was about to do.

"It must not end this way," he hissed at himself, his voice lost in the maddening cacophony of fire in his skull and the flames that burned in every cell of his body. "*It cannot...*"

Rigah-Lu'orh watched in amazement as her shrekka struck the stone pillar on which Reza had been impaled. The weapon shattered uselessly against the rock, a prelude to the roar of surprise that rose from the watching multitude.

Reza was gone, vanished.

The Empress leaned forward, eyes wide in amazement and swift acceptance of what She had seen, what She now felt stirring in the fabric of the Way.

Beside Her, Tesh-Dar gasped in surprise as she saw Reza's body vanish, leaving behind only the shimmering air of a desert mirage. As her eyes beheld the spectacle, her blood suddenly burned with a surge of power that struck her like a reflected shock wave. In that instant, she knew. If he demonstrated the will and the wisdom required of what was to come, what must come, the Ancient Ones would protect him, as they would Esah-Zhurah. Both had proved themselves worthy of one another and of the Way, and the Ancient Ones could give them powers that Tesh-Dar had studied her entire life to master. And more. What the peers were witnessing now was only the beginning.

"And so is The Prophecy fulfilled," the Empress murmured wonderingly. She closed Her eyes and listened to the song of Reza's soul as it danced through the darkness beyond time, waiting to return to the bloodied sands before Her and claim his final victory.

Rigah-Lu'orh whirled around in search of her vanished opponent, but he was nowhere to be seen. "Where has he gone?" she cried angrily, feeling cheated of her triumph. "What kind of trick is–"

A brush of air against her back, like the tiniest of zephyrs, was the only warning she had before Reza's armored body slammed into hers, carrying them both to the ground.

As they fell to the sands of the arena, Reza was clamped tightly to her back, trying to reach his arms around her neck for a chokehold. Securing his grip, he applied pressure, but Rigah-Lu'orh made no attempt to resist him.

Then he saw why. The other short sword she had been holding, waiting for his attack, was now protruding from her back, pointing like a bloody finger at the sky above. Totally surprised by Reza's attack, she had fallen on her own weapon. Only by a narrow margin had it missed piercing his own armor over his vulnerable heart.

The arena went silent after a collective gasp of surprise.

Reza lay atop Rigah-Lu'orh's lifeless body for what seemed like a long time, fading in and out of consciousness. Finally, realizing that he still had one last duty to perform before joining her in death, he struggled to his knees. Crawling across the sand like a dying crab, he gathered up the sword that bore his name and began the long trek toward the dais where the Empress and Tesh-Dar awaited him.

He finally brushed against the stone stairs that led up to the dais. With a groan of effort, he got to his knees and peered up with one sparkling green eye, the other now scarlet and blind.

"May this one forever dwell in Thy light, my Empress," he rasped for what seemed like the hundredth time this day, blood from his punctured lung trickling from his lips, "for in Thy name... did she follow the Way."

"And so may it always be," Tesh-Dar finished from the step above, having come down from the dais to meet him. The few warriors within earshot of Reza's weak voice were still muted by shock.

Reza slid forward, his broken hand hanging useless at his side as his good hand held onto the grip of the great and battered sword for support, the point of the weapon's blade buried deep in the sand under his weight.

"My priestess," he whispered, tilting the weapon toward her in invitation as he slumped toward the ground, "let it be finished." Letting go of the weapon, he waited for her to complete the experiment begun so long ago; nicked and scarred as it was, in Tesh-Dar's hands the sword would still make quick work of his neck, and the story would be finished.

But the expected blow never came. Instead, Reza felt hands gently touching his face, and he found himself staring into the eyes of the Empress. It was a privilege very few had been granted over the ages.

"In My name have you fought and suffered," She said, Her words barely audible as his body lapsed into shock, "and in My name shall you live. When you awaken, you shall be as one with My children."

As Reza collapsed into the sovereign's arms, Tesh-Dar heard the eternal whispers of the Ancient Ones stir in her bones. With life granted to Reza and Esah-Zhurah, they had broken the silence of their spiritual vigil.

The blood that would break the curse of their people had at last been found.

* * *

"I would not have believed it, had I not witnessed it with My Own eyes," the Empress said. She watched as the healers hovered over Reza and Esah-Zhurah, anointing their bodies with healing gel. They applied it carefully to the wounds in Reza's chest, and the Empress watched their hands brush the gleaming black metal of the Collar of Honor that now hung around his neck. When he awoke, he would no longer be an Outsider. He was Hers, now. "To vanish before an enemy, and then to reappear as he did is a feat known only to the ancient orders, such as your own. Never has a tresh done such a thing, in all the time since She... Keel-Tath left us. Never."

"He has been given a tremendous gift," Tesh-Dar acknowledged, kneeling beside Her. "Her blood gave voice to the song of his spirit, and the Ancient Ones have given him the power to use it." She lowered her head. "And I would give him the knowledge, if you would bless it, my Empress."

"You would accept him as your successor, and teach him the ways of the Desh-Ka?" The sovereign considered the thought for a moment before she answered. "Many firsts has this day brought upon us, Tesh-Dar," She said quietly. "I can see no reason to deny yet another. And, should you wish it, I give my blessing to the daughter of My Own blood; she is yours, as well."

Tesh-Dar lowered her head to her chest in gratitude. In all the thousands of generations of warriors who had worn the order's rune upon their necks, never had a priestess been given such an honor as to bring more than a single disciple into the fold of the Desh-Ka as a priestess... or a priest. Had she been capable of tears, she would have wept with love and pride.

"In Thy name," she whispered huskily, "it shall be so."

Sixteen

When Reza awoke from the curing sleep induced by the healers, he was immediately aware of something cool and sleek around his neck. His probing hands found not the rough steel band of a slave that he had worn since childhood, but the Collar of Honor, made of living steel attuned to his body, and half a dozen pendants. Five inscribed his name, with the glittering runes poised relative to each other, as were the Five Stars in the night sky. The last pendant proclaimed him the victor in his final Challenge, an honor made all the greater because it had been fought to the death. It was an honor to which precious few warriors could lay claim.

The week that followed was one of quiet but intense celebration. In pairs and threes, sometimes singly, the tresh made their way to his bedside to pay their respects with a salute on bended knee. There was no mockery here, no false pretenses. Their sincerity was as real as the sound of their fists hammering against their breastplates as they knelt beside him. He was a part of them now, and they felt and accepted the new voice that sang in the choir of their souls as one of their own.

Beside him, Esah-Zhurah recovered quickly, the horrible wounds in her back fading into oblivion under the care of the healers, leaving not even the smallest scar in their wake.

As they both healed, they lay quietly together, saying little except when the priestess paid them a visit to check on their progress. At night, when the healers had retired for the evening, they held each other close, but they did not make love. The spirit was willing, but the flesh was yet weak.

They had time now.

They could wait.

* * *

"The priestess would see you, Reza, Esah-Zhurah," the young tresh announced as she knelt and saluted. The two who stood before her – both Kreelan, now – were no longer tresh. The Seventh Challenge was the demarcation line between the learning cycle begun in the Nurseries and the beginning of one's true service to the Empire. Esah-Zhurah and Reza were now warriors.

"Thank you, Te'ira-Khan," Reza replied. "We shall come at once."

As the young tresh trotted away, Reza appraised Esah-Zhurah with a raised eyebrow. It was a gesture she had once tried to imitate to humor him, but the ridge of solid horn that served as her own eyebrows was entirely immobile. Instead, she had stuck out her tongue.

"An assignment?" he asked.

"Possibly," she replied, walking beside him as they made their way toward the priestess's quarters. She knew how much Reza wanted to begin his service. Night after night, as they lay close to one another in the infirmary, he spoke to her about his hopes and dreams. Of venturing into the wastelands in search of the unknown, of traveling to the stars of the frontier, of spending endless days in the halls that held the Books of Time to learn of his adopted culture and of so many other things.

And each night she was warmed by her dreams and by his gentle touch. She knew that she would take him to see the stars. But her hopes stood on a trembling foundation of fear, for she dreaded the possibility of their separation. At no time since the death of the First Empress had tresh been assured of serving together. Some did by a twist of fate, but most spent their entire lives separated one from the other, to live, serve, and die in Her name without the comfort of the companion with whom they had shared most of their young lives.

She had no way of knowing that the Empress had expressly forbidden their separation in service. It was not an act of charity on Her part; She was simply doing what She could to ensure that The Prophecy would be fulfilled. Neither Esah-Zhurah nor Reza knew of their role in the fate of the Empire, nor would they until the time came that such knowledge was necessary. For now, only Tesh-Dar, the Empress, and a handful of others truly understood. In any case, the Empress was determined that wherever the Way took them, they would go together.

But Esah-Zhurah did not have this knowledge from which to draw reassurance as they entered the priestess's quarters. They could easily be ordered to opposite ends of the galaxy. Esah-Zhurah's heart trembled.

They found Tesh-Dar alone, waiting for them. After paying their respects with a salute, they knelt before her.

"The time has come for you both to make a decision," she told them. "You have completed your obligatory training here, and are within your rights to claim your entry into service of the Empire. But I ask you to consider another option."

"What other is there?" Reza asked, puzzled.

"I wish you both to accept the ways and powers of the Desh-Ka," she told him, "to become members of my order." Reza and Esah-Zhurah both gaped at her in shocked amazement.

"For as long as our people have walked the Way," Tesh-Dar told them, "the ancient orders have preserved and strengthened the Empire with their blood and skills. The priestesses have led their children in battle, and in their twilight years have taught the young ones the fundaments of the Way, as I have taught you.

"And for the service that we render unto Her, we are given one right that no other – even the Empress – is granted: we may choose our own successors, those to whom we would pass the stewardship of the order. It is a thing we may do only once in our lifetime, for when the torch is passed, no longer do the powers we shepherd dwell within us. We are left as we were as young tresh, but older, waiting for Death's embrace. It is the greatest gift we may give, but it is still a gift; no one may force you to take it, and you must be sure in your heart that it is what you desire. It is a responsibility and a burden only for the most worthy and dedicated of warriors.

"Tradition demands that a priestess pass her legacy on to only one other. My order, the most ancient of all, predating even the First Empress, has only one keeper remaining: myself. Of all the young warriors I have seen in my many cycles, you are the most deserving, but not one over the other. Together have you loved and suffered; together may you receive my offering, as the Empress has granted."

Reza and Esah-Zhurah were silent for but a moment. But when they spoke, it was with a single voice. "We accept, my priestess," they said, their lips moving in unison.

Tesh-Dar felt a tiny bit of tension fall from her shoulders. This was the last and, in some ways, the most important of her duties to the Empress. The ways of the Desh-Ka would not die with her, and these children, who had yet to realize their own importance to the Empire's future, would be much better equipped to survive the rigors of the Way. For survive they must, she thought to herself. "It is done, then," she said quietly. "Gather your things and say your farewells, for we shall be leaving on the morrow, and shall not be returning to this place."

* * *

Reza walked slowly, his arm held out in support of the ancient woman who shuffled beside him. Overhead, the Empress Moon glowed warmly, lighting the sky with its emerald light, illuminating the path before them. The kazha was quiet, most of the tresh having retired for the evening after reviewing the day's lessons and having their evening meal. The only sounds came from the stables, where a handful of tresh were preparing several beasts for the long journey that lay ahead for the priestess and her two disciples.

"Proud am I of you, young one," Pan'ne-Sharakh said in her raspy voice. "Far shall you go upon the Way, and well shall it be for those who tread in your footsteps."

"Thank you, mistress," Reza said, humbled by her words. "But I am saddened greatly by leaving you behind. More than any other, you have shown me kindness. You have left me with a debt I can never repay."

Pan'ne-Sharakh patted him on the arm. "You are one with us, child," she said. "That is payment a thousand-fold over anything you received from this living relic. The blood of the chosen flows in your veins, and great glory shall you bring to the Empress, you and your tresh." She leaned a bit closer. "Your mate."

She paused for a moment, thinking. "I only regret that my Way comes to an end, for I would have liked to craft the first set of armor for your children."

Reza stopped in his tracks. "But, mistress... Esah-Zhurah was born of the silver claw," he said quietly. "She is barren."

Pan'ne-Sharakh looked at him blankly with her blind eyes, an unsure look on her face. Then she blinked, and her features turned downward into a frown. "The truth do you speak," she said, as if acknowledging an argument that carried the superior weight of logic. "This, I had forgotten. Such is the trouble with age." She continued to shuffle along, and Reza had to take an extra large stride to regain his place next to her. "But the dream remains. And perhaps..."

"Perhaps what?" Reza chided her gently. "This, even the Empress cannot change."

Pan'ne-Sharakh looked at him sharply. "The powers of the Empress are legion, child," she told him, "and you would do well to never underestimate Her strengths. She presides over the world of the living and the dead, and is forever stronger than all the priestesses who have ever set foot upon the Way. I, an old mistress who long has served Her, know not what will come to pass for you and Esah-Zhurah, for the future and Her desires are far beyond my sight. But Her will is the river that carves the Way from the rock of Time, and it shall not be denied. It shall not."

Reza knew that the old woman spoke the truth, but what Pan'ne-Sharakh had implied was simply too much to hope for. He had lived a life of shattered dreams and hopes, but had at last found a home and a love that could carry his spirit forever, and he dared not ask any more of Fate. He consciously pushed her words from his mind. He was content with what he had.

When they reached the overlook to the valley, Pan'ne-Sharakh sat down on one of the stone benches with a heavy sigh, beckoning Reza to take a seat beside her.

"Tired am I," she said softly as she sat, her head slumped forward as she waited to catch her breath.

After a moment, she looked up at Reza. "Something I have for you." Reaching into her robe, she extracted a leather box that looked about the size and shape to hold a small dinner plate, or perhaps a shallow bowl, about as big across as Reza's hand spread wide. Handing it to Reza, she said, "Long have I worked upon this, in hopes that this day would come. Many hours have I spent in the great halls, poring through the Books of Time. I knew that which I sought existed, but I had to be sure, to find a record of it. And so I did," she finished with the impish smile that he had come to know so well.

"What is it?" Reza held the box carefully in his hands, almost afraid to know what lay within.

"Open it, child, and see."

Reza undid the clasp, which itself was ornately decorated with silver and gold, and slowly lifted the lid. "Oh, mistress..." he breathed.

Inside, surrounded by the softest black felt lining, lay a tiara the likes of which Reza had never seen. Black it was, with mystifying swirls of color that were ever-changing under the light of the moon and stars. Its edges were crowned with gold inlaid into the dark metal, and as Reza held it up, he could just see the tiny runes that made up an ancient prayer to the Empress in the Old Tongue, which he had not yet been taught. And in the crown of the tiara were two sets of the Five Stars displaying the names of Esah-Zhurah and Reza in diamonds against emerald sunbursts. He held it in shaking hands, wondering at the time Pan'ne-Sharakh must have spent in creating it, hunched down over her worktables, her dying eyes lending what aid they could to her nimble fingers. She had known this day might come. Somehow, she had known.

"A custom it was, long ago," Pan'ne-Sharakh explained quietly, her voice barely a whisper, "for the suitor of a warrior priestess to present her such a gift, in the days when suitors were to be found. Thus speak the legends of the time." She placed a gentle hand on his. "When upon your collars is inscribed the rune of the Desh-Ka, then will be the time to give it to her, and she may wear it with the Empress's blessing. It is the last work I shall do in Her name, my child, and in my heart I know it is my best. It is my gift to you and your mate."

She paused, and Reza felt her hand squeeze his tightly. "May thy Way be long and glorious, my child."

He turned just in time to catch her as she slumped forward, a soft sigh escaping from her lips. As he held her he saw that her eyes were closed, her face serene. In his heart, Reza felt a slight change in the spiritual chorus that had become a cherished part of him in these last days: the trembling of a single spirit crossing the threshold from this life into what lay beyond.

Pan'ne-Sharakh was dead.

* * *

"We are nearly there," Tesh-Dar said as she halted, pointing out the overhang that jutted from a peak high above. Atop it was perched a large structure that overlooked all but the snow-capped ridge above.

Thirty-four days had passed since they had laid Pan'ne-Sharakh's body on the funeral pyre and departed the kazha, and their travels had taken them farther than Reza had ever been on this world, or any other. The journey had been a long but uneventful one, the caravan of three warriors and their half dozen animals making its way through the great forests west of the city and into the mountains that lay beyond.

"We shall be there before sunset," the priestess told them before urging her magthep forward along the rough trail. The ancient path was barely visible, so overgrown was it with clinging vines and ferns. It suddenly occurred to Reza as he guided his beast upward that the trail had not been used in a very long time: a young warrior named Tesh-Dar had been the last to go this way before them, nearly two hundred human years before.

At last the magtheps struggled to the top, their chests laboring in grunting heaves as they sought to leach more oxygen from the thin atmosphere.

Reza, too, suddenly felt his breath stolen away, but not from the thin air. As they topped the last rise to the overhanging plateau, the temple – barely visible from the trail up the mountain – suddenly came into full view.

It was an enormous complex of structures, the largest greater in size than even the great amphitheater in the city far behind them. The buildings had been hewn of a hard green stone that had once boasted beautiful ornate carvings of warriors engaged in battle, but now were worn with age, the green faded by countless millennia of sun and storm, the carvings dulled to illegibility. The arenas had not been the simple rings lined with stone pillars that he had come to know so well; they had been elliptical domed structures of various sizes, each apparently tailored to suit a particular function, although he could not imagine what. In its day it must have been a place of indescribable magnificence. But the temple had fallen into ruin with the inexorable march of time and all it entails, and there was no longer a host to maintain it.

"Long has it been since the stone was cut from the mountains," the priestess told them in wonder and awe, "and harsh has Time been upon its ancient skin. But the temple still stands, as I pray it shall for all time. For this is where my ancestors learned the Way, and this is where it is reborn in the spirits of Her children."

With mounting anticipation, Reza and Esah-Zhurah stripped the magtheps of their harnesses and provisions for the return trip to the city, stashing them in a stone cellar that Tesh-Dar somehow opened. Once the priestess closed the enormous doors with little more than a wave of her hand, no animal would ever be able to gain entrance to sample the food they had brought to sustain them.

The priestess led them inside the only building that had been left standing intact, an enormous dome that resembled an enclosed coliseum. They entered through an ancient wooden door, thicker than Reza was tall. Yet it yielded easily to Tesh-Dar's touch, moving aside as if pulled from within.

They entered into a chamber of utter darkness.

"Wait," the priestess ordered. Reza felt more than heard her move off into the blackness. He exchanged a glance with Esah-Zhurah, who only gave the Kreelan equivalent of a shrug, her head tilting just so to one side. They waited silently.

Suddenly, a warm glow arose from ahead of them, and soon they stood bathed in a gentle light that seemed to be coming from the walls themselves.

"Come," commanded the priestess's voice from beyond the end of the corridor in which they stood. They moved forward quietly, their footsteps echoing softly. Their eyes roved the walls and ceiling, taking in the ornate beauty that lay in the carvings there, untouched by the ravages of time. This part of the temple, at least, still lived on.

They found Tesh-Dar standing atop the central dais, although this one was as much a thing of beauty as it was utilitarian, the decay that was so evident outside utterly absent within. The dome crested far above her, seemingly much higher than the building should have allowed, disappearing into darkness as deep as the night sky. Around the great arena lay thin windows that curved gracefully from near the ground toward the apex. Seven doorways, each appearing to have aged not a year since they were made, stood at equal intervals around the arena.

The priestess gestured to one of the semicircular stone pads that encircled the dais and bade them to kneel.

"This place has been the home of the Desh-Ka since before the days of Keel-Tath, before the changes that altered the destiny of our people," the priestess said in a distant voice. Her eyes were on her two acolytes, but her mind lay very far away. "This is one of the five birthplaces of what we know as the Way, built by our hands untold centuries ago, and where the first ritual bonding was performed. The temple lies in ruins, but its spirit lives still.

"I have brought you here to teach you the Old Ways, the ways which were passed on to me by my priestess, many cycles ago. Many have been my disciples since my coming to teach the Way, but I have not found any worthy of this place, save you who now kneel before me." She paused. "In accordance with tradition, I may pass on my knowledge to only one who follows me, but because you are as one in your hearts, both shall learn. So has She willed.

"But I beg that you learn well, my children," she said, her voice a soft, sad command, "for I may not pass this way again." She nodded at the corridor from which they had come. "Once more will I step through those doors into the sunlight beyond, and then will I be forever barred from returning here." She gazed upon them each in turn. "Having accepted the legacy I am about to bestow upon you, you will be the keepers of the keys to the knowledge that was born and lives in this place. Should you survive what is to come, you also shall someday have the honor of passing on what you will learn here to another. Do you have any questions of me?"

Reza and Esah-Zhurah signed no, they did not.

"Then let us begin," Tesh-Dar commanded.

* * *

In his dream – if it indeed was a dream – the three knelt in a tight circle upon the dais. To Reza's right was Tesh-Dar, her eyes closed in meditation. To his left, he found Esah-Zhurah staring at him, wide eyed. When he ran a hand across his cheek, he found not the smooth skin to which he was long accustomed, but a full beard that flowed in a brown and gray cascade to his waist. Looking more closely at his hands, he saw that they were stronger than in his youth, yet weathered and aged.

Esah-Zhurah, too, had changed. Her face and the skin along her body not covered by her armor bore more scars than he remembered. Each of them had come to know the other's body with surgical intimacy, their hands and fingers cataloging the other's skin each night in a ritual of the tresh, coming to know their bodies well since long before they had become lovers. But the most striking thing was her hair. The braids, coiled neatly at her side, were much longer now than they had been when they had first entered the temple.

For if all was as it seemed, they had been here, in the temple, for at least ten great cycles: twenty-five years or more, as measured by the human calendar.

As he turned to the priestess, to ask her what magic this was, his skin prickled with a knowing sensation that had been cultivated in him for many years, but that suddenly seemed so much more powerful than he had ever known. It was a sense of premonition and understanding that existed independent of its subject, as if he were able to grasp the plot of a book without ever actually having read it. The sensation told him that they were not alone. In the darkness that fell like a velvet curtain just beyond the dais, Reza could see shadows of regular outline. Occasional glimmers of gold and platinum and ruby caught his eye, and he instantly recognized the pendants that hung from around the necks of the phantoms arrayed beyond the glowing amber light thrown down upon the dais from high above. As he became more accustomed to them, they became more real, their existence more of substance than imagination. In only a few moments, he saw them – all of them – clearly in his mind, even while his eyes were still blind in the darkness. Thousands, tens of thousands of them were gathered around, kneeling, waiting. Reza instinctively understood what – whom – he was seeing. These were the spirits of the Ancient Ones who had once bound themselves in blood to this place, those who wore the peculiar rune that adorned Tesh-Dar's collar, and who had died fulfilling Her will on the long journey that was the Way of the Empire.

"It is time, my children," Tesh-Dar whispered.

As if with a will of their own, Reza's hands extended outward, palms up, to Tesh-Dar.

Esah-Zhurah did the same, a look of serene anticipation on her face. Like Reza, she was aware that much time had passed in what seemed like the blink of an eye. But she also knew that she was ready, although for what, she did not quite remember, nor did she care to try. It had been a dream time, when great secrets had been revealed, and many Challenges fought, but which the conscious mind was not yet prepared to recall. It would take time to learn, she knew. Time to understand, to become something new...

Tesh-Dar held aloft a knife whose blade bore the markings of the First Empress in the Old Tongue. Reza's eyes widened at the knowledge that he understood what the symbols meant: during the years they seemed to have lost, he had been taught that arcane but revered language, and could only guess at what other knowledge now lay hidden in his mind.

"In the name of The One Who first blessed us," Tesh-Dar was saying, "and All Who have come after, do we accept Thee," Tesh-Dar intoned in the Old Tongue, its lilt and measure pleasing to Reza's ears. She drew the knife across each of Reza's palms, then Esah-Zhurah's. Finally, she forced the blade into her own palms before placing the knife into a waiting hand that had appeared from the darkness, and that vanished as mysteriously as it had come.

The three of them joined hands, and Reza felt an electric surge flow through him, a fierce tingling sensation – much like what he had experienced with Esah-Zhurah when they had shared blood, but so much stronger – pulsing up his arms in fiery waves.

As he watched Tesh-Dar's face, he felt the dais tremble, and suddenly its center seemed to drop away to infinity, leaving behind a circular abyss that stared at them like a sightless eye. The trembling continued, and suddenly a circular pillar began to rise from the abyss before him, within the triangle formed by their outstretched arms and joined hands. Slowly, as if its weight was an enormous burden for whatever force propelled it, the pillar arose from the pit, stopping as it reached the level of Reza's eyes. Beneath them, the trembling ceased.

The tingling in Reza's arms had become almost painful now, as if jolts of energy were striking his nerves like tiny, ferocious needles. Reza looked at Esah-Zhurah, wondering if it was having the same effect upon her.

But Esah-Zhurah's attention was focused on something far above, and Reza followed her openmouthed stare toward the dome's dark ceiling. A pinpoint of electric blue fire was hurtling down at them like a comet, and Reza knew that it was coming from much farther away than the ancient dome's ceiling could have allowed. He suddenly felt heat upon his face, and knew that the shooting star was about to strike. He tried to cover his face with his hands, but they were beyond his control, locked in a clasp of bonding that was unbreakable by any mere physical force. As the heat became unbearable, and his ears were about to burst from the hellish roaring, Reza opened his mouth to scream–

There it sat, cupped by the precisely made hollow in the top of the extended pillar. Reza stared at the glowing gem, the scream caught in his throat. Slightly larger than his own head, it was shaped roughly like a teardrop, and glowed like a blue flame. Gradually, he became aware of Esah-Zhurah and the priestess. The three of them still held hands. The circle had not been broken.

"In Her light are all things purified, are all things made new," the priestess said, looking first at Reza, then Esah-Zhurah. "And so shall it be this day, my children." She looked upward, and Reza saw that there was now a circular opening in the dome above them, and that streaks of sunlight pierced the darkness of the great arena to form a circle of light just to one side of the dais. "When the light of Her sun strikes the Crystal of Souls, we shall be changed forever. Much pain shall you bear, for what cleanses best of all is fire, and Her fire shall blaze within every cell of your body. Death may come; there is no guarantee of life. But if life finds you afterward, forever changed shall you be in body and soul, crafted to Her will. The strength of ten and talons of ebony did I inherit many cycles ago, when I endured the pain of the crystal. The wonders of The Change are impossible to predict, but I wish no lesser gifts for you, my children. For when you again awaken, you shall be the standard-bearers of the Desh-Ka, and it shall be my honor to teach and serve you for the remainder of my days." She looked at the rapidly advancing pool of light, focused by the great dome as if it was a magnifying glass, now just touching the crystal's sparkling facets. "Soon, now, the Crystal of Souls shall shine. Do not avert your eyes from its fire, do not cry out in pain from the touch of its light, or death will take you swiftly. For in its light lies Her light. In its fire lies Her touch. So has it ever been, so shall it always be. In Her name, let it be so."

The sunlight rapidly swept over the dais toward the crystal. Reza watched, fascinated, as the light seemed to be drawn into the enormous gem; the pool of light that had existed only a moment ago beside the dais had now become a cone focused precisely on the crystal. The hair on the nape of his neck stood to attention, and he felt as if he were standing on a spot about to be struck by lightning. The electric pulses through his joined palms were suddenly overshadowed by a charge that seemed ready to strike his entire body.

And then the crystal exploded with a light that first consumed the pillar on which it stood, a blazing cyan cone that slowly swept upward and outward toward the three joined warriors surrounding it, filling the air with the smell of scorched stone and ozone.

Reza watched as the blue flame crept toward him, eating up the stone floor that separated the light from his knees. The desire to flee was tremendous, but one look into Esah-Zhurah's eyes was all he needed to redouble his courage. She needed him, needed his courage in addition to her own. They needed each other. Forcing himself to be strong, he gripped her hand tighter and held his eyes steadily on the advancing fan of light.

When it touched him, it was all he could do to keep from screaming. Never had he felt such searing agony as when the light crept upon his knees. He felt as if every cell in the flesh touched by it was exploding into flame. Tears flooded from his eyes, but his mouth remained clamped shut, his voice still. Beside him, Esah-Zhurah and Tesh-Dar also fought against writhing in the pain that was enveloping them, and all three of them used all the control they had ever mastered to keep their eyes upon the blazing crystal.

Faster and faster did the light sweep upward over their bodies, consuming them with the agony of burning flesh. Reza felt himself toppling over the edge of sanity, the light having consumed his body below his neck like a ravenous predator. As his bulging eyes fixed one last time upon the crystal, his last conscious effort to follow Tesh-Dar's command, the flame swept over them, and the world disappeared in an explosion of cyan.

* * *

Somewhere, deep in the infinite labyrinth of neurons, an electrochemical impulse burst across the chasm that was the synapse. The command instruction that it evoked followed a journey that would take it far from its birthplace. Slowly, very slowly, more synapses began to fire, discharging their energy in the infinite darkness of the surrounding tissue, carrying their messages into the unknown wilderness.

Far away, after traveling a lifetime, the first impulse was received by a receptor that decoded the messenger's instruction and issued a command of its own. Nearby, a muscle fiber twitched feverishly, contracting as hard as it could, the only way it understood to respond to the nerve's command.

More nerves in the area received the frenzied, sporadic impulses from the Command Center, immediately issuing their own instructions to their subordinate muscle fibers. Hundreds, then thousands, then tens of thousands of the tiny fibers were called to action by the desperate rain of impulses from the Command Center, ordering the muscles around them to contract... *contract*...

A finger twitched. The effort had been Herculean, temporarily exhausting many fibers, damaging a few. But the Command Center was not content with such sacrifices; it demanded more. The darkest recesses of the entity that controlled all within its Universe were slowly alighting. A cascade of impulses exploded along the neural pathways that led away to its lieutenants, associates in life whom it controlled and brought to its will, but who in turn kept it alive in a miraculous symbiosis. Millions upon millions of messages were encoded and dispatched, received and decoded. Slowly did the Command Center come to grips with the status of its domain, and as new information was received, more messengers were sent forth: more commands, more demands for information. The Command Center was not the least bit hesitant to use the authority granted it by nature, and it had an insatiable appetite for information.

Over and over was the cycle repeated, and gradually, within the lifetimes of only a few million of the cells under its unquestioned authority, the Command Center was satisfied that all was prepared for the next step on its programmatic cycle. Under a barrage of impulses, the great gathering of special muscle fibers that was the heart contracted, then released. Another barrage of impulses was rewarded with a second beat, then a third. As the heart warmed to its work, the Command Center allocated the supervision of this most vital of tasks to a subaltern within itself. Thus, it freed the remainder of its resources to concentrate on reviving the many other organs of The Body.

It would be some time yet before the Command Center would begin to apportion effort to analyze the unaccustomed condition from which it had recently emerged. In its haste to make The Body serviceable again, it did not notice, nor pause to contemplate, the changes that had taken place within the living quilt of its domain.

In the meantime, Reza began to breathe.

* * *

"Reza."

He blinked, then opened his eyes fully. Tesh-Dar's face was close to his, her hands on his shoulders.

"Yes, priestess," he murmured. His face tingled, the muscles tight as if he had been forced to hold a smile for several hours on end. The rest of his body was the same, tingling and burning at the same time, his nerves feeling as if someone had tried to electrocute him. And had very nearly succeeded.

Looking up at Tesh-Dar, he saw the traces of a similar level of discomfort. Her eyes, normally clear and sharp as silver-flecked diamonds, wore a glassy cast that made them look almost hazy, slightly opaque.

"Esah-Zhurah?" he asked, allowing Tesh-Dar to help him to his knees. Neither his balance nor hers would allow them to stand up all the way.

"I do not know," she breathed, winded from the effort. Her hands trembled as they touched him. Together, they crawled around the pillar, empty now of the strange blue crystal, to find Esah-Zhurah sprawled upon the far side of the dais.

"Esah-Zhurah?" Reza called her name several times with mounting urgency as he cradled her head in his hands. He felt behind her ear for a pulse, but his own fingers betrayed him: his sense of touch was still virtually useless. He fumbled with her breastplate, trying to get it off so he could listen to her heart. His fingers turned black with the carbon of the scorched metal and burned leatherite, both so resilient that only the heat of white-hot coals could affect them. Out of frustration he simply tore the plate from its weakened bindings, brute strength prevailing where simple procedure had failed. He brushed the remnants of the undergarment – like the armor, burned to ashes – to find her skin unmarred, pristine, without a single scar of the many combats she had fought. Kneeling down, he put his ear to her breast and listened intently. After a terrifying moment of silence, he was granted with a slow *lub-dub*. Then another. And another. "Her heart beats," he whispered. And as he did, her chest rose gently as her lungs pulled in a shallow draught of air. "She is alive."

Only then did he notice what had become of the collar she wore. In its center, over her throat, was affixed one of the sparkling eyestones they had taken from the genoth they had killed. The scale had been meticulously polished and shaped into a precise oval. And on its face was carved the ancient rune of the Desh-Ka. He felt his own throat, and his numbed fingers told him enough to know that he wore the stone's companion.

"Priestess," he murmured, "how is this possible?"

But Tesh-Dar did not hear him. She was holding one of Esah-Zhurah's hands in hers, staring at it with a look of awe.

"What is it?" Reza asked, suddenly worried that something was not right.

"Her talons," Tesh-Dar whispered, turning Esah-Zhurah's hand so that Reza could better see it in the soft light that now permeated the great dome like a gentle mist from the sea. Instead of gleaming silver, her talons now shone a fiery red, a bright crimson the color of oxygenated blood.

"Is there something wrong with them?" he asked worriedly. "Are there not talons only of silver and of black?"

"Now, in these times, this is so," she answered cryptically. "But long ago..."

Tesh-Dar did not have time to finish her answer before Esah-Zhurah's lips moved and she called out in a weak, strangled voice, "Reza."

"I am here," he told her, running his hand over her forehead to comfort her.

Beside him, Tesh-Dar reluctantly released Esah-Zhurah's hand. But the image of the crimson talons stayed in her mind. Only one such aberration had been known throughout the Empire's meticulously recorded history, and the significance of their emergence in Esah-Zhurah from The Change could hardly be coincidence. As she turned her attention to her adopted daughter, her mind was cast into a whirlwind of possibilities.

And then Esah-Zhurah opened her eyes. They wandered aimlessly for a moment before fixing on Reza's shocked face. "What... what is it?" she whispered weakly. "At what are you staring?"

"Your eyes, child," Tesh-Dar answered for him, her voice filled with awed wonder. "They are green, now. Green as your mate's. Another gift of The Change."

Esah-Zhurah brought a hand to her face, as if her fingertips could themselves see color, could take the measure of what the others saw in her eyes. Then she reached out to Reza, who took her hand gently and held it to his lips.

"It is true," he told her, amazed at how brilliant the jade green of her irises was against the cobalt blue of her skin, even as he marveled at the fact that the beard he had grown in his dream – or had it been real? – was now gone.

"And what of me?" Reza asked, curious that there seemed to be no outward differences such as his mate's. "I assume I do not look different, nor do I feel changed in any way."

"The Change is often very subtle," the priestess told him, leaning back against the pillar to rest. The crystal's flame had left her with little strength, and she knew that her days of glory on the field of battle were over. She had given up much of what she was to her inheritors, and would never again tap the Herculean strength and most of her ancient powers that she had accepted from her own priestess; these powers were now in the custody of the two young warriors before her. "The changes in the body are sometimes obvious, sometimes not. Only time will tell of that. But the greatest changes lie within your souls and minds, yet shrouded in unknowing. It will be my duty from this day on to teach you both of your inheritance, to use it wisely and well. This I shall do until the end of my days, in my last service to Her. And someday, you will do the same for another, that the ways of the Desh-Ka may continue unbroken."

* * *

Reza lay awake, thinking. Hours uncounted, unnoticed, had passed since the crystal had worked its strange miracle upon them. Shortly after Esah-Zhurah had revived, the priestess had fallen into a deep, exhausted sleep. Her two adopted children worried over her for some time, concerned that all might not be well. But the priestess breathed steadily, if ever so slowly, and they could sense that her blood still sang, though not as strongly as before. The Change had greatly weakened her, but she had many cycles yet to live.

After making sure she was well, they turned their attention to one another. Quietly, so as not to awaken the priestess, they made love, the lingering numbness in their bodies from the crystal's fire fleeing before the heat of passion that set their flesh aflame yet again. The need to be quiet only served to heighten their passion, and Esah-Zhurah's involuntary cries were spent muffled against Reza's chest.

Some hours later, Reza lay awake as Esah-Zhurah slept with her back cradled against his chest. He pulled her slightly closer to him, and she moaned softly in her sleep. He wondered at all that had transpired since they had entered the dome. He had remembered the image of his great beard and their outgrown hair, signs that many years had passed. He and Esah-Zhurah had discussed this as the priestess slept, but there had only been one way to be sure. The two of them had found the door through which they had entered the temple. It yielded easily to their touch. In the world beyond the doorway they found that only an hour or so had passed from the time of their arrival. The magtheps grazed in the same spot in which they had been left, their grazing trail easily gauged. The sun's glow had given way to a brilliant twilight that colored the great mountains with violet and orange rivers. Above, the Empress Moon had just risen, about to take its rightful place among the Five Stars.

Now, lying next to Esah-Zhurah, he thought again of the Empress Moon as it rose above the mountains and of the priestess's last words before she had fallen silent with sleep.

"Tomorrow," she had said, "we must go before the Empress. You have both come of age as warriors, and accepted the ways of the Desh-Ka. It is now time for you to hear Her will, and to seek the next step of your Way."

Listening in wonder to the vast chorus of voices that now sang within him, voices that he now understood, Reza waited for the dawn.

* * *

The next day passed in a whirlwind of activity. When they made their way out of the temple, a shuttle was already waiting for them, perched precariously on the cliff like a peregrine clutching to a limb. Reza had been frightened at first, for he had not seen such advanced technology since his boyhood, and the memories he had of such things were not pleasant ones. But the comfort of Esah-Zhurah's guiding hand overrode his fears, and in but a few minutes they found themselves within the palace. There they were fed and their scorched armor replaced before they were shown to the Empress.

"The Empress would see you now," a warrior announced to Tesh-Dar, bowing deeply as she did so.

It was time.

The trio followed the warrior to where the Empress waited, standing among the very trees and flowers where she and Tesh-Dar had once discussed Reza's fate. They knelt in greeting and rendered the salute of respect to their sovereign.

Acknowledging their presence with Her gaze, She first spoke to Reza.

"*My son*," She said softly. "My son. So wondrous a feeling is it to speak those words, for they have not passed the lips of an Empress for many, many thousands of generations. Even though you were born of an alien race, My blood flows in your veins as through those of the children of My body, and I hear your song in My heart.

"And you, child," She said, turning to Esah-Zhurah. "Comely are the changes that have been worked upon you by the first of the Seven Crystals, the most holy relic of the Way. The eyes of your mate are now yours, as are the claws of crimson for which we have waited many, many cycles to see."

"My Empress," Esah-Zhurah said, bowing her head to her chest, "I do not understand. The priestess would not speak of it; I can only wonder at your meaning."

"I believe you are the one to fulfill The Prophecy, My child," the Empress said gently. "I believe that there shall come a day when the collar that I now wear shall be yours. And with your ascent to the throne, so too shall return the spirit and power of the First Empress, so long lost to us. Its fulfillment would end the curse that has befallen us these many cycles and bring back the spiritual power of the First Empress, bring Her back from the darkness to which Her soul fled in anguish and rage so long ago."

"But, my Empress," Esah-Zhurah murmured, "I was not born of the white mane, nor of the ebony claw. How can I ascend to the throne?"

The Empress ran a hand through Esah-Zhurah's hair. "The Change has deceived you, child," She said. "Already can be seen the white of the snows of Te'ar-Shelath in the roots of your hair. And the silver of your claws is gone, replaced by the crimson that belonged to Keel-Tath alone, for as long as the Way has been. Someday, your voice shall ring with Her wisdom and power, and the spirits that now dwell in My soul shall serve you.

"But there are many cycles ahead of you before you set aside your name and don this robe and the collar now about My neck. Your generation is graced with a race of worthy opponents, and combat and conquest are our heritage. To them you shall go to seek your fortune and show your honor, and from the priestess shall you learn the ways of the Desh-Ka, that their way of life and knowledge are preserved."

Reza suddenly had the sensation that the ground beneath his feet had dropped away, leaving him spinning downward into a dark, bottomless chasm.

"My Empress," he said slowly, already knowing from the chorus that was now clamoring in his heart what Her answer must be, "can we not show our love to You among the unknowns of the frontier?"

The Empress looked at him curiously, and a frown of concern suddenly began to etch its way across Her face. "You wear the trappings of warriors, not the robes of the clawless ones who explore the frontiers. To fight is your calling, and fight you will. I cannot allow it to be otherwise." She paused for a moment. "This is My will, warrior priest."

Tesh-Dar and Esah-Zhurah were staring at him, an identical look of confusion on their faces as their own hearts registered this unexpected turn of events.

"Reza," Esah-Zhurah said softly, "what is wrong? I know you dreamt of going to the frontiers, but..." She fell silent at the agonized expression on his face.

To Reza, the world had suddenly changed. Images from the past, pale alien faces whose names he could no longer remember, whose voices he could no longer understand, loomed large in his mind. And then alien words, spoken by his own tongue, echoed not in that forgotten language, but as a pure thought: *I will not fight against my own kind.*

The Empress immediately sensed the cause of his hesitancy. "You must choose, My son," She told him, Her own heart aching at the answer She knew would come from his lips. "To stay with us, with Esah-Zhurah, you must fight. Else you must return to the people from whom you were born. There can be no in-between, no compromise."

"Reza," Esah-Zhurah said, her voice filled with desperation as she put her hand upon his shoulder. From him more than any other could she feel and sense the melody of the Bloodsong. His soul was entwined with hers, now, and the mournful dirge in his heart terrified her. "Do not leave me."

Reza began to shudder. The sudden rage he felt at fate, the anguish of making the decision he knew had to be, the fear of what lay ahead, all collided within his mind. His fists clenched so hard that the talons of his gauntlets cut through to his palms, and blood began to weep onto the floor. With all his heart did he wish to remain here; he loved and honored the Empress and the people to which he now belonged. But to destroy those with whom he shared a common heritage – all of humanity – would be to break the most sacred oath he had ever made, and would taint his honor in the eyes of all who ever looked upon him. There could only be one answer.

"Then I must leave, my Empress," he choked. He wanted to scream. He wanted to die.

Esah-Zhurah and Tesh-Dar were silent, stunned. They could only stare at him, the black trails of mourning marks already making their way down their faces like ashen tears.

"Reza..." Esah-Zhurah whispered, her face contorted with pain and disbelief.

"You choose the course of honor, My son," the Empress said sadly. "Deeply does it grieve Me that this has come to pass. This, I did not foresee. But if you cannot obey My will, it must be so."

"But," Tesh-Dar said, fighting through the pain that was tearing at her heart, "what of The Prophecy? What shall become of us?"

"I know not, priestess," the Empress answered quietly, the ageless spirit that dwelled within Her wracked with confusion and gloom. She looked at Esah-Zhurah. "Perhaps it is only that his role is complete, that he has given us what he had to give. Or perhaps it is not yet time and we were wrong in our judgments of what we have seen. But the Way shall not be denied."

The Empress took a small ebony box from its place on a nearby pedestal. "I was going to give you this parcel of memories from your past as a gift, that you might cherish them before they found their way into the Books of Time. Now I give it to you in hopes that the things within shall ease the burden of your return to the blood of your birth." She handed him the box.

Inside, Reza found a folded sheet of paper: the letter of introduction an old man had once written for Reza to get into the Marine Academy. On top of it lay a blackened crucifix on a chain that had once been bright silver, a token of affection from a girl he had once loved, but whose name and face were long lost among his memories. They were the most precious things he had possessed in his lifetime as a human, and their appearance now brought a sob from his throat as hot tears of bitter anguish fell from his eyes. He closed the box with shaking hands.

"Thank you, my Empress," he whispered.

The Empress regarded him with great sadness in Her eyes, mourning marks touching Her face, casting a shadow upon Her soul. She wished with all the spirits that dwelled within Her that She would not have to banish him from the Empire, but there was no alternative, and it could not wait. With his decision to return from whence he came, so did he lose everything She ever could have offered him. She closed Her eyes, and after a moment visualized a place where he might find his Way among those who were beyond Her light, Her love. Because so now, was he.

"When must I go?" he asked.

"This moment, My son," the Empress replied. "I cannot tolerate division among the spirit of My people, Reza." She held out Her hand to him. In it were two black rings. "These shall you place around the first of your braids, that which is woven as the Covenant of the Afterlife. One ring shall remain with you for as long as you live, to bind your spirit to you. The other shall bind the covenant after your knife does its work. When you are gone, this will be all that shall remain of your body and spirit among us, and shall be Esah-Zhurah's until the day she dies." She looked at Reza with eyes that would have wept had they been able. "If you cannot do My will, My son, I cannot shed My light upon your soul. When the knife makes its cut, no longer will you feel the Bloodsong of the peers. No longer will you feel My love. Your memory shall live on forever in the Books of Time, for you have done no dishonor. But you will be alone from this day forward, and when you die, your spirit will fall into Darkness for all Eternity."

She stood before him for a moment, feeling the pain that welled from his heart like lava flung from a volcano. She loved him so much, but there was nothing She could do. If he could not be obedient to the Way of the Empire, the Empire could not give him its love in return. It was a relationship as simple as it was – in this case – tragic, and She offered him the only comfort She could.

She put Her hands on his shoulders. "I beg that you remember this," She whispered. "You are of My blood, the blood of an Empress. And although you have chosen a Way that will take you to be among our enemies, you do so with honor. And thus shall you forever be remembered in the Books of Time. From this day onward you shall never again feel My love, but know that I do love you, and I pray that glory shall forever follow in your footsteps. Farewell, my son, and may thy Way be long and glorious."

At last turning away, the Empress made her way into the garden, her white hair and robes trailing behind her like wisps of cloud.

The three of them stood as the Empress departed, but remained silent for what seemed an eternity.

"I must go." Reza said finally, looking at Esah-Zhurah, then at Tesh-Dar. Their faces were black in mourning, and he could feel the hot sting of tears on his own face. They seemed to be ghosts from a swiftly fading dream. He felt so empty, so alone.

The priestess stepped forward and grasped him by the forearms, the traditional way of parting among warriors. After a long moment, she let go, then handed him the short sword she had worn at her side since long before he was born. The blade bore the names of all who had carried the weapon, written in the Old Tongue that only now, after The Change, could he understand. There were very few spaces left. His, he saw with a painful surge of pride, was the last inscription.

"I am old and my Way grows short," she told him, her voice sounding fragile, ancient to his ears. "This I would leave to you. It has been among the Desh-Ka for over a thousand generations. Now, it is yours. You wear the rune of our order, now also do you bear a weapon in its name." Her eyes were soft and vulnerable. He had never seen her this way, and he suspected that few others ever had. "Good-bye, my beloved son," she whispered. "Go in Her name. May thy Way be long and glorious."

"Farewell, Mother," he said softly. "I love you." He saluted her, bowing his head to his priestess. She bowed her head in response, as befitted her rank, resisting the impulse to take him in her arms, to hold him as if he were but a young child. Then she stood back, her head bowed, waiting for what must come. She looked and felt old, defeated, and it broke Reza's heart to see her so.

Then he turned his attention to Esah-Zhurah, who stood quietly by his side, as fragile as a mirage. He reached out to touch her, suddenly afraid that she would simply vanish and that he would wake up, his entire life having been spent in a dream. But her flesh was firm under his hand. He dropped his gauntlets onto the ground at his feet, wanting nothing so much as to touch her one last time. She did the same, and he saw her hands: they were black with the mourning marks, so great was her pain.

He could stand it no longer. He began to cry as he pulled her to him, crushing her against his chest. She kissed his neck, her fangs streaking the skin. Her talons dug furrows into the metal of his armor as she clung to him.

"Please stay," she whispered, and he felt the echo of the pain in her heart in his own.

"Do not ask me again," he pleaded. "I beg of you. For we both know that I cannot. I must not."

"How shall I live without you?" she whispered, her arms tight around his neck. "My heart shall die when you are gone."

He pulled her away just far enough to see her face. Her green eyes were so bright they seemed to glow. "You must live," he told her, the desperation plain in his voice. "Live for me. All that sustains me even now is the hope that someday, somehow, I shall see your face again. You must believe that it will be so, that someday our Way shall be one again." She nodded her head, but her eyes and the keening in her blood betrayed the hopelessness that dwelled in her soul. He held her to him again, and kissed her softly, running his hands through her hair one last time.

"I have one last gift for you," he whispered into her ear. Reaching into the satchel at his feet, the leather bag that contained all his worldly possessions, he withdrew the box in which lay the bejeweled tiara. Extracting it carefully with his shaking hands, he held it up for her to see. "This was Pan'ne-Sharakh's last gift to us," he told her, "a token of my faith in courtship of a warrior priestess. I was going to give it to you when we met with the Empress, but..." He could not finish. Instead, he carefully placed it on her head, fitting the crown to the woman he would love unto death.

Even old and blind, Pan'ne-Sharakh had divined in metal and minerals a kind of beauty that was the stuff of dreams, beyond the reach of mortals such as himself. The tiara seemed to become a part of her, and he wanted to weep at how beautiful she looked with it on, but his tears were finished. Only pain and the uncertainty of what the future would bring remained. "Priestess of the Desh-Ka," he whispered, "forever shall my heart be yours."

They embraced a final time. Then she pushed herself away. Her eyes had clouded over, becoming hard as she fought to be strong. But he could see that her resolve was brittle, frail. They gripped each other by the arms as warriors. Then it was time for her to play out the last act of his departure from the Empire. Trembling, she separated out the first braid of his hair. Sliding the two black rings down the braid toward his scalp, she tightened them like a tourniquet only a finger's length from the roots. She took the knife that had once belonged to the reigning Empress and put the blade's edge between the rings. With her own hand trembling, she guided Reza's palm to the knife's bejeweled handle. "This," she said, her voice trembling, "is my gift to you, my love."

Reza took a deep breath. His eyes were closed, and his heart stopped. He did not know what to expect. "It is Her will."

Esah-Zhurah closed her eyes.

Reza gritted his teeth, and with a swift cut, the long braid came away, falling to the ground.

"Reza!" Esah-Zhurah screamed as pain ripped into her heart, the voice of Reza's spirit suddenly having been silenced. "No," she whispered. "It cannot be. It cannot." His Bloodsong was gone. The melody that thrilled her in her dreams and when they touched, that gave her strength when she fought, was no more. She wanted more than anything simply to plunge a knife into her breast. But she could not deny Her will. Even her love for Reza could not prevent her from obeying the call of the Empress.

She felt something being pressed into her trembling hands. "This is yours, my child," Tesh-Dar said shakily, as if from a thousand leagues away.

Esah-Zhurah knew what it was. Tenderly, she took the long braid of Reza's fine brown hair into her hands and pressed it to her face, taking in the scent and touch that she would never again feel. Then she opened her eyes to look upon him once more before he was taken away.

But there was nothing for her to see but the garden and Tesh-Dar's grieving form. Except for the bent blades of grass upon which he had been kneeling, there was no sign of him.

Reza was gone.

CONFEDERATION

Seventeen

"It's going to be light soon."

The statement was more than simple fact. Coming from the young Marine corporal, whose left leg ended halfway down his thigh, the bloody stump capped with crude bandages that now reeked of gangrene, the words were a prophecy of doom. Like many of the others clustered around him, broken and beaten, he was beyond fear. He had spent most of the previous night taken with fever, whispering or crying for the wife he would never see again, the daughter he had never seen beyond the image of the hologram he held clutched to his lacerated chest. There were dozens more just like him crammed into the stone church, waiting for morning. Waiting to die. "They'll be coming."

"Rest easy, my son," Father Hernandez soothed, kneeling down to give the man a drink of water from the clay pitcher he carried. "Conserve your strength. The Lord shall protect and provide for us. You are safe here."

"Bullshit."

Hernandez turned to find Lieutenant Jodi Ellen Mackenzie, Confederation Navy, glaring at him from where she kneeled next to a fallen Marine officer. Her foul mouth concealed a heart of gold and a mountain of determination, both to survive and to keep the people who depended on her – now including these Marines – alive. Momentarily turning her attention from Hernandez, Mackenzie closed Colonel Moreau's eyes with a gentle brush of her hand.

Another life taken in vain, Hernandez thought sadly. How many horrors had he witnessed these past, what, weeks? Months? And how many were yet to come? But he refused to relent in his undying passion that his way, the way of the Church into which he had been born and raised, and finally had come to lead, was the way of righteousness.

"Please, lieutenant," he asked as one of the parish's monks made his way to the side of the dead Marine colonel to mutter the last rites over her cooling body, "do not blaspheme in my church." He had said the very same thing to her countless times, but each time he convinced himself that it was the first and only transgression, and that she would eventually give in to his gentle reason. He was not, nor had he ever become, angry with her, for he was a man of great if not quite infinite patience and gentleness. He looked upon those two traits and his belief in God as the trinity that defined and guided his life. They had served him and his small rural parish well for many years, through much adversity and hardship. He had no intention of abandoning those tenets now, in the face of this unusual woman or the great Enemy, the demons, that had come from the skies. "Please," he said again.

Mackenzie rolled her eyes tiredly and shrugged. "Sure, Father," she said in a less than respectful tone. "Let's see, what is it you guys say? *Forgive me, Father, for I have sinned?*" She came to stand next to him, the light from the candle in his hand flickering against her face like a trapped butterfly. "The only sin that I've seen is you and all your people sitting around on your butts while these poor bastards," she jabbed a finger at one of the rows of wounded that now populated the church, "throw their gonads in the grinder for you." She saw him glance at Colonel Moreau's body, now covered with a shroud of rough burlap. "She can't help you anymore, priest," Mackenzie muttered, more to herself than for his benefit. Moreau had been as sympathetic to Hernandez's beliefs as much as Jodi was not. "I guess I'm in charge of this butcher shop now." She closed her eyes and shook her head. "Jesus."

Hernandez regarded her for a moment, taken not so much by the callousness of her words but by her appearance. Even exhausted, coated with grime and smelling of weeks-old sweat (water conservation and Kreelan attacks having rendered bathing an obsolete luxury), she was more than beautiful. Although Father Hernandez and the other dozen monks who tended to the parishioners of Saint Mary's of Rutan had taken the vows of celibacy, he could not deny the effect she had on him and, he suspected, on more than one of the monks under his charge. Even for a man of sixty-five, aged to seventy or eighty by a rough life on a world not known for its kindness, she was a temptation for the imagination, if not for the flesh. Hernandez did not consider himself a scholar, but he had read many of the great literary works of ancient times, some even in the original Latin and Greek, and he knew that Helen of Troy could have been no more radiant in her appearance. He could hardly intuit the heritage that gave her the black silken hair and coffee skin from which her ice blue eyes blazed. In his mind he saw the bloodlines of a Nubian queen merged with that of a fierce Norseman. Perhaps such was the case, the result of some unlikely but divine rendezvous somewhere on the ancient seas of Terra.

"You're staring, father," she said with a tired sigh. *It was always the same*, she thought. Ever since she was ten and about to bloom into the woman she someday would become, she had been the object of unwanted interest from men. The boys in her classes, sometimes the teachers; countless smiling faces had flooded by over the years, remaining as leering gargoyles in her memory. The only man she had ever truly loved had been her father, who had been immune to her unintentional power: he was blind from birth, beyond even the hope of reconstructive surgery. Jodi was sure that the fate that had placed this curse on him had been a blessing in disguise for her and for their relationship. He had never seen her beauty beyond what the loving touch of his fingers upon her face could reveal, and so he had never felt the craving or lust that her appearance seemed to inspire in so many others. He had always been wonderful to her, and there were no words to describe her love for him.

Jodi and her mother had been equally close, and with her Jodi had shared her feelings, her apprehensions, as she grew. But while her mother could well understand

Jodi's feelings, she had never been able to truly grasp the depth of her daughter's concerns, and in the honesty they had always shared, she had never claimed to. Arlene Mackenzie was a beautiful woman in her own right, but she knew quite well that Jodi was several orders of magnitude higher on whatever primal scale was used to judge subjective beauty. Jodi was only thankful that her mother had never been jealous of the power her daughter could wield over others if she had ever chosen to, which she never had. Jodi had always been very close to her parents, and she reluctantly admitted to herself that right now she, Jodi Mackenzie, veteran fighter pilot of the Black Widow Squadron, missed them terribly. The priest's appraising stare only made her miss them more.

"What's the matter, father?" she said finally, her skin prickling with anger. "Did you get tired of popping your altar boys?"

Red-faced, Hernandez averted his gaze. A nearby monk glanced in their direction, a comic look of shock on his face. The Marines lying on the floor beside them were in no condition to notice their exchange.

"Please," Hernandez said quietly, his voice choked with shame, "forgive my trespass. I cannot deny a certain weakness for your beauty, foolish old man that I am. That is an often unavoidable pitfall of the flesh of which we are all made, and even a hearty pursuit of God's Truth cannot always prevent the serpent from striking. But I assure you," he went on, finally returning her angry gaze, "that the vows I took when a very young man have been faithfully kept, and will remain unbroken for as long as I live." Hernandez offered a tentative smile. "As beautiful as you are, I don't feel in need of a cold shower."

Jodi's anger dissipated at the old joke that sometimes was not so funny for those in Hernandez's position. More important, she appreciated the priest's guts for admitting his weakness with such sincerity. That, she thought, was something rare on the outback colony worlds, where men were still men and women were still cattle.

"Maybe you don't," she told him, her mouth calling forth a tired but sincere smile of forgiveness, simultaneously wrinkling her nose in a mockery of the body odor they all shared, "but I could sure as hell use one."

Visibly relieved and letting her latest blasphemy pass unnoticed, Hernandez took the opportunity to change the subject. "Now that you are in command," he asked seriously, "what do you intend to do?"

"That's a good question," she said quietly, turning the issue over in her mind like a stringy chunk of beef on a spit, a tough morsel to chew on, but all that was available. She looked around, surveying the dark stone cathedral that had been her unexpected garrison and home for nearly three weeks. Shot down by Kreelan ground fire while supporting the Marine combat regiment that had been dispatched to Rutan, she had bailed out of her stricken fighter a few kilometers from the village of the same name, and that was where she had been stranded ever since. She had never worried about being shot at while floating down on the parachute, watching as her fighter obliterated itself against a cliff face five kilometers away, because in all the years of the war, the Kreelans had never attacked anyone who had bailed out. At least, that is, until the unlucky individual reached the ground.

In Jodi's case, friendly troops happened to reach her first, but that was the beginning and the end of her good fortune. As she was drifting toward the black-green forest in which Rutan was nestled, the *Hood*, her squadron's home carrier, and her escorts were taking a beating at the hands of two Kreelan heavy cruisers that a few days earlier had landed an enemy force to clean out the human settlement. After destroying her tormentors in a running fight that had lasted nearly three days, *Hood* had informed the regimental commander, Colonel Moreau, that the ship would be unable to resume station over Rutan: her battle damage required immediate withdrawal to the nearest port and a drydock. The captain expressed his sincere regrets to Moreau, but he could not face another engagement with any hope of his ship and her escorts surviving. There were no other Kreelan ships in the area, and Kreelan forces on the planet were judged to be roughly even to what the regiment could field, plus whatever help the Territorial Army could provide. On paper, at least, it looked to be a fair fight.

But neither *Hood's* captain, nor the Marines who had come to defend the planet had counted on a colony made up entirely of pacifists. Normally, the two thousand-strong Marine regiment would have been able to count on support from the local Territorial Army command that was supposed to be established on every human-settled world in the Confederation. In the case of Rutan, that should have been an additional five to eight thousand able-bodied adults with at least rudimentary weapons, if not proper light infantry combat gear.

Unfortunately, the intelligence files had contained nothing about the colony's disdain of violence. But that was hardly surprising, considering that the information contained in the files was for an entirely different settlement. Only the data on the planet's physical characteristics – weather, gravity, and the like – happened to be correct. Someone had called it an administrative error, but most of the Marines had more colorful names for the mistake that was to cost them their lives. They were bitter indeed when they discovered that what should have been a comparatively swift human victory through sheer weight of numbers rapidly became a struggle for survival against the most tenacious and implacable enemy that humans had ever encountered.

Now, a month after the Marines had leaped from the assault boats under protective fighter cover from Jodi's Black Widows, the proud 373d Marine Assault Regiment (Guards) had been reduced to twenty-two effectives, eighty-six walking wounded, and nearly five-hundred stretcher cases, most of them crammed into St. Mary's. The rest of the original one thousand, nine hundred and thirty-seven members of the original Marine force lay scattered in the forests around the village, dead. Among the casualties were the regiment's surgeon and all thirty-one medics. The survivors now had to rely on the primitive skills of the two local physicians (Jodi preferred to think of them as witch doctors), plus whatever nursing Hernandez and his monks could provide.

The remainder of the population, on order of the Council of Elders and with Hernandez's recommendation, had holed themselves up in their homes to await the outcome of the battle. Jodi had often pondered the blind luck that had led Rutan's founders to build their village in the hollow of a great cliff that towered over the forest, much like an ancient native American civilization had done over a millennia before on Terra: it had been the key to their survival thus far. An ordinary rural settlement, situated in the open, would have forced the defenders to spread themselves impossibly thin to protect their uncooperative civilian hosts.

On the other hand, Jodi thought, depressing herself still further, the human contingent was now completely trapped. While the village's natural defenses helped to keep the enemy out, and the sturdy stone construction made its dwellings almost impervious to the small arms fire the Kreelans occasionally deigned to use, they also left no escape route open to the defenders. There was only one way in, and one way out.

She thought of how close victory could have been, had the villagers cooperated. But Colonel Moreau and her Marines had dished out punishment as well as they had taken it, inflicting at least as many casualties as they had themselves taken. Jodi was convinced that even now a completely untrained and moderately motivated militia, led by the few remaining able-bodied Marines, could take the field. They were the defenders, and in this battle of attrition the humans had at least one advantage: they knew where the Kreelans would attack, and when. The enemy did not apply the principles of Clausewitz or Sun Tzu to their tactics and strategy. In fact, it was not entirely clear at times if they really had either, or cared. This confused the bulk of their human opponents, who were conditioned to deal with "logical" objectives like capturing terrain or severing enemy lines of communication, all of which – hopefully – would help accomplish some particular strategic objective.

More often than not, however, the Kreelans simply preferred a stand-up brawl that was more typical of the knights of Medieval Europe than the technologically advanced race they otherwise were. Rarely did they seek a decisive advantage, mostly preferring to duke it out one-on-one, or even conferring a numerical or qualitative edge to the humans. They used their more advanced weapons to strip the humans of theirs, lowering the level of technology employed on the battlefield to not much more than rifles, knives, fists and claws.

The humiliating – and frightening – thing, Jodi thought, was that they usually won, even when fighting at a disadvantage.

Here, on Rutan, Jodi knew that even now the remaining Kreelans were massing for an attack on the village. The first shots would be fired at dawn, as they had for the last three weeks. She also knew that this would probably be their last fight. There simply were not enough able bodies left to cover all the holes in their flagging defenses. Once the Marine line finally broke, the civilians who cowered in their shuttered homes would be massacred.

"Father," she said, trying to drive away the oppressive desperation of their situation, "I'm going to ask you this one last time: will you please at least let people, anyone who wants to, pick up a weapon and help us. You don't have to ask for volunteers, just let them do whatever–"

"And I have told you, Lieutenant Mackenzie," he replied, gently but firmly cutting her off, "that I shall permit no such thing." Jodi, her cheeks flushed with frustration and rising anger, opened her mouth to say something, but Hernandez waved her into silence. "I grieve terribly for the deaths and suffering of these courageous people," he went on quietly, "but we long ago set aside violence as a part of our lives. Rutan has not had a violent crime committed in nearly a century, and neither I nor the council will condone our people taking up arms for any reason, even our own self-preservation. We did not ask you to intercede on our behalf; you came of your own accord, uninvited. I am truly sorry, but this is how it must be."

Jodi just stared at him for a minute, trying to calm herself down. It made her so mad to know that her demise – as well as that of the Marines around her – could have been so easily prevented. She wanted to scream at the old man, but she was too tired, too worn out. "This is probably going to be it, you know," she told him quietly so the others nearby could not hear. Most of them knew that their number was going to come up this morning, but she did not see any sense in advertising the fact. "They're going to get through us today, and then you're going to have a real bloodbath on your hands, father. All your little sheep, hiding in their comfy houses, are going to get more than fleeced. They'll be slaughtered to the last child."

"I am an old man," he told her solemnly, "but I am still young enough at heart to believe, to have faith in God. I don't believe that divine miracles disappeared with the passage of Jesus our Lord from the earth. God has already granted us one miracle in our time of need: your coming to protect us as the enemy was knocking at our gates. I believe that He has not yet abandoned us."

Jodi regarded him coldly. She liked him, respected him. Deep down, she wanted to believe him. She wanted to throw herself on her knees and beg forgiveness if only things would just be all right, if the enemy would just disappear, if someone would wake her up from this nightmare. But she knew it was an illusion. The enemy was not about to simply be sucked into some miraculous celestial vacuum cleaner. The wounded and dying around her and the bloody carnage outside the village gates was clear evidence that, if there was a God, His benign interests were obviously elsewhere, not worth expending on the inhabitants of this insignificant grain of dust in the cosmos. No, she thought grimly. The Kreelans would not just go away, whisked to some never-never-land by a momentarily preoccupied God. They had to be fought and killed to the last warrior, hacked to pieces, exterminated. Only then would Jodi feel justified in thinking about tomorrow.

"The only miracle," she told him, "would be if you and your people suddenly got some balls." Turning on her heel, Jodi stalked away toward the rear of the church to get her equipment ready for what she already thought of as Mackenzie's Last Stand.

Father Hernandez stared after her, not knowing if he should be angry or ashamed at the woman's words. His leathery face shrouded in a frown, he bent to his work, doing what he could to comfort the wounded.

God has not abandoned us, he told himself fiercely. *He has not.*

Amid the cries of the wounded and the dying, Father Hernandez prayed.

* * *

Jodi picked up the ancient-looking pitcher and poured some cold water into the hand-made clay basin. After soaking a worn strip of cotton cloth, she wiped her face and neck, scraping off some of the grime and dirt that had accumulated since the last time she had allowed herself such a luxury. She considered undoing her uniform and wiping down the rest of her body, but decided against it; not out of modesty, but because she did not have the time.

Here, alone in Father Hernandez's private quarters submerged beneath and far behind the altar, she could have danced nude had she wished. Hernandez had donated his tiny rectory to the female officers, insisting that they take any necessary moments of privacy there. Jodi had originally resented it as a sexually oriented distinction that she initially found offensive, but Colonel Moreau had accepted, if only to mollify the headstrong priest. But now, Jodi was glad to have this little room to herself, just to be alone for a little while. There were no other occupants. She and Jeannette Moreau had been the last two, and now Moreau was gone. That left Jodi as not just the last surviving female officer, but the last surviving officer, period.

She looked for a moment into the palm-sized oval of polished metal that Father Hernandez used for a mirror, studying the face she saw there. She was not afraid of having to lead the Marines in what was probably going to be their last battle, for she had been doing that since shortly after she had been shot down and Moreau had needed her to fill in for Marine officers she had lost. Jodi had not had the Marines' specialized training, but she was tough and quick, both mentally and physically. It had not taken her long to prove that she was more than just another pretty fighter jock, and the Marines had quickly adopted her as one of their own. The Marine NCOs had given her a crash course in how to fight that made a mockery of the self-defense training she had received as a part of her pilot training. And, fitted with a Marine camouflage uniform and armor, she was indistinguishable on the battlefield from her rival service colleagues, such was her courage and tenacity. She had put their teaching to good use and had somehow survived, keeping as many of her people alive as she could in the process.

She set the mirror down. She could handle the upcoming fight, win or lose. She was ready, except for the one thought that nipped at her heels like a small but vicious dog: she was afraid to die. Unlike many of those in her profession, she was terrified not just of how she died, but of death itself. The courage to face the end of life – or at least to ignore the possibility that death would someday come – was the one thing neither her parents nor the years she had spent fighting the Kreelans had given her. Her only religion was flying, but it was little consolation when faced with the prospect of the end of one's existence. Jodi was and always had been an atheist, despite her parents' best efforts, and it had made her life somewhat more straightforward, if not necessarily easier. It was only when one contemplated the end of the line that things became complicated. Not surprisingly, Father Hernandez had taken up the challenge with his customary gusto, but Jodi had argued him to a standstill, as she had with other would-be converters. A belief in any afterlife required a kind of faith that Jodi just did not have, and their intellectual sparring had left them consistently deadlocked, if for no other reason than Hernandez could not prove to her that there was a God or Devil, Heaven or Hell. Her beliefs, of course, did not require proof of anything except the given facts of human existence and the inevitability of death.

Therefore, she had little trouble defending her own views while easily finding logical faults in his. Faith, virtually by definition, transcended logic and empirical knowledge, which always made it vulnerable to attack. Still, Jodi respected the man's vehemence in his beliefs, and was even a little afraid on a few occasions that maybe – just maybe – he might have something. But then he would go on about his "miracles" or some other patent silliness, blowing away any thoughts Jodi might have had of more closely examining her own beliefs.

Despite his apparent latent lecherous tendencies, for which Jodi easily forgave him, she liked the old man, and knew she was going to miss talking to him about things most of her regular companions took for granted.

But the person she would miss the most was her squadron commander, with whom Jodi had fallen hopelessly in love when they met four years before. Jodi tried desperately to push from her mind any thoughts of the woman she loved for fear that she would break down and cry now, just before her last battle. But the image of the woman's face and the imagined sound of her voice were more powerful than the fear of failure, even the fear of death. Jodi knew that the lover of her dreams would never look upon her as anything more than a close friend, because she had chosen a different way of living, finding whatever solace she required with men. Outside of one very tentative advance that was gently rejected, Jodi had never done anything to change her love's beliefs, and had done everything she could to remain her closest and best friend, no matter the pain it had sometimes caused her.

Jodi knew she would never see her again.

"Come on, Mackenzie," she chided herself as she wiped a threatening tear from her eye. "Get a fucking grip."

Grimacing at the opaque water left in the basin after rinsing out the rag, Jodi forced herself back to the present and bent to the task of putting on her armor, donated by a Marine who no longer needed it.

The candle on the washbasin table suddenly flickered, a tiny wisp of black smoke trailing toward the ceiling as the flame threatened to die. Then it steadied again, continuing to throw its melancholy light into the rectory.

Jodi, concentrating on closing a bent latch on her chest plate, did not need to look up. She had not heard the door open, but had no doubt that the regiment's acting sergeant major had come to fetch her.

"I'll be there in a minute, Braddock," she said, smiling. She liked the crusty NCO, lech or not. "If you want a peek or a piece of ass, you'd better try the monks' quarters." She finished dealing with the recalcitrant latch on her breastplate, then grabbed her helmet and turned toward the door. Braddock had been almost like a big brother to her since she had fallen from the sky, and she was going to give him one last bit of hell before they plunged into the real thing. "This is off limits to enlisted scum–"

There was someone – some *thing* – in the rectory with her, all right, but it was not Braddock. Looming in the shadows just beyond the candle's reach, she saw that it was neither a Marine nor one of the church's robed inhabitants. In fact, it did not appear to be human at all.

Her hand instinctively went to the pistol at her waist, but she never had a chance. With lightening speed, so quick that it was only a dark blur in the dim candlelight, the thing covered the two or so meters between them. Before Jodi's hand was halfway to the gun she sought, her arms were pinned to her sides in a grip of steel as the Kreelan warrior embraced her. As she opened her mouth to shout a warning to the others, a gauntleted hand clamped down over her lips, sealing her scream in a tomb of silence and rapier-sharp claws that rested precariously against her cheek. She struggled, throwing her weight from side to side and flinging her knees upward in hopes of catching the warrior in the crotch and at least throwing her off balance, but it was to no avail. It was like she was being held by a massive slab of granite. The pressure around her ribs suddenly increased, crushing the air out of her lungs and threatening to break her upper arms. Gasping through her nose, she closed her eyes and relented, helplessly surrendering herself to the inevitable.

But Death did not come. Instead, the pressure eased to a bearable, if not exactly gentle, level. Then she felt the hand over her mouth slowly move away. She wanted to scream, but knew it was probably futile. The warrior now holding her was stronger than anything or anyone she had ever encountered, and she had no doubt that with a single determined twitch the arm still around her chest could crush the life out of her. She bit her lip, stifling a moan that threatened to bubble from her throat. Her eyes were still closed; she had seen enough Kreelans close up to know that there was nothing there that she wanted to see. It was sometimes better not to look Death in the face.

She heard a tiny metallic click in the darkness. So quiet that normally she would never have noticed it, the sound echoed in her skull like a thunderclap. It was a knife, she thought. Or worse. Involuntarily, cursing her body for its weakness in the face – literally – of the enemy, she began to tremble. She didn't want to be afraid, now that her time had really come, but she was, anyway.

Something touched her face. She tried to jerk her head away, but realized that she had nowhere to go. Her breath was coming in shallow pants, like an overweight dog forced to run at his master's side under a hot sun. The dark world behind her closed eyes was beginning to spin, and suddenly the most important thing in that tiny world seemed to be that she was on the verge of losing control of her bladder.

She felt something against her face again, but this time she did not try to draw away. She knew that it must be a knife, drawing a pencil-thin bead of blood down her cheek, painless because it was so sharp. Strange, she thought, that the Kreelans so often used knives and swords when they had such weapons built into their bodies. Of course, she absently reflected, as she imagined the skin of her face being carved away, they used their claws often enough, too.

The knife – *What else could it be?* she wondered – slowly traced the bones of her cheeks, then moved along her proud and intelligent brow, pausing as if to investigate the anomaly of her eyebrows, of which the Kreelans had nothing but a ridge of horn. Then she felt it spiral around her right ear, then move to her lips.

God, she thought, *there won't be anything left of me*. She wanted to cry at what must be happening to her once-beautiful face, but she stifled the urge. It would avail her nothing. Surprisingly, she neither felt nor smelled any blood, which should by now be pouring from her wounds and streaming in rivers down her face and neck.

Whatever it was continued to probe at her lips, gently insinuating itself into her mouth to brush against her teeth. Like some absurd dental probe, it dallied at her canines. Then the thing – a finger, she suddenly realized – extracted itself, leaving Jodi to ponder the tracks and swirls upon her skin that were now burned into her memory.

Again, she waited. She wondered how much time had passed, hoping that someone would come looking for her and burn this alien thing into carbon. But a hasty reflection revealed that only a minute or two, if that, could have passed since the thing mysteriously appeared. And how–

Her thought was suddenly interrupted by a sensation she instinctively recognized, and it jolted her with the force of electricity. She had no idea what had run its course over her face only a moment before, but what touched her now was immediately recognizable. A palm, a hand, gently brushing against her face. She could tell even without seeing it that it was rough, callused, but warm and almost timid in its touch.

Unable to control her curiosity at what was happening, and against her better judgment, she forced her eyes open.

What she saw in the dim candlelight stole her breath away: a face that was unmistakably human. The skin, while not exactly any easily catalogued shade, was obviously not the cobalt blue of the enemy. She could see eyebrows where there should be none, and hair that was somehow of the wrong texture – a bit too fine, perhaps – and undeniably not the ubiquitous black found among the Kreelan species. It was instead a dark shade of brown. Even the general shape of the face was different, slightly narrower in a jaw that did not have to accommodate large canines. He even smelled human somehow, if for no other reason than the almost-sweet musky smell of Kreelan skin was absent from the air.

But even with all the other differences immediately noticeable, the most obvious giveaway was the eyes. They were not the silver-flecked luminescent feline eyes of the Kreelans, but displayed dark, round pupils surrounded by irises that were an unusual color and brilliance of green, easily seen even in this murky light and with the pupils dilated fully open. The eyes were not exactly cold, but were nonetheless inscrutable, impenetrable, and she could see that the intelligence that lay behind those eyes was not human, not by any measure.

There was another difference, too. It was more difficult to pin down until she noticed the shape of the chest plate against which she was pinned. The creature – human or otherwise – that now held her captive was male. It was not just the chest plate's lack of the two protrusions that customarily accommodated the females' breasts that grabbed her attention. It was also her instinctive understanding of the signals that defined sexual orientation on a primal level, the way one could tell if an unseen speaker was a man or woman. And the individual now holding her was unmistakably male.

She blinked once, twice, to make sure she was not just seeing things, but the human apparition in Kreelan garb remained. It – *he* – stared at her, unblinking, as he gently ran his hand over her face, acting as if he had never seen another of his own kind.

It was then that she saw the wet streaks on his face. He was crying. That sight shocked her more than anything else.

"Who..." Jodi whispered, trying not to speak too loudly for fear of frightening her captor into using his powerful grip to silence her, "... who are you?"

His hand stopped its inquisitive caressing, and he cocked his head slightly, his face silently voicing the obvious fact that he did not understand her words.

Jodi slowly repeated the question, for lack of any better ideas at the moment. "Who are you?" she asked him again, slowly.

His lips pursed as if he was about to speak, but then he frowned. He did not understand.

Awkwardly, her movements hampered by his arm around her chest, she began to raise a hand toward him. His grip tightened at her movement, eliciting a grunt of air being pushed out of her lungs, and his eyes flashed an unmistakable warning. But Jodi was unperturbed, and after a moment of indecision, he allowed her to continue.

"I'm not going to hurt you," she said, hoping that she sounded convincing. She did not really know what she should – or could – do in her present situation. On the one hand, she desperately wished that one of the Marines outside would suddenly burst in and free her from this surreal rendezvous. On the other, she found herself oddly captivated by this... man. If he was what he appeared to be, a human somehow converted by the Kreelans, and not one of the Marines playing out a cruel joke at the eleventh hour, his discovery might be terribly important. Assuming, of course, that any of the humans here survived long enough to tell someone about him.

And that he would allow her to live.

Tentatively, she touched the hand that had been exploring her face, feeling a tiny jolt of excitement, almost like an electric shock, as her fingertips touched his skin.

"Please," she said, her trembling fingers exploring his opened palm, "let me go. I'm not going to hurt you. I promise." She almost laughed at the words. Here she was, pinned by a man who had extraordinary strength and whose intentions were entirely unknown, saying that she was not going to hurt him. It was ludicrous.

But, much to her surprise, it worked. Slowly, his other arm fell away from her, and she breathed in a deep sigh of relief. He was holding her hand now, gently, as if he was afraid of damaging it, and his blazing green eyes were locked on her face, waiting. It was her move.

"Thank you," she said, taking a small step backward, giving herself a little breathing room, but not moving so far as to arouse any suspicion that she might be trying to flee. Besides, with him between her and the door, and only a tiny dirty window looking to the outside behind her, there was nowhere for her to escape to.

Taking his hand, she held it to her chest, just above her breasts. "Jodi," she said, hoping to convey the idea of a name to her uninvited guest. She felt slightly foolish, because she had no idea if Kreelans even had names. No one knew the answers to even the most mundane questions about their culture. "Jodi," she repeated. Then she moved his hand to his armored chest, gingerly, shocked at how warm the ebony metal was, and asked, hoping her tone might convey her message better than the words themselves, "Do you have a name?"

He looked at her for a moment, his brow furrowed in concentration. Then his eyes cleared. In a quiet tenor that made Jodi's flesh prickle with excitement, he said, "Reza."

"Reza," Jodi repeated, smiling as she felt a shudder of nervous relief through her body. Perhaps he was not going to kill her after all. At least she had some hope, now. She might yet leave this room alive. Surely he would not bother with this little game if he had come only to kill her. But then again...

"Say my name, Reza," she said, moving his hand back to her chest. "Jodi," she said.

"Jo-dee," he managed. Even that simple utterance was nearly lost to the guttural accent that filtered his speech.

"Good," she said, elated by this tiny success. She edged slightly to one side, trying to move closer to the door without him becoming suspicious of her intentions. "Come on, now. Say it again."

He did, and she nodded, breathing a little easier. As she looked at him, forcing herself to ignore the door that was only a few feet away, but still so far out of reach, she was taken by the moist tracks that ran down his face. With her free hand, she touched them, feeling the wetness against her fingertips. "Why are you crying?" she whispered wonderingly. She did not expect an answer.

Reza worked his mouth, as if he wanted – or was at least trying – to say something more than just repeat her name, but a change flashed across his face, a look of such cunning and knowing in his expression that it frightened Jodi. His eyes narrowed suddenly, and he took hold of her and spun her around in his arms like they were on a dance floor, whirling to some insane waltz. In the blink of an eye, she found herself facing the door to the rectory, staring into Gunnery Sergeant Braddock's surprised and confused face as he opened the door.

"You, ah, all right there, ma'am?" the regiment's acting sergeant major asked quietly, a frown of concern turning down the corners of his mouth as his hand gripped his rifle a little tighter.

Jodi spun back around to where Reza was and found... nothing. She was alone in the rectory.

"There was..." she began, then shook her head. "I... I mean... oh, shit." She looked back at Braddock, her face pale, then reddening from embarrassment. She was shaking. "I think I'm flipping out, gunny," she said with a nervous smile. "I could've sworn I was just talking to a Kreelan that looked like a human, a man."

"That'd be a bit odd for you, wouldn't it?" he joked, poking fun at her sexual preference, but he got only an uneasy grimace in return. *Jeez*, he thought, *she's really spooked*. He came up to her and put a hand on her shoulder, offering her a sympathetic smile. "Look," he said quietly, "I know what you mean, lieutenant. I've had some pretty freaky spells myself lately. We're just strung out a bit thin, getting tired and a little jumpy, is all. You'll be okay." He handed her the helmet that had been sitting on the priest's tiny bed. "We've still got a job to do, ma'am. Morning's on the way, and our blue-skinned lady friends will be along any time, now, I imagine. I'll get the troops started along while you get your stuff together. Maybe we can have one last formation before the carny starts."

"Yeah, sure," she said, trying to control the trembling that was shaking her so hard that her teeth threatened to chatter as if she were freezing. "Thanks, Braddock," she told him.

Favoring her with a compassionate smile, he left her in peace. A moment later she could hear him barking orders in the main part of the church, rousing the remainder of the able-bodied Marines to yet another fight, their last. Shaking her head in wonder, Jodi rubbed her eyes, then stopped.

Her fingertips were noticeably moist. With her heart tripping in her chest, she looked at them, saw them glistening wetly in the candlelight. Cautiously, she put a finger to her lips, tasted it with the tip of her tongue. It was not water, nor was it the bitter taste of sweat. She tasted the soft saltiness of human tears.

"Jesus," she whispered to herself. "What the hell is going on?"

* * *

She met Father Hernandez as she was moving toward the front of the church and the roughly aligned ranks of her gathered command.

"I see that, yet again, you refuse to have faith, lieutenant," he said somberly, his eyes dark with concern. He had said the same thing to all of them every morning that they had gone out to fight, hoping that someone would accept his wisdom as the truth and lay down their weapons to let God do the work of feeding them to the Kreelans' claws. "If only you would believe, God would–"

"Please, father," she said, cutting him off more harshly than she meant to. But the incident, hallucination, or whatever the hell it had been back in the rectory had really rattled her, and she did not need his well-intentioned mumbo-jumbo right now. "I don't have time."

She tried to push her way past him, but he held her up, a restraining hand on her arm. "Wait," he said, studying her face closely. "You saw something, didn't you?"

There was no disguising the look of surprise on her face at his question. "What the hell are you talking about?" she blustered, trying to pull away.

"In there, in the rectory," Hernandez persisted, his eyes boring into hers with an intensity she had never seen in him before. He gripped her arm fiercely, and she suddenly did not have the strength to struggle against him. It reminded her too much of what had happened only a few minutes ago. "I know when people have seen something that has touched them deeply, Jodi, and you have that look. Tell me what you saw."

"I didn't see anything," she lied, looking away toward the crucifix hanging above the altar. The wooden statue of Christ, forever pinned to the cross by its ankles and wrists, wept bloody tears. A shiver went down her spine as she imagined the statue's eyes opening, revealing a pair of unfathomable green eyes. "Please, father, let me go." She looked at him with pleading eyes that were on the verge of tears. "Please."

Sighing in resignation, the old priest released her arm. "You can close your eyes and ears to all that you might see and hear, you can pretend that it never happened, whatever it was, but He is persistent, Jodi," he said. "Even you cannot ignore God's Truth forever." He leaned forward and kissed her lightly on the forehead, surprising her. "Go then, child. I do not believe in what you do, but that will never stop me from praying for your safety and your soul."

Jodi managed a smile that might have been more appropriate on the face of a ten-year old girl who had yet to experience the pain and sufferings of adult life. "Thanks, father. For whatever it's worth–"

"Lieutenant!" Braddock's voice boomed through the church over a sudden hubbub that had broken out near the great wooden doors that led to the outside. "Lieutenant Mackenzie! You better take a look at this!"

"Now what..." Jodi muttered under her breath as she made her way through the rows of invalid Marines, running toward the doorway.

"What is it?" she demanded as she pulled up short next to Braddock.

Her voice was all business now, the acting sergeant major saw. She had it back together. *Good*, he thought. "Look," he said, pointing through the partially opened doors toward the village gates. "Just who – or *what* – the hell is that?"

Jodi looked toward where Braddock was pointing. The village gates were at the apex of the semicircular stone wall that formed Rutan's external periphery beyond the cliff into which the settlement was recessed. The church, located under the protective shelter of the cliff itself, was in line with the gates and elevated by nearly fifteen meters, giving anyone at the church's entrance an unobstructed view of the approaches to the village. The only approach of concern to the Marines had been the stone bridge that spanned the swift-flowing Trinity River. It was there, along the deforested stretch from the river to the village gates, that most of the battles for Rutan had been fought. The Kreelans had taken refuge in the thick forest on the far side, unable to find any suitable ground closer or to either side of the village, and it was from across the bridge that they attacked each morning. It had not been so in the first week or two, when they had engaged in fluid battles away from the village. But after the humans' heavy weapons and vehicles had finally been knocked out, the Kreelans had set aside their more powerful war machines and contented themselves with a small war of attrition, virtually forcing the humans into daily fights at close quarters, often hand-to-hand.

"I don't see..."

Then suddenly her voice died. There, facing the bridge and the Kreelans already advancing across it, was the man who had come to her in the rectory, standing like an alien-inspired Horatius.

"Reza," she whispered. She suddenly felt very, very cold.

Braddock was staring at her. "Is... is that him?" he whispered incredulously. "He was real?"

"Looks that way," Jodi replied hoarsely. She did not have enough energy for anything more. "I, ah, think we better get out there and get ready. Don't you?"

"Yeah," Braddock replied absently as he pulled out his field glasses and held them up to his eyes, focusing quickly for a better look.

But neither of them moved. Behind them, the Marines murmured among themselves, unsure and afraid at their leaders' strange behavior. A few of them were standing up on pews to see what was happening, peering out the narrow windows and reporting the action to their fellows. The church grew uncharacteristically silent, even for a holy place filled with the injured and dying.

Nearby, Father Hernandez watched the two figures peering out the door. A curious smile crept onto his face.

Fascinated into inaction by what they saw, Jodi and Braddock watched the Kreelan phalanx converge on the mysterious figure that awaited them.

* * *

La'ana-Ti'er stepped forward from the group of warriors who had come in search of combat. Kneeling, she saluted her superior. Behind her, the other warriors kneeled as one.

"Greetings, Reza of the Desh-Ka," she said humbly. "Honored are we that you are among us, and saddened are we that your song no longer sings in our veins." She bowed her head. "To cross swords with you is an honor of which I am unworthy."

Reza regarded her quietly for a moment. He was chilled by the emptiness he felt at no longer being able to hear in his heart what she and the others could, at being unable to feel the Empress's will as a palpable sensation. Although he had possessed that ability for only a brief period, its absence now was nearly unbearable. The severed braid that had been his spiritual lifeline to the Empress throbbed like a violated nerve.

"Rise, La'ana-Ti'er," he told her. They clasped arms in greeting, as if they had known each other their entire lives, had been comrades, friends, as if they were not about to join in a battle to kill one another. "It is Her will." He was left to interpret Her desires from his own memories of what once was. With his banishment to this place, wherever it was, all he had left were his memories and the single, lonely melody that sang to him in the voice of his own spirit.

La'ana-Ti'er looked upon him with respectful and sympathetic eyes. She did not pity him, for pity was beyond her emotional abilities; she mourned him. "Should you perish on the field of battle this day," she told him, "it will bring me no joy, no glory. I will fight you as I have fought all others, but I pray to Her that mine shall not be the sword to strike you down and cast you into darkness." She dropped her eyes.

"My thanks, warrior," he told her quietly, "and may thy Way be long and glorious." He drew in a breath. "Let it begin."

* * *

Jodi blinked at the sudden violence that erupted on the bridge. One moment, the Kreelans who had come to finish them off were all bowing in front of the strange man who had come to her. In the next there was nothing to see but a whirlwind of clashing swords and armor. A memory came to her from her days as a child on Terra, when a neighbor boy released a single black ant into the midst of a nest of red ones. The savagery and intensity she had seen in that tiny microcosm of violence was an echo of the bloody chaos she was witnessing now. The church reverberated with the crash of steel upon steel, the cries of blood lust and pain raising gooseflesh on her arms.

"What the hell's going on?" Braddock whispered, his eyes glued to the binoculars. "Lord of All, they're fighting each other!"

"Can you see him?" Jodi asked. Her eyesight was phenomenal, but the distance was just too great to make out any details in the raging rabble that had consumed the old stone bridge. All she could see was a swirling humanoid mass, with a body plummeting – *hurled* might be a better word, she thought – now and again from the bridge like a carelessly tossed stone. She had lost sight of the man after the first second or two as he waded into the Kreelans' midst, his sword cutting a swath of destruction before him.

"Yeah... No... What the hell?" Braddock wiped his eyes with his hands before looking again through the binoculars. "I see him in one place, then he just seems to pop up in another. Damn, but this is weird, lieutenant." He turned to her. "Should we go take a closer look?"

"How much ammo have we got?" she asked.

Braddock gave her a grim smile. "After we redistributed last night, three rounds per rifle and a handful of sidearm ammunition that isn't worth shit. Everybody's got their bayonets fixed for the rest of it."

Jodi sighed, still concentrating on the scene being played out on the bridge. It was no worse than she expected. "Let's do it."

Braddock turned to the Marines now clustered behind them. "ALL RIGHT!" he boomed. "MOVE OUT!"

Twenty-two Marines and one marooned naval flight officer burst from the safety of the church's stone walls and began to move in a snaking skirmish line toward where the unexpected battle still raged at fever pitch.

* * *

Reza paid no attention to his eyes and ears, for he had no real need of them at the moment. His spirit could sense his surroundings, sense his opponents far better. He was living in a state of semi-suspended time as the battle went on, his opponents appearing to move in slow motion, giving him time to analyze and attack with totally inhuman efficiency, his body and mind acting far outside the normal laws that governed physical existence. His fellow warriors knew that they would die at his hand, but none of them would ever have dreamed of turning their backs upon an opportunity to face a Desh-Ka in a battle to the death. It was unspeakably rare to engage in such a contest since the Empire had been born; the Empress had sought external enemies to fight, allowing Her children only to fight for honor among themselves in the Challenge, without intentionally killing one another except in the most extreme of circumstances. To face one so skilled, regardless of whether they lived or died, would bring much honor to the Empress and their Way.

Now their blood keened with the thrill of combat, and as they died, slain upon Reza's sword, their spirits joined the host that awaited them and welcomed them into the Afterlife. By ranks they charged the warrior priest who for the briefest of times had been a part of their people, throwing themselves into his scything blade like berserkers bent upon self-destruction. Time and again they converged upon him in a ring, swords and axes and pikes raised to attack, and time and again he destroyed them. There was no sorrow in his soul for their passing, save that they would no longer know the primal power of battle, and never again could bring glory to Her name through the defeat of an able foe.

At last, it was over. His great sword still held at the ready, Reza surveyed the now-quiet scene of carnage around him. There were no more opponents to fight, no one else to kill. The bridge was slick with the blood that still poured from the dead Kreelans' veins, blood that turned the churning white water of the river below to a ghastly crimson swirl. La'ana-Ti'er's lifeless body lay nearby, her hand pressed to the hole in her breast, just above her heart, where Reza's sword had found its mark.

Replacing his bloodied weapon in the scabbard on his back, he knelt next to her. He saw Esah-Zhurah's face on the woman sprawled beside him, and a terrible realization struck him. He knew that he would see his mate's face upon every warrior he fought, and would feel the pain of loneliness that now tore at his heart, that burned like fire in his blood, for every moment of his life. Worse, he knew that she would be enduring the same pain, and would never again sense his love, or feel his touch.

He had touched her for the last time but a short while ago, and already it seemed like an eternity.

He bowed his head and wept.

* * *

"My God," someone whispered.

Only a few minutes after Jodi, Braddock, and the others had reached the village wall, only a hundred meters or so from the church, the battle was over. The Marines who now overlooked the scene on the bridge were not new to battle and its attendant horrors, but none of them had ever witnessed anything like this. Even Braddock, a veteran of eight years of hard campaigning ashore and on the ships of the fleet, had to look away from what he saw. Fifty warriors, perhaps more, lay dead upon the gore-soaked bridge, or were now floating downstream toward the distant Providence Sea. They had ceased to be a threat to the inhabitants of Rutan, and Braddock seriously doubted that there were any more to contend with, except maybe injured warriors who would only kill themselves to prevent capture.

Braddock turned to Mackenzie. "Looks like Father Hernandez got his bloody miracle, doesn't it?"

"Yeah," she whispered, still not believing the incredible ferocity and power of the man who now knelt quietly among the dead. "I guess so." Somewhere down the line of Marines, huddled against the stone of the chest-high wall, someone vomited, and Jodi fiercely restrained the urge to do the same.

"What do we do now?" Braddock asked, clutching his pulse rifle like a security blanket.

Jodi licked her lips, but there was no moisture in her mouth, her tongue dry as a dead, sun-bleached lizard carcass.

"Oh, shit," she murmured to herself. There was only one thing they could do. She began to undo her helmet and the web gear that held her remaining weapons and ammunition. "I want you to keep everyone down, out of sight, unless I call for help," she told him.

"What are you going to do?" he asked, suddenly afraid that she really had flipped. "You're not going out there by yourself, are you?" he asked, incredulous. "After what we just saw?"

Shrugging out of her armor, glad to be free again from its clinging embrace, Jodi smiled with courage she didn't feel inside and said, "That's the point, Braddock. After what I just saw, I have no intention of giving him the idea that I'm a Bad Guy. I don't know how he's choosing his enemies, since he just waxed a wagon-load of what I suppose are – were – his own people. But walking up to him with a bunch of weapons in hand doesn't seem too bright." Finally free of all the encumbrances demanded by modern warfare, she fixed Braddock with a look of concern that failed to mask her fear. "If he polished off that crowd by himself," she said quietly, "we wouldn't stand a chance against him should he decide to turn on us. I don't know who – or what – he is, but he scares the piss out of me, and I want to do everything I can to try and get us on his good side before he starts looking for some more trouble to get into."

Standing up, she put her hands on top of the wall. She did not have the patience to walk the fifteen yards to the bolted gates. "Give me a boost, will you?"

"You're nuts, el-tee," Braddock grumbled as he made a stirrup with his hands to help lift her over the wall.

"Look at it this way," she told him as she clambered to the top. "At least he's human. Besides," she went on with faked cheerfulness as she dropped to the ground on the far side, "I know his name. Maybe he'll take me out for a beer."

Worried like an older brother whose sister has a date with a known psychopath, Braddock kept an uneasy watch through the sight of his pulse rifle. He kept the cross hairs centered on the strange warrior's head, as Jodi slowly made her way toward the bridge and the silent, alien figure that knelt there.

The closer she got to the bridge, the faster Jodi's forced upbeat attitude evaporated. She was excited, which was good in a way, but she was also terrified after what she had just witnessed. The memory of this man holding her captive only a little while ago, holding her closer than she had ever allowed a man to hold her, overshadowed all her other thoughts. It was also a sliver of hope: he had not harmed her then, and she prayed to whatever deity might listen that he would not harm her now.

As she stepped onto the old stone blocks and saw more closely the destruction that lay just a few meters away, she stopped. The thought that one individual, wielding what she had always considered to be a very primitive weapon, a sword, had shed so much blood in so brief a time, was beyond her understanding.

But looking at Reza now, she saw no trace of the monstrous killing machine that had slain her enemies only minutes before. He appeared bowed under, crushed by some incredible pressure, as if his spirit was that of an old, broken man.

Stepping gingerly around the ravaged Kreelan bodies, Jodi slowly made her way toward him.

"Reza," she said quietly from a meter or so away, trying not to startle him.

After a moment, he slowly lifted his head to look at her, and she cringed at the blood that had spattered onto his armor and his face, coating him like a layer of crimson skin. He stared at her with his unblinking green eyes, and she began to tremble at what she saw there, not out of fear, but with compassion for another human being's pain. Kneeling beside him, she took the sweat-stained bandanna from around her neck and began to gently wipe some of the dark Kreelan blood from his face. "It's okay now," she soothed. "Everything will be all right now."

Reza did not understand her words, but her feelings were as plain to him as if they had been written in stone. He had found a friend.

Eighteen

Fleet Admiral Hercule L'Houillier was not by nature an excitable man. Small in stature, but with the courage – or so some said, and he would sometimes allow himself to believe – of a lion, he had survived many long years of combat by maintaining his composure and his wits in the most desperate situations. His war record and an instinctive political savvy eventually had placed him in the position of Supreme Commander of the Confederation High Command, the highest military posting in the human sphere.

But today, during the emotional discussions and heated arguments that had swept over his staff and the other assembled notables sitting around the table, his normally placid demeanor had been shaken with the possibilities and responsibilities that now lay before him. Around him, the other members of the hastily assembled commission continued to argue while L'Houillier remained content to listen. He would take the floor when he judged the time was right.

"I tell you, this is the first and only opportunity of its kind! We must take full advantage of it, regardless of the consequences for a single individual." Major General Tensch, a notable conservative on the crisis council that had been convened to review the situation, had echoed his sentiments with the dedication of a modern-day Cato. "The destruction of–"

"Yes, general, we know," interrupted a woman with close-cropped blond hair who wore an extremely expensive – and attractive – suit of red silk. "'The destruction of the enemy is the first and only priority,'" Melissa Savitch, a delegate from the General Counsel's office, finished for him, rolling her eyes in disgust. "Your single-minded approach to the issue has been well noted on numerous occasions, general. However, there is more at stake here than the information you can pull from this man like juice squeezed from a grapefruit. Until we have all the facts at our disposal, we just don't know what we're dealing with, and this office will not support the kind of action you are advocating." Looking around the table, careful to make eye contact with every one of the people gathered around her, she went on, "I would like to remind you, all of you, that we are discussing the future and well-being of a Confederation citizen here, not one of the enemy."

"I think that has yet to be determined, Ms. Savitch," interjected T'nisha Matabele, a young aide to Senator Sirikwa. She was standing in for the senator who was at the moment dozens of parsecs away on Achilles and unable to return in time for the meeting. "There is no evidence to prove beyond a shadow of a doubt, as your office loves to quote, that this – what's his name – Reza Gard was forcibly abducted by the enemy." She paused, confident now that she had everyone's attention. She did not bother to feel foolish for momentarily forgetting the subject's name. That wasn't important. "At this point, there is no way at all to prove his identity, even if we had a DNA sample right here. All we have is a report that he presented local Marine Corps authorities with a letter allegedly written by a war hero who died over fifteen years ago in an enemy attack that has never been explained in terms of motive or method. Any records on this Reza Gard were destroyed there, and the chances of stumbling across any validating birth or orphanage records on another planet are slim, to say the least. In my estimation, the entire affair is simply too convenient. I think the enemy is trying to lead us on somehow." She looked around the table, daring anyone to contradict her assessment of the situation. "While I sympathize with Counselor Savitch's position," she went on smoothly, wearing her conceit like an overpriced perfume, "I firmly believe, and am going to recommend to the senator as our course of action, that a deep-core brain scan is the best approach to deal with this... problem."

"I agree," said General Tensch, obviously satisfied with her reasoning, and certainly with her conclusion.

Melissa Savitch noted with dismay that more than half the heads in the room and on the far end of the holo links bobbed their assent. *Some of the fence sitters just took a side,* she thought. She was about to make a rebuttal when another voice intervened.

"Poppycock."

As one, the three dozen heads, real and holo projections, turned toward a huge bear of a man in a dress black Navy uniform who sat in the shadows at the periphery of the gathered luminaries. The gravelly voice, barely understandable through a carefully cultivated Russian accent, belonged to Vice Admiral Evgeni Zhukovski, one of the Confederation's most brilliant officers and an unabashed Russophile. His left breast boasting more ribbons and decorations than most of the others in the room had ever seen in their lives, Zhukovski had more than paid his dues to humanity. Glaring at Matabele with his one good eye, the High Command's Chief of Intelligence did not try to conceal his contempt for her and some of the others in the room. After facing the Kreelan enemy so many times in his life, the potential opponents arrayed around him now seemed entirely laughable, save that they had a great deal to say about their race's survival. It was what continually terrified him away from retirement.

Squinting theatrically at the table console, Zhukovski said, "Obviously, I have been remiss in my understanding of what was said in good Lieutenant Mackenzie's report, as well as progress of war in general," he paused, glancing at Counselor Savitch, "and articles of Confederation Constitution in particular. Perhaps review of facts may help eliminate ignorance of old sailor.

"Fact," he said, thrusting his right index finger into the air as if he was poking out someone's eye. "Since war began long ago, certain humans have tried to betray their own kind – for whatever insane reason – and Kreelans have never accepted them."

He paused, glaring at Matabele, then at Tensch. "Never. In fact, from what little is known from exposed cases, would-be betrayers fare even worse than normal victims, getting nothing for their trouble but slow and painful death. This is no war of nation against nation, fighting over land or competing ideologies, where at least some participants of both sides may find something in common, even if only greed, and therefore find reason to betray side they are supposed to be on. We have nothing in common with Kreelans. Or, if we do, we do not know what. Nearly century later, we know nothing of their language, culture, customs; nothing of their motivations, their weaknesses: only their name – and even that we *assume* from what dying Kreelans have said before death. We know much about their biology, but we cannot explain what we see. And their technology, which covers such wide scope, we do not understand on anything other than strictly application level, and sometimes not even that. They build incredibly advanced starships to come and find us, and then use swords and spears to kill us."

He had to pause for a minute, taking a dramatically noisy gulp from his water glass. "Please excuse," he said, cutting off one of Tensch's supporters before he could open his mouth, "I am not finished yet." After another gulp, he went on. "Now, where was I? Ah, yes. So, we know nothing of importance, really, about our enemy, which makes basic tenet of most human martial philosophies, 'know your enemy,' rather useless, *da?*

"Another fact: over fifteen years ago, planet Hallmark blows up. Poof. No distress signals, no evidence that orbital defenses worked, nothing. No people left, all blown to little pieces. We know it was Kreelan handiwork, because navigational traces were found in system and orbital defenses destroyed, but we do not know how or why. Bigger question is why did they only use this weapon that one time? Why not use it on all human planets? And why use it on defenseless Hallmark, world of orphan children, in first place? Could they not find better target? What were they doing there, and why did they not want us to find out about it, why cover their tracks with such vigor?

"Now, fact that brought us together today." He pointed at the console and the display of Jodi Mackenzie's report. "Less than twenty-four hours ago, strange young man masquerading in Kreelan armor shows up on tiny settlement where Marines are, shall we say, not doing well. According to young Lieutenant Mackenzie's report, he somehow appeared inside and somehow got out of small room that had only one door, and that was watched by remnants of Marine regiment on far side – all without being seen." He jabbed his finger in the air again. "Then he appears on field of battle and proceeds to kill over fifty Kreelan warriors by himself in close combat in only minutes."

"So what, admiral?" Anthony Childers, another senatorial aid filling in for his master, asked. "First of all, how do we know this Mackenzie is reliable and not just coming up with some nutty concoction to get back to her ship or something? Frankly, I find it hard to accept this magical mumbo-jumbo about popping in and out of rooms like a cheap magician." Heads nodded around the room, with several hands covering not-so-innocent smiles. "Secondly, this guy killing a bunch of his own doesn't prove anything. He could have done that just to get into the confidence of those grunts down there on the colony, and from the way this drippy report reads, he did a damn fine job."

Zhukovski could do nothing but glare at the man. The admiral lost his arm and an eye nearly ten years before after ramming his dying ship into a Kreelan destroyer, and he now regretted not having taken up the surgeons' suggestion that he get a prosthetic. He would have liked to strangle Childers, but would have needed two hands to grasp the man's fleshy neck. "I will ignore insulting comments to men and women of military services," he growled, his accent deepening. "Not having served any time in military sometimes makes people say and do unkind things to those who have, instead of truly appreciating their sacrifice."

Childers reddened at the insult. It was not a widely known fact that he had obtained an under-the-table exemption from mandated military service through the intercession of his powerful shipping magnate father, and he would have preferred to keep it that way, especially in this crowd.

Zhukovski knew that he had just made yet another enemy by humiliating the man, but he did not care. What could they do, retire him? He shrugged. Childers had more than deserved it.

"But, comrade," Zhukovski went on, "to answer question, I have reviewed Mackenzie's records in detail. I have no reason at all to believe that what she said is not so. As for this Reza Gard pulling off so-called 'snow job,' I do not believe it. As Chief of Intelligence, I cannot and will not rule it out as possibility, but it goes against what few hard facts we have obtained, and – more importantly – nearly century of deadly experience."

"Then what exactly do you believe, admiral?" Melissa Savitch asked. Based on previous encounters with the man, she had long regarded Zhukovski as another conservative military hard case whose brain functioned on one level only, if at all. But she got the feeling that she was in for a surprise.

Zhukovski regarded her quietly before he answered. *What a strange world I live in*, he thought to himself, considering that this woman, who usually was in vehement opposition to his position, now appeared to be his only potential ally. He had noticed the shift in the room, seeing that the likes of Tensch and Matabele now had clear control of those who would allow others to make their decisions for them, and those who simply wished to be politically correct.

"Yes admiral," Tensch prodded acidly, "please enlighten us."

"Very well," Zhukovski replied, biting his tongue to keep from telling Tensch how much he needed to be enlightened. "I believe that we must take this Reza Gard at face value until or unless he shows us otherwise. He perhaps is only one who can answer our questions, even if only about his own personal history, about what happened to Hallmark and why."

"So why the big argument, admiral?" Matabele interrupted, even more impatient and self-important than Tensch. She flashed a quick glance at Childers, just to let him know that she had usurped his influence, and was immune to attack, at least from that angle: she had done her time in the Territorial Army. "Why worry about whether he's for real or not, when a core scan can tell us all we need to know right away?"

"Two reasons, young lady," Zhukovski sighed as if he was speaking to a complete idiot. "First, while I confess I am not overly moved by Counselor Savitch's emotive arguments, I nonetheless support her position. This is not because I am great humanitarian that you know me to be," he noticed Savitch suppressing a smile, "but because of something she herself commented upon very early in our meeting today. It is something all of you have so far overlooked or ignored: I believe Reza Gard is not a spy, something for which our enemy has no use, but some kind of emissary from the Empire."

The room suddenly became a maelstrom of gesturing hands and animated faces that matched the flurry of conversation that erupted at the admiral's statement. Melissa Savitch was impressed not only by what the man had said, but by the contrast in effects between when she had brought up the idea this morning and now. Her attempt had been solidly brushed off by everyone who cared to comment on it. But after Zhukovski's delivery into the vacuum left by all the arguing and fighting that had gone on all day, the delegates at least were willing to shout about it.

The man has timing, she had to admit to herself.

Admiral L'Houillier let the pandemonium continue for a few moments before he brought the meeting back to order with several raps of the gavel upon the table. "Order!" he called. "Order!" The conversations rapidly tapered to silence.

The admiral directed his attention to Zhukovski. "Evgeni, you said there were two reasons to take this individual at his word. You elaborated on the first. What was the second?"

"The second is that he presented to good Lieutenant Mackenzie what I believe to be authentic letter written by retired Marine Colonel Hickock, may he rest in peace." Again he studied the transmitted image of the yellowing letter, his old friend's distinctive scrawl immediately recognizable. *Wiley*, he thought sadly, *whatever became of you?* "Kreelans," he went on, not wanting to think of how few old friends he had left, "have never shown interest in our literature and correspondence, even military signals as far as we can tell, approaching fray each time as if they were rediscovering us. There is no reason to suspect that he was given letter with intent to use it as *bona fides* for espionage. Besides, if that was truth, why would he appear in guise that was so obviously Kreelan? Because they do not know how to spy on us properly? Bah." He shook his great head. "I believe letter is real, and that Reza Gard knew Colonel Hickock at some time before he came under control of Empire. And, if estimate of Reza's age is good to within few years, only place they could have met would have been on Hallmark when he was young boy."

"Which we can't prove," said Melissa. It was not an attack against Zhukovski's reasoning, but a statement of unfortunate fact.

"Da. Which we cannot prove. For now, anyway."

Tensch was shaking his head. "I'm sorry admiral," he said, "but all that's fantasy, as far as I'm concerned. I understand your respect for Colonel Hickock, but that has nothing to do with the subject of this meeting. We're talking about a human being who was indoctrinated into the Kreelan Empire, and then returned to the human sphere for reasons unknown. I believe he poses a serious security threat and I think he should be dealt with accordingly. Assuming he cooperated, it might take years to reintroduce him to humanity, and that's time that we just don't have." Tensch's expression hardened. "If he has to be sacrificed, so be it."

Zhukovski leaned forward like a cat about to pounce. The balance of power in the room had shifted again, with most of the delegates on the fence again, and he was determined that Tensch and his band of reactionaries would not have their way. Zhukovski had a gut feeling that the young man now waiting in a monastery on a faraway colony could be the deciding factor in humanity's continued survival, and he was not about to let a mistake here seal the fate of Zhukovski's great-grandchildren. His gut instincts had seldom steered him wrong, and he was not about to dismiss them now.

"Then perhaps you will be one to carry out deep-core on him?" he hissed. Tensch looked shocked. "Surely you, much-decorated general of the Marine Corps, will have no difficulty in getting man who slaughtered fifty Kreelan warriors single-handed to willingly submit to excruciating procedure that will leave him as permanent vegetable?" He swept his hand around the room, then banged it against the console in front of him so hard that the entire table shook. "You do not seem to understand, my friends. If half of what Mackenzie's report says is true, you may not have any choice but to accept him for what he claims to be, because we may not be able to control him – *may not even be able to kill him* – otherwise."

The room was dead silent. Very few of them had considered the problem from that angle. They had been so concerned with the end result that they had ignored the difficulties of how to achieve it. Clearly, assuming the report from Rutan was credible, if Reza did not want to submit to the deep-core scan, it was extremely unlikely that he could be convinced or coerced into doing so. Jodi Mackenzie had not reported any trouble with him, but she had been treating him well. So far, it seemed that her approach of kindness and respect was paying off.

"What is it that you suggest we do, Admiral Zhukovski?" L'Houillier's question told the others in the room that Zhukovski's recommendation would be undersigned by the Supreme Commander. L'Houillier had listened patiently to all the arguments during the day, not because he did not have his own views, but because a committee had to be allowed the latitude to discuss what it might in order to reach a workable consensus. It was the chairman's job to keep it on track without crushing it with his or her own bias. But there came a time when discussion had to end and a decision had to be made. Zhukovski's arguments, judging by the expressions on the faces of those around him, had carried the field. They had also convinced the Supreme Commander. There might still be opportunities for some of the others to dissent

L'Houillier's decision to go with Zhukovski's recommendations, but not in this room, and not today.

No, L'Houillier thought. If anyone wants to take it up later, they will have to do so with the president himself.

Inwardly relieved, but not showing it except for a surreptitious wink in Melissa Savitch's direction, Zhukovski said, "I propose that we do exactly what Colonel Hickock originally intended, admiral. I believe that Reza Gard should be inducted into Marine training and put into military service, at which he appears to excel already, at earliest possible convenience."

Tensch was about to interrupt when L'Houillier angrily hammered the gavel against the table. Tensch visibly jumped, startled by the sound. His face reddening with anger, the general bit his tongue as he gave L'Houillier a glare the admiral returned until Tensch, thinking better of it, looked away.

"As I was saying," Zhukovski went on, allowing himself only a moment to relish Tensch's humiliation, "this will serve several purposes. It will let Gard do what he apparently wishes, which will make him easier, perhaps, to deal with in near term.

"Second, military training centers are good place to indoctrinate people into Confederation. Long ago, concept was called 'school of nation,' and it is no less applicable in this case. He will learn language and customs, how to be more human and less alien.

"Third," Zhukovski continued, "military service will make it easier for us to watch him without him feeling like he is being watched. There will always be someone – superior, subordinate, whoever – nearby. If he is not who he says, or does something untoward, it is more likely to be noticed than if he is given job selling flowers on street corner or reading poetry on mall.

"Finally, we will learn much more from him if he willingly cooperates, which I feel is based in large degree on what we decide today, how we treat him in future. That way, we get much more information over time. I know that time is factor, because it translates directly into lives lost. I have children, grandchildren, and great-grandchildren, and many members of my family have already given their lives to our cause, and I understand this well. But war has gone on for century already, and I doubt there is knowledge in his head that will let us win in week, if at all." He nodded to Tensch. "Also, those who would like to do core scan on brain forget one very important thing: we have no Kreelan linguists and thought interpreters to go through what might come out of your *chekist* machine. We have never successfully interpreted their language, and know nothing of their cultural images. I do not think Gard's brain will provide convenient translation for data thus extracted."

L'Houillier nodded, satisfied with the intelligence officer's reasoning. "Very well, admiral," he said. "Please meet with the operations officer and work out the details as soon as possible, beginning with the retrieval of Reza Gard and the Marines now on Rutan. That operation has uncompromising priority over all other tasks for the fleet, and the operations orders will carry my signature. Once that has been arranged, I want you to work out a long-term development plan for this young man and have a draft copy to me by twelve-hundred hours the day after tomorrow. After I have reviewed it, we will brief your plan to the president and Special Council as soon as possible." He made a few quick scribbles on the table's scratchpad, putting notes in his daily log file for later retrieval in the privacy of his office. Then he looked up and surveyed the committee members. "Ladies and gentlemen, does anyone have anything else to add?" Aside from a few disappointed looks, no one did. They were all anxious to get back to their parent organizations and agencies to hatch their own operations. "Very well then. This meeting is hereby adjourned."

The gavel pounded the table a final time.

History, Evgeni Zhukovski thought somberly to himself, *has just been made*. He prayed to God that they had made the right decision.

Nineteen

"This just came in, ma'am." A young Marine handed Jodi a message.

Jodi took it and gave the man a quick nod. "Thank you, corporal."

Braddock saw her face light up. "What is it?"

"Task Force-85 is on its way," she told him, "ETA thirty-six hours." It was not their home task force, TF-1051, but it would do.

"Hot damn!" Braddock cried. "Man, that's the quickest reaction I've ever seen from fleet."

Smiling with excitement, she read him part of the message: "As of 2385.146.1958T, prior regimental mission and priorities rescinded, repeat, rescinded. New priority as follows: imperative that safety and well-being of subject Reza Gard be maintained until arrival TF-85. Regiment is to stand down except for security details until relief arrival."

She turned to Reza, who knelt quietly on the ground nearby, watching her and Braddock's conversation as if he were a dog listening to its masters talking to one another, intensely interested, but unable to understand.

"Well, my friend," she said happily, "it seems as though somebody thinks you're awfully important."

"Yeah, enough to send a whole frigging task force!" Braddock announced.

Reza cocked his head at her words, his expression intense but unreadable, and she found herself pierced by his gaze. *The hearts you could break with those green eyes of yours,* she thought to herself, then smiled. She knew that hers would not be among them.

* * *

"Nothing's ever easy, is it?" Braddock sighed.

Jodi looked through the trees to the village walls and the several thousand heads peering over it. They had thought that the news of the task force's approach would make everyone happy. While the Marines had been elated, the Rutanians had taken a somewhat different approach to the news. A hastily called council meeting that had excluded Jodi and the Marines had ended with demands that Reza be brought into the village for what Hernandez had called an "inquisition."

Had her orders not been so out of the ordinary and Hernandez's request not so blunt – it was very obviously a demand – Jodi might have considered taking Reza into the village herself so Hernandez and the others might meet the instrument of their salvation that morning.

But, in light of the strange circumstances and fearing for Reza's safety – and that of the villagers – Jodi had managed to follow orders for once and refused. Much to her surprise, Hernandez had stalked away, silent with what could only be rage.

Not long afterward she heard Father Hernandez on the steps of the church. He was shouting something about "the Antichrist," and she ordered Braddock to have his Marines keep the townspeople back behind the wall while she took Reza to a secluded stand of trees where they could be fairly comfortable, yet inconspicuous. They were out of sight of the townspeople, but Jodi could still see out to keep an eye on things.

After seeing to the positioning of his Marines, Braddock had joined her, careful to let Reza see that he had no weapons. Reza accepted his presence without any comment other than his unblinking stare.

"I hope these people don't decide to do anything rash," Braddock murmured, looking back toward the city gates. Through his field glasses, he could see that the number of gesticulating hands and angry, frightened faces had multiplied considerably since his last observation. "Tomlinson," he said into his comm link, "what's the situation over there?"

Lance Corporal Raleigh Tomlinson's voice crackled back through the receiver in his ear. "I don't like it, gunny. These people are starting to look a little ugly, if you know what I mean. I'm not a Christian, but I know that some of the stuff they're saying isn't real nice. They're starting to get pretty hot under the collar, and I heard some saying stuff about crossing over the wall, mention of heretics, and so on. Looks like the old priest is making it into a religious hocus-pocus thing, talking about 'signs' and the Antichrist and such. He and some of the others on their council have been shouting garbage like that at me for the last couple hours." He paused. "I don't know, gunny, looks like refusing to let them talk to whoever you've got there might have been a bad idea. It kind of reminds me of when we were on Dehra Dun a couple years ago."

Braddock frowned. "Okay. Keep me posted, and for God's sake don't feel bashful about singing out."

"Roger. Tomlinson out."

"What about Dehra Dun?" Jodi asked, having heard the conversation through her own comm link. "What happened there?"

The gunnery sergeant looked at Reza, then at the gates, before he turned to face her. "Two years ago, when the regiment was due for some R-and-R, the task force dropped us off on Dehra Dun before moving off to a rendezvous to take on the regiment scheduled to replace us in the line. Dehra Dun wasn't described in the info bulletins as a garden spot, but it didn't look too bad." He shook his head slowly. "Man, were we in for a surprise.

"About a week after we arrived, me, Tomlinson, and a few others from my old squad were wandering around the capital when we saw an inter-city bus cream some poor kid that just ran out in the road. We were gonna try and see if we could help, but we couldn't get near the accident. It seemed like people all of a sudden just appeared out of nowhere and surrounded that bus like a human wall. They didn't do or say much of anything at first, like they were only rubbernecks or something. Then somebody shouted something and it set them off. First it was only murmurs and grumbling, but in a few minutes they were all shouting and angry as hell, buzzing around that bus like a bunch of hornets. It wasn't long after that when they started in, attacking those poor bastards in the bus. Even then, the driver might have been able to get away, but he waited too long. He never should have stopped." The memory gave him the shivers. "The crowd ripped open that bus like an army of red ants tearing into a caterpillar. They dragged all those people off, maybe a couple dozen, and beat every last one of them to death. They took the driver, who was probably already dead, and trussed him between a couple of skimmers. They took off in different directions, and that was the last of him." He smiled grimly. "Then they turned on us."

Jodi silently wondered if he had ever told this story to anyone before. She had only known the man for several weeks, but she felt she knew him well. In the daily battles they had fought, she had never seen him show fear; he had been an idyllic leader to his Marines, fierce and courageous, and a welcome support for her. It was difficult to imagine him being any other way. But, listening to his tale, she caught a glimpse of something else, of a time when Gunnery Sergeant Tony Braddock had indeed been afraid.

He looked back at the crowd that was beginning to gather at the city gates. "I had already gotten my people moving back down the street, away from the trouble, but it wasn't soon enough." He made a nervous laugh that caught in his throat. "You can't imagine what it feels like to be running like hell, with the ground shaking under your feet and your ears filled with the screaming of a few thousand pissed-off indigs chasing after you. Lord of All," he said quietly, "I've never been so scared by anything, before or since."

"Why were they after you guys?" Jodi asked. "You didn't do anything."

Braddock shrugged. "Who knows? I guess it was because we were there, and we were different. Just like the people on that bus. They happened to be Muslims on their way through a Hindu town to somewhere else. But, from what we read later about the place, it just as easily could have been a bunch of Hindus in a Muslim town. Wouldn't have mattered a bit.

"Anyway, we managed to get away with a few cuts and bruises from bottles and rocks, running fast enough to leave most of the rioters behind to look for someone else to beat up on. A few minutes later, a bunch of Territorial Army guys were heading back down the street to bust some heads and get those people under control, but it was too late for the people on that bus, and almost too late for us." He shook his head. "The news reported that eighty people died and over three hundred were injured in the rioting that day. That's what you get when religious fervor mixes with fear and hate. A bloody frigging mess."

There were over four thousand adults in the village of Rutan, Jodi thought. What if Father Hernandez's zealous pacifism was fired into righteous anger and fear?

Jodi, while not an ardent student of history, had read enough to know that some of humanity's bloodiest wars had been fought in the name of one god or another. And the Rutanians outnumbered her Marines by about two hundred to one.

"Jesus," she whispered.

* * *

For one of the few times in his life, Father Hernandez was truly enraged. He was angry that he and his people were being held like prisoners within their own walls by the people who allegedly had been sent to protect them from the Enemy, from the powers unleashed by Satan upon the Universe. How ironic, he thought: the miracle for which he had prayed, and which he at first thought had been answered this very morning, appeared to be only an agent of the Evil One, a demon under whose enchantment the Marines beyond the gates had fallen. When he had seen Jodi's face that morning, he knew that she had seen a sign, but he had been so sure that it had been from God that he had never even considered the possibility of Satan's deceitful treachery. That morning he was certain that his call to God for help had been answered, and that an angel had been sent to save and protect them from the demonic hordes that had descended unbidden from the skies.

But it had not been so. As the last of the Marines followed the young Navy lieutenant down Waybridge Street toward the city gates, Father Hernandez had finally allowed himself the privilege of gazing firsthand upon the miracle God had delivered. At first, he was sure that his eyes were deceiving him, but then it became clear: an angel had arrived, no doubt, but it was not from above. As the thing made some unholy communion with its fellow demons, Hernandez understood that the angel before his eyes was the Angel of Death. He became sure of it as the beast suddenly turned upon its own kind in a ritual of slaughter designed to seduce the Marines in a demonstration of power, of a kind they could easily understand and accept.

Now, as he stood at the gates, he knew that Satan had won the hearts of these strangers with his clever tricks. The unbelievers stood now facing the thousands of Hernandez's flock, uniformed victims of a plague that needed no rats to spread. He felt pity for them, especially Mackenzie and Braddock, whom he had come to like and admire a great deal. But they apparently had never had the strength of faith possessed by Hernandez and his people, and so they were unprepared for Satan's insidious assault. God's miracle would indeed come, but it would be wrought by the hands of His faithful servants. It was a thought that repelled Hernandez and his fellows because they so abhorred violence. But it also thrilled them that God was giving them this opportunity to strike back at Satan, using their own hands as the divine instruments of the Evil One's undoing.

Still, Hernandez was a stubborn man, even in carrying out God's just vengeance. He had spent most of the years of his life saving souls, and he would not be content with himself until every avenue into the hearts of the weak had been tested. Not every man and woman on Rutan had died in the last half century with the Savior in their hearts, but none of them had died without hearing Hernandez's voice at least once in their lives, begging them to open their hearts to Him and be saved. He had encountered Satan's mark many times over the years, and only on a few occasions had he been forced to concede defeat or resort to the staff and rod. He knew his enemy was tenacious, and he was determined to be no less so.

"Corporal!" he called to the nearest Marine on the other side of the wall. "You must allow us to see the thing, that we may know if it is Satan's messenger!" Hernandez was as conscious as Corporal Tomlinson of the townspeople's increasingly agitated state, but he viewed it from a different perspective. What Tomlinson saw as religious fervor about to explode into undirected violence, Hernandez viewed as the gradual massing of God's power within his people. It was the means to slay the embodiment of Evil that had arisen, as champion of its own kind in a contest to be fought not for blood, but for the souls of Hernandez's people. "Please, corporal, you must let me speak with Lieutenant Mackenzie!"

He saw the Marine speak into his communications device, but knew that this meant nothing. He was merely sending information to be used by the Evil One cowering among the trees. Around Hernandez, men with crude weapons – hoes, scythes, axes – quietly began to move from the rear of the crowd toward the wall, to act as the vanguard of God's army.

Dread and excitement competing for dominance in his heart, Hernandez waited.

* * *

"I think we've got what's called 'a situation,' el-tee," Braddock said. "Farm tools and axes may not be much, but it's more than a match for whatever force we can muster against them."

"I don't want that to happen, dammit," she hissed. Tomlinson's last report had been the first page in the last chapter of tranquility; the next move would be a very short-lived battle between the Marines and a few thousand frenzied villagers, and she and Braddock both knew that the Marines would not be among the victors. "Tomlinson," she called over the comm link.

"Yes, ma'am," answered the young corporal's voice, a bit uneasily.

"Tomlinson, tell Father Hernandez that he and one other person – only one – of his choice, can come out here. Tell him, again, that we don't want trouble, but that we're dealing with something – someone – that's very dangerous and his people need to stay where they are for their own good. You got that?"

"Roger, ma'am. Right away. Out." He sounded relieved.

Jodi watched through her binoculars as Tomlinson called out to the priest who waited by the gates.

"Here they come," Braddock said as Father Hernandez and a somewhat younger man whom Braddock knew to be on the council quickly passed out of the gate and came toward them at a brisk walk. Hernandez, in fact, was walking so fast that the other man occasionally had to trot to keep up. The gunnery sergeant went out to meet them.

"Listen, Father–"

"No, my son, there is no time for talk!" Hernandez brushed by Braddock as if he were a pocket of cold air. "I know that Satan has already worked his powers upon you, and that you are now his unwitting servant. My only hope is that you can yet be saved from his clutches!"

"Wait!" Braddock cried, torn between tackling the old man and risking the consequences or letting him charge into the tines of Reza's claws. He decided that he had no choice but to opt for the latter.

Storming into the little clearing, Hernandez found only Jodi. "Where is he?" Hernandez demanded, his eyes darting into the shadows of the trees that lay around him like the bars of a cage. "Where is the servant of the Antichrist?"

"Father Hernandez," Jodi said evenly, straining to control the anger and fear that sought to creep into her voice, "if you turn around, very slowly, you'll see."

"Enough games, child!" he said angrily. "There is no–" He felt a tap on his arm, and turned to find his companion staring at something behind them, his eyes wide with disbelief.

Following his companion's gaze, Hernandez found what he had come for. "Mary, mother of God," he whispered as he crossed himself.

Backlit by the sun, Reza was an animate shadow that soundlessly stepped a pace closer to the elderly priest and the councilman. Jodi had not seen or heard him get up and move to where he stood now, even though he had been right beside her a moment before. More fascinating, however, was that when she did not look directly at him, if she looked at Braddock or the priest and Reza was only in her peripheral vision, he completely disappeared, as if he were an illusion, not really there.

"Please, father," she said quietly, keeping her eyes riveted on Reza, "don't make any sudden moves or threaten him. He has been very cooperative, but he's a complete unknown. Anything might set him off."

"What has he said to you, child," Hernandez said through his astonishment at the apparition before him, "to convince you that the ways of Darkness are best?"

Jodi shook her head. "Father, he hasn't said a word other than what I believe to be his name, which is Reza. I don't think he knows our language, or if he does, he's either forgotten it or has just chosen not to communicate with us."

"Foolish child," Hernandez chided softly. "So easily have you been led astray." He held up the wooden crucifix that hung from around his neck on a length of ivory cord. "As darkness flees from the light, so too does Evil retreat from the sign of the cross." Like a mythical vampire hunter, pushing the stunned councilman aside, Hernandez stalked toward Reza, the crucifix thrust before him just like the weapon he believed his faith to be.

"Father, no!" Both Jodi and Braddock reacted instantly, trying to stop the priest from carrying out this lunatic act of self-destruction, but they may as well have been miles away. In a movement so swift that it barely registered in Jodi's brain, Reza's sword sang from the sheath on his back, the ornate blade reflecting the glory of the sun as it sought its target. The air was filled with the ring of metal striking bone, and Father Hernandez crumpled to the ground at Reza's feet. As he fell, the tip of Reza's sword caught the cord of the crucifix, deftly lifting it from around the priest's neck and prying the cross from Hernandez's powerless hands. With a tiny flick, the cross flew into the air to land in Reza's outstretched fingers.

The councilman dropped to his knees and began to pray for deliverance with eyes tightly closed as Jodi and Braddock knelt beside the fallen priest.

"Oh, shit," Jodi cried. "You stupid old fool, I tried to warn you."

"I don't see any blood," Braddock remarked quietly. His eyes and hands worked over Hernandez's body, but there did not appear to be any sign of injury. "Reza's sword was so bloody fast I didn't even see where it hit him," he muttered. But then he saw the swelling near Hernandez's hairline, where the flat of Reza's sword must have hit the old priest's head.

Hernandez moaned, and his eyes flickered open. "Has the beast fled?" he whispered.

"Father," Jodi said, relieved that he seemed to be all right, "just be thankful you're still alive, although I can't figure out how. Where are you hurt?"

"My head," he groaned, his face wrinkling in pain, "but that is not important. Where is the child of Satan?"

"At the moment," she told him, taking a quick glance at Reza, "your demon is giving your crucifix a good looking over."

That was something Hernandez did not expect to hear. "That cannot be!" he exclaimed. Struggling mightily against the hands that sought to gently restrain him, he propped himself up on his elbows to see for himself.

There, as Jodi had told him, stood Reza, raptly staring at the crucifix in one hand, his sword held easily at his side in his other, the shimmering tip held just above the ground. He turned the old wooden cross over in his taloned hand with great care, as if it were a priceless family heirloom that had survived generations of hardship to arrive safely in his hands. Then, as if noticing the others for the first time, he leaned over Hernandez and dangled the cross by the cord from his fingers. Speechless, the old man reached for it with one trembling hand, and the cross came away in his fist.

"This cannot be so," he whispered. "All my life, I have believed that evil must flee from God's sign, but Satan has somehow transcended even this."

"Have you ever considered," Jodi told him, "that maybe you're not being confronted with something evil? Just because he's different, he's not necessarily the work of the devil, you know. Braddock and I are different from you, but you didn't seem to have too much trouble accepting us."

Hernandez shook his head, stubborn to the last. "It is not the same."

"No," Jodi said, "it's not. It looks like he's more like you than we are."

"What does that..." His voice died as he watched Reza pull something from a black leather pouch at his waist. Looking at it carefully, as if not sure of what he was seeing, an almost-human expression – longing, perhaps – crossed his face before the inscrutable alien mask descended once more. Squatting down, Reza held out his hand to Hernandez, palm up. Something small glittered on his palm.

Slowly reaching forward, careful to avoid the rapier claws at the ends of Reza's fingers, Hernandez came away with a chain that was attached to a small crucifix that might be worn around one's neck. The metal of the crucifix and the chain had long since oxidized to an inky blackness, but the few spots where the original material showed through left no doubt that it was made of silver. Rubbing his fingers over the surface of the cross, he was rewarded with a dull glimmer of beauty. Holding the cross from the chain, he looked at Reza. "This is yours?"

Reza seemed to concentrate for a moment, then slowly and deliberately nodded his head.

Hernandez could not say what lay in the green eyes that were fixed upon him, but he could not honestly tell himself that he believed this stranger was lying to him, or was in any apparent way an instrument of evil.

Perhaps Jodi is right, he thought. Although Satan could choose any form he wished, why would he choose such an easily penetrated disguise? Were there not better forms in which to deceive the simple folk of Rutan? The chameleon seeks to blend in with its surroundings, he thought now, not to stand apart from them. Hernandez's people had been segregated from the human sphere for many years, making Rutan a place where different ways of any sort were viewed with skepticism, especially since the harshness of life ruled heavily in favor of community over individuality. Just as Jesus had shown his disciples the need to seek out and touch those who were wretched in the eyes of their fellow men, so too had Hernandez striven to reach out to others. Not with his staff or a scathing tongue, but with his love and compassion. He was not yet ready to dismiss his fears that this Reza was an instrument of the Devil. But he was prepared to consider the alternative, that this was a man like any other in the eyes of God, flawed and imperfect, molded of the same clay by His hands. For Hernandez, that was still a great leap of faith, but it was a chasm he was sure – in time, at least – he could cross.

But for now, holding the tiny crucifix in his hand, he could not restrain himself from asking one more question of the stranger looming over him. "Do you believe in God?"

Reza cocked his head to one side in what Jodi now thought of as some kind of Kreelan gesture or body language, and then he looked to her and Braddock, in turn, as if for help.

"I don't think he understands the question Father," she said. "Sometimes, it's almost as if he can sense your thoughts or feelings and react to them, and not the words you say. But that's only been with very simple or obvious things. What you're asking now, especially after what he must have lived through in the Empire, goes well beyond the simple and obvious, even if you just want a yes-or-no answer."

Hernandez nodded, favoring Reza with a smile that was sincere, if not entirely trusting. "So true," he said. The priest was more inclined to believe in Reza now, because he was sure that a demon under Satan's power would have tried to deceive the priest with an answer, be it yes or no, because Hernandez wanted so badly to hear it.

Somewhat relieved, he would be content to wait for the Truth to be revealed.

* * *

As evening turned to night, the trio began to tire under Reza's unflinching gaze. It was not long after four bedrolls were brought from the village and a fire started that all of them were ready for sleep.

All, that is, except Reza. Eschewing the bedroll and the fire's warmth for the lonely chill of the nearby darkness, he knelt on the ground at the edge of the grove and stared into the star-filled sky.

"Do you suppose he is praying?" Father Hernandez asked. The possibility that this strange man knew of the existence of God was quickly becoming an obsession with him. Hernandez was aware that he was falling into that spider's web, but he was powerless against the force that propelled him into it.

"He might," Braddock said. "But it looks more to me like he's homesick as hell... ah, sorry padre."

Hernandez waved it off "I am used to it by now," he sighed, gesturing at Jodi, who rolled her eyes. "But what makes you think he is homesick and not simply praying, perhaps confessing for killing those on the bridge this morning?"

Jodi frowned, not so much at Hernandez's curiosity at Reza's beliefs, but that he automatically seemed to equate the killing of anyone or anything – regardless of the circumstances – to some form of murder. She was not happy to have to kill anyone, either, but there were circumstances that justified, even necessitated, the taking of another being's life. In the war against the Empire, the Kreelans had laid the ground rules: fight and have a chance or die. Even among humankind, the score was often the same. Jodi had been forced to kill a man once as he brutally assaulted and then tried to rape a woman in a suburban park on Old Terra. Jodi had not known either of them, she had only been a casual stroller-by, but her duty then had been every bit as clear as the duties she had sworn in her commissioning oath to undertake on the part of her race. She had felt terrible after the fact, was sickened by the knowledge that one human being could do something like that to another when the survival of their entire race was in jeopardy in a much larger war. But she had never, not once in all the years that had passed, regretted shooting the man when he turned with a knife to fight her off. He had been an enemy to everything Jodi believed in, perhaps even more so than the Kreelans were. To Jodi, not having tried to help the woman would have left nothing inside her but intolerable guilt. Perhaps if Father Hernandez underwent a similar experience, he might gain an appreciation for what lay beyond the idealistic cloak of his pacifism.

"Before I joined the Corps," Braddock told them quietly, not noticing the momentary glare Jodi leveled at the priest, "I spent my whole life in a little town on Timor. I worked as a mechanic after I got out of secondary school. I did all right, but I never would have gotten rich at it." He smiled wistfully, suddenly remembering how awful it had been, how wonderful it had been. The long hours, the hard work, the ribbing he had taken from his friends because he studied in his free time instead of playing pool at the local bar. The loves he had had, had lost. It had been his home, and he knew it always would be. "I never saw anywhere else on that whole planet, just that little town. Doing or seeing other things was something I didn't think about much, because I didn't really have time for it, not when you have to do all you can just to get food on the family's table.

"But then my draft notice was posted, and I decided to join the Marines. I figured it was a better shot than the Navy. No offense, ma'am." Jodi shook her head. The two of them had shared times that had long since dissolved any seriousness in jibes about their rival services. "After the papers were signed, I felt good about it. My folks and little sister would have money to make ends meet, and I'd get to see something of the outside, which really began to appeal to me after a while. And fighting, that was something I'd always been good at, since I was a little kid. And if I was going to be fighting the Blues, so much the better."

He looked at Reza. "It wasn't like I thought it would be, though. Boot camp went by in a flash, all of us so busy we didn't have time to think about anything but making it through the next day.

"But when I reached the regiment and saw what the war really meant to a grunt like me, to all of us, I suddenly realized that I'd probably never see home again, except maybe in a box. It hit me just like that. That night, while we were waiting to ship out to the fleet, I went off by myself a little ways and knelt on the ground, just like Reza there. I looked up at the sky, but damned if I could figure out which star was home, where Mom and Dad and Lucille were. All I wanted then, more than anything in the world, was to be at home, sitting in the kitchen and having dinner with my folks, or maybe having a beer with Dad out on the porch, a thousand other little things. I wanted to be home so bad that I just started bawling like a baby." Braddock was silent for a moment, taking the time to look at the stars himself. "Since then, Father, I've seen a thousand other guys and gals do the exact same thing. He might be praying all right, but if he is, my money says that it's not inspired by guilt from his work this morning. If he's praying, it's a wish to wake up from all this and be at home, wherever his home might be, tucked into a nice warm bed."

The three of them were silent with their own thoughts for a while.

"Well, folks," Braddock said, finally breaking the spell and stretching out with obvious pleasure on the heavily padded bedroll, the first real chance to sleep that he could claim to have had for the better part of a month or more, "I think I'm going to shut down for the night. I don't know about you, but this Marine needs his beauty sleep real, real bad. 'Night, all."

"Goodnight, my son," Hernandez replied. He, too, was tired from the ordeals of the last weeks, and today especially. His mind was wound tight as a clock spring, but his body needed rest. "I think I will avail myself of sleep, as well. Goodnight, Jodi."

"Goodnight, Father, gunny." Jodi sat at the fire by herself for a while, still thinking about what Braddock had said. That Reza might be homesick had not occurred to her. She had naïvely assumed that Reza would be happy to be back in the Confederation, among his own people. She saw how precious the old letter from

Colonel Hickock was to him and the respect he had shown Braddock after Reza understood that Braddock was a Marine.

But believing that Reza should be happy to be "home" again had been silly, she understood now. Whatever Reza was thinking, it could hardly be from a perspective akin to hers. After all, how long had he been under the Empire's influence? Since early childhood? Since birth? And what – if anything – was left inside him that someone could point to and say, "That is human"? What did he really have in common with anyone in the human sphere, other than his genetic origins?

It was these questions that brought on a sudden wave of compassion for the dark, silent figure kneeling a few meters away. In the short time since he had been among them, he had demonstrated powers that made Jodi wonder if her disbelief in the supernatural, benign or otherwise, might be unjustified, and she wondered with uneasy curiosity at what other secrets might yet lay cloaked behind his green eyes. But for all that, he still boasted at least some of the frailties of his kind. He could shed tears of sadness, although she did not know exactly why he might be sad. Looking at him now, she knew that he could feel loneliness, too, just as Braddock had thought. Severed from the culture he had grown up in and whomever he might have been close to, how could it be any other way?

Quietly, so as not to disturb Braddock or the snoring priest, Jodi got up from her bedroll and went to sit beside Reza.

"Listen," she said softly as he turned to her, the pendants on the collar around his neck glittering brightly in the glow of the fire, "I know you can't understand what I'm saying, but I want you to know that you don't have to be alone." She reached out and found one of his hands. With the armored gauntlet and its rapier claws, it seemed huge and menacing against her tender flesh, but she held it anyway. "I don't know why you're here, or what or who you left behind. I hope that maybe you'll tell me those things someday, when we can speak in a language we both understand, because I really would like to know. Because I care. And there will be others who will care about you, too, and will be your friends." She touched his face with her other hand. There were no tears there now, just his glowing eyes. "I'm sure life won't be easy for you," she went on. "It never is for people who are different from the others around them, and you're different from every other human being who has ever lived. But you're still human, and that's what counts most. It'll be enough. I know it will."

She heard a tiny click, the same strange noise as when he had been holding her in the rectory, as he took off one of his gauntlets and clipped it to his waist. He took her hand in his, flesh against flesh, and did what Jodi thought was the most extraordinary thing.

Shyly, like a bewildered teenage boy on his first date, he smiled.

* * *

Jodi dreamed. Her nose was filled with the heady aroma of meat cooking over an open fire, and saliva flowed in her mouth like the warm waters of a deep subterranean river. Her stomach growled in her dream, and she moaned with almost sexual pleasure at the prospect of feasting on a thick, juicy steak, even one out of the shipboard food processors.

The dream, strange though some might have considered it, was rooted in one of Jodi's deepest desires since she had been marooned on Rutan. Penned up within the village walls for most of their stay, unable to hunt because of the threat from the Kreelans, the Marines had been eating little more than the stored bread, beans, and some vegetables of dubious origin. The Rutanians, being vegetarians, found this no great hardship, but Jodi and many of Colonel Moreau's people had become almost desperate for the taste of meat, especially when edible game was so plentiful in the nearby forest. Father Hernandez had chided her that it was an addictive vice akin to overindulgence in alcohol, and Jodi had not argued the point. If he and his people were content to live eating nothing but what came directly from plants grown and harvested by their own hands, Jodi would be the last to condemn them. But she and many of the others wanted something more.

She turned over on her side as the object in her dream floated into crystal-clear focus: a thick tender sirloin, this time not lean and healthy, but edged with a centimeter of delicious fat. Its plate-sized sides were streaked with the charring marks from the grill and carried the scent of the rare mesquite charcoal used to cook it.

Her stomach growled so loudly that it woke her up. Up to that point, the dream had been more satisfying and pleasurable than any sexual fantasy she could recall, if not because of its vividness, then perhaps because she had not eaten since the afternoon two days before.

"Oh, shit," she moaned, putting one hand over her empty belly, wishing she were back in the village rather than out here. But even though the villagers had all peacefully returned to their homes and the village was quiet, there was still a great deal of uncertainty regarding Reza. In light of that and Jodi's unusual orders regarding Reza's safety, she, Braddock and the priest had decided to remain in the tree grove – surrounded by the remaining Marines – to await the arrival of TF-85 and keep Reza company.

The culinary dream fading, Jodi came fully awake, her stomach grumbling even louder. The bedroll next to hers, where she had finally convinced Reza to lay down and sleep, was empty. "Where's–"

As she turned toward the fire and where Braddock and Father Hernandez had made their beds, her breath caught in her throat. Not five feet away, suspended on a spit over red-hot coals, was a forest gazelle. The aroma of cooking meat was nearly overwhelming, and she realized that this is what had prompted the dream about the steak. Her mouth suddenly was awash in saliva in anticipation of biting into the golden brown meat.

"Maybe there is a God," she murmured.

"To hear such words from your lips," came Father Hernandez's cheery voice from somewhere on the other side of the roasting animal, "makes me think that you are not quite as stubborn as me after all." His head popped up, his cherubic smile clearly visible through the smoke of the mystery barbecue. "Would you care to be baptized in the river this morning, good daughter?"

"Very funny, pious priest," she said. She was not sure which was worse, being baptized into something she had never understood, or having someone dunk her in the freezing glacier water of the nearby river. She had always thought that was a truly moronic idea. "Where's Reza? And where did this come from, besides heaven?"

"Reza and your *gunny*," he said, as always emphasizing the term as if he had never heard it before, "headed off toward the river a short while ago, presumably to take a refreshing dip while leaving me temporarily in charge of this most awful effort." He made a show of rotating the carcass a quarter turn on the spit, his face a tight grimace of disgust. "I awoke to this horrid vision when dawn broke. Reza must have killed the poor thing some time during the night and prepared it for your culinary pleasure."

"You just don't know what's good for you, Father," she said, taking one last look at the savory meat and wondering how Reza could have done all that without any of them waking up. Then again, they were all exhausted, and Jodi knew she probably could have slept through a hailstorm. "Since you're doing such a good job, I'll let you be and check out what the boys are doing down at the river."

"Wait! Don't leave me with this... this thing," Hernandez called, but Jodi paid him no attention as she trotted toward the sound of the rushing water. "Lord, forgive me for saying this," he muttered, glaring at the roasting beast, "but great should be my reward in Heaven for enduring such trials."

Jodi found Braddock sitting on the bank, a slender blade of grass protruding from his lips. Beside him Reza's armor and clothing lay in a meticulously ordered stack, but its owner was nowhere to be found. "Where is he?" she asked.

Braddock pointed to a group of rocks in the middle of a swirling mass of white water a few meters from shore. "In there somewhere."

"What do you mean?" she asked, panicked. "Can he even swim?"

Braddock chuckled. "He's already been to the far side and back. Underwater the whole way on a single breath. I don't think we have to worry about him drowning any time soon."

Jodi eyed the river, gauging its width. She figured she might make it a quarter of the way to the far side in one breath on a good day with a tailwind, but certainly not in the current that flowed here. "Shit," she said.

"Yeah," Braddock agreed.

Sitting down beside him, she asked, "Why didn't you wake me up?"

"Officers get cranky when they don't get enough sleep," he said lightly. "And you haven't had much sleep since you bailed out over this rock."

"So, are you saying that I'm cranky?"

Braddock laughed. The atmosphere around them had changed; the battle was over, the pressure was off. Reza's appearance was an enigma, but no immediate threat had materialized from him. Braddock felt like a human being again, instead of a cornered animal fighting for its existence. "No comment."

"Braddock," she said, serious now.

"Yeah."

"For whatever it's worth, thanks for keeping me in one piece."

He nodded, then gave her a mischievous smile. "It's only because I kept hoping you'd go straight and surrender to my masculine charms."

Jodi laughed so hard that her stomach began to hurt. "I'm sorry," she said finally, trying to control the spasms when she saw his face redden slightly. He had said it as a joke, but she could tell that there had been more than a grain of truth to his words. "Tony, really, I'm sorry. I didn't mean to... well, you know. Make you feel bad. I mean, off-duty, I'd like to be friends," she shrugged, "as much as officers and NCOs are supposed to be, anyway. But that's all I can ever be with you."

"Oh, hell, Mackenzie," he sighed wistfully, "I know that. It's just wishful thinking, is all. I won't hold it against you. Too much."

"Thanks," she said, patting his arm. He was a good man, a rare commodity on any world, and a good friend, which sometimes was even more difficult to find.

He suddenly nodded toward the water. "There's our boy."

Jodi looked up to find Reza standing chest-deep in the water, his gaze fixed on her.

"Hey, I think he's got the hots for you, too."

"Oh, stop it," Jodi chastened him, but she wondered if what Braddock said wasn't at least partially true. While Reza seemed to have bonded to Braddock and at least tolerated Father Hernandez, he related to her almost like a newborn chick that had imprinted itself on a surrogate mother. The bond did not seem to be sexually motivated; then again, there was no way for Jodi to really know, either way. Until Reza could be taught Standard – or he could teach someone Kreelan – only the most rudimentary communications could be exchanged. "He's only interested in me for my mind."

"Oh, Christ," Braddock moaned, "he can't be that desperate."

Reza watched them curiously, then energetically gestured at them with an outstretched hand, beckoning them to join him.

"Looks like he wants some company," Braddock said, shaking his head and holding up his hands in deferment. "He tried to get me in there earlier, but this is one I'll pass on."

"What's the matter? Is tough old gunny afraid to show off his wares?"

Braddock snorted. "Come on. You know how cold that water is. One step in there and I'd be groping around for a week trying to get a grip on myself again. If Reza can swim around like a beluga whale, power to him. I'll just sit nice and dry and stinky for right now, thanks very much."

"You better turn around, then," she told him as she began to undo the catches on her combat smock. "No free peeks unless you do the same."

"Jodi," he cried, "are you crazy? You'll freeze in there!"

"I know," she sighed as she made him turn around to face the sloping wall of the river bank, "but they don't heat the water in the village, either, and I'd rather not be the star of another peepshow for Hernandez's monks. I found the little hole they drilled in the wall of the bath." After this little discovery, the priest had been livid with his charges, and a severe tongue-lashing left them suitably terror- and guilt-stricken. But that was all ancient history now, having taken place soon after Jodi had bailed out, when such luxuries as personal hygiene had still been possible for the human combatants. "I figure I can jump in, scream, rub off some of the scum and get some of the shit out of my hair, and then jump back out and dry off with my smock and get dressed again before I turn into a popsicle."

"You're nuts," Braddock said, exasperated, as he faced the opposite direction. He heard the whisper and rasp of the heavy combat uniform against Jodi's skin as she undressed behind him. With a subtle movement, he extracted a small mirror, much like those used by dentists before more sophisticated scanners became available, from a cargo pocket on his uniform. He had used it on many occasions to see around corners without exposing his head to attack, and the seemingly primitive device had saved him from becoming a headless wonder on more than one occasion. He had to smile to himself. The young Navy lieutenant was going to have to work harder to outwit this Marine.

Holding it up in such a way as to not be too obvious, he took a surreptitious look at the scene behind him. He let his breath out slowly at what he saw when Jodi's undershirt and panties slid to the ground. Braddock had intimately known more women than he sometimes cared to admit, but none of them compared to this one. A non-practicing Christian, he marveled at how Jodi could look at herself in a mirror and still not believe that the Universe was a divine creation.

Feeling a rush of heat, he decided that he better put the mirror away.

"You can look after I get in the water," she told him firmly.

"Whatever you say, ma'am," he replied innocently.

Jodi gingerly stepped toward the water, suddenly wondering if this was not a serious error in judgment on her part. "What the hell," she sighed as the icy water touched her feet, bubbling around her ankles. Reza watched her patiently. "Here goes," she cried, diving headfirst into the water.

There was cold, and then there was *cold*. Jodi's reaction left no doubt as to what her body thought.

"Shit!" she cried as her head broke the surface. Her heart was pounding and she could barely breathe, but she was still alive. As she stood precariously on the bottom, resisting the swirling currents around her, the water came to just above her breasts. "God, Reza," she exclaimed, "how can you stand this?"

Reza, of course, did not reply, but watched with great interest as Jodi began to rub her skin with her hands and then rinse out her hair to clean off some of the accumulated grit and grime.

As she was dunking her head under, coaxing water into her hair, a sudden surge of the current knocked her off balance. Her arms flailing desperately, she lost her footing and was pulled under. She opened her mouth to cry out, but there was nothing but water, and it eagerly rushed into the void between her parted lips.

But just as suddenly as the crisis arose, it was put to an end. She felt a pair of strong arms gently grasp her around the chest and pull her away from the current. Her head broke the water, and the first thing she saw was Braddock, quickly wading into the water toward her, his face torn with concern.

"Are you all right?" he yelled.

"Yes," she managed, spitting water from her mouth. Luckily, she had not inhaled any water. "I'm okay."

"Goddamn stupid officers," he grumbled as he watched, unsure if it was necessary to go any further into the water. "Never have a lick of sense." After another moment of hesitation, he decided that Reza could handle her safety better than he could, and he beat a hasty retreat to the shore, already wet up to his waist and feeling every inch of it.

As Braddock was trudging back to dry land and comparative warmth, Jodi turned to Reza, who had one arm around her torso and the other under her legs, holding her like a groom carrying his bride across some watery threshold. She thought she could feel the heat of his body where his skin touched hers, although she knew that was impossible in water so cold. The muscles of his arms and chest, difficult to see in the water, felt as hard and resilient as his armor.

"Thank you," she told him. She kissed him on the cheek, just below an old scar that ran down his face over his left eye. Wrapping her arms around his neck, she let him carry her from the water, overseen by the ever-watchful gunnery sergeant.

"Hell," Braddock muttered, "I should have just gone skinny dipping." He was soaked past his waist and already shaking with cold, and now had no dry clothes to change into.

"We can dry off near the fire," Jodi told him as they reached the bank, "while we're having something to eat."

"Amen to that."

"Is everything all right?" Father Hernandez appeared from the direction of the camp. "I came to tell you that this barbarian ritual of *barbecue* appears to be nearing..." His voice trailed off and his eyes grew suddenly wide. "Sweet Mary, mother of God," he whispered.

"What's wrong, Father?" Jodi asked as Reza set her down. She thought for a moment that he was looking at her, but he was not. As alluring as any man might normally have found her, particularly naked, the old priest's eyes were firmly fixed on Reza. She turned to see what he was looking at. "Is Reza well-hung, or some... thing..."

Following Hernandez's gaze, she saw that Reza's skin boasted some differences that she at once found fascinating and repellant, things that she could not have seen with his armor on. For one thing, he had no hair except on his head. His groin and underarms were bereft of even a single pubic hair, and she could not see a single strand on his chest or arms, either, even a patch of downy fuzz. And on his face, there was not even a trace of a beard's shadow.

But that was not what really caught her attention. It was the scars. She had seen the half-dozen or so on his face, of course, and had thought it unfortunate that such a handsome man had to carry such terrible marks, especially the long one that ran over his left eye. But the highways of pinkish tendrils that coiled and meandered over the taut muscles of his body was like nothing she had ever seen. It was like a catalogue of pain and suffering, from the tiny puckers that seemed little more than oversized pinpricks to the scar in his side that looked like someone had skewered him like the gazelle now roasting on the fire. Leaning to one side, she caught a glimpse of a matching scar in his back. She had seen enough entry-exit wound combinations to know what one looked like. He had been stabbed clean through with what must have been a sword, just below the heart, and had lived to tell about it.

Urged on by morbid fascination, forgetting both her nakedness and the cold water that clung to her skin, she slowly circled this stranger, marveling at the unspeakable cruelty he must have endured.

"My God, Reza," she whispered, "what did they do to you?" She gently touched his back where seven jagged scars remained where the Kreelan barbed whip must have once struck him. Running a finger over the scar where another sword had pierced him, she traced the gnarled tissue that was as long as her palm and almost as thick as her hand.

"Yeah," Braddock said quietly, "he carries quite a history, doesn't he?" He had already seen the scars, when Reza undressed to go swimming. Braddock had seen enough scars to not be shocked by Reza's appearance, but he was still impressed that a man, any man, could endure such punishment and still function. "Look," he went on, "I don't know about you all, but I'm heading back to the fire. I'm freezing my ass and I'm starving." He looked at Jodi until they made eye contact. "And I'd recommend you get dressed and do the same."

"I will... ah, prepare some dry things for you," Father Hernandez said quickly. He had gotten an eyeful of Reza, and was not about to stay long enough that his attention wandered to the other exposed body standing on the river bank. He hurried back toward the camp, trailed only slightly by Braddock, who was now so cold his teeth were chattering.

Entranced as Jodi was by the tale seared into Reza's skin, her own body finally made known its own needs. "We'd better get dressed before we freeze," she said. Despite the warmth of the morning air, the cold water had penetrated to her core, and the last thing she wanted was to catch pneumonia just as the task force arrived and she had to start answering a lot of questions. She hurriedly wiped herself off with the battered smock. "Here," she said, turning to hand it to him. "I know it's grungy and a little wet, but you can still dry yourself off..." She felt her knees turn to rubber as she turned back around to him and saw what was happening. The camouflage smock dropped from her hand to the ground at her feet.

Reza still stood beside her, except that now wisps of steam were streaming from his skin and hair like cold water evaporating from hot pavement. She could feel the heat radiating from him like she was standing near an open fire.

"This is impossible," she whispered, reaching out to touch him. His flesh was hot, much hotter than any fever a human being could survive, and painful to her touch. "Reza, what are you?" she whispered.

Never letting her eyes wander from the spectacle, she managed to dress herself, her only oversight being that her undershirt was on backwards. When the steam stopped streaming from Reza's body, he, too, began to dress. His body completely dry, he put on his clothing in a precise ritual that Jodi found utterly fascinating. Watching his hands and the rest of his body move through their motions was like watching a precision drill team performing a ballet.

As she led him back to where Braddock was carving the meat from the cooked gazelle, Jodi wondered about the man who walked beside her, thinking that maybe Hernandez's first thoughts, that he was some kind of messenger from God, might not have been too far from the truth.

TWENTY

Commodore Mauritius Sinclaire was known and loved by his sailors as a jovial man who was not above the occasional bout of wildness that had been part of naval tradition since men had first set sail upon the seas of Earth. The red-haired commander of one of the Confederation's finest task forces was claimed to have shared a pint or two, and sometimes a glass of something more sturdy, with the lowly sailors of his command, and was even reputed to have lost a game of poker now and then. Or so the senior chiefs would boast in front of the wide-eyed young sailors who had just set foot on the steel-plated decks of the task force's men-of-war.

Unlike so many of his peers, Sinclaire spent as much time as he could prowling the lower decks of the ships of his command. He sought out contact with the men and women who only bore a few red or white stripes on their sleeves, listening to what they had to say, telling them the things he thought they deserved to hear and reassuring them that what they did really mattered. Having started his naval career nearly thirty years before as a lowly machinist's mate on a long-dead destroyer, Sinclaire was a firm believer in the extraordinary strength and wisdom of the common man and woman.

He liked to laugh and tell jokes, and was as colorful and alive as his family's clan heritage had destined him to be. More than that, since the day he pledged himself to the Navy at the tender age of sixteen he had seen enough of death to know how precious life was, how dear and worthwhile, and he was loathe to squander it wastefully, or to see it so disposed. Honest to a fault and just as outspoken, his thoughts and tongue had cost him more than one promotion, but it was a price he was more than willing to pay to maintain his personal and professional integrity. He was certainly no angel, but no god could deny that Sinclaire had always tried his best to do what was decent and right.

And doing that was just what perplexed him now. "Blast it, doctor," he growled, "I understand your point, but my orders – *our* orders – say that we are to treat him as an ambassador until the powers-that-be decide just where this lad's supposed to fit into our way of doing things."

"That's all fine and good, commodore," said Deliha Rabat, the chief of the army of scientists, philosophers, clerics, diplomats, and seemingly countless other last-minute arrivals that had swarmed aboard the battlecruiser *Aboukir* for this mission. "But the Council expects a lot in the way of results out of this group before we reach Earth, and the only way that's going to happen is if we approach this from the scientific standpoint that it clearly warrants." She frowned theatrically. "I'm not talking about putting him in a straight jacket, for the love of All. But you have to remember: we're dealing with a complete unknown here, and – in my professional opinion – you would be well advised to follow my recommendations on this and keep him in a suitably appointed cell in the brig where he can be observed properly and kept under control." She paused a moment, waiting just until Sinclaire was about to speak. "Remember, commodore," she interjected as he was opening his mouth to reply, "you have the crew of the *Aboukir* to consider, as well. This man could prove quite dangerous."

Sinclaire clamped his jaws shut. If there was one thing he could not stand, it was when someone tried to use his vested concern for those under his command as leverage to influence him into making a particular decision. "I thank you for your concern for Captain Jhansi's crew, doctor," he said coldly, noting with satisfaction the rise of color in Rabat's olive cheeks, "but I've my orders, and nothing you've said has convinced me that there's any reason to deviate from them. Any results you want to present to the Council will have to be the fruits of your own hard labor and Reza Gard's willing cooperation. You'll get no support for coercion of any kind from me. Thank you, doctor, and I'll see you in the landing bay at fourteen-hundred sharp." With that, Sinclaire returned to studying his data terminal.

Deliha Rabat, Ph.D., M.T.S., etc., etc., had been dismissed.

The commodore did not have to look up to feel the hateful glare he received before she whirled around and stalked out of his day cabin.

* * *

"That's where we're going," Jodi told Reza, pointing out the shuttle's small viewport at the rapidly growing bulk of the *Aboukir*, orbiting majestically against the backdrop of the blue-green sphere of sunlit Rutan. She watched as he peered intently through the clear plastisteel, leaning further and further out of his seat until his nose bumped against the glass and he recoiled slightly, like a dog discovering a see-through door for the first time.

How much like a child he seems, she thought. There was so much she would have liked to know about him, but she knew that the knowledge would be someone else's to learn first. Jodi was a fighter pilot, not a trained interrogator, diplomat, or liberal arts teacher, and her home was with her squadron on the *Hood*. She had been informed that a shuttle had been prepared to take her to Ekaterina III where *Hood* was being repaired and refitted after her last mauling; Jodi should arrive there just before the battlecruiser was ready to sortie once again. She looked forward to returning to her squadron-mates and flying duty, but she could not shake the feeling of envy toward whoever would come after her and tap into the treasure trove of information now sitting beside her.

In the seats opposite sat Braddock and Father Hernandez. Braddock, sound asleep, snored open-mouthed in a ritual of fighting men and women that went back centuries: the delight of sleep after a battle fought and won.

Father Hernandez also had his eyes closed, but for an entirely different reason. Born on a planet without indigenous spacecraft – or even the most primitive of atmospheric craft, for that matter – he had developed a sudden and dramatic case of motion sickness when the shuttle lifted from Rutan, and had kept his eyes closed and his mouth moving in quiet prayer ever since. Jodi was sure his handprints would be left ever afterward in the shuttle, permanently embedded in the plastic armrests of his seat.

Those who had sent the task force had not planned on his coming with them, nor had it been planned by anyone on Rutan other than Father Hernandez himself. In what Jodi took to be a shocking course of action for one of their people, he had insisted on coming with them.

"But Father," Jodi had tried to explain as Hernandez strode up the shuttle's ramp amidst the survivors of Braddock's regiment, clutching the leather satchel that contained his Bible and few worldly belongings, "this isn't a taxi service. If you come with us, there's no telling when you'll be coming back. This task force is bound for Terra, and not many ships happen out this way–"

Hernandez waved her off. "So much the better, child, that I may see St. Peter's and the other great cathedrals of Terra with my own eyes." He tried to smile, but she was not returning it. For once, her irreverence had disappeared, replaced with a businesslike attitude that would have been well placed on a pit-bull terrier. "My child," he went on softly as the Marines trudged by behind them, "my time in this life wanes, and my service to my parish is nearly complete. Only next year was young Father Castillo to take my place at the altar. While there was a time when I looked forward to quiet contemplation and study of the scriptures to pass my days before Judgment, it holds promise for me no longer." He gestured toward the hatchway where Braddock had already led Reza to get him settled in for the flight up to *Aboukir*. "God has offered me something more, a final challenge for my mind and my faith before I come before Him. There are things I must know about this young man's spirit, things that will forever consume my curiosity if I do not make this journey of discovery, a journey perhaps not much different than his own. I realize I am not a distinguished scientist or scholar as are those of the group you have told me await him, but I am in no less need of the knowledge that they also seek, and I am determined to find out what I must know. If I cannot go as a priest and friend, then I will go as a representative of the planet Rutan, of Reza's chosen place of redemption."

Slowly, Jodi nodded. "All right, you nutty priest," she said. "I just wanted to make sure you knew what you were getting into."

Hernandez smiled. "The Lord does make some allowance for fools, young lady."

"That He does," Jodi said under her breath as she helped Hernandez with his bundle of belongings and led him into the beckoning interior of the shuttle.

Returning her thoughts to the present, she asked, "How are you doing, Father?"

Hernandez hazarded a peek out of one eye, immediately snapping it shut again. "I am fine," he announced flatly.

"Liar." Grinning, she turned to the viewport again, trying hard not to laugh at all the nose prints Reza had left on the clearsteel.

"It won't be long now," she told him, reaching out to hold his hand, careful to avoid the razor-sharp talons.

Outside, a great cavern appeared in *Aboukir's* starboard flank as the shuttle's course brought them in sight of one of the battlecruiser's enormous flight bays.

* * *

"Attention on deck!" As the hundreds of officers and assembled crew of *Aboukir* snapped to attention, fifty Marines and the same number of seamen, all in dress uniform, filed down each side of the red carpet that had been rolled up to where the shuttle's main gangway was just now lowering. Unseen by most of the assemblage was the reserve gangway on the vessel's opposite side through which the regiment's wounded were already being taken off to sickbay. Sinclaire had orders to treat Reza as if he had diplomatic status, but he would never put protocol before the care of the injured.

The commodore, accompanied by *Aboukir's* captain and Dr. Rabat, waited at the end of the honor guard as a kind of abbreviated receiving line. Rabat's presence there rather irked Sinclaire, but there was nothing he could do about it. She was the Council's designated diplomatic liaison in this matter, in addition to being the research team chief. Besides, it was all he could do to limit the number of official greeters to the three of them: Rabat had wanted her entire team there, plus a boatload of people from the Department of State. On that score, however, Sinclaire had been firm, and Rabat had reluctantly conceded the point. The other members of her team were stuck in the ship's compartments set aside for their research, jealously watching the closed circuit feeds scattered around the flight bay.

The gangway hissed to the floor, and Sinclaire felt his fists begin to clench. So much could go wrong, from the inconsequential to the horribly disastrous. He had wanted to greet Reza with a very small party of people in a neutral atmosphere. Rabat had conjured up a circus, and this time he had been almost powerless to resist her demands.

"Present... ARMS!" The honor guard snapped their rifles in a salute and the ten-person band began to play *La Marseillaise*, the Confederation's official anthem, just as Braddock stepped down the ramp, a wobbly Father Hernandez on his arm. The gunnery sergeant was obviously mortified, returning the salute with as much dignity as he could muster. Father Hernandez smiled beneficently and waved at the receiving party with his free hand.

"What a bloody cock-up," Captain Jhansi muttered.

Braddock quickly dragged Hernandez down the carpet, his borrowed and badly fitting uniform and Father Hernandez's simple cassock contrasting poorly with the bright scarlet of the carpet and the immaculate uniforms of the honor guard. He came before Sinclaire and brought himself to attention, snapping a smart salute to the task force commander. "Commodore," he said formally, trying to see past the absurdity of it all, "may I present Father Hernandez of Rutan."

"Father," Sinclaire extended a hand in sincere greeting. From what he had heard, Hernandez could be something of a character, and he genuinely looked forward to talking with him. But that would have to be later.

"Thank you, commodore," Hernandez said sheepishly. "I apologize for what I gather was a breach of protocol, but I could stay on that machine no longer."

"Quite all right, Father," Sinclaire said, turning to Braddock. "And you, gunny, welcome back to the fleet. You and your people did a damn fine job."

"Thank you, sir–"

"Excuse me," Deliha Rabat interrupted impatiently. "With all due respect, we aren't here for you gentlemen. Where's Reza Gard?"

"Take a look," Braddock said coldly, pointing toward the shuttle, wondering who this egotistical woman might be. He would have liked to tell her to take a hike instead, but he doubted the commodore would have approved.

On that count, however, Braddock would have been quite incorrect.

"Where?" She snapped. "I don't see – oh..."

A sudden hush had fallen over the flight bay. The band stopped playing, the instruments falling into silence as if on a prearranged cue. Every individual present had been told what to expect, most had even seen holo movies as children depicting such fiction as men or women under Kreelan influence, but no one ever expected to see it as part of undeniable reality.

With Jodi holding one hand, reassuring him that those he was about to encounter meant him no harm, Reza stepped down the ramp. The blue rune of the Desh-Ka burned like a star on his breastplate and in the eyestone of his collar, the medallions that made up his name glinting like diamonds in the bay's harsh lighting. He paused a moment to take in his surroundings, his eyes roaming around the huge bay, the brilliant lights and strange mechanical shapes, and the colorfully dressed humans who apparently were there to greet him. He gathered that this spectacle of warriors and the humans with instruments that made strange noises – *a band*, he suddenly remembered – were for his benefit, and he felt honored by the display.

Sinclaire watched as the young man released Jodi's hand and stepped from the gangway onto the red carpet, and was suddenly struck by how fitting it seemed for him to be cast against such a background, a prince from some exotic and faraway kingdom here on a state visit. The silence magnified the dignity and grace of Reza's approach, and he was thankful that the band had ceased its playing of the Confederation anthem.

After an initial assessment of his new environment, Reza turned his attention to the three figures standing at the head of the warrior line, evidently serving as his immediate destination for the rendering of greetings. Two men and a woman, Reza instantly knew that these three were in their own different ways the most powerful beings on this vessel. The swarthy red-haired man was empowered to take or give life to those who served him; he was the one whose words guided the others, whose power extended beyond the walls of this ship to realms somewhere beyond. The man next to him, with skin the color of night and with little flesh on his bones, was of lesser stature than the red-haired one, but held similar powers over those within the confines of this ship. He was the vessel's master. Lastly, there was the woman, who seemed at once to be the least powerful of the three among all the souls Reza could sense around him now, but who perhaps carried more influence than the other two with authorities even higher. He could also sense that while the men were extremely curious about him and somewhat fearful, the woman had some keener interest that instantly set Reza on his guard.

With this one, he told himself, *you must be careful.*

"Commodore Sinclaire," Jodi announced officially as she led Reza to the end of the carpet and a new way of life, "let me present Reza Gard." For a moment, she considered adding "formerly of the Kreelan Empire," but thought better of it. For one thing, she did not wish to put words in Reza's mouth, especially when they could not speak the same language yet. For another, she did not know if it was true. "Reza," she said, "this is Commodore Sinclaire, the Commander of Task Force 85."

Sinclaire extended a paw toward Reza. While the shaking of hands was hardly the standard greeting among all humans, it was Sinclaire's. "In the name of the Confederation people and government, I bid you welcome Reza, welcome home."

There was an uncomfortable moment as Reza simply stared at Sinclaire. An air of tension began to build from the earlier excitement, and several of the Marines in the honor guard clenched their fists in worry as they threw sidelong glances toward where Sinclaire and Reza faced one another. Marine sharpshooters in the distant shadows of the flight bay tightened their fingers slightly on the triggers of their weapons, all pointed at Reza's head.

Much to everyone's surprise – and relief – Reza did not accept the commodore's offered hand. Instead, he knelt down on one knee and made what could only be a salute, bringing his left fist over his right breast.

"Well, I will be damned," Sinclaire breathed. "Come on, now, lad, get on your feet." With sinewy grace, Reza rose to his full height, turning toward Captain Jhansi. "This is Captain Michel Jhansi," Sinclaire said, exhilarated by this living enigma and what he might represent, "commander of the *C.S.S. Aboukir*, the vessel you're now on."

Reza nodded respectfully, but did not salute. He did not render the traditional Kreelan greeting of gripping arms to any of them, for they were not of the Way, and to do so was forbidden.

"And this," Sinclaire said, managing a neutral tone in his voice, "is Dr. Deliha Rabat, the diplomatic representative of the Confederation Council and head of your debriefing team."

Sinclaire felt a sense of grim satisfaction in the way Reza stared at her, and he thought that there was just an instant when something recognizably human passed over his face. Suspicion.

The commodore smiled to himself. *The boy hasn't but set eyes on her,* he thought, *and already he's made her game.* If he understood things right, Dr. Rabat was in for a real tussle.

With the initial pleasantries out of the way, Sinclaire led the *Aboukir's* little diplomatic group out of the landing bay to the ship's conference complex where Reza's reintroduction to humanity was to begin without delay.

Behind them, the dead and wounded Marines from Rutan continued to pour from the shuttle.

* * *

"Are you sure you won't change your mind?" Braddock's question was as much personal as professional. He might never get a chance to be her lover, but he still liked her more than just about anyone he had ever met. Even if she was an officer. "I mean, I'm sure the commodore could find some way to keep you on for a while. The *Aboukir* could use another hot jock, or so I hear."

"No," Jodi said quietly. "I need to get back to the *Hood*. They'll be deploying again in not too long, and I want to be on her when she does. Besides, I can't stand to be on the same ship as that Rabat bitch." It had taken as long as the time needed for Jodi and Braddock to shower, clean up, and change into clean uniforms for the New Order to emerge: Rabat had literally ordered Sinclaire to get Jodi, Braddock, and Hernandez out of her way. Regretfully, he had been forced to oblige. And that meant no more contact with Reza until Rabat deemed it necessary and acceptable. Jodi wanted to spit. "There's nothing more I can do here now, I'm afraid." She smiled then. "Look, playing Marine was fun, but I'd prefer to leave it to the pros. I miss flying too much." *And my commander*, she added silently to herself

"Lieutenant," a flight-suited petty officer called from the interior of the fast cutter that would take her to the *Hood's* drydock on Ekaterina III, "any time you're ready ma'am."

Jodi was grateful for the interruption. She hated protracted good-byes. No, she corrected herself. She hated good-byes, period. Too often they were permanently sealed with the mark of Death. "Time to go," she said, extending her hand. "Take care, gunny."

"You, too, el-tee. Drop me a line sometime." He shook her hand, his big and callused paw swallowing her trim and efficient palm. After only a second of consideration, he drew her close and hugged her. Jodi returned the affection with a tight squeeze of her arms around his neck.

"That's a promise," she said, fighting back tears. She picked up her gear bag that held a souvenir Marine uniform and some other tokens the men and women of the regiment had given her, and walked up the gangway into the cutter.

Braddock waved to her, but she did not turn around to see. The bay's outer door closed, and a moment later there was a subtle thump as the little ship left its berth for open space.

Frowning, he began the long trip back to the barracks bays where the remnants of his regiment were bedding down.

On board the cutter, Jodi sat in the cramped passenger cabin adjoining the two-person cockpit. There were no other passengers for this particular flight. In her hands was the wooden crucifix, his own, that Father Hernandez had given her as a parting gift. She had always disdained the existence of any Supreme Being, no matter what the name or religion. But something – she was not sure if it was hope or fear of what Reza might bring to the human universe – drove her to do something she had never honestly done in her entire life.

She prayed.

* * *

Father Hernandez sat alone in the ship's chapel. As on all ships of the Confederation Navy, it was an All-Faith chapel that welcomed the worshippers of all humanity's religions. It was so universal, in fact, that not even the most common objects of Earth-descended faiths were displayed. Instead, a single word adorned the pulpit that stood before the plastisteel pews: *Welcome*. Services were delivered every day of the week for each of the major denominations on the ship. While this meant that some religions were not always attended to directly, the ship's chaplain was skillful enough that all who wished to worship in public and with their fellows found a place in his words. Depending on the service being given, the walls that were now a soft white could be altered to show the inside of a great cathedral, a mosque or synagogue, or any of a thousand other places of faith, even an open mountaintop with white clouds and blue sky. Hernandez had been struck dumb the first time he had seen the wizardry that made such miracles possible. No such technology existed on his world.

Since Rabat had exiled him and the others from Reza's company, he had had one thing he had not wanted: too much time to ponder his own fate. While he was confident that there would come a time when he would have his chance to ask Reza the questions upon which he had become fixated, his obsessive interest held no patience to wait. And yet, he must, for there was no alternative. He was virtually a captive aboard this ship now. While he was free to roam throughout all but the most restricted areas, he could not venture beyond the confines of the metal hull; he could not return home.

But Hernandez was not sure, thinking about it for the thousandth time, if he even wanted to return home. To gaze from the steps of his church to where Reza had fought the invading demons to a standstill, to see the grove of trees where the young man had taken an old man's foolishness in good humor when he could just as easily have taken his life. Each day would only bring the same unanswered questions, the same nagging thoughts about things of the spirit that only Reza could answer. For if he, raised somehow by these horrid alien beings, perchance believed in the one God, was there not the chance for peace in the name of fellowship?

Besides, to return to Rutan prematurely would only be to disturb the simple but fulfilling way of life that his people had worked so hard for so many years to preserve. He was an outsider now, possessed of alien, perhaps even heretical thoughts that would pollute the pure stream from which he had been spawned. They would welcome him back with open arms, of course, but he would be forever lost to their way of understanding.

In his hands he held the tiny silver crucifix, which he had asked to borrow from Reza and had not been able to return. It had been a measure of spite on his part that he had not mentioned it to his present keepers, and guilt nagged at him for still having it. He consoled himself that it would be well taken care of until it could be returned. His own he had given to young Jodi, in what he knew were vain hopes that she would come to her senses and realize that there were greater things in the Universe even than the alien hordes that sought to destroy God's work. He was fond of the young woman, and hated terribly to see her go. But he knew that her work was important to defend Creation against the monsters that had raised Reza.

And now, the more he thought of it, the more he became convinced that Reza was genuine, that some spark of goodness, of godliness, had led him home, to stay raising his hand against those of his own kind. Perhaps, he thought wonderingly, Jodi was right when she said that different was not always evil, not always bad. To judge by outward appearances had led them to the brink of disaster before Reza had literally beaten sense into Hernandez, and the old priest vowed to change his ways, to never repeat that most human of mistakes.

* * *

Deliha Rabat watched silently as the young petty officer struggled to get back into his uniform, nearly laughing as he fell over backwards onto the bed while pulling his pants back on. He was fifteen minutes late for his duty station on the bridge.

"You'd better slow down, dear," she chided, thinking that he had been even more comical in bed. And just as hurried. Deliha was still well within her prime and attractive to both sexes, and when the fancy took her, she allowed her body the occasional pleasurable tryst. Unfortunately, it always seemed that her taste in bed partners was even worse than her choice in professional associates. None of them ever seemed to measure up. It was a paradox whose solution consistently eluded her.

"I'll, uh, I'll see you later?" the man stuttered as he finished dressing and hurried for the door.

"Don't be ridiculous," Deliha said absently, already having dismissed him from her mind. He had rated very low on her bedroom scale; masturbation would have provided a lot more enjoyment than his frenzied thrusts, and without the resultant mess. That he was now conveniently leaving behind.

With an unsure wave, he disappeared into the corridor, and the door swished closed behind him.

"Imbecile," she muttered.

As she rose to go to the bathroom and clean herself up, she contemplated her situation with a sense of frustration. Their voyage was almost over, with Earth only a few days away, and she felt she had very little to show for it. Oh, yes, the dietary team was ecstatic: they now knew what Reza liked to eat (nearly raw meat and a particular lager originally brewed in Earth's Australia), had studied his body's fantastic metabolism (but did not know how he achieved it), etc., etc. The linguistic team, led by Dr. Chuen, had made what even Rabat had to admit was phenomenal progress in teaching Reza Standard, although it was clearly due to Reza's learning skills, not Chuen's teaching.

But there had been no reciprocation on Reza's part. No matter how hard any of them tried, he refused to utter a single Kreelan word or discuss anything dealing with the Empire. Of greater annoyance, even granting his limited vocabulary in Standard, was that he refused to divulge the reason for his returning to humanity. It was as if he had simply been born again right out of his mother's womb and had no idea what they were talking about.

But that, Deliha was sure, was rubbish. Reza understood precisely what they were after, but was simply refusing to part with any information any more than he would part with his clothes: no one could convince him to stop wearing his Kreelan garb and dress in something a little more... fashionable. That and his habit of staring at people with the strange alien expression he always seemed to wear became unsettling after a while.

No, she thought, *the bastard is hiding something. No*, she corrected herself, *he's hiding everything*. And that was where most of her anxiety was focused, because that was her field, and thus her responsibility: psychoanalysis. It was her job to find out what made Reza tick, how he thought, what he thought, and why. She was fascinated at the prospect of his having psychological aberrations – and possibly superior abilities – that mirrored his physical ones, but he refused to cooperate with her at all. He would not let anyone get near him with any kind of physical probe (they still had been unable to draw a basic blood sample), and he became silent as a stone when she entered the room. It was as if he hated her personally, or at least despised her, and she could not understand why. It was small consolation that there were others on the team with whom he acted the same.

At least Dr. Chuen was able to deal with him, she thought sourly. Fool that the man was, his talent with languages was as unequaled as it was genuine, and she had to admit that it was good fortune that he was in the pool of lucky people Reza had chosen to open up to. But even Chuen was not immune to Reza's stubbornness, she thought, smiling to herself. His "human Rosetta stone" remained silent about the Kreelan language that Chuen had been so hoping to understand.

"What am I doing wrong?" she asked herself aloud. While she was at the top of her field in several esoteric areas of psychological research, her bedside manner left much to be desired, not that she particularly cared. She was more at home dealing with drugged criminal patients strapped into deep-core machines than she was with a highly intelligent and alert individual. Mentally, she went over every step and action she had taken with him, looking for some clue as to why he was holding out against her, but she could come up with nothing. Except spite, perhaps.

She finished her business in the bathroom and returned to the bedroom, this time sitting behind the desk monitor. It showed Dr. Juanita Feron, one of her team, sitting with Reza and giving him what Deliha recognized as one of the simplified versions of the Baumgartner-Rollmann intelligence tests that didn't depend on language.

"Good luck, you idiot," Deliha sneered as she called up a cup of hot tea from the food processor, recalling her own miserable luck while attempting to administer a similar test, several times. When she had laid out all the test pieces, of which there were nearly two hundred, each of which had to be arranged precisely within a defined work area, he had simply turned his attention to the room's viewport and ignored her. She had done everything short of physically touching him (she had wanted to throttle him, she thought angrily) to get him to pay attention, all to no avail. Now, she decided she was going to sit back and watch Feron's humiliation at the hands of this beast. "Go ahead, Juanita, lay it all out for him so he can spit in your eye." It occurred to her that this was Feron's first chance at him. She was not one of Deliha's protégés, and had been near the bottom of the access list. *So much the better*, Deliha thought savagely. This should be a good introduction for her to Kreelan manners.

Deliha leaned forward, watching Feron's lips move as she explained what she wanted Reza to do in a way she hoped he could grasp with his limited – albeit rapidly expanding – understanding of Standard. Rabat had turned down the sound during her little interlude with the awkward petty officer, and she had no interest to hear the test explained again. She had already heard it a thousand times. And so had Reza.

She took another sip of her tea, closing her eyes and pondering why Fate had cast her such a difficult nut to crack. Things would have been a lot smoother and more effective if the Council had just authorized a deep-core scan. Such a pity.

When she looked at the screen again, she was so surprised at what she saw that she spilled the tea in her lap.

"Dammit!" she snarled as the hot liquid burned her upper thighs. "You bastard!" The puzzle, which normally took someone with a genius-level IQ almost five minutes to complete, was half done in little over sixty seconds. Deliha wanted to vomit at the sight of Feron's overjoyed expression, completely overlooking the enormous significance of what Reza was doing.

Cursing every god and person that came to mind – Reza most of all – Rabat threw on some clothes and headed for the conference center, leaving the mute screen and Reza's contemplative face behind.

TWENTY-ONE

Jodi was never so glad to get off of a ship as she was to leave the *Aboukir's* cutter. While the crew was a good one and the ship was fast, the voyage to Ekaterina III had taken what had seemed like forever. The fact that Jodi had not been allowed by the cutter's captain to get any cockpit time had not helped.

But thoughts of the cutter – indeed of the last few months – faded with every step she took toward Berth 12A, where *Hood* was tied up for repairs in Ekaterina's huge orbital shipyards. While Jodi had been sorely tempted to take one of the shuttles, she decided to stretch her legs after being so cramped in the cutter. It was worth the hour-long walk to get back to the ship.

At long last, there she was: *C.S.S. Hood.* The shipwrights of Trivandrum had built more than legendary striking power into their metal leviathan. The *Hood,* among humanity's most powerful warships, was also a beauty to the eye. Unlike many of her sister ships-of-the-line, she was not a collection of angular plates and protrusions that gave so many vessels an insectile appearance. *Hood* was a collection of finely modeled curves, streamlined and sleek, as if her destiny was to navigate through some terrestrial ocean as had her namesake centuries before. But in that beauty also lay strength, both in the armor that made up her thick protective hide and the weapons that bristled from her hull like the thorns of a rose.

But her last battle had severely tried her strength, as the carbonized craters and streaks, the breached hangar deck and ruptured gangway hatch attested. Most of her damage had already been patched, but there would be some ugly scars that would endure with the ship until her retirement by age or by fire.

You're still a tough old bitch, Jodi thought admiringly.

Pausing on the ramp just before reaching the new gangway hatch, Jodi snapped a salute to the Confederation flag suspended nearly a kilometer away on *Hood's* stern, before stepping up to the ensign who was the officer of the watch and rendering the same courtesy. "Lieutenant Mackenzie, reporting aboard."

The young woman's eyes lit up as she returned the salute. "Yes, ma'am," she said cordially. "Welcome back. The captain pays his respects, and will see you when he returns from shore leave."

"Thanks, ensign." As Jodi made her way over the decks she had come to know so well, greeting the few members of the crew who were not on rotation down to the planet surface, her excitement began to build. The sounds and smells of the great ship, the thrum that she knew was there but could not quite hear: all the many things that made the ship a living thing. It was her home.

There was a moment, just a tiny fraction of a second, as she was approaching her destination that she was afraid, terrified, that one tiny thing might have changed. Holding her breath, she approached the door and read the names on the assignment placard. There were two. One was hers. The other was...

Jodi burst through the door, knowing that her roommate and commander would be there. She always was.

"I'm back!" she shouted like a giddy teenage girl who had just been asked to the prom by the most sought-after male – or female, as the case might be – in school.

The woman inside, dressed in her duty fatigues, practically fell out of the chair where she had been writing performance evaluations of her pilots.

"Jodi!" her commander cried as she fell into Jodi's embrace. "*Mon Dieu*, I was so worried about you! Are you all right?"

"Yes, Nikki," Jodi said, "I'm okay. Oh, God, am I glad to be back."

Later, there would be many stories exchanged for the time they had been away from one another. But for now, Nicole Carré was content to hold her only real friend tightly, both of them crying tears of relief that the other was still alive and, for the moment, out of harm's way.

* * *

Ekaterina III boasted one of the strongest military forces in the human sphere, both in terms of its ground forces and the naval squadrons patrolling her system, guarding the enormous orbital shipyards. If there was a safe place in the known human galaxy, with the possible exception of Earth itself, it was here.

And that was how Jodi felt now. Safe, content. She was still riding an emotional roller coaster that alternated between the exhausted depression of the furious fighting she had seen on Rutan and the hyperventilated feeling of knowing she was back with the woman she loved. The fact that her love was unrequited, that Nicole Carré had long ago made it clear that she could never be more than a close friend, did not – and never had – been an obstacle for Jodi's tacit affection. It was enough to know that Nicole cared, loving Jodi as a friend. That they had never shared a passionate moment together was something Jodi had decided she could live with. The physical expressions of her love for Nicole were discretely diverted toward others who were more than happy to receive them, and who willingly did their best to satisfy Jodi's needs in return.

As for Nicole, Jodi knew that she had been with men on a few rare occasions, but nothing had ever come of any of these relationships. Nicole's life was her job, and Jodi doubted that there was anyone in the Fleet who did it better: Nicole Carré lived and breathed fighters. Living so long in such a lethal profession was beyond the ability of all but a very few. Nicole Carré was among them. Her mastery of technique and relentless aggression in the cockpit had quickly earned her commander's stripes and a squadron command, and she was now on the verge of putting on another stripe and taking over *Hood's* entire wing. Her cold demeanor had earned her the call sign *Ice Queen* since early on in flight training. But Jodi knew there was more, much more, beneath the flawless porcelain skin of her commander.

Nicole's professional and personal aloofness gave Jodi a certain sense of security, the feeling that she would always be the one to whom Nicole would turn in times of need. And so it had been for the years they had known each other. Jodi, her own flying skills having proven quite lethal to the enemy, had sacrificed promotions and choice assignments to stay with Nicole. Jodi obstinately refused her friend's pleas – and several direct orders – to take her own command and develop her career, and at last Nicole had given up after Jodi had laid her heart bare. It was then that Nicole fully realized how dependent she was on Jodi for support, lover or not; Nicole could not deny the fact that she herself was only human, and needed someone by her side. That someone just happened to be Jodi Mackenzie.

Still, Jodi could not help but be sad for her friend. She needed love just as a flower needs the light of the sun, but would never find it. As much as she wanted Nicole for herself, she would have been happy to see someone sweep her off her feet, to love her like Jodi would have loved to. That was the measure of Jodi's love.

"Jodi, what is wrong?"

Nicole's question caught her off guard. "Nothing," Jodi said, pushing away the thoughts of what could never be. "I… I was just thinking how good dinner was." She smiled. "It's been a long time since I've had food like this." She laughed nervously. "It'll probably make me barf."

"Do not be silly," Nicole said, letting Jodi's white lie pass for the time being. She knew that if something was bothering her, she would speak up about it sooner or later. Fishing for a little humor to brighten up her friend, Nicole made a theater out of looking over their plates, at the devastated remains of an authentic lobster dinner that had cost Nicole half a month's pay in the best restaurant in the port. It had been worth every credit, both for the food itself and to help welcome Jodi home. "The day you become sick from good food is the day the goat becomes the gourmet, *oui?*" Leaning forward, she took one of Jodi's hands in hers. "I am glad you are back, my friend."

"Me, too," Jodi rasped. She was afraid that she would break down and start bawling with joy. She squeezed Nicole's hand tightly.

Nicole smiled. She so much wished that Jodi would find someone she could be truly happy with, for she had so much to give. But Nicole knew that this was not going to happen any time soon; Jodi had made that quite clear. Sitting across from her, Nicole was painfully aware just how attractive Jodi was to the people around her. From surreptitious glances to unabashed stares, easily a dozen people close by were more than casually interested in her friend. If only…

But it was not to be. Not yet, anyway. Jodi was content with the way things were and, as fate would have it, so was Nicole. They were a good team.

"Jodi," Nicole asked, "what is that?" She had seen a strange bit of jewelry hanging from Jodi's neck that she had not noticed before. It looked like nothing more than a loop of twine or very fine rope cascading down into her ample cleavage.

"Oh," Jodi said. "It's a gift from someone I met on Rutan." She looked sheepish as she held up the small wooden crucifix that Hernandez had given her.

"May I see it?" Nicole asked, curious as to the origins of this token and who had gotten Jodi Mackenzie, of all people, to take up religion.

"Sure," Jodi slipped it from around her neck and handed it across the table.

"Does this mean you are a believer?" Nicole asked, curious as she examined the cross in her hands.

"No," Jodi answered immediately. "Yes. Maybe." She threw her head back in exasperation. "Hell, I don't know. I prayed on the way here from Rutan, on the shuttle. Can you believe that? I meant it, too. But now, I don't know. How can anyone believe in any God when the universe is as fucked up as ours is?"

"That is what faith is supposed to be about, or so they say," Nicole answered distantly. "To believe in something you have accepted to be true, but that sometimes seems to go against all that you see." She was quiet for a moment as she turned the old cross in her hands. "I used to have one of these, given me by my mother. That, and the clothes on my back, was all that was left to me when my parents died. There was a time when I believed in such things as God, but that was a long time ago, when I was very young, before the realities of life showed my beliefs to be painfully foolish."

"What happened to it?" Jodi asked softly, more to draw the pain out of her friend than to satisfy any sense of curiosity. Nicole had never spoken much about her childhood. But Jodi figured that this was a harmless question now. "The cross, I mean. Do you just not wear it anymore?"

Nicole shook her head and smiled, but Jodi could see that her eyes were misting over. She had never seen Nicole like this. "Nikki," she said quickly, "I'm sorry, I didn't mean to upset you. You don't have to–"

"It is all right," Nicole told her as her mind paged back to those distant years of her youth. "It has just been a very long time since I have thought of it, that is all. When I was a young girl, after my parents died and I was put into an orphanage, I had a friend. A boy who was very special to me. Since I was older, I was able to leave the orphanage before him, to go to the academy. I gave my crucifix to him to keep for me, the only special thing I had for the person I held most dear."

"What happened?" Jodi asked, watching Nicole turn the wooden cross over in her hands. "He blew you off, didn't he?"

"No," Nicole said with a force that startled Jodi. "No," she went on more softly now, "he would never have done that. Never. We wrote each other often, and I counted each passing day toward the time when he could join me. I would have been a senior by the time he could have come, but we would have had some time together. I knew even then that we were terribly young, mere children, but still, I had hopes and dreams for the two of us, and I knew he did, too.

"Then, in my first year at the academy, I was going back to visit him when I found out that the orphanage had been attacked, that the entire planet had been wiped out." She smiled bitterly. How many times had she relived that day in her nightmares? "The silver of my mother's cross burned away with the rest of Hallmark's atmosphere. Along with him."

Looking up at Jodi and seeing her shocked expression, Nicole apologized. "Jodi, I am sorry for bringing up such unpleasant a subject." Pretending she had something in her eye, a convenient excuse to wipe away a tear that threatened to fall, she asked, "Did you wish to go see the show tonight at Wilmington's, or... Jodi, what is wrong?"

"Did... did you say *Hallmark?*" Jodi rasped.

"Yes," Nicole said, confused and growing concerned at her friend's alarming change in expression. She looked like she was going into shock. "Jodi, tell me what's–"

"What was his name?" Jodi demanded suddenly.

"Jodi, why–"

"Dammit, Nicole, what was his name?" Jodi practically shouted from across the table. Around them, conversations ceased as people turned to stare.

"Reza," Nicole said, looking at Jodi as if she had gone mad. "Reza Gard. Why? What does it matter? What is wrong with you?"

Jodi felt her heart hammering in her chest, and she was becoming lightheaded to the point of dizziness. "What did he look like?" she asked, licking her lips and leaning forward as if she were physically starving for the words that were to come from Nicole's lips.

"He... he was just a boy then–"

"Did he have green eyes that you couldn't turn away from?"

That shocked Nicole. "Yes," she said, her face knotting with concern. "How–"

"Did he have a scar over his left eye, like this?" Jodi ran a fingernail over her left eye, just touching the skin of her forehead and cheek. "And dark brown hair?"

"Yes. Yes," Nicole croaked. A strange sense of déjà vu was creeping over her, leaving her skin tingling and a distinctly unpleasant feeling in the pit of her stomach. "Jodi–"

"Did your mother's cross have '3089' engraved on the back of it?"

"Yes. That was the year my parents were married." She suddenly reached for Jodi's hands. "Jodi, what is going on?"

"Oh, God, Nicole," Jodi said, fighting hard to contain her excitement, oblivious to the crowd of onlookers who had forsaken their dinner to watch the spectacle these two were providing. "He didn't die on Hallmark," she blurted, her words rushing forth in a stream. "He showed up on Rutan, carrying an endorsement letter from some Colonel Hickock and your mother's crucifix. He was brought up by the Kreelans, as one of them. He taught me his name. He's on his way to Earth right now aboard–"

"That is not possible!" Nicole shouted. *But how else could Jodi possibly know these things?* she demanded of herself. *And who else could it be?* Jodi began to fade behind a curtain of swirling black spots that suddenly began to pool in Nicole's vision.

"Nicole, it's true! I swear!"

"Reza... alive?" Nicole, wide-eyed, shook her head as the blood drained from her face.

"Nicole, I'm sorry, but – Nicole? Nicole!"

But Nicole could no longer hear what Jodi or anyone else was saying. Her eyes rolled back to expose the whites, and she fell from her chair to land at the feet of the shocked restaurant manager who had just emerged from the kitchen to see what all the fuss was about.

* * *

Jodi sat in a chair next to Nicole's bed, keeping watch over her friend as the sleep drugs did their work. In what had seemed like a trek born of a novel of the surreal, Jodi had somehow gotten Nicole back to the *Hood*. The chief surgeon examined her and put her on bed rest for twenty-four hours with a diagnosis of emotional trauma. Jodi felt awful.

But as she sat there, holding Nicole's hand, she realized why Nicole had reacted so strongly to the news that Reza had not died, but had been raised by their enemies: even though she had been so young, she had never let go of him, never stopped loving him. She had taken on the occasional lover, but never had she allowed the relationship to blossom into something more substantial than the satisfaction of the most basic primal needs. Somehow, inside, she had gone on believing that he could not really be dead, that somehow he would return like a fairytale hero to claim her heart, a modern Prince Charming, snatched from the jaws of Death. While Jodi knew that Reza was not – or at least did not seem to be – bent on the destruction of humanity, and perhaps just the opposite, his Kreelan upbringing and all the negative implications that lay therein could not be ignored. And to Nicole, who had not yet given Jodi time to explain all the things that had happened on Rutan, it must have seemed like her long-lost knight in shining armor had returned as some infamous Black Knight, corrupted and evil. The Reza Jodi had seen would be nothing like what Nicole remembered. She was bound to be taken aback, Jodi thought, perhaps even horrified.

"It's not that way, Nikki," Jodi said quietly, although she knew Nicole could not hear her through the narcotic fog that had been required to sedate her shocked brain. "I just wish you could have been there to see him. Maybe, maybe when that stupid bitch Rabat finally gets done with him, you'll get your chance. But..." Jodi sighed.

Despite the guilty feelings that the thought evoked, Jodi could not help but wonder if such a meeting would be a good thing for her. Reza represented a change in the equation of her relationship with Nicole, and that was something she was distinctly uncomfortable with.

On the other hand, if the two of them did share something, it would be so much more than Nicole had now.

An idea suddenly congealed in her mind, and she acted on impulse, calling the captain's yeoman.

"Yes, ma'am?" the young man answered.

"I'd like to speak to the captain as soon as possible," she said. "Please tell him it's extremely urgent."

"Just a moment." The boyish face was replaced by the *Hood's* coat of arms for a moment.

"Yes, Mackenzie, what is it?" The captain's face suddenly appeared, his short-cropped gray hair forming a silvery helmet on his head. From the rough leather jacket she saw on him, she knew he had just gotten back from shore leave, and his face made it clear that whatever she had to say, it had better be good.

"Sir, I'd like your permission to go to Earth with Commander Carré. She has knowledge that is vital to an ongoing Confederation intelligence project..."

Twenty-Two

Deliha Rabat was her usual flawless self. Despite too little sleep and horrendous stress, most of it produced by her own imagination, she was outwardly calm and collected. But under the plastic veneer she wore in front of her masters, there lurked a seething core of disappointment with herself and resentment toward the successful members of her team, her jealousy at their success a mountain that towered beyond the shadow of her own failure.

Now, standing before the Council and the president, she had to submit herself to what many lesser souls would have considered the final humiliation, the results of the debriefing that they had conducted on the *Aboukir* on the way to Earth. But to her, it was a challenge, and one that she eagerly accepted. She knew the human mind well, in all its various malignant forms, and was thus well prepared for her time before the Council.

The other researchers had told the Council their golden tales of success: of how phenomenally Reza had scored in language, spatial concepts, and certain types of mathematics; of his superhuman physical strength and mental acuity; of how his physiology was still basically human, yet fundamentally different in ways that were not entirely understood, as if Reza were the product of an extremely successful genetic engineering project that was well beyond human means to fully understand, let alone duplicate. Even the things at which Reza did not excel, but was merely human and thus flawed, were laid at the Council's feet where they were examined with the enthusiastic but often myopic vision of those disposed to power but often ignorant of the value of the individual.

Needless to say, they were entranced by the work that had been accomplished in the short trip to Earth, and none of the notables present commented on the lack of personal success on Rabat's part. This, of course, only fueled the fire of her malice.

Following the completion of Dr. Chuen's impassioned presentation, the last of her team chiefs to speak, she stood up and took her place at the podium that stood like the hub of the half-wheel of padded chairs from which the eyes of the Council looked down upon her.

"Mr. President," she said in her best subordinate voice, "ladies and gentlemen of the Council, let me conclude the research team's statements with some observations that may serve as food for thought as the Council considers the subject's place and future within the Confederation."

Rabat did not notice the Navy yeoman who entered through the room's rear doors like a stealthy field mouse and hurriedly sought out Admiral Zhukovski, who sat beside Melissa Savitch in the small audience arrayed well behind the podium. Zhukovski listened to the man for a moment, then dismissed him. Melissa noted the fleeting impression of a smile across his face, but he refused to answer her signaled question: *What was that about?*

"As you have already heard," Deliha went on, "while the subject has adapted extremely well to Standard, he has not uttered a single word of his adopted language, nor has he given any insight whatsoever into Kreelan customs or capabilities outside of those with which he, personally, is endowed.

"In short, he has consciously withheld information that is vital to the security of the Confederation, despite the clear understanding on his part of our need to learn of his experiences. Further, the physiological alterations to the subject apparently have been accompanied by no less significant psychological changes, which undoubtedly are responsible for the subject's genius level scoring in several areas of the psychological test battery and a phenomenal score in the extra-sensory perception portion of the tests."

Several of the council members raised their eyebrows at that. It was common knowledge that some individuals possessed a certain "sixth sense," in some cases active at a level that could be measured with the appropriate scientific techniques. However, Reza's test results weren't simply phenomenal; they were literally off the charts.

"Finally," Rabat continued, "it is my professional opinion and conclusion, as leader of the debriefing mission, that this physiological and psychological transformation was indeed deliberate on the part of unknown powers within the Kreelan Empire, and was done with malignant intent toward the Human Confederation. This leads me to recommend to the Council that the subject be treated as a significant threat to Confederation security, and should be peaceably confined while a much more thorough interrogation is undertaken using all measures appropriate to the potential threat."

The room fell into a quiet, uneasy murmur. While at home or at meetings dealing with the social welfare of their frequently embattled worlds, the members of the Council generally were predisposed to show dignified compassion. But in matters of security, brought up in the dark times of a seemingly endless war that had cost billions of lives and dozens of worlds destroyed, a more callused eye was focused on matters such as those at hand; conflict did little to instill trust in those besieged.

It's happening again, Melissa Savitch thought to herself as she saw the mood of the room swing from nearly awestruck interest to fearful muttered musings. Rabat had even managed to play Reza's strengths against him, Melissa saw now, using his superior abilities to highlight the fears Rabat was trying to draw out. Melissa's spine became a rod of iron as she made to stand up and take a stand against this insanity. This was not about any threat to Confederation security, it was not about Reza's right to be human if he so chose. It was about power. "I object to–"

"Ladies and gentlemen," Zhukovski rumbled, his good hand unobtrusively drawing Melissa back down into her seat, its strength communicating her need to cooperate quickly, "*Gospodin Prezident* and Council, I would like to speak, if I may."

Without another word, Melissa sat down.

"By all means, Admiral Zhukovski," the president said pleasantly, but with a poker face to conceal any thoughts of his own. While Zhukovski was one of the only people in the room whose judgment he truly trusted, the president also had to be a politician, which sometimes forced him to ignore good advice for far less noble purposes. They were on far more delicate ground than even Zhukovski probably realized. Mistakes here could trigger political repercussions that could topple the present government, and the president chose not to think about what would happen to the Confederation as a democracy if that happened.

Zhukovski bowed his head to honor his commander-in-chief before he began to speak. "It seems we find ourselves balancing future of entire race on outcome of one man's knowledge, and yet again are tempted into quick solution based on scant knowledge we ourselves possess. And all of this based on premise that Reza is not necessarily Confederation citizen, that he is different, not one of our *kollektiv*, and thus may be treated in any fashion found desirable and convenient, even unto death.

"But this... rationale, it would seem, now has – how do we call it? – litmus test." He held aloft the message the yeoman had left with him. "It has come to my attention that certain young Navy officer has personal knowledge of Reza Gard as youth on Hallmark."

This caused a stir of surprise in the audience and across the semicircle of the Council.

"Do you mean to say, admiral," boomed Senator Borge, the president's chief rival from the Opposition Party, "that this person knew Reza from before the Kreelan attack?"

"Exactly so, honorable senator," Zhukovski told him. "And to answer any question of how viable is her knowledge, I submit that it would be in best interests of all concerned if this officer was allowed re-introduction to Reza in hopes of verifying his identity, and to perhaps help build personal and cultural bridge he may cross to join our culture." He glared at Rabat and Major General Tensch, who still openly advocated a deep-core procedure on Reza, whether he was found to still hold citizenship or not. "I would also suggest that reintroduction be made here, for all members to witness. Only a few who now sit in this room have ever laid eyes on young man whose fate we charge ourselves with deciding. It would be only fair to him." *And to ourselves*, he added silently. "I am sure Dr. Rabat's host of experts can provide Council verification of Admiral L'Houillier's officer, that she is telling truth both about what she knows and about whatever may take place should Council agree to such meeting between her and Reza."

"Do you feel confident that this is so, Dr. Rabat?" the president asked.

Rabat seethed at the way Zhukovski had boxed her into a corner, but there was no alternative, for the moment, at least. She had to cooperate or she would look like that fool Tensch.

"Of course, sir," she admitted evenly. "I think even Reza has been baselined enough to know if he is telling the truth." This was the best compromise statement she could make without leaving herself open to charges of outright lying; in all the time the team had worked with Reza, not one single time had he lied or even bent the truth, to the best of their knowledge. If he did not wish to address something, he would simply remain silent. Apparently, silence or the complete truth were the only options available to his tongue. "And the officer Admiral Zhukovski has mentioned should be easy enough to deal with."

Neither Zhukovski nor Admiral L'Houillier liked the open conceit in her voice, but there was nothing to be done about it at present.

"Very well," the president said briskly. "Admiral L'Houillier, Dr. Rabat, set this up as soon as possible. Ladies and gentlemen, this meeting is adjourned until then."

Two raps of the gavel, and it was over.

* * *

The president. Reza mulled over the word and its significance. The humans did not have an Empress as did his own people. This they had told him, the words sparking dim memories of things he might at some time have known long ago. But seeking the knowledge of the human child who lay somewhere deep within him was by and large fruitless, for he was no longer a boy, nor was he truly human any longer. He had to learn everything anew.

Although it was very difficult in the beginning, he understood most of what they spoke to him now, and he could answer intelligibly. He felt their frustration when they asked him about things that dealt with the Way and his people, of the Empress and Her designs, and he became mute. Those things were not privy to any not of the Way, and although he no longer was bound to Her and his sisters in spirit, he did not feel compelled to cast aside his vows and beliefs. His honor was Kreelan, as was his soul, and these things he pledged to forever uphold as inviolate. He had tried to communicate this to the "scientists," but they had not taken his words as final. There were things he could tell them, perhaps, that would not endanger his honor or bring shame before Her eyes. But he sensed that the time was not yet right, that those who had swarmed around him in the bowels of the great ship like starving carrion eaters were but lackeys to a greater power.

The president. Undoubtedly not endowed with Her powers or divine grace, Reza understood that this person was the most high among humanity, the giver of laws, the maker of war, the one with final responsibility for all that happened or did not happen in the human realm. It was initially difficult for Reza to accept that the leader of humanity was a male. He had thought the scientists had been telling him a joke, as they periodically were wont to do to test his understanding of the concepts he was relearning, human-style humor not least among them. Doubting their words, Reza had demanded that they produce a likeness of this person, and they did so, presenting him with a small life-like image of a stately, if not quite regal, man wrapped in brightly colored scarlet cloth, with vibrant insignias and other ornaments around his neck and arms. His hair was a silvery gray, a handsome contrast to his skin, which was nearly as black as Reza's armor.

"This is President Nathan," they told him.

"Why," Reza had asked, perplexed not by the man's color or garments, which he knew were diverse among humans, but by how he had been addressed, "does the president have a name, and is not simply the president for always?"

This, in turn, confused them. "He – or she, as the case may be – is not president forever," one of the scientists had replied, deeply curious as always at anything he said or asked, "but only for the time he has been elected by the people, the voters. Then he is replaced by someone else, again selected by the people. That is the way a democracy works."

"And his spirit lives on in whoever follows, to help guide... him, or her?" Reza had asked.

At this, the researchers began asking him questions that he could not answer for fear of revealing more than he was able of the Way and his Empress. The researchers were intensely interested in all his beliefs learned while among the Children of the Empress, but there was little he could tell them. He fell silent, his own question unanswered.

Had Jodi or Braddock, or especially Father Hernandez, been at hand, Reza was sure they would have answered without expecting information in return as the scientists often seemed to. Of all the humans he had met so far, those three and the red-headed one called Sinclaire were the only ones he trusted, for their hearts were true, if strange in their own way. But they all had been barred from him for reasons he did not understand.

But now, he thought, he would be able to see the president himself.

"This way, sir," one of the four Marine warriors who attended him said, gesturing to the left, down yet another corridor in the great building that was the ruling place of the "government," another concept that he had vaguely understood as a child, but that now eluded him entirely. The Kreela had no similar thing, only the Empress and Her will.

Now, approaching the great wooden doors to what could only be a throne room, it was time to see the essence of that for which he had given up all that he cherished and loved, to his very soul.

The Marines stopped abruptly and stood to the sides of the door. The commander of the guard, a highly decorated staff sergeant, opened the door, then stood aside.

"Please, sir," he said, motioning Reza through the portal. He was to meet the president without a formal guard.

The president was a man of courage, Reza thought. Perhaps, a man of honor.

He stepped over the threshold into the main Council chamber, the same room where the closed-door session had been held several days before. Now, as then, it was full of people, all of them staring silently at Reza as he stepped into the room.

Uncertain, he stopped a few paces from the doors, sensing them closing behind him. He did not feel threatened, only uncomfortable, as might a tiny scree lizard, cupped in curious hands.

Reza knew, however, that he was far more powerful than such a tiny creature, and in this knowledge he drew comfort.

He surveyed the room and drank in the strange mix of emotions that floated here like the smoke from Braddock's cigarettes. He sampled the unfamiliar smells of different perfumes, was amazed at the dazzling array of colorful clothing. Standing in his armor and weapons, having stolidly refused the flimsy human garments endlessly pressed upon him, he felt as if he were the only solid, tangible object in the room. Everything else before him was as much an illusion as had been the small holograph of the president.

Suddenly, as if on an unseen signal, the assemblage in the room stood and turned to face him. A female whom he had never met before stepped forward.

"Welcome, Reza," she said, beckoning him to come closer, to the center of the raised semicircular dais at which the human elders sat, observing him closely. "My name is Melissa Savitch, and I'll do what I can to help you communicate with the others." *And keep you from being thrown to the wolves*, she added silently to herself. Rabat had been outraged that Savitch should suggest – demand – that she herself be by Reza's side during what Savitch knew was in all respects an interrogation, but Savitch had held firm. Without her to keep the less constitutionally scrupulous at bay, she knew that Reza would soon find himself strapped to a table, an electronic probe sticking out of his skull. "Mr. President, members of the Council," she said, turning to face the elders, "may I introduce to you Reza Sarandon Gard of Hallmark."

And there, standing but a few paces away, was the president himself.

"Welcome home, young man," he said. President Nathan had wanted very much to have himself and the entire Council down there, on the floor, to welcome Reza in a more personal fashion. But the Secret Service had been adamant that they remain separated, and more than a few of the senators had voiced their own personal objections. An unknown quantity, armed and known to be extremely dangerous to his opponents, Reza posed an incalculable threat to the core of the Confederation government at close quarters; the Council was quietly protected by an invisible force field immune to any attack Reza could make. Or so the Secret Service hoped. "I bid you welcome home to the Confederation, on behalf of all of humanity."

"My humble thanks, my president," Reza replied formally as he knelt and brought his left fist over his breast in salute. "My sword is yours to command."

This caused a few raised eyebrows and hushed murmurs in the audience.

"Young man," President Nathan said, "you need not kneel before me. I am not your king, your lord, or your emperor. I am chosen by the people of the nation of humanity to serve and to lead. Yet, I remain but a citizen myself. Please, be at ease."

Reza relaxed slightly from his position of subordinate humility and looked at the dark man, who smiled.

"Sit, and be comfortable," he said.

Finding no skins laid out on which to sit, only the awkward and uncomfortable human-designed furniture, he simply knelt on the shiny wooden floor right where he was, resting his armored hands on his knees.

For a moment, he thought he had done something wrong. The elders suddenly seemed confused, as if some form of vital protocol had not been adhered to.

But the president quickly resolved the matter. Smiling with good nature at Reza and the others in the room, he said, "Ladies and gentlemen, let us all be comfortable in our own way." Reza heard some laughter at that before everyone sat down.

The woman who had first spoken to him appeared again beside him, awkwardly sitting down on the floor with her legs pressed close together and folded beneath her, as if she were afraid of showing the parts of her body beneath the tube of fabric she wore from her waist.

"I guess where you come from they don't use chairs," she said, smiling.

"No," he answered, noting the sense of genuine concern this woman held for him. "Animal hides are much more comfortable."

"I'll see what I can do," she replied in a whisper as the president cleared his throat.

"Are you sure you want to sit on the floor, Miss Savitch?" the president asked amicably.

"I'm fine, sir."

"Very well, then," Nathan said, nodding. "Reza," he went on, his voice deepening in pitch with the gravity of his words, "your return to human space has posed a number of very complex challenges for us. While we would like to think otherwise, that we are wise enough and powerful enough to know all there is to know about anyone or anything, there are some questions that only you can answer for us. Unfortunately, these questions are the most serious of any we have had to consider in your case.

"Fundamentally, Reza, we are concerned about your loyalties after so many years in the Empire. For example," he held up a yellowed piece of paper, the one Wiley Hickock had written so many years before, "you presented this to military representatives of this government, offering it as proof of citizenship and declaring your interest in joining the Confederation Marine Corps. Further, while you have been extremely cooperative in most instances, in not one case have you divulged a single scrap of information about the Empire, a fact we have found most disturbing."

Nathan paused a moment to look at Reza carefully, assessing for himself if the young man understood the importance of what was being said. If he did not make some kind of showing now, Nathan would have little choice but to give in to the increasing pressure by certain members of the Council and the High Command to use more serious methods of interrogation.

All he received was Reza's unnerving alien stare.

"Reza," Nathan said, "as most who know me understand, I am not one who enjoys long speeches with great fanfare, and I also do not wish to tax your understanding of our language on so critical an issue as this. But you must understand that a great deal – your future, and perhaps ours, as well – rests on what you say and do now, here in this room. I realize that once more you must find yourself in a strange new world with strange customs, and have had to relearn your native language in but a very short time. But these people," he gestured with his arms, indicating the senators sitting to either side, "indeed all of the Confederation, need some reassurance that your presence among us is of your own free will, and that your loyalty now is – and always will be – to this Confederation of Humanity."

The room became deathly silent except for the occasional creak of a chair as someone unconsciously leaned farther forward in their seat, the better to hear what words Reza might utter, or to see what he might do in response to those of the president.

"Take your time answering, son," Nathan said quietly.

"Reza," Melissa whispered beside him, "think carefully before you answer; but, whatever you say, it must be sincere enough to let these people understand that you're with them, that you're one of them. If you feel you need help of any kind, ask me – that's why I'm here with you now." That really was all she could say. The president had laid the ground rules, and the ball was deep in Reza's court. It was now up to him to play out the game.

"Mister President," he began slowly, his deep voice resonating in the hushed room with the accent of the language in which he dreamed – the Old Tongue – heavy on his words, "there is no secret to why I am here. I am neither the devil some see, nor a god. When first I came to the Empire as a boy, I promised myself that I would never fight against those born of human blood. This was a promise I have kept for all of my life." Reza looked at each of the senators sitting around the dais, his green eyes boring into each of them with a look of such uninhibited animal power that several of them had to turn away. "You ask me why you should believe my allegiance to this Confederation, why you should accept and value my honor, why you should trust my words and my silence. In answer I tell you this: everything dear to my heart, all that made my life worth living, all that I suffered for, have I sacrificed to return to this realm, to serve you with my sword rather than slay you. I can offer you nothing of substance in proof, for there is nothing I can give save my word and my life."

He withdrew the knife that had once graced the palm of the Empress, and had since bound his life to Esah-Zhurah's.

There was a collective gasp from the audience, and several Marines and Navy officers rose from their seats, reflexively reacting to the potential threat, but none were quite ready to challenge the armored figure sitting quietly before the dais. President Nathan did not flinch or change expression.

"You ask me why you should trust me," Reza said quietly. While he hardly understood anything about these people and the culture they had built around themselves, he realized that only the greatest sacrifice would prove to them that he was not a "traitor," a term for which he himself had no reference from living among the Kreela. He would die, but at least his name would not be held in contempt, and his honor would be preserved among humans as well as his sisters in the Empire. "I tell you that you are all I have now," he said, "that there is nothing for me but to serve you, to offer you my life. I can never return to the Empire, for my Way there is finished, my bond to Her Children severed." He held the knife in both hands as if it were a platter, offering it toward the president. "You ask for proof of my honor; I offer you my life."

"No," Melissa gasped as Reza turned the knife's glittering blade toward his throat. She grabbed at his arms in an attempt to thwart his suicide, but her best efforts had as much effect as if she were grappling with a giant redwood.

The room broke into a pandemonium of unfocused noise and movement as those who could see what was happening leaped out of their chairs with cries of astonishment, and those behind them acted similarly because they could not see what was taking place. Those seated at the dais were on their feet, with the president trying to calm both Reza and the panicking assemblage, but his words were lost in the din. To the left, opposite the doors through which Reza had entered, a troop of Marines burst in, weapons at the ready.

Reza took it all in calmly, absorbing both the words and feelings of those around him as he might take a breath of air before diving deep under water. He fastened his mind upon the image of Esah-Zhurah that never left him, that caused his blood to boil in his veins, and prepared for the final leg of his journey. He steeled himself for the frozen emptiness that awaited his soul like the river in which he had once almost lost his life.

It is time, he told himself, and the blade that Pan'ne-Sharakh had crafted long before he was born shot toward his throat, aimed at the flesh that lay exposed above the collar that bore his name. In his mind's eye, the gleaming metal traveled ever so slowly, and the panicked humans slower still. There was yet a lifetime to ponder things that had once been, and things that might have been...

"Reza."

The blade stopped just as its tip touched the skin of his neck, drawing a small bead of blood. It was not the cry of his name that had stopped him, for the sound of the voice was lost among the many others echoing about him. It was the feeling behind it, the wave of empathy that crashed upon him so unexpectedly, with the force of desperate love.

And there beside him, where the one who had called herself Melissa had been, knelt a woman whom he had never before seen, a stranger who was yet oddly familiar to him. She wore the black dress uniform of a Navy officer, with gold trim around her sleeves and crimson piping down the sides of her perfectly tailored pants. The almond brown eyes, caring and frightened, seemed on the verge of tears. Her face was perhaps nearly his age in human time, but somehow seemed so very, very much younger. It was as if hers was a face from the past, from a time that came to him only in odd dreams now, when he once knew her as...

"Nicole," he breathed, the sound of her name, unspoken for so many years, startling him with its sudden familiarity.

"Yes, Reza," Nicole whispered hoarsely as she touched his face with a trembling hand. "*Oui, mon chère, c'est moi...* it is I."

As everyone watched in silent amazement, Reza let the ornately inlaid knife slide to the floor as he embraced the woman who had returned for him from the past to help him step into the future.

Twenty-Three

"This is madness, Job, sheer madness," Senator Borge declared to his longtime friend and political rival. Ice cubes clinked in the tumbler that was now nearly empty of the expensive Scotch that President Nathan kept especially for his friend and opponent. The president's personal living quarters, built on the site of what had once been the United Nations building in Old New York City, were sparsely but tastefully decorated with priceless original silk batiks depicting the rise, decline, and eventual rebirth of Nathan's native Masai tribe.

Strom Borge detested the room. "It's completely irresponsible of you as Commander-in-Chief to allow such a thing. Over twenty billion people have died in this damned war. And here you are, worried that we might be infringing on one person's rights, for the love of All."

Looking out the enormous pane of plastisteel that served as the room's east wall, facing forever into the rising sun, Job Nathan sighed in resignation. He was tired of arguing, but he was not about to alter his decision. "We've talked about this enough, Strom. And don't play your guilt trip scenario about war casualties, either. Believe me, my friend, as much as you might like to believe otherwise, I have felt each of those deaths as if they were members of my family. Unlike your hero of twentieth century Eurasia, Joseph Stalin, I don't accept those figures as simple statistics; they are all human beings – every single one of them. And making Reza Gard another statistic is not going to help the war effort." He turned away from the window, his face creased with age and the strain of leadership. "We're losing this war, Strom, as I am sure you are well aware. It may take a number of years for that to become clear to the general populace, but the fact remains that we cannot replace our losses as fast as they are incurred. We don't trade planets with the Kreelans; they take them from us after bloody fighting, as if there is no end to their resources, which maybe there isn't. They never give us a chance to return the favor. And our losses have been accelerating over the last few years."

He turned to look out the window again, his eyes taking in the ocean waters that once had been poisoned, but that had in the centuries since been restored to sufficient purity that the water once again was teeming with life. "Reza represents what may be our only chance, Strom, and our decision now must be the right one, and not simply for his sake. If I were confident that your methods were the best for the situation, I would have acted upon your suggestions and those of General Tensch. I would sacrifice one life, a thousand, a million to end this war. But that is only wishful thinking, and I will not punish someone who has committed no offense

– other than being in the wrong place at the wrong time as a child – for the sake of fantasy."

"So," Strom said quietly, watching the president with an almost predatory gaze, "you are confident that Reza is actually going to pan out as a Marine, then?"

Nathan shrugged. "I think it will be an interesting experiment in culture shock," he said. Borge smiled politely, but obviously was not amused. Going on in a more serious voice, the president said, "General Tsingai has taken responsibility for getting Reza prepared for Quantico and overseeing his training there, and Zhukovski's recommendation to have Mackenzie and Carré assigned there as temporary duty instructors was accepted by L'Houillier, with my endorsement. As for how well he will adapt to his new environment – or it to him – who can say? The most important thing is that the matter is settled unless or until something untoward happens."

Strom Borge looked at his friend with an expression that was calculated not to show his true feelings. "You realize, Job, what will happen if you're wrong, if Tensch, the others and myself are vindicated?"

"Yes, my good senator," Nathan replied coolly, raising his brandy snifter in a mock toast. "I will be slated for early retirement, or worse. Would you have me thrown in prison? Shot, perhaps? Then you, Strom Borge, will be the next president of this Confederation."

Borge smiled thinly. *That will only be the first step*, he thought to himself as the last of the scotch slithered down his throat.

* * *

General Tsingai and his newly acquired special aides – Carré and Mackenzie – had done their best to prepare Reza for his introduction to the Marine Corps at Quantico. Quantico was the Confederation Marine Corps' primary training facility, located almost five hundred light years from Earth and the North American city after which it was named. Tsingai, a veteran of many campaigns, was the post commandant. It was a far more significant assignment than it had been on Earth, for Tsingai's domain encompassed not only the planet of Quantico, but the rest of its star system, as well.

Despite the tremendous resources at his disposal, however, Tsingai remained somewhat at a loss as to how to deal with his latest, and in many ways most significant, challenge. Reza had been among other humans for several months now, but unlike most humans who came to live in a culture different from the one into which they had been born, humanity had made virtually no cultural impression on him at all. He could speak the language well, he understood the things he was being taught, but he consistently failed to adopt anything that would have made him a bit more human. Even the best efforts of Carré and Mackenzie, who appeared to be the only two who could draw anything at all from him, failed to get him to open up to human ways and loosen his tongue about his experiences in the Empire.

"Well," Tsingai said to both of them as they all stood watching the induction about to begin in the massive courtyard below, "I guess we've done what we can. Now we wait to see if he sinks or swims."

"He will be all right," Nicole said quietly beside him.

"Yeah," Jodi added. "It's the others who had better watch it."

Tsingai grimaced inwardly. "You're sure that he understands that he is not to act like some warlord down there? We're risking a lot of lives by letting him keep his weapons. If he harms anyone..."

"He will harm no one who does not threaten him with death, General." Nicole strained to see the dark figure in the crowd below, but could see nothing but a mass of bodies, slowly aligning like iron filings trapped in a magnetic field. "This he promised me, and it is a vow he will keep."

Frowning, Tsingai watched the crowd of inductees as the drill instructors, the DIs, began forming them up. He hoped the two women beside him did not notice the white knuckles of his clenched hands.

Somewhere down below, they heard a DI bellow.

* * *

"Line up on the white lines, NOW!"

Reza stood like an ebony pillar among the crowd of inductees who filled the courtyard outside Quantico's main in-processing building. The other would-be Marines favored him with wary, sometimes frightened, glances and quiet mutterings. He wore his armor and weapons, and carried his few precious belongings in the hide satchel that had accompanied him as a gift from the Empress, for it contained all the few material things he treasured, besides his weapons. He had politely refused the general's request to adopt some form of human dress after learning that what little off-duty time he had would be his own; he would proudly wear the uniform of the Corps, but he found the civilian clothing unattractive and ill-fitting. Most difficult for the general to accept, of course, had been Reza's refusal to surrender his weapons to anyone, for any reason. He was a warrior, and his weapons were a part of his body, his soul. He also refused to cut his hair, but never explained why. General Tsingai had grudgingly agreed to these unusual accommodations, but only after very intense arguments from both Jodi and Nicole.

Reza looked at the men and women around him. They ranged from a youthful seventeen to a trim forty, of all different colors, shapes, and ways of life. They were clothed in a bewildering variety of clothes that Reza found somewhat comical and completely alien to the ways of the Kreela. But the diversity in clothing only underscored the fact that Quantico, and the other installations like it, served as temporary melting pots to even out the gaps inherent in the regimental system.

Apparently, Reza was perhaps more diverse than some of his companions could handle. He met their stares, could sense their unease like the predatory animal he was. These were the same feelings he had encountered from almost everyone he had met so far in the human sphere, most especially from those in the high council chamber in which he had been judged, and apparently found worthy. Part of him wanted to reach out to those around him, to tell them that he bore them no ill will, that he had come to fight for them, with them.

He was jostled from behind, and he reacted instantly and instinctively, whirling about with the claws of one hand ready to slash at the eyes as his other hand went for the blade of the short sword that had been a gift from Tesh-Dar.

"I'm sor–" a young inductee, a gangly boy about the same age as Reza, apologized before his face blanched and his eyes bulged from their sockets with surprise and fear at the whirling apparition before him.

Reza stopped his defense and counterattack, relaxing his body instantly. He regarded the young man quietly, noting the complete lack of threatening feelings from this mere child. He noticed the sniggering that took place in the row of people behind the boy, and understood that they had pushed him into Reza to see what kind of reaction they could get.

"Really really I'm sorry I didn't mean to bump into you I–" He was babbling in a steady, fearful stream.

"What is your name?" Reza asked quietly of this young human who evidently had volunteered to be a Marine. While military service was compulsory, service in the Marine Corps was rarely enforced by draft placement; the Corps had all the volunteers it could handle. What courage might lay beneath the surface to make this timid creature want to seek his Way in the Marine Corps?

"Uh... Eustus... Eustus Camden. Look, really, they pushed me I didn't–"

"Be still, Eustus Camden," Reza said, and the boy instantly quieted. Reza watched and felt the emotion's of the young man's tormentors, gauging their reactions. What courage this boy may have, he thought, was ten-fold what they possessed. "I was told that trainees may choose their room-mates," Reza went on, fighting through the accent that he physically could not suppress from his speech. "I choose you." Ignoring the stupefied gasp of his new human tresh, Reza turned back around toward the front rank.

Behind him, Eustus Camden turned to the three recruits behind him – his tormentors since childhood – to give them his best version of a withering stare, but they sniggered and made faces at him.

"Looks like you got a new buddy, Eus," one of them hissed.

"Go to Hell, you bastard!" Eustus spat in reply.

"You there!" a voice burst through the ranks. "I MEAN YOU, BOY!"

Eustus felt like shrinking into a tiny ball and evaporating as a DI that looked like a human fireplug with a built-in PA system instead of vocal chords stormed up to him and began berating him for talking in formation.

Dear Lord, Eustus thought. What have I gotten myself into?

As the DI reviewed some fascinating aspects of Eustus Camden's heritage, a ripple of excitement went through the crowd. The doors to the in-processing building had been thrown open. It was time.

Things had changed little over the centuries in how new blood was brought into the military. Each rank was filed in with mechanical precision, aided where necessary by the DIs and a liberal application of psychological pressure that would become all too familiar to the recruits over the next sixteen weeks.

The lines filed into the front of the main administration building quickly and in good order. Almost all the trainees had several months of prior training conducted by local training centers. Some, mostly those who were coming from Territorial Army units to join the Corps, had considerably more.

Reza soon was lost in the flurry of questions, computer scans, and the rest of the modern paperwork required to become a Marine. Most of the forms, Reza had to leave blank or nearly so. Nicole and Jodi had anticipated this and had researched what they could to help him fill in the information. He meticulously wrote in the names of his parents, which he had been unable to remember but that Jodi had discovered in his mother's service records. And then, something that meant a great deal to him, Nicole had thought when she coached him through it, he signed his name, *Reza Sarandon Gard.*

Next was the physical exam. Every recruit bemoaned it because they had all gone through at least one in the previous months and were tired of being scanned, probed, and poked.

"Strip!" shouted a short Filipino sergeant major with a face like parched leather and a voice that pierced the group's ears like a squawking parrot. The group of about a dozen recruits, which included Reza, was already undressing. Men and women were examined in the same room at the same time, for the war had left little room for the modesty of earlier periods; it did not take into account race, creed, color, or sex, nor did the Corps.

After seeing what the others were doing, Reza began to unclasp his armor, carefully putting the pieces in the plastic bins provided for the purpose. While he had refused any medical examinations while on the *Aboukir*, Nicole and Jodi had said this was required to become a Marine, and he had decided to allow it. Only his collar and its pendants remained as he slipped the last of three bins into the wall lockers where they would stay until the in-processing was finished.

"In the name of God," Eustus uttered from behind him. He was staring at Reza's back, his mouth hanging agape, as was everyone else's who could see.

The nearby recruits took a few steps back, shocked speechless by the tendrils of scar tissue that undulated across Reza's body.

"Looks like he got caught in a tiller," quipped a dark-skinned woman who appeared to be quite unimpressed.

"Gross," hissed a woman with blond hair cut nearly down to her skull. She turned away, making a face of disgust.

"C'mon, goddammit," growled the sergeant major. "None of you are any better looking!"

Putting away their feelings toward Reza in hopes of avoiding any more serious action by the sergeant major, the recruits slowly shuffled to the exam booths set up around the room. The ones who had to stand in line waiting for the medtechs continued to gawk at Reza.

When he came to the head of the line at his station the female medtech carried out the requisite tests with hardly a look at any part of his anatomy other than what happened to be of immediate clinical interest. He watched her intently, intrigued by the compact high technology equipment with which she worked.

His interest made her nervous. The unblinking stare from his sharp green eyes was beginning to upset her, but she did not become really upset until she saw the results of his gene and DNA scans on the computer. This was the first time that Reza had allowed anyone close to him with medical probes, and it appeared that the machine had decided that he was not really human, delivering a message proclaiming "species unidentified."

"Stay here," she ordered tersely. She got up to speak with the sergeant major. "This is all wrong," she told him quietly, glancing nervously at Reza. "And I know there's nothing wrong with my equipment. I just calibrated it this morning."

"I know, corporal," the sergeant major replied. "Just log the results and pass him on to the next station. The... discrepancy was anticipated."

The medtech hastily finished the remaining details and let Reza go with the others, relieved that she no longer had those predatory eyes burning into her.

The naked recruits gathered up their things and followed their Filipino chaperone to the next stop, the quartermaster. There, each was measured and fitted for the camouflage combat uniforms they would wear for the duration of their stay. They would not receive a dress uniform until graduation. That was the first and only official function – other than a possible court-martial or two – that they would attend during basic training.

Reza received his uniform with a mixture of curiosity and apprehension. He was intrigued by the weave of the fabric, yet he was concerned at how little it offered in the way of protection. His armor was a second skin to him, and he was not enthused by its replacement.

They finally got to their last stop before the noon meal was to be served: billeting. In this one respect, things had perhaps become more civilized, less regimented, in that there were only two trainees to a room. In active duty units the troops often lived in open bay barracks, usually with thirty or forty men and women to a bay, but Quantico had been laid out differently at its inception for reasons no one quite remembered, and the quarters had never been updated. But one thing that both the Quantico dorms and open bay barracks had in common was that they were entirely coed. The women were billeted with the men, whether they were in barracks or semi-private rooms. This often caused a stir among the troops from the more conservative worlds, but it could not be helped. The time of sexual equality had, more or less, finally arrived.

"Gard, Reza!" called the Marine sergeant handing out the billeting assignments. Reza stepped forward, still chafing at the feel of the training center uniform he now wore. He carried his armor and satchel in his arms. The young man handed him a key. "Room 236. Across the courtyard, second floor, turn right."

"I wish to specify Eustus Camden as my roommate," Reza said.

The Marine glowered at him. "Move out!" he shouted.

Reza left as the man called out the next name, assuming that the sergeant had granted his request.

As luck would have it, he did.

"Remember, people, chow at twelve-hundred. That's twelve o'clock for you civilian and Territorial Army pukes!" someone shouted from the room behind him. He assumed that "chow" meant food, but he was not sure. Shaking his head in puzzlement, he joined the stream of new recruits making their way to the rooms they would be sharing for the next six weeks.

* * *

"Battalion, ten-HUT!" The Filipino sergeant major brought the recruits in the auditorium to attention. "Listen up, trainees," he began. Reza frowned to himself. He had a terrible time understanding the man's accent; he was not alone. "Your first week is now over," the sergeant major continued. "It was easy. You had a day to rest. That was easy. Now you will begin to learn how to be real Marines, not just boys and girls in ugly Quantico uniforms." He smiled, his perfect white teeth blazing from his rawhide face. "That will be very hard. Not all of you will make it. Some of you might even get yourselves killed, and more than a few will cry for their mommies and daddies." There were a few nervous laughs in the captive audience, but the sergeant major was quite serious. "But whoever finishes will be worthy of the uniform you will receive when you graduate. That will be a real uniform, not the toy soldier costumes you wear now.

"You already met your classroom instructors last week. Most of them are officers or NCOs who are on a break between combat assignments. You will see some of them again during your advanced courses. Providing you make it that far." Aquino's flawlessly polished black boots clicked on the polished wood of the stage as he strutted to the side that held a podium bearing the Marine Corps emblem, a galactic swirl overlaid by crossed sabers. He was so short he would have almost disappeared behind the podium had he been speaking from it, but the medals on his khaki uniform dispelled any notions about his size affecting his combat abilities. "Instructors, POST!" he barked.

Five people marched out onto the stage and assumed parade rest facing the trainees. The sergeant major gestured toward the screen behind him that held the new week's schedule. "Starting tomorrow, you will do PT for three hours, starting at oh-six-hundred. Every day." The trainees groaned. "Captain Thorella will be your primary instructor."

An ox with arms and legs instead of four hoofed feet stepped forward from the line of instructors. His uniform was specially cut to accommodate his enormous frame of hardened muscle. He snapped his hands to the creases of his trousers as he came to attention, a fierce grimace on his face.

The trainees groaned again.

"Oh, no," Eustus muttered beside Reza. The good captain was already well known to everyone in the group, and Eustus and Reza had become two of Thorella's personal favorites during their break times between the intro week classes.

"Pipe down," Aquino ordered. "If there's anyone out there who's better qualified, step up." He glared at the trainees. The moaning abruptly ceased. No one came forward. "In combat," Aquino continued, "there is no substitute for proper physical conditioning. Captain Thorella will ensure you are ready."

Thorella smirked at his new victims. "See you at The Bridge tomorrow, ladies and gentlemen," he announced to more groans and muffled curses before he stepped back into line. The Bridge was a log across a creek where Thorella "instructed" trainees in the arts of gravity and physical humiliation. It was well-known from its brutal reputation.

"You will have two instructors in common skills and small unit tactics," Aquino went on. "Staff Sergeant Taylor and Gunnery Sergeant Walinskij." The two stepped forward. "Common skills will be every other day for three hours during block one of your training. Small unit tactics will be on the remaining days during the same time period. Short duration deployments for field exercises to try out what you have learned will be announced later.

"Light weapons training will be by Gunnery Sergeant Grewal Singh." Singh broke the tradition of the preceding cadre by smiling as he stepped forward. Singh was well versed in the fine art of being an asshole, but he preferred other, more palatable methods of getting his points across to his students whenever possible.

"And, a special guest to Quantico, Navy Lieutenant Jodi Mackenzie will see to your close combat needs." She snapped to attention, stepped forward exactly seventy-five centimeters, and stomped her right foot down at her new posting. She did not smile, nor did she scowl. Her face bore the neutral calm of a complete professional. Someone in the audience whistled. Mackenzie paid them no attention. She would undoubtedly find out who it was during hand to hand exercises. They would not be whistling then. "While Lieutenant Mackenzie is by trade a fighter pilot, she has the benefit of recent experience during the Rutan campaign, where she fought with and eventually came to command the 373d Marine Assault Regiment."

The sergeant major did not have to mention that Nicole Carré was a classroom instructor, whose instruction blocks included military history and battlefield automation. The recruits had already gotten a dose of her curriculum, and most of them were still reeling. She was sitting in the back row of the auditorium with the other instructors who had already been introduced to the recruits.

The sergeant major nodded, and Mackenzie resumed her place in line. "All of the instructors here have at least one full year of combat experience. Carré, Thorella and Mackenzie have received Silver Stars in the line of duty, and the rest have received citations for gallantry. Some of you out there have combat experience. I expect you to put it to use here. If there is a point of contention between you and an instructor, I will moderate it myself. If you have an idea to improve our tactics or training," he paused and looked directly at Reza, "I want to hear it. We are training you not only to fight, but also to complete your mission, whatever it may be, and hopefully to survive. You are no good to the Confederation dead; make the Kreelans die for their Empire instead.

"But I don't want any pissing contests," he went on after a slight pause and a less-than-surreptitious glance at Reza to see if his earlier words had gotten any reaction, which – somewhat to his disappointment – they hadn't. "You are here to train. If you knew it all you would be in the Fleet Admiral or Marine Commandant's chair. You aren't. Remember that. Are there any questions?" He looked about the auditorium. "No? Good. That concludes the morning brief. Drill sergeants," he called to the DIs interspersed through the hall, "take charge of your platoons and get them to their training..."

* * *

The next day, at The Bridge, Eustus stood in a momentary daze as the blood from his broken nose pattered into the water that slowly passed under the log on which he and Thorella were standing. Each held a pugil stick, a pole about a meter long with a bulbous pad at one end and a padded hook at the other.

"Awww," Thorella said theatrically, "what's the matter, recruit? You need mommy to wipe your nose for you?" He laughed as the younger man's face set itself into a mask of venomous ferocity. "That's better, you queer," Thorella sneered as Eustus came toward him. "It's nice to see you show some balls for a change."

Thorella had been the king of The Bridge since his arrival at Quantico. He loved it. He was a towering mountain of a man, his flexing biceps larger around than most of his contemporaries' thighs. His face was molded in a permanent grin that would have made his face very attractive except for the black, darting eyes that were without depth, without feeling. He was cunning, intelligent. He was a killer, and he enjoyed his chosen profession. No matter what the prey.

This was the first day on The Bridge for this batch of recruits, the morning after Sergeant Major Aquino's briefing. Thorella requested the cadre put Reza up first, but they had opted for tradition. Thorella took his place as King of the Bridge and waited for voluntary opponents. If no one came forward to challenge him, names were called alphabetically. Two of the recruits voluntarily came up to try their hand at knocking Thorella from his perch, but both wound up with soaking uniforms and splitting headaches.

In a short time he had worked his way through the trainees to Camden, who now stood on the opposite end of the bridge.

"Take it easy on me, kid," he smiled, his little obsidian eyes glittering with anticipation. He had something special planned for this one.

"Fuck off, sir," Camden hissed through his bloodstained teeth. He did not know how to swim, and even though he knew the water below was not deep and there were instructors standing by to pull people out, he was not thrilled with the prospect of being knocked down – semiconscious, undoubtedly – into the cold stream. He gripped his weapon tightly, hoping to anticipate Thorella's moves.

Thorella waited casually for Eustus to come within range before feinting a blow to Eustus's feet, then he hit him in the face just hard enough to split his lip, but not so hard as to send him spinning from the log. As Eustus fought to recover, his face now streaming with blood from his violated nose and now his mouth, Thorella slammed him hard in the stomach, driving the wind out of him.

Gagging and dripping blood, Eustus fell to his hands and knees, barely retaining his grip on his useless weapon.

"C'mon, recruit," Thorella complained, "you're disgracing my uniform by even wanting to call yourself a Marine. Some blue-skin is going to use you for a tampon if you fight like that. You'd probably like it, just like your buddy Gard."

Eustus did not take Thorella's last insult lightly. His family had been raised on a very small outpost settlement not far from Quantico 17. Too small to support even a single regiment, it more than made up for its small size by the devotion to duty of its inhabitants: the Camden name had appeared proudly on a succession of Marine uniforms. Eight gold stars now hung in his widowed mother's house for his father and the sisters and brothers who had died in the line of duty. Only Eustus and his youngest brother, Galan, remained, and his little brother would volunteer for service when he turned seventeen. That was the way things were. And when Galan finally finished school and left to join the service, his mother intended to finish her days helping the sons and daughters of other families in the sector military hospital. She expected to outlive her two remaining sons, but that would not stop her from continuing her contributions to the war effort.

His heart in a cold rage now, Eustus lunged into a fierce but technically uninspired attack that the captain easily defeated. Drawing Eustus into the trap, Thorella moved very close to him, first driving the hooked end of the stick into Eustus's crotch behind the screen of his body. As Eustus gagged and began to sag to his knees, Thorella hit him in the face again with the padded end, bruising his right cheek.

As the young trainee toppled backward, Thorella snagged his left foot with the hook and yanked it toward him. Eustus hit the log with a loud crack; had he not been wearing a helmet, he probably would have fractured his skull.

Grinning like a death's head, Thorella contemptuously kicked Eustus's unconscious body off the log, sending him tumbling into the water below where he was retrieved by two waiting trainees who had already taken their plunge.

The sergeant major frowned slightly, but said nothing. He held his silence not because Thorella was an officer – Aquino's power as senior enlisted man in this camp on Quantico far overshadowed the captain's – but because he believed that a bloody nose here and there helped to toughen his trainees for the deadly fighting that awaited them among the stars: if they couldn't handle this, they would never be able to handle combat. The captain had overstepped the bounds somewhat with Camden, but not so far that any action could really be taken against him. But Aquino would be watching. And he wished that Thorella did not appear to enjoy himself so much.

"Buddha," Reza heard someone whisper in the silence that fell over the trainees who waited their turn with the troll who guarded the bridge. It was the first remark of a hushed torrent of resigned commentary: "This is bullshit." "I can't believe they're letting this guy get away with this." "Oh, man, we're going to get our asses creamed."

And, what Reza understood to be the classic epithet: "Oh, shit."

He considered their comments, as well as what he had just seen. He himself was not overly impressed with Thorella's method, as it was trivial gameplay in terms of his own experience. What offended him was the reasoning behind Thorella's tactics: it was not to instruct or inspire, to make the trainees more competent in battle. Even in Reza's first days in the kazha, while the tresh were often cruel, they did not spar with him without useful purpose. No, he thought, Thorella's actions were born of his personal hatred and contempt for those around him. More specifically for Eustus and, as he was well aware, for himself.

Thorella made a theater of yawning and stretching before he called out, "Who's next? Darman! Get out here. I–"

Before the young woman, who was clearly trying to mask her fright, could step up, she felt Reza's hand on her arm, gently pushing her aside as he stepped forward.

"I request the honor to fight you, captain," he said formally. Reza had decided that a lesson in humility was in order.

"You understand the rules, trainee?" the sergeant major said before Thorella could reply to Reza's challenge, but it was more a statement than a question. He did not want a bloodbath on his hands, regardless of who started it. Thorella was much bigger than Reza, but he was not sure that size and the captain's appreciable skill would make up for the unknowns that presented themselves with the younger man.

"I believe I understand Captain Thorella's rules, Sergeant Major Aquino," Reza replied carefully. "I shall obey them."

Aquino's eyebrow arched. Captain Thorella's rules, he thought. This should be interesting. "Very well. Continue."

"All right, you little slime-bag half-breed," Thorella whispered under his breath. "Let's see just what color blood you've got."

Reza ignored the stick one of the other trainees offered to him.

"Take your weapon, Gard," Thorella ordered.

"I have no need of it," Reza replied as he stepped onto the log. He felt clumsy in his combat boots and exposed wearing the flimsy camouflage uniform rather than his armor, but he thought he would be sufficiently agile for the job at hand. He waved away the helmet one of the trainees offered him.

"This is more like it," Thorella said, impressed, as he removed his own helmet, tossing it aside. Even if Gard was a loser, he thought, at least he knows how to go down right. But he was also eager to see how Reza would look after the unpadded grip of the metal bar had been smashed across his shoulder blade. Or the side of his exposed skull.

Reza walked about a third of the way out onto the log and stopped, his eyes never leaving Thorella. His scarred, tan face was calm, his callused hands hanging at his sides.

"Well, come on, freak," Thorella said, his mouth a cruel smile that split the lower half of his face like a crevasse.

Reza offered him a hand gesture that he had seen used by some of the other trainees. He did not know what the extended middle finger meant, but understood that it was entirely offensive in nature.

"You arrogant little prick," Thorella said as he made a lightning-quick thrust at Reza's midsection. Had it connected, he probably would have broken some ribs.

But Reza had somehow disappeared, and Thorella found himself flying through space, propelled by the enormous force he had put behind his own attack. "Shit!" he hissed as he fell, face-first onto the log, scrabbling desperately for a grip before he fell into the water. The hooked and padded stick slipped from his grip and disappeared into the stream with a splash, accompanied by a series of gasps from the watching trainees.

Quickly regaining his feet, Thorella found Reza standing casually a couple meters away, *behind him*, watching with that stare of his. But now he also wore a slight smile – something he had relearned from Jodi – on his face.

Thorella was incensed, but he kept it well beneath the surface, in the same place he kept all the feelings that seethed within him that could not be exposed to the light of public scrutiny. "Not bad, punk," he said amicably as he flashed a wolfish smile at the onlookers. *I'm going to tear your guts out for that*, he screamed to himself.

Reza said nothing as he waited.

Thorella moved forward cautiously, his body fluidly transitioning into his favorite hand-to-hand combat stance, edge-on to Reza, his arms raised to their strike/defend positions.

Aquino was growing concerned. Thorella's stance was not one he wanted to see practiced here: the technique he was intending to use was for killing only, and was only learned and practiced under very carefully supervised conditions. Still, he hesitated to say anything. Just as much as everyone else, he was curious as to what Reza would do.

Thorella was nearly within striking range. He was not planning any feints or drawn-out sparring contests. He wanted to hurt Reza, hurt him bad, hurt him *now*–.

Thorella's cruel smile vanished, to be replaced with the feral snarl of a rabid animal. He darted forward with agility amazing for so bulky a body, making a vicious thrust at Reza's midsection with his left hand, closed in a rock-hard fist.

Reza deflected the blow without discernible effort and stepped aside, his booted feet solidly balanced on the sloping side of the log. He felt it roll slightly and compensated for it; the log was not fixed in place. A few chips of wood fell into the running water below.

In this way Reza entertained Thorella for a while, parrying the larger man's thrusts while allowing himself to be pushed toward one end of the log, ostensibly cornered.

"Stand and fight, you bastard," Thorella snarled. "You've got nowhere else to run, now."

The fist that lashed out like a knife toward Reza's throat would have killed or crippled him had it found its mark. Instead, it found the wall of Reza's palm, his fingers closing around Thorella's larger hand like a vise. The sound of the impact echoed over the streambed like a rifle shot. Thorella tried to pull away, but quickly discovered that to do so was impossible: it was as if his hand had been set in concrete with reinforcing steel around it. He had never encountered a grip so strong.

"What is wrong, captain?" Reza inquired politely. He began to increase the pressure on Thorella's fist, simultaneously canting it at an angle that began to force the captain to lose his balance on the log or risk having his wrist broken.

"If you let me go now," Thorella whispered threateningly, "I'll let you off easy. Otherwise..."

"Do not threaten me, child," Reza said contemptuously. "Your lack of honor and courage disgrace your bloodline, your peers. Were I not bound by my honor to the strange laws of your people, I would slay you as the beast that you are. Beware, captain."

Thorella's eyes bulged with outrage. "Why, you little motherfu–"

He did not have enough time to finish the sentence as Reza flicked him from the bridge as if he were no more substantial than a wad of paper. Howling obscenities, Thorella flew through the air until he hit the water, throwing up a tremendous splash that would be the subject of delightful recounting among the trainees for weeks.

There was another collective gasp among the recruits. Thorella had never been dropped by anybody, and Reza did it his first time on the bridge. With his bare hands. For a moment, there was total silence.

Eustus was the first to react, clapping and whistling his approval. "Way to go, Reza!" He was quickly joined by the rest of the trainees.

"What a belly-flop!" someone exclaimed amid the chorus of laughter from the trainees. Some of the instructors smiled. The little leather-faced Aquino nodded, impressed, and that did not happen very often.

"You mean to tell me that somebody finally got that asshole?" Reza heard a voice in the group ask, incredulous.

"Couldn't have happened to a nicer guy," said another.

Thorella suddenly burst from the water, sputtering with rage. He slapped at the surface in impotent fury at having been bested. When he finally contained himself, he looked up to where Reza stood on the bridge, silently watching him. Thorella put on his smile again, the lower half of his face smeared with blood from his tongue where he had bitten it as he hit the water. The blood made him look like the water had washed away the skin of his face to expose the red muscle tissue and ivory skull underneath. He pointed a finger at Reza in warning. "Watch your back, freak," he hissed. "Watch your back." He winked like they had a mutual secret, and then he moved off toward the shore.

The hatred Reza saw in the man's eyes left little doubt as to the future. He knew that someday he would probably have to kill him.

* * *

"What's the matter, Marine?" Thorella sneered. "Can't you take it?"

Ever since Reza had tumbled him from the bridge, Thorella had made even more of an effort to make their lives completely miserable. Sometimes he enlisted other officers and NCOs – and even some trainees – to aid him in his mission, but mostly he preferred to administer his harassment personally. The post command staff, while conscious of his singling out Reza and Eustus for special attention, generally made no move to interfere as long as Thorella kept his actions within the unwritten limits of cadre deviltry. For the most part, he complied. Grudgingly.

Eustus cursed to himself as he tried to keep from collapsing into the gravel. He had been doing pushups now for five minutes straight after a grueling five kilometer full-pack run with the rest of his platoon, and his traitorous arms were shaking like the bass strings of a harp, about to give out. His hands were bleeding from the jagged rocks under him, the edges of the sharp granite shards of The Pit doing their best impersonation of razor blades. He looked up at Thorella's square face.

"No pain, no gain, sir!" he huffed in a less than respectful voice.

"Yeah, Camden, but in your case it's no brain, no pain." Thorella got down, right into the younger man's face, so close that a drop of sweat from Camden's nose trickled onto Thorella's. "You drop out on me, you start eating gravel, and we're gonna take a nice long run through the bogs to warm up your legs, Camden. A nice long run." The bogs were a notorious hell for the trainees, a series of ankle deep patches of soft ground and reeking standing water that made running more of an excruciating experience than it normally was. Thorella knew without a doubt that Camden wouldn't be able to hack it after everything else he had been through that morning.

"Fuck off, sir!" Eustus hissed enthusiastically through clenched teeth.

"Keep it up, dickhead," Thorella warned quietly, the ubiquitous smile etched onto his face. Eustus wanted to barf right between his eyes, but he didn't have the strength to spare. "Let's see how your buddy's doing over here."

Reza was as solid as stone, Thorella noted despairingly. The big captain looked around for some sandbags or something to pile on the smaller man's back, but he could find nothing nearby, and it wasn't worth the effort to go looking too far. He might miss something. "How do you feel, freak?" He tugged on Reza's hair like he might an animal's tail. Someday he was going to cut it off and put it with the other trophies in his collection, he thought smugly.

"I am well, Captain Thorella." Reza refused to call him "sir".

"That's good, freak. Know why? Your buddy over here's starting to look a little tired, and I was thinking you might want to help him out. Camden!" He barked. "Recover and get your ass over here!"

Eustus heaved himself up and staggered to attention in front of Thorella.

"Stand on his back," Thorella ordered. Eustus just looked at him, his face a question mark. "I'm talking to you, trainee dickhead. Mount up. Now."

Eustus opened his mouth to tell Thorella just where to take it when Reza interrupted.

"Go ahead, Eustus."

"No way, Reza. This is totally–"

"Just do as I ask of you." He looked up. "Go ahead." Eustus shook his head and did as he was told, placing his booted feet carefully on Reza's back. He threw a look at Thorella that left few doubts as to his thoughts. The captain only smiled more.

"All right, Marine. Start knocking 'em out. I'll count cadence, trainee dickhead here will count repetitions. In cadence, exercise! Ooooooooone..." Reza lowered himself to the ground, his arms like hydraulic pistons. "Two..." He raised himself back up. "Threeeeeeeee... four."

"One," Eustus spat, enraged that this kind of thing was allowed to go on. He looked around, careful not to upset Reza's balance. No other instructors were in sight. Unless they wanted to fight Thorella – he had no doubt that Reza could hammer him to the ground, but they would both get tossed in prison – they were stuck.

The pushups were brutal, a slow count down, a pause at the bottom, and a fast push up to be in time for the next repetition. If you got behind, you found yourself starting from zero all over again.

"Thirty." Eustus was amazed at Reza's strength. He was lifting most of his own body weight, plus the additional eighty kilos Eustus boasted. He imagined that someone as big as Thorella could maybe do something like that, but Reza was almost half the larger man's size.

Thorella was beginning to get impatient, but he reminded himself of the old adage that good things come to those who wait. His smile became a toothy grin in anticipation. "Ooooooooone... two... threeeeeee... four."

Reza made it, but he was beginning to slow down. His pace was just slightly off. "Thirty-one."

"Bullshit," Thorella snapped viciously. "It's zero, trainee. Zero."

Eustus snarled and was about to leap for Thorella's throat, damn the consequences, when another voice joined in.

"That is enough, Thorella!" he heard Nicole bark. "Camden, get off of him! Reza, on your feet." Greatly relieved, Eustus stepped down. It was like getting off a sheet of spring steel. He leaned down to help Reza get up.

Reza nimbly got to his feet, not even breathing hard, as Nicole stormed across the field like a miniature whirlwind, her normally neutral expression distorted with a very unprofessional look of anger. "What the hell is going on here? Reza, are you all right?"

"Yes, ma'am." The lactic acid that remained in his muscles was already dissipating. But he was ravenous from the temporary change he had made to his metabolism. He would be making several passes through the mess hall line this afternoon.

"I'm not through here, ma'am," Thorella tried to bully her. The only time the two of them came in contact was over Reza and Eustus, and then it was a clash of the titans, at least from Eustus's point of view. "If you recall, I am in charge on this field."

"Not anymore, captain," Nicole snapped. "If anything like this ever happens again, I will put you up on charges."

"Well, well," Thorella chuckled, not the least bit intimidated. He stepped closer to the petite Navy officer, his bulk looming over her like a freight train beside a bicycle. "Not only is she going to pull rank on me, she's going to write me up next time. Maybe I'll get a spanking, too?"

Sadly, his intimidation was not having the desired effect. Nicole did not budge.

"You can do whatever the fuck you please. Ma'am," he told her, finally giving up on simple intimidation. "But on this field, I am in charge, regardless of what you say. And if you interfere in my business again, I'll write *you* up." He rendered her a mock salute and stomped away like a prehistoric beast, screaming at other gasping trainees doing grass drills, ordering them to recover for a quick run through the bogs before they hit the showers.

Nicole saw the blood on Eustus's hands, then took one of Reza's hands in hers, looking it over. She was shocked at how callused it was. The gravel had not made any indentations in the skin. "Both of you, I want you to go to the infirmary and get checked out. And I want you two to stay together so you can protect one another. I do not trust him."

Reza did not trust him either, but he did not understand the depth of emotion Nicole felt. Perhaps, he thought, it is only a protective instinct. He turned back to her, his eyes blazing with a cold fire that had been ignited under an alien sun. He made an expression that might have been a smile except that his teeth appeared poised to tear something apart. "Do not worry, commander."

"What a shithead," Eustus mumbled as they walked back toward the compound. Reza frowned at his friend's description, trying to conjure up a suitable image in his mind. After a moment, he smiled.

Twenty-Four

"C'mon, Reza, I can't believe you're not going to take this pass." Eustus watched him with disapproving eyes, hands on hips. He had fashioned himself into a credible ersatz younger brother in only a few weeks.

Reza shrugged as he pulled on the black undergarment over his naked body. His skin tingled with delight as the smooth material glided on. He was always tempted to dress and undress several times simply for the pleasure of the sensations, of the memories that it evoked. But not now. "Thank you for your concern, my friend, but it is not how I would spend my free time."

His roommate threw up his arms in frustration and sat down on Reza's bunk, watching him dressing in his Kreelan armor. No matter how many times he watched Reza do it, it never failed to give him the creeps to see him change so totally into an alien.

"Look," Eustus pleaded, shaking off the thought, "you've got to get out and see something of the universe around you, Reza. You've got to learn to have a little bit of fun instead of being so morose all the time. We've got a chance to go to town! Don't you realize what that means?"

Reza smiled. "'Booze, babes, and booze,' as I heard someone say. Some others said 'Booze, beef, and booze.' I believe I would prefer the latter. The mess hall does not know how to prepare meat correctly. Perhaps the town has good beef, but I prefer to hunt my food myself."

"No, no, Reza," Eustus said impatiently. "That isn't the kind of beef they're talking about. They're talking about *beefcake*."

"And what is wrong with that? Can you not still eat it?"

Eustus shook his head, blushing. He was raised in a liberal home, but public talk of any kind about sex still embarrassed him. The thought of Reza and "beefcake" together in the same context was too much. "It means guys, Reza, guys! Men, not animal meat. It's, well, a kind of reference to, uh, manliness, I guess." He sighed. "Look, never mind. You just ought to come with us. You might enjoy yourself for once. All the time you're sitting with your nose at the vidscreen or down in the armory messing with the weapons or just sitting in here in some kind of a trance. You never have any fun, Reza. We could have a few drinks, maybe see a kino or even a live show. We might even meet some girls or something. That'd be kind of nice, wouldn't it? I mean, the female trainees are nice, but..."

He trailed off as he saw Reza stiffen and shudder slightly, almost dropping his breastplate.

"I have no need for females," Reza whispered hoarsely. He recovered quickly, fastening the armor into place with a vicious snap.

Eustus panicked. He had never considered the possibility that Reza might be homosexual. While he did not care for it personally, it was a widely accepted practice in many parts of the Confederation. "Reza... I mean, uh, if you like guys, well, I guess that's okay, too, but..."

"No." He turned to his friend, smiling weakly. "I am not that way. I just need to be alone."

Eustus saw tears welling in his friend's eyes. "Hey, are you okay?"

Reza shook his head. "No, but there is nothing to be done about it. And I will speak no more of it." With a quick yank of a leather strap, he secured the short sword to his back. "I wish you a good time, my friend. I will see you when you return."

Then he padded silently out of the room without turning back.

Eustus watched him go, wondering exactly what was bothering his friend so much.

* * *

While Eustus and most of the other trainees were piling into the buses that would take them to the nearby towns, Reza was running through the forest as fast as his legs would take him, which was far faster than any human being had ever run. He whispered between the trees, faster than the wind, taking in the scents of the forest animals and trees, all descended from Old Terra after Quantico had been terraformed. He smelled a rabbit, several squirrels, and some larger predators: a fox and two wolves. The sun had set and it was time for them to hunt. Like them, Reza's vision in the darkness was as keen as those born of Kreelan flesh: another gift of the Change.

He opened his mind, going beyond mere sight and smell. He could sense the birds overhead in their nests, the strange creatures that burrowed underground that he had never seen but knew were there, the insects that clung to the ground and the leaves of the trees.

At last he reached a spot that suited his spirit, a deep cove of trees with a small creek running through it. He knelt next to a rock and became one with it, thinking nothing, sensing everything. Time passed...

When the sky was completely dark, Reza stirred. He wanted to see the stars. He lay down on his back, wondering at the countless points of light that brightened the night sky.

"Where is she?" he asked the sky in the Old Tongue. There were so many questions he wanted to ask, but there was no one to answer. He had made the only decision his Way allowed, thereby damning himself to an eternity of spiritual solitude and Esah-Zhurah to... what? He prayed to the Empress to carry his love to Esah-Zhurah in her dreams. At this moment he would have given anything to be with her, but even the Devil that Father Hernandez so feared would not be lured into making such a bargain.

Sleep finally carried him to the faraway land he had once called home.

* * *

Dawn came.

A deer neared the creek, thirsty for a drink. Reza rose silently from his sanctuary and approached it. It did not run away, for it sensed nothing to fear; he appeared only as an insubstantial shadow, no more a threat than was the mist. That was how Reza preferred it. He wished the animal no pain. Death, when it came, was instantaneous.

This was the first time he had been able to make an unhurried hunt since leaving the Empire. Reza constantly craved meat, but there was no accommodation to be found in the mess hall. Instead, he was forced to hunt in the occasional spare hour or so that was not taken up by training or commander's call. He knew his abnormal need for meat was a result of the Change, but it was one he welcomed; it was another means of preserving in his mind the heritage he had earned, the love he now missed.

He cleaned the deer carefully and stripped it of meat, cutting it into strips to carry back with him, where he would dry and salt it. What little was left of the carcass he carried away from the stream, that the other animals could have their share, and that the water would not become fouled.

He laid out the hide and began to cure it, fortunately a swift process using the methods Esah-Zhurah had taught him long ago. Getting the proper ingredients had been very difficult, but he had finally convinced a pharmacist at the hospital to make up what he had requested. When asked what Reza was going to use the concoctions for, he had told the man, explaining the process in halting Standard, the technical terms of curing a hide not coming to him easily. Strangely, the man had not believed him, but had indulged his request anyway, the ingredients being harmless ones. Reza shook his head in silent wonder at how humans so often mistook the truth for deception.

In any case, Reza was eager to have a skin to sleep on again, even one as thin as this. The human-fashioned bed in his room was unbearable.

* * *

"Hello, *mon ami*," Nicole said as she leaned against the entryway. Reza had left the door standing open to let fresh air flow through the room from the window. "May I come in?"

"Of course, commander," he said, coming gracefully to attention. He had been sitting on the deerskin, reading another technical manual. He had felt her approaching long before she reached the door, but he reacted as if he had not known this. He had discovered that certain of his abilities unnerved those around him, and he had gotten into the habit of screening himself with more human reactions, difficult as they often were to emulate. "You are always welcome here."

"Please, Reza," she said as she stepped into the room, quietly closing the door behind her, "we are off duty now. You can relax and call me by name."

Reza nodded, noting her clothes and the light makeup that adorned her face. She was dressed in a close-fitting scarlet blouse of pure silk, skin-tight black pants, and a gold sash tied around her petite waist. A slim gold chain hung around her neck, and her feet were wrapped in soft black leather boots.

"I thought you had gone into town with the others yesterday, when I did not find you here," she said casually, knowing full well that Reza would not have gone. This was the first and only free weekend the trainees would have during their basic training. Very, very few chose to pass up the opportunity to go into one of the nearby towns and get their fill of booze, gambling, and sex before returning to the discipline of the barracks. Jodi had begged Nicole to go, but she had refused, insisting that Jodi go on with some of the other instructors for an outing probably every bit as wild as those the trainees had in mind, Nicole claiming she had some work to finish that could not wait.

While she did not say so, Jodi had suspected otherwise.

"No," Reza said lightly, smiling as he shook his head. "After Eustus explained to me the merits of 'booze, babes, and booze' and the controversy over 'beefcake,' I decided to forego such pleasures for simpler pursuits." While Eustus was sometimes an awkward young man, his vigor in any endeavor he set his mind to was not to be underestimated. "No, Nicole," he said, his smile fading slightly, "I have no need of these things. I went hunting instead."

Nicole sat down on Eustus's bed, and Reza folded back into his sitting position opposite her, his legs resting on the freshly cleaned and cured deerskin that lay atop a collection of blankets that he had scrounged from somewhere. He had removed the bulky bed frame, having found it intolerably uncomfortable. Along with his long, braided hair, it was written off as an acceptable – barely – deviation from the norm, and therefore exempt from inspection as long as it was kept orderly and neat, which of course it was.

Nicole shook her head. Very few things he did now surprised her. Or so she liked to think. "It looks very comfortable," she said, silently wondering what the animal fur might feel like against her skin. She felt the stirrings of heat in her body and a flush rising to her cheeks, and she quickly changed the subject, groping for a more delicate way of approaching him.

"I have spoken several times with Eustus," she said as she compared the two sides of the room. Eustus had the maximum number of allowable personal effects displayed: a holo of his mother and father, another of his whole family – so many children! – and a real photograph, tastefully framed in luminous black metal, of a famous singer with the woman's autograph.

But on Reza's side, there was nothing but bare wall and – she stopped. That was not quite true. The silver crucifix she had given him when they were children hung from a pin directly above his bed. It made her flush with a combined sense of pride and guilt, of conflicting duty and impatient desires.

"He thinks the world of you, Reza," she told him. "And, from what the other instructors have said, not only he but your whole platoon has been performing and learning better and faster than the others, thanks to you."

"All of them have the warrior spirit," Reza said, proud that others had thought and spoken well of him. It was a far cry from what they had said in his first days among them, and there remained those who would never trust him because of his unusual heritage and the collar he wore. "They simply have not yet learned to use it and control it. But this shall come, in time."

He looked at Nicole, who seemed to be studiously examining the portrait Eustus treasured. "Nicole," he said quietly, sensing the turmoil within her, "what is wrong?"

"I am afraid, Reza," she said, still averting her eyes. "There are things I would like to say, to do, but I..." She shook her head, a bittersweet smile on her face. "I am so silly, Reza," she told him. "I have waited all this time to have you alone to myself for a while so that we could... get to know one another again. I thought it might be good to talk of things other than the war, or what you can tell us of your time in the Empire. To get away from all the things of official interest. But now I find my courage has gone. I do not know what to do, what to say." She looked up at him then, her brown eyes brimming with tears. "Would you hold me?" she whispered.

Reza held his arms open for her, and she knelt next to him, wrapping her arms around him in a fierce embrace, her head against his shoulder.

"What is it in the world that could frighten you so?" he asked softly.

"Oh, Reza," she whispered. "Ever since the day that I found out Hallmark had been destroyed, I knew that you had not died. I simply could not accept it. You were... special in my heart. I had dreams that someday we might... be together. Something in me knew that you would come back, that you would be with me again. Years passed, and still I waited for you. There were times... there were times when it seemed that the thought of your return was all that sustained me.

"But I have not always been faithful to your memory. I know we were only children then, but it seemed more real than anything I have since felt, as foolish as that may sound." He felt her quiver in his embrace, holding him tighter, drawing him closer. "I sometimes listened to the advice of others and the wants of my body; I slept with a few men, but it was never right for me. Never." She brought her face close to his, her eyes glowing with a passion he suddenly realized no one else had ever witnessed. "May God forgive me, Reza," she whispered, "but I love you. I have always loved you."

He felt the sudden heat of Nicole's lips pressing against his, parting for the velvet tongue that yearned to touch his own. He felt the strength of her emotion, was almost overcome by it as she pressed herself against him, the warmth of her breasts burning through her flimsy silk blouse, searing his own chest with the heat of her need.

"Nicole," he managed before she pulled him to her again.

"Make love to me," she whispered urgently between kisses as she pulled him down on top of her. Her hands began to work on the bindings of his clothes. "There is nothing in the world I have ever wanted so much as I want you now."

Confused and alarmed, his nervous system afire with sensations he was powerless to control, Reza somehow managed to gently disengage himself from her embrace. "Nicole, please, I cannot do this," he said softly as he rolled over, gently pushing her away.

"Reza, what is wrong?" she asked, her voice trembling. "You do not want me, do you?"

Reza sat up, an expression of pain and misery on his face. "Nicole..." He shook his head, his mind swirling with confusion as his blood began to burn with desire for the one his heart held most dear, and whom he could never again hold close to him, could never again touch. It was physical agony. "Nicole," he rasped, fighting against the roaring pain that surged through him, "I love you as a friend and kindred soul more than any other, for who you once were in my eyes and my heart, and for who you are now. But I cannot give you the love you seek, the true love of my heart, for that forever belongs to another."

Nicole felt like she had been stabbed through the heart, and Reza felt her pain in his own. "Who?" she asked, bitter and angry, not at Reza, but at fate. *Why?* she cried to herself. *Why must it be like this, after waiting so very long?* "Who is it? One of the trainees? Jodi?"

Reza shook his head slowly, rubbing the scar in his hand where Esah-Zhurah had shared her heritage with him, consummating their love with blood. "No," he replied. "No, if only our lives were that simple, but it is not so."

Nicole watched the skin of his face tighten as his jaw set. His eyes closed, and his head bowed, as if a heavy burden had just been dropped upon his shoulders. He was in pain, terrible pain. She sat up next to him, her sudden anger at his rejection overtaken by concern. She put a hand to his face simply to touch him, to reassure him. His skin was on fire, almost too hot for her to touch.

"*Mon Dieu*, Reza," she gasped, "are you... are you all right? You are burning up."

"It shall pass," he whispered fiercely as he fought to control the trembling that swept his body. "I get this way when I think of her. It has been... the most difficult thing for me to deal with. Her face is seared into my brain, and my blood burns at the mere thought of her."

"Who is she?" Nicole asked again softly.

Reza's hands tightened into fists of iron. "Her name is Esah-Zhurah," he whispered. It was the first time he had uttered her name aloud since leaving the Empire.

"A Kreelan," Nicole whispered, incredulous.

"Yes," he said mournfully, opening his eyes again to face her. "She has the key to my heart, but I shall never see her again. I am banished from her, as I am from the Empire."

"Tell me about her," Nicole asked quietly as his skin began to cool under her touch. She wrapped her arms around him, holding him close. "I want to know who this... woman... is, what she means to you. Please. I know you have sworn not to reveal the secrets of the Empire, but this is very important to me. I must know."

How to tell her? Reza wondered dazedly, acutely aware of her body against his. How could he share with her what he had been, what he had known, what he had felt then and now? He was not concerned with staining his honor with words spoken of the Empire where Nicole was involved; he was worried more about how to convey to her all that made the love he had shared with Esah-Zhurah what it was.

Then he knew. Perhaps he was wrong to even think what now ran through his mind, but he could imagine nothing more fitting. And the more the thought took hold, the more he knew it to be the right thing, almost as if some unknowable power had suddenly dictated this course in his life. "Will you trust me, Nicole?" he asked. "Will you trust me with your spirit and your life?"

A chill ran up Nicole's spine at the sound of Reza's voice. It was not malevolent, not chilling, but held a note of power and understanding that seemed ages beyond his years. The intensity of his gaze proclaimed it as a challenge, daring her to follow where no others of her kind save the man kneeling beside her had gone.

"*Oui, mon ami,*" she said evenly, trying to keep the sudden surge of excitement out of her voice, "I trust you."

Moving away from her, Reza turned to the precisely arranged stack of his Kreelan things and withdrew a particularly beautiful and deadly looking knife. Nicole suddenly wondered what Reza was going to do, but she had given him her trust, and was not about to take it back.

"Give me your hand," he said, holding up his own in the space between their bodies as he had done before with Esah-Zhurah. He put the knife between their joined hands, the blade now flat and cold against their palms. "This is one of the most ancient and sacred rituals among my people," he said, his soft voice a marked contrast to the sparkling fire that danced in his eyes. "In our blood lies our spirit, our honor, our soul. In sharing our blood," Nicole suddenly felt the warmth of blood upon her skin as Reza drew the knife across their palms, but she felt no pain, lost now in Reza's eyes and the lilt of his voice, "we share ourselves with one another, that we may become one. In Her name, let it be so."

Nicole felt Reza's hand close tightly with hers, and she silently wondered at what a silly thing this was, for what could come out of pressing two bloody wounds together? Surely blood did not really flow from one to the other? But why did she feel no pain, for surely the knife had cut her deeply?

"Reza," she gasped as a tingling began in her hand, a warm, prickly feeling the likes of which she had never before felt. The feeling raced up her arm like an incoming tide, then spread through her body like the warmth from a glass of good brandy on a chill evening. "I feel... dizzy," she said, watching as Reza's face began to swim before her, and the light in the room faded toward darkness.

"Come," she suddenly heard him say in a language she had never heard before, but somehow understood. "Come with me."

He stood there, waiting for her, dressed in the gleaming armor that she recalled had once disturbed her, had found threatening somehow. But now it seemed normal, as if that is the way he always had been, and always would be. Behind him she could see a great city of stone and spires, with a brilliantly colored moon hanging in the sun-filled magenta sky. She stopped and stared in awe at a world that no human had seen and survived except Reza. He held his hand out to her, and she took it, barely noticing the talons on her hands and the blueness of her skin, for that was the way she had been born, a daughter of the Empress. And within her, she felt the endless chorus of voices that sang the melody of Her will and love. She felt the power of her own spirit there, a tiny but wondrous drop in an endless ocean of souls.

"Our Ways again are one, my love," she said, feeling as if sunlight bathed her heart, as if the Empress had caressed her soul with kindness.

"In Her name, may it always be so," he said, tenderly kissing her on the lips. "Yours shall my heart always be, Esah-Zhurah."

She smiled as he spoke her name, and walked with him toward the great gates and the wonders that lay beyond.

* * *

"Nicole!"

Nicole sat up at the vaguely familiar voice, blinking at the light that illuminated her surroundings. She fought to say something, but her body did not understand the words her mind wanted to form. Her lips moved, but no sound came.

"Nicole," Jodi said urgently, "are you all right?"

Nicole? Was that her name? She looked at her hands, at the rest of her body, confused by their pale color. Where were her talons? *My name is Esah-Zhurah. No*, she thought again, as the dream rapidly faded, *that cannot be. My name is Nicole. Nicole Carré, not Esah-Zhurah.* That name belonged to another. She frowned, unable to remember who the other woman might be.

"Nicole?" Jodi asked again, her hands on her friend's shoulders, her eyes wide with concern. "Say something, will you? Do you need the surgeon?"

"*Non*," Nicole rasped, finally locating her voice. "I... I am all right." She managed a weak smile that did nothing to reassure her friend.

"You look like hell, Nikki," Jodi said, reluctantly releasing Nicole to sit up on her own. "My God, you were having some kind of wild dream, woman, let me tell you."

"Did I say anything?" Nicole asked, her mind still in a deep fog. She caught fleeting glimpses and sensations flashing across her memory that seemed totally alien, yet somehow familiar...

"The only thing I could understand was when you said Reza's name," she replied quietly. "The rest was gibberish as far as I could tell." *God*, Jodi thought, *and I thought I had a wild time last night.* What had Nicole been doing? She had been crying Reza's name over and over, as if she was never going to see him again. Well, she thought, somewhat bitterly, at least her suspicions were confirmed: Nicole was in love with him. Even if she was risking a lot by fraternizing with a trainee, Jodi conceded that at least Nicole had managed to fall for a decent guy this time.

Nicole looked at her palm. Where there should have been a bloody gash from the knife there was only a scar that looked as if it had been there for a long, long time.

"Jesus, Nicole, how did you get that?" Jodi yelped, taking hold of Nicole's hand to get a better look at the scar. She knew her friend's body fairly well from living together for so long, and knew that this had not been there the day before. But if that was so, she thought, confused, how could there be a scar now? They didn't just form overnight.

"A long time ago," Nicole mumbled noncommittally, pulling her hand away. She was still dazed, confused, and wanted only to be alone to think. She looked at the clock. It was almost oh-seven-hundred. Time to get up. She groaned, feeling as if she had run a full marathon. No, she corrected herself. She felt as if she had lived a lifetime in a single night. The only problem was that she did not remember now whose life it had been. "A long time ago," she repeated absently as she pushed herself out of bed and headed toward the bathroom and a long shower, wondering silently what had really happened last night.

"A long time ago?" Jodi murmured after Nicole had closed the door between them. "Bullshit."

* * *

"Reza," Eustus puffed as he ran with his friend through the obstacle course that took up nearly three hours of their morning every other day, "you know Commander Carré, right?"

"Yes," Reza replied as he led Eustus over a water obstacle. Both of them cleared it with room to spare. They were almost halfway through the course, with about half their classmates ahead of them. Reza chose to pace Eustus, for he himself had never found the obstacle course particularly challenging. He was breathing now only slightly faster than normal, which was practically not at all. "I knew her when we were children. She was... special to me then. And she is a good friend now."

"Oh," Eustus grunted as he leaped up and heaved himself over a ten-foot wall that shook as if it was undergoing a perpetual earthquake. Scrabbling like a rat, he gripped the top and hurled himself over and down the other side, rolling as he landed.

Reza was already on the ground waiting for him, as if he had simply walked through the wall. "Why do you ask?" he said.

"Well," Eustus breathed as he fought to keep up with Reza's relentless pace, "I heard some of the instructors talking when I was passing by their table in the mess, when the commander wasn't around." He paused as they navigated a series of barbed wire mazes. They were very primitive, but very effective for focusing one's attention on one's surroundings. "They said she's been acting a lot different than she normally does."

"How so?" Reza asked, curious. The training schedule had been so busy that he and Nicole had not had a chance to speak to one another since she had come to his room three nights before. Sharing himself with her had somehow released him from the horrible pain that came with thoughts of Esah-Zhurah, the furious burning in his blood. He had not realized what agony it had been until, later that night, after he had led Nicole back to her room and put her to bed, he had dreamed of Esah-Zhurah in his sleep. He had awakened in tears, longing for her, but the pain was no more than a dull throb, as if Nicole had taken away the bulk of the pain by sharing his burden. Nicole, in her turn, had seen and felt the world he would forever call home, voyaging through Reza's spiritual memories as Esah-Zhurah, viewing it as she might, knowing his love for her. But those memories would only visit her in her dreams – she would never be able to relate them to another soul.

Eustus blushed slightly, not knowing how Reza would take what he had overheard. How did you tell someone like Reza that one of Nicole Carré's colleagues said she was acting "like she'd found a really good lay"?

"Well," Eustus said, searching for a somewhat more tactful phrase than the original version, "I guess she seems abnormally cheerful and outgoing, like she's suddenly taken normal pills and stopped being so, you know, aloof, I guess." The two of them sprinted across a worn wooden log laid over a mud-filled bog. "They think she's sleeping – you know, having sex? – with someone, but they can't figure out who it is." He cast a sideways glance at Reza. "It wouldn't happen to be you, would it?"

Reza did not answer, instead throwing himself and Eustus to the ground as the brush nearby erupted with a volley of liquid "bullets" fired by patrolling robots at the trainees running the obstacle course. Any trainee having the telltale red stain on his or her fatigues at the end of the course was in for remedial reaction training and two dozen pushups per "hit." The technique was an effective attention-getter.

Satisfied that Reza and Eustus had reacted properly by quickly rolling into the nearby foliage after hitting the ground, the two rovers moved out of their temporary hiding spot and further back down the trail in search of other victims.

"Damn, but I hate those things," Eustus muttered, again thankful that Reza usually ran with him. He always seemed to know exactly where the lunatic machines were. Eustus only worried about what would happen in combat, when Reza probably would not be by his side.

They went on running, gaining speed for the next set of obstacles – the surprise set – that was different every time and lay around a few more bends in the trail, still out of sight.

"You haven't said no," Eustus said, trying to pick up where he had left off.

"I have not had sex with Commander Carré," Reza replied quietly, almost toying with the truth. While their bodies had never touched in that way, the cache of memories she held in her subconscious included the times he had lain with Esah-Zhurah. In her dreams, Nicole would remember them as had Esah-Zhurah herself after they had been joined in blood. "She is a friend and superior officer, but she is not my lover, nor has she ever been." He smiled to himself, hoping against hope that his touch had brought her some happiness, that perhaps she no longer would have to live her life as the cold and quiet Ice Queen. While he had not touched her body, he had touched her heart, and had found it tender and warm, wanting but afraid to love. She, in her turn, had granted him release from much of the pain he felt merely at the thought of Esah-Zhurah. What magic this was, he did not know. All he knew was that his heart had been lifted and that he could fulfill whatever destiny awaited him. "If she has found freedom in her heart," he went on, "I rejoice in her happiness."

Eustus smiled at his friend's words, not because of the stilted way in which Reza often spoke, but because everything he said was sincere. Eustus, who would have given his eye teeth to have the attentions of someone like Nicole Carré, could not help but admire Reza's complete lack of jealousy toward whomever Carré's lover might be.

"You're such a sap sometimes, Reza," he said lightly as they rounded the bend and saw the set of obstacles that Thorella and his minions had devised for them today. "*Oh, shit...*"

* * *

With few exceptions, the sprawling Quantico headquarters compound was asleep. The command and communications watch centers, deep below the planet's surface, maintained their vigils, humming with matters of insignificance and importance both. Above, trainees pulling guard duty at their posts stamped their feet to keep warm in the chill night air, waiting impatiently for their watch to be up so they could return to their bunks and the religious comfort of sleep. Overhead, no stars showed through the solid cloud cover. The sweet smell of rain, creeping in among the reek of ozone and bitter oil of sleeping war machines, promised an early morning downpour.

Only a few lights were visible throughout the complex. The warning strobes on communications towers blinked on and off, warning away any incoming ships. Guardhouses located along the roads leading onto the base glowed softly. Then there was the bright pink neon sign over the post's premier NCO club. It was a gaudy aberration that somehow had survived long enough to become an icon of the Corps. And, of course, there were lights illuminating the entrance to the bunkers where the post's weapons and equipment were kept.

Many considered the lights a danger, believing that they would only serve as an added target signature in case of a Kreelan attack. This argument was countered by the belief – demonstrated in many drills – that without the lights, it took a great deal longer for the trainees and Marine Corps regulars who staffed the base to get to their assigned bunkers in the massive confusion of an attack. Moreover, in all the years that humans and Kreelans had been fighting, never once had any Kreelan ships even ventured near Quantico, let alone attacked it, despite the fact that the base was on well-established transit routes between colonies that had repeatedly fallen under attack over the last several decades. Some thought it was almost as if the Kreelans were intentionally avoiding the base and its young warriors-in-training.

Now, under one of those lights next to the yellow and black striped blast door that served as the entrance to bunker 175, a red indicator showed on the entry panel: the bunker was occupied. Inside, through the second set of blast doors and the man-sized inset hatch that now stood open, the interior was dark, save for the light of a single hand-held lantern. Carefully balanced on one of the armorer's worktables, its narrow beam was focused on one of the many suits of heavy combat armor that was the primary item in this bunker's inventory. The armor, different from the light armor that Jodi had become accustomed to during her time on Rutan, was of far sturdier material. Completely airtight and equipped with its own maneuvering system, and combined with the heavy armament it allowed the wearer to carry, the armored suit transformed a single human being into a weapon of awesome firepower. Their expense and complexity made them a rare item outside of Marine fleet units.

Not coincidentally, the trainees of Reza's company were to use these very sets of armor in an upcoming exercise that served as the final exam before they received their regimental assignments. Combining all of what they had been taught here, with a great deal of "ingenuity enhancers" thrown in, the final exercise – or "ENDEX" as many called it – was more than a canned field problem that everyone was expected to pass: in ENDEX, failure often meant sudden and violent death.

That was exactly what the sole occupant of bunker 175 was concerned with, although not in nearly so generic a sense. The man smiled as he worked with gloved fingers that seemed far too large for the nimble work they were engaged in now.

Almost finished, he thought placidly as he fitted the auxiliary access panel, about the size of his palm, back to the right thruster pack that bulged from the armor's backplate. Beneath the panel lid, amid the extremely complex but solidly reliable jet control system, a pair of circuits had been slightly altered, their metallurgical and electronic properties not quite what they had been before. When the thrusters had been used a preset amount of time, about half as long as it took for a Marine to hit the ground from an exo-atmospheric combat drop, the right side thruster would fire at maximum burn until it had exhausted its fuel supply. And the left would be disabled, useless. The wearer, faced with a hopeless asymmetric thrust situation, would be left falling, helpless as he spun like a top into the ground. Any remaining fuel and the few live weapons the individual would be carrying would explode, eliminating any physical evidence of tampering.

That was the first modified circuit's intended function: to cause the failure. The second one was somewhat more devious: it sabotaged the miniature telemetry system through which the suit's functions could be monitored by Navy ships or other Marines tied into the same data net. It, too, would fail, just before the thruster fired for the last time. There would be no indication of what had gone wrong.

"A terribly unfortunate accident," he murmured to himself as the panel clicked into place and sealed.

Replacing the heavy armor on its storage rack, he shone the light over it to make sure that nothing appeared amiss. No, he thought, no one would notice a thing. The light paused a moment on the name that had been written in temporary stencil on the armor's breastplate.

"PV-0 GARD," it read.

Happy landings, he thought as he left the bunker, closing the doors and reactivating the alarm and access recording system behind him. Even the computers would not know he had been there.

Whistling a tune he had made up himself, he briskly walked the almost two kilometers back to his quarters, noting with pleasure that the trainee sentry there, ensconced in the warmth of the tiny lighted cubicle outside the officer cadre's quarters, had fallen asleep. Passing up the spontaneous urge to berate the young woman for her dereliction of duty, the man silently passed on, unheard and unseen, to a sound sleep and pleasant dreams of what was soon to come.

Twenty-Five

To an untrained eye, the hangar deck was the epitome of confusion as would-be Marines in full combat gear poured from the ready rooms and into the cavernous launch bay of the old auxiliary carrier, their feet hammering an urgent tattoo as they double-timed their way into the waiting drop ships. Overhead, klaxons bleated and eerily calm voices issued instructions and warnings over the ship's PA system as the launch sequence began. But the apparent chaos was an illusion: every movement, every order, had been rehearsed for days before the recruits had set foot on the ship.

Inside Boat 12, Reza's platoon was settling in, securing their weapons and themselves into the dropship's harnesses for the bumpy ride that doubtless lay ahead. Dressed in powered assault armor that made Reza feel more like a trapped animal than a human killing machine, they were about to do what Confederation Marines got paid for: taking the fight to the enemy. Only this time, the enemy would be human, fellow trainees from another battalion, and the energy bolts would not hurt them. Too much.

"Stand by for launch," Nicole told the trainees in Boat 12's cargo section. Then she reported in to hangar deck launch control. "Pri-Fly, this is Delta One-Two, standing by."

"Roger, Delta One-Two," the controller replied. "You're first up. Launch on green." Outside Nicole's viewport, a series of lights that a race car driver might have found familiar cycled from red to amber. "Launch," she heard the controller say as the light went green.

Even with the little ship's gravity and acceleration controls, the catapult launched the boat with enough force that Nicole could sense it. Ahead of her, the catapult tube seemed to peel away to reveal the stars. As the boat was released from the launch field, she took control and smoothly maneuvered it toward their target, one of Quantico's continents that had been established as a massive training range.

"Delta One-Two, this is Eagle One," came Thorella's voice through the comm link. He was flying ahead of them in a fighter that had been modified to carry the assault group coordinator and an assistant, in addition to the pilot. Today, Thorella was serving as assault group coordinator, with Sergeant Major Aquino observing. This jump, the last before graduation, was going to be their toughest – in training, at least – and Aquino wanted to be there to see it.

Jodi, as usual during the exercises of the past few weeks, had the great misfortune of being Thorella's pilot.

"Delta One-Two," Nicole acknowledged.

"Delta One-Two, you are point for first wave. Note that local target defenses are active; no deep-space systems or fighters noted." That meant that Nicole's ship probably would not have to worry about being seared out of space by any simulated enemy weapons, but nearer the ground the Marine trainees would have to contend with flak. The Kreelans were never known to use anti-aircraft fire, as they preferred their opponents to get to the ground in one piece. But it never hurt to train for the unexpected.

Thankfully, Thorella had chosen not to throw any enemy fighters into the scenario. Yet, at least.

"Did you copy, Reza?" she asked.

"Affirmative," he replied through the boat's intercom. During each exercise, trainees would be chosen at random from within each platoon to fill the leadership positions in the company. Reza had drawn the position of "platoon guide" for this drop; not being qualified NCOs or officers, the designated trainees were ostensibly unfit to be termed "leaders." Be that as it may, in his distinguished post Reza was tied into the drop group's command nets and was responsible for the orders and reports that concerned his platoon.

Reza looked at Eustus, his acting platoon sergeant, who nodded vigorously, eager to get on with it.

"We are ready, commander," Reza reaffirmed.

Nicole could not help but smile at his voice. Despite Thorella's best efforts, his endless harangues and futile attempts to provoke him, Reza had excelled during his training, and was now ranked at the top of his class.

Behind and to either side of Nicole's boat, eight other similar vessels now flew, carrying the first company of Reza's trainee battalion, one of thirty active at any given time on Quantico. In a real drop, the Marines normally deployed in battalion or full regiment strength, and there would be hundreds of ships – assault boats, gunships, fighters – swarming toward the surface.

For the trainees, however, the exercises focused on platoon and below training and tactics. Training for anything more was deemed a waste of time for men and women who likely would either be dead or out of the service before they reached company command or higher, and who needed now only the basics of how to survive in combat. Besides, many a trainee had noted wryly, it would have been too expensive to mount such exercises on a continual basis for a Confederation that had been surviving economically on good-faith War Bonds for nearly half a century.

Reza surveyed his command with a calculating eye. While the Way was one of glory through individual combat, Her Children were not unfamiliar with the tactics and strategies that accompanied mass warfare. Her blood united them, eliminating the need for the complex command, control, and communications – "C3" – systems that the humans relied on for relaying orders and reports between those doing the fighting and those who were directing the battle. Reza had tasted that uniting force for but a fleeting instant in the span of his own lifetime before being severed from that spiritual lifeline; now, among humans, he had only his wits and training such as this to guide him, and he found that it was a poor substitute.

He clicked over to the platoon's command net, reserved for the platoon guide (or leader) and the platoon "sergeant," and asked Eustus, "Did Scorelli replace the loose ammunition feed housing on her weapon?"

"She should have," Eustus said through his suit's external speaker. Unlike Reza, everyone else already had their helmets on. "I told her to, anyway." He glanced back at the nervous looking woman who clung tightly to her weapon, one of the platoon's four auto pulse rifles, very similar to the one a soldier serving under Reza's father's had used a lifetime before.

Reza smiled. "I can hear it rattling, my friend," he said. More than anything else, the other trainees had learned from Reza how valuable the art of stealth was. An enemy that could not be heard, could not be seen, and could not be found, was extremely hard to kill.

"Sorry, Reza," he said sheepishly. Reza did not have to remind him that, as platoon sergeant, he was responsible for making sure that the platoon leader's directions were actually carried out. Eustus shook his head, disgusted with himself. Over the muffled roar of the dropship's engines, he had heard nothing. "I'll take care of it."

Eustus clicked over to First Squad's net and quietly, without making a scene, corrected the deficiency. Scorelli hurried to oblige.

"Suit up, Reza," Nicole said from the cockpit, looking at the telemetry displays for her passengers, which showed his suit helmet still not attached. She knew how much he hated the armor, but there was no getting around it: they were almost at the drop point.

Grimacing, Reza did as he was told, hefting the helmet from where it sat between his feet and jamming it on his head. He heard and felt the hiss of air as the suit brought its own environmental systems on-line, isolating him from the universe beyond its layers of flexible ceramic and fibersteel. Of all the things he could say he loathed, being confined in this suit was one of the worst. In his Kreelan armor, he was completely free, the leatherite and Kreelan steel conforming perfectly to his body and its motions. His eyes and ears, his nose and tongue, were all free to tell his mind of the physical world around him as his spirit sought out things that lay far beyond. But in the suit, there was only the bitterly dry air and the tasteless water held in the recycling system, which also required pure distilled water, and could not tolerate the waters from the streams from around the base with which Reza had become familiar and now cherished. Worse, although there were packets of dried and salted meat in his external pouches, there was no food within the suit for him to eat; he found the concentrates simply intolerable, inedible. If he were forced to remain in pressurized armor for the entire exercise – a full week – Reza would be very hungry indeed. Simply ducking out of sight for a quick bite to eat was not only unthinkable to Reza as a form of cheating, it was also a technical impossibility. The telemetry data links that tied every set of Marine space armor to anyone able and interested in receiving the information would know if a suit had been opened. And that certainly included the exercise umpires.

In front of his eyes, his helmet, the power to it now enabled, glowed in a panorama of virtual reality, displaying his environment in a user-selected palette of shades and colors that rendered the differences between dark and light, rain and smoke, completely immaterial. While the virtual reality systems, tied into sophisticated suit sensors and able to receive external inputs from other suits or vehicles – even ships – did not have limitless range in a tactical environment, they gave the human soldier a distinct edge against a Kreelan opponent. When the suits were available.

But even that technology, Reza added silently and with a note of personal pride, was not equal in battle to a Kreelan warrior priestess... or priest.

He examined the projected drop zone again, just to confirm that what he held in his memory was perfect, for when they reached Quantico's surface they probably would not have the advantages of the space armor indefinitely, and he refused to rely on the computerized battlefield intelligence systems. The general plan was to make the initial landing and assault, and then hold a critique of the operation, while armorers prepared the suits for the next class cycling through. From there on in, the trainees would fight their mock battles with the kind of basic armor that Jodi had used on Rutan, and which was the mainstay of Marine personal armor everywhere.

"This should be a lot easier than the last one," Eustus commented, tapping into Reza's view of the terrain. The drop zone was in an area of rolling hills, dotted with tree groves and covered with knee-high scrub, and promised few landing injuries, although it left little in the way of cover for the attackers. "Landing in that rocky stuff last time really stunk."

Reza nodded grimly. There had been fourteen injuries, two of them serious, in their previous landing in the training area's desert zone, a wasteland of sharp, irregular granite rock formations that had been a literal hell to jump into and then fight out of. Reza's battalion had lost nearly two-thirds of its strength – on paper – by the time the administrative critique was given. It had not been a glowing one.

In only a few more minutes, the appointed time had arrived. "Prepare for drop," Nicole announced from the flight deck. An illuminated bar that ran the length of the cargo compartment suddenly turned red. "Two minutes."

Unlike many ships and atmospheric craft, Marine dropships had no designated jump- or loadmaster. That was the responsibility of the senior man in the jump group. There was simply too little room aboard to spare.

"Stand up!" Reza bellowed as he moved aft toward the jump doors that had now cycled open. Beyond the eerie blue sheen of the force fields that kept the air in the compartment from exploding into the vacuum beyond, Reza could see the cloud-shrouded outline of the target continent. A blinking red cursor in his helmet visor informed him of the drop zone's exact location in the middle of an enormous expanse of green vegetation.

The men and women of his group unharnessed themselves and checked over their equipment and themselves one last time. Once they had stepped through either of the two doors at the rear of the compartment, they would not get another chance before they hit the ground. And mistakes made now could make that one long, hard step.

"Sound off!" Reza barked.

"First squad, ready!"

"Second squad, ready!"

"Third squad, ready!"

"Heavy weapons, ready!"

Eustus nodded inside his helmet, the movement invisible to anyone outside. "That's it then," he said.

"Reza," he heard Nicole's voice one more time on the platoon command channel, "thirty seconds..." She paused. "And please, *mon ami*," she said quietly, "be careful."

"Roger," he replied. "And I will."

"Don't worry, ma'am," Eustus's lighthearted voice broke in. "I'll keep his butt out of trouble."

The flight status strip above their heads turned from a mournful red to a brilliant green.

"Go!"

In twos, the Marine trainees shuffled out the doors and fell into the infinite void of space.

* * *

"There they go," murmured Jodi as she saw dozens of new blips appear on her sensors. Normally, the countermeasures devices on all the ships and the suits themselves would be active, trying to erase their signature from any electronic or thermal detectors. But even here at Quantico, some small compromise was made for safety. Each suit had a beacon built into it to make finding the trainees easy. The only combat jump Jodi had ever made was when she ejected over Rutan, and that had been enough. "Bon voyage, guys."

"Cut the chatter, pilot," Thorella snapped from the seat behind her. "Come to course three three two mark eight seven and reduce your throttle to station-keeping. I want to stay close to them during descent."

"Sure thing, Markus," she replied casually. While he was the acting group coordinator, he did not outrank her. She was senior to him in time in grade, and it amused her to goad him by addressing him on a first name basis.

Sergeant Major Aquino remained silent.

* * *

Reza maneuvered slightly to his left to get a better view of his platoon's dispersal. A series of four wedges representing each of the squads under his command was spread over a few kilometers now, with one squad ahead of him and the rest behind. Eustus, the platoon sergeant, was between the third and last – heavy weapons –

squads. Behind and above his own silently falling formation, five hundred and twelve other figures in space armor floated and jetted about as they sought to reach their individual falling stations within the battalion's designated thousand cubic kilometer maneuver zone.

For once, Reza was thankful for the computers that calculated where everyone should be on the way down. Exo-atmospheric drops were always a challenge in geometry: extra distance between individuals and units was better when they were still high up, to keep losses to a minimum in case the enemy brought any heavy weapons to bear on them. But later, as they entered the atmosphere – if there was one – and neared the ground, their formation needed to tighten up considerably if they were to maintain vital unit integrity. A combat unit that landed together and intact could fight. One that did not was nothing more than meat waiting for the Kreelans' swords.

That, Reza told himself, *we are not.* This would be their best jump, he thought, and his blood began to sing at the devastation – simulated though it might be – they would inflict on their enemies waiting below. His comrades, while lacking many of the benefits of a martial upbringing such as his own, nonetheless would prove worthy opponents for Her Children when the time came. For a species intellectually dedicated to the pursuit of peace, humans were finely adapted for the art of making war.

The altitude display on his visor continued to unwind toward zero as they approached their target, the miniature field generators of the suits deflecting the friction heat of the upper atmosphere as they plummeted downward. With a little more than eighty kilometers of altitude to cover, and a slant range to the drop zone of about one hundred and fifty, they only had a few minutes of flight remaining.

High above, the drop ships were returning to the carrier to bring down the next battalion that was scheduled to jump. Only the group coordinator's fighter remained with them, its rakish hull barely visible to Reza's naked eye.

He clicked down to the platoon's common net, listening for any idle chatter. There was none. There were only a few clipped words as people maneuvered to keep position, informing their neighbors they were moving, and where to, with their actions echoed in their helmet data displays.

Reza smiled. It was going very well. Their training was paying–

The thought was torn from his mind, as he suddenly felt crushed within his suit and a shrieking roar filled his skull. The planet rushing up at him suddenly began whirling, faster and faster, until it was nothing more than a kaleidoscope of color that alternated with the black of space and the shining stars. He heard voices calling to him on the comm link, but he could not make out the words over the roar of what he realized must be his suit's maneuvering jets. Worse, he himself was unable to speak, the air crushed out of his lungs by the induced g-forces as he spun out of control. His arms and legs felt like they were about to rip out of their sockets as he spun around and around, faster and faster, and his vision began to narrow to a tiny tunnel, then vanished into a gray mist.

In only a few seconds, Reza blacked out.

* * *

"Reza!" Eustus cried as he watched his friend's suit spin crazily out of control, one of its thrusters firing like a roman candle. He desperately clicked over to the emergency frequency, biting on the control so savagely he caught his tongue. A sudden taste of salty copper filled his mouth. "Mayday! Mayday!" he shouted. "This is First Platoon. Reza's suit looks like it's had a malfunction. He's heading down and out of control!"

"I've got a lock on him, First Platoon," Jodi's controlled voice came back. "Moving to intercept."

"Negative," Thorella's voice interjected coldly. "I've got over five hundred other people out here to watch over, and this ship isn't capable of making a pickup. We don't have suits on."

"Then what the hell–"

Another voice, accented by his native Tagalog, broke into the conversation. "Camden, designate someone to take over your platoon and break formation forward of your group," Sergeant Major Aquino ordered tersely. "Pilot, rendezvous with Camden as quickly as possible."

"Roger," she said thankfully. *Fuck you, Thorella*, she thought.

In about fifteen seconds she had Eustus in sight. "Now what?" she asked.

"Camden," the sergeant major said, ignoring her, "what I have in mind is going to take some guts. Can you handle it?"

"We're wasting time, sar-major," Eustus replied quickly. "Let's have it."

Aquino nodded to himself. The boy had dedication. And a set of brass balls. "Behind the cockpit is a recess that you should be able to squeeze yourself into. It is outside the fighter's gravity control system, so you will have to hold up to the gee's we pull. Understood?"

"On my way." Eustus was already jetting toward them. In a few seconds, Jodi heard him clambering over the hull behind them. "I'm here, sar-major. Let's go."

"Find Gard, Lieutenant Mackenzie," Aquino ordered before he told Eustus the rest of what he planned. He did not tell either of them that his interest in Reza was far more than academic. He was an old friend and confidant of one Admiral Zhukovski, who had provided Aquino with information that someone within the cadre was going to try and kill Reza. Where he had gotten such information, he would never say. However, Aquino was almost sure it was Thorella, although there was certainly no shortage of other likely candidates. But he had no evidence. Yet.

Jodi rammed the throttles forward, momentarily forgetting that Eustus had no protection. "Shit," she hissed to herself as Eustus yelped, and she dropped the thrust back to something she thought he might be able to handle. "Sorry, Eustus," she said. "You still with us?"

"Barely," he breathed, his fists clenching even harder to the recessed handholds. Had it not been for the augmented strength the suit gave to his own body, he would have been left behind the leaping fighter. *That was close*, he sighed to himself.

Scanning her instruments, Jodi picked out Reza's tumbling form. "Reza," she said over the comm link, "do you read me? We're coming to get you. Hang on."

Not surprisingly, he didn't answer. Jodi bit her lip, wondering if he was even still alive. As puny as the thrusters were on those suits, they were still plenty powerful. At least it had finally burned itself out of fuel, she thought bitterly, wondering how such a thing could happen. The armored space suits the Marines used were probably the safest pieces of military hardware next to the common rock. While a thruster lighting off like that was not impossible, it was sure damn unlikely.

Behind her, Captain Markus Thorella sat silently.

The short time it took to close on Reza's spinning form passed like hours, and their time was quickly running out. "Altitude, ten kilometers," her ship's computer reported in Nicole's voice.

"I know, goddammit," she hissed, trying to keep the fighter stable in the increasing buffeting from the atmosphere. She followed the little blip on her head-up display like a bloodhound, but she could not yet see Reza visually, and she could not go much faster for fear of losing Eustus. "C'mon, Reza," she whispered to herself "Where the hell are you?"

There! A tiny speck became visible right off the fighter's nose, tumbling against the backdrop of the rapidly approaching ground as Jodi dove straight down toward the planet surface.

"Got him in sight," she said, easing the throttles forward a little more, but not too much: if she was going too fast when she reached him, her ship would overshoot, and there would not be time for a second pass before Reza hit the ground. "Stand by, Eustus."

"Any time," Eustus breathed. He was getting sick from being bounced around while hanging onto the fighter's back like a parasitic insect, and his hands were beginning to cramp from holding on for dear life to the thin bar aft of the cockpit, even with the suit augmentation.

"Altitude, five thousand meters," the computer warned. "Warning... warning," it went on as a steady warbling tone sounded in Jodi's headset. If she did not pull out soon, she never would.

Steady, now, she breathed to herself as she crept up on Reza's windmilling form. *Now!*

"Go, Eustus!" she shouted.

Without hesitation, Eustus flung himself into the air stream screaming around the fighter, trusting that his suit's screens would keep him from being smashed into jelly against the ship's hull. At the same time, Jodi separated away in the opposite direction, leaving him tumbling in her wake.

"Holy Jesus," Eustus breathed as he felt himself being grabbed and pummeled by the atmosphere. A beep was going off in his ear. Altitude. Quickly righting himself with his thrusters, he pointed himself like an arrow at Reza's inert form and shot toward him, closing the dozen or so meters between them in only a few seconds.

"Gotcha!" he huffed triumphantly as he grabbed one of Reza's flailing arms. Pulling his friend to him, he linked their suits together at the waist with the built-in safety tethers. Then, fumbling at Reza's sides with his hands, he fought to separate the bulk of the equipment attached to Reza's suit. If he could not get rid of it, they would be too heavy for his own suit's jets to put them safely on the ground. "Come on," he muttered angrily as the altitude warning tone sounded faster and faster. When the tone become a continuous sound, the suit's thrusters would not have enough time to slow them to an acceptable landing velocity, and the most elementary laws of physics would take over. They would be splattered like eggs over the ground below.

With a sudden snap, the molded combat pack and the fifty or so kilos it represented popped away.

"Burn!" Eustus shouted into his helmet, initiating the preprogrammed firing sequence that Aquino had told him to use. Canted at a ridiculous angle to account for the asymmetrical thrust condition imposed by the weight of Reza's body, the two jets of Eustus's suit flared and fired at their full thrust.

Grunting at the force of the suit's thrusters, Eustus kept his eyes glued to the suit visor and the scene beyond as he and Reza continued to plummet toward the ground. "Please, Lord of All," he hissed through clenched teeth over the roar of the straining jets and all of six gees, "Come on... come on..."

The whirling numbers that indicated their descent velocity gradually slowed as the jets fought against the force of Quantico's gravity. They flashed through one thousand meters, still falling like a rock. The trees and hills below, so beautiful from higher up, held all the beauty now of a trap of sharpened bamboo stakes.

Through his faceplate and his rapidly dimming vision, his blood drawn away by the force of the thrusters, Eustus caught a glimpse of Jodi Mackenzie's fighter nearby as she brought it down in a matching spiral descent.

Well, he thought with a detached part of his panicking consciousness, *they won't have long to wait.*

At five hundred meters, the fuel caution warning began sounding in his ears. The jets were going to run out of fuel before they hit the ground. "Shit," he muttered bitterly. He closed his eyes.

A few seconds later, the jets flared one final time and died. Eustus felt himself seized by the sickening sensation of free-fall. They weren't going to make it–

With a roar of snapping branches, he found himself tumbling through the middle of a stand of trees, their limbs tearing at his arms and legs, hammering his back, and whip-cracking against his helmet. Before he had any time to react, he found himself in a short free-fall again.

He hit the ground. Hard. The wind was knocked out of him like a child who had fallen from a swing, and Eustus fought back tears of surprise and pain.

But he mostly felt relieved. He was alive.

* * *

"How's your head?"

Reza blinked away the stars that clouded his vision, only to see Eustus's concerned face.

"Fuzzy," he answered quietly as he took stock of his body. Obviously, they had survived their fall. "What happened?"

"I don't know, exactly," Eustus said as he removed the palm-sized mediscanner from Reza's forehead. It did not register any damage more serious than a very mild concussion and some hellish bruising. "It looked like one of your thrusters went berserk and sent you tumbling. Sergeant Major Aquino came up with the idea of me hitching a ride on Lieutenant Mackenzie's fighter to come pick you up. And, well, here we are." He smiled sheepishly.

"I owe you my life, my friend."

"Stow it, Reza," he said, smiling more brightly now. "I promised Commander Carré I'd keep your butt out of trouble, remember?"

Reza nodded, tried to smile at his friend's humor. "What are we to do now?"

Eustus snorted. "Well, I already reported that you looked like you were going to be okay, at least according to this thing," he held up the scanner. "Captain Thorella said that unless you needed a medevac out of here, we're supposed to move our butts back to the battalion op zone or we'd have to E & E through Second Battalion when they land." A wry smile curled his lips. "A mere forty klicks away, and through Second Battalion's training lanes."

Reza frowned. "E&E" was better known as escape and evasion, a convenient acronym for one of the most hellish aspects of Marine training. As part of the ENDEX, all of the trainees would have to go through a ten-kilometer long stretch of "enemy territory," doing whatever they could to keep from being captured by the mock enemy forces that would be gunning for them. Not surprisingly, very few ever made it through without being bagged. Everyone who was caught had to spend the remainder of the E&E exercise in a mock prisoner of war camp, undergoing unpleasant but harmless "torture" and lectures on how to do better next time, in the real world. The best motivator, however, was the fact that the Kreelans did not take prisoners. In combat, anyone who was caught was killed. Period.

"I take it then," Reza said slowly as part of his mind began directing his body toward repairing itself as rapidly as possible for the long travel ahead, "that we had best move quickly and soon?"

"That would seem the prudent thing to do, if you're up to it." Despite the reassuring signs the mediscanner gave him – apparently enough to satisfy Aquino, as Thorella could not have cared less – Eustus was not at all sure Reza was really up for this. They had a long way to go.

"Do not worry, my friend," Reza said, sensing Eustus's mood as he collected up his rifle – which miraculously had survived undamaged – and other gear. The now-discarded armored suits would be left where they were until one of the dustoff crews came to pick them up. "Come, Eustus. We are wasting time, and have far yet to go."

* * *

"They've finally decided to get a move on," Thorella muttered to himself as he watched the two icons representing Eustus and Reza move off toward their battalion's drop zone. He frowned to himself as he stood up from the display and stretched his cramped back muscles. Aquino had gone back to the main base in a shuttle after determining that Gard was all right. Thorella knew that the little Filipino bastard was going to try and pin something on him, but there would not be anything for him to find. In the meantime, Thorella had to play out the game as it was scripted. It would not do to call too much attention to himself by trying to take Gard out again. For now.

"You know something, Thorella," he heard a silky voice behind him, "you're a real fucking sleazeball."

"One of these days, Mackenzie," he said just loud enough for her to hear, "I'm not going to have to take that from you anymore." Unfortunately, Thorella did not have control over the cadre roster. Mackenzie seemed forever glued to him, a thorn in his side. But someday...

"Is that a threat, you ox?" she challenged in the comparative silence of the empty command post. Only she and Thorella were on duty right now, the rest of the cadre out wreaking havoc among the struggling trainees. She knew Thorella could probably beat her in a hand-to-hand match, but not by much. She was good, and had had a good teacher. She wished that Tony Braddock were here with her now. "You know, I just don't understand why Tsingai doesn't just send you to the rock pile where you belong. You hate your own people as much or more than you hate the Blues, and yet they just keep bailing you out of all the trouble you seem to make for yourself. Now, why is that?" She didn't expect more than an epithet in reply.

But Thorella obliged her with what she had to consider an intellectual tour de force, at least for him. "There are a lot of things I wouldn't expect you to understand, Mackenzie," he replied calmly. "But I would think that the fact that our race needs people like me to survive against an enemy like the Kreelans would be self-evident, even to you. The trouble is that you're soft and malleable, like wet clay. I realize that people like you would like nothing better than for the rest of us to just roll over or turn the other cheek as the Kreelans send in their seed to poison us, but that's not how it's going to be." He turned to face her, his face a cold mask of hatred. "There are a lot of people who never wanted that half-breed to contaminate our population, to disgrace the Corps, and I'm one of them. Where there's one, there's more, and pretty soon we'll be overrun with half-breeds spreading their ideas and their genes through our population." He leaned closer to her. "And I'll do anything I can to stop that from happening."

Thorella's use of "half-breed" was not lost on her. With black skin and blue eyes, her own racial lines were far from any measure of purity people like Thorella seemed to find acceptable. But her own personal anger took second place to her growing suspicions that Reza's mishap had not been an accident. "Does that include murder, captain?" she asked quietly, waiting tensely to see if Thorella would attack her.

Slowly, he smiled. "I don't know what you mean, lieutenant. And if you accuse me of anything, I certainly hope you have a lot of evidence to back it up. Because if you don't," the smile evaporated, "you can kiss your career goodbye."

"No," Jodi said as she casually began to step away from him, "just wondering." *He's insane*, she thought. But his warning struck a chord of truth in her. How had he managed to stay out of trouble, despite the numerous allegations of disgraceful conduct that had been levied against him, all of which eventually were dismissed? He must have some sponsorship from higher up the chain. The question was, how high? And could they get away with trying to kill Reza, or anyone else, for that matter? "I think I'll just go and check on my ship, if you don't mind."

"Not at all," Thorella said flatly.

Watching her go, he knew she would have to be taken care of. When this little exercise was over, he would have to talk to his mentor again. He would know just what to do.

Smiling like the Dark Angel, he busied himself with the exercise unfolding around him, seemingly oblivious to Reza and Eustus. One of them he hated, the other was simply in the way.

* * *

Senator Strom Borge's face was a mask of contemplation. It was the face he often wore while jousting with his colleagues over the many issues of state and war the Confederation Council faced each day. The men and women he secretly loathed. They were weak and foolish, leading the Confederation into genocide at the hands of the blue-skinned alien horde. But he knew better, and worked diligently each day to set things right, biding his time until the day that he would no longer feel compelled to conceal his true goals, his real ambitions. Power was his sole reason for existence, and to exercise unlimited power was his ultimate goal. Someday, he thought. Someday soon.

A small sheaf of genuine paper slipped from the slender fingers of his hands as he gazed out the window that took up the entire wall of his office suite in the Confederation Plaza, as his thoughts wandered among the myriad lights that shone in the evening darkness outside. The paper contained a message from his protégé in the military, Markus Thorella, requesting guidance as to how to pursue the matter of dealing with Reza Gard. Thorella's initial attempt at quashing their unsuspecting enemy, while imaginative and seemingly foolproof, had nonetheless been thwarted, and the senator was not willing to put Thorella at risk again. At least, not yet.

Tapping a finger to his lips, an idea came to him. "Maria," he said.

"Yes, senator," the disembodied voice of his secretary outside answered immediately from unseen speakers in the room.

"Inform General Tsingai that Reza Gard is to be assigned to the Red Legion," he told her, "on order of the Chairman of the Confederation Council's Military Oversight Committee."

"Immediately, senator," she replied.

He sat back, smiling. Tsingai would protest, of course, but he would not press the issue after he, Senator Strom Borge, threatened to expose his little ongoing extramarital affair in public. Borge knew everything about everyone, and considered no one beyond his reach or influence.

Outside, his secretary carried out his instructions, silently wondering at the terrible fate that awaited Reza Gard.

Twenty-Six

The day Reza had looked forward to as a boy, and then again when he rejoined humanity, had finally come. He stood at parade rest, hands clasped behind his back, alongside his peers. The four companies of the graduating training battalion stood in mass formation on the parade ground as the post commandant gave his graduation speech, but Reza paid him little attention. His thoughts focused on the single stripe now on his sleeve that, lowly in rank as it was, signified that he was worthy to be a Confederation Marine. He had made good Wiley Hickock's faith in him from those bittersweet days that he had once forgotten. Past that, he thought of the future, of the time – soon, now – when he would be cast into battle and his blood would again sing in time with his sword.

The pomp and ceremony of graduation finally came to a close, the last comments and speeches rendered. It was now time for the trainees' last act as a battalion.

"Battalion..." he heard Eustus's voice boom over the field. He had been chosen as battalion trainee commander for this final day, and had loved every minute of it.

"Company..." each of the trainee company commanders echoed.

"Atten-SHUN!" Over five hundred pairs of boots stomped the ground, heel to heel, as the battalion came to attention.

"Dismissed!" Eustus's final command was drowned out by a sea of jubilant cries as the former trainees voiced their thanks that the hell of the last weeks was finally over. Hundreds of hats flew into the air, and the once orderly formation broke down into a riotous mob that surged toward the barracks area to prepare for whatever Fate had in store for them.

No longer old or young, man or woman, rich or poor: they were Marines.

* * *

Reza's platoon stood at attention before Sergeant Major Aquino in what they knew was a private ceremony he conducted for every platoon that graduated under his tutelage. Out in a far corner of the post, arrayed before an abandoned storage building that was away from any prying eyes, he began the ritual.

"Listen up, Marines," he bellowed in the tinny, heavily-accented voice that they had all come to respect, a note of pride in his words that he was no longer addressing recruits, but young warriors ready for battle.

"Some of you now will be going on to more training, to be specialists of some kind. The rest of you will be going straight to a combat regiment somewhere. But all of you, sooner or later, will be out in the fleet. And in the fleet there is no room for petty personal problems or grudges. Life, as you will soon find, is too short for that, and there is no room for it on a warship or in battle."

He held up an electronic notepad that they already knew was their unit roster. "When I read your name, you are to go into the building," he nodded to the door behind him, "and wait. Then anyone who wants a piece of you will get their chance, and all of you can get any hard feelings out of your systems now and leave them here, where they belong. We want you to take out your aggressions on the enemy, not on each other." He paused, surveying his audience, looking for squeamish faces. He saw none. Good. "When you're done, come back out and take your place in formation, then we will go on to the next one. I will observe to make sure no one gets carried away. Any questions?"

There were none. While the ritual they were partaking in was officially prohibited, it was a longstanding tradition that would survive anything less than outright murder, and Aquino was not about to let anything like that happen on his watch. "Very well," he said, focusing on the roster. "Alazarro!"

Jose Alazarro broke ranks and double-timed into the building.

"Anyone want a piece of him?" Aquino challenged. Four Marines nodded. "What are you waiting for?" the sergeant major snapped. The three men and one woman hustled through the door, followed by Aquino. There followed a few minutes of muffled grunts and groans, after which all five Marines, three of them with bloody noses or lips, returned to the formation. Together.

And so it went.

Reza stood in the building after his name was called, wondering about this strange practice as he took his turn being "on the spot," as some of the others called it. Eustus, called long before him, had cleared up some things with the young men who had once bullied him, and who now had broken noses and bruises, plus some respect, for their one-time scapegoat.

But such things held no interest for Reza. He loathed some of his companions – he did not consider them peers – disliked a few more, was neutral toward most, and genuinely liked a very small few. Despite any negative feelings he held for any one of them, however, he had no reason to assert himself. He was a priest of the Desh-Ka, and any matters of import would not be settled to his satisfaction outside of the arena and the clash of sword and claw. And this, to be sure, was not the arena.

He turned as two figures entered the building, their footfalls soft on the stained concrete floor. He nodded at Aquino, who took his place to one side in the role of officiator to make sure things did not get too ugly, and the older man nodded back gravely. Reza understood that his situation was somewhat different than that for the others. He would have to meet a higher standard of "satisfaction." Reza would be happy to oblige. His only real challenge would be to prevent himself from seriously injuring or killing his challenger.

Washington Hawthorne stepped forward. A towering pillar of ebony muscle, Hawthorne made a mockery even of Thorella's imposing form.

"I don't have anything against you personally, Reza," he said, "but I wanted to know if I could take you on man to man, without all the usual bullshit. You understand?"

Nodding at the man's candor, understanding him perfectly, Reza stepped up to meet him. Hawthorne's motives, while not particularly wise, were nonetheless honest and understandable, at least to Reza. He made a note that this was a man who might someday make a valuable ally and friend.

"When you are ready, Marines," Aquino announced.

Hawthorne nodded, happy not to be disappointed. He had not worked very closely with Reza, but he had heard about how great he was supposed to be in close combat. He wanted to find out for himself without wearing all the protective gear and playing by all the stupid rules the instructors sometimes – but not always – required. He raised his fists like a pugilist and moved in, anxious to see how Reza would react. Reza was a lot smaller, probably more agile than Hawthorne, but he was certainly a lot more vulnerable to any blow that the larger man could deliver. Hawthorne smiled.

The contest began as a black fist the size of a cantaloupe shot toward Reza's face with all the force and speed of a jackhammer...

Reza gave Hawthorne the feeling of a real fight without really offering him one. He easily dodged the larger man's blows, and only when Hawthorne began to feel frustration and anger at not being able to get a solid hit against his opponent did Reza finally bring the match to a close. Dodging another of Hawthorne's Herculean strikes, Reza nimbly stepped forward to deliver a carefully placed blow to the larger man's solar plexus, dropping him without doing any damage. Reza was hardly using his true combat skills, but Hawthorne was not an enemy.

"Son of a bitch," Hawthorne gasped as he collapsed, doubled-over with the pain that had exploded inside him. After gagging and choking for a few moments, effectively paralyzed from Reza's single strike, he looked up through tearing eyes to find a hand extended toward him.

"You fight with spirit, my friend," Reza said, "and shall prove a worthy opponent for your true enemies, whom we shall face together. Come, let us leave this place."

Nodding slowly, his curiosity satisfied at the expense of a slightly bruised ego, Washington smiled as he took Reza's hand, allowing the smaller man to help him up. "I just had to find out for myself, Reza. I'm just glad you're on our side."

Together, the two of them headed back outside where they would await the completion of their platoon's unofficial farewell party.

A much-relieved Sergeant Major Aquino followed them out.

* * *

The newly appointed Marines stood in murmuring groups in the main hall, waiting for the harried cadre officers to post their orders. One after the other, they were called forward to the rows of tables at which the officers and NCOs sat, presenting and explaining each trainee's first official orders. There was no reason for people to be doing this, of course: the trainees could have their orders posted just as easily by electronic mail, and very few actually needed anyone to explain orders. But the Corps had developed a tradition of seeing their people off to their first assignment with a human face and a word of encouragement, rather than a sterile electronic beep followed by an equally lifeless form letter.

Nicole and Jodi stood beside Reza as they all waited for Eustus to return with his orders. Nicole was nervous, Reza could tell, and also touched with sadness. She did not want to leave him again.

Eustus came running back, weaving his way toward them through the throng of fellow Marines, some of whom were cheering at their orders, others groaning with dismay. He held them clutched in his hand, the slender plastic seal still unbroken.

"Well, dummy," Jodi blurted, "where are you going?"

"I want to see what Reza's say first," Eustus panted excitedly. "I've been... well, kind of hoping we'd get assigned to the same unit."

"Don't hold your breath, bucko," Jodi told him seriously. "The fleet's a big place, and the Corps is spread all through it and on hundreds more planetary garrisons besides. The chances aren't too good."

"Yeah, but I figure that we're probably going to be assigned to an orphan regiment, right? I mean, my homeworld never had any regiments of its own, and Reza technically doesn't have a homeworld for regimental assignment. So that makes the chances of us being in the same orphan regiment that much greater, right?"

Jodi looked at him skeptically. "Orphan" regiments were so named because the homeworld that originally raised them and kept them supplied with recruits had either been decimated or destroyed by the Kreelans. When that happened, the regiment's colors and organization remained intact, but it got whatever replacements could be sent to it, regardless of the source. Planets that did not have enough people to raise a complete regiment of its own and did not have an agreement with another world to supply replacement personnel had their Marines put into orphan regiments as replacements, fresh blood. While this was not a problem in most cases, in some it could be disastrous. In one case, an entire regiment had to be forcibly subdued after the military personnel – MILPO – office had unwittingly assigned a large block of replacement Marines to it, not realizing that the fresh troops, from a conservative Muslim colony, were likely to clash with the regiment's indigenous Hindus. It took three other regiments to put down the resulting insurrection and mutiny.

"Well," Jodi said, "I'll give you an A-plus for imagination. But I still wouldn't get your hopes up too high."

Eustus looked to Nicole for support, but she only shrugged. She did not know either. She had asked, of course, but the MILPO officer had stonewalled her for some reason, and she suspected that Thorella probably had something to do with it. "I do not know, Eustus," she said simply.

"Gard, Reza!" one of the NCOs shouted over the low din in the room.

"Hurry up, Reza," Eustus said, anxious to find out if they would get their assignment together.

Reza made his way forward and came to stand at attention before Sergeant Major Aquino, who had taken Reza's orders packet from the sergeant at the table and now held it in his hands. The older man looked up at him with his piercing black eyes.

"I am not surprised that you made it this far, Gard," he said as he handed Reza his orders, "in light of what you went through before you came to us here. I hope you go far in the life you have chosen, and in the Corps." He gestured to the sparkling new Marines around him and said quietly, "I wish all of them were half as good as you." He stuck out his hand. "Good luck, Marine."

Reza nodded as he shook the smaller man's hand. He had always liked Aquino. "Thank you, sergeant major. I shall do my best."

"That is all I ask. Carry on."

Reza quickly walked back to where the others were waiting, the orders burning in his hand. He wanted to get out of this world of "discipline" and make believe combat and into the world where he belonged, where his sword would sing with honor to Her glory, even though She no longer saw him in Her heart. The thought depressed him until he saw Jodi, Nicole, and Eustus. They and the Corps were his family now, and he would do his best to bring honor to them all.

"Well?" Eustus asked. "What is it? Where are you going?"

Reza opened his orders and scanned them. "I have been posted to the 1st Battalion of the 12th Guards Regiment," he told them.

"That's the Red Legion, isn't it?" Jodi said, shocked. Nicole's mouth dropped open. The Red Legion was infamous throughout the Corps as being a dumping ground for every undesirable individual and bloody mission in the service. It was the High Command's garbage disposal. "My God, Reza, that unit's a meat grinder!"

Eustus tore his orders open. "Dear Father," he whispered. He looked up at Jodi, then Reza. "What is it they say about not wishing for something, because you might get it?"

"You received the same assignment?" Nicole asked, aghast. "This is absurd! There must be some mistake–"

"There's no mistake, commander," a familiar voice spoke from behind. They all turned to find Thorella standing there, an angelic smile on his face. "Those orders came from on high, or so I hear. I hope you enjoy your duty stations, gentlemen. Now, if you'll excuse me–"

"You fucking piece of shit," Jodi snarled. "You know they don't deserve that. Even you can't hate them that much. The Red Legion isn't anything more than a marching coffin."

"My, my," he said, shaking his head theatrically. "You Navy types do have a way with words. I know you won't believe this, Mackenzie, but it actually wasn't my idea. But you're right: the Red Legion is a meat grinder, although it isn't listed as such. But that makes it all the more fitting for a traitor and his sidekick."

Eustus made to step forward, his fists clenched, but Reza held him back. "No, Eustus," he said before turning to Thorella. He stepped close to the larger man, and was rewarded with the sharp tang of fear that suddenly erupted from his pores. "There will come a day of reckoning for you, Markus Thorella. And I pray I am there to witness it."

Thorella snorted derisively, but Reza could tell he was still afraid. "Say your prayers for yourself, half-breed. You and your little buddy here will have your hands full as it is." He looked at Eustus. "I was thinking of getting you a jar of petroleum jelly for when you get there, Camden. I hear the NCOs in the Red Legion don't like their little boys dry."

"That is enough, captain," Nicole hissed. Her anger had called forth an unfamiliar burning sensation in her body, as if her blood was on fire. Her conscious mind was afraid that if Thorella did not shut up, she would find herself lunging for his throat. "Leave us. Now."

"Yes, ma'am," he sneered. He threw a mock salute, turned on his heel, and sauntered away through the crowd.

"Motherfucker," Jodi called quietly after him.

Nicole turned to Reza and Eustus. "I will see if I cannot get in to see General Tsingai about this," she said. "He may be able to–"

"No," Reza said firmly. "At least, not for me. I thank you for your concern, Nicole, but I have received my orders, and I shall do my best to carry them out." Jodi opened her mouth to protest, but Reza silenced her with his eyes before he spoke. "I do not do this purely out of respect for orders which, I suspect, are not entirely legal. But I have also heard of the Red Legion, and perhaps – for me – it is the best place. I believe that I probably would fit in better with a group of misfits than I would in a regular unit." He held up a braid of his long hair to illustrate his point. He was the only Marine any of them had ever seen whose hair was not the regulation crew cut. And that was the least of his differences.

Jodi scowled furiously, the normally crystal smooth skin of her forehead wrinkled like aged parchment. "What about you, Eustus?" she asked.

"I'll go with Reza," he said decisively, pocketing his orders. "A Marine's job is going to be tough no matter where he is. And I figure that sticking with Reza makes my chances of staying alive and doing my job well that much better." He had glanced at Reza's orders and compared them to his own. They were slated for the same company, and he could only hope that they would be assigned to the same platoon.

"*Oui*," Nicole said resignedly, trying to keep the sadness from her voice. Not only was Reza leaving her again, he was probably going to be sacrificed as undesirable cannon fodder on some rock in space that had nothing more than a number for a name. "I guess that is that, then."

They all stood there for a few minutes, as if not quite sure that the play they were acting out was real or only a bad dream.

It was Eustus who finally broke the spell. "Well," he said, "I guess we'd better get packing. The transports start loading at fourteen-hundred, and we've got a long trip ahead of us." The Red Legion was scattered over a sector of space nearly two months' hyperlight travel from Quantico.

Nicole held back her tears as she walked with her friends toward the barracks, wondering if a year from now any of them would still be alive to remember this day.

Twenty-Seven

Six Years Later

Captain Reza Gard sat at a nondescript desk in the small cubicle that served as his company's CQ and administrative office, trying valiantly to deal with the paperwork that he could not in good conscience leave for his adjutant, Corporal Alfonso Zevon. Zevon, who only recently had been transferred to A Company, 1st Battalion of the 12th Guards Regiment (Red Legion), had transformed the company's paperwork, which Reza considered to be a small slice of Father Hernandez's Hell, from an unqualified mess into a real system. It was a gift that Reza was endlessly thankful for, especially since Zevon also happened to be an expert marksman and a good fighter. What terrible thing he had done to earn himself a posting to the Red Legion, Reza did not know, and would never ask.

He looked up as his First Sergeant poked his head through the door. "Reza," Eustus said, "there's a message coming in for you on channel five. It's from Nicole."

Reza's skin tingled at the sound of her name. It had been months since he had last heard from her, but he had felt recently that something was different in her life, something good had happened. He felt it in his blood, the blood he had shared with her. "Thank you, Eustus. I'll take it in here." Eustus smiled and ducked back out.

Reza shook his head as he thought about his friend. Eustus had insisted on staying with him in the bloody machine that was the Red Legion, despite receiving several offers to be posted to other, more "reputable," regiments. He had also received several offers – strongly supported by Reza – to go to officer candidate school, but that, too, he had refused. "Why would I want to become an officer?" he would ask, seemingly perplexed. He had risen through the enlisted ranks on his own merit, and now served as the senior enlisted man in his company. He was honored to serve Reza, and Reza was equally honored to have him.

Washington Hawthorne, too, had joined the Legion – by choice, amazingly enough – two years after graduating from Quantico. He had survived long enough to become Reza's executive officer, and would soon be up for command of his own company, an event that Reza awaited with anticipation and pride in his friend's abilities.

As for Reza himself, his start in the Legion as a much-maligned rifleman who had spent nearly as much time fighting his fellow Marines as he had the Kreelans had changed five months after his arrival to the unit. At the Battle of Kalimpong, half of their battalion was wiped out in an ill-planned attack against a Kreelan mining operation that had been discovered in the system's asteroid belt. Reza had managed to rally the survivors in time to beat back a fierce Kreelan counterattack that had come very close to destroying their ship, the old cruiser *Pegasus* (which not long after, Reza lamented, had been burned into vapor by a Kreelan battlecruiser). For that action, Corporal Reza Gard had won the Confederation Medal of Honor and a trip to Officer Candidate School, where Nicole pinned on his gold second lieutenant's bars three months later. He had returned to his battalion to take over A Company's 1st Platoon, and ten months later had assumed command of the company itself after the acting company commander and executive officer were killed in action. Four years ago, that had been. Four years. A lifetime...

Gratefully shoving aside the data pad that been monopolizing his time, Reza turned his attention to Nicole's message. "Play," he ordered the console. After a short pause, Nicole's face appeared in the screen, and his heart warmed at the sight of her. She looked as beautiful as always, and was – he was not able to describe it exactly – warmer, somehow, more vibrant. *Happy*, he thought. For perhaps the first time since they were children, she looked happy.

"*Mon ami*," she began, almost hesitantly, "I hope all is going well for you, that you are safe there on the Rim. Jodi and Father Hernandez are fine, and asked me to say hello to you; I am sure that you will soon receive messages from both of them, but I told them to wait until I had brought you the news.

"Reza..." she paused, unsure how to continue, and he found himself leaning closer to her image, as if he could somehow sense something from the electronics in the console, "I do not know how you will feel about what I am going to tell you. I hope you will not be angry with me for not talking with you about it before, but these messages are often delayed – I can only pray that you receive this one in time – and I could not bring myself to wait any longer to make a decision." She looked down at her hands, obviously nervous. It was a state he had never seen her in before. She looked back up. At him. "Reza, Tony Braddock asked me to marry him. I told him yes."

Reza felt his mouth drop open in surprise. Jodi had sent him a message some time ago, saying that Braddock had been medically discharged from the Corps after receiving a near-fatal wound in combat. He had then turned up on Earth as the Council Representative from Timor, of all things, and quickly made something of a reputation for himself on the Confederation Council. Nicole had met him through Jodi, and – Reza now surmised – one thing had led to another. Jodi had gone on to say that Braddock had asked Nicole out on several dates – with Jodi watching over them like a zealous parent – but that was the last he had heard over the last several months. Until now.

"*Mon chère,*" Nicole went on, "I can only hope that you receive this in time, because I want more than anything for you to be here, to be with me when I take the vows. It has been two years since you last went on leave, when we last saw each other for but two days on Solaris. I know that it may not be possible, for this is war, but if you can, my brother, please come. With my father gone, I would like for you to be the one to walk down the aisle with me, to give me away to Tony. Please."

Reza's chest tightened as he saw Nicole brush away a tear. She wanted so much for him to be with her. This is what he had been feeling in his blood for the last couple of months. It was the song of her happiness.

"There is a file attached with everything you should need to get here, transport schedules and so on. I do not know how, but Jodi found enough priority-one transit vouchers to get you from the Penlang La transit station on the Rim back to Earth." She forced a smile, and he could imagine her fears that he would never receive the message, or get it late, or not be able to come back to Earth. Or be dead. So much could go wrong over distance and time, through bloody war. But his blood burned brightly, his spirit calling to her, to reassure her that her message had found its way to him.

"Take care, Reza," she said. "*Je t'aime.*" The screen faded to black.

* * *

Jodi waited alone at the crowded spaceport terminal. Nicole and Father Hernandez had wanted to come, but Jodi had insisted that they stay and get ready for the wedding that was to take place this evening. She had arranged Reza's transport schedule as well as she could, but getting people from the Rim to the Core Worlds on any kind of real schedule was impossible. Jodi was nervous, worried that Reza wouldn't make it, because he had not appeared on any of the earlier flights today, and the shuttle coming down now would be the last one scheduled before the wedding was to start. They were cutting it awfully close.

To add to her consternation, the trash-hauler (a less-than-affectionate name most pilots held for the ugly little orbital shuttles) was late, as usual. To make matters worse, she had no idea if Reza was on it, or even if he had made transit aboard the transport the shuttle was now returning from. She had tried to find out two dozen times over the last week if Reza was on the rosters of any of the seven different ships he had to board to get from the Rim back to Earth, and she had drawn a blank on all of them. The harried transportation people had tried to be helpful, but it hadn't changed the fact that she knew no more now than she had a month ago.

"Trying to track things down on Rim transits," one of the agents had told her with a shake of her head, "makes finding a needle in a haystack look easy." Jodi had no idea what a haystack was, but she'd gotten the picture. She decided to just go to the terminal and wait, because if Reza wasn't on this shuttle he was going to miss the wedding, anyway.

Finally, the transport arrived, its squat shape heaving into view while it jockeyed for position next to the extending boarding tube. The repeller field shimmered against the ground as the gaily painted – in red, white, and blue, no less – shuttle settled on its seven landing struts.

After what seemed to Jodi to be an interminable wait, passengers began to trickle from the gateway. She tried to get closer, but a solid wall of babbling people prevented her from seeing anything more than bobbing heads.

"Goddammit," she muttered in annoyance as a Navy commander pushed past her to embrace a squealing woman from the shuttle. The two of them, oblivious to the rest of humankind, solidly blocked the aisle with their wet and sloppy reunion. Jodi thought she was going to gag.

"Pardon me, please," a deep voice said from among the debarking passengers trapped behind the commander and his bimbo. The request had been gentle, but was nonetheless the voice of one accustomed to being obeyed. The babbling among the nearest waiting friends, relatives, and others suddenly ceased as the man, now revealed as a Marine captain in dress blue uniform, stood silently, waiting.

The commander released his significant other and gave Reza a hard stare. "Aren't you forgetting something," the commander said, pointing to the three full gold rings around his sleeve, "*captain?*"

"Not at all, commander," Reza replied, returning the man's stare. He pointed to the single ribbon – a cluster of white stars set against a field of azure blue – that made up its own row above the seven other full rows of combat decorations, five more rows than the Navy officer could boast, that adorned his uniform.

The Navy officer stared at the ribbon for a moment, before slowly lifting his right arm in a salute. While he outranked Reza, centuries-old tradition dictated that a bearer of the Medal of Honor was entitled to a salute first by his or her fellow service members, regardless of their rank. In the war against the Kreelans, there had been many Medal of Honor winners; unfortunately, since most of them were awarded posthumously, pitifully few recipients survived to enjoy the courtesy that tradition granted them.

"Good day to you, sir," Reza said pleasantly as he smartly returned the salute and stepped past the man and his open-mouthed companion.

"Reza!" Jodi cried, throwing herself into his arms, burdened as they were with his two flight bags. He didn't even have time to utter her name before she covered his mouth with hers in an unexpectedly passionate kiss. Reza could not see, but behind him, Jodi made sure that the Navy man saw the three stripes on her sleeve as she put her arms around Reza's neck. When they made eye contact, Jodi gave him a wink. A moment later, she drew away from Reza, who still stood there, stunned.

"Jodi!" he breathed, his face flushed with – mostly, he knew – embarrassment. "What are you–"

"Just welcoming you home, is all," she said, a devilish smile lighting up her face as she took him by the elbow and led him into the main terminal.

"Commander Mackenzie," Reza said with a smile as he sensed the Navy officer behind him fuming in embarrassment and not just a little bit of jealous envy, "you are a bloody liar."

Jodi laughed. "No doubt. But hey, let's get a move on – we're late and we've got a long way to go."

* * *

"So," Jodi said when she had gotten him settled into her skimmer, "how was your trip?"

Reza grunted. "Long. Boring. And I am convinced that not one single galley in the entire human fleet – outside of my own ship, of course – can properly prepare meat for a Kreelan warrior."

Jodi laughed. "Well, don't get your hopes up here, either. Tony bought one of those silly barbecue contraptions not long ago. I guess he didn't like the processor food, and now he's convinced himself that he can cook with the thing." She shook her head. "I guess you can eat anything if you put enough of that weird sauce of his on it, though."

Reza made a face. "I will cook," he said with determination.

The skimmer shuddered lightly as it pulled away from the ground. A moment later, the landing gear retracted and Jodi turned the craft southwest. Reza watched the ground fall away. The spaceport complex soon faded from view as the skimmer gained speed and altitude.

But his mind was not on the lush trees and velvet green landscape rushing by below. He was thinking of Jodi. The happiness that had bubbled from her at the spaceport seemed to have evaporated. Beneath the crumbling veneer he saw fear and, more than that, a growing mountain of loneliness. There was silence between them for a time, but Reza could feel her pain, and it reminded him of the wound that still bled within his own heart.

"What are you going to do, Jodi," he asked quietly, turning to her, "after Nicole is wed?"

"I... I don't know, Reza," she said, trying to keep her voice even as she switched on the autopilot. "I know that three's a crowd, but I haven't had any brilliant flashes of insight as to what I'm going to do with the rest of my life. Not after... not after she leaves me."

"They would let you stay–"

"Yeah, right," Jodi interrupted. "Come on, Reza, what am I supposed to do? Be the live-in nanny for the kids they want to have? How about Tony's public relations rep? Or maybe Nicole's manicurist. Yeah, I can see that one: Jodi Mackenzie, shoots down alien fighters by day, does nails by night." She was silent for a moment, and then hammered a fist against the flight console. "Fuck it," she shouted angrily. "Just fuck it all to hell!"

She made to pound on the unoffending console again, but her fist found only Reza's palm, which gently enveloped hers. He drew her to him with irresistible strength and held her as the tears came.

"I know that she doesn't want me," she said as she fought against the painful tide in her heart, "but in my mind I kept thinking that, maybe someday she'd come around. I mean, not even to sleep with me – I knew from the first that that was always going to be just a fantasy. But I thought that maybe I could be her companion, someone she could share her life with." She closed her eyes and buried her face against Reza's chest, her tears streaking his uniform. "But now, it's all over. Sure, we can still be friends," she said bitterly. "And what the fuck does that mean, Reza? That maybe she'll remember my name after the first tour we have to spend apart? That maybe we can squeeze in a quick lunch now and then – if we happen to be in the same star system – so she can tell me all about Tony and their oh-so-wanted kids? It's not enough for me, Reza," she choked. "It's just not fucking enough."

She shuddered against him, holding him tighter, and she could not see the tears in his own eyes as he thought of Esah-Zhurah. He had never stopped thinking of her. Never. The pain was not so great as it once was, but it ebbed and flowed like the tide.

After a while, her sobbing eased, then stopped. Her arms loosened slightly from around his chest, but only a little. "I doubt I'll be lucky enough to grow old, Reza," she whispered, "but if I get that chance, I don't want to grow old alone."

"Jodi," he told her, "the loneliness you fear is what has filled my heart since I left the Empire... since I left behind the woman who owns my heart. The only things that have sustained me since then have been my memories of her and the friendship I have been shown, by you more than any other. You are right when you say that it is not enough, to just be friends when your heart cries out for something more. But sometimes it has to be enough. Fate is neither kind nor fair; it simply is. But no matter what happens, remember that I will always be there for you. No matter how many stars apart we may be, I will always be there..."

* * *

Tony Braddock did everything he could to resist the urge to pace back and forth before the altar. The patient beauty of the chapel that had been the gleaming centerpiece of the otherwise bland Ridgeway Military Reservation was in stark contrast to the anxiousness he felt. The chapel had stood on this spot for over four hundred years, silent witness to countless baptisms, weddings, and funerals. But to Tony, waiting for the remaining members of his tiny wedding party to arrive so he could finally marry the woman he loved, the last forty minutes had seemed every bit as long as the chapel's four centuries.

"Where can they be?" he wondered aloud for what must have been the tenth time. He glanced yet again at his watch before looking out at the guests who now filled the many pews behind him. Neither he nor Nicole had many friends here, and they originally had wanted a small, private ceremony. But by the time they had invited their few real friends, Nicole's squadron-mates, and finally made the obligatory invitations to members of the Council – plus the spouses of all of the above – the chapel had been filled to capacity, with nearly five-hundred people in attendance.

Such an event, of course, also drew the attention of the media. Nicole's combat record, and her current score of nearly two hundred kills, was well known, and Tony was a member of the Council. While their wedding was not exactly considered the gala event of the year, there was a healthy interest in getting some shots of the bride and groom, plus any other notables who might pass before the lens. Besides, the editors had reasoned, there might always be the odd opportunity to gather a bit of smut in the process. In any event, two junior but competent reporters had been dispatched to take in the scene. One was from the Confederation Times, the other from the Navy Journal. They had already circulated amongst the guests for interviews and any tidbits they might pick up while people were still arriving. But right now the two were standing at the back (there was nowhere for them to sit), looking much like everyone else was at the moment: impatient.

Father Hernandez, too, looked around worriedly. While the people here seemed good-humored and were certainly willing to put up with certain inconveniences, there was always the question of how long was too long. Jodi was to be the maid of honor, and Reza was to play a dual role, giving away the bride as well as being Braddock's best man. As such, their absence constituted something of a problem.

He sighed heavily. "Well, I will see what your bride wishes to do," he said.

Braddock watched him disappear through one of the doors that let onto the dais that held the altar, trying not to feel silly as he stood there alone, waiting.

"Jodi," he muttered under his breath, "I'm going to strangle you..."

Meanwhile, Hernandez bustled back to the room where Nicole had been getting ready. Knocking on the door, he called, "Nicole. They have not yet arrived. What do you want to... do...?"

At that moment she opened the door and stepped into the corridor. She wore a white wedding gown that made her look like a princess from a fairy tale. The porcelain skin of her face glowed beneath the veil she wore, and her eyes glittered like jewels, showing no concern, only joyful anticipation.

"They are coming now, Father," she told him. She could always tell when Reza was near, always knew how he felt. "Trust me," she said after he gave her a look of acute disbelief.

"Now, child," he began, "I know you're nervous on this magnificent day, but you should not let your imagination–"

A door swinging open at the end of the hall, followed by the sound of running footsteps, interrupted him.

"Oh, Jesus – oh, shit, sorry, didn't mean to say that, Father – Reza's shuttle was late and we..." Jodi's explanation tapered off when she saw Nicole standing there next to the old priest. "Nicole," she breathed. "God, you look so beautiful."

"I only wonder if the good councilman will be able to properly appreciate such beauty," Reza said with a smile from behind Jodi. "It is good to see you again, Nicole."

They embraced, Nicole putting her arms around Reza's neck as he lifted her from the ground, holding her tightly against his chest.

"Reza," she breathed as she kissed his cheek, "I am so glad you could come. I knew you would."

"All the warriors of the Empire could not have kept me away," he told her. "I am so happy for you, Nicole. I only wish... that I had more time to be with you than we have had over the last few years." Almost unwillingly, he lightly set her down again. "But–"

"Do not speak of it, *mon ami*," she told him, putting a finger against his lips. "You are here now. That is all that is important. Nothing more."

Hernandez cleared his throat. "Nicole," he said, "I think perhaps that it is time to begin."

* * *

The music was not traditional; Nicole's concession to tradition had been her wedding gown. Nonetheless, the chapel's ancient pipe organ – bringing to life a composition by Jules de Clerc, from Nicole's native La Seyne – declared the occasion one of joy. Everyone was now standing, turned toward the rear of the chapel. The time they had spent waiting for this moment was forgotten as the moment of truth – and beauty – arrived. Tony Braddock stood nervously at the head of the maroon carpet that would guide his bride to him. Father Hernandez stood by the altar, his eyes beaming.

Jodi came down the aisle first, bravely holding back the tears that were at once a sign of joy and sorrow. Her dress whites sparkled in the sunlight admitted by the chapel's two-story high windows as her feet made a precise seventy-five centimeter stride toward the altar. She took her place just to the left of where Nicole was to stand. She smiled at Tony's happily anxious face, and the two of them waited for the bride to emerge.

The music changed tempo, slowing slightly, the major chords now as bright as the sun outside. As one, the guests turned toward the rear of the chapel, expectation plainly written on their faces.

Reza, his dress blues a vivid contrast to the regal white of Nicole's wedding gown, led her arm-in-arm down the aisle. He ignored the sudden murmuring of those who noticed the Kreelan collar he wore and the length of his hair; in fact, he ignored everyone except the woman who walked beside him and his friends standing at the altar. He rejoiced at the happiness he could feel in her heart and in Tony's, and the pride he felt in Father Hernandez's. Inside, though, he wept at the pain he felt in Jodi's heart, pain that was so much like that in his own. But on his face he wore the mask that he showed to the world when he did not wish to show the truth inside.

Nicole glanced over at him, a cloud of concern flashing across her face. She momentarily felt a pang of guilt at the pain she could sense deep inside him, a melancholy chord that ran through her blood. She felt as if she was abandoning him by marrying Tony. But she had offered herself to him long ago, she had wanted to love him, but he had gently turned her away. Their eyes met for a moment, and their minds linked for just that fraction of a second.

It is my Way, Reza's eyes told her. Yours is upon a different – I pray happier – path.

Is it indeed, my brother? her own eyes replied, echoing the doubt in her mind.

Reza turned away. Nicole wanted to hold him to her, to force him to look her in the eye once more, but the moment was gone and the altar now stood before them. What had gone unspoken was lost now forever, she understood sadly. She could feel the rhythm of his soul in her blood like faint sighs in the night, but she knew that from this moment on he would never open himself up to her as he once had, would never let her look into his eyes like that again. Not because he was jealous or angry about the vows she was about to take, but because he loved her, and did not want to endanger the happiness she might find with another, with the man she was about to marry.

"I love you, Reza," she whispered.

Reza stood in silence beside her as the music drew to a close; they had reached the end of their journey to the altar.

"Good people," Father Hernandez said, standing before them, "let us pray." Among the guests heads lowered and eyes closed. Reza, respectful of but untouched by Hernandez's God, silently studied the figure of Christ hanging from the cross upon the wall over the altar as Hernandez offered a prayer to Him:

"Holy Father, we have come together this day to seek Thy blessing for this couple who would be married in Your house, with Your love. Father, dark are the times in which we find ourselves. The demons run rampant upon the field of stars that shine in the night sky. But we ask Thee to smile upon these two who stand before You now, to protect them and let their love grow in your heavenly light for all the days of their lives. In Jesus' holy name we pray, amen."

"Amen," echoed the gathering.

"Please, be seated." Hernandez waited until they had settled themselves in the pews before he continued. "Brothers and sisters, we are gathered this day to witness the ceremony that, among my priestly duties, has without exception been my favorite to administer. To unite two hearts, two souls, in the eyes of God is like presiding over a new creation in His Universe, playing a hand in the birth of something unique and wonderful.

"In the case of the man and woman who today have come forward to declare their love for one another through the bond of marriage, I must say that I am especially pleased. I have known Nicole Carré and Tony Braddock for years, not as warriors and servants of the Confederation, but as friends. And it is now with great gladness that I would ask them to step forward to take their vows before the Almighty."

With a nod, Reza released Nicole's arm, and she stepped forward to where Tony stood waiting. They turned toward each other, shyly, like children about to experience their first kiss, and Tony carefully lifted her veil and smiled at her lovely face. Together, they turned toward the elderly priest.

Reza took a place two paces to Tony's right, mirroring where Jodi stood next to Nicole. He met Jodi's eyes briefly, and they both tried to smile, but it was all either could do to hold back their tears: Jodi for what she was about to lose forever, and Reza for all he had lost long since.

"Anthony, with the Lord as your witness and the love of Christ in your heart, do you take this woman, Nicole Carré, to be your wife, to love her and nurture her, to entwine your soul unto hers, to become one with her for all Eternity?"

"Yes," Tony said, his voice carrying through the chapel like a bell, "I do."

"Do you offer this woman a token of your love, Anthony, and of your devotion to the vows you take this day?"

"A ring, Father," Anthony said. He turned to Reza, who deftly placed a wedding band in his hand. But it was no ordinary ring, and this was the first time that anyone but Reza had seen it: it was made not of gold or silver, but Kreelan metal that Reza had fashioned for her. Sparkling like diamond but far stronger, it bore an intricate pattern that he had managed to fashion in the short time he had to work on it before leaving for Earth. The design was based on what Pan'ne-Sharakh had created for Esah-Zhurah's tiara many years before; it was Reza's homage to his old mentor, and to his love.

"Reza," Tony gasped, "it's beautiful." He had a backup ring in his pocket that he would have used had Reza not made it to the wedding, but it could never compare to what he now held in his hand. The ring Reza had fashioned glittered and shone as if it were alive; and, in a way no human would ever understand, it was.

Reza only nodded, gratified at how wide Nicole's eyes got when she saw it, sensing the surge of joy in her heart.

Smiling, Tony passed the ring to Father Hernandez, who held it in one of his age-spotted hands as if this, made of the strongest substance known, was but a fragile flower.

"And you, Nicole Carré," Hernandez continued, "with the Lord as your witness and the love of Christ in your heart, do you take this man, Anthony Braddock, to be your husband, to love him and nurture him, to entwine your soul unto his for all Eternity?"

"I do," she answered softly, her voice nearly gone from nervous anticipation.

"And do you offer him a token of your love, and of your devotion to the vows you take this day, Nicole?"

"Yes, Father, a ring," she said, turning to Jodi and holding out her hand.

Jodi felt her face go slack. *The ring!* What did she do with it? Where could it–

She suddenly sighed with relief as she felt a small object pressing against her left breast. She had put it in the inside uniform pocket over her heart. With an embarrassed grin, she reached into her coat – after undoing two of the buttons – and got the ring for Nicole, who only smiled and shook her head. "I love you," she mouthed silently.

She had no idea how those tacit words pierced Jodi's heart.

Hernandez took the ring – a plain but thick gold band – and held both rings up so the well-wishers could see them. "The ring," he said, his voice filled with wonder, as if this were the first time he had ever uttered these words, "is a symbol of life, without beginning, without end. It is a symbol of perfection to which we may aspire in our love for one another, and all the more so between husband and wife. It is a covenant of love between you; shall it never be broken or cast aside." He handed the Kreelan metal ring back to Tony, the gold one back to Nicole, and they placed them on each other's wedding finger, and remained holding hands.

Hernandez looked out upon the audience, his eyes beaming, yet perhaps with a trace of fire. "Is there one among you who would come forth to speak against this marriage, that it is unjust in the eyes of God?"

Jodi felt a sudden mad urge to scream, to shout, "Yes! Yes, damn you! I don't want her to marry him!" But she held her tongue and smiled, and after a moment the giddy feeling passed.

Hernandez nodded, pleased. It rarely happened, but there had been times when objections were raised, and of course that had upset the course of the ceremonies in question.

"Very well, then," he said. "May this union as witnessed by God and Man never be broken." He looked down at Tony and Nicole, spreading his arms wide as if to catch the drops from a spring rain. "I now pronounce you husband and wife." With a huge grin on his face, he leaned toward Tony. "Well, what are you waiting for, young man? Kiss the bride!"

The two of them embraced and kissed as if they were auditioning for a movie love scene, and the onlookers – even the two jaded reporters – whistled and cheered their approval...

* * *

Jodi was not sure how many hours might have passed since the end of the reception, since the new Mrs. Nicole Braddock had been whisked away with her adoring husband in a sky-limo to a week-long honeymoon on the beaches of the old French Riviera. Actually, now that she tried to think about it, the only thing Jodi was really sure of was that she was totally, utterly drunk.

"Drunk right off my little black ass," she chuckled humorlessly to herself as she took another swallow from the half-empty bottle of champagne. Two empties already lay on the floor beside her like spent lovers. Which, she supposed in the hazy realm that had become her thoughts, was probably about as close as she was going to get to true love. "Too bad they don't make 'em with batteries." She laughed at the thought until she cried, but there were no more tears to be shed. Her body had none left to give.

Jodi couldn't recall much about what happened after the wedding, even when she really tried to. Nicole had been happy, smiling and chatty as a teenage girl after being asked to the prom by the school hunk, which was totally out of character for her. She was so happy. And Jodi had found herself drifting away to the far side of the room, trying to keep her pecker up, as they say, but also trying to shield the world from the fountain of jealousy that had sprung up within her. And that, of course, had only made her feel worse, because she loved Nicole and she adored Braddock. When the two of them had left the reception, Jodi knew that Nicole had been looking for her to say good-bye. But Jodi had hidden herself away in one of the hotel's anterooms until Nicole and Braddock had finally had to leave. Jodi simply couldn't bear to talk to Nicole just then, because she knew that she would do something, say something, that she would regret for the rest of her life. So she had made herself disappear. She had chickened out on her best friend in her hour of glory.

But not Reza, she remembered with sudden clarity. No, not poor Reza. She knew that he was trapped in his own little hell, letting himself be ripped apart by memories of whatever life he had known before, thoughts of the woman and the love he himself had left behind somewhere in the Empire. But he had let none of it show. No, not him. Not the Kreelan warrior priest trapped in flesh that was all too human. Jodi was sure he must have ground his teeth to nubs in his effort to mirror the happiness of his friends, dutifully playing out the role he had drawn in this particular play. He had even treated the two curious reporters with something like respect as they barraged him – this strange Marine who wore a Kreelan collar and had long braided hair – with questions, hoping to find some kind of interest angle in an otherwise smut-free VIP wedding.

No, she thought ruefully, Reza had been a pillar, while she had melted and flowed like sullen lead. At least he had been until Nicole and Tony departed and he had been left alone in a crowd of strangers, mingling like oil in water until the revelers headed home or to another stop on their party venue.

It was after they had all gone that Jodi had finally returned from her coward's hideaway. She found Reza sitting alone in a corner of the great reception hall, with no company other than the cleaning bots that were disposing of the evening's detritus. He was clutching a mug – no doubt filled with that evil brew he sometimes concocted – in his hands, and was staring silently into some other time, some other place. His face, which had never seemed to age since the first time she had seen him in Hernandez's musty room in the church on Rutan, was now drawn, haggard. It seemed that he had aged fifty years in the course of an evening. His strong shoulders were rounded, as if he had been whipped, beaten into submission. Defeated.

He must have known that she was standing there, watching him, but he did not acknowledge her presence any more than he did the cleaning bots. Jodi was just about to walk over to him, to try to say something, anything, when he absently set the mug down and then staggered out of the hall. Jodi could not believe her eyes: Reza was drunk, or at least he acted like it.

After that, she surmised wearily, she must have gathered up some bottles of booze from a nearby table and wandered back here to her room. Fortunately, she and Reza were in the same hotel where the reception had been, so at least she had not had to publicly embarrass herself by finding some form of public transportation. Her private disgrace was quite enough, thank you very much.

She took another deep swallow, spilling champagne down her uniform, trying to make it all go away, trying to drown out reality. But her conscience was nagging at her enough now that the alcohol was no longer providing the yearned-for numbing effect. It just tasted bitter.

She slammed the bottle down in frustration, ignoring the fountain of foam that suddenly spouted from it like a gleeful ejaculation. She turned to the comm panel and ordered the ever-patient computer to connect her with Reza's room.

"One moment, please, madam," responded a pleasant automated female voice.

"Hurry the fuck up," Jodi grated, not knowing how much longer her courage might last.

"There is no answer, madam," the computer finally replied.

"Is Reza Gard in his room?"

"The room is currently occupied," the machine answered, refusing to give out any other information on who might be there.

"Try again."

"One moment..." There was a longer pause this time. Jodi figured the computer must have been programmed to try and accommodate idiots like her by trying longer the second time. Jodi wasn't going to bother with a third. "There is no answer, madam. Would you like to leave a message?"

Jodi didn't bother answering. She was already halfway to the door, a full bottle in hand.

She hadn't bothered to check the time, partly because she wouldn't have cared, and partly because she was too drunk to think of such a thing. But she was happy that it was late enough for the hallways to be empty. She knew she must look like hell – her uniform jacket gaping open, champagne spilled all over her blouse, her hair going wild – but she couldn't have cared less. In fact, had she encountered someone who would have made so much as goo-goo eyes at her, she probably would have tried to whack them over the head with the bottle that she was working on even as she shuffle-staggered toward Reza's room. They were on the same level, but in different towers, and it took her a while to realize that she had already passed his room twice.

"Christ, Mackenzie, you couldn't find your ass with both hands and a compass," she muttered to herself as she finally reached his room, number 1289. She pounded on the door, eschewing the more polite method of using the call panel. "Reza!" she shouted, heedless of the people in four adjacent rooms whom she had just succeeded in waking up. "I know you're in there! Open this fucking door!"

She waited. Nothing. She was about to pound on the door again, when a sudden flash of inspiration brightened her alcohol-shrouded mind. She pressed her hand against the access panel, hoping that Reza had keyed her into his room's access list.

Apparently, he had. The door hissed open to reveal nothing but darkness. Jodi staggered inside just as someone two rooms down poked his head out into the hallway to see what the fuss was about. The door whispered closed behind her.

She stood there a moment, leaning against the wall of the foyer, fighting against the sudden sense of vertigo that was a gift of the alcohol coursing through her system and the total darkness of Reza's room.

No, she thought, it wasn't totally dark. Toward the far side, through the ridiculously large – at least, it seemed that way to someone used to a warship's spartan accommodations – living room suite, she could see some faint points of light: stars in the sky, showing through the sliding clearsteel door that led onto the balcony outside.

"Reza?" she called. No answer. The room was totally, almost unnaturally, quiet. "Reza, are you here? Answer me, dammit!" She groped forward in the darkness, not thinking to turn on a light. The silence in the room was unnerving, and she felt little pricks of fear along her spine. It didn't feel as if no one was here, she thought. She just wasn't sure who was, and suddenly she thought that she had made a bad move by coming here.

Her shin suddenly came in contact with something very hard-edged and quite unyielding, and she let out a yelp of pain that she was sure had somehow given her away, as if her earlier shouting had not.

She was just about to turn around and bolt for the door when, out of the corner of her eye, she saw him. At least, she thought it was him: a dark figure kneeling in the middle of the expansive balcony. He was in his Kreelan armor, its black surface mirroring the stars in the sky above. But his head was not turned toward the stars; it was bowed as if in prayer.

"Reza," she said quietly as she stepped onto the balcony, ignoring the throbbing pain in her shin where she'd hit the coffee table, "are you okay?" She still felt a tingle of fear, and she now knew why: the Reza she was looking at was a Kreelan warrior priest, not merely a captain in the Confederation Marine Corps. That is why she had felt so strange just a moment ago. Something inside her had known that he had let slip his human mask.

She shook the feeling off, trying to concentrate as she knelt beside him. "Honey, what's wrong?" she whispered, tentatively reaching out to touch his arm. It was so hot that it was painful to her touch.

"I... I cannot go on," Reza rasped through gritted teeth. "The pain, Jodi... I thought I had banished it forever with Nicole's help, but the pain has returned. My blood is fire, my heart an angry wound, for I cannot clear the memory of my love's face from my mind. I would rejoice for Nicole's happiness, but it has brought back too many memories. Molten steel sears my veins... it is too much."

It was then that she saw the knife that he held with both hands. It was the weapon he was most fond of, a beautiful but deadly dagger that she had never known him to let out of his sight.

"So what are you going to do?" she asked bluntly. "Just kill yourself and be done with everything? Is that how Kreelan warrior priests get out of tough spots – just ram a knife through their throats?"

Reza turned to glare at her, and without the booze she might have wilted under such a withering assault from his swirling green eyes, but not now. Not tonight.

"Let me tell you something, tough guy," she went on, moving closer to him, their noses only a hand's breadth apart, "you don't have a monopoly on heartache. How do you think I feel after watching the only person I've ever really loved marry a good friend? And how do you think I feel about being jealous as hell of him, so jealous that I couldn't even bring myself to say goodbye to either of them before they left for their honeymoon? And I was her maid of honor! What a fucking joke that is!" She tried to laugh, but strangled on a sob as she reached out and grabbed him by the shoulders, ignoring the heat that burned its way into her palms from the metal armor and his searing flesh beneath. "So I don't want to be hearing any of this shit about how your heart is tearing itself to pieces, Reza, because mine is, too, and I need you now, damn you, I need you so much, you're all I've got left. You promised me you'd be there when I needed you, Reza. You promised me, dammit! Don't you leave me, too. Don't you dare..."

Then she reached for him, wrapping her arms around his neck as if she were drowning, just as she had when he had pulled her from the river on Rutan so many years ago, and he was honor-bound to save her. Careful not to tear her clothing or skin with the talons on his gauntlets, he drew her to him, shielding her with his arms as he commanded his body to cool while fighting a savage battle with the loneliness that burned in his blood. The knife he laid carefully beside him. He still longed for its cold metal touch, for the release from the hell that his existence had once again become. He was so happy for Nicole and Tony, but what he felt reminded him too much of his life with Esah-Zhurah, as if he had been forced to relive it. And with those thoughts, those feelings, once again had come the burning agony of loss that was as powerful as when he had first left the Empire.

Silently, he cradled Jodi in his arms as she cried, doing his best to isolate himself from the past, closing off the universe beyond this woman, his friend, to whom he owed a debt of love.

Jodi didn't realize that she had fallen asleep until she noticed that she no longer felt the hot steel of Reza's armor pressing against her. Instead, her body was nestled against something warm and firm, but made of flesh, not metal.

She opened her eyes to find herself still out on the balcony with him, but he had taken off his armor and gathered her up to lay beside him in a padded chaise built for two. He had one arm wrapped around her, holding her to him, with her head resting on his powerful shoulder. The night air was warm enough that she didn't need a blanket, Reza's body providing all the warmth she needed. Above her, the stars still shone, and she guessed – hoped – that only a little time had passed, and that the night had not yet begun to wane toward morning.

"Reza," she whispered, "are you awake?"

"Yes," he replied, instinctively holding her just a bit tighter. "I have not yet found... sleep."

Peace, she thought he meant. He had not found the peace he was looking for, and probably never would. Just like her. A thought, quite alien to her way of thinking, began to uncoil in the back of her mind, stretching like an awakening lion. She reached out and touched Reza's face, much as he had done to her on the day that he had first appeared before her like an unholy apparition in Father Hernandez's rectory. How lonely he had been then; how lonely they both were now. "Tell me about her," she said, gently turning his face toward hers, "tell me about the woman you love."

Reza hesitated, but only for a moment. *What does it matter?* he told himself through the red haze that had settled over his mind like the acrid smoke that is all that is left after a fierce battle, one that leaves no one alive, no victors, only the vanquished. Telling her of his love was certainly no betrayal to the Empire. And, perhaps – just perhaps – sharing his pain with her might in some way help rejuvenate the emotional shield that Nicole's blood in his veins had provided him over the years, that now had failed him in the face of an onslaught of memories that he could not control.

"Her name," he said, forcing his tongue to work within the numbed orifice his mouth had become, "is Esah-Zhurah..."

Jodi listened intently as Reza wove the tale that had been his life with an alien woman whom he had once hated, yet had finally come to love with all his heart.

He and I have so much in common, she thought in the depths of her mind. *There is so much in common between us, and yet so little in common with those around us.* She realized then that she wanted Reza to heal her, just as she wanted to heal him. She wanted the pain to be gone, if only for a moment, for both of them.

In that moment she did something that she never thought she would do: she kissed a man. Not as a friend, or as a stunt, but with passion, with desire. She thought she could only want a woman, but Reza was so different from all the other men she had ever known, and that difference somehow made it seem right to her. She pressed her lips to his as she pulled him against her, wrapping her arms around his neck, entwining her fingers in the braids of his hair.

"Jodi," Reza rasped as he tried to pull himself away, "I cannot..."

"I don't want to have to explain this to you, dammit," she sighed as she again pulled him to her, harder than before. "I need an escape, Reza, and you're it. Just pretend... pretend that I'm Esah-Zhurah. I don't want you to fall in love with me. I just want you to hold me, to be... a part of me for a while. To take the pain away. And let me do the same for you. Just for a little while..."

Reza suddenly shuddered against her, as if he were fighting off a terrible fever.

But then she sensed a change in him, perhaps a kind of acceptance of what was, what he wished could be. Their lips met again, but this time it was Reza who kissed her. Her body tingled as she felt his powerful hands touch her, tentatively at first, but then with growing confidence as they sought out the catches to her clothing.

Jodi sat up to help him, straddling his waist as she did so, and she could feel the heat rapidly building within her as she took off her uniform, throwing it carelessly aside. Her heart began to race and she bit back a sigh as Reza's hands tenderly cupped her now-exposed breasts. She fought to pin him down, wanting to tear away the black Kreelan clothing from his body so she could feel his skin against hers, but her efforts had no more effect on Reza than if she had been trying to restrain a volcano. She gave up completely the instant that Reza's mouth closed over one of her nipples, and she cried out in surprise and delight as an orgasm unexpectedly swept through her like a rogue wave upon the ocean, coming from out of nowhere and carrying her away. *My God*, she thought, just before her body went into convulsions of delight, *he didn't even have to touch me anywhere else...*

Reza felt his lover climax, and sensed his own body soaring toward those heights as the woman he held – he knew it was Jodi, but in his mind, behind his closed eyes, he could only see and feel Esah-Zhurah – finished her own pleasure and had set about bringing him his. He felt her unsure but eager hands at work upon his manhood, stroking him, teasing him into involuntary sighs of pleasure. And then... and then he was inside her. In no time he felt himself tearing upward through the sky as his body suddenly melted away, dissolving in a geyser of passion that had come to claim him from the hard bitterness of reality.

Later, Jodi smiled at Reza's sleeping form. Pulling up a blanket she had retrieved from inside to cover their nakedness, she thought that things had worked out just fine. Her eyelids grew unbearably heavy as she snuggled next to him, her head on his shoulder, and her last thought before sleep took her was echoed by her lips.

"Thank you..."

* * *

She awoke to the sun and a gentle morning breeze. She stretched her body, remembering the night before with a sharp but pleasant tingling between her legs. She suddenly wondered if Reza was up to another bout of lovemaking.

But that hope evaporated as soon as she opened her eyes. Reza was no longer next to her, and she knew that he would not be found in the suite behind her, either. His shuttle wasn't due to leave until around noon, but she knew instinctively that he was gone.

That, however, was a disappointment she was prepared to deal with. Last night they had given each other something that both had desperately needed. It was something she could always feel good about, could always look back on to help warm her heart.

With a sigh of resignation, she rolled over, and was confronted with something she had not expected. A single red rose, the most perfect and beautiful she had ever seen, waited for her upon a small stand that Reza must have placed next to the chaise that had been their bed last night. Gingerly, careful to avoid the thorns, Jodi picked up the rose and smelled its fragrance.

"Be careful, Reza," she whispered to the sun that was yet rising over the city. "And remember that I'll always be there for you."

* * *

Hernandez was waiting for him in the transit lounge, as Reza knew he would be. He felt a pang of guilt at not having spent as much time with the old priest as he would have liked, but the same could be said for all of his few other human friends, save Eustus, who served beside him. There had never really been enough time for friends in this age of war, and he knew there never would be, least of all for a warrior like himself. "Peace" as humanity fought and died for was a concept as alien to him as was the blue skin of the Kreela to them. And in that, he thought, perhaps they had found a higher purpose than he himself could ever aspire to, for the Kreela fought only to bring glory to Her, while the humans fought for their future, and the future of their young. It was a novel concept, but clearly one that he did not fully appreciate.

Father Hernandez, still as animated as ever, was nonetheless losing his battle with age. He rose unsteadily to his feet with the help of a walking staff – he had steadfastly refused anything so elegant as a cane, and certainly would not accept any "modern medical hocus-pocus" – and made his way from the chair where he had been waiting.

"Greetings, my son," he said warmly as he grasped Reza's outstretched hand with fingers that could yet make one's knuckles pop.

"Hello, Father," Reza replied, trying to ignore the sudden resemblance in spirit between this man and Pan'ne-Sharakh, now long dead, but not forgotten to Reza's heart. "You did not have to come to see me off. It is much too early in the day for such a late sleeper to be roaming about."

Hernandez scoffed at Reza's light humor. Both of them knew full well that Hernandez had risen before the sun every day of his life, on Rutan or any other of the several worlds he had visited since leaving his old parish, no matter how many or how few hours were in their days. "Well, young man, I had to make sure that someone would be here to get you on the proper shuttle. The Lord indeed knows that even Marines need a shepherd, and most especially you!"

"Indeed you are right, Father," Reza told him with a smile. In the background he heard the sterile female voice of the starport announcing that his flight would be boarding in five minutes.

Hernandez scowled at the voice. "She sounds like my mother," he muttered. Then he turned again to Reza, seriously now. "You won't be seeing me again, you know. I'm an old, old man, and by the time you get back from your next adventure, wherever it may be, I fear I shall be long gone."

"Father–"

Hernandez held up his hand, cutting Reza off. "You know it is true, Reza, and that is the way of things; it is how things should be. And, believe me, after seeing the likes of this world, I cannot but yearn for the next.

"And that brings me to you, young man. While I haven't learned everything about you that I would have liked, I do know that you are troubled spiritually, and even if you had never given me a clue in words, I could tell from your eyes. You offer the world around you the eyes of a hunter, Reza, but I see something deeper: I see fear. Not fear of anything living or dead, and not even fear of Death itself; you are afraid of what comes after, of what becomes of your soul when your body turns to dust." From the suddenly haunted look on Reza's face, Hernandez knew he had been right.

I only wish that I had had more time with this one, he complained to his God. Over the years they had never really had a chance just to sit down and talk, and for the most inane of reasons, it seemed to Hernandez now. But he could not turn back the clock, and his own time among the living was swiftly winding down. *No matter*, he thought, *I will make do with what is given me.*

"Reza, tell me. Let me help you reach for what lies beyond that threshold. If you are willing to open your eyes and your heart, Salvation awaits you."

"Father, I have studied your God, and the gods of many other religions. But salvation for me lies with none of them, for I am merely a part – painfully separated – of a greater being, the Kreela. Perhaps the Empress answers to your God, for in truth I do not know if I consider Her to be 'the Creator,' as you believe of your God. All I know is that Her blood is in my veins, and for a short time I could hear Her voice, and the voices of the billions of Her Children, singing in my blood, in my heart. We were one as I never was before, and have never been since. She commands the living and the dead of Her people, Father – all who have ever lived and died with Her blood in their veins."

That, indeed, was a revelation to Hernandez, but he had no time to contemplate its meaning. Behind him, the cool female voice announced, "Shuttle APX-954, now boarding for transit to *C.S.S. Hera*. All passengers are to report to Gate 73B..."

Reza gathered his flight bag and a smaller one that contained gifts – souvenirs and chocolates – for Eustus and his troops.

Time! Hernandez cursed. Would you not give me just a few precious minutes, Lord? No, of course you wouldn't!

"Reza," he said hurriedly, stepping closer and dropping his voice slightly so as not to be overheard by the passengers streaming by toward the gate, "in my profound ignorance, I once accused you of being the Antichrist, of being Satan's instrument. I know that I was terribly wrong, but now I must wonder if you are perhaps the opposite. Many think of angels – even Christ Himself – as being always kind and peaceful, menacing toward none. But that is not really true. Some of the angels are warriors, Reza, and the Prince of Peace has powers of destruction that defy imagination." He looked Reza in the eye, knowing this would be the last chance he would have in this life to try and understand this miracle/curse that had changed his simple existence forever. "What are you, Reza? What are you really?"

"I am no angel, Father, nor am I your Messiah. If anything... if anything, you may think of me as Adam without his Eve, cast out of the Garden with no hope of ever returning." Reza smiled the best he could and extended a hand to Hernandez. "Take care, Father," he said, "and may your God smile upon your soul."

Hernandez watched him as he left, swallowed up in the slogging torrent of military and civilians who were still crowding onto the shuttle. "Goodbye, my son," he said sadly. "You shall always be in my prayers."

He stood there, alone, and waited until the shuttle lifted its squat bulk into the sky. As its contrail finally disappeared from the sky, it struck him that perhaps Reza's words were truer than the young man had himself believed.

"An Adam without his Eve," Hernandez muttered as he shuffled toward the far distant exit to the terminal. He stopped then, turning his attention again toward the sky and the invisible stars beyond. "Or the prodigal son who is yet to return home?"

Twenty-Eight

Over a year after Nicole's wedding, Reza found himself in a predicament whose resolution eluded him, and he did not have either Nicole or Jodi from whom he could draw strength. In what Reza considered a wretched twist of fate, his company, reinforced with a battery of artillery and a tank platoon, had been ordered to Erlang on a "civil unrest" mission. His job was to ensure that the flow of metals and minerals from the planet's mines to Confederation shipyards continued uninterrupted. He had been briefed that the two major political and demographic factions on the planet had been having troubles getting along for the last few years, but recently tensions had risen sufficiently to arouse Confederation concerns, enough to sponsor the mission Reza found himself stuck with. Since it was an undesirable duty and the Red Legion happened to be in that area of the Rim, it was assigned to them. And, since "shit rolls downhill," as Eustus was so fond of saying, Reza's company got the job.

Civil unrest, Reza thought acidly, a growl escaping his throat. No one had bothered to tell him that the planet was about to erupt into open civil war, with him and his Marines trapped in the middle. On one side there was the Ranier Alliance; on the other, the Mallory Party. Both seemed very similar at first glance, but as with many things human, it was the underlying details that led to disagreement, bitterness, and – eventually – bloodshed.

From what Reza had been able to piece together from the wildly diverging accounts of the colony's existence that he had extracted from the library database, a colonizing expedition led by one Ian Mallory had landed on Erlang nearly two hundred years ago. The colonists numbered over fifty thousand men, women, and children from the Grange Cloud asteroids. They had decided to risk all they had for the prospect of something better and had pooled their money to buy an outdated ore hauler from a bankrupt Grange mining firm. They refitted it themselves for the seven-month voyage that would take them to the Promised Land. Reza was not an expert in the art of starship construction, but he had to marvel at the courage of these people, that they had traveled so far in what was no more than a hulk awaiting the breaker's torch.

But they paid a steep price for their dream. The old ship's engines were not as reliable as the colonists had hoped, and by the time they finally made planetfall over a year after they left the Grange, nearly five thousand of them had died of starvation and disease.

Abandoning the ship in a stable orbit from which it later could be tapped for raw materials and its few remaining supplies, the colonists descended into their Eden in the landing barges they had brought for the purpose. Miraculously, all but one landed safely.

Unlike so many similar expeditions, which often suffered countless hardships only to meet with ultimate disappointment and, in many cases, death, the Mallory expedition had truly found the Garden of Eden. A sister to what Earth must have been in the age before *homo sapiens*, their new home – Erlang – was a priceless and beautiful gem of blue skies and green valleys, of towering mountains and seas teeming with life. Despite the losses of their loved ones and the nightmare of the long voyage, the Mallorys had found their dream, and over the years their colony grew and prospered.

Some three hundred years later, the Raniers arrived. Unlike the Mallorys, Therese Ranier and her fifteen-thousand followers were upper-class descendants of the shipbuilders of Tulanya who had decided to emigrate to a newly-discovered world, even farther-flung from the human-settled core worlds than Erlang had been.

Unfortunately, their ship, despite being generations newer and designed from the outset to transport a colony expedition, had an engine mishap that fortuitously left no permanent casualties in its wake other than its primary stardrives. By no small miracle, they happened to be close enough to Erlang's system to make it there in a few months on their auxiliary drives. Had the stardrives failed much before or after they did, Ranier and her group surely would have perished in the vast wasteland of space that separated Erlang and her closest neighbors, for there would have been no ships nearby to heed their distress calls.

The arrival of the Ranier ship signaled a change in the peaceful agrarian life of Erlang's inhabitants. It did not take the newly arrived minority long to determine that the Erlangers – the Mallorys, as they eventually came to be called – knew and cared little for the capitalistic concepts in which the Ranier group had been raised and took for granted. When they came, the Raniers found little more than a barter economy, with virtually nothing in the way of industry except for textiles and the manufacture of basic farming implements. And while they deeply appreciated the Mallorys' open invitation to make Erlang their home, the new arrivals knew that they had not invested so much and traveled so far simply to work the land like the simple peasants they took the Mallorys for. Regardless, their decision, after a suitably short debate, was unanimous: they would stay. Of course, with their ship disabled they had no other choice at the time, but Erlang offered too much profit potential for them to pass up.

Over the next century or so, the two groups worked to mold Erlang into the vision of what each thought it should be. Unfortunately, their visions and plans for their bountiful world soon diverged. The Mallorys were content to live with what they had, celebrating the anniversary of their landing each year with a feast and the knowledge that they had been saved through divine grace, no matter which divinity one chose to believe in. They were farmers and hunters, whose only profit was for their children to grow up strong and well on a world that would provide for all their needs for as long as any of them could imagine.

The Raniers, on the other hand, saw the enormous potential of Erlang as an economic power in this far-flung sector of space, and soon saw the Mallorys as a key ingredient in their budding plan for exploiting the planet. It did not take long for the newcomers to begin opening shops and businesses, to establish the roots of a real economy in the various Mallory settlements. And in but a few years, the Raniers had discovered the minerals that they knew would someday make them rich. It was hardly surprising that most of the backbreaking labor was later to be undertaken by Mallory hands.

Many years had since passed, and the dreams of Therese Ranier had come true in more ways than she could have imagined had she stood among her people today. With the first visits by enterprising merchant ships, Erlang quickly became the leader of a loose economic coalition of rim worlds. Her mineral wealth had put her very close to the top of the list as a resource for everything from gold and diamonds to the many ingredients that went into constructing starships, starships that soon came to visit the planet with reassuring regularity, despite Erlang's remote location. And those families who had invested in this vision of the future – virtually all Raniers – had grown rich beyond the wildest dreams of their predecessors.

But there was a darker side to Erlang's success. Only a hundred years after the Ranier ship had arrived, the way of life that had been cherished by the Mallorys was all but gone. The simple but effective system of barter and goodwill that had seen them through the many winters since their forebears arrived had been replaced by the specter of the bank and the company store. When once a person only had to turn to their neighbor for help or food, now they had to pay for it with money they often enough did not have; and if they did not, they had to find work from a Ranier, usually in the mines. At first, work in the mines, being paid for it, seemed like a good thing, a way to better their families' lives. After all, many of them had thought, did their forefathers themselves not make their way in the mines?

But they had forgotten the hardship and eventual abandonment by the owners of the mines that had forced their forebears to seek out Erlang in the first place.

Worse, the Mallorys quickly lost their political power in a new system that the Raniers had promised would give one person one vote. Unfortunately, they neglected to inform the Mallorys that the only votes that really counted would be from Raniers, who in later generations became classic practitioners of the Golden Rule: whoever has the gold makes the rules. This was an alien concept to the Mallorys as a group, as they had practiced the most basic kind of democracy since they landed on Erlang: anything that impacted on the whole colony was voted on by the whole colony, and on any part by those who stood to be affected. It was a tradition that had stood the test of time in many years of hard living.

But now most Mallorys lived in poverty, engaged in hard labor in the mines or cutting down their once pristine forests to make barges and ships to haul minerals to the Mallory spaceport. Exhausted from their daily fight to stay alive, they had lost the battle for civic equality, if not their pride. And their pride is what sustained them, along with a burning will to survive and overcome. It was the same strength that had carried their forefathers across light years from hopeless despair to find God's gift. And their sons and daughters vowed that they would someday reclaim what they somehow had lost.

Then, of course, the war with the Kreelans had come. While Erlang had never itself been attacked, the planet had nonetheless felt the impact of the war as the newly formed Confederation – of which Erlang had unanimously become a member – sought to tap the resources, human and material, of its constituent worlds. Erlang was not yet large enough to raise a combat regiment of its own, but the Confederation sponsored it with equipment to form a powerful Territorial Army and Coast Guard to protect its vital mineral wealth. Virtually all the Territorial Army personnel were drawn from Ranier families, a slight that the Mallorys fought to overlook in the best interests of their world. Then, fifty years later, the first regiment was raised for the Marine Corps for service on worlds that no Mallory and few Raniers had ever seen or heard of; the enlisted ranks were filled by the sons and daughters of Mallory families, the officers all drawn from Raniers. And so the Mallorys saw their children bleeding and dying under alien suns, but weren't trusted to serve in defense of the world that was their home.

It was the final insult, the spark that ignited their long-suppressed rage into open violence. A series of strikes and riots ensued that were quickly and savagely put down by the Ranier-controlled Territorial Army and police forces, and thereafter the Mallory townships had lived under virtual martial law.

The emergence of outright oppression, however, only fueled the determination of the Mallorys to overcome the domination of the Raniers. Mallory township elders and activists set about organizing themselves into a political underground that became known simply as the Mallory Party. The party was illegal in the Houses of Parliament that were dominated by the Raniers and puppet Mallory leaders who made up the Ranier Alliance. But the Mallory Party had gradually gained strength in numbers and weapons until its leaders felt they could force the Ranier Alliance to accept it as a viable political entity and return some sense of equality to Erlang. The Mallorys had hoped that the Confederation would assist them in their efforts to achieve political equity on their homeworld. But the Confederation government, preoccupied with an endless war and besieged with the pleas of worlds under attack, had little time to deal with what the Council saw as little more than petty political squabbling.

This, of course, did nothing to make the Mallorys – or the Raniers, for that matter – any more receptive to Reza's newly arrived Marines. As he always did before landing his people, Reza had made a reconnaissance of the spaceport where he had intended to land his troops. He found that it was encircled by two rings of people, each invisible to the other. On the inside were police and Territorial Army troops facing out toward the landing zone's electrified perimeter; on the outside, facing in, hundreds of people Reza could best describe as partisans lay in wait, as if planning an ambush for the incoming Confederation forces. Reza reached out his mind to them, and his initial observations were confirmed. Armed with hunting rifles and homemade bombs, the civilians hiding in the forest had every intention of attacking the spaceport in hopes of driving the Marines away before they could become established.

Reza was impressed by their courage. Even if there had been no Ranier troops between the waiting Mallorys and the incoming Marines, any battle would have been swiftly decided. There would have been many dead Mallorys, and his Marines would still have landed.

Realizing that the landing could not go as planned, Reza had decided to make a tactical landing on a ridge overlooking Mallory City and its spaceport, about five kilometers distant. The colony's president, who had sponsored a welcoming parade for the first Confederation Marines to visit Erlang in nearly ten years, had not been happy about the unannounced change in plans.

"What in blazes are you doing, captain?" President Belisle's voice crackled over the comm link. "You are only cleared to land at the spaceport, not–"

"Forgive me, Mr. President," Reza cut him off quietly, "but I believe a more neutral location would serve my purposes better. I apologize for ruining your welcoming plans, but it cannot be helped. I will be in contact with you again as soon as we have completed our landing." He disconnected just as the president's reddening face contorted with a reply.

That had been two hours ago. He watched the holo tactical display that had been set up in a large room of an abandoned equipment building as his troops finished deploying into a defensive perimeter. Until Reza could sort out who their enemies were and who were their allies – if indeed there were any – he would trust no one. The landing boats and the carrier that had dropped them here had already left orbit and jumped into hyperspace. The Marines were on their own.

"We're ready, sir," Hawthorne reported from where he hovered over the company's command and control console, monitoring everyone's progress while Eustus walked the perimeter outside, making sure everything was being done right. "Everyone's in place, and the arty's sited behind the ridge." For this mission, they had received a battery of six multiple rocket launchers – MRLs – that Reza had targeted against the local Territorial Army garrison and the city's three aerospace defense sites. Just in case.

Hawthorne paused a moment, nodding to someone who was speaking into his headset. "Walken says he's ready when you are." First Lieutenant Rudi Walken commanded the mechanized detachment: one platoon of armored skimmers and one of tanks that Reza had been given from the regiment's armored battalion. Like the artillery, it was a choice luxury that filled Reza with suspicion. Such units were very precious, especially in the Red Legion, and were not allocated without a great deal of forethought by regimental command. While the detachment was small in size, there likely were few weapons on Erlang that could destroy the armored skimmers, and nothing that could touch Walken's five tanks.

"Very well," he said, grabbing his helmet and rifle. While officers were supposed to only carry sidearms, ostensibly to force them to lead the fight instead of acting as another rifleman, Reza carried both. Sometimes having an extra rifleman made the difference between victory and defeat. As always, the Empress's dagger clung to his waist, while the Desh-Ka short sword given him by Tesh-Dar lay sheathed at his back. "You have the con, captain."

"Aye, sir," Washington acknowledged. While the exchange was a Navy tradition, Reza had become fond of it and had adopted it for when he delegated his authority to one of his subordinates to take command of the company in his absence. "Good luck."

Reza frowned. He feared that they would need it. "Come with me, Zevon," he said as he passed the younger man, who stood at attention for his commander.

"Sir," he said, following at Reza's heels. In his left hand he carried the plastisteel case that contained the computer interface and the other materials he needed to keep the administration of the company together, as well as some more mundane items with which he took notes and drafted messages for his commander. In the other hand, he carried his rifle. While at any given time he was the company clerk, commander's adjutant, or one of a hundred other things as needed, he was a rifleman first and always.

Outside, Reza quickly surveyed his company's positions. As he knew it would be, all was in order. "Captain," Eustus said as he met Reza beside the armored skimmer that would carry him into the city, "be careful."

Reza suppressed a smile at his friend's words. Eustus had turned out to be what some of his troops had termed a perfect mother hen.

"We will be back before dusk," Reza said. Eustus nodded and stepped back as Reza and Zevon squirmed through the skimmer's hatch, Zevon closing it behind them.

"Rudi," Reza said through his helmet's comm link as he folded himself into one of the skimmer's seats, fighting the claustrophobic reaction he always suffered when he had to ride in armored vehicles, "it is time."

"Roger," Walken replied. The convoy was made up of the skimmer carrying Reza, Zevon, and a rifle squad, sandwiched between the two tanks of the tank platoon's light section. The other three tanks and seven skimmers would remain here with the company. Content that everything was in order, Walken spoke into his helmet microphone. "Convoy Alpha, this is Alpha One. Move out."

The heads of over two hundred Marines swiveled in unison to watch the little convoy depart. The air crackled and the ground shook as the two tanks lifted on their anti-gravity screens. Titans of surface warfare, each massed over two hundred tons and carried enough firepower to level a small city, with armor that protected them from all but the most horrendous weapons the enemy could bring to bear. A legacy of mankind's self destructive age, the modern tank had no equal in the armory of the Kreelans, and it was behemoths like these that had turned the tide in many a battle from disastrous defeat to life-preserving victory. Alas, their great power came only at an astronomical cost in labor and resources, and there were never enough of them to go around.

As the two turreted monsters began to move forward, the bottoms of their armored hulls borne a meter from the ground, the much lighter and more agile skimmer lifted and quickly took its place between its larger cousins, its thinner hide protected by their bulk and potential menace.

* * *

"They're coming down The Lane, now," Mallory City's mayor, the Honorable Crory Wittmann, said from the balcony as he watched the Marine vehicles thunder down the main thoroughfare of the city, which fortunately was wide enough for the tanks. People had poured out of buildings at the noise, thinking perhaps that an earthquake was in the making. Such was their surprise when they saw the house-sized shapes rumbling past their shops and apartments, the camouflaged flanks of the vehicles adorned with the seal of the Confederation followed by the word MARINES in tall black letters. "God, look at the size of those things!" he said excitedly, like a young boy seeing his first parade.

President Belisle glowered from his chair, his face a cherry red that reflected the anger still boiling inside him. *What else could go wrong?* he thought acidly to himself as he considered berating Wittmann for being such an impressionable imbecile. The Ranier Alliance was in trouble, big trouble, and people like Wittmann were too stupid to see it. First the Mallorys began to think they were equals instead of just the laborers they had always been, holding strikes and forming their own underground political party, as if any of the brutes understood what politics was really all about. Then the Territorial Army, which Belisle and his predecessors had gone to great lengths to maintain as a club to keep the Mallorys in their place in the mines, had begun to mutiny in the provinces after having to carry out a few jobs against the workers there. *No bloody stomach for it,* Belisle thought savagely, cursing the weaklings who had been in charge. A few summary executions had settled that issue – for the moment, at least – but Belisle and the Alliance were no longer content to rely on the Territorial Army outside of the colony's major population centers, including Mallory City.

He pursed his lips as if he had just sucked down a lemon. *Mallory City.* The name made him want to spit, but it had been a necessary compromise when it had been chosen. *Bloody beggars.*

All that was bad enough, he thought. But being snubbed by an arrogant Marine – a captain, no less! – was far, far too much. He was going to send good Senator Borge a very choice set of words as thanks for the support he had promised. The cargo ships that streamed through Erlang's ports to carry away their loads of metal and minerals for the Confederation must not be worth very much to the man and the Council if they could only spare a niggardly company of Marines to help keep the Mallorys at work. Taking into account the ships that carried away cargoes for personal consumption by certain political figures, the tiny contingent he had been apportioned made little sense, indeed. Belisle's face tightened, his mouth compressing to a thin line. The Marine captain was going to learn a lesson or two about how to deal with the sovereign leader of Erlang.

The Marine tanks took up station on opposite ends of the square in front of the parliament building. The skimmer pulled up to the steps of the Assembly Building in front of an assemblage of shocked legislators who had been awaiting the arrival of a ceremonial procession, not a tactical deployment.

Three stories below the balcony on which Wittmann stood, four heavily armed and armored Marines emerged from the skimmer and took up deceptively casual positions beside the vehicle, their weapons at port arms, their eyes in constant motion, alert for any sign of trouble. Reza and Zevon followed them out and silently returned the gaze of the speechless legislators until Reza finally spoke.

"Will you take me to President Belisle, please?" he asked a man in a dull gray woolen suit that passed for high fashion in Erlang's capital city. The man looked around for a moment, as if expecting someone to come to his aid. After no one made any sign of addressing the situation, he turned back to Reza.

"Er, this way... captain," he said, resigned to the fact that he had been charged with the irritant that had enraged the president, and Belisle was not known for his kindness toward bearers of bad news.

"Thank you," Reza said with as much courtesy as he could muster in what struck him as an intolerably arrogant atmosphere. He did not need his special senses to tell him this was the case. It was plainly written on their faces.

Leaving the rest of his escort with the skimmer, Reza and Zevon (who reluctantly left his rifle in their vehicle) followed their unwilling guide through the gawking crowd, whose mood had soured to the point of outright surliness. Zevon shot a deadly glance at someone who muttered something about his parentage. The man shut up and turned away.

After leading them upstairs, their unwilling guide paused at a set of enormous and outrageously ornate doors that looked entirely out of place in the building's modern architectural style of whites, grays, and blacks, of classic geometric shapes. Two nervous Territorial Army soldiers stood guard outside.

"The president is through these doors," their guide said curtly. "You will, of course, excuse me if I don't accompany you." As if afraid that he was going to be physically beaten for some unnamed transgression, the man quickly disappeared down the hall, leaving Alfonso and Reza looking at each other.

"Sir," Zevon announced quietly, "these people give me the creeps."

Reza's only comment was an arched eyebrow. "Let us meet the President of Erlang, then, shall we?"

Ignoring the two soldiers, Reza opened the massive door and entered the room beyond.

"Captain Gard, I presume," Belisle's voice boomed from behind his desk, situated in the middle of a room as large as some flight decks Reza had been on. Directly overhead was a crystal chandelier that must have weighed at least five hundred kilos and cost more than some colonies had in their vaults. The walls were adorned with shelves of books that climbed to the ceiling, which itself was glorified with a painting that appeared to depict the taming of Erlang's forests. "So nice of you to join us."

"Mr. President," Reza said formally, as he and Zevon crossed the two dozen paces to Belisle's desk. "I offer my apologies for spoiling your plans, but–"

"*But?*" Belisle interjected hotly. "But what? I should have you charged with reckless navigation and wanton destruction of government property, your Navy ships and Marine vehicles tearing up Helder Ridge. You were sent here to do what I want, what my government wants, and so far you aren't measuring up very well. You're supposed to keep the mines open, and keep those damned Mallorys at work!" The older man rose from his desk, his face redder than ever, his eyes narrowed into dark slits.

Wittmann, who had come over from the balcony with the intent of shaking Reza's hand in welcome, shrank back behind the one individual on Erlang who wielded very close to absolute power.

"I ask for a regiment and *men* to do the job," Belisle spat, "and what do I get? A stinking company of misfits!" He walked around the desk, coming face to face with Reza. The two men were about the same height, but Belisle was much paler from never having worked in the sun. His hair, gray from age, was full and perfect, perhaps too much so. His body was in good shape, although a far cry from Reza's near-perfect form. When Belisle opened his mouth again, Reza was assaulted by the strong smell of cognac. "Who the devil do you think you are, mister? Captain Gard, I have half a mind to strip you of your rank and take your men and equipment for the Territorial Army."

Reza's eyes narrowed. Beside him, Zevon could feel the sudden heat from Reza's body, and his hand lowered just enough that his palm touched the butt of the blaster that hung at his hip, his trusty rifle's temporary replacement. Without moving his head, his eyes scoured the room for any trace of treachery.

"To attempt such a thing would be most unwise, President Belisle," Reza said, his voice masking the sudden flames that had erupted in his blood. "As you well know, you have no direct authority over me or my Marines, and any attempt to do what you are suggesting would be met with the stiffest resistance. Further," he took a step closer to Belisle, until their noses almost touched, "you do not seem to understand my orders, sir. They are to ensure that the flow of material from Erlang is disturbed as little as possible. They do not say to oppress the Mallorys or support the Raniers. I have been given complete authority in how to proceed." One minor and ironic advantage of being in the Red Legion, Reza thought: unless at least an entire battalion was participating in an operation, subordinate commanders detailed to missions like this one were given a free hand in determining its outcome. It was only natural, since many officers and units did not survive the tasks assigned to them, anyway.

"Is that a threat, captain?" Belisle hissed.

"No, sir, it is a statement of fact. I wish to cooperate with you, but I will not be coerced or browbeaten. I am a Marine, my people are Marines, and we will not be used as a political tool by either you or the Mallorys."

Belisle laughed, a coarse bark belonging to a heartless predator. "Big talk for a man who only has a couple hundred people behind him," he sneered. His voice turned cold. "Let me tell you something, little man. I make the rules on this world, and people either play by them or they get hurt. Badly. The Mallorys would love to get their hooks into a bleeding heart do-gooder like you, but I'll warn you now against it. You were sent here to help me to keep the mines open, and that's what you're going to do."

"I believe we are agreed that keeping the mines open is the objective," Reza said, "but what if I do not 'play' by your rules to do that, Mr. President?"

Belisle smiled like a hyena. "Captain, at the snap of my fingers I could have ten-thousand troops on that mountain where your beloved Marines are, and they wouldn't be up there just to pick mushrooms. Your people wouldn't stand a chance."

Wittmann watched in wonder as a smile crept upon Reza's lips.

"The view from your office is truly magnificent, Mr. President," Reza said admiringly as he moved past Belisle and out onto the open balcony, a structure that extended a dozen meters to his left and right around the curved face of the building. His eyes scanned the view for a moment until he had found what he was looking for. "I see that your people have a fondness for history and remembrance," he said, gesturing toward a tall mountain directly to the east of the capital that bore the inscription in enormous numbers of the dates on which the Mallorys and Raniers arrived. Below the dates, carved into the mountain face years ago, was the first scar of what was to be a giant likeness of Belisle. Today, fortunately, no workers were there. "Perhaps you also have a fondness for the future."

"What's that supposed to mean?" Belisle growled. He did not hear Zevon whispering something into his helmet microphone, but Wittmann did. "Karl," he stuttered, using Belisle's first name, "they're going to–"

Whatever the mayor had intended to say was to go unsaid forever as the mountain face suddenly erupted into a boiling mass of exploding rock and burning dust, the result of a single bolt fired from one of the tanks in the Marine encampment. It took ten seconds for the sound of the detonation to reach the capital, and it was still so loud that it shook the building like rolling thunder in a gale wind.

By the time the sound had died away, the mountain lay shrouded in a black cloud of dust and smoke.

"A great pity," Reza said, genuinely sad at having to destroy part of what had been a magnificently beautiful mountain, even after human hands had immortalized their own conceit with hammer and chisel. When the smoke cleared, there was only a smoldering crater where Belisle's likeness was to have been.

He turned back to Belisle, who was now as pale as the inside of his mistress's thighs. "Do not threaten me or my people again, Mr. President," Reza said quietly, his deep voice cutting through the city's sudden silence like the fin of a shark in dark water. "You will think on these things this night, on how you wish to solve your problems here, with or without my assistance. We will speak again tomorrow."

He and Zevon departed, leaving Belisle and Wittmann to contemplate the ramifications of what they had just witnessed.

* * *

"I tell you, Ian, our time has come," the man said passionately. "Surely it was a sign we saw today, that the days of the Raniers are numbered!"

There were nods of assent from people around the crowded room, visible in the low lamplight through air choked with pipe smoke and the salty smell of sweat clinging to bodies that had been laboring hard only hours before. Numbering one hundred and thirty-eight souls, they were the elected cell leaders of the Mallory Party, each of whom represented the interests of thousands of people.

But this meeting was not a normal one, by any means. It was the first time in over five years since representatives of all the groups had gathered to discuss the future of their people. The last time they had met, they had been betrayed by a young fool with a loose tongue, and many of their number, including the speaker's father, had been arrested, tortured, and then executed as traitors by the prefecture police and Territorial Army. No event since then had warranted the risk of another such meeting. Until now.

"Perhaps the mountain was not a warning to us," the man went on, "but to the Raniers. Perhaps the Marines–"

"They are here to help the Raniers!" a woman with a face of angry leather shouted from the other side of the gathering. They were men and women of all ages, tall and short, but all with the callused palms of those who labored for a living, and the hollowed eyes of those who lived in despair but who dreamed with hope. "Our first plan was best, to kill the Confederation dogs before they set foot on our soil. Now they'll turn their weapons on us, on our children, to keep us in the mines, digging like rats! I say we walk away from these damned pits. Blow them up. Collapse them for good. If they want the lode, let them dig it out themselves, and their Marines be damned!"

There were angry murmurs and more nods. Some were from different people than before, and some from those who had earlier agreed with the man's words. They were afraid, angry, and confused by the events of the day. They had known the Marines were coming, and had done their best to lay an ambush for them, believing that they were here to act as a whip for Belisle. But after the Marine ships suddenly diverted to the ridge, and then destroyed the site of Belisle's effigy in stone, the Mallorys' original determination to openly rebel had wavered. The seniors had called a meeting, and every group from every province had managed to get a representative here by nightfall. It had been a terribly dangerous gamble, but was considered worth the risk. But until the meeting ended and they were all safely away, more than one wary eye would be fixed on the approaches to the hideout, and local Mallory agents were in contact with spotters outside the nearby mines, watching for trouble.

"No."

In unison, all eyes turned to the owner of that voice. Enya Terragion, all of twenty-three years old, had not been with the Committee very long, but had early on won its respect.

"We must fight the wrongs we have suffered with right, with justice, not with spite," Enya told them. "Yes, we could destroy the mines, but where would that leave us? The Raniers would take their fortunes and themselves and leave us behind to rot in poverty worse than we know now."

"Fine, then!" someone shouted. "Good riddance to them!"

"We don't need their damned money to live!" added another.

"No, we don't," Enya said, her voice rising above the shouting. "But consider this, all of you: we remember stories of what it was like when the first Mallorys came here, how Erlang provided for them, how they carved their lives from the soil and the forest. But we can't go back." Her words hung like rifle shots in the suddenly silent room. "*We can't go back.* Look at yourselves: to right and left, and across from you. Who do you see? Do you see someone who can hunt in the forest, till soil and plant grain, spin wool into yarn and weave, someone who can provide for so many of us?" Many eyes dropped to the floor, many fists clenched in frustrated realization of the truth. The years had taken away their skills and given them a population that could not be sustained by a simple economy. "When was the last time any of you had something to eat or wear that did not come from the company store? How many of you have a plow, or know how to make one?" Her challenge was met with a resentful but contemplative silence. "And even if we could go back to the old ways, do we want to go back, when we could go forward? My father could not read, but he saw to it that I could, and I vow that any child of mine shall also. Gerry's boy," she nodded to a woman who sat a few seats down, "was born blind, but the doctors at Kielly's Hospital gave him his sight. Are these, and so many more, things we want to give up?" She paused again, her deep brown eyes touching each face in the crowd. "You all think that the lives of our first blood on this world were grand and full of joy, and for them they were. But that was their world, their time. This is our time, and we must make Erlang our own world, with our own vision, and not that of our forebears."

"So what do you suggest, girl?" a man who wore a patch over one eye and had a mass of scar tissue over the right side of his skull said sarcastically. "That we just say 'pretty please' to President-By-God's-Holy-Right Belisle and ask him to give us our lives and freedom back? We've tried that approach, many times, but it doesn't work. These people only understand what comes out the end of a gun, and we've got enough now to give it to 'em."

"What about the mountain?" Enya said over the chorus of agreeing voices. "Do you think our tiny, outlawed hunting rifles are a match for their pulse guns? Will our gasoline bombs stop their tanks or thwart their artillery?"

Silence.

"Good people," she said, "even should the Kreelans never show their terrible faces on this side of the Grange, we have many an enemy in our own kin, in the Raniers who oppress us, in the Confederation Council members who rob our world of its riches for their own gain. We are a remote world, far from the center of human consideration. It is time we sought out some friends, if we can, and show them that we are not the mindless brutes the Rainiers claim we are."

"Regardless of the cost?" the leather-faced woman asked.

Enya shook her head slowly. "No. But at least we can find out the price before we pay in blood, perhaps needlessly."

"And you think these Marines may help us?" Ian Mallory, a direct descendent of the original Mallory, said. He held his position solely through due democratic process in his ward and through his own abilities, not by his name. Longest surviving member on the Committee, he served as its leader.

"All of you heard earlier what Milan told us of Wittmann's horror at what happened to the mountain today, at what the Marines did to it," she said. Milan was the Mayor's servant and a Mallory spy. "Whoever these Marines are, whatever they came to Erlang for, it was not to be solely for Belisle's pleasure. Will they help us? I do not know. But I am willing to wager my life that it is worth the risk to find out. And if my way does not succeed, no other alternatives are closed away from you."

Ian Mallory nodded, his gray beard slowly bobbing against his barrel chest. He was a strong man, and proud, but held out little hope for a successful armed rebellion of his people against Belisle's Territorial Army. It had been tried before, and failed. As then, many Mallorys would be slaughtered, and Erlang would still remain under Ranier control. More than that, his people would be driven inextricably from their roots, from their heritage of honest work for an honest wage, the helping hand of a neighbor, a government that said "yes" to its people, not "no." He hoped beyond hope for a settlement that would restore his people to their rightful place in an environment of forgiveness and of looking to the future, where perhaps Raniers and Mallorys could someday simply call themselves Erlangers. But it was a difficult road. The past held so much bad blood, but his heart grew weary from the burden of hate that it bore. His wizened eyes sought out the gaze of his friends, his people.

"The time has come for talk to end," he said. "Does anyone have anything else to say on this matter, over what has already been spoken?"

No one did. Unlike many committees convened over the ages, the Mallorys did not have the luxury of talking and not acting. Every meeting ended in a vote and action.

"Then it is time to have a show of hands. All in favor of letting Enya speak to the Marines on our behalf, raise your hand." Roughly two-thirds of those present, some after a moment's hesitation, raised their hand above their head. "All those against?" The remainder raised their hands. There were no abstentions in a Mallory Committee vote. The right was too precious to waste.

"And what if she fails?"

Ian frowned. It was an unpalatable prospect, but an all-too realistic one. "If that happens, we'll have no choice but to destroy the mines and fight the Raniers and the Marines face to face." *And die*, he thought grimly.

TWENTY-NINE

"Captain," Zevon said from the dim red glow of the command post, "a personal message just came in for you from Tenth Fleet. I thought you might want to see it."

"Thank you, Alfonso," Reza said, instantly awakening from a restless sleep. He was not tired, particularly, except that dealing with the unfathomable intricacies of human politics drained him terribly. He would never become accustomed to a dark art that was unutterably alien to him and the ways of his people. *His* other *people*, he chided himself.

Reza took the proffered electronic notepad from Zevon, who immediately turned away and left him in privacy, closing the curtain of thick canvas between Reza's personal area and the company HQ.

Keying in his personal code, Reza was rewarded with Tenth Fleet's emblem and a video message. It was from Jodi.

"Hi, Reza," she said warmly, her face as beautiful as ever. It had been over three years now since he had last seen her or Nicole in the flesh. "I know I only wrote you last week, and you probably get sick of me sending these things all the time." Reza smiled. While the two of them had religiously exchanged letters every two weeks for years, only half of them ever got through. Looking at the date, he saw that this message had been posted three months ago. *Electronic miracles, indeed*, he thought sourly. "But I had some news for you, and I'm afraid it isn't good." Reza could see a veil of sadness fall over her face. "Father Hernandez died two days ago in Rome, here on Earth. I guess he was on another one of his trips between Rutan and the Vatican to tie things up with the Church again when his heart finally gave out. From what Monsignor Ryakin said – he called me this morning – Father Hernandez died in his sleep." She paused as she brushed away a tear. "I know you won't be able to come to the funeral or anything – it'll probably be long since over by the time you even get this – so I ordered some flowers for the ceremony in your name. I hope that's okay with you."

Of course it is, my friend, he thought sadly. He had liked Father Hernandez a great deal, and often thought how good it would have been to spend more time with him. But that was not part of Reza's Way. He only hoped that Hernandez had found whatever it was in life that he had been searching for, and that his God would look after his soul as Reza wished the Empress might, but could not, after he himself died.

"Well, now that I've got you depressed, I can at least say that there's some good news. Tony and Nicole are doing great. Big surprise, huh? Nicole's in charge of one of the training squadrons at the Red Flag range now (I'm her exec), and it seems that

Tony's been making quite a splash as a member of the Council. Seems like he hasn't forgotten to be a Marine, anyway, the way he gives some of those candy-ass senators a good tongue-lashing.

"Anyway," Jodi went on, her recorded image taking on a smile that was radiant despite her evident sadness at the changes time had brought, "all three of us will be going to Father's funeral, along with some of the others in your old welcoming committee. Even that stupid Rabat bitch loosened up enough to say she was going. Probably some kind of publicity stunt, I suppose.

"So, I guess that's it for now." Her piercing blue eyes turned serious. "Please, Reza, take good care of yourself. Tony says he's going to write you soon, too. And Nicole... well, Nicole seems to know when to write, so she'll do it when it's time. Tell Eustus I said hello, and Nicole promises to send him some more chocolate from Paris next month. I miss you, Reza. All my love to you." She blew a kiss at him. "Bye until next time."

The transmission ended.

Reza sat in the dark, alone with his thoughts. He wondered what would happen to him when all his friends were gone. Because he was so different from the others of his chosen kind, it was very difficult to make even friendly acquaintances, let alone meet someone with whom he could share a deeper relationship. Most of those in his graduating class at Quantico toward whom he had felt any kinship had either died or received medical discharges. Those to whom he was closest – except for Nicole and Jodi – were here with him, and had miraculously survived the perils they had faced over the years. But that could not last forever; they were stunning aberrations beside the Red Legion's massive casualty statistics.

A sudden surge in the activity beyond the canvas drew him away from his melancholy reverie.

"Captain," Hawthorne, his executive officer said, pulling the makeshift door aside with one tree-trunk sized arm. "Sir, you'd better come check this out. We've got a visitor at the perimeter."

"Show her in." Reza had sensed the young woman approaching the encampment some time ago.

Hawthorne only nodded, registering no shock or curiosity that Reza knew it was a woman who had come to visit them. He had long ago learned that his commander's seeming lack of curiosity about elaborating information did not mean he was not interested; it was just that somehow he already knew. "Yes, sir."

As Hawthorne relayed the orders, Reza put his uniform on over the silken black Kreelan garb he had worn every day of his adult life, the collar of his heritage and standing among humanity's enemy prominent above the neckline of his battle dress uniform. Carefully positioning the ancient dagger at his side, he went out into the pale yellow light of the command post.

* * *

"You don't understand, senator," Belisle said urgently, desperately restraining his growing fury as he spoke to the life-size holographic image of Senator Borge. "This man destroyed one of the capital city's landmarks, and threatened the entire colony with destruction if we didn't deal with him."

Borge's face took on a fatherly look that Belisle found maddeningly patronizing. "Karl, Karl, please, calm down. It is not that I doubt you, old friend. It is just that I find it difficult to believe that the people I dispatched to Erlang would do such a thing. The orders I laid down were very specific, and the command personnel chosen were, shall we say, of the highest reliability. I can only assume that there was a breakdown somewhere in the military chain. Please, rest assured that your interests are my interests, and I'll do everything in my power to rectify the situation."

Belisle nodded. Borge was a man of his word, as well he should be. He had profited enough from Erlang's riches. "What do you intend to do, then?"

"Well, first I need to know the unit that's causing you all the trouble, so I can track down where things went wrong and fix the problem." He smiled like a wolf, except wolves did not smile with malevolence. "And if you could provide me the name of the officer in charge, I can... effect a change in his career development profile, as it were."

"A summary court-martial and execution would be nice," Belisle muttered.

"That could be arranged, I suppose. Now, who are these people?" Borge's effigy motioned for someone to take a note.

"I don't know what unit it is. They never bothered to tell me." His mouth puckered momentarily in a sudden fit of anger, then he went on, "But the officer in charge is a Marine captain by the name of Gard. I don't know his first name."

For a moment, Borge did not speak, but his eyes widened perceptibly. "You said 'Gard?' Did he have long, braided hair and a Kreelan collar around his neck?"

Belisle thought about that a minute. "Yes," he said, suddenly feeling like an idiot. He had been so angry when Gard arrived that he had not noticed any obvious oddities. Perhaps because of the helmet he had been wearing? "Yes, by the Lord of All, he does. How in the devil did you know?"

"Never mind," Borge said grimly. "Karl, this man is extremely dangerous to our plans, and it is only the worst of luck that put him in charge of the Marine contingent I ordered to help you. I'll be sending help immediately. In the meantime, do whatever you have to do to cooperate with him. Make whatever concessions are necessary."

"But that would mean–"

"Just do it, Karl. Remember that it is only for as long as it takes for me to repair this misfortune. Any compromises you make can be undone easily enough. Am I right?"

Belisle thought about it a moment. Giving in to the Mallorys would not be an easy thing, even for a short time. On the other hand, if he agreed to a "compromise," he just might be able to lure their leaders out into the open and finish them off for good, an opportunity he had missed only by a hair five years ago. His mouth curled into a satisfied smile.

"Yes, of course, Senator," he said. "And this may give me the opportunity to finish some other long overdue... housecleaning."

"Good. I'll have someone on this right away, and they will be in touch with you regarding the plans as soon as they are in motion." Borge's projected face nodded once in farewell, then the image faded into random sparks and disappeared.

His spirits lifted, Belisle went to bed and his waiting mistress.

* * *

"Please, sit down," Reza told the young woman standing between a pair of his Marines who, while no taller than she, appeared enormous beside her in their combat gear. He nodded to them, and they quickly and silently left the command post.

"Thank you, captain," Enya said, having difficulty taking her eyes off him. He was so different from what she had expected. A tall man, lithe and strong, his body was well-muscled, yet sinewy like a cat's. He would not have seemed that much different from many in his company were it not for an alienness that clung to him. She saw the collar around his neck and his long braided black hair, but was taken most with the jade green eyes that seemed to swirl with color in the dim lamplight. Groping for the chair that was poised across the table from where Reza stood, she nearly tripped and fell as she sat down.

"You have nothing to fear here," he told her, as he sat down on another of the simple folding field chairs. "You have come representing the Mallorys." It was not a question.

Enya could only nod. Having seen the arsenal that lay in this camp, and now the quiet power in this man's eyes, she suddenly understood the seriousness of what she was undertaking. If these people were to turn on hers, no Mallory would ever again know freedom. The fear that welled up within her at the thought only served to fuel her determination: she must not fail.

"Yes," she said, taking a deep breath and staring Reza right in the eye, which took much more willpower than she had imagined it might. Not to look at him, but to occasionally look away. "I am Enya Terragion, a member of the Mallory Party Committee. I am empowered to speak with you on their behalf."

"You are the ones who sought to ambush my troops at the spaceport?" Reza asked, curious to know if she would speak the truth. If she did not...

Enya did not hesitate. "Yes. We feared that you had come to further oppress us, and the Committee decided to try and defeat you before you could add your firepower to that of the Territorial Army."

She heard a quiet snort off to one side, and turned to see a hulking black man who looked quick as a tiger, shaking his head as he turned back to whatever he had been doing.

"I believe Mister Hawthorne is saying that you were very... fortunate, Enya Terragion," Reza said, "that such an incident was avoided."

Enya nodded somberly. "We realized that today, when you destroyed the mountain. All of our people near the spaceport would have been killed, would they not?"

"If not all, probably most," Reza said simply. It was a fact beyond dispute. "I am glad things turned out differently." He smiled. With his eyes.

Enya blinked, trying to break the mesmerizing hold he seemed to have on her. "What do you intend to do here on Erlang?" she asked quietly. "Will you help Belisle herd us into the mines?"

"That depends on you," Reza said as Zevon, as if on cue, poured coffee for Enya. Suspicious that it was a trick, she only looked at it. Reza reached over and took a sip to prove it was safe, forcing the bitter liquid down his throat. He had always hated coffee. He set the cup back down on the table.

"My orders," he said through the bitter aftertaste, "are to ensure that the flow of minerals from the mines to Confederation shipyards continues without interruption. As I am sure you are aware, Erlang is virtually irreplaceable to the shipyards in this sector." He looked at her pointedly. "Those are my orders. How I carry them out is largely up to President Belisle... and you."

"Meaning what?" she said coldly. She pushed the coffee away. "That Belisle calls your superior and orders you to do his bidding, and we are worse off than ever before?" She shook her head. "Do not play games with me, captain. We are willing to talk with you, but we will not sacrifice everything for which we have lived and suffered without a fight. We know that you blew up the mountain to frighten Belisle, and perhaps us; you succeeded on both counts. But what are we to do now that you have put the fear of God in us all? Our only real weapon is our willingness to work the mines, and it is a weapon we are ready to use, and will use – to the death, if necessary – if it is forced upon us."

Reza's brow furrowed in thought for a moment before he spoke. "I pledge to you, as I have pledged to my Marines, that we will not turn upon your people, no matter our orders." Not surprisingly, disobeying orders was almost a Legion tradition, and it did not grieve Reza to ignore orders that conflicted with either his instincts or sense of rightness, corrupted with Kreelan influence as some thought it was. Good fortune, however, had seen to it that he had only rarely had to act in such a fashion. "My people are warriors, not murderers, and I will be perfectly honest with you: my mission cannot succeed without cooperation from both your people and Belisle."

Enya twisted her face into a scowl of skepticism. "And how," she said, "are we to go about doing that?"

His green eyes fixing her like a deer in a beam of light, he said, "Your people and Belisle will negotiate, and quickly. The plans you make shall be your own. I will guarantee neutrality. You will do what all humans seem to love to do: you will talk. You will reach a consensus."

"And if we don't?"

Reza shrugged. "Then you both shall suffer. If your workers strike or destroy the mines, you destroy Erlang's greatest defense against the Kreelans, which is providing raw materials to the shipyards for building warships that can protect you. As rich as your world is, by colony standards you have almost no ground defenses against a fleet assault. Worse, your Territorial Army seems more adept at police actions than waging war against the Empire. You would also push Belisle to vengeance, and his wrath would drive him to murder. The Territorial Army would be unleashed to slaughter Mallorys on a scale that I could not prevent." He shrugged. "On the other hand, Belisle has every interest in keeping the mines open, regardless of the cost. Erlang's economy and his own wealth depend on it. More than that, he cannot leave here with such blood on his hands. He will be exposed as a petty tyrant, a criminal and – if it comes to it – a mass murderer. No planet in the Confederation would take him."

Enya shook her head. "Belisle will never agree to it, no matter how little or how much we ask of him. The lines of hatred run too deep."

"He has no choice."

And what choice have we? Enya thought. What Reza said, while glossing over a great many smaller issues, was essentially true. If the Marines protected the Mallorys from punitive action by the Territorial Army and the police, and if enough changes could be made quickly...

There was hope, she decided. There was terrible risk, but no more than they faced already. Mallorys had already placed charges on all but the smallest mines, enough explosives in the right place to collapse the shafts and destroy much of the equipment. But if the mines were destroyed, there would be no limits to Belisle's retribution. And the outcome of a civil war between the Mallorys and the TA was not worth a moment's contemplation.

"On behalf of my people," she said formally, "I accept your offer of neutrality and negotiations with Belisle. What are we to do?"

* * *

To his visitors, Belisle appeared furious, yet resigned to the fact that the time for change had finally come. Having arrived in one of the armored skimmers, again escorted by two of Walken's tanks, the Mallory representatives had walked into the president's conference room and taken their appointed seats opposite their Ranier counterparts. Reza stood at the end of the table.

"I wish to make perfectly clear my position in this matter," he said. "I now act as an impartial third party mediator to your dispute until the proper authority has arrived from the Confederation Government."

"And who might that be?" Belisle asked, smugly thinking that he already knew the answer: a full regiment of Marines who would answer to *him*.

"Someone who is much more adept at these matters than am I," Reza said. "General Counsel Melissa Savitch."

Belisle's mouth hung slack as the blood drained from his face. "That's not possible," he squeaked.

The Mallorys, as well, were stunned.

"Isn't she the senior Confederation Counsel?" Enya asked incredulously. "Flattering as it is, why would she take an interest in this matter? Because of the mines?"

"No," Reza said, shaking his head. Melissa had stayed in touch with him over the years, and had become a welcome and cherished face in his small circle of friends. She had risen steadily until she had reached the pinnacle of achievement in her chosen field, now designated the highest-ranking member of the Confederation's judicial wing. "It is because I asked her to come, and she agreed. It is good fortune that she was on a visit to Nathalie when my message reached her. She will be here in five days. I am acting local counsel until she arrives."

"You bastard," Belisle suddenly spat. "You bloody freak."

"You test my impartiality, sir," Reza said coolly, but the look in his eyes was close to what Belisle had seen just before his own likeness on the face of Haerding Mountain had disappeared.

For a moment, Belisle did not know what to do. But then he remembered what Borge had told him before about anything done being undone easily enough. *Let the good counselor come*, he thought icily. He was sure that something fitting could be arranged. "Get on with it, then," he said in only a slightly more cordial tone.

Reza looked at him suspiciously, his mind ringing with alarms of intended treachery. But until Belisle exposed his intentions, Reza could not be sure, nor could he act. He decided that he would be very careful with this slippery serpent.

"Mr. Mallory," Reza said to the leader of the Mallory Party who represented two-thirds of the souls on this planet, "please, sir, begin."

Slow and rocky though it was, they took their first steps upon the road toward a true democracy.

Thirty

"Are you sure you wouldn't like to come along with us, captain?" Enya asked. "It's a truly beautiful place."

Looking up from the paperwork Zevon had forced upon him, Reza shook his head. "No thank you," he told her, smiling. "I appreciate your offer, but I have much to do here." He knew quite well that she fervently hoped he would say no, for purely personal reasons of her own. "Perhaps another time."

"Are you sure, captain?" Eustus asked valiantly, also hoping against hope that Reza would say no, but he felt honor-bound to ask. "Zevon always has you doing too much paperwork crap, you know."

Reza fought to keep from smiling. Sometimes, he thought, being able to sense the emotions of others must be more interesting than actually reading their thoughts. Eustus was helplessly, hopelessly in love with the young woman standing close beside him, and Enya felt the same about Eustus. The Marines had only been planetside for two weeks, but the changes had been little short of miraculous, especially after Counselor Savitch had arrived to oversee things. Sensing something malignant in Belisle's mind, Reza had assigned two of his best Marines to be her bodyguards, despite Savitch's vehement protests. They went with her everywhere, including the bathroom (both Marines were female). He had since gotten the sense from Belisle that whatever he had been plotting would not be put to the test, but there was something else about him that Reza was missing, something the man knew that fueled an inner fire of arrogance and patient vengeance. But what?

"That *crap*, as you're so fond of saying, First Sergeant," Zevon said tiredly, interrupting Reza's chain of thought, "is what keeps all of us paid, fed, and loaded with ammo. If you want me to cut your paycard loose–"

"No, no! Not that!" Eustus cried with mock horror, raising his hands to his face as if to ward off some nightmarish creature.

"First Sergeant," Reza said formally.

"Sir?" Eustus asked, suddenly confused by Reza's tone of voice.

"Dismissed."

Smiling, relieved, Eustus saluted. "Aye, sir," he replied.

"Captain," Enya said, bowing her head.

Watching the two of them leave together, Reza felt a sudden weight upon his heart. Where was Esah-Zhurah now? What was she doing? Was she thinking of him? Was she even still alive?

But there were no answers to his questions. He pushed her beautiful face from his mind and forcibly immersed himself in the jumble of paperwork that Zevon pushed at him to sign.

Outside, Eustus and Enya mounted the horses that waited patiently near the command post. Riding through the company compound, Enya smiled at the Marines who went about their daily routine. Some exercised or practiced hand-to-hand combat, others washed or shaved, several groups were clustered around the gigantic tanks that now lay in great pits dug into the ridge, working noisily on some mysterious mechanism inside the huge vehicles. Yet others, those who were off-duty and on free time, simply lay in the sun, getting tanned and doing what soldiers often loved above all else when granted the time: sleeping. Still others, whom she did not see here, had passes to go into Mallory City and take advantage of whatever hospitality offered itself.

Eustus had chosen to spend his two-day pass entirely with her.

Once outside the perimeter, Enya took them to an easy trot, leading Eustus into the woodlands that had once provided all the needs of her people. They rode on, paying no attention to time, but taking in the sights, smells, and sounds of what had to be one of the most beautiful worlds in the Confederation, if not in all the galaxy. They spoke in the language of those who knew they were in love, but had not yet confessed it to one another. Idle banter, mostly, that avoided hinting directly at what they felt inside. The day was warm, the air clear as it always had been for as long as any human had known, and both were having some of the happiest days of their lives.

At last, they came to Enya's favorite place, a small crystal lake, surrounded by majestic conifer-like trees that lay next to a sheer rock face that rose hundreds – perhaps thousands – of feet above them, its top hidden in a wreath of clouds.

"My father used to bring me here all the time," she explained as they dismounted and left the horses to graze in the hardy grass. Brought by Therese Ranier's settlers as pets, the horse had been their single greatest positive contribution to the lives of the Mallorys, who kept stock of their own in the forests beyond the Raniers' reach.

"Enya, this is absolutely fantastic," Eustus said in awe as he looked up at the rocky face. It soared up... and up... and up. Finally looking down into the water, he only saw the rock face again, this time reflected from the water's smooth surface, for there was no wind, not even the slightest breeze. "I've never seen anything like this in my life."

Enya smiled, taking his hand and leading him along the shore of the lake. "We were told as children that this is a magic place," she said as she plucked off her shoes so she could walk barefoot in the cool, wet sand along the water's edge. "Sometimes you can hear voices, my father used to tell me. I've heard them, too, singing in the rock. They always sound so sad."

Eustus looked at her skeptically. "Voices in the rock?" he said.

Enya smiled, tossing her head playfully, her silken hair brushing Eustus's shoulder. "I know it's only the wind moving through some kind of tunnels or something. But when you hear them... it... it doesn't sound like the wind at all. They sound like sirens in mourning, or maybe lamenting a lover's loss."

Eustus stopped, conscious of the warmth of her hand in his. "Sounds romantic," he said as she stepped close to him, her breasts brushing his tunic.

"Yes," she breathed, "it does, doesn't it?"

The kiss, when it came, was all that Eustus had anticipated, and more. They held each other for what seemed a long time, and when their lips finally parted, Enya silently led him by the hand to a bed of soft grass, pulling him down to lay on top of her.

"Are you sure...?" Eustus breathed between her increasingly passionate kisses.

"Stop procrastinating," she whispered in his ear just before her lips and teeth began to work their way down his neck, her hands unfastening the clasps of his uniform.

Eustus raised himself up enough to bring his fingers to bear on her blouse. Cursing his own clumsiness, he finally exposed her breasts and their erect nipples, and Enya sighed as his lips made contact.

They continued to wriggle out of their clothes like two butterflies, struggling to emerge from cocoons that were bound together, their frantic breathing echoing across the still water and the towering rock beyond.

"Ow!" Enya gasped, rolling over so quickly that Eustus toppled over onto his back beside her, his pants shoved down around his knees.

"What's wrong?" he asked, terrified that he had done something to hurt her. "Did I–"

"No, no," she said, shaking her head. A scowl on her face, she reached underneath herself with one hand, feeling around until she had found what she was looking for. She held up her hand to Eustus and smiled. "Just a dragon's claw."

"A what?" Eustus said, taking the object from her hand. It was the length of his index finger and really did look like a claw, curved and pointed, except that it was flat and completely black. The surface was fairly smooth but pitted, like a piece of rock or metal that had been sandblasted or weathered with age.

"A dragon's claw. People have found them all around here. Nobody knows exactly what they're made of. Some kind of weird rock, I guess. They're supposed to bring good luck." She paused as Eustus looked at the scythe-like piece of rock. "Do you feel lucky?" she whispered huskily, one of her hands stroking Eustus's flagging erection back to life.

"Yes, ma'am," he said, his eyes alight with renewed desire as he tossed the dragon's claw aside, "I surely do."

* * *

The warmth of the sun and the heat of their lovemaking made for two sleepy lovers, and Eustus had fetched the blanket Enya had brought. "For a picnic," she had told him. Now, lying awake on the soft flannel, Enya's head resting on his shoulder, his mind and heart skirmished over the future.

I've done my three required combat tours, he told himself. While that was not enough to retire from federal service, it was sufficient to get himself a posting to a non-combat position or Territorial Army assignment. He could stay here, he thought. With Enya. While he had only known her these two weeks, he felt as if he had known her all his life. He had known infatuation before, but never like this. He loved her, he admitted to himself. He had never really loved anyone before; there had never been time. But here...

Beside him was the crumpled heap that was his uniform, and the crimson dragon of the regimental insignia stared at him as if saying, "Traitor." The men and women of the company beside whom he had fought and lived, whom he had helped to survive and who had helped him – how could he simply walk away from them? They were not the riffraff they had once been. No matter what the raw material, they were the best Marines in the service. Reza had seen to that.

Reza. He almost groaned to himself. What of him? How could he turn his back on Reza? Deep inside, he knew that Reza would understand the burning in his heart, the desire to stay with this woman who was now a part of him. Eustus had served him well, and they had long been close friends; more than that, they had developed the bond that only those who live through times of extreme hardship know, the knowledge that they can rely on each other, no matter what.

But that only seemed to make things worse. Reza would go on and on, until finally he was alone. And alone he would die, with no one to watch over him, with no one to be there for him, to remind him that he was human and not the half-alien beast that so many believed he was.

His thoughts sinking to despair, he turned his head to look at the cliff that soared into the noon sky. A glint of light from the ground nearby caught his attention, and he reached out and retrieved the dragon's claw from where he had dropped it. Turning it over in his hand, he examined it closely in an effort to push thoughts of the future from his mind. One of his fingers slipped, rubbing across the curved edge of the "rock," and he saw a line of red appear on his finger.

Some lucky charm, he thought sourly as blood began to seep from the half-inch long wound that was like a huge paper cut. He set the rock down carefully, avoiding the edge on which he had cut himself, and sucked on his finger to get the bleeding to stop. He knew that rocks and minerals of various types could be sharp either naturally or with a little help from busy hands, but the dragon's claw Enya had given him seemed to have an extraordinarily good edge.

As he thought about it, checking his finger to see if the bleeding stopped, something about the dragon's claw nagged at him. There was something vaguely and disturbingly familiar about it, but he could not put his finger – which by now had stopped bleeding – on it.

One of the horses suddenly looked up from where it had been contentedly stuffing its face with grass, its ears pricked forward. The other one did the same. Both of them began snorting, their nostrils flaring and eyes widening in alarm.

Eustus had been with Reza long enough to trust his own instincts and those of others, especially animals.

"Enya," he said, rousing her from sleep, "wake up."

"What is it?" she said, her eyes snapping wide open. She was a deep sleeper, but when she woke up, she was fully awake almost instantly. She sat up beside Eustus, drawing the blanket up to cover her breasts.

"The horses are spooked," Eustus said quietly, reaching for the blaster that normally hung low on his thigh, but was now nestled in the pile of clothing beside him. The feel of the weapon, nearly as long and large around as his forearm, steadied and comforted him. No predator of the forest could survive its firepower. He raised his nude body into a wary crouch, his eyes scanning around them, a tingling sensation running up his spine as his scrotum contracted, drawing his testicles into a less exposed position. He looked at the horses. They were staring straight across the lake, their eyes fixed on the cliff. "Something over there is spooking them," he whispered, "but I can't see any–"

And then he heard it, a keening sound that appeared at the uppermost range of his hearing and slowly moved down the scale.

"The sirens," Enya whispered excitedly. "The horses heard them before we did."

Eustus's blood chilled at the sound as it evolved into a chorus of haunting voices that alternately boomed and whispered over the lake, the sound reverberating between the cliff and the trees around them.

"Jesus," he whispered, but the name of the Christian Savior was swept away on a melody of sadness and mourning that was like nothing he had ever heard. The song evolved into a complex harmony that would have been the envy of the most accomplished chorus, the notes washing over Eustus and Enya like gentle but urgent waves upon two tiny reefs.

And then, as rapidly as they had come, the voices ebbed away, their mournful song fading into notes so low that Eustus and Enya could no longer hear them. The two sat, transfixed, until they noticed that the horses had resumed their eating, the sound no longer audible even to their more sensitive ears.

Eustus swallowed, then sat back down, the strength drawn from him as if someone had sucked it out with a straw. The blaster slipped from his numbed hand to fall harmlessly onto the blanket.

"I told you," Enya whispered into the sudden silence as she pulled herself close to him, wrapping her arms around his chest. "Isn't it incredible?"

"That's hardly the word for it," Eustus said, wincing at the sound of his voice, as if it were an unworthy intrusion to his ears after what he had just heard. "Come to think of it, I don't think there is a word to describe it."

Enya nodded. "That's the third time I've heard it. The first was when I was nine. The last time was five years ago. And it's different every time, as if you're hearing different parts of the same song."

"Has anyone ever tried to find the caves or whatever it is that makes the sound?"

"People have tried to find the source for a long time," she said, "but I've never heard of anyone finding anything except little caves and such that didn't lead anywhere, and had no strange acoustic properties that would account for the sound."

He looked at her. "Care to do some exploring?"

She eyed him slyly. "Why? Haven't you done enough cave exploring for one day?"

He pulled her close and kissed her, feeling his body react to the warmth and softness of her skin, the smell of her body. "You're right," he said as he lay down, pulling her on top of him, her legs straddling his waist. "Maybe I should get some more experience here first."

"Excellent idea," she breathed as he slid inside her.

* * *

Eustus trailed behind her as she made her way along the rock ledge like a mountain goat. Extremely agile himself, the result of Reza's training more than any intrinsic ability on his part, he still felt clumsy as he watched her fluid movements.

"Watch your step here," she warned, pointing to a spot on the ledge that was crumbling. Enya easily stepped over it, seemingly oblivious to the fact that they were a hundred meters or more above the lake.

Eustus peered down quickly, then up, before he stepped over the crumbling part of the ledge. While it had looked sheer from their earlier vantage point, the cliff face had an undulating series of ledges that was almost like a secret staircase, wide enough to walk comfortably without turning sideways against the cliff.

"Are you sure that the place you saw was this far over?" Eustus asked, silently cursing himself for not bringing his binoculars so they could have gotten a better look at the mountain before they started up.

"Yes," Enya told him. After they had decided to abandon – temporarily, at least – their amorous pursuits, she had taken a good look at the cliff and noticed a dark spot where there should not have been one. Below it were streaks of dust and debris, as if part of the cliff face had sloughed off, revealing... what? "It shouldn't be much... Eustus!"

"What? What is it?"

"We found it," she said, her voice alive with childlike excitement. "It's a cave, just like I told you!"

Coming up behind her, Eustus saw it: a ragged opening that looked just big enough to crawl through. The ledge they were on, he saw, ran just to the edge of the hole. The rest of it had been taken down by the loosened rock that had fallen to expose the cave, and now lay somewhere under the lake's placid surface far below.

"Enya," he asked seriously, "do you think this is safe? I mean, whatever caused the rock to fall might happen again."

She paused a moment, considering. "They were doing some blasting at the MacCready mine not too long ago – that's on the far side of the mountain. I imagine that's what must have caused it. But Ian told me they weren't going to be doing any more explosives work for a while." She frowned to herself. *Unless Belisle betrays us,* she thought. "It should be fairly stable, as long as you don't go firing off your gun or something."

Eustus grinned. "I already did that."

She laughed, then began to move toward the cave entrance. Eustus, concentrating hard now, followed close behind her.

"Let me have your light," she said.

Out of long habit, Eustus carried a variety of essential items on his pistol belt everywhere he went when dressed in his combat uniform. His blaster, of course; but he also carried a handheld light, comm link, basic medical kit, and his combat knife. Unclipping the light from his belt, he handed it to her. "Be careful," he cautioned.

Nodding, she turned on the light and shone it as far as she could down the cave mouth. "Well, it's not just a pocket, anyway." She turned the light off and clipped it to her pants. Then, judging the distance carefully, she half stepped, half jumped from the end of the ledge into the low mouth of the cave.

Eustus followed quickly behind her, willing himself not to look down as he crossed the small gap. Enya took his arm and steadied him in the low opening. Crouching down, they made their way forward in a duck walk, Enya shining the light ahead of them. After a few meters of scrabbling over rough rock, they emerged into what seemed like a larger tunnel, big enough for them to stand upright with plenty of room to spare.

"Look at this," she said, shining the light around the tunnel. "This looks like it's been bored out."

Eustus looked back at the section that led outside. The walls there were much rougher and rocky, almost as if someone had pressed a cap of debris into the main tunnel. "Could it be an old mine that your people dug out some time ago?"

"And be covered over with rock like that?" Enya shook her head. "No. I know we could bore a hole up this high if we really wanted to, but it would be bigger than this. A lot bigger. Besides, the rock that was covering this up looked like part of the cliff, not just debris pushed back down the shaft. If that were the case, this cave would have been filled with rocks and dirt, but it's not. It's too clean."

"An airshaft?"

"With no opening to the outside?" She shook her head. "And it's so smooth." She knelt down and brushed away some of the dust on the floor. "It's almost like glass. Our boring machines are good, but nothing like this."

Eustus frowned. None of it made much sense. *It's almost as if someone had bored out the tunnel almost to the cliff face from the inside*, he thought. "Well, I guess there's only one way to find out what it is," he told her.

Enya leaned over and kissed him on the cheek. "I love a man with a sense of adventure," she told him.

Wondering what they were getting themselves into, he followed her into the cave.

"This is unbelievable," she said after they had gone about three hundred paces into the tunnel.

"This thing's as smooth and straight as a pipe," Eustus said quietly as he followed the slight downward angle of the floor. The echo inside was becoming increasingly eerie, and he had to fight back the urge to grab Enya and head back toward the rapidly fading light behind them. "Has any evidence been found of any other sentient races having lived on Erlang before your people arrived?"

She shook her head as she walked onward, following the white beam of light from the flashlight.

"No, nothing. People have looked, of course." She did not add that only the Raniers had had the time and money for archeological pursuits. "But only animal bones and such things have been discovered. No paintings, carvings, pottery, or any of that kind of thing, and certainly no tools or other signs of a sentient race."

Eustus frowned. His brain knew something, he could sense it, but he just could not quite make out what it was. *I've got all the pieces*, he thought, *I just can't put them together right*.

Something hard and sharp in his pants cargo pocket rubbed against his leg.

The dragon's claw.

A tunnel made neither by human hands, nor by nature.

The dragon's claw. A weird rock that was sharp enough to draw blood.

"Oh, my God," Eustus groaned as he shuddered to a stop, the hair on the back of his neck standing at stiff attention.

"What?"

"Give me the light, Enya!"

Her eyes wide with concern in the pitch darkness, she handed the tiny torch to him.

Grabbing it from her, he shone it on the dragon's claw he had carefully extracted from his pocket. "Oh, shit," he murmured. "I knew I'd seen this before."

"Eustus, it's just a rock," she told him with utter conviction.

He looked up at her, his face creased with fear, something she had never seen him show before. "No it's not, Enya. It's Kreelan metal, a blade from what Reza calls a *shrekka*, the most lethal blade weapon the Kreelans have. They can penetrate armor that'll stop a pulse rifle cold. You said these things have been found all around here?"

Enya nodded. "Yes. I mean, it's not like thousands have been found, or anything, but all the ones that I know of – probably a few dozen over the years – have been picked up around the valley outside. Eustus, are you sure?"

"Yes, I'm sure. Once you've been tagged by one of these, or seen someone else get hit with one, you don't soon forget. I would've recognized it sooner, except that it's in terrible condition, and the center hub is missing." He thought about that for a moment. "Enya, this thing must have been here for a long time. An incredibly long time. Kreelan blade steel is the toughest material known. It lasts forever and stands up to practically anything. Some metallurgists are even convinced that it's some kind of quasi-organic material, able to reshape itself, to maintain its edge and balance without any kind of sharpening." He looked at her. "We've never been able to duplicate or reforge it." He looked down at the blade he held gingerly in his hand.

"This thing must have been here for thousands of years." He looked up at her. "Maybe longer."

Enya was very quiet for a moment, until the eerie silence in the tunnel made her afraid not to speak, just so her ears could hear something. "So, you think this tunnel was made... by them?"

"That would seem to fit," he said quietly, turning the shrekka blade over in his hand.

"Then what is this place?" Enya asked. "And if there were Kreelans here at one time, where did they go? Why did they leave?"

"I don't know. But I guess nobody can say anymore that the Kreelans have never ventured beyond the Grange. Because they were here, all right. At least they were when our ancestors were still learning how to finger-paint on cave walls."

"Could... could they still be here... down there?" She tilted her head toward the darkness of the tunnel.

Eustus shook his head in the reflected light, but with less conviction than Enya would have liked to see. "If there had been any still alive here, I'm sure your predecessors would have met up with them. I've never known Kreelans to be particularly shy around humans."

"What should we do?"

"I think we should go back and get Reza. He's the only one who could make any sense of this, and–"

He broke off as Enya collapsed. Her hands covered her ears, her mouth open in a silent scream of pain. Even as he made a motion to help her, the sound erupted in his skull like an explosion, knocking him to his knees. The flashlight fell from his hand, went out as the switch hit the smooth rock, plunging them into darkness.

The voices had returned. The keening wail rapidly grew and multiplied into the chorus that he had heard outside, but in the tunnel it was so loud that his teeth rattled.

"Come on!" he screamed into the gale of sound, his words carried away as they left his lips. Staggering to his feet, he felt in the darkness for Enya, suddenly terrified that something had happened to her. But his desperately groping hands found her arm, and frantically he seized her and pulled her to her feet. Dazed and deafened by the sound that was now so powerful that it seemed to be jarring his insides loose, he ran through the tunnel, dragging Enya behind him, trusting his feet to guide him down the center of the curved floor, running toward the distant light.

The sound only grew stronger, until he was sure that his eardrums must burst.

"Not much farther!" he shouted to himself, even though he was unable to hear his own voice.

Suddenly, he stumbled and fell sprawling into thin air. "What–" he cried. The fall was not far, less than a meter, but the rock he fell upon struck him a stunning blow, and Enya landed right on top of him. The two of them lay there, dazed, as the voices ebbed and flowed, then slowly died away into silence.

After a few moments, he finally had enough strength to do more than hold his eyes open. "Enya?" he croaked. He was struck with surprise at being able to hear his own voice through the ringing in his ears. He thought he would be totally deaf.

"Here," came the muffled reply. She was lying beside him now, breathing steadily.

"Are you all right?"

"I think so," he managed. His head hurt like hell, he had a split and bleeding lip, and he might have twisted an ankle, but nothing was broken. "You?"

"I'm all right. But there are better ways of getting me to fall on top of you in the dark. Where are we?"

Now there was a good question, Eustus thought, smiling at her humor. She was tough. He liked that. "I don't know. I thought I was running toward the entrance. I could see a light. But... I guess I must have run the other way, deeper into the tunnel."

Pause. "You saw a light? At the far end?"

"Yeah. But now that I think about it, it wasn't the right color. Too cool, not yellow like the sun. Bluish, sort of." He found her face with his hands, held her to him. "I guess the tunnel just ended here... wherever here is."

"Where's the light?" she asked. She kissed his hands, glad they were both alive, but increasingly curious about where they were. *What was this place?*

"Dropped it in the tunnel. We should be able to find it on the way out."

Still trembling from the force of the voices – or whatever it was – that had struck them, Enya raised herself to her knees, trying to orient herself in the darkness.

But it was not completely dark. Somewhere in front of her, it was impossible to tell just how far, she could see a dim bluish glow like a smudge of watery blue paint on a black canvas. "Is that the light you saw?"

Eustus turned over so he could look where she was, orienting himself with her body. "That must be it, but it was a lot brighter when I saw it. It was a point of light, like a star, not like it is now."

"What could it be?"

"Some kind of fire, like methane burning? That burns with a blue color, doesn't it?"

Enya shook her head in the darkness. He felt her hair brush against his hand. "No, we should be able to distinguish the flame clearly. This looks like the light is being diffused, or something. I'm going to see what it is."

"Wait," Eustus said, digging into his utility pouch. "We don't have the light, but we can still get some light in here. I don't smoke, but this is too handy an item not to carry. Here, use this."

Enya heard a clicking sound, then saw Eustus's bruised face in the yellow light of the tiny flame of his cigarette lighter. Behind him, she saw something else. She pitched backward, screaming, her eyes wide with terror.

With reflexes honed through years of combat, Eustus drew his blaster, rolled in the direction of the threat, and fired three times. Only after the crimson energy bolts flashed from the weapon did he get a glimpse of what he was shooting at.

A Kreelan warrior.

He fired twice more for good effect before he noticed that there were others, all around him. His nerves jangling with dread, he reluctantly took his finger from the trigger. If they had wanted to kill him, he would have long since been dead.

"Give me the lighter," he said in a shaking voice, still holding his pistol at the ready. His nose filled with a strange odor from the work his blaster had done, but it was not the customary stench of charred meat. It was more like burned dirt or dust, with a tang of molten metal.

Enya reluctantly surrendered the tiny lighter, then scrambled to her feet, following Eustus as he stepped closer to the warrior he had killed.

They saw immediately, however, that she was already dead. Long dead.

"Lord of All," Enya whispered as she stepped around Eustus, kneeling beside what remained of the corpse. "It looks like a mummy."

The skin, where it showed through the extensive armor the Kreelans wore, was desiccated and shrunken over the bones. The eye sockets were empty, the silver-flecked orbs that had once filled them long since shriveled to nothing. The hair, still meticulously braided after all this time, clung tenaciously to the skull. The hands were skeletal, making the talons look all the more deadly.

"Let's look at that one," Eustus suggested, interested in examining a whole specimen. The one he had shot was missing its entire torso, and the smell, while not terrible, was very unsettling.

"Why are they still standing?" Enya asked quietly. As far as the light could reach, there were corpses standing at attention in what looked to be a circle, facing inward. Facing what? "Did someone somehow prop up the bodies?"

"From what I've seen, they were probably this way when they died," Eustus said. "I'm sure no one touched them after they were dead. Kreelan anatomy's a lot different than ours. It could be that their skeletal structure is more durable after they die, breaks down slower, maybe." *They sure seem that way on the battlefield*, he thought. "Besides, Reza told me once that the Kreelans remove the collars from their dead, kind of a last rites thing. These ladies still have their collars on."

"Except, my love, that these aren't ladies," Enya said.

"What? Of course they–"

"Look at the breastplates," she said, pointing to the dust-covered armor of the nearest intact warrior. The dark metal followed the contour of the massive rib cage that once must have supported a formidable mass of muscle, but the form was clearly that of a male. "No breasts there."

"Hold this," Eustus said, handing her the lighter, his heart pounding with excitement. Humans had never encountered a male Kreelan, even a dead one.

"What are you going to do?"

"Check this guy out," he said, taking his knife from its sheath and cutting away the armor from the mummy's waist. "I'll be damned," he breathed. "Will you look at that. This Kreelan has an honest-to-goodness mummified pecker. The Confederation Academy of Sciences is going to love this."

"What does it mean?" Enya felt slightly embarrassed, looking at the alien's exposed genitals, shriveled though they were. Remarkably similar to a human's, this one must have boasted a penis in life that would have been any man's envy.

"Well, for one thing, we might be able to figure out how the Kreelans reproduce and how often. Kind of give us an idea of the Empire's demographics, I suppose." He shrugged. "Hell, I don't know, except that it's something no one's ever seen before."

"After seeing what you've got, I'm not very interested in an alien mummy's privates," Enya said lightly. The knowledge that they had found a potentially very important piece of the answer to the puzzle posed by the enemy thrilled her beyond the fear that still nagged at her from being in this strange chamber.

"Yeah," Eustus quipped, "especially since mine's a first sergeant."

They both laughed, shedding some of their fear in the process. They were on an archeological dig now, not running for their lives from some unknown terror.

Now that they knew their would-be enemies were dead and crumbling with age, incapable of attacking them, Eustus held the light up and turned around slowly so they could see what else lay in the chamber. "Look at that," he said, pointing to what looked almost like a tapestry of Kreelan runes that ran from the chamber's floor to disappear in the darkness beyond the light's reach. "We've got to get Reza in here. He could read this for us."

"Eustus," Enya said, thinking aloud, "have you ever read much about Terran archeology?"

"No," he admitted.

"My father made me read things on every subject he could find a book on," she told him. "He had me read them to him aloud, because he wanted to learn, too, but he did not know how to read himself." *Another legacy of the Raniers*, she thought bitterly. "In one of those books," she went on, "there was something about the old Egyptians on Earth, and what they called the pyramids. That's where they buried their royalty, in big chambers inside the pyramid, usually with everything the priests thought the king or queen would need for the afterlife. Food, clothes, everything. And I think some of them even had soldiers, or replicas of soldiers, buried with them to protect them, or something. I can't remember it all anymore." Those days were a long time ago, before the police murdered her father during a "routine" interrogation.

"That's what you think this place is? Some kind of burial vault for royalty or something?"

"Well, it has the right feel to it. I mean, who – or what – would be important enough to the Kreelans that all these warriors would stand around it, guarding it, I guess, until they themselves died?"

"But then," he asked, "what happened to the others, the ones who brought these warriors here? There must have been some, right? And why did they leave?" He thought for a moment. "Wait a minute. Maybe not all of them did. If pieces of shrekkas were laying around, maybe there was some kind of battle here?"

"But then who are these people? The winners, or the losers? Or maybe someone else?"

"Who knows?" Eustus said. "But we haven't found your king's – or queen's – body, yet."

"Let's move toward the center of the room."

"Okay, but be careful."

With Enya still holding the light, the two of them slowly moved toward where the center of the chamber should be, at least according to the facing of the long dead Kreelan sentinels. There were a lot of them, probably hundreds.

"This room is really big," Enya whispered as they moved through the darkness to a point where nothing was visible around them but the floor, which had been inlaid with colored stones or tiles that had remained like new, polished and free of any trace of dust. The lighter's flame, tiny though it was, cast enough light that they could no longer see the blue glow that lay somewhere in front of them. "How long will this thing last?" she asked about the lighter.

"A few hours," Eustus said. "I fill it up every time I use it. It runs on some kind of high-tech..."

Enya did not have to ask why his sentence abruptly ended. It didn't matter, anyway. She would not have been paying attention. She had seen what had cast Eustus into sudden silence. "What is that?" she whispered.

Before them lay the treasure over which the ancient male warriors had been standing silent guard for countless centuries. Atop a spire of something resembling clear and slender glass sat what looked like nothing so much as an opaque crystal in the shape of some living thing's heart. And at its center shone a faint blue glow.

The two of them stood there for a moment, transfixed by what they saw, by the simple but undeniable elegance and beauty of the structure before them, which itself stood only as high as Eustus's shoulder. The crystal heart itself was a bit larger than a man's fist.

"This is where the light was coming from, then," Eustus said quietly as he moved closer. "The color's right, but it's so much weaker now. You can hardly see it at all."

Looking more closely at the glassine pillar on which the heart was poised, Enya said, "I don't know much about the Kreelans, but they must have incredible artisans. I'm not much of an art expert – Mallorys aren't even allowed in the few good museums here – but my personal opinion is that there was an incredible talent and genius behind whoever made this."

"So, this is our – what did they call them? – pharaoh, a piece of sculpted crystal with a blue glow in it. A radioactive isotope maybe?"

"Cherenkov radiation?"

"What kind of books did your father let you read, anyway?" Eustus asked, smiling. "I thought you were supposed to be a dumb miner or something. Cherenkov radiation... I don't know, maybe."

Enya stepped closer to the spire, the light now playing crazily through the glass. "What could it be?" she whispered to herself as she extended a hand toward the crystal heart.

"Enya," Eustus warned, "maybe you shouldn't–"

It was too late. As her fingers brushed the crystal's surface, Eustus's ears were filled with the crackle of electricity and his nose with the smell of ozone as the crystal heart suddenly pulsed with light, a blue flame so bright it left spots swirling in his vision.

"Enya!" he shouted, grabbing her by the shoulder and whirling her away from the crystal that had begun to pulsate erratically. "Are you all right? Answer me!"

She only trembled in his arms, as if she were in a state of shock. Her eyes were wide open, staring at the crystal, her lips trembling but mute.

Eustus half dragged, half carried her back toward the entrance. He noticed in the sudden explosion of light that there were six other tunnels leading down here. He was not confused as to which one to take because of the pile of smoldering bones that was the Kreelan warrior he had shot, whose shattered remains now served as a gruesome trail marker.

Behind him, the crystal heart began to pulse more rhythmically, and the light coming from it grew with every beat, so intense that Eustus did not need any other source of light as he frantically made his way down the tunnel.

Something is going to happen, his mind screamed at him. They had to get out...

"Eustus," he heard Enya rasp.

"I'm here," he told her as he propelled her along, ignoring the pain in his foot from when he twisted it entering the chamber. "We're getting out of here!"

His ears began to tingle, and he realized that the voices were coming again. And he suddenly realized what the sound really was: it was the voices of the warriors standing guard over that thing. Eustus did not believe in ghosts, but he knew with absolute certainty that what they had heard was not the sound of wind through caves, or anything artificial. Those dead mouths back there might not be moving, but that's where the sound originally came from. Where it came from now, he did not know, nor did he wish to find out.

The light continued to brighten, much faster now, and Eustus was almost blinded even facing away from it. Worse, he felt like his neck and arms were getting sunburned.

It's some kind of bomb, he thought suddenly. That only made him move faster.

The voices, when they finally came, were every bit as loud as before, but Eustus was ready for the pain, at least psychologically. What he was not ready for was the song itself. No longer a mournful dirge, the voices seemed to be elated, filled with joy at something that Eustus probably would never understand.

Behind him, even as the voices rose, he could hear the snapping and popping of flames as the mummies began to burn in whatever supernatural flame Enya's touch had sparked. He could hear the air crackle with heat, a wind rising in the tunnel as the heated air sought freedom outside, rushing up behind them like a frenzied locomotive.

"Eustus, what is it?" Enya cried. "What is happening?"

"I don't know," he screamed over the rising chorus of the dead warriors and the crackling hum growing behind him like a rapidly approaching storm. "Hang on!"

With a final leap, they hurled themselves into space, falling from the cliff face through the afternoon air toward the lake. They hit the water just as a stream of blue light, bright as any sun, exploded from the shaft and into space.

Far below, Eustus and Enya struggled toward the shore of the lake and sanctuary from the power of the alien beacon that now reached out toward the stars.

* * *

Reza stood in the company headquarters, thinking, waiting. Suddenly he felt a tingling at the base of his skull, unlike anything he had ever felt before. A warning?

"Alfonso..." he said to Zevon before getting to his feet and going to the door. Opening it and looking outside, he noticed nothing amiss. All was as it should be. Freeing his spirit, he searched around the encampment for any threat to his people, his mind's eye scouring every rock and tree.

"Sir?" Alfonso asked quietly, his rifle at the ready to protect his commander. He knew Reza probably did not need it, but that would not keep him from being prepared.

"I do not know," Reza said as he completed his mental sweep of the area. Nothing. But the tingling continued, grew stronger. "Something feels... wrong? Different? I am not sure."

Zevon scanned the area, as well. He happened to be looking at the enormous mesa a few kilometers away when seven streams of electric blue light erupted from it and shot through the sky.

"Captain! Look at that!" All around the bivouac, Marines were leaping to their fighting positions, regardless of what they had been doing.

But Reza did not hear him, nor did he see the blazing blue lances Zevon was frantically pointing out to him. He did not have to. At the instant the beams erupted from the ancient cavern, Reza felt as if a set of electrodes had been inserted into his brain and an invisible switch thrown.

Convulsing but a single time, Reza's eyes rolled up to expose the whites before he collapsed to the ground.

* * *

Eustus fought to keep his footing as Enya helped him run through the forest and Hell erupted behind them. He still couldn't believe they had managed to survive the fall from the blazing tunnel into the lake. They had struggled to shore and started running for their lives.

"Look!" she shouted above the roar of the cataclysm behind them.

Turning his head just enough to peer back through the canopy of smoldering trees, Eustus could see that the shaft of blue light behind them had changed its position. Sweeping slowly in a horizontal arc through the mountain, the beams – he could see others now, too, lancing toward the horizon – were slicing the rock apart, as if they were consuming the upper half of the mountain. Sheets of flame and rock, molten and vaporized to plasma, shot out and upward. The lake was now a boiling pit, the trees at its edge bursting into flame from the heat of the ash and rock that spewed from the disintegrating mountain. Beneath them, the ground shook with the force of an earthquake, the trees around them swaying precariously over their heads.

"Come on!" he shouted, pushing her forward, "We've got to get out of here!"

"Where are the horses?" she cried.

"Long gone, if they've got any brains at all. Run!"

They staggered onward, forcing steadily hotter air into their lungs. Eustus felt like the steam that was now roiling from the doomed lake was poaching them. Above them, he could hear the crackling of the treetops as they burst into flame. And everywhere was the rain of ash and glowing blobs of molten rock.

Behind them, the great beams continued to circle the mountain, faster now, grinding and burning it away to expose the pulsing core that Enya had somehow brought to life.

"Look out!" Enya screamed as she shoved Eustus aside, both of them toppling over a rock outcropping. A huge chunk of burning rock smashed to the ground where they had just been, burning a hole into the earth. "What are we going to do?"

Eustus didn't have a good answer. The smoke-filled air was so hot it was almost searing their lungs, and flaming debris was raining all around them. As slow as he was moving now, limping along on his injured ankle, they didn't stand a chance of escaping the fire.

"Enya," he pulled her close so she could hear him shouting, and also so that he could feel her next to him one more time, "I'm not going to make it. Can't run fast enough. You've got to go on alone, try to–"

"No! I'm not leaving you! We both go or we both stay!" The look in her eyes left no room for argument as her hands tightened in his.

He turned away, not wanting Enya to see the look of hopelessness on his face. He expected to die in the Corps, but he never thought it would be like this. And not with the woman he loved beside him.

He looked up to the sky, now so clouded with smoke and ash that the sun was no more than a dim disk in the darkness, searching for inspiration. Instead, he saw salvation.

"Look!" he shouted, pointing at the glinting metal shape that was rocketing toward them. "They've found us! They must've homed in on my comm link!" Eustus had tried to call the company and warn them of what was going on, but could hear nothing over the din crashing all around them.

Weaving through the flaming treetops, the hail of liquid rock spattering dangerously on its lightly armored sides, the "jeep" – one of a dozen light utility skimmers in the company – settled half a meter above the ground beside them, the troop door already open. Eustus saw a fully armed and armored figure with the name ZEVON stenciled on the helmet, frantically gesturing for him to get on board.

"Get in!" he shouted at Enya, who needed no further prompting. Zevon hoisted her aboard with one arm, his other still clutching his rifle, aiming it out beyond Eustus. With a grunt of effort, Eustus threw himself in after her, slamming the hatch shut just as a shotgun blast of debris hit the outside of the door.

"That was close, Top," Zevon said through gritted teeth as the jeep's pilot raced upward and away from the burning forest as fast as the little vehicle could take them. The debris outside sounded like hammers were being thrown at the skimmer, and Eustus's nose filled with the smell of charred clothes, skin, hair, trees, rock, and metal. "What the fuck – sorry ma'am – happened?" Zevon asked.

Eustus and Enya exchanged a strained look. "We don't really know," Eustus said as he took a long drink from the canteen Zevon handed him. He gave another to Enya.

"The Kreelans have been here," Enya told him. "It was a long time ago, probably hundreds or maybe even thousands of years. There was what looked like a tomb or something deep in the mountain." She cast her eyes down. "I think I touched something I shouldn't have."

"Yeah," Zevon said, looking worried, "looks like it."

"Back off, Zevon," Eustus warned. "It wasn't her fault."

"It doesn't matter to me, Top," the younger man replied. "But you two are going to have to explain to the XO why the company commander is in a coma."

"What the hell do you mean, he's in a coma?" Eustus demanded. "What happened to him?"

"He got some kind of funny feeling just before those beams lit off," Zevon explained. "Said he felt like something was wrong or different, but he didn't know what. We went outside to look. A minute later, all hell broke loose back there where you were, and the next thing I know the captain stiffens like someone hit him with a cattle prod, and he falls to the ground like a sack of potatoes." Zevon was silent for a moment. Reza had been like a father to him, and he was not able to deal with the situation as well as he would have liked. "The medtechs have been working on him, but all they know for sure is that he's in some kind of coma."

Eustus closed his eyes. "Sweet Jesus, what have we done?"

Enya leaned close against him, tears in her eyes.

"Eustus, I'm so sorry. It was stupid. I–"

He put a finger to her lips. "It wasn't your fault. There was no way for us to know. I should have dragged us out of there the instant we figured out it was Kreelan, and gone to get Reza."

The jeep emerged from the cloud of smoke and spiraled in to land at the Marine firebase, now fully alerted to a disaster the magnitude of which had yet to become apparent.

Thirty-One

Lieutenant Josef Weigand sipped at a cup of scalding, bitter coffee as he struggled to stay awake and alert.

Lord of All, he thought, *how I hate this job*. He almost laughed at himself. He thought the same thing at least a hundred times a day, but he had refused every opportunity to give it up.

He took a moment to look through his ship's forward viewport, giving his eyes a rest from scanning the battery of instruments that surrounded the command console, as if he would notice anything before the computer did. Outside lay a seemingly endless nebula of swirling gas and dust that danced to a rhythm measured in millennia, giving off light and radiation in brilliant displays that surely could have been the inspiration for Dante's *Inferno*. This was why he always decided to sign on for yet one more tour, one more mission as a scout: the bloody view.

Weigand was one of eight men and women crammed into a tiny ship that only had a number, SV1287, for a name. At least that is how she appeared on the Navy's ship registry. But to her crew, she was the *Obstinate*, a name that applied equally well to her maintenance and operation, as to her defiance in the face of the enemy.

Defiance, however, was not the mission of *Obstinate's* crew. A scoutship, she was a specialist in the fleet, packed with every passive scanning instrument her tiny hull could accommodate. Her unarmored skin bristled with dozens of telescopes and antenna arrays to pick up the faintest trace of the enemy without betraying her own position. She carried no weapons, and the only time she activated any radiating sensors or shields was when she was in friendly space or in the direst emergency. Her job was to watch and listen, but to be neither seen nor heard herself. The only contact she had with human space was through the secure tight-beam communications gear she used to communicate with the STARNET intelligence network and fleet command.

Another benefit of scout work, Weigand thought wryly as he refocused his attention on the signal monitors. There was no brass to worry about, no additional duties to drive a junior officer crazy, no ass-kissing. Nothing but him, his little crew, his ship, and the stars. And if the Kreelans wanted to find him... well, they'd have to catch him first. *Obstinate* was one of the fastest ships in the human fleet, and with her big ears and eyes, she would know long in advance about any Kreelan ship coming her way.

He heard a few muffled moans coming from the back and smiled. Stankovic and Wallers again, he figured. With eight people crammed into a tiny tin can for three to six months at a time, some allowance had to be made for romance. Or outright lust. Whatever. At least that's the way Weigand looked at it. As long as things didn't get out of hand and jeopardize their mission – which he did, in the end, take seriously – he let nature take its course. Personally, he preferred to remain celibate while on patrol, not out of any lip service to some mythical superior morality, but because it was simply too complicated. People who thought they loved one another or just wanted to play grab-ass one day all too often hated each other the next, and the last thing a scoutship commander needed was an overly neurotic crew. And the crew could not afford a commander who was a few newtons shy of full thrust mentally, or involved in some emotional skirmish with one or more crewmembers. The possibilities for disaster were simply too great out here, all alone. Among the crew, he had his ways of straightening things out, just as long as he didn't get involved himself.

No, Weigand preferred looking out the viewport to wrestling under the covers, at least until port call and the mandatory month-long crew stand-down. With a sigh, he chose to exercise his only viable option: he would have to make do with the ship's coffee. It was a poor trade for months without sex and a decent drink, but there was nothing to be done about it.

More moans, louder this time. *Buddha*, he thought, *didn't these kids ever sleep?*

Then he heard the thunk of a boot against a bulkhead panel and another voice admonishing the young lovers to keep it down in language that was far from romantic.

Here we go again, Weigand thought. The other seven members of *Obstinate's* crew were all in the crew section, trying to sleep – or whatever – through the transition shift. Weigand preferred to have his little crew rotate shift partners periodically, to keep anyone from either getting too attached or too hateful of any one person. The transition shift was when he made them all eat, sleep, and crap on the same schedule for twenty-four hours until the new cycle came up and they switched partners. He took the twenty-four hour duty himself, while the crew battled it out in back. It was his favorite part of the cruise: he got to be alone for a whole day, to sit and watch over the computer as it sniffed through the thousands of cubic light years around them for traces of the enemy.

He glanced at the main intel display, which presented the computer's slow-witted human controllers with an easily assimilated visual representation of the space around them, and whatever it had found within it. Scouting was a lot like fishing, he thought, checking out each fishing hole in turn to see if you got a bite. He had been on some missions where they had not spotted a single Kreelan ship or outpost in three months. Other times, they had to extend the tour weeks on end to wait out Kreelan warships that prowled the scout's patrol area. But most patrols were somewhere in between, with Kreelan activity present in some spots, and absent at others.

In this case, a few light years into the QS-385 sector – a quaint name for a zone of space that no one otherwise cared about, far beyond even the human-settled Rim colonies – Josef Weigand the interstellar fisherman had gotten more than a nibble. After jumping into the nebular cloud to conceal her arrival, *Obstinate's* sensors had immediately picked up three separate sets of Kreelan activity, all within a radius of about fifty light years. Two were clearly warship flotillas by their rapid movement across the sector, apparently en route to the third, which appeared to be some kind of outpost or settlement with vessels already in orbit. This was the kind of find that the crews of other ships like the *Obstinate* hoped to discover. Fleet command was keen to go on the offensive somewhere – anywhere – in hopes of drawing the Kreelans away from human settlements, following the maxim that a good defense comprised a good offense. With that in mind, "indigenous" Kreelan outposts such as this one were at the top of the list. Several such worlds had been found, but most were too far away or too well-defended (as far as the scoutships could determine) to be attacked without taking too much from defensive campaigns on human-settled worlds that already stretched Navy and Marine resources to the limit.

From the looks of it, Weigand thought dejectedly, this world fell into the same category. While the computer had only been able to identify three of the dozen or more ships out there by class, what it told Weigand was depressing: they were all dreadnoughts. Battleships, and big ones, too. Even if a human fleet could get here, he told himself, they would have a hell of a fight ahead of them before the jarheads even hit dirt.

He watched another display in silence as the computer busily worked away at identifying the remaining ships, comparing their signatures with known Kreelan ship profiles and playing an extraordinarily complicated guessing game for those that did not fit. Unfortunately for Confederation Navy analysts, the Kreelans did not build their ships in classes – each comprising one or more ships of similar construction and characteristics – like the humans did. It was as if they hand-built every ship from scratch, tailoring it to serve some unknown purpose in an equally mysterious master plan. Some tiny ships carried a tremendous punch, while a few of the larger ones were practically defenseless. And so, the analyst who needed to categorize the Kreelan ships as something settled for a generalization: fighter, corvette, destroyer, cruiser, battleship, super-battleship, and so on. The only advantage to their ships being unique, of course, was that once identified, they could be tracked just as men in ships and submarines on long-ago Earth had tracked one another, using the unique sonic signature produced by each vessel.

None of these ships, however, matched any of the thousands of entries in the computer's database. *More depressing news*, Weigand thought. *More ships we've never even seen before. More ships to fight.*

The display flashed three times to alert him that it had completed another identification, showing him everything it had determined about the ship and its postulated class.

"Oh, great," he murmured. "A super-battleship this time. Isn't that special." That made it two battleships identified in one flotilla, plus another battleship and this super-battleship in the second. He pitied the human squadron that ever had the misfortune of running into either of these groups. And the Lord of All only knew what was in the squadron orbiting the outpost.

"Well," he said, reluctantly setting down his coffee in the special holder someone had glued to the console, "I guess it's time to phone home and tell mommy and daddy the bad news." Super-battleship sightings qualified for immediate reporting, regardless of where they were or what other activity was going on. Short of invasion alerts, they were the Navy's highest priority.

He was just calling up the STARNET link when an audible alarm went off.

"Warning," the computer said urgently in the sultry female voice Weigand had programmed in, "radical change in profile for targets Alpha, Bravo, and Charlie. Vector analysis initiated."

Weigand ignored the flashing STARNET access screen, alerting him to the fact that he was accessing a controlled military intelligence link, and that any unauthorized use could result in fines, imprisonment, or both. "Highlight profile changes," he snapped.

The main holo display split into three smaller holos, each zoomed in on one of the three Kreelan targets. "Targets Alpha and Bravo" – the two maneuvering flotillas with the battlewagons – "are executing near-simultaneous course changes toward a similar navigation vector. A new maneuvering target is separating from target Charlie; designating new target Delta. Target Delta is accelerating rapidly along a similar vector as Alpha and Bravo."

Weigand watched as the two designated flotillas hauled themselves around in what he could see was more than a casual maneuver: the ships were cutting the tightest circle in space that they could. The third flotilla, coming out of orbit, was accelerating at what must be full thrust to get far enough away from the planet's gravity well to jump into hyperspace.

"Warning," the computer bleated again, "Targets Alpha and Bravo have executed hyperspace jump. Calculated time for target Delta is thirty-six seconds."

Those ships were going somewhere and fast, Weigand thought. He hit the ship's alert klaxon. Stankovic and Wallers would have to finish their little party some other time.

"Crew to general quarters!" he snapped over the intercom.

Golda, his exec, was in the seat next to his before the klaxon finished its third beat and automatically switched off. There was no need for big-ship sounds in a scoutship. "What's going on, Josef?" she asked as she strapped in and scanned her console.

"Alpha and Bravo just hauled around to similar vectors and jumped," he told her as he started the computer feeding information to STARNET while he began composing a manual report for the intel types on the other end. "A new crowd came zipping out of orbit–"

"Target Delta has jumped into hyperspace," the computer said, "at time nineteen thirty-seven-oh-four Zulu."

"Computer," Golda said, ignoring the bustle of the other six people on board who were now cramming themselves into their respective positions throughout the tiny vessel, "can you project navigation vectors to potential targets?" Unlike in "real" space, where a ship could alter course at will, in hyperspace it was restricted to linear motion along its last vector until it dropped back into the Einsteinian universe. That being the case, the ship's vector just before it jumped could be used to plot potential destinations. Of course, there was always the chance the ship would drop out of hyperspace somewhere, maneuver onto a different vector, and jump again in a completely different direction.

"The only human target along projected axials for all three target groups is Erlang, trans-Grange Sector," the computer said immediately.

"What's on Erlang?" Weigand asked as he watched the computer pump information into the STARNET buffer before it was sent in a subspace burst to a receiver many light years away.

"Population one point five million. Terran sister world. Responsible for seventy-five percent of strategic minerals and metals for trans-Grange shipyards."

He and Golda shared a glance. "Estimate the probability of Erlang vector being initial course only, and not the final destination."

The computer was silent for a moment. "Probability is non-zero."

"What the hell is that supposed to mean?" Golda asked.

Before the computer could reply with its own explanation, Weigand said, "It means that whoever's on Erlang is going to be hip-deep in shit."

* * *

Those were the same sentiments of the young Marine STARNET watch officer. Buried in the special STARNET processing and analysis center two kilometers beneath the surface of Earth's moon, she glowered at the reports from three different scoutships. They were in far flung regions that read the same except for numbers and types of ships: a massive Kreelan battle fleet, probably the largest ever seen during the entire war, was headed for Erlang.

"Send a FLASH to Tenth Fleet," she ordered the yeoman sitting at the fleet communications station, "and get confirmation that they have this information."

While the analysts behind her were busy piecing together what information they had, she turned to her own console and hit a particular button. After a moment when all her screen said was "Call in Progress: Line Secure," a bleary-eyed but alert face finally appeared.

"Admiral Zhukovski," she said, "STARNET is declaring an impending invasion alert for Erlang, in the Trans-Grange sector."

A man all too used to these calls in the middle of the night, Zhukovski's expression hardened, a reflection of his soul as it readied itself for more bad news, the announcement that yet more human lives were about to be lost.

"Brief me, captain," was all he said before he sat back, his good eye fixed on her image as he listened to her report, his good hand clenched tightly out of view of the monitor.

Thirty-Two

Enya sat quietly in the semi-darkness of the hastily completed command bunker, shielded from the ops section by a blanket hung over a cord strung between two walls. She was maintaining a vigil over Reza. Three days after she had touched the crystal and started the mysterious reaction, Reza still lay unconscious. His heart beat very slowly, his breathing slower still. In fact, were it not for the sophisticated medical instruments available to the company medics, they probably would have thought him dead.

In the meantime, the rain of ash from the disintegrating mountain had finally stopped, most of it consumed by the cutting beams originating in the center of the mountain. Finally spinning so fast that the beams became a nearly solid disk of energy, they began to sweep upward, forming a rapidly narrowing cone of brilliant cyan that quickly destroyed what was left of the mountain. They swept the debris up and away into the upper reaches of the atmosphere where it formed a cloud that easily rivaled the one on Earth after the explosion of Krakatoa centuries before. The area around the mountain had experienced horrendous winds that had done much damage to Mallory city and the nearby townships. But those, too, had finally subsided, leaving amazingly few casualties in their wake. After the beams had done their work clearing away the mountain top, they also disappeared, leaving behind a perfectly smooth bowl, a gigantic crater, that now radiated a ghostly blue glow, much less intense than the cutting beams, from its center into the dark heavens above.

"Any change?" Hawthorne asked quietly.

Enya shook her head. They had kept Reza here in the company firebase instead of moving him to the hospital in Mallory City mainly because Washington Hawthorne seemed to trust Belisle even less than the Mallorys did. Besides, Hawthorne had figured that it would not make any difference. A Mallory General Hospital neuro specialist had come and examined Reza, but could not make heads or tails of his vital signs and the basic changes in his physiology that had been wrought in the Empire. He wanted to run a quartermaster's list of tests on him, but Hawthorne had politely refused and thanked the man for his time. He knew that the tests would only help satisfy the surgeon's curiosity, and not help Reza to recover.

"No," she said quietly, shaking her head dejectedly, "no change yet." They had assured her that this was not her fault, but it was. If only she had not touched that... thing.

Washington put a massive hand lightly on her shoulder. "Don't worry," he said. "Reza's a tough bastard. He's breathing. He'll be okay."

"Oh, Mister Hawthorne," she asked, "what have I done? What is that thing out there?"

"Your guess is as good as mine, probably better, because you seem to know something about most anything, or so Eustus tells me." He smiled to make sure she knew it was intended as a compliment, and not sarcasm. She only managed a weak parody of a smile in return. "Look, why don't we take a break and get some coffee? Eustus'll be back pretty soon from checking on Counselor Savitch in the city, and I'd feel awful bad if he had to see you like this."

"Thank you, but–"

"Enya, give it a rest. You can't take the whole universe on your shoulders. Please, trust me. He'll be all right. Erlang will be all right. I promise."

She knew that he could not possibly keep such a promise, but his saying it seemed, for now, enough. "All right. I'll take you up on it. But only if you find me some tea; your coffee is terrible."

Hawthorne laughed quietly as he followed her out of the tiny cubicle and into the red and green glows of the equipment in the ops section.

* * *

"What is thy name, child?" a voice softly asked from somewhere near, somewhere far away, speaking in the Old Tongue.

"Reza," he said, wondering if he had somehow been blinded by whatever had struck him. All around him was darkness, cold. And then he realized he had no eyes. No body. He floated in Nothingness, a spirit without form. "Where am I?" he asked, strangely unafraid. *Thus has Death come*, he thought.

"You are... here," the voice said. "You are with Me."

"Who are you?" He could sense the spirit that spoke to him as his feet sensed the earth: he could judge only that it was there, but not how great it might be.

"I am She," the voice began with a flare of pride and power before it faltered. "I am... Keel-Tath." Reza sensed time beyond his understanding in the brief pause that followed, time that spanned millennia. "Long has it been, my child. Long have I waited for you, for The One."

Reza felt a spark of excitement, a tremor of fear. *The One, who was to fulfill The Prophecy*. "Keel-Tath," he thought/spoke Her name in awe.

"Yes," She said. "Yes, that is – was – my name before the Ascension, before... the Darkness." He felt Her touch as might two clouds brushing against one another in the sky, their forms distinct, yet one. "Lonely have I been, My child, waiting for you to come, to awaken Me, with only the songs of the Guardians to keep Me company here, in this place of mourning." Her spirit shimmered against him, a touch of leather, a touch of silk. Power. Curiosity. Love. Sadness. "But that time is past," She said, Her spirit brightening as the sunrise over a tranquil sea. "You and I shall become as One, and all shall be forgiven."

"My Empress," Reza whispered, his spirit electrified by Her touch, and terrified of revealing the truth to Her, "I am not the vessel to bring you forth once again into the world."

Curiosity again, so intense that he shrank back in fear, but there was nowhere for him to retreat to, for She was everywhere, everything; She was the Universe itself. "You were not born of My womb, yet you are of My blood," She said as the eyes of Her spirit probed to his very core, all that he was and was not laid bare before Her inquisitive gaze. "You wear the collar of My honor, yet you are shunned by the peers. You are of the Way, yet you are apart, lost to the love of She-Who-Followed... and to She-Who-Shall-Come. A warrior priest of the Desh-Ka, the greatest order that ever was, that ever shall be, and who never again shall see his temple. You are The One, child."

He felt her curiosity continue to swarm over him like a mass of inquisitive insects, hovering, darting, drawing out all that lay within his heart, his mind. He cried out in fear and pain, anguish and rage at what could have been, but would never be. He begged for Her to hold him, to comfort him against the pain. He begged for Her to destroy him, to cast him into the pit of Oblivion and the darkness of the damned.

At last Her curiosity was satisfied, for She knew of him all there was to know. "Child," she said, enfolding him in warmth, "you need not fear My wrath, for your heart and courage are worthy of My love, and the lonely melody of thy blood is joy to My ears, a song that shall forever live in My heart. I know the measure of thy Way, and that the time of My return draws near. You are The One who shall redeem the sins of others, and who in turn shall return to grace."

She held him in Her heart that he would know Her love, and told him, "Do not fear the Darkness, My child. For while in this lonely place My eyes are blind to what is, to what will be, there shall come a day when I again will open My eyes to the light of the sun of the world of My birth, and smell the scents of the garden of the great palace that was built in My name. And on that day, My son, shall you be saved."

Reza would have spoken then, but She held him, stilled him. "Until that day, you must live according to the Way you have chosen, for the glory and honor of She-Who-Reigns."

She withdrew from around him, fading into the Nothingness from which She had come, into the voices of those whose spirits had comforted Her mourning heart through the ages. "Rise, My child," she commanded from afar. "Awaken."

Thirty-Three

"President Belisle, I demand an explanation." Counselor Savitch was more than furious. She was outraged.

"I'll be honest with you, counselor," Belisle said, a sneer on his face as he looked out the closed French doors onto the still ash-covered balcony of his parliament office. The two of them were alone. Despite their protests, Savitch and Belisle both had insisted that her Marine bodyguards remain outside the door. "Your coming here was, shall we say, an unpleasant surprise," he told her. "I had asked the Council for Marines to help the cowards in the Territorial Army keep the Mallorys in their place, but no one ever counted on getting a half-breed traitor like Reza Gard and that motley band of thugs in Marine uniforms." He grimaced. "That was a mistake that no one was able to foresee."

Melissa Savitch shivered at the hatred in the man's voice, wondering what anyone could ever have done to him to make him so completely devoid of compassion toward a fellow human soul. *But he didn't think of Reza as human, did he?* she thought.

"Yes," he went on, almost as if to himself, "he really took me by surprise, and calling you in made it a damned bleeding liberal party." He turned from the glass doors to face her, a sly, serpentine smile on his face. "But that's all in the past, let me assure you."

"Just what is that supposed to mean?"

"It means, counselor, that your services are no longer required," a new voice said. Behind her, the door to one of the three anterooms adjoining Belisle's office had opened, and a Marine whom she had never seen before silently stepped into the room.

"I'd like you to meet Colonel Markus Thorella, commander of the First Guards Marine Assault Regiment," Belisle said as he began backing away from her.

She was about to say something when her eyes caught sight of the dark metal shape in Thorella's hand.

"Sorry, counselor," he said. His voice did not sound particularly apologetic.

Thorella's predatory smile was the last thing she saw before the blast from his pistol vaporized her skull.

* * *

"Sir!" shouted the comms technician from her console. "We've got trouble!"

"What now?" Washington Hawthorne growled, covering the distance to the lance corporal's position in three great strides.

"Sergeant Bayern radioed 'Black Watch,' then she went off the air," the comms tech said as her fingers flew over the console's controls. "I haven't been able to raise her again. No contact with PFC Morita, either."

Hawthorne's face grew tight, his fists clenching tight. "She didn't get out what it was?"

"No sir," the comms tech told him. "But I heard what sounded like firing, pulse guns." She paused. "Two shots. I think Bayern was already hit when she called in."

Hawthorne's blood ran cold with anger. "Goddamn," he hissed.

"What happened?" Enya asked quietly, afraid of what she might hear. "What is 'Black Watch?'"

Hawthorne turned to her, his eyes angry white orbs in his black face. "That's a shorthand code for what we call a losing proposition, when Death has you by the collar and you've only got time to get out a word or two. Two Marines, and probably Counselor Savitch, are gone. Dead."

"My Lord," Enya whispered, getting unsteadily to her feet. "Why? What could have happened?"

Hawthorne turned on her, his voice savage not because he wanted it to be, but because he needed the truth, and fast. "Were any of the Mallorys planning anything against Belisle or Savitch? Anything?"

Enya shook her head, shocked that he would even consider such a thing. "Of course not," she said angrily, her own fears boiling up inside. "We had everything to gain from the Counselor's intervention, and literally nothing to lose. None of the Mallorys, even the farthest fringes, planned anything but cooperation with her. We did not trust Belisle – as I see now was wise – but we were not planning anything against him. We have suffered too much and waited too long for what the counselor promised to deliver. Only now it looks as though it was all in vain."

Hawthorne nodded, relieved. "I'm sorry Enya, but I had to know."

She nodded that she understood. "What will you do?" she asked.

"I'm not sure yet," he said, uncomfortable with the situation. His choices were extremely limited. It had been bad enough sitting a few kilometers from some kind of Kreelan-induced cataclysm, the full effects of which they could not even guess at. Now he had to deal with what appeared to be treachery and murder on the part of fellow humans. "It looks like we'll have to send a recon patrol in to find Savitch, but–"

"Reza!" Enya suddenly exclaimed as she saw the Marine captain emerge from behind the curtain that separated his sick-bed from the ops center. His face was extraordinarily pale, even in this dim light. She ran over to help him as he began to slump against the wall. Hawthorne was close behind. "You should be in bed!" Enya told him as she helped him up. "You look terrible."

He shook his head, a look of impatience on his face.

"Captain," Hawthorne said as he took over from Enya in helping Reza, wrapping one tree-trunk of an arm around his commander's waist.

"Washington," he rasped as his exec settled him onto one of the metal chairs clustered around the tactical display, "we are in grave, grave danger."

"What do you mean, sir?" Hawthorne handed Reza a canteen, from which Reza drank greedily. He was soaked with sweat, dehydrated.

"First, tell me exactly what happened when I passed out."

Hawthorne turned to Enya, who guiltily explained everything that had happened in the mountain and since then. Reza listened in silence, his eyes focused on the wall, on something only he could see.

"What does it mean?" she asked when she was through. "What will happen to us? To Erlang?"

"Very likely," Reza said, "this world will be destroyed." They sat in stunned silence as he went on. "You have stumbled upon something that has been lost to the Empire for over one hundred thousand years, something that they value over all else in the Universe: the tomb of the First Empress. She was the most powerful of their kind who has ever lived." He paused for a moment, taking another drink. "I have no doubt that every available Kreelan warship within hundreds of parsecs is heading here at this very moment."

"Can we capture or destroy it?" Washington asked, groping for some kind of leverage, something he could fight the enemy with when they came. "Maybe even take it hostage?"

Reza shook his head. "You cannot take a spirit hostage, nor can it be captured or destroyed." He nodded toward the wall display that showed a panorama of the outside and the glowing bowl that once had been a mountain, and was now only a reflector of the crystal heart's mysterious aura. "Anyone or anything who is not of the Blood and ventures into that light will perish as surely as if they had set foot upon the face of a star."

"And if you think that's good news," Hawthorne said grimly, "you're going to love this..." He told Reza about what had happened to Bayern and Morita, and his suspicions that Savitch was dead.

Eustus suddenly appeared through the tunnel entrance to the bunker, his back soaked with sweat: the air conditioner in his skimmer was not working.

"Reza!" he blurted. His eyes were wide with relief that his friend and commanding officer was alive. But his enthusiasm dimmed when he saw the look on everyone's face. It was the expression of the Damned. "What's wrong? What the hell is going on?"

"Eustus," Enya said, coming to embrace him openly in front of his fellow Marines, something she had promised him she would never do, "I fear I have killed us all."

"What–" He never got a chance to finish.

"Captain," the corporal at the comms console interrupted, her face ashen, but for a different reason, "Sir, I think you'd better come over here."

Reza did as she asked, walking unsteadily the two meters to her position. "Yes, corporal?"

"It's a call for you, sir," she said, stepping away from the terminal.

And there on the visual display was the grinning face of Colonel Markus Thorella.

"Well, well, well," he said, "if it isn't my favorite captain." The smile grew wider, more menacing. "It's been a long time, Gard."

Reza's blood trilled with fury at the man's face, Belisle just visible behind him: the mysterious deaths of his two Marines had just been explained.

* * *

The two men glared at one another for a long time, Reza struggling to restrain the fire in his blood, Thorella smiling with unconcealed smugness.

"What did you do to my Marines?" Reza asked in a voice as cold and empty as the depths of space.

"I was just going to ask you about that, captain," Colonel Thorella said conversationally. "It would appear that the civil authority here," he nodded to Belisle, "seems to think they got a little out of hand. What was it you said, Mr. President?" he asked rhetorically. "Ah, yes. Murdering Counselor Savitch. I'm afraid my troops and I weren't quite fast enough to keep *your* troops from committing that heinous crime, but we were able to prevent Erlang's lawful president from coming to harm." His smile became the hard-mouthed frown Reza had learned to be wary of during his time on Quantico. "And then there's this fascinating incident with the mountain, or what's left of it. I'm afraid you've got some explaining to do, captain."

"And what of the Mallorys in the Parliament Building?" Enya blurted out from behind Reza.

"Ah," Thorella said brightly. "You must be the young and witty Enya Terragion. I'm terribly sorry, my dear, but your friends have been arrested as accomplices to murder. Even as we speak, the rest of your illegal council is being arrested. But don't worry. We'll be by soon enough to take care of you, too." He turned his attention back to Reza, who stood shivering with rage. "And you, captain, should not have been so stupid as to try and be the great righter of perceived wrongs," he said as if he were speaking to a child who had done something wrong, but who should have known better. "You were foolish to the last, and now you're going to pay the price. Hawthorne!"

"Sir," the big man said, reluctantly moving toward the screen. He knew what was coming.

"So nice to see you again, Hawthorne. It's too bad you didn't choose another regiment, though. You might have one day made a good regimental commander. As it is, you'll go no higher than your friend." To whom he turned his attention once again. "Captain Gard, as senior Marine officer on Erlang, I hereby relieve you of your command. Hawthorne, you are now in command of your company. Do you understand me?"

"Yes, sir," he rasped, his eyes narrowed to angry slits.

"That's good, because I have orders for you. First, you are to place Captain Gard and Enya Terragion under arrest and confine them until representatives of my regiment pick them up for holding pending court-marital for the captain and civil arraignment for Ms. Terragion on charges of conspiracy to commit murder. Second, you will order your company to stand down and prepare for immediate transport off-planet, as per President Belisle's fervent wishes. You've done enough damage here already. We don't need any more. Is all of that crystal clear, captain?"

"Yes, sir."

"Good. Carry on." And the screen went blank.

It was a long time before anyone said anything. It was Enya who spoke first.

"Reza," she whispered, placing a hand on his still-shaking arm. "I am so sorry."

"That murdering bastard," Eustus spat at where Thorella's image was no more than a memory. "Can't we send a message to Fleet?"

"And say what?" Reza asked quietly. "Whom do you think they will believe? A captain raised by their enemies, a man who is largely hated by his own kind, or a regimental commander of excellent standing who obviously has tremendous political force behind him?" He shook his head. "No, my friends, there will be no help from outside. But we are overlooking the real problem."

"What's that?" Hawthorne asked.

"The Kreelans," Reza replied. "They are on their way."

* * *

"I can't believe they will cooperate so easily," Belisle said after Hawthorne had radioed back that Thorella's orders had been obeyed. "That bunch is like a cult of personality focused on Gard. They won't give him up so easily."

Thorella smiled and waved his hand dismissively. "My dear president, don't be so apprehensive. I hate that half-breed traitor with all my heart, but I do have to admit that he does have a sense of honor, to a fault. He realizes that he's in a box, and the only way his company can get out unscathed is if he cooperates."

"You're going to just let them go, then?"

"Of course not. But their cooperation will simplify their demise. One assault boat can hold all their personnel. We'll have them leave the vehicles and heavy equipment behind, as I'm sure the Territorial Army could always use it." He shrugged as he stepped on a spot of blood that had once belonged to Counselor Savitch, the coagulated liquid having penetrated deep into the office's huge genuine Persian rug. "I hate to lose a boat and the flight crew, but it's a price I'm willing to pay."

Belisle nodded, satisfied. He liked this man, and was beginning to think that he might just request Borge to have Thorella posted here permanently.

"Now," the colonel mused as he stepped toward the glass doors that looked out onto the glowing crater, "we'll just have to find out about this little puzzle, too, won't we?"

* * *

"They're here." Eustus turned away from the tactical display, his face pale and drawn. Outside, the skimmer from Thorella's regiment that had come for Reza and Enya had just touched down.

Reza emerged from behind the blanket that served as a door to his impromptu quarters. Enya, who had been sitting beside Eustus while they waited, not holding hands but wanting to, gasped.

The Marine uniform was gone. In its place he wore his Kreelan ceremonial armor, the great rune of the Desh-Ka a flame of cyan on the black breast plate. The talons of his gauntlets gleamed blood red, reflecting the crimson light of the tactical display. The great sword given him by Pan'ne-Sharakh was sheathed at his back, and at his waist hung the short sword Tesh-Dar had entrusted to him, along with the most valued of all his possessions, the dagger that had been his gift from Esah-Zhurah. On his upper left arm clung three shrekkas like lethal spiders.

"Do not be frightened," he said in a voice that none of them had ever truly heard before. It was not the voice of a company commander. It was the voice of a king.

"Why... why are you dressed like that?" she asked. He looked exactly as the warriors in the tomb must have before they died. She shivered involuntarily.

Reza smiled thinly. "I have worn the Marine uniform with honor for years," he told her. "I will not wear it while I am under suspicion of such acts as I have been accused, for that would be to disgrace all who wear it honorably." He looked at the others. "Thorella has always treated me as the enemy, as a Kreelan warrior. I do not wish to disappoint him."

"Isn't there anything we can do, Reza?" Hawthorne asked quietly as the command post guard shouted that Thorella's people were waiting.

Reza turned to him. "Get our people off this planet if you can, my friend. But do not trust Thorella. He will try to destroy all of us to eliminate the evidence pointing to his crimes."

"What about Enya?" Eustus asked, in a way ashamed of his concern for her when he had an entire company of his own people to look after. But he could not help it any more than he could still his own heart.

Reza put a hand on his shoulder. "I swear that no harm shall come to her from Thorella's hand, my friend. I cannot make the same promise for when the Kreelans come, but Thorella shall not harm her."

"And what of my people?" Enya asked quietly, bitterly. "Belisle will murder them, finish what he tried to do five years ago."

"I cannot see the future," Reza told her softly. "But we shall do what we can."

He looked around him then, at the people who had been his friends and fellow warriors for so long. "Go with honor, my friends," he said simply. There was no more time for good-byes.

After a quick embrace and a last kiss from Eustus, Enya turned to follow Reza through the dark tunnel to the even darker world beyond.

Thirty-Four

"What is that thing, Gard?" Thorella asked as he stared at the blue glow streaming from the crater, pouring its light forth into space. He could see the movements of his regiment's skimmers and tanks as they took up their positions around the city and partway up the ruined mountain. He and a few of his most trusted troops had come in first to deal with Gard and Savitch, landing over the horizon and coming overland in a skimmer to avoid detection. The rest of the regiment had been landed soon after Gard had been taken into custody. Thorella would have liked to kill him straight away, but his sponsor had convinced him that a gory show trial, followed by Gard's execution, would be much more satisfying.

Reza remained silent. He would kill Thorella, no matter what the cost, he had decided, but the time had not yet come. He had also decided to kill Belisle, as well. Despite Nicole and Jodi's best efforts to educate him that society alone was best left to judge the crimes of others, he knew that it was not always so. These two men had committed murder and would continue to do so with impunity unless he stopped them. Too much power lay behind them, power that lurked in the shadow of the pillar civilization had built to Justice, power that crushed its victims without remorse, without compassion; the laws of society could not reach them. For Bayern and Morita, killed by fellow Marines; for Melissa Savitch, who had answered his call for help and died for her trouble; for the Mallorys who had died and those who would soon die, he would kill Thorella and Belisle. He was the only instrument of Justice that might prevail. He alone could avenge the fallen.

"You know," Thorella said quietly, "you could be a bit more cooperative. I would hate to see Ms. Terragion accidentally abused during her interrogation."

Reza said nothing, but kept staring at Thorella, who sat behind a wall of armorglass. Reza retained his weapons because no one dared challenge him for them, and Thorella was content to let him have his way, as long as he himself was safe.

So you believe, Reza thought, imagining the look on Thorella's face if Reza stepped through the wall, as he easily could. Part of his mind was with Enya, who sat in a large interrogation room downstairs with a number of her friends. If Thorella decided to go ahead with his threat, Reza's period of waiting would be over.

"No," Thorella said after a moment's consideration. "The only women you ever cared about were Carré and Mackenzie, the frigid bitch and the dyke. Maybe I'll make Ms. Terragion my mistress while I'm here. That would make Camden happy, I know. At least, until it comes time to execute her." He smiled. "You're going to the gallows, Gard. You know that don't you?"

"I shall not go alone."

Thorella laughed. "No," he said, ignoring the implicit threat, "no, rest assured that you won't. There will be plenty of Mallorys swinging beside you. But that's beside the point." He leaned closer to the glass. "I just want to know what that thing is out there, that could chew up half a mountain. We've probed it and run drones around it, and it doesn't even register. Some kind of Kreelan energy source?"

You could say that, Reza answered silently. "I have nothing to say to you, Markus Thorella."

"Guards!" Thorella suddenly barked. Six of Thorella's best men, Reza's guard force, stepped forward from where they had their weapons trained on Reza's back. "Put him with the others. If he tries anything, kill them all." That was what Thorella believed would be an effective tool to enforce his will on Reza: the threat of death to the others.

As he turned to leave, Reza glanced again at the unearthly glow of the mountain.

Soon, he thought. *Very soon.*

* * *

"We're starting over it now, sir," Emilio Rodriguez reported as he began to turn his skimmer over the top of the glowing crater. He had been circling it for ten minutes, gathering more information – *which meant no information,* he thought sourly – before actually flying over it.

"Hurry it up, Rodriguez," Major Elijah Simpson, the regiment's intel officer, snapped. Many said that his intelligence was directly proportional to his patience. He was a very impatient man.

"What an asshole," Lauren Nathanga, a tech from the regiment's intel company who was Rodriguez's passenger, said over the intercom.

"No arguments here," Rodriguez sighed.

Their little jeep crossed over the lip of the crater about one hundred meters above the glass-smooth rim.

"This is really incredible," Nathanga said. "The power it must have taken to do this, and yet we don't have a single reading except some residual heat from whatever cut through the rock."

"Anything yet?" Simpson interjected.

"Still scanning, sir," Nathanga replied, shaking her head. "We're... What is that?"

"What's going on?" Simpson demanded over the radio, but neither Nathanga nor Rodriguez heard him.

The two explorers had suddenly found themselves encased in a web of blue light that seared their flesh. They thrashed and writhed, screaming in agony as their skin began to burn, as if they had suddenly been cast into a furnace. The last thing Lauren Nathanga saw was Rodriguez's smoking body bursting into flame. Then Nathanga was herself consumed by the cleansing fire.

Back at the command post, Major Simpson watched and listened in horror to the screams and the nightmarish video coming back across the comms link. First Rodriguez, and then Nathanga suddenly exploded into human torches, burning so bright and hot that the jeep's control panel must have begun to melt, because the video abruptly cut off. Thankfully.

Simpson got exactly two paces across the regimental command post before he retched on the floor amid the other shocked members of the intel section.

Undamaged except for the crew compartment that lay smoldering from the flames that had left only husks of carbon where once there had been human beings, the skimmer continued on its way across the crater, eventually crashing into the ocean over two hundred kilometers away.

* * *

"So," Nicole said, "what you are telling us is that we will be too late."

The *Gneisenau's* chief intelligence officer nodded grimly. "I'm afraid that about sums it up, CAG. Even if the Kreelans don't have any ships heading to Erlang that might be closer than the ones our scouts have detected, the estimated on-orbit time of the first enemy battle group will still be at least an hour ahead of our own ETA."

The faces around the table, real and projected, frowned. That meant the Kreelans would have time both to start their assault on the planet and array their ships in a defensive posture for a Confederation counterattack that they knew must be coming. While the humans still had some degree of tactical surprise on their side, it probably would not be enough to make a difference. While the Tenth Fleet task force – of which Sinclaire's *Gneisenau* was the flagship – had eleven battleships, two carriers, and a host of cruisers and destroyers, the Kreelan defenders would hold most of the cards in what was shaping up to be the biggest fleet engagement in decades.

If only we had more bloody ships! Sinclaire cursed to himself. "What do you think, Nicole?" he asked her. He hated calling Fleet Captain Carré "CAG" – Commander, Aerospace Group. He respected the position and the tradition, but to him the acronym sounded like some kind of affliction.

"It all depends on what we are up against," she said, noting the *Hood's* CAG nodding agreement. Nicole and Jodi had only recently completed their tours as instructors at the Fighter Weapons School on Earth, and had both accepted combat assignments on the newest fleet carrier, *Gneisenau*. Jodi had taken over one of the new ship's squadrons, finally accepting the responsibility and grade that she had so long avoided, while Nicole had assumed the post of senior pilot and aerospace group commander. "We have one-hundred sixty-three fighters and attack ships on *Gneisenau* ready to fight, plus another one-hundred and thirty-five on *Hood*. But we have no idea what the enemy will show up with other than the seven capital ships – two in the superdreadnought category – that STARNET was able to confirm before the Kreelans jumped. And we do not know, out of those, how many carry only guns and how many carry guns and fighters both."

"I would venture to say," said Captain Amadi, *Gneisenau's* commander, "that we should expect the worst. There is some compelling and unknown reason why the Kreelans are going to Erlang. They have never done this before, spontaneously converging on a colony from so many different quadrants. I suggest that we go in with the fighters and destroyers screening forward, followed by the main combatants in wedge abreast, and the attack ships and cruisers held in reserve to the rear."

Sinclaire nodded. It was a standard tactical formation, and for good reason. It would give them a lot of flexibility in an unknown situation, meaning that they could bring a lot of power to bear in any quadrant very quickly. *Or retreat with a minimum of losses*, he thought grimly. "Comments?"

"What about sending a recon in ahead of the van?" the captain of one of the destroyers, a young woman who was always looking for a fight with the enemy, said.

Sinclaire smiled at her eagerness. She was a good destroyer captain, aggressive and fearless, one of a breed that was increasingly hard to find. Destroyer captains and their crews did not usually live very long. "Given that we know little of what we'll be facing," he said, "I don't think we can afford to give the enemy the least advantage over us, more than they have already. Surprise is all we've got right now, and I won't surrender it without good reason. Maybe next time, Captain Dekkar."

The woman frowned, disappointed, but she nodded understanding.

"Have we been able to contact the colony yet?" someone else asked.

"No," the intel officer answered. "The comms people believe that the subspace signals are being blocked by an ion storm that came up within the Grange cloud. Until we're past it, we won't be able to reach them."

"Any other ideas? No? Then that's it. We'll go with the overall attack plan as suggested by Captain Amadi. The flag ops officer will issue formation and launch orders to your commands by twenty-two forty-five Zulu for the jump in-system at oh-five seventeen tomorrow." He looked at the chronometer on the wall of the conference room. "That gives us a tad over nine hours from now until we arrive at Erlang, people. Let's not waste a second of it."

* * *

"Brooding isn't going to help," Enya said.

Reza opened his eyes and looked at her. He seemed utterly calm. "I am not brooding," he said quietly, offering her a gentle smile. "I am thinking." He looked to Ian Mallory, who sat against the wall across from him. Mallory's left eye was swollen shut, his split lip still bleeding slightly. The Territorial Army contingent that had arrested him and the other seniors of the Mallory Council had beaten them badly. "We must find a way to get a message to your people," Reza told him. "They must get out of the cities and towns, away from anywhere the Territorial Army or Thorella's troops might stand and fight the Kreelans."

"What difference would it make?" the older man said quietly, his open eye blazing with anger and bitterness. "They'll be slaughtered either way. I'm not like most of this flock," he said, gesturing with a hand that boasted two broken fingers. "I've been off-world. I've seen what happens during a Kreelan attack. The TA has oppressed us for many years, but I can't justify asking our people to abandon the only hope they may have for survival. The Territorial Army troops are the only defense any of my people have."

"Listen to me, Ian Mallory." Reza said urgently. "If they do not leave, if they are anywhere near troops who will fight the Kreela, you condemn them to certain death. The Kreela do not come to your world now to fight as they usually do, seeking to honor the Empress in battle. They come to take the First Empress home. Any resistance will bring instant devastation. There will be no landings or ground battles. Kreelan warships will simply obliterate every defensive position on this planet from orbit, and every defended human settlement will be annihilated. This is more important to them than any other event in the last hundred thousand years, and they will take no chances. They will spare nothing, no one, who raises a hand against them."

"And they'll spare unarmed people?" someone scoffed. Reza had noticed that the mood of the Mallorys had changed dramatically since he had appeared in his Kreelan garb, the aura they projected verging on open hostility. Only Enya's word and their own fears of what he might do in retaliation held them in check.

"If you do as I say, yes, your people will be spared." He looked at Ian. "But there is a price that must be paid."

"I knew there must be a catch," Ian grumbled. "How much blood need be spilled?"

"Seven hundred," Reza said. "If you wish your people to live, you must find exactly seven hundred souls who are willing to fight and die for the rest. Men or women, it makes no difference. They must assemble in a single line upon the plain on the far side of the mountain of light, with no weapons other than those that may be hammered in the forge or carved from wood."

"Why seven hundred?" Enya asked. "And what are they supposed to accomplish other than satisfying Kreelan bloodlust?"

"There must be seven hundred because that is the number of the host that accompanied the First Empress here after she died, after her spirit inhabited the vessel, the crystal heart that was awakened by your touch," Reza explained. "The Seven Hundred who brought her here were the ones you found in the burial chamber, the Imperial Guard. The number will not be lost on the warriors who are coming here; they will understand." He looked around at the others in the room. "As for what your volunteers are to accomplish, they will fight for your world," Reza said, "against an equal number of Her warriors, similarly armed. Theirs shall be a sacrifice for the rest of your people, those who survive the destruction of the cities."

"We could not hope to win against trained warriors," Ian said.

"It is not a battle that is meant to be won, Ian Mallory. It is a sacrifice, a showing of the honor of your people, that the Kreela will understand and respect."

"I take it, then," Ian asked darkly, "that the seven hundred who go forward onto the Plain of Aragon may all expect to die?"

Reza nodded. "It is the only way."

The room was deathly silent. As they spoke, the others of the Council had gathered around the trio, the uninjured helping those who were. Even imprisoned and under sentence of death without a formal trial, the Mallory Council still held the future of their people in their hands.

"I say we put it to a vote," Enya said, looking at Ian. "We've got nothing left to lose, except the lives of everyone on this planet, Raniers and Mallorys alike."

"Let the Raniers die!" someone hissed like acid eating through metal.

"Don't say that!" Enya retorted. "Not all of them are like Belisle. There are–"

"You cannot save them," Reza said quietly. "If you give them warning, Belisle will find a way to turn it against you. He would confine the Mallorys in the cities where they would be killed, and evacuate the Ranier families to the forests, although that would not save them in the end. Only those who choose to fight on the plain have the power to save your world, but the Raniers must also bear their share of the price of your planet's survival; it is they who shall be sacrificed to the guns of Her warships."

The faces around him were grim. Even the most hardened of the Mallorys here knew that there were innocents among the Raniers, people who had helped them in some way, or who simply had no control over the planet's course as Belisle led them through tyranny. Men, women, children, they would all die in the cities. They would have to, that the rest of Erlang's people might live.

"I say do as he says," growled an older woman who had suffered more hardships than she cared to recount. "Better to make a stand than to just wait and get shot, either by the aliens or by our own."

Ian nodded respectfully. Her words were well thought of in this circle. "And you, Markham?"

"Aye," a big man, an equal in physique to Washington Hawthorne, said easily, as if he made these kinds of decisions every day. "I'll raise an ax and a little Cain any day. All the better that it be for a good cause."

"Waverman?"

"Aye."

And so it went, around the room. The vote was unanimous. They would fight.

"Does that meet with your satisfaction?" Ian said to Reza after the last of the council had nodded her head. "Will that be enough blood for you?"

"Ian!" Enya said, dismayed. "He offers us a way to survive, after trying to help us against Belisle. You have no right to treat him that way."

"We're the ones who'll be dying, girl. He has no stake in this."

"You are wrong, my friend," Reza said gently. He could feel Ian Mallory's pain and trepidation, and was not resentful that he was the focus of the man's anger. Mallory did not – could not – understand the Way or the fulfillment of the Prophecy. But there was no other course for them to take.

"How's that?"

"Because I am the one who will lead your people into battle."

Ian only looked at him.

"Why you, and not one of us?" someone else demanded.

"Because only one who wears the collar of the Empress may declare such a combat," he explained.

"How much time do we have?" Enya asked in the silence that followed.

"I do not know exactly," Reza said, "for I do not know where the closest Kreelan warships might be. But I would say that we only have a few hours to act."

"A few hours isn't enough time," Ian said pointedly.

Reza fixed him with a stony gaze. "It is all that you have."

* * *

The next step, getting the Council's instructions out of the Parliament building and to the Mallorys outside, was not as difficult as Thorella or Belisle would have liked. One of the guards was a Mallory sympathizer known by Ian to be trustworthy, and he was passed a message in code, written on a stained sheet of paper that had once been a shopping list for the company store in Laster, a town far to the north. The guard, in turn, passed it to the servant of Mallory City's mayor, who passed it to someone heading out of the building. In less than an hour, the instructions had been transmitted over the inter-city communications networks to every village on the planet.

The orders were viewed with incredulity by many, but there was no mistaking Ian Mallory's coded signature, and they knew that he would die long before he revealed it to Belisle's minions. While there were a few who refused to believe it, thinking either it was a trick or that the Council simply did not know any more what it was doing, the vast majority of Mallorys did as they had been instructed.

It was fortunate that the message had been sent late in the evening, for it gave the Mallorys the cover of darkness to carry out their instructions. Evacuation plans were on hand for every township, and in the darkness the Mallorys began their exodus, taking with them only a prescribed bundle of things essential for survival – a few tools, a good knife, some food – to avoid arousing too much suspicion from the periodic Territorial Army patrols. Since most of the townships were ringed by forests that the villagers had known since childhood, finding their way to the designated rendezvous points was not a problem. Moving in silence, carrying the very young and the old or infirm who could not walk or keep up, the Mallorys disappeared by the thousands from their homes.

By first light, when the horns blared at the mines signaling the start of another twelve-hour shift, only the Ranier shift supervisors had appeared, wondering what had happened to all their workers. In the meantime, the miners who were streaming from the mines headed quickly toward their ramshackle homes... and then vanished.

THIRTY-FIVE

"What the devil do you mean, 'No one's showed up to work?'" Belisle shouted into the comms terminal.

The man at the other end shrank back. "Just what I said, Mr. President," he stammered. "There was no one at the gates except the supervisors, and the miners working the night shift practically ran home. We tried to find them, even sent in TA patrols, but there wasn't anyone there. Anywhere. The whole township's empty."

"That's impossible! People can't just vanish into thin air! Where did they go? Surely you idiots can find a few thousand people wandering about!" He stabbed at a button on the comm link, and the man's image disappeared.

"I'm afraid it's worse than that, Mr. President," Wittmann, the mayor, said quietly behind him, as if afraid he would be beaten for bringing more bad news.

"How can it?" Belisle snapped angrily, his mind unconsciously figuring the monetary losses for every hour that even a single mine lay idle.

"I just got a report from the chief at Promontory Mine," Wittmann said uneasily. "He reports the same thing. The Mallorys are all gone. They just vanished into thin air. Food still on the tables, fires burned cold in the kitchens with pots still hanging over them. That sort of thing."

Belisle just stared at him. *Promontory Mine.* That was Erlang's most productive source of income. Even the time that they had spent standing here talking had cost them over a million credits. "Find them!" he yelled. "Find them and get them back to work, or you and your family will be down there breaking rock!"

He turned to Thorella, who sat casually in one of the office's chaise lounges, a look of contemplation on his face. "They've finally gone and done it," Belisle said, spittle flying from his mouth. "They're openly rebelling. What are you going to do about it, colonel?"

"Well," he said casually, scrutinizing the nails of one hand, "there's not much we can do with your miners until they've been found." He smiled in spite of himself. The planning it must have taken to allow hundreds of thousands of people to disappear overnight under the nose of the Territorial Army was indeed impressive, even to Thorella. Hunting them down would be a real challenge, he suspected, which was something he always enjoyed. "But we can certainly inquire among your friends in the basement about the matter, as I'm sure they have something to do with it."

"That's impossible," Belisle spat. "The cell they're in is impossible to breach. They couldn't get out a whisper."

Thorella frowned. This man could sometimes be so ignorant. "You underestimate your opponents, my friend. I'm sure your staff has its share of sympathizers. I reviewed some of the recordings of the goings on in the cell not too long ago, and discovered that certain portions had been... edited. And whoever did that could just as easily get a message out to warn the Mallorys." His frown grew deeper. "The question is, warn them of what?"

"Retaliation by the Army and police, of course," Belisle said impatiently, thinking Thorella an imbecile for not coming to that conclusion right away, and also wondering who on his staff could possibly have betrayed him. It was unthinkable. "And rightly they should be afraid. There will be reprisals."

"But would that be cause for evacuating the whole Mallory population?" Thorella thought aloud. "And if they were openly rebelling, wouldn't they have tried to destroy the mines? Why did the miners just disappear?" He was not concerned about Belisle's threatened reprisals. That was a job for which the Territorial Army was well suited, and did not concern him or his Marines. But was there some other threat, of which he and the Raniers were unaware?

There was one way to find out. "I think, Mr. President," he said, "that we need to ask your Mallory friends some questions." He turned to the guard who stood nearby, a Territorial Army sergeant. "Have Ian Mallory and Enya Terragion brought up here immediately."

"Yes, sir," the sergeant replied, saluting before he left the office to carry out his mission. Thorella had no way of knowing that the man was a Mallory sympathizer.

"Sir," Thorella's adjutant called from where he had installed himself in one of the anterooms, "Major Simpson's on the line. He has an emergency – the recon of the crater."

Now what? Thorella wondered, annoyed, as he went to take the call and learn about the disastrous reconnaissance mission over the glowing crater. *Could nothing go right today?*

* * *

Thorella and Belisle had been counting on the explosive device set in the holding pen to be a deterrent to any unwanted actions by Reza or the others. It was a sophisticated device, and might even have worked, had Sergeant "Pippi" Hermutz not disabled it earlier, leaving the arming light glowing threateningly to reassure anyone who took an interest that the device was still viable. He was also responsible for destroying the recordings of their vote to evacuate the Mallorys, as well as sabotaging the surveillance gear for the rest of the short time it would matter to anyone.

"Wait here," he told the other guards as he keyed open the outer lock to the cell. "I'll bring them out."

He went inside, waiting for the outer door to close before he opened the inner one. He immediately picked out Ian and Enya, sitting close to Reza in the group of thirty or so, all of whom got to their feet as he entered. Until he had carried out the message Ian had drafted, none of the others had realized he was one of them, even though his heritage was Ranier. He was simply one of a growing number of people who had grown tired of Belisle's kind of leadership and oppression of others. He noted the tension in their faces. They wanted to know if their families were safe.

"Everything seems to have gone according to plan," he whispered to Ian. "I don't know about the rest, but at least Promontory and Sheila townships were evacuated all right. And Charlotte" – a woman he only knew by her code name – "told me that the volunteers you asked for are in place and with the equipment you said to bring." Charlotte had not bothered to tell him that it had been inordinately difficult to send only seven hundred to the plain: nearly every man and most of the women who heard of the chance to stand and fight had wanted to go.

"Thank you for your help, Pippi," Ian breathed. "We all owe you a debt we probably will never be able to repay."

"It's just nice to feel like I'm doing something right, for once," Hermutz sighed. "Belisle and his kind are no friends to anyone but themselves. But that's for another time." He looked at Enya, then back to Ian. "That Marine colonel, Thorella, wants you and Enya for interrogation. Belisle thinks the Mallorys are gone because they're afraid of reprisals, but Thorella suspects something more. What should we–"

Reza visibly stiffened, his eyes widening slightly.

"What is it?" Enya said, putting a hand on his armored shoulder, feeling him quiver beneath it.

"They have come," he told her. He could not sense those of the Blood, ever since the Seventh Braid, his link to the spirit of his people, had been severed the instant before the Empress exiled him from the Empire. But he had cast his mind's eye upward, into the human ships that orbited overhead, and had heard their cries of surprise as the first of the Kreelan battle groups converging on Erlang had arrived in-system. Those cries soon turned to screams of panic and pain as the great Kreelan warships began the devastation above that would soon begin here, on the surface. He focused on Ian. "We have no more time," he told him. "We must leave at once, or we will be caught in the coming holocaust."

"I might be able to get a few of you out," Pippi said, glancing over his shoulder to see if the other guards were becoming suspicious. They were looking through the viewport. Pippi waved. "But there's no way I can get everyone out. The parliamentary guard force would cut you all down before you got a foot past the cell block doors."

Reza thought for a moment. No matter what powers he had, he would not be able to kill every guard before the shooting began. Some, or many, of those with him now would be gunned down. "Then take Enya and Ian with you," he said. "I will see to the rest."

"But–" Enya began.

"Go now," Reza said. "I will meet you on the knoll that overlooks the plain. Go."

Reluctantly, Enya and Ian let themselves be prodded out of the cell. As the door closed behind them, Markham, the man who could have been Hawthorne's twin, said, "So, Gard, what are we supposed to do? Just sit here until the Kreelans start shelling Mallory City?"

Reza looked at him, a grim smile on his face. "Yes," he said.

Markham did not think it was funny.

* * *

Pippi Hermutz could not get away with escorting the two prisoners by himself, he knew, and there were no other sympathizers here who could help him. So, out of necessity, he chose a man he knew to be a strong supporter of Belisle to help him. It would make killing him a little easier on his conscience.

After the four of them crowded into the elevator that would take them upstairs to the president's office, Pippi turned to his Territorial Army colleague and subordinate, Hans Miflin, and shot him between the eyes with a low-power pencil beam from his blaster. Just strong enough to penetrate the man's skull, it turned his forebrain into bloody steam. Twitching like a pithed frog, he collapsed to the floor of the elevator.

Enya jammed the STOP button. Ian and Pippi propped up Miflin's body beside the door in a sitting position so it would be harder for someone outside the elevator to see him.

"My God, Pippi," the elder Mallory breathed. "How can we kill one another like this?"

Pippi looked at him as if he were a child. "Too easily, Ian. But at least he was armed. Most of the people he's killed in his lifetime weren't. Keep that in mind the next time you feel like shedding a tear for the likes of him." Checking that none of them had any blood on their clothes, he said, "Take this." He handed Ian his blaster, and then picked up Miflin's gun, handing it to Enya. "Keep them hidden unless you need them. Go straight out the back door, through the kitchens on the first level. You can't miss them. Someone should be waiting for you there with transportation."

"What about the others?" Enya asked.

"Reza will have to deal with that," he said impatiently. "I've done all I can."

"What about you, Pippi?" Ian said.

He nodded at the blaster in Ian's hand. "You have to shoot me, to make it look like an escape. Injure me enough to make it convincing."

"But aren't you coming with us?" Enya asked, incredulous. "Pippi, the Kreelans are coming!"

"I have to think of my family," he said. "I can't leave the building before my shift is up without drawing notice to myself. And if Belisle or his people ever find out that I've helped you, my wife and children..." He shook his head. Sympathizers were treated far more harshly than Mallorys. His entire family would probably be imprisoned, and he would be executed. "You owe me this, Ian."

Clenching his jaws, Ian raised the pistol, aimed as carefully as his trembling hand allowed, and shot Pippi in the head, through his helmet. Their rescuer collapsed, and Enya quickly knelt and put a hand to his neck.

"He's still alive," she whispered as the stench of smoking flesh turned her stomach. She had to get out of here or she would vomit.

Ian carefully placed Pippi's body on the other side of the door in a position similar to Miflin's. "Thank you, my friend," he whispered, a hand on the man's shoulder. He knew there was no way either he or his family would make it out of the city alive when the Kreelans came. He should have saved him the pain and simply killed him, he thought sadly. Standing again, he turned to Enya. "It's time."

Nodding, she pushed the RUN button, and the elevator lurched upward toward the first floor.

It stopped and the doors swished open. Ian had been praying fervently that there would be no one standing there when it did. Thankfully, no one was.

"This way," Enya said, leading him to the left, behind the twin staircases that were the centerpiece of the foyer. This early in the morning, few of the Parliament's bureaucrats and other functionaries were about. They saw two guards, but they were half asleep, inattentive.

Turning down a long corridor, Enya saw the silvery doors that led to the main kitchens. In the job she had once held as a runner for one of the more moderate Ranier representatives, she had often come down here to get him food to satisfy his compulsive eating habits, his only vice.

There were three cooks getting ready for the morning meal service in the main dining room, but they did not see the two refugees as they stole past a row of gleaming copper and stainless steel cookware along the far side, away from the steaming urns.

The back door loomed ahead. Enya opened it, only to find a Territorial Army uniform blocking her way.

"Hey!" the man said, raising his rifle.

Enya shot him in the chest.

But that was not the end of their troubles. Ten meters away stood a big Marine transport skimmer and a group of camouflaged, armored figures with their weapons pointed directly at them.

"Don't," Ian said as she raised her pistol. "It's useless," he said, defeated.

Tears of frustration in her eyes, Enya threw down her weapon and raised her hands. Ian did the same.

Suddenly, a familiar face peered out through the skimmer's personnel door. "Don't just stand there," Eustus shouted. "Get in!"

"Eustus!" Enya cried as the Marines bundled her and Ian into the troop carrier, hiding the Territorial Army soldier's body in a nearby trash bin and retrieving their weapons from the pavement before someone noticed something amiss, unlikely as that was in the darkness of this early hour.

Inside the vehicle's armored hull, Enya and Eustus kissed and embraced. "What are you doing here?" she asked.

"One of your people came and tipped us off to your little breakout," he told her. "But let's save that for later. Where are Reza and the others?"

"They're still being held," Ian told him.

"We've got to get them out of there quickly. Belisle and Thorella are expecting us for interrogation, and they'll be getting suspicious."

"Well," Eustus said, "we should be able to do something about that. But I'm not sure what we're going to do afterwards. We don't really have anywhere to go, and we'll have Thorella's entire regiment on our ass."

Ian and Enya looked at each other. "What about the plain on the far side of the mountain?" she asked.

Eustus looked at her blankly.

"The messenger didn't tell you?" Ian asked. "That the Kreelans are coming?"

Eustus's eyes widened. "They only told us that you guys were going to make a break and that you'd need help getting away. Nobody said anything about Kreelans."

That would figure, Ian thought. The courier had only told them what he had been ordered to; his cell leader would have given him only the information he absolutely needed for that specific task.

"When, where, and how many?" Eustus asked.

Quickly, Enya and Ian explained what was about to happen to their world.

* * *

When the door to the cell whined open, Reza and the others were ready and waiting.

"It is good to see you again, my friend," he said as Eustus came through the doorway.

"You, too, sir," Eustus said as he ushered some of his Marines forward to help with the people who could not move on their own. Some of the interrogations had taken more of a toll than others. "But I wish I'd known about the Blues being on the way."

"The squadron in orbit is already nearly finished," Reza told him. He had drawn away his mind's eye from the carnage above. He had seen more than enough. "Did you get a message to Hawthorne?"

"Aye, sir. The company's volunteered to stand on the plain. That should give the Kreelans a bit more–"

"It cannot be so, Eustus," Reza told him as they led the group to the bank of elevators, past the limp bodies of the guards whose only sign of injury was the lack of a pulse. "Only Erlangers and myself may stand upon that field. You and the company must stand aside."

"And just what the hell are we supposed to do?" Eustus said angrily. He was not about to leave Reza to die with a bunch of miners who had never been in a battle bigger than a beer hall brawl. "We've got a boat, but if the squadron upstairs is catching it, where does that leave us? We may as well fight and do some good." He thought of how Thorella had ordered them into that boat, and how amazed Eustus had been at the number of ways Hawthorne had found to stall him. While they would never know it for sure, he knew that Hawthorne's tactics had saved all their lives. They figured Thorella was going to plant an explosive among their equipment for a convenient accident, but it had never come to pass. And never would.

"More of our forces are on the way," Reza told him. "Nicole is coming." He could feel her, just barely. She was preparing to do battle, and her Bloodsong, faint though it was, rang clearly in his heart. "They will arrive soon. And when they do, you and Hawthorne must take the company to safety. Just remember: you must not fire on any Kreelan forces or you will be destroyed. If you offer no resistance, they will not attack you." *If all goes well*, he thought.

"I'm not leaving you," Eustus said stubbornly as they filed through the kitchens to the back door, the cooks staring at them wide-eyed. The Parliament's Territorial Army guards had been no match for Reza's Marines, who now moved quickly to get everyone out before a more general alarm was called.

Reza pulled him aside by the arm. "I leave you no choice, Eustus," he said. "There are... rules to the engagement I am planning that forbid me to allow any but those who have lived in the shadow of the mountain to fight for their right to remain. If those rules are not obeyed to the letter, the battle is forfeit, and every soul on this planet shall perish." Eustus turned away, unable to look him in the eye. "I shall not forget you, my friend," he said gently.

"You're not planning on coming back, are you?" Eustus asked hoarsely.

"No," Reza said. "I have no illusions about what is to come. The Mallorys, for all their courage, cannot win. They will die, and I with them. But perhaps that will be enough to spare the rest." He glanced up at the parliament building. "Besides, there is some personal business I must attend to first that would make my future service to the Confederation... awkward." He smiled solemnly. "I have put away the uniform of the regiment forever, my friend." He pointed to the armored skimmer and Enya's face peering intently through the still open door, past the two Marines who stood warily on guard. "There is the best reason of all for you to go," he said. "Her love is true. You would be wise to ask her to be yours. Take her with you, Eustus."

"Reza–"

"Go." Reza's voice turned to steel. There was no more time. "That is an order, First Sergeant."

"Yes, sir," Eustus rasped, standing tall and rendering his commanding officer and best friend a sharp salute.

Reza returned it as a Kreelan warrior, his left fist against his breast. He watched as Eustus clambered into the heavily loaded skimmer after the watchful Marines, the door hissing shut behind them.

As the carrier sped away, Reza went back inside, bearing the long sword that was inscribed with his name before him like a flaming torch to ward off the darkness.

* * *

"No one answers downstairs, sir," the Territorial Army orderly said matter-of-factly.

"What?" Belisle snapped. His mind was on the brink of raving insanity after receiving report after report of vanished Mallorys and idle mines. Virtually every single worker had disappeared on him, and none had yet been found. "Don't tell me the guards have vanished into thin air, too?"

"You may inspect their bodies, if you wish," Reza said from an alcove in the far wall. There was no door behind him. "Yours shall join them shortly."

Belisle whirled around at the voice as the soldier drew his pistol. It was not halfway out of its holster when a shrekka ripped through his chest. A geyser of blood followed it as it flew across the room, embedding itself in the far wall. Clutching at his savaged ribcage, the man crumpled to the floor.

"What do you want?" Belisle whined. "Money? I've got millions of credits in the vault in this office. I can give you anything you want! I–"

"Oh, shut up, Belisle," Thorella's calm voice called from the anteroom. "It only makes you look more like the coward you really are."

Reza eyed Thorella carefully. An enemy who acted calmly in the face of seemingly overwhelming force was one not to be underestimated.

"I suppose," Thorella went on, stepping further into the room, "that since the explosive in the basement did not go off when I pushed the button, all of your traitorous friends managed to escape?"

Reza did not favor him with an answer. Thorella was hiding something. His eyes narrowing in concentration, Reza swept the room with his senses, but could detect nothing that seemed overly threatening. Yet something was wrong...

"What does he want, Thorella?" Belisle hissed.

"He's come here to kill us, Mr. President," Thorella said nonchalantly.

"Yes," Reza said as he leveled his sword at Thorella, the blade steady as the stones of the ancient Kal'ai-Il in his hands. "The world has no need for such as you. Too much blood is on your hands, and there is no one – not even the Confederation's senior Counsel, whom you also murdered – to avenge the lives you have wrongly taken, the pain you have caused."

"Please don't kill me!" Belisle pleaded, his hands clasped like a repentant sinner.

Reza suddenly swung his sword in an arc that appeared as a golden ring in the office's mild light. Belisle's mouth continued to move for a moment as it tumbled from his neck, bright arterial blood spurting to the ceiling from the torso, creating its own gruesome fresco.

"Bravo!" Thorella applauded as Belisle's headless body at last collapsed, still twitching, to the carpet.

"Excellent swordsmanship, as always, Captain Gard. I'm sure the General Staff will enjoy watching it."

Reza looked up sharply, eyeing Thorella more closely. The colonel walked through a sofa as Reza might through a wall.

It was a hologram.

"Yes, that's right, you fool," Thorella's image said as recognition dawned on Reza's face. "You didn't think that I would let you get anywhere near me, did you? Even during the interrogation, I wasn't behind the glass. It was only a projection with an appropriate olfactory representation to fool you. And it seems to have worked quite well, eh?"

Reza's anger threatened to boil over like a volcano, but there was nowhere to direct it. Wherever Thorella was, he was safely out of Reza's reach. How could he have been so foolish?

Because, Reza thought savagely, cursing himself, you thought that even Thorella would have had enough courage to face you and not run away like a terrified rat. Or a cunning one.

"Well, my friend," Thorella went on, "I'm afraid I have to go now. Your blue-skinned friends are getting a bit too close for comfort." His smile faded. "One word of advice, Gard: die here, now, or turn your coat again and go back with the Kreelans. Because if your face is seen again in Confederation space, you'll be arrested and charged with murdering a sovereign planetary leader, not to mention a host of other lesser offenses." A contemplative look. "I might even be able to arrange it to have you charged with the murder of the General Counsel." He laughed. "People will hate you so much that they'll curse your name in their sleep. And your friends will suffer their share of society's rightful vengeance on your treasonous life."

"In Her name," Reza whispered, his blood a burning river of fire through his body, the power that flared within him stayed only by the knowledge that he did not know where to strike, "I shall somehow get you for this. If I die here, my spirit will reach you from beyond the Darkness, Thorella. My spirit and my vengeance shall haunt you until the day you die."

"How thrilling," Thorella said, amused. He looked at him as he might a steer that was being sent to the slaughter. "Good-bye, half-breed."

Somewhere beyond the city, Reza knew, Thorella was probably lifting off in an assault shuttle, trying to join up with the incoming human fleet.

His soul burning with impotent rage, Reza fled the Parliament building and Mallory City just as the first salvoes of the Kreelan bombardment began to fall.

THIRTY-SIX

Seven hundred men and women stood on the Plain of Aragon in the shadow of the crystal heart's mountain crater, watching their world burn. As Reza had foretold, the Kreelan battleships now orbiting close to the planet were devastating every human defensive position, turning the cities around them into rubble and flames.

They watched the sky glow bright orange and red as huge crimson, green, and blue bolts of energy crashed into Mallory City from the great Kreelan guns. The waiting Mallorys knew there could be no survivors.

"Surely, Sodom and Gomorra saw no greater wrath from the Lord," someone said quietly as fire rained down from the skies.

The bombardment went on for what seemed like a long time, the ground trembling with salvo after salvo as the Kreelans pulverized the settlements. The ridge where Reza's Marines had landed was no more than a smoldering scar in the earth; Walken's tanks, the artillery, and the First Guards troops that had taken over from Reza's company were gone, annihilated.

The smoke that poured from the smoking ruins of Mallory City and the Territorial Army garrisons blotted out the sun. A rain, a black rain, fell for a while and left behind an oily mist that swirled about the great plain like a funeral shroud. The Mallorys, cold and frightened, waited for whatever was to come.

"Where is he?" Markham asked. In his enormous right hand was the ax he often used to split logs as big around as a man's chest. He figured it would kill a Kreelan just as well.

"I don't know," Ian said, shivering in the wet chill. "He said he'd come. He'll be here."

"I suppose it doesn't matter," Markham said after a while. "One hand more or less isn't going to change things."

"I am here," Reza's voice flowed from behind them. From the glow of the flames that shimmered through the mist, Reza strode toward them like a wraith in human form. The people parted before him as he made his way to the place of leadership, to the front.

"I was beginning to worry about you," Ian said.

"Belisle is dead," Reza told him. "Thorella escaped my hand, but justice shall someday find him." He only half-believed the words. In the human world, people such as Thorella as often as not lived their lives through without the justice they deserved.

"I'm sorry," Ian told him sincerely. "I know how much your Marines and Counselor Savitch must have meant to you. To see the one responsible for their deaths escape is a hard thing."

Reza nodded in acceptance of Mallory's condolences before pushing the matter from his mind. There was much yet to do this day. "Are your people ready as I instructed you?"

Ian nodded. "Axes, knives, picks, anything we could lay our hands on that wasn't a gun or bomb. I don't know what good we'll be, but if nothing else we're fighting with things we've held in our hands all our lives."

Reza fixed him with a searching gaze. "Are they afraid to die, Ian Mallory?"

Ian looked around him. While he could not see every face among the crowd that had gathered around them, he knew all the names. And when his gaze touched them, they seemed to stand taller, their eyes brightening in the dim light. These people, some from Mallory City, some from a long distance away, many from in between, were his people, his friends. And he knew why they had come, why thousands more would have come if they could. "They didn't come here to be cowards," he said proudly, his heart swelling with love for the people he gladly called his own. "They came to protect what is theirs. There won't be any Mallorys running yellow from the Plain of Aragon today."

Reza nodded. "Then let it be done," he said. "Form them in a line, arm's length apart, facing as I do. Our wait shall not be long, for the enemy shall soon be with us."

He stared into the mist as Markham bellowed his instructions across the field, Ian Mallory standing thoughtfully beside him. The Mallorys, long used to teamwork in the mines where one man or woman's life depended on another, had already formed themselves into subunits that reacted quickly to Reza's commands.

It was amazing, Reza thought, that such fierce warrior spirits dwelt in people who so cherished peace.

In only a few minutes they were ready, the ends of the skirmish line just visible in the mist on either side of Reza. There was no need for a modern Napoleon or Wellington this day, for there would be no maneuvering and no need for tactical genius. When the battle was joined, it would be warrior against warrior, human against Kreelan, in a battle fought with courage and ferocity that only one side could win. A battle to the death.

"They come," Reza said, the softly spoken words carrying amazingly far. Beside him, men and women gripped their makeshift weapons tighter, adrenaline flowing through their bodies as they prepared to defend the right of their people to exist.

"Where?" Markham growled. "I don't see–"

"There," Ian said, nodding to their front. In the early morning mist, shadows danced in the glowing light of the rising sun, gradually taking form as the line of Kreelan warriors strode forward to meet them.

"Good Lord," Markham whispered. He had never seen a Kreelan before, and suddenly wished he were not seeing them now.

"Are you afraid, Markham?" Reza asked him.

"Naw," the big man said. "I'd much rather be in the pub, but I'm not afraid. If they get me, fine, but I'll take a few myself."

The Kreelan advance stopped. They waited.

"Markham," Reza said, "you will wait here with the others. Ian, you must come with me, as my First."

"What are you going to do?" Markham asked.

"We must greet them." He turned to the big man, who was obviously uneasy about letting Ian get so close to the enemy. "Do not fear; treachery is alien to the Kreela. The greeting is part of the ritual."

"Be careful then," Markham said, still not pleased.

"We'll be back, Nathaniel," Ian told him.

While Markham issued orders for the line to hold fast, Reza and Ian set out across the no-man's land separating the two forces, moving toward their opposite number.

As they got closer and more details of the two approaching figures, their opposites from the Kreelan line, became apparent, an uneasy feeling began to stir within Reza. There was something familiar about the leader. Something...

For just a moment, he faltered, his heart stopping with realization.

"What's wrong, Reza," Ian asked. "Reza?"

The two Kreelan figures continued to advance, slower now, and Ian saw that one of them had hair that was completely white, the snowy braids coiled around her upper arms like stately serpents around gleaming ebony trees. As they got closer, he could also see that her face was black below the eyes, as if she had cried in tears of ink.

Reza watched as she came to within arm's length, but his mind refused to believe what his eyes told him. His heart had begun to beat again, but with the surge of warm blood through his limbs also came the heat of tears to his eyes as he looked upon the woman he thought he would never see again.

"Esah-Zhurah," he whispered, unable to believe his eyes. "Is it possible?" he said in the Old Tongue, "Can it truly be you?"

For a moment, she only stood there, her deep green eyes searching his, her mind grappling with her own disbelief. "Your eyes do not deceive you, my love... my Reza."

They reached out to one another in the greeting of warriors, of peers, clasping their arms tightly. Each was afraid that the other was only an illusion, that a mere touch would shatter the dream. But they were real. They were together.

Reza reached a hand toward her face, the armored gauntlet seemingly invisible to the nerves in his trembling fingers as they made contact with her skin. Her own arms reached for him, cupping his face in her hands, his skin where she touched him burning with a wondrous fire.

"How I have thought of you each day of my life, my love," she said as they drew closer, the world around them fading to nothing, the Universe itself contracting into haunted, loving eyes, the touch of flesh upon flesh. "The pain of your banishment has never left me. The mourning marks have never gone away."

"My own heart has been empty without you, Esah-Zhurah," he whispered as her face came close to his, and his senses, denied the communion of blood that he had given up when he left, drowned themselves in her touch, her look, her scent. "I have lived each moment in hopes of someday again seeing you, touching you, one last time before Death came, but I never believed it would come to pass." With her face so close that he could feel the heat of her body like a roiling flame, he said, "I love you."

Their lips touched, just barely, and Reza felt the hard and terribly lonely years that had come between them melt away like soft steel in a white-hot furnace. A kiss more gentle, more passionate, there had never been.

They ran their hands along the braids of the other as their lips pressed together more firmly, their tongues greeting like the old lovers they were. Time kindly stood aside to let them enjoy this one moment that it could not, in good conscience, deny them.

As one, as if the union they had once made in spirit and blood had never been broken, Esah-Zhurah and Reza pulled themselves away from one another with no less reluctance than two planets overcoming their mutual attraction to spin away toward opposite ends of the galaxy. Shivering with the power of desires and needs that could never be satisfied, their hearts crying in anguish at the hand they knew Fate would this day deal to them, they stood face to face not as lovers, but as warriors.

As enemies.

"You would defend them, Reza?" Esah-Zhurah asked, fighting to control her trembling voice.

"Yes, Esah-Zhurah," he said unsteadily, his tongue leaden in his mouth. "Long have they lived in this place, and much have they suffered for it. According to the Legend of The One, in Her name I claim the right of Challenge."

Esah-Zhurah surveyed the human who had accompanied Reza, noting that he had already suffered physical harm before coming to this place. But she felt no fear from him, only determination, courage. Behind him, standing silently in the swirling mist, were the others who had come to serve the Challenge. Males and females, large and small, dressed in rags and without armor to protect their fragile bodies, she sensed that they had come here with no intent to flee. Their hearts beat quickly, but with anticipation, not with fear. "You choose your companions wisely, my love," she said. "The right is yours," she said quietly. "I accept your Challenge."

Reza bowed his head deeply. The sacrifice the Mallorys were about to make would not be in vain. Their people would be spared.

"In Her name," Esah-Zhurah said, her heart filled with bitter ashes at the knowledge that Reza had come here to save the kin of these people who offered themselves up to her, that he had come here to die, "let it be done."

With a final embrace, their hearts broken by the weight of duty and the injustice of Fate, the two separated, turning back to begin the short march to their respective lines.

"Who is she, Reza?" Ian asked uncertainly.

"She is... my wife," Reza replied with an effort to keep his voice even. It was the closest relationship he could imagine in human terms to describe his relationship with Esah-Zhurah.

Ian did not hide his shock well. "I can't ask a man to kill his own wife," he said. "This is our land, and we'll pay for it, Reza. There's no need–"

"It is as it must be," Reza told him woodenly. "Pray to your God that I may have the strength to do what must be done." Reza knew that the only sword on the field that could slay Esah-Zhurah was his own, and that to save any of the seven hundred Mallorys who had gathered here this day he would have to kill her.

"I don't know how to thank you for all that you've done, Reza," Ian said quietly, "but your name will never be forgotten on Erlang."

They took their place in the center of the line, a few paces in front of the rest.

Reza drew his sword, holding it easily in his right hand, the blade shimmering in the sun. "Let it begin," he whispered.

As one, with hearts beating cadence to their marching feet, the fourteen hundred warriors of the two battle lines started forward.

Thirty-Seven

"Stand by for transpace sequence... Five... Four... Three... Two... One..." The ship's klaxon sounded twice to announce that *Gneisenau* had reentered normal space, and the swirling starfields of hyperspace resolved themselves once more into individual points of light.

In the massive port launch bay, Nicole sat in her fighter, impatiently waiting. "What is the matter?" she snapped into her comm link. "Why have I not been launched?"

"Standby, CAG," the chief of the bay advised. "We're showing some problems with your catapult."

Nicole could feel the thumps in the hull as the ship's other catapults began to hurl the fighters into space. They were not able to launch in hyperspace, of course, since the fighters had no hyperdrives themselves, and if they went outside the hyperspace field of the mother ship, they would find themselves left far behind in normal space.

Merde, she thought, suddenly furious with a passion that frightened her. She needed to get out there! "Pri-Fly," she said, "get my ship out of here. Now."

"CAG, the inductor circuit's fluctuating way outside the safety norms," the ops chief told her. "I can't launch you until–"

"Get this ship into space, damn you!" she shouted. "That is a direct order!" Her body felt like it was burning up with fever, and her only thoughts were those of the battle that awaited her beyond the obstacle of a mere piece of machinery.

"Wait one." The chief had known Nicole for only a month, and suddenly wished he had never met her. He turned to his exec, who shrugged.

"Looks like the thing's back on-line," the younger woman said. "Green across the board, now."

The chief frowned. He did not like it when machines decided to be finicky. It got people killed. His gut told him not to launch the CAG's fighter, but he was not left with much of a choice. "Stand by, CAG," he said. "You're up."

Nicole's heart rate picked up as she anticipated the launch. She eagerly watched for the visual signal from the control booth that hung down from the ceiling of the launch tunnel. Red. Yellow. Green.

Her ship suddenly accelerated away from the blast gates, the tunnel rushing past her in a blur as the stars outside seemed to grow larger, tantalizingly closer.

Something went wrong. Without warning, the magnetic field that accelerated the ship, and that was also responsible for ensuring the craft's safe passage down the center of the catapult tunnel, lost its integrity. Nicole's fighter slammed against the catapult tunnel wall, the Corsair's right stub wing disintegrating in a hail of sparks and electrical discharges. The ship yawed further to the right, the slender nose of its hull crumpling under the force, the metal screaming but the sound lost to vacuum. In the cockpit, Nicole reeled from the violence of the impact, the dampers in her ship unable to completely compensate for the horrendous forces that had taken hold of the fighter.

Long before humans could react, the launch safety computer intervened. Terminating the failed launch field, the computer activated emergency dampers that rapidly slowed Nicole's ship, bringing it to a stop twenty meters short of the tube's gaping mouth. Blast vents snapped open in the floor and ceiling of the tube; should the fighter explode, most of the force would be directed out the mouth and through the blast vents, lessening the force on the blast doors far behind that led to the vulnerable insides of the ship.

"CAG, can you hear me?" the launch chief asked tensely. He had seen this before. And worse. "Please respond."

"*Oui*," she said numbly. "I am... all right."

"Get her out of there," the chief said to the emergency crew that was already pouring through one of the tunnel's service entrances. "Move it."

Nicole Carré would not be doing any dogfighting this day.

* * *

"Sir," the intel chief said quickly, "it looks like we're facing two squadrons. One with a heavy division of two battleships and a heavy cruiser, and a second division with three cruisers."

Sinclaire nodded grimly. The odds were in their favor. For now. Turning to his ops officer, he said, "Order Mackenzie to take out the three cruisers. We'll handle the other lot."

"Aye, sir."

A few moments later, Sinclaire's orders reached Jodi as she led two Corsair squadrons from *Gneisenau* toward the enemy fleet.

"Roger," she acknowledged tightly. She was still unsettled by what had happened to Nicole. She had heard her over the common channel, screaming as her fighter was torn apart in the cat tube. Jodi had bitten her tongue so hard it had bled, as much to keep herself from tying up the channel with her own voice as from fear that Nicole might be hurt. But then the emergency crew had come. Nicole had been all right, just a little shaken up and with a mild concussion.

With difficulty, she pushed the thoughts of Nicole from her mind. Fifty-three other pilots from *Gneisenau* were depending on her now; as the second most senior pilot, she was in command. She was now the fighter force strike leader.

"Rolling out of your line of fire now," she told the controller on *Gneisenau*. She did not want her fighters anywhere near the massive gunfights that would soon erupt between the opposing capital ships.

Like a massive living thing, the two squadrons behind and to either side of Jodi's Corsair swept toward the three Kreelan cruisers that had the misfortune of being separated from the other ships of the Kreelan fleet.

As Sinclaire watched Jodi's fighters clear the field, he turned to Colonel Riata Dushanbe, the commander of *Gneisenau's* Marine regiment, the Fifty-Eighth African Rifles. "What is it, colonel?" he asked.

"Admiral," she said urgently, "we've finally gotten through to the colony, to some Marine forces there."

"What?" Sinclaire asked, incredulous. "When the hell did Marines arrive there? Why the hell didn't MARCENT inform us?"

Dushanbe shook her head. There was no way for her to know that Thorella's regiment had been dispatched outside of Marine channels in extreme secrecy, and Reza's contingent – a reinforced company – was so small that probably no one had bothered to report it as being on Erlang. No one had been expecting trouble like this. "I don't know, sir. Apparently, however many there were, there is only a company left, now. Alpha Company of the Red Legion's First Battalion, with a First Lieutenant Washington Hawthorne in charge. They've only got a single boat to lift their company and some injured civilians."

"What about the rest of the civilians?" Sinclaire asked. "There are supposed to be over a million people down there!"

"I asked him that, sir. He said he didn't know other than that the capital and probably the other settlements had been bombarded from orbit and completely destroyed." She paused. "He also felt sure that a lot more Kreelan ships would be headed this way, and quickly."

"How the bloody hell could he know that?" Sinclaire muttered to himself.

"Admiral," Captain Amadi said, "main batteries are within range, sir."

Sinclaire scowled. *Too many irons in the fire*, he thought. *As always*. He turned to his ops officer. "Have Mackenzie pull off a flight to provide escort to the Marines down there. Coordinate it with Dushanbe here." Then to Amadi, he said, "Captain, you may commence firing."

* * *

Jodi had just pulled out of her first attack run, her weapons crisscrossing the lead cruiser with splashes of light and a few minor explosions, when she received her new orders.

"There are still Marines down there?" she asked, mortified. Much closer to the planet than the rest of the fleet, she could see the damage the Kreelans had done to the surface: the blackened pockmarks where cities used to be, clouds of smoke streaking across the emerald surface like rivers of crude oil.

"Commander Mackenzie?" a voice suddenly interrupted on the link. "Is that you?"

"Eustus? Eustus Camden?" she asked, the muscles in her jaws tightening up. Where there was Eustus, there was... "What the hell are you doing here? And where's Reza?"

"It's a long story," the voice came back, scratchy in her earphones. Jodi could sense the strain in it. "Reza is... gone. Lieutenant Hawthorne's in charge down here, but he's in back trying to get some more wounded on board. There aren't many people that survived the attack on Mallory City. Jodi, we've got to get out of here, fast."

"Wait one, Camden," she said, hauling her fighter up and away from the three enemy cruisers. From here they looked like rakish beetles surrounded by enraged wasps. "Day-Glo, Snow White, Whip," she said, "form on me after you've made your runs." In perfect sequence, the three pilots acknowledged, and had formed on her wing in less than a minute. "Hangman," she called to the remaining senior pilot, "you're in charge. Finish those bastards off."

"Roger," Hangman, the second most senior pilot replied. "Good luck, Commander."

"All right, Camden," she said after switching back to the established air-to-ground link, "where's your beacon?"

As the four fighters screamed down through the atmosphere, the warships above them grappled like scorpions in a bottle, engaged in a fight to the death.

But Jodi could not push Eustus's words from her mind: *Reza was gone.*

Thirty-Eight

In the clearing mists that hung over the Plain of Aragon, the battle raged for the fate of Erlang. Like a living thing in agony, the mass of clashing humans and Kreelans writhed and twisted, their even lines having dissolved in the fury of battle. Battle cries and the screams of the injured and dying filled the air, accompanied by the crash and echo of sword against ax, wooden club against steel armor. The bitter smoke from the ruins of Mallory City swept over the once beautiful plain, masking the coppery scent of human and Kreelan blood that now splashed under the feet of those who remained standing, fighting. The humans fought for their home and their loved ones, the Kreelans for the honor of the First Empress for whom they had come.

Ian Mallory stood in a tiny eddy of the stream that was the battle, his breathing coming in harsh gasps as his eyes sought out another of the enemy to join the one that he had just slain. He turned in time to see Nathaniel Markham searching for his own prey. The big man's gaze fell on Ian, and he offered his old friend a smile that was cut suddenly, tragically short by the blade that suddenly exploded from his chest like a great silver tree from bloody earth.

"Nathaniel!" Ian screamed as he watched his best friend's face contort in puzzlement as his eyes took in the length of the sword that had just taken his life.

But then those eyes, normally those of a peaceful man, filled with a killing rage. As the Kreelan warrior who had struck him the mortal blow fought to withdraw her weapon from his body, he whirled around, seizing her by the hair with one great hand. Then, like a dying Thor, brandishing an ax rather than a hammer, he took his opponent's head from her body with a turn of his great weapon. Holding the severed head high above him, he let out a roar of triumph that boomed over the raging battle.

Before Ian Mallory could take a step toward his friend, Nathaniel Markham's voice died away. Without another sound, he collapsed to the earth, the Kreelan's head still clutched in his hand.

Like an all-consuming fire, the battle swept onward. And at its center were Reza and Esah-Zhurah, locked in their own battle of a higher order, refined well beyond the uncontrolled chaos that whirled around them like a great tornado of slashing steel and bleeding flesh. But while they stood as titans beside their warriors, they were evenly matched against one another, each denying the other the quick victory that would have spared lives on either side by the honor that bound them to the Empress and to one another. And so it was that their own private hell raged on in time measured by the blood spilled upon the ground from those around them, each dreading the blow that would kill their beloved.

The two circled and crashed together like beasts fighting for the right to mate, oblivious to the small ship that leaped from the forest but a few kilometers away, carrying Reza's company and a few Erlangers to the comparative safety of the human fleet.

* * *

"You look like hell, captain," Sinclaire told Nicole as she walked onto the bridge. While his comment seemed brusque, his voice was filled with concern.

"Thank you, sir," she said flatly as the lights suddenly dimmed and a deep thrum shook the ship as the main batteries fired again. One glance at the tactical display told her that she might as well forget about asking for another fighter. There would not be much to shoot at for much longer. Two of the three cruisers that Jodi's fighters had attacked were already destroyed. The third was severely damaged and obviously out of control. The battleships that had devastated Erlang from orbit were far from finished, but their efforts now were more out of spite than anything else. The guns of *Gneisenau*, *Hood*, and the other heavy ships would soon finish them, as well.

"Nicole," Sinclaire said, "I'm just glad that you're alive. I know you're upset about not being able to lead your people today, but I'm not one to push luck too far."

"I know, sir," she said, looking down at her shaking hands. "I am sorry." To herself, she thought, *He just does not understand*. It was more than just wanting to lead her people; combat had become an addiction, a craving that she had to satisfy. It often terrified her, but she did not know what else to do. Worse, since she had awakened in sickbay from the minor concussion she had received, passing out as the emergency crew freed her from her wrecked Corsair, she had felt terribly odd, as if ants were crawling on her body. She saw visions, flashes of some kind of battle, two warriors fighting, and felt her muscles twitch in time with movements other than her own. As she was coming from sickbay, she felt a horrible pain in her upper left arm, as if it had been torn by animal claws. She had nearly cried out, it had been so intense and shockingly sudden, but her tongue had remained silent. The pain had gradually faded to a dull throb, but her breathing remained abnormally rapid, and she could swear that she smelled her own blood. Turning away from Sinclaire, she stared at the viewscreen and the battle that raged there between human and Kreelan ships. But her eyes were far away. A muscle twitched in her face.

Sinclaire regarded her quietly as the bridge continued to bustle with the hectic activity of the battle.

He had seen the signs before, too many times. She had lost her edge. While it was a great regret for him, he would have to post new orders for Fleet Captain Carré. Her days of combat were over.

* * *

The sands of the hourglass in Reza's mind had run out. His Marines were well away, and he knew in his heart that Esah-Zhurah would beg the Empress to spare the people of this planet on his behalf. There was no point in prolonging the battle further, for that would only leave more Erlangers dead and increase the risk of harm coming to Esah-Zhurah, the one thing that he could not allow. He also knew that she would not attack him with his guard down; he would have to trick her.

With the ferocity of their sparring, it did not require much. Warrior priest and priestess, each was able to sense which attacks would fail, and which might not. Thus far, their only injuries had been mere trophies, a gash here or there for the healers to mend to a scar that would be a remembrance of this combat.

It was time. Esah-Zhurah lunged forward with her sword in an attack she instinctively knew Reza would deflect. But he surprised her by holding his sword arm downward at the last instant, leaving his torso completely exposed.

Esah-Zhurah's weapon did as it was designed, piercing Reza's breastplate just below his heart. The armor, sturdy as it was to a slashing attack, gave way like warm butter to the sharp tip of the sword's living steel.

Reza's vulnerable bones and flesh offered no resistance to the hurtling blade, whose blood-streaked point emerged out Reza's back, the armor peeled back around it. With a morbid thump, the sword's pommel slammed to a stop against Reza's breastplate.

* * *

Colonel Dushanbe was just informing Admiral Sinclaire that the boat carrying Hawthorne's Marines and its four-ship escort had landed in the starboard landing bay, when Nicole Carré suddenly screamed in agony. Clutching her hands to her chest, she crumpled to the deck and lay very still.

"Lord of All," Sinclaire boomed, rushing to his fallen officer and friend, "get someone from sickbay up here on the double!"

Carefully turning her over onto her back, he saw that all the blood had drained from her face. Her eyes were open, but Sinclaire hoped never to see whatever she was seeing: it was as if she was staring into Hell itself.

* * *

Esah-Zhurah's shocked eyes swept across the blade of her weapon as it protruded from her lover's back, covered in his blood. Her nose, far more sensitive than any human's, was flooded with its coppery tang. She heard, dimly, the sound of his sword dropping to the ground, and felt the weight of his sagging body as he wrapped his arms around her neck, his head falling to rest on her shoulder. All around her, like sails sagging under a dying wind, the Kreelan warriors suddenly lost their ferocity, their hearts torn by the force of Esah-Zhurah's emotional shock.

The humans, too, felt something change, and accepted the break Fate had given them. Confused and exhausted, they backed away from their Kreelan opponents by a pace or two, many of them dropping to the ground, chests heaving with pain and exertion.

"Pull it out, Esah-Zhurah," Reza whispered into the sudden stillness, speaking in the Old Tongue. His hands clutched at the armor protecting her back, his talons issuing a high keening sound as they sought purchase in the metal of her armor.

"No," she whispered. Her sword's blade had a serrated upper edge. It would tear out his heart if she tried to remove it. "No. Reza, I cannot... The healers will take care of you. They can remove it without–"

"You must," he breathed, a trickle of blood escaping his lips. "Please, Esah-Zhurah. You know I cannot return... home." He felt hot tears burning his face. "Let this be done... Let it be over... Now."

"Reza," she rasped. Her voice was an echo of the agony that seared her soul. She held him tightly with her free arm, thinking desperately for another way – anything – but there was none. She smelled the salt of his tears mingling with the scent of his blood, and suddenly wished she could cry with him. For him. The black of the mourning marks she had worn since he had gone so long ago just did not seem to be enough. "Forgive me, my love," she rasped as she closed her eyes. With one smooth motion, her sword hand drew back with all the strength she had, freeing itself with a ghastly grating sound against Reza's armor and the shattered bones of his ribcage.

Reza cried out before he slumped against her. She threw her sword to the ground and held him with both arms, her teeth grinding with anguish, her heart cold in her chest, dead with pain. Gently, with Syr-Kesh's steadying hands, she laid him on the ground, cradling his head to her breast.

"Reza," Esah-Zhurah whispered mournfully. There was so much to tell him, so much wonder that he would never know. "Why did you do this?"

His eyes, still gleaming with the life that faded rapidly within, fastened on her. He struggled to free his hand from the armored gauntlet, finally succeeding with Syr-Kesh's reverent help. Unsteadily, he reached for Esah-Zhurah's face. She took his hand and held it to her, kissing his fingers.

"You well know why, Esah-Zhurah," he said, softer than a whisper, barely a sigh. "You are the successor to the throne... on you the Way shall someday depend." He shuddered, suppressing the cough that would rend further his violated lungs, his damaged heart. Already it slowed, nothing more than a leaky valve as it sought in vain to pump more blood into the ruptured lungs where it rapidly pooled, and would soon drown him. "My life is nothing beside yours. I only ask that... in my memory, the Empress let live the people of this world."

"So much do you care for them," she said in a trembling voice as she watched her lover's life ebb away, "that you would utter your last words on their behalf?"

Reza smiled. "Not so much as that," he told her, his trembling fingers stroking her face. He could no longer feel anything below his waist. "My last words I save for Thee, Esah-Zhurah. While I love the Empress with all that I am, I love Thee all the more." He labored for another breath, knowing it would be his last. His chest was warm, too warm. "I shall... take my memories of you... to the Darkness that falls upon me. Your face and love shall keep me... for Eternity."

She watched helplessly as his eyes fluttered, closed. His hand, the hand that had held her, that had touched her as they made love, lost its strength, the fingers relaxing in her grip. His breathing stilled.

Shutting away the Universe from around her, she held him close as she had the child she had born to him, the son who had never felt his father's Bloodsong, the son whom Reza would never know.

On the Plain of Aragon, Esah-Zhurah wept without tears.

* * *

"Your orders, sir?" Captain Amadi asked quietly.

Sinclaire scowled at the tactical display. Thirty Kreelan warships, none of them smaller than a heavy cruiser, had just jumped in-system. There was nothing Sinclaire's task force could do to save the people down below. They did not have enough ships to hold them all, even if they had time to evacuate them. The first of the new Kreelan arrivals would be in orbit in less than thirty minutes. Sinclaire had recalled all the fighters, and the last of them were landing now. In one of the starboard landing bays, the last of Reza's Marines were carrying wounded civilians from their hijacked boat. They were lucky to be alive.

"Turn the fleet around, captain," he growled. "There's nothing more for us to do here."

Nodding sadly, Amadi quickly began to carry out his admiral's orders.

* * *

"What's wrong with her, doc?" Jodi had come to the sickbay the instant she had gotten free of the flight deck. She stood in the sickbay's anteroom with the doctor, her face still sweaty and marked with the outline of where her helmet had been pressed against her skin.

"I don't know," the surgeon said uneasily. "She's in deep shock, like she experienced some kind of massive physical trauma, but there's no evidence of any injury. Not a thing."

"Please," Jodi said, "I need to see her."

She was not ready for what she saw. For all she could tell, Nicole was dead, for nothing but a corpse could look so white. Her eyes were all that seemed to be alive. But they frightened Jodi: they were the eyes of the insane. She took Nicole's hand. It was freezing. "Nicole," she breathed, "can you hear me?"

Nicole's eyes pivoted slightly, then again, as if the muscles were no longer capable of the rapid and fluid movements they once had been. "Jo...di." The sound seemed alien coming from her blanched lips.

"I'm here, Nikki," Jodi said again, holding her friend's hand tightly, running her other hand across Nicole's chilled brow. "It'll be okay. Can you tell me what's wrong? What happened?"

"Reza," Nicole uttered, a little more clearly. "Help him."

Jodi fought back the tears that wanted to come to her eyes. She knew that others often saw them as a sign of weakness, but it was how she coped with things that otherwise would break her heart and crush her spirit. "Honey," she said gently, "Reza's..." She paused. It was so hard for her to say it. "He's gone, Nicole... dead. There's nothing–"

"No," Nicole said with such force that Jodi blinked. "No… help him… must not… let him die."

"Nicole, I know this is hard for you, but he's gone. Let him go. Besides, we've got to leave. There are more Kreelans coming and–"

Nicole's grip on Jodi's hand suddenly tightened, so hard and quick that Jodi let out a yelp of pain and surprise. "Nicole!"

"Help him," Nicole said through gritted teeth. The skin of her face was stretched tight, exposing the outlines of her skull through the bleached skin. Her eyes burned with ferocious intensity, like a wolf making its final leap before the kill. Jodi felt her knuckles grating together as Nicole's hand clamped down on them like a vice. "Save him." It was not a request, or even an order. It was a commandment.

Suddenly, the energy that had taken her over vanished, and she faded into unconsciousness, her heart beating erratically, her breathing shallow and unsure. Her hand, limp now, fell away from Jodi's. Her eyes rolled up to reveal the whites, then closed.

"Jesus," Jodi muttered, looking with widened eyes at the surgeon, who only shook his head; he was as shocked as she was. "If there's no real trauma," she said shakily, "she can't die, right?"

One glance at the vital signs monitors would have told her otherwise.

The surgeon shook his graying head. "I wish saying it made it so, but it doesn't. If I can't figure out what's causing her to be like this, I don't think she'll make it another two hours. Her body is just shutting down."

"Take care of her," she told him decisively before turning to the door. There was a certain Marine first sergeant she needed to see.

* * *

Eustus stared at the landing bay portal, as big around as a football field and filled with the stars and vacuum, safely on the other side of the force field.

"Eustus," Jodi said urgently, "it's Reza we're talking about."

"It's mutiny," Eustus snapped back. "More than that, it's suicide. You weren't there when the bombardment was coming down. You didn't see a whole planet get flattened. I did. And the fact that there's a whole shitload of Kreelan ships coming down our throats doesn't thrill me, either." He turned to Jodi, mindful of the blue eyes in her ebony face blazing at him. "Look, Jodi, I loved Reza as much as anybody ever did. I fought for him. I gladly would have died for him. But it's over. He's gone, along with the rest of them. He told me himself that he had no intention of coming back." He looked at Enya, who tended to some of the wounded, most of them Raniers. She was the real reason he did not want to go, he thought, ashamed in a way. Enya was worth more to him now than anything or anyone had ever been, and he was not going to just throw that future away. "I'm sorry, Jodi. But I'm not going. Maybe Hawthorne will–"

"Come on, Eustus!" Jodi nearly shouted, causing a few heads – Enya's among them – to turn in their direction. She lowered her voice. Slightly. "Hawthorne's no good for this and you know it. He's too straight to pull a stunt like this, and besides, he's too damn big. I couldn't get both him and Reza into the rear cockpit." She stared at him, willing him to come. "It's you or nothing, Eustus. I can't do it by myself."

"Can't do what?" Enya asked from behind them. "What are you up to, Eustus?"

"Nothing," he said, shaking his head.

"Commander?" Enya asked, a look of concern on her face. "What is it?"

"I think Reza's alive down there," she told her quietly. "And I need help to bring him back." She looked pointedly at Eustus.

Enya's brow furrowed. "How could he be alive? He was going to the Plain of Aragon to fight, I know, but... How do you know this?"

"Captain Carré – she's in sickbay right now – told me. She and Reza have some kind of special bond, they seem to know things about each other when there doesn't seem to be any possible way." She glared again at Eustus. "Nicole's dying, and the surgeon doesn't know why. I think it's because she's linked to Reza somehow, and is reflecting whatever's happening to him. I think he's important in some way that we don't understand. And if what Nicole said is true, and we don't do anything about it, we'll live to regret it. And Nicole will die."

"Could you make it through all those Kreelan ships?" Enya asked quietly. Eustus opened his mouth, but was smart enough not to say anything.

"We'll never know if we don't try." Jodi looked at Eustus again. "Time's up, jarhead. What's it going to be?"

"Eustus," Enya said quietly, "go with her."

"But–"

Enya raised a finger to his lips. "You must have faith, Eustus," she told him. "Our prayers brought your captain to our aid, and my prayers brought your heart to me. We don't know what has happened to our people. Maybe they are all dead. Maybe none of them have been harmed save those in the cities. But we do know that your Captain Gard is directly responsible for saving anyone who is still alive, and perhaps that kind of power is something worth the risk Commander Mackenzie is asking."

"Enya, it's suicide."

She nodded, biting her lip. This was the hardest thing she had ever done, sending the one man she had ever really loved off to die. "It well may be. But can we afford not to try?"

Eustus closed his eyes, hoping that it would all go away. Instead, he felt Enya's warmth press against him, her lips gently kissing his. "Go quickly," she said. "And may the Lord of All watch over you."

* * *

Master Chief Petty Officer Clarence Mahan was enjoying what was, ironically, the quietest period during a war cruise. As chief of the starboard catapults, he was responsible for getting *Gneisenau's* fighters and attack ships off the deck. Recovering them was someone else's job down in Pri-Fly. Now that the fleet was hauling itself around toward its jump point, it was only recovering fighters, not launching them. The standard four-ship alert had already been spotted on the outboard cats, leaving the rest of his watch free of major problems. Or so he had hoped.

"Chief," one of his assistants called, "we've got engine start on the number three alert bird."

"What?" Mahan said. The alert pilots were not normally kept in the cockpits, but in a ready room a few paces behind the blast shields. "Denkel, if you're pulling my leg, I'll–"

"No, chief, I'm not shitting you. Look." On the big board that made up the main display for the starboard catapult system, one of the alert ships was indeed powering up.

"Goddammit," Mahan snarled, "somebody'd better have a good explanation for this." He snapped the intercom circuit open. "This is cat control to Alert Three. Shut down immediately and get your ass out of that cockpit. Respond, over."

"Chief, this is Commander Mackenzie. I don't have time to explain, but I'd really appreciate a cat launch. I hate bolting down these tubes on manual."

"I'm sorry commander, but nobody said anything to me about any launches," Mahan said, wondering what the hell was going on. "I need to check with Pri-Fly on this one."

"Don't bother, chief," Jodi said as she brought the engines up to ninety-five percent power. The blast shields behind her automatically slid into place to prevent the fighter's engines from vaporizing the adjoining part of the hangar bay. "Pri-Fly won't know anything, either. See you later, Mahan."

"Commander–" He did not bother saying anything else. Her fighter was already gone: Mackenzie had guided it down the catapult tube manually. *Goddamn bloody dangerous stunt*, Mahan cursed silently. "Get me the bridge," he said to his assistant. "Somebody's going to be really pissed over this one."

* * *

"Jodi, this is insane," Eustus said. He was not qualified to fly as a back-seater on this ship, but he also was not an idiot. The holo display that was projected on the console and on the bubble canopy around him told him enough. There were Kreelan ships everywhere, although none had fired on them. Yet. "Even if we make it down there, how are we supposed to find him?"

"Do you know where this Plain of Aragon is that Enya mentioned?"

"Not exactly," he said, calling up a map display of Erlang on the computer. "It's supposed to border the ocean, on the far side of the coastal mountains where that glowing crater thing is. Hmmm... Due east of Mallory City – what's left of it – looks like that might be the place to start, anyway."

Jodi quickly evaluated the information that was echoed on her display. "Make you a deal," she said. "If he's not there, we'll split back to the fleet, and I'll think up some bullshit about bending you to my will." She grinned to herself. "I'll tell them I suddenly went straight and just had to have wild sex in the cockpit with you. No one else would do. What do you think?"

"No joy, commander," Eustus said, ignoring her attempt at humor as he clumsily called up the scanner data on what he hoped was the right place. "We've gone past the point of no return. We either come back with Reza or we don't come back at all."

Jodi nodded grimly. Around them, more warships of the Kreelan fleet sped toward Erlang.

* * *

Reza was in the temple, kneeling before the crystal that was the spirit of his order, the host of the cleansing fire that burned away the old to reveal the new. The crystal was light and warmth, wisdom and power. All else was darkness, without order. Chaos.

He was not alone. Sitting across from him was a warrior whose face he could not see but for her glowing silver-flecked eyes. Her hair was white as the snows of Kraken-Gol, her talons the color of his own blood.

"It is not yet your time, child," came the voice of Keel-Tath

Reza looked at his body, his eyes widening when he saw the armor of his breastplate, untouched, gleaming as when it was first made by Pan'ne-Sharakh.

"Pierced was my heart, Empress," he said, uncomprehending, knowing that he should be in Darkness, the place that was beyond all, where Time itself did not venture. He was dead.

"This I know, young priest," She replied. Her hands reached out to him above the crystal, and he took them, his flesh against Hers. "I have seen The One who shall inherit my spirit, who shall be the vessel of my Resurrection, the guardian of your heart. But She-Who-Shall-Ascend is only a part of the whole of which you are the other half. If you die, so shall she, in spirit and heart, if not in body, and the Great Bloodline shall come to an end. My Children shall perish from the world."

Reza felt his very soul chill at her words. "Can this be?" he whispered.

He saw the look of sorrow in Her eyes. "Indeed it can, My son," She said. "The cycles are few that remain to the Empire under the curse I set upon them so long ago. Soon it will be that no longer shall they bear any male children, and those who must mate will perish of the poison in their blood, and those who are barren shall witness the destruction of their race. Only in The One is there hope for the future, for My Children."

"What must I do?" Reza asked softly. Even in the dim light just beyond the crystal's glow, he could see the mourning marks that flowed down her face, so much like Esah-Zhurah. Even the immortal First Empress, he saw, could know remorse and compassion.

He felt the pain of the blade across his hand, the flesh of her palm pressing against his. The crystal glowed brighter, pulsing in time with Her heart. He felt the tingling of Her blood in his, felt the warmth, the fire. He heard only Her voice in the song that took his blood, but it needed no accompaniment; it was a universe unto itself.

"You must live," She said.

* * *

"I've got something at one o'clock," Jodi announced as she guided the Corsair through the debris-choked clouds, trusting her sensors to keep her from smashing into the mountains she knew lurked nearby. Below lay the burning pyre that had once been Mallory City.

"Just don't fly anywhere close to that blue glow, Jodi," Eustus warned, keeping his eyes fixed on the eerie light that penetrated even the smoke of the burning city.

"Trust me," she answered. She had no idea what it was, but nothing and no one could convince her to go closer to it than she already was.

Ahead loomed the last of the coastal mountains, and Jodi pulled the Corsair's nose up to clear them. Beyond lay the coastal plains and the ocean.

"Oh, shit," Jodi hissed as her ship squawked an alarm. "We're being tracked. There's a Kreelan ship down there, some kind of assault boat."

"Don't fire on it," Eustus told her. "Are your shields up?"

"Of course they are–"

"Drop them."

"Eustus–"

"Drop them!" he ordered. "Dammit, do as I tell you."

Cursing under her breath she dropped her shields, leaving her ship naked to attack by anyone hefting a fair-sized rock, let alone pulse weapons.

"Look!" Eustus said. "Down there!"

Jodi looked in the direction Eustus was pointing. "Holy shit," she whispered. On what must be the Plain of Aragon, she could see hundreds of human figures through a light mist. Most of them, she could tell, were not interested in her fighter, but in the perfect circle of Kreelan warriors, hundreds of them, who knelt on the plain itself. And in the open center of the Kreelan circle, she could see three figures.

One of them, she knew, had to be Reza.

"Why aren't they firing on us, Eustus?" she asked as she circled over the warriors, who seemed to pay her no attention.

"I don't know," he said, "but we'd better hurry up and get this over with before they change their minds."

"Roger that," she said quietly. She started the landing cycle, lowering the Corsair's landing gear and transitioning to hover mode. "If anybody ever told me when I was in flight school that I'd be pulling a damn fool stunt like this..."

Jodi set the fighter down smoothly just outside the circle of warriors, some of whom, she could see now, had taken a sudden interest in the new arrivals.

"All right," she said, her heart hammering, "let's do it." Leaving the engines idling, she cycled open the clearsteel canopy and disconnected the umbilicals linking her suit and helmet to her ship. She left her helmet on the shelf over the control panel. Eustus followed her out. "Let's take it slow and easy," she suggested.

"Good idea," Eustus said uneasily. His blaster weighed heavily on his hip, but he knew his life expectancy would be measured in tenths of a second if he reached for it. He followed Jodi out of the cockpit, clambering awkwardly down the diminutive crew ladder that had popped out of the hull.

By the time both were firmly on the ground, the warriors around them were on their feet, and there was no mistaking the hostility on their faces. "I'm beginning to have second thoughts," Eustus murmured.

"Stay here until I call you," Jodi told him. She was looking at the three warriors in the ring's center. One, with white hair that Jodi had never seen on a Kreelan before, was cradling Reza's body, oblivious to everything around her. A shiver ran down Jodi's spine. *I know who you are*, she thought to herself.

The other one, with the regulation black hair, stood by like some kind of bodyguard, her hands poised over her weapons, her eyes locked on Jodi and Eustus.

Moving slowly, her arms outstretched, palms open to show she was holding no weapons, Jodi made her way toward where Reza lay in the white-haired warrior's arms. The bodyguard moved through the surrounding ring of warriors to block her.

"I've come for Reza," Jodi said slowly and clearly. She had no idea if any of them understood Standard, but they should certainly understand his name. "Reza," she said again, pointing to his lifeless form.

The bodyguard looked confused, suspicious, perhaps, but did not move. Jodi decided to play her ace. It was all you could do when you only had one card left in your hand. Addressing the warrior with the white hair, she called, "Esah-Zhurah."

The bodyguard's eyes widened at that. The woman behind her, holding Reza, slowly lifted her head. She fixed Jodi with eyes that were as green as his, and so full of pain that it made Jodi's heart ache, no matter that this was her sworn enemy, an alien. She said something in a raspy voice to the bodyguard, who saluted with a fist over her right breast and stepped out of Jodi's path.

Jodi made her way past the warriors, who parted before her, and knelt down next to Reza. "I've come to take him home with us," she said gently, hoping Esah-Zhurah would understand.

"His home," Esah-Zhurah said slowly in Standard, the alien words coming to her only with difficulty after so many cycles of disuse, "is in my heart." Her eyes turned to his face, peaceful now, and pale, the thin line of blood from his mouth almost dried. "But you are right," she whispered after a moment. "It was for your kind that he denied himself before the Empress and parted with all he once loved; it was for your kind that he gave his life. His body, his ashes – even the collar of his honor – I grant you, for he died without Her forgiveness. He died not one with our Way."

Reaching out with a bared hand, Jodi gently touched Esah-Zhurah's face. "I'm so very sorry," she whispered. "I... I know how much he loved you. All these years, he never loved anyone but you."

"Did you love him?" Esah-Zhurah asked quietly, her magnetic eyes fixed on Jodi's face.

Jodi flushed with a sudden pang of guilt and embarrassment, but she did not look away. This was not the time for modesty. "I cared for him greatly," she said. "I... I held him once, at a time when I think he would have died from loneliness, without you. When he slept, he cried out for you. He told me about you, about your love. That's how I know your name."

Esah-Zhurah nodded. "Thank you for your kindness," she whispered. "Will you honor his memory?" she asked.

"Always," Jodi answered. "He will not be forgotten."

"Then he is yours," Esah-Zhurah said, her voice trembling. She carefully laid his body down, smoothing back the hair from the face she so loved. Gently, she kissed him on the mouth. "Fare Thee well, my love," she whispered in her own language.

Esah-Zhurah stood up and nodded toward Eustus, who walked quickly to where Jodi was kneeling. "You must go quickly," she told Jodi.

"Jesus," Eustus said upon seeing the gaping wound in Reza's chest. He saw the weapon that caused it lying in the grass nearby, its serrated edge festooned with gore. His last delusions about Reza still being alive quickly evaporated, regardless of what Nicole may have said.

"Come on, Eustus," Jodi said, trying not to look too closely at the wound, "we've got to hurry."

Esah-Zhurah turned away as Jodi and Eustus struggled with Reza's body. The smell and taste of Reza's blood were still strong, too strong, and she feared they would always be with her. She watched the blue glow of the First Empress's pulsating heart, still resting in the mountain crater, and prayed to Her for salvation, for forgiveness. For her own heart was dead, and never would live again.

Eustus was now acutely aware of why Jodi had needed someone's help. It took both of them to get Reza's body to the ship. Jodi danced up the ladder to the aft cockpit, standing on the edge of the hull to help Eustus as he climbed up behind her, Reza over his shoulder in a fireman's carry. After a few minutes of precarious balancing and brute force, Eustus was secured in the aft seat, holding Reza's body.

"Let's get the hell out of here," he said as Jodi dropped down into the pilot's seat and began the takeoff sequence, slapping on her helmet as the canopy whined into place.

Thirty seconds later, they were airborne.

* * *

"We're reading a ship ascending from the surface, sir," the intel officer reported. "Checks out as a Corsair."

"Mackenzie," Sinclaire growled.

"Looks like it, sir."

Sinclaire only grunted in response. On the tactical display, a tiny blue wedge detached itself from the planet and set course for the fleet, now hundreds of thousands of kilometers away. And everywhere, crowding the display, were red wedges accompanied by a few lines of elaborating data that identified the Kreelan ships that were appearing around Erlang like salmon about to spawn. "How many Kreelan ships, now?"

"Eighty-seven major combatants, sir, plus scores of smaller ships," the intel officer reported. "STARNET is reporting as many more still on the way."

"Bloody hell," Sinclaire whispered. It was the largest Kreelan battle fleet that had ever been assembled in Sinclaire's lifetime, and more ships were still arriving;

humanity would never have been able to amass such a fleet in one location so quickly. "How long to the jump point?"

"Nine minutes and forty-seven seconds, sir," Captain Amadi replied.

"And how long for Mackenzie's ship to reach us?"

Intel shook her head. "Almost eleven minutes, admiral, at the Corsair's top speed."

A little over a minute too late, he thought glumly. "Has anyone been able to contact her yet?"

"No sir," Amadi said. "Nothing since she left the ship." They had no way of knowing that Jodi had disabled the command datalink in her fighter that might have allowed Sinclaire to recall it on autopilot, overriding Jodi's own commands. And along with the datalink went the voice and video communications.

"She's on her own, then," Sinclaire said. "I won't risk the fleet for a single person."

"Sir," a yeoman called from the FLEETCOM position, "it's Commander Ivanova. She's in trouble."

* * *

Commander Ludmilla Ivanova, captain of *C.S.S. Gremlin*, a destroyer guarding the fleet's rear as it withdrew, was more than in trouble.

"Admiral, we're taking heavy fire from a cruiser that just dropped in-system," she said quickly as her ship rocked under the impact of another salvo.

"Captain!" the engineering officer reported, "We've lost the starboard aft-quarter shields!"

"Helm, roll us nine-zero degrees to starboard!" she ordered quickly. The destroyer responded immediately, rolling its exposed side away from the withering fire from the heavier Kreelan ship. "Make your course zero-five-zero mark eight-zero. All ahead flank!" While *Gremlin* was outgunned and out-armored, she was still faster and more maneuverable, and had her own set of fighting teeth.

Focusing again on Sinclaire's concerned image, she said, "We'll try to draw them off, sir." She smiled. "Wish us luck, admiral."

"Good luck, Ludmilla," he said. It was a paltry farewell to the captain and crew of a good ship. Both of them knew that *Gremlin* would not be returning to port. The Kreelan cruiser had the uncanny luck to have dropped in right behind the retreating human fleet, where none of the heavy ships could bring their main batteries to bear, and where they themselves were most vulnerable to enemy fire. It was *Gremlin's* job to hold off any Kreelan ships long enough for the fleet to jump out; if she could not, and Sinclaire was forced to turn any of his other ships to face the oncoming threat, he stood to lose a lot more than a single destroyer. "Godspeed, captain."

On Ivanova's display, his image faded, disappeared.

An explosion rocked the ship, throwing her forward against the combat restraints of her command chair. "Damage report!" she shouted into the chaos that was the bridge.

"Hull breach in engineering!" someone replied. "Main drives off-line!"

"Weapons," she ordered the crew manning the weapons stations, "ready torpedoes, full spread, home-on-target mode."

"Torpedoes ready, captain!"

In the main viewer, she could see the Kreelan cruiser gaining rapidly. Her skin tingled as she could almost sense the enemy ship's main batteries charging, almost ready to gut her wounded destroyer...

"Shoot!"

Just as the Kreelan cruiser's guns erupted with lethal energy, *Gremlin's* eight torpedo launch tubes jettisoned their own destructive cargo. Seven of them cleared the ship before the final Kreelan salvo tore into the thinly armored destroyer, boring into its reactor core. The *Gremlin* disappeared in a huge fireball that consumed Ivanova and her crew.

The eighth torpedo, not quite free of its tube, suffered minor, but significant, damage to its guidance system before it cleared the blast and debris that was all that remained of the *Gremlin*. As its siblings began their dance of death with the Kreelan cruiser, the eighth torpedo wandered off on its own. Its electronic brain damaged, no longer able to distinguish friend from foe, it circled through space, looking for a target.

Any target.

* * *

"Somebody just bought it," Jodi said as she watched the fireball fade to the residual glow that was all that was left of whatever ship it had been. Not far from it, she saw several smaller explosions silhouette a larger ship that passed through the first fireball, only to explode in its own turn. *Torpedoes*, she thought to herself. *Somebody nailed that Kreelan fucker*.

"How much farther?" Eustus asked. He had loved Reza as a friend and commander, but was losing patience with him as a corpse. His uniform was soaked with Reza's blood, and Reza's crushing weight in the already cramped cockpit was giving him a case of claustrophobia. The smell was none too pleasant, either.

Jodi checked her instruments. It was going to be a lot closer than she cared to admit. And the margin was not in their favor. "About six minutes," she said. She was not about to worry him with details, like they were going to be almost a minute short of the fleet's projected jump-out time. Unconsciously, her left hand pressed forward on the throttles, which were already pegged against their stops. The Corsair was giving her all it had.

All around them, the weapons of the dozens of Kreelan warships in the area were trained on them, but none had fired.

A warning buzzer suddenly went off in Jodi's ear. "Oh, shit," she hissed, craning her head, scanning the space around her.

"What is it?" Eustus asked, looking around frantically, although he did not even know what he was looking for.

"A torpedo's got a lock on us," Jodi said urgently. "There it is!" Highlighted on the holo display as the ship's targeting computer calculated the weapon's trajectory, the torpedo was coming at them from almost directly ahead. "Son of a bitch! It's one of ours! Hang on!"

She pulled up in a wrenching, twisting corkscrew, hoping to throw the torpedo off, to make it break its lock on her ship. She watched in the display as it passed beneath them, swung around, and began tracking them from astern.

Goddammit, she thought angrily. She could clearly see the human ships now, *Gneisenau's* enormous drives shining like a friendly star. But they were too far, much too far away.

"Jodi!" Eustus cried. He was propped up in his seat, looking aft at the torpedo. Forgetting for a moment that he was looking at his own death, he was mesmerized by the sight of the thing, the weapon's speed sufficient to induce fusion of the hydrogen in space on a molecular level, generating a bow wave of ghostly reddish radiation.

He did not see Reza's eyes flicker open.

Jodi did everything she knew to shake the weapon, but to no avail. She knew that their time was up.

"I'm sorry, Eustus," she said as the cockpit filled with the blood-red fusion glow from the approaching torpedo. "I'm so sorry."

Neither she nor Eustus noticed as metal claws took hold of them, just as the torpedo exploded above the cockpit.

* * *

Sinclaire turned away, sickened at the lives he had just seen wasted. And he probably would never know why Mackenzie had done what she did, or even what she was trying to accomplish. But it did not matter now. "That's it, then," he said angrily.

"The fleet reports ready for jump, admiral," Captain Amadi said quietly. Commander Mackenzie had not been with him for very long, but he had enjoyed her company greatly. Her loss, and the effective combat retirement of Captain Carré, was indeed tragic.

Sinclaire nodded. "Let's be off, then. If you need anything or there's any news, I'll be in my cabin." Two of his finest officers, a good destroyer and her crew, a full Marine regiment, and over a million civilians on Erlang, all written off. He wished he was planetside already, where he could find a nice dark pub and get thoroughly, utterly drunk. He kept his hands close to his sides, hoping that no one would notice that they were shaking.

"Aye, aye, sir." Amadi turned and began issuing the instructions that would take the fleet home.

* * *

In the landing bay, the Marines had been watching the holo display, howling their support of Jodi's run through the Kreelan lines as if they were at a Marine-Navy soccer game, evening up the score. But the bay was filled with shocked silence as the display showed the icon representing Jodi's fighter wink yellow and then disappear after her desperate attempts to get away from the brain-damaged torpedo. She and Eustus were gone.

A moment later, the display cleared entirely as the fleet jumped into hyperspace.

The Marines who now belonged to brevet Captain Hawthorne turned away, sadness and exhaustion etched on their features.

Enya found a corner to herself where she slumped down and rested her head in her hands, too tired even to cry. Her world was gone, her people gone, and now Eustus was gone, too. She had nothing left.

"Hey," she heard someone say, "do you feel that?"

"Feel what?" someone snapped angrily. "Your hand on my butt?"

And then she felt it, too. The air had suddenly grown heavy and still, as if they had dived under water. Her ears popped. As she looked up she was blinded by a searing blue-white flash.

"Explosion in starboard bay!" someone shouted in the maelstrom of lights that clouded her vision. She heard an alarm braying and running feet guided only by flash-blinded eyes. But there had been no sound, just the flash, and then the heavy feeling in the air disappeared as mysteriously as it had come.

As the others crowded their way out of the bay, fearful of a hull breach, Enya stayed in her corner, her eyes shut, waiting for her vision to clear. She did not know the bay like the Marines did, and could just as easily find herself running out the shielded landing door.

After a moment that seemed like forever, she opened her eyes. And there, in a heap of tangled arms and legs on the floor, looking wide-eyed at their surroundings as if they had never seen this place before, were Eustus and Jodi, with Reza's torn body between them.

"Eustus!" she cried as she leaped to her feet and ran toward them, throwing her arms around his neck and kissing him. The remaining Marines, shocked by what they saw, slowly gathered around the new arrivals, looking at them as if they were ghosts, the result of a mass hallucination.

"Lord of All," someone whispered.

"Get Captain Gard to sickbay, now," Jodi managed, still in shock. She was conscious only of two totally unrelated things: that Reza was somehow still alive, and that she had peed herself. The change of laundry, she decided, could wait; Reza came first. She struggled to her knees as helping hands pried Reza's talons from her numb shoulder and Eustus's thigh before they carried the stricken captain at a run to the sickbay. She did not try to dissuade the hands that picked her up, carrying her after him. Eustus, helped by Enya and a babbling Washington Hawthorne, trailed dazedly behind.

Final Battle

THIRTY-NINE

The world was strangely white, so unlike the darkness of Death, so unlike the place where the First Empress's spirit had waited all these generations for Her awakening, and where only he, among all mortals, had ever been. He could not imagine the power, the wonder that must come to the Empire upon Her return, and his heart stopped beating for a moment as he thought of Keel-Tath's spirit encased in Esah-Zhurah's body. He would have given anything, everything he had ever had, to see her in the white robes and slender golden collar, high upon the throne, the most powerful Empress his people had ever known. His only regret would be that he could never again call her by her birth name.

In the whiteness that was now the Universe, he saw strange shadows hovering above him like odd birds fluttering above a snow-covered field. Their jerky movements were accompanied by noises that were sharp and purposeful, but not threatening. Were they other spirits, perhaps?

But he knew that this could not be; the place of the banished was forever dark and cold, and all those who dwelled there did so in eternal solitude. Or did they?

The world seemed to turn slowly, the white turning to gray, the strange noises drifting away into silence.

He slept.

* * *

If any time had passed, he was unaware. Dreams of life, and things that were beyond life as any other human had ever known, came to him, played their parts upon the stage that was his slumbering mind, and left to wherever such dreams go. While he would never be able to recall the exact moment, at some point he became aware that he did, in fact, possess a body. He gradually became sure of this because of what his mind perceived with gradually increasing clarity: pain. It was not the sharp, excruciating pain of a weapon cutting flesh, the kind of pain that he had been trained and toughened to withstand, to endure; it was the slow, throbbing pain of his body struggling to heal itself. This pain also was something he was well accustomed to. But this was deep, to his very core, and he realized in that instant that he was still alive.

The shock of that realization was sufficient to send enough adrenaline through his sluggish body to bring him to the threshold of consciousness. He opened his eyes. He was still in the white place, but saw no shadows.

"Reza," said a voice, so softly that he could barely hear it. "Can you hear me? Squeeze your right hand if you can. Do not try to talk."

Not questioning the instructions, Reza tried to carry them out. Sluggishly, he traced the nerves from his brain to his right hand, commanding it to close. Nothing. He concentrated harder, ordering his hand to obey. At last, he was rewarded with a slight twitching of the muscles in his forearm, causing his fingers to move fractionally.

"Can you feel this?" the voice asked with barely contained excitement. Reza felt a gentle pressure around his fingers, the squeeze of another's hand. He replied with another feeble movement of his fingers.

In his vision, he saw a shadow appear above him that gradually resolved into something that, after a moment, he recognized. It was a human face.

Nicole.

He tried to speak her name, but somewhere in the complex chain of physical operations that made speech possible was a breakdown. His lips, feeling swollen and numb, parted. The tip of his tongue curled toward the roof of his mouth, behind his teeth, to its accustomed position for making the "n" sound. But that was all he could do. His lungs were too weak to force enough air into his larynx to make the sound of her name. He tried again, hard.

"Ni...cole," he breathed faintly.

"Please, *mon ami*," she said softly, placing a finger gently against his lips, "do not waste your energy trying to talk. We will have plenty of time for that later."

She smiled, and Reza saw tears brimming in her eyes. It took him a moment, but it finally struck him that she looked exhausted, haggard. Her face was pale and drawn, her normally flawless ivory skin creased and sallow. Her eyes were bloodshot, with dark rings beneath them.

She mourns, he thought absently. But that was at odds with the light that shone in her eyes now. They were joyful, relieved.

"You will be all right, now," she said. It sounded to Reza as if the words were more to reassure herself. "We were very worried about you for a while. You were hurt very badly."

"How... long?" he asked, ignoring her pleas to conserve what little strength he had. His range of vision began to constrict, the periphery of his world turning to a dull, featureless gray until all he could see was Nicole's exhausted face.

She hesitated for a moment, and Reza sensed a general feeling of unwillingness to tell him the truth. His senses were terribly dulled, blunted like a rusty sword, but they told him that much.

"Six months," she said finally, her eyes questing, hoping the news would not send him into shock. When she saw that he was not fading on her like he had so many other times over the last months, she went on, "It has been six months since we left Erlang. After you got Eustus and Jodi to *Gneisenau* – however it was that you did it – the surgeons worked on you for many hours." Her smile faded with the remembrance of how agonizing that time had been. She herself had to be anesthetized, to shield her from the pain that Reza was feeling as the surgeons worked on him, trying to reconstruct his shattered body. "You never came out of the anesthesia, never fully regained consciousness," she went on. "Until now. You have been in a coma all this time." Her own recovery from the psychologically-induced trauma had taken two months, and the news that she was being forcibly retired from combat duty sent her into a bout of depression that she had still not entirely recovered from.

"You... all right?" he whispered.

"I am... better, now. I know I must look awful, but I have not been able to leave you." She looked down at her hand holding his. "I had a great deal of leave built up, so I decided to take some. To be here for you, when you woke up."

Reza's heart ached for her. He sensed the long, lonely hours she had spent at his bedside for months, wondering each moment if the next he would be dead, or would never wake up at all. "Thank you, my friend," he sighed.

"I could not leave you here alone," she whispered. Tony had understood, and had supported her after *Gneisenau* had returned to Earth on Fleet HQ's orders. He himself had spent many hours beside her, beside Reza. The two men had not seen each other in a long time, since the wedding that had made Tony and Nicole husband and wife, but there was a bond of trust between them that went far beyond the measure of their acquaintance.

"Erlang?" he asked as his strength began to wane, his range of vision narrowing again.

"The Mallorys, and what few Raniers are left, are well," Nicole said, still marveling at how that was possible. While the cities and major townships had been totally destroyed with grievous losses among the population, the vast majority of Erlangers – almost exclusively Mallorys – had survived. The Kreelans, after retrieving whatever it was that they had come for, had mysteriously departed without inflicting further harm. "Several convoys of ships have taken them the things they need to help rebuild. Ian Mallory sends his hopes for your recovery, and his thanks."

She did not add that he had also petitioned to be a witness in Reza's defense at the court-martial that had long since been planned for him. He was charged with multiple counts of murder, including those of President Belisle of Erlang and Chief Counselor Melissa Savitch, as well as high treason against the Confederation.

Reza sensed that there was something deeply wrong, something that she was not telling him, but his body demanded that he rest. "I am glad that Ian lived," he said quietly

The last thing he felt before his eyes closed was the gentle warmth of Nicole's lips pressed to his.

* * *

Tony Braddock was a troubled man. Someone to whom he owed his own life and that of his wife was in a dire situation, and there did not seem to be any way for him to help. While he had told Nicole that Reza had been charged with murdering President Belisle, Counselor Savitch, and an Erlang Territorial Army soldier, plus what he took as nothing more than a gratuitous and hate-inspired charge of high treason, he had not told her how extensive was the evidence against him. Not only did Colonel Markus Thorella claim to have been a witness (by remote, naturally), the man had also produced an especially damning piece of evidence in the form of a recording of the soldier's and Belisle's murders. The holo had been validated by the court in the last months, meaning that it had been declared devoid of tampering, was genuine, and would be admitted as evidence in Reza's court-martial. The alleged murder of Counselor Savitch was based entirely on Thorella's say-so, but considering the other evidence in hand, Tony Braddock knew that almost any military or civilian court would convict Reza out of hand. Politically, as the war went on and worsened, they could ill-afford not to. The public wanted a scapegoat for the pillaging of their civilization, and they would have one. And who better than Reza, who was caught between two worlds?

Worse – *How could it be worse?* Tony asked himself – since so much time had passed and no one was sure if Reza would ever come out of the coma, they had dispensed with the pre-trial preliminaries that might have given him some sort of due process, at least in terms of technicalities. Most of the witnesses for his defense had been released to fleet duty, their sworn testimony recorded for the proceedings. But it was not the same as in-person testimony, Braddock knew, especially when Reza's chief accuser, Colonel Thorella, had conveniently been ordered to a posting on Earth after he had somehow explained away the annihilation of his own regiment on Erlang.

While Tony had no proof, he had no doubt that there were some dark forces moving things along. He suspected Senator Borge and his increasingly large and vocal militant following of having a hand in it, but there was no way to prove it. And even if that were true, what could he do? Go to the president and accuse Borge of subverting the legal process in the military?

He smiled bitterly. Even with evidence as solid as Kilimanjaro, that would be foolhardy, at best. Borge had few remaining political enemies except the president and a few older and more powerful senators who still remembered what democracy was like, and who cherished the ideal above the rhetoric of their office.

And there were still a few young fools like Tony Braddock.

He rolled over, careful not to disturb Nicole, sleeping beside him. She seemed so much better now, after the months she had spent recovering from whatever had come over her, all the while distraught over whether Reza would survive. Tony had found it maddening sometimes, but he had done everything he humanly could to be there for her, to comfort her and try to lighten her burden. He knew she had been, and still was, deeply depressed at being assigned a non-combat position, but he was relieved that she had finally been taken out of harm's way. She had done more than her share, and it was time for them to have some time together as man and wife, and perhaps to ask themselves again if they were ready to become father and mother.

He heard her whisper Reza's name in whatever it was that she dreamed. His heart used to darken out of jealousy, wondering if perhaps she did not really love Reza more than she did himself. But over time, his fears had subsided. She loved Reza, yes, but as a sister might a brother or close friend. Perhaps there had been a time when she had wanted it to be something more. But he knew, from both Jodi and Nicole, that Reza would never have accepted anything more than platonic love from her or any other human woman; Reza's heart lay elsewhere, deep in the Empire.

Braddock had also listened to Jodi tell him of her suspected "psychic link" between Nicole and Reza, but he had never believed it until Admiral Sinclaire himself had told him of what had happened to Nicole on *Gneisenau's* bridge when Reza was wounded.

Braddock would have to learn more about that, and many other things, come morning, he thought, as well as bring an old friend some very bad news. He would go and visit Reza, not as a friend, but as his legal counsel in a trial that he knew could only result in Reza's execution.

* * *

"...and that's where you stand, Reza." Having finished outlining his friend's situation, Tony sat back in the chrome chair next to Reza's bed, feeling drained. A week had passed since he had first resolved to visit Reza, but the doctors had refused any visitors other than Nicole, who seemed to be a catalyst in Reza's recovery. But after seven days the patient's condition had improved enough that the doctors had finally allowed Reza one additional visitor. His defense counsel.

Reza showed no reaction, but continued to stare out the window as he had the entire time Tony had been talking.

Braddock frowned. "Reza, did you hear anything that I just said?"

"Yes," Reza said, at last turning to face him, his face an unreadable mask. "I heard and understand."

Braddock's temper flared. "Dammit, Reza, they're not just trying to throw the book at you, they're trying to dump the whole library on your head! Everyone who knows you knows that you would never have committed these crimes, but the court will–"

"I did, Tony," Reza said quietly, his eyes glinting in the light.

Braddock's mouth hung open for a moment. "What?" he said. "What did you say?"

"I killed Belisle and the Territorial Army soldier," Reza went on, his voice not showing the keening in his blood. "The killing of the soldier was unfortunate, an act of self-defense, but I killed Belisle with forethought." He paused, noting the blood draining from Braddock's face. "And if I had to do it again in front of the Confederation Council itself, I would. He was an animal, a murderer. Had I not killed him, or had the Kreela not come and destroyed the city, many of Erlang's people would even now lay dead at his hands. As for Melissa Savitch, her death was Markus Thorella's deed. And I shall yet find a way to avenge her."

"Can you prove that Thorella killed her?" Braddock asked, seeing his case to defend Reza foundering as surely as a scuttled ship. But perhaps there might be enough to hang Thorella for murdering Savitch. At least that bastard could swing beside Reza on the gallows.

"None but my word."

"That's not good enough, Reza."

Reza nodded gravely. In the world in which he had been raised, the world of the Kreela, one's word was a bond stronger than steel, a commitment backed by one's very life. Among those of this blood, among humans, however, it often meant little or nothing. Especially if one stood accused in a court of law. "I would have taken his head, as well, had he not outwitted me," Reza told him, describing Thorella's scheme and what exactly had happened in Belisle's office. "He shall not deceive me again."

No, Braddock thought, *he won't: you will be a dead man and he will go free.* "Reza," he said, leaning forward to emphasize what he was saying and shocked that Thorella's accusations were even partially true, "confession is only going to earn you a quick trip to the gallows. The only way I can help you is if there are some mitigating circumstances, maybe by having some Mallorys testify as to Belisle's misdeeds. We might be able to get that charge reduced to a crime of passion in the UCMJ, or even dropped altogether if we can get the Council to cede jurisdiction to Erlang."

Reza was warmed but amused by his friend's determination to keep him from the hangman's noose. He shook his head. "My friend Tony, you know far better than I that the Council will do no such thing. They cannot. I killed Belisle and the soldier, but not Melissa Savitch. To try and convince anyone otherwise would be to lie. And what of the charge of treason?"

Braddock shook his head, wishing that this were all a bad dream and that he would wake up in a warm bed next to Nicole. Even if he could get the murder charges dropped or reduced, the treason charge would not be let go. "How could you have done this Reza?" he asked more to himself than his doomed friend. All Tony could do now was to ensure that due process was given and the procedures themselves were legal. "You don't have a prayer with the judges. You may as well have just stayed there and died."

"I tried," Reza said quietly.

Braddock frowned. "The only other alternative I can think of is to ask the president to pardon you. I mean, since you are the only real authority on Kreelan affairs, maybe–"

"Impossible," Reza said quietly. "I am accused of capital crimes, Tony, two of which I am guilty by my own admission. How can it be that your society, which claims to hold justice so high, could simply allow me to go free? I do not well understand the politics of the Confederation, but I do not see how even the president could manage such a thing without devastating repercussions. He would not pardon me; he could not. And I do not wish it. I knew what I was doing when I took Belisle's head. I simply did not intend to survive to receive the punishment I must under Confederation law."

"You could escape," Tony said quietly. He was not suggesting it as a counsel, but as a friend. He knew that Reza would not have done what he did without good reason, but that would not hold up in a court, especially if Reza confessed. "It would be easy for you," he said. He knew as well as anyone that Reza could disappear like a ghost if he wished.

Reza shook his head. "And go where, Tony? To the hills of this planet? To the desert? Even if I could whisk myself to Eridan Five and dwell among the saurians there, I would not. What would be the point? Even without a trial, I am an outlaw among your kind, having forsaken the cloth of the Corps and the Regiment, and I cannot return to my own people without disavowing the oath I made that banished me. And that is something I can never do, even at the price of my own head."

Braddock did not say anything for a while. He felt like his guts had been ripped out and stomped on.

"What about Nicole?" If Reza had resigned himself to death, then so be it. There was nothing more he could do for him. Now he had to worry about Nicole. His wife. "How will she handle your death?" Tony asked, imagining the metal cable tightening around Reza's neck, Nicole writhing in agony as it happened, filling her with the same grisly sensations that Reza would feel. "What is this bond, or whatever it is, between you going to do to her?"

Reza had been devoting a great deal of thought to that, but he had no answer. He simply did not know. Even the memories of the Ancient Ones that only seemed to unlock themselves in his dreams had left him no clue. "I do not know," he said helplessly. "There is no way to undo what has been done."

"Does this link still exist?"

Reza shook his head. "I do not know. I have not sensed her since I awakened, but that means nothing. The Blood that flows through her is much diluted, for there is little enough in me. The bond has always been little more than a filament between us. Perhaps the shock of what happened broke it..." He shrugged helplessly at Braddock's uncertain expression, his own heart filled with fear on her behalf. "Tony, if there was any way at all to guarantee her safety, I would do it. But I just do not know."

"Sometimes, when she dreams, she speaks in a strange language. Would that be the language... your people speak?"

Reza nodded. "It would be the Old Tongue," he explained, "the language used in the time of the First Empress. She would only speak it if the bond was unbroken."

Braddock's heart sank. He was afraid that would be the case. "She spoke that way last night."

Reza closed his eyes, his heart beating heavily in his chest with grief. "Then I fear that whatever I feel, so shall she."

"She'll die, Reza."

Opening his eyes, Reza looked his old friend in the face, his own twisted in a mask of emotional agony. "I know," was all he could say.

* * *

"Now tell me, Markus," Borge said cheerfully, "isn't this far better, even after having had to wait so long?"

Markus Thorella smiled as he cut a strip of sirloin that was among the usual delicacies served at Borge's table. "Yes, your Honor," he said honestly. "I have to admit that I thought you were wrong all this time, but now..." He shrugged. "I was wrong. Publicly humiliating Gard has been more fun than I possibly could have imagined."

In many ways, an outside observer might have thought that the two were like father and son. It was a comparison that would not have been lost on Borge, although Thorella would have chosen to ignore it. Borge had sponsored the younger man, getting him out of trouble when required – as in the nasty incident on Erlang – while developing him into the political and military tool that he needed. He was daring, ruthless, and bloodthirsty, all characteristics that suited Borge's needs most satisfactorily. It had been a lengthy struggle to keep Thorella from following his passions when he should have been following orders, but it had been worth it. Borge's plans demanded such an individual, and the time was drawing near for him to put Thorella to his ultimate use.

The fact that he would eventually have to kill Thorella was entirely beside the point. He could never allow such a powerful weapon to exist after its usefulness had ended.

"So," Borge asked, "tell me, how goes the war?"

Thorella looked startled. "You haven't heard?"

Borge shook his head as he carefully set down his fork. He was not in the mood for surprises. He never was. "What's that supposed to mean?" he said. "Is there something the General Staff hasn't been telling us?"

"I don't know, Senator. But Admiral Zhukovski–"

"That Russian bastard," Borge hissed under his breath. *I'll make Zhukovski eat gravel one day*, he vowed to himself. "He's a meddler and a fool."

"Well," Thorella went on, "my little network found out that there's been something strange going on. Zhukovski's people apparently believe that the Kreelans have slacked off heavily in the last few days in their overall offensive, and a lot of their fleet units have mysteriously disappeared."

"Are you telling me that those witches are retreating?"

"I don't know, sir," Thorella said carefully. He was not about to stick his neck out on the basis of someone else's information, no matter how valid it might be. "But that was the word I got. Unfortunately, I assumed that it would have already made its way to the Council by now."

Borge nodded. He was furious, boiling inside, but not with Thorella. The Council should have been informed immediately, and he was determined to find out why it had not. "Not your fault, colonel," he said graciously, actually meaning it, "not at all. But I am afraid that this will cut our dinner date a bit short."

"I understand, sir," Thorella said, relieved that Borge's wrath would be directed away from him. Without hesitation, he rose from the table after Borge and followed him to the hall that led to the front door of the senator's mansion.

"Be standing by, Markus," Borge said. "I may need your services very soon."

"It will be my pleasure, your Honor," Thorella replied, shaking the older man's hand before he put on his cap and opened the door to leave. The smell of coming rain was strong in the night air. "You know where to reach me."

As the younger man walked to his waiting speeder, Borge returned to his study to contact his staff. They all had a great deal to do tonight.

* * *

"Blast it," the president said, "how did he find out? The entire bloody Council and Senate is up in arms, screaming that the Executive has withheld vital defense information from them without due cause. Borge has asked for an emergency Council session this morning, and no doubt putting my head on the chopping block will be the topic of discussion." He had no doubt what the result would be if Borge somehow managed to push through a vote of confidence.

Zhukovski shrugged. "Is not so difficult that he found out, given nature of information," he said. "Anyone gets idea that Kreelans are backing off, word spreads like fire, and to devil with security."

"That does not help us, Evgeni," Admiral L'Houillier said, exasperated. "The fact that your people came up with some analysis like this on the war and were not able to keep it secret–"

"What do you propose I do, admiral?" Zhukovski retorted before his superior could finish. "Shoot my entire staff, their families and friends? Everyone wants war to end, and is willing to pass on good news to others, rules and regulations be damned. But leak of Kreelan 'withdrawal,' as good Senator Borge might say was, perhaps, premature."

"Meaning?" the president asked sharply.

Zhukovski called up a galactic map on the table's holo system. "Information that Borge received was initial analytic conclusion," Zhukovski explained in his rumbling voice. "Young analyst of mine saw pattern of sharply increased losses among Kreelan ships and ground forces in battles over last few days, without apparent reason. Further, she found that far fewer Kreelan ships are now in human space than week ago, and offensives on and against many of our colony worlds have suddenly and inexplicably collapsed." He frowned. "It is as if Kreelans have suddenly lost will to fight. This is information she initially reported informally to me, and I presume is same information received by Borge."

"I sense a large 'but' coming up, Evgeni," L'Houillier said.

Zhukovski turned his good eye on the senior admiral, nodding his head gravely. "Indeed, it is so. Analyst continued her good works, and discovered what I believe to be Truth, with large T." The other two men were silent. "Her analysis of STARNET reporting shows that large number of Kreelan warships have passed through trans-Grange and Inner Arm sectors on what looks like converging vectors."

"Well, where?" the president said impatiently. "Dammit, Evgeni, spell it out!"

"We have only been able to plot location to spheroid of about eight-thousand cubic light years, centered toward galactic hub, past Inner Arm rim worlds." He sat back, waving his hand dismissively. "But that is immaterial."

"Why, Evgeni?" L'Houillier asked him.

Zhukovski eyed him closely. "Because, my dear admiral, if projections of my analyst – completed as of this evening – are correct, as I believe they are, no fewer than three thousand Kreelan warships are massed in that sector for what can only be final chapter in this war: total destruction of humanity. And those are ships we know about. There could be more. Many more."

The other two men sat silent, dumbstruck.

"Three thousand," L'Houillier whispered finally. "Evgeni, that is impossible! How could they mass that many ships, and so quickly? We do not have half as many warships in our entire fleet!"

"Exactly my point," Zhukovski said as he took another sip of the over-sweetened tea. "Why Kreelans suddenly die like flies in combat, like drunkards or fools, I do not know. But with three or four thousand ships, even drunkards or fools can destroy Confederation Navy and every colony populated by *homo sapiens*."

"Lord of All," President Nathan whispered, "what shall we do? Evgeni, even if you are completely wrong – which, unfortunately, I doubt – if that information were to reach the press, we'll have an interstellar panic on our hands. The government will collapse."

"Borge will not hesitate to use it against you, Mr. President," L'Houillier said. While he was supposed to be apolitical, the Grand Admiral had no illusions about Borge's own lust for power, and had no doubt that he would use any tool available to further his own cause. "Nor can we legally keep the information from the Council, even if there were no leaks."

Nathan nodded. His political position had just disappeared, vanished into a bottomless morass. But that was not his real concern; the people of the Confederation were. "I'll have to strike a bargain with him."

"Better to be bitten in throat by venomous snake," uttered Zhukovski, not relishing the president's position. He himself despised Borge and his sycophants, avoiding them whenever possible. Unlike L'Houillier, he made no effort to disguise his personal or political likes and dislikes.

"Believe me, Evgeni," the president said, "I would much rather jump into a pit of such snakes than give Borge this kind of leverage." He thought of how long he and Borge had been friends, before Borge had changed, been consumed by a lust for power that had made him into something alien, despicable. *It's strange*, Nathan thought, *how well I thought I once knew him. I wonder what ever made him change into something so evil?* "But I don't have any choice, do I?"

The two military men looked at each other, then at the president – their commander-in-chief – for whom they had worked for many years. They could not exactly call each other friends, but they were close and respected one another.

"No, sir," L'Houillier said flatly, wishing there was some other way out, "you do not."

"And what of the Kreelan fleet?" Nathan asked. "Is there anything we can do?"

"I have already taken liberty of calling operations officer," Zhukovski said, exchanging a look with L'Houillier. The woman, competent though she was, was a political animal who would jump at any chance to get ahead. "I gave her 'hypothetical' scenario to model on command computers, to see what best fleet reactions would be." He winked at L'Houillier. "I explained that Grand Admiral was most interested in such extreme cases to get more money for fleet expansion, and would be most grateful. Results should be available in another hour."

"Evgeni, you are incorrigible," L'Houillier said with a wry smile. "You are worse now than as a midshipman."

They were silent then, each of them turning Zhukovski's grim news over in their heads.

"Well," the president sighed, "I guess there's not much for it. Thank you gentlemen, and please keep me apprised of the results of the simulations. If you'll excuse me, I have some calls to make."

The two Navy officers got up, saluted, and left the president as he called in his aide and began to prepare to meet Borge's onslaught.

"You realize, admiral," Zhukovski said quietly as the two of them walked down the corridor to the elevators, "what simulations will say?"

"Of course, Evgeni," L'Houillier said glumly. "Despite Laskowski's best efforts to show that she can come up with a plan for victory, the computers will show that we are about two thousand ships short. Even if we concentrated every battle group in a single place to defend against a massed Kreelan attack, we would still be outflanked and destroyed, no matter how poorly the enemy fought."

As they made their way back to Joint Headquarters, Zhukovski wondered about the Kreelans' sudden lapse of fighting spirit. He made a note to ask someone who might just know.

* * *

Reza stood perfectly still in the center of the room, naked except for his collar. His long black hair was again carefully braided in a cascade down his back, a startling contrast to his pale but now healthy looking skin. Starting with his left little toe, he began to flex each muscle in his body, working up his left leg to his waist, then back down his right leg. Then he began to work on his abdomen, then his upper body. He noted with dismay how weak he had become, how quickly his muscles tired, but that only fueled his determination to rebuild both his body and his spirit. It was all he could do, and so it is what he did.

He performed the exercises of body and mind that he had learned as a boy and young man, taking himself to his present limits, slightly beyond, then resting. Even though he was a prisoner shortly to be condemned, the hospital still viewed him as a patient, and so he had no trouble getting the food he needed for the repairs his body was making to itself. At one point, he had even considered asking for his Kreelan clothing to be returned to him to wear, but there was no point; the shape of his body had altered so much that nothing would fit, or so he believed. If necessary, he would wear no clothes at all rather than disgrace himself in ill-fitting armor.

He was just completing the first cycle of calisthenics, vaguely similar to human tai chi, when a knock came at the door. He closed his eyes, looking beyond the metal confines of the room as he ran an impromptu test of his weakened psychic abilities.

Evgeni Zhukovski, someone he had not seen in many years. And he had a very, very troubled mind. He put on a plain white robe for the admiral's benefit.

"Come," he said as he turned toward the door.

He heard the electronic buzz as the security lock was released, and Zhukovski quickly pushed through with his good hand.

"Welcome, admiral," Reza said, taking Zhukovski's hand. "This is a pleasant surprise."

"I wish I could say same, Reza," Zhukovski said sadly. "You as man condemned does not appeal to me. Counselor Braddock has told me of your situation. I wish there were something I could do. I am sorry."

Reza nodded. Zhukovski understood him.

"I know this is unfair, Reza," Zhukovski went on as the two of them sat at the tiny table in Reza's room, "but something has come up, and I find I must ask your help."

"I will try," Reza told him.

The admiral nodded, and over the next few minutes explained what he and Admiral L'Houillier had discussed the previous night.

After he had finished, Zhukovski said, "Well, how do you think?"

Remaining silent, Reza stood up and walked to the armored window that looked out over a tree-filled courtyard. It was also backed with an invisible force field. While he was still technically a patient, he was very much a prisoner, at least in the minds of his keepers.

"Something has gone wrong with the Ascension," he said quietly, his fists clenching at his sides to keep them from trembling with anxiety. "The Empress is in distress."

"What does that mean?" Zhukovski asked. "Is she sick? Dying?"

Reza shook his head. "It is not so simple as that," he told him. He had never spoken to anyone of the Empire, save for what he had told Nicole and Jodi. But now, after hearing what Zhukovski had told him, he felt the old admiral had a right to understand. "The Empress is really two entities, one of flesh, the other of spirit. Her body is that of a warrior who is determined in life to be the vessel for Her spirit. When the reigning Empress is near death, the Ascension takes place, and the spirit is passed from the old Empress – whose body then dies – to the chosen vessel. That process has not been interrupted in over one-hundred thousand Standard years... until now."

Zhukovski was shocked not so much by the event itself, but by the longevity of the unbroken chain. *One-hundred thousand years*, he thought to himself with amazement. So long ago, early humans had not even scrawled primitive paintings upon the walls of their caves, and these aliens already had a global, perhaps even interstellar, empire. "What could have caused this?"

"I cannot be sure, but it must have something to do with what took place on Erlang. You see, there is another, a third entity, that of the First Empress, whose spirit fled to what you might call Purgatory many, many centuries ago. It was said in legend that someday Her spirit would return to us; that, joined with the reigning Empress, She would grace Her Children with the ancient powers which had for so long been lost to us." He turned back to Zhukovski, a look of genuine fear on his face. "She has returned. I know this to be true. But something has gone wrong."

Zhukovski did not know what to make of Reza's explanation, Kreelan religion holding little interest for him, and the rest sounding like fantasy from ancient legends. He was interested only in its effects. "Is this why they fight so poorly?" he asked. "They are... preoccupied with these events?"

"'Preoccupied' is hardly the word, admiral," Reza told him, fighting the nausea that rose from his stomach. *Esah-Zhurah*, he wanted to cry out, *what has happened?* "The will of the Empress is their will, their motivation, their reason for existence. They are not telepathic as you might understand it, but there is a psychic bond that links every heart in the Empire together unless, as in my case, it is intentionally severed by Her hand. If the Empress is in distress... if the vessel of Her spirit has died prematurely... they will not know what to do. They will be lost." With difficulty, he managed to find the chair opposite Zhukovski, slumping into it like a dying man.

It was difficult for even Zhukovski's natural cynicism to stifle his growing excitement. "If what you say is true, now could be our opportunity. If we struck at them, at their homeworld..." He slammed his fist against the table. "But we do not know where to strike! We know where their ships are gathering, which must be around their homeworld, but our information is not yet accurate enough."

"Do not ask me to help you find the Homeworld, admiral," Reza told him, his voice no more than a hoarse whisper. "For even if I knew how to guide you there, I would not."

Zhukovski shook his head. "I would never ask you such a thing, Reza," he said apologetically, alarmed at how old Reza suddenly looked, how tired. How afraid. "I am sorry that you are caught between humans and Kreelans like deer between charging tigers. I do not envy you. But as human, I can only hope worst for your people, that your Empress is dead, that they will be helpless before us for just this once."

Reza nodded sadly, his fingers caressing the eyestone on his collar, on which was engraved the rune of the Desh-Ka. He bit back the tears that burned his eyes, for he knew how uncomfortable it would make his guest, bearer of bad tidings though he was. "Please do not wish Her dead," he whispered. "Wish the Empire all the ill will your heart may conceive, but do not wish my Empress dead."

Zhukovski leaned back in his chair. "Reza, I know Empress is leader of your religion and government, as it were, but–"

"She is also my wife," Reza rasped, his green eyes burning with fearful longing. "She was to ascend to the throne. If the Empress lies dead, so, too, does she."

The admiral felt a sudden pang of shame and guilt for his words. "I am sorry, Reza," he said sincerely. "I... I did not know. Please, forgive me."

Reza nodded slowly, his eyes falling closed, his mind turning inward to wonder about Esah-Zhurah's fate, his heart calling out to her. In vain.

Evgeni Zhukovski laid his hand on Reza's shoulder for a moment before he got up and left the room, quietly closing the door behind him.

* * *

Nicole awoke from her nap with a start. Her chest felt as if it was being held in a giant vice, making her heart thunder in her ears and her lungs heave against air that had suddenly become as thick as water. She was not in physical pain, but she sensed a hurt far deeper than any lance could make, an echo in her brain from someone calling her from far away.

"Reza," she said aloud.

"Nikki?" she heard from the other room. "Are you okay?" Jodi's concerned face peered through the door.

"*Oui*," she said with more energy than she felt. "I am all right."

Jodi was not convinced. She came in and put her hand on Nicole's forehead. "And I think you're a lying sack of shit. You look terrible."

"Complimentary, as always," Nicole murmured, trying to brush Jodi's hand away. "Please, Jodi, do not pester me."

"Pester, my ass, woman," Jodi said, straightening up. She had been staying with Nicole and Tony while she completed some of the non-resident courses for the Command and General Staff College. She was still on flying status, occasionally going to the Fighter Weapons School for refresher training and to help beat the new crop of fighter jocks into shape for the real thing, but she spent most of her time with Nicole, who was still on medical leave. She knew that Nicole resented someone keeping an eye on her, but that was just too bad. "You just don't know how good you've got it. There are a lot of people who'd pay to have me telling them they're full of shit. Now that I think of it, that's what the Navy does."

"You are impossible," Nicole said, managing a weak smile. "Now, get yourself out of my way. I need to visit Reza."

"Need to?"

Nicole sighed. "I *wish* to. Is that good enough?" Jodi was still frowning. "*Merde*, commander, get out of my way!"

"Aye, aye, ma'am," Jodi saluted as Nicole made her way past her to the bathroom. "Mind if I tag along? Maybe those stupid jarheads guarding him will let me through this time..."

The trip into the city did not take long. Someone from the twentieth century would not have recognized New York City, or any other major city of that time, for a very simple reason: they no longer existed as they once had. Earth had largely been depopulated in the twenty-second and twenty-third centuries through a combination of famine, regional warfare, and then mass exodus soon after interstellar travel had finally been made practicable. It was only after humans had finally begun to explore the worlds in their galaxy up close, discovering just how inhospitable most of them were, that they realized what a priceless treasure their own birthplace had been. In the twenty-fourth century a program was begun to revitalize Earth as something more than a breeding ground for *homo sapiens*. While much of what had been done in centuries past could never be undone, the new caretakers did the best they could, and in their hands Earth had been reborn. Humans still lived here in great numbers, but with swift and clean transportation available to go anywhere on the globe, they were able to widely disperse themselves, minimizing their impact on the again thriving world. The great cities, which had been so instrumental both in humanity's early development and in the catastrophic consumption of its resources, had gradually been dismantled into smaller townships and villages, and much of the land returned to a natural state that had brought back the luster to planet Earth.

The automated shuttle dropped them off at the central entrance to Kennedy Memorial Hospital before speeding off to fetch more passengers. They made their way through the warmly lit corridors and elevators to the penthouse level: the isolation ward.

"Captain," the Marine in charge of the security detachment said politely as Nicole showed him her ID. "I hope you didn't come for a smile, ma'am. He hasn't been very happy since Admiral Zhukovski left this morning."

"Admiral Zhukovski was here?" she asked, looking at Jodi, who only raised her eyebrows. "Do you know what about?"

The Marine, a first lieutenant, laughed. "No, ma'am," he said. "Admirals usually don't confide their business to the likes of us. We're just the hired help around here."

Jodi took the opportunity to thrust her ID forward. The Marine verified with a quick retinal scan that she was who she was supposed to be, then checked his approved visitors list, which was very, very short. "Sorry, commander, but I can't let you in. You're not on my list."

"Oh, come on–"

She shut up as Nicole gestured for her to be silent. "Lieutenant," Nicole said, "Commander Mackenzie is a very close friend of Captain Gard." The Marine started to shake his head, but Nicole persisted. "I know it is against the rules to let her in, but the last time she saw him was in sickbay on board the *Gneisenau* when we all thought he was going to die. I would appreciate it if you would consider letting her in long enough just to greet him. I will vouch for her conduct."

Jodi could see that he was hesitating. "Please," she said. "Just for a minute."

The lieutenant looked at the other five Marines, all enlisted, who made up the guard detail. They were astutely looking in any other direction but at him and the two Navy officers. *Why is it*, he asked himself, *that this always seems to happen on my watch?* "All right," he relented, "but so help me God, commander, if you–"

"I'll be a perfect angel, lieutenant," she said. "I promise."

"All right," he went on, "I'm sure I'll live to regret this. Step into the lock, please." The two women stepped into the security lock that was both a physical safeguard against escape and a scanner that looked for concealed weapons or other contraband. Satisfied, the lieutenant passed them through. "Five minutes," he said pointedly Mackenzie.

She nodded, then opened the inner door.

Reza stood before them, bathed in sweat from the exercises he had been doing to focus his mind. Other than his collar, he was again naked.

"So much for modesty," Jodi said lightly. "At least you know how to greet a girl in style." Without hesitating, Jodi embraced him, sweat and all. "I'm so glad to see you. That you're all right," she said, kissing him on the neck, on the lips.

"And you, my friend," he said, returning her embrace with moderate pressure, his effort rewarded with a light popping sound from her ribcage.

"Your Marine friend out there gave me a few minutes with you," she told him, surprised that his strength had grown so quickly. "Nicole sweet talked him for me. But I can't stay long."

"So true," Colonel Markus Thorella said as he stepped through the security lock. "I just had a little discussion with our Marine lieutenant outside. I don't think he'll be making any other security breaches again for quite some time."

"I take full responsibility for Commander Mackenzie's presence, colonel," Nicole said, cutting toward him like a destroyer. "The lieutenant–"

"Spare me, please, Carré," he snorted. "The lieutenant is my concern, not yours. He was negligent, and he'll pay the price."

Jodi felt the muscles in Reza's back flex like steel springs. With feline grace he separated himself from her embrace. "You should not have come here," he hissed, his blood singing in his veins as he prepared to attack.

"Reza, no!" Nicole shouted as she tried to get between him and Thorella, bracing herself to protect someone she hated so much from someone she so loved.

But she need not have bothered. As Reza's fury peaked, something inside him seemed to break, as if his brain was no longer able to command his body. His eyes wide with surprise, he collapsed in a heap on the floor, completely paralyzed.

"What the fuck did you do to him, Thorella?" Jodi snapped as she knelt next to Reza, feeling for his pulse. It was there, his heart beating rapidly to clear the adrenaline from his system. His eyes were still open, but they stared straight ahead, unblinking. "What did you do?"

"Not a thing, commander," he said, a surprised smile on his face. "And I would remind you not to address me like that ever again. I don't care if you like me or not, but I am a superior officer."

"Then let me say it, Markus," Nicole growled like a leopard, her nose not an inch away from his, "what the fuck did you do?"

"I already told you," Thorella said, obviously pleased with whatever had happened. "While I know you won't believe me, I did absolutely nothing. It just appears to me that your traitorous friend there has not fully recovered. Such a pity."

"Reza, can you hear me?" Jodi said urgently, looking into Reza's glazed eyes. The pupils were dilated wide open. "Nicole, I think you'd better get the doctor in here. There's something–"

As she watched, Reza's pupils suddenly began to contract to something close to normal for the light in the room. He blinked and tried to speak.

"Well," Thorella said merrily, "I do have to leave now. I just wanted to check on our temporary guest, pending his trial and execution." He stepped back toward the door, then turned around as an afterthought. "And Commander Mackenzie, please don't stay more than sixty seconds after this door closes behind me, or I'm afraid I'll have to have you arrested." He smiled, and was gone.

"Nicole–"

"I know, Jodi," she said, kneeling down beside her as Reza began to recover from whatever had happened to him. "You had better do as he says. I will take care of Reza."

"But–"

"Go," she said. "He means it. We can ill afford more trouble now."

Furious, Jodi did as she was told. As she stepped through the outer lock of the holding cell, she noticed the Marine lieutenant standing at stiff attention, eyes boring a hole in the far end of the corridor, staring after the retreating Marine colonel who had just promised to destroy the younger man's life in the military. "Lieutenant," she said to his pale, emotionless face, "I'm terribly sorry. I'll see... I'll see if there's anything I can do..."

He said nothing, did not even acknowledge her presence.

Feeling like a fool and plagued with guilt, Jodi turned and walked away, the sound of her boots on the marble floor echoing hollowly in her ears.

Forty

Commodore Denise Marchand was quietly elated but openly confused. Her tiny scouting squadron, consisting of the heavy cruiser *Furious* – her flagship – and three destroyers, had stumbled upon a much superior Kreelan force of three heavy cruisers forty-three hours earlier. Much to her surprise, the Kreelan ships had not only failed to engage her, but had split up and run without making anything more than half-hearted attempts at defending themselves. Not by nature a cautious sort, Marchand had split her force, sending two destroyers after one cruiser, the *Furious* and the remaining destroyer after another, while temporarily ignoring the third enemy vessel. That was as much prudence as she was able to muster at the time.

In a matter of minutes, the first Kreelan cruiser had been reduced to a flaming hulk by torpedoes from the two pursuing destroyers, which immediately wheeled about to rejoin the flagship and her escort, which were still racing after the second fleeing Kreelan vessel. Not long thereafter, that ship finally came within range of the guns of the pursuing *Furious*, which wasted no time in breaching the enemy's hull with a series of accurately placed salvos. The enemy cruiser exploded in a swirling fireball.

Then Marchand turned her attention to the surviving Kreelan cruiser, which had wisely used the time bought by its companions to try and escape, for now it was completely outnumbered and outgunned.

But this ship, or its commander, was different. While it hardly showed the fearless courage normally shown by Kreelan warships, its captain fired back, keeping both the *Furious* and the darting destroyers from nipping too closely at her heels as she fled deeper into Kreelan space.

Marchand was still wary of some sort of elaborate trap, but that would be totally out of character for the enemy. The Kreelans did not run, nor did they normally play games of cat and mouse. At least, not until now. Besides, she thought, why would anyone sacrifice two cruisers – three, if she caught up to this one – in exchange for a cruiser and three destroyers?

No, she told herself, this was something else, and it fit with the recent intelligence reports of sharply decreased resistance on the part of Kreelan forces everywhere.

"Commodore," the flag communications officer reported, "we have an answer from Fleet."

Eager to see what headquarters had to say in response to her request to follow the enemy cruiser into what was, except for the silent scoutship patrols, unknown space to human ships, Marchand called up the message on her console: *Pursue enemy at own discretion. No supporting forces available. Godspeed.*

It was just what she wanted to hear. She had been in the Navy – and had survived – for nearly twenty years. She was tired of always being on the run, turning her stern to run away from what always seemed to be a superior enemy force, or rushing to save some colony from destruction, only to arrive a little too late. While her squadron hardly constituted a major battle fleet, they were good ships with good crews, and this time she was determined to take the fight to the enemy.

"Captain Hezerah," she asked of the *Furious's* captain, "what's the range to target?"

"One-hundred fifty thousand kilometers and steady," he said instantly. "Zero closure rate." At flank speed, the human squadron was making only enough speed to keep up with the Kreelan, not enough to overtake her. "Commodore," he said quietly, "we won't be able to keep this up much longer. *Tai Mo Shan's* main drive is near the breaking point, and our own core passed the red line three hours ago. If we don't slow down soon, we may never get home."

Marchand frowned. She had known this was the case since *Hotspur*, one of the other destroyers, had blown a deridium converter over twelve hours before. Somehow, her engineers had kept her going, but that would not last for much longer.

She looked at the red icon that was the Kreelan ship they were hunting, wondering for the thousandth time why it had not jumped into hyperspace. The only reason she could imagine was that there was something wrong with the enemy ship's hyperdrive. For the pursuing human squadron, that was both a blessing and a curse. Had the ship jumped, Marchand would have been forced to turn back. It was impossible to actively track a ship in hyperspace, and this entire area of space was uncharted. Marchand could not afford a jump that might drop her squadron back into normal space in the center of a star. On the other hand, drawn out, high-speed chases through normal space were hard on ships and their crews. And in Marchand's grim estimation, any ship losing its main drive this far into enemy territory would have to be written off the naval registry as another casualty, for they could hardly expect to return home.

"We're so close," she whispered angrily through her teeth. "Are they still headed for that nebular formation?"

"Yes, ma'am," Captain Hezerah replied uneasily. "Right for it." In all his years in the service, he had seen nothing quite like it. Like a giant fog bank in space, or some gigantic ball of wispy cotton, it hung before the racing ships like a siren's lair on the seas of old. Much sensor probing and more discussion had not given them any more understanding of it than that it appeared to exist; it was real. He dearly would like to chalk up the remaining cruiser to the squadron's score, but there was something unsettling about the cloud toward which they were heading, something unnatural that sent a shiver up his spine. He silently wished that Marchand would call an end to the chase. He did not want to take *Furious* in there.

In the main viewer there was a sudden flare where the Kreelan ship – otherwise invisible to direct observation – raced in front of them.

"Captain!" shouted the chief gunnery officer. "Looks like they had a core breach! She's losing way!"

"Thank the Lord of All," Hezerah breathed. "How long till she comes in range?"

"If their projected deceleration curve holds up, thirteen minutes, sir," the navigator replied.

"Will she have reached the nebula?" Marchand asked quickly, her eyes fixed on the little red icon in the holo display that was now ever so slowly losing ground to her own pursuing hounds.

"On the current velocity curve, she'll come within about three-hundred thousand kilometers of it by the time we're in range."

"Close," Hezerah muttered.

"Order the destroyers to flank her at their best speed," Marchand ordered her operations officer. The destroyers could make slightly better speed than the larger cruiser, and Marchand felt it worth the risk of pushing their drives past their already strained limits. "They are not to get within range, just keep her penned in. I don't want her to get away from us now. Captain," she said to Hezerah, "you are to commence firing as soon as we are in range."

"Aye, aye, commodore," he said. Anything to keep from having to go into that so-called nebula, he thought.

The minutes crept by as the human squadron, the destroyers now pulling ahead and slightly to the side, gained on the fleeing Kreelan ship. The human sensors recorded the debris the enemy cruiser left behind, silent mementos of the explosion that destroyed enough of her drive capacity to leave her far too slow to escape, to make it into the looming mist. It reminded the humans of how easily they could become marooned in this strange area of space.

Marchand watched with barely contained impatience as the main battery range rings on the holo display slowly converged on the enemy ship. At last they overtook the fleeing prey, flashing a set of gunnery data that was echoed throughout the ship's weapons stations.

"In range, captain," reported the gunnery officer.

"Commence firing!"

The lights on the bridge dimmed to combat red as the energy buffers of the main guns siphoned off all available power that was not used by either the ship's drives or her shields. Seconds later, the energy was discharged into space in the form of a dozen crimson blasts from the cruiser's main forward batteries, stabbing out toward the ever-slowing enemy ship.

"Three direct hits," the gunnery spotter reported. She need not have; the extra long range and precise resolution of her special instruments were not required in this case. The Kreelan ship had long since come into view on the main screen at a medium magnification, and the hits were plainly visible.

"Fire!"

Again the main batteries fired, and it was obvious that the gunnery section had found the Kreelan cruiser's range. Every crimson lance hit home, flaying the enemy ship's vulnerable stern into flaming wreckage. The stricken ship began to yaw off course, a secondary explosion setting her tumbling about her long axis. A sudden flurry of shooting erupted from turrets along her battered hull as the human ships came into their line of fire, but the firing was erratic, poorly aimed. She posed no threat.

"Fire!"

The third salvo blasted the cruiser amidships, breaking her back. The stern section, two of the six drives still burning bright with power, broke free of the shattered midsection to drift uncontrollably until it exploded in a fierce fireball. The sleek bow section, still resplendent with the runes with which all Kreelan ships were decorated, tumbled end over end, trailing incandescent streamers that were the ship's burning entrails.

Captain Hezerah was about to order the *coup de grace* when the chief gunnery officer spoke up. "New contact! Looks like a small cutter or lifeboat separating from the bow section."

"What the devil?" Marchand asked, watching on the viewer as the tiny ship separated from the twisted wreckage of the cruiser. It wasted no time, heading straight toward the nebula at flank speed.

"Commodore?" Hezerah asked, waiting for her instructions. The guns were trained on the cruiser, waiting to finish her off. The escaping cutter was another matter. Unless they took it under fire right away, it had every chance of making it into the nebula.

Marchand had no time to consider. Something strange was afoot, and she was determined to get to the bottom of it. "Captain, you may finish off the cruiser," she told Hezerah shortly. Turning to her operations officer, she ordered, "Have *Zulu* intercept the lifeboat, or whatever it is. She is not, repeat not, to open fire on it. I want it – and whoever might be on board – in one piece if at all possible."

"Aye, ma'am." The man turned away and quickly relayed her orders. Like a greyhound on the scent of a rabbit, the destroyer *Zulu* hauled her bows away from the dying cruiser to pursue the much smaller prey.

But as the *Furious* quickly finished off the remains of the Kreelan ship, it became clear that *Zulu* would not be able to get close enough to the escaping lifeboat to fix her with a tractor beam.

"Dammit," Marchand hissed *Nothing could ever be easy*, she thought acidly, *or even just difficult but straightforward*. More and more, she wanted that ship, and whoever or whatever was on it.

It suddenly had become an imperative for her, an obsession. It was a hope for explaining the strange twists of fate that had brought them farther than any humans had ever been into this sector.

To the flag operations officer she said, "Tell *Zulu* to maintain contact and continue to close, if possible."

"They're to proceed into the nebula, ma'am?" he asked, his eyebrows raised. Their sensors had not been able to penetrate the milky whiteness, the likes of which no one had ever seen before. They would be running blind.

"Negative," Marchand sighed. She was well aware of the dangers, and was not about to risk one of her ships in there. She had another idea. "She is to proceed to the mist's edge only. And have the other destroyers patrol around the nebula. I don't want us to be surprised from the far side. Captain Hezerah."

"Ma'am?"

"Take your ship to the mist's edge," she told him. "And have the Marine detachment commander report to me immediately in my ready room. I have some work for them to do."

As he carried out her orders, Hezerah silently thanked the gods that he would not have to go in there.

He also said a silent prayer for the Marines who would.

* * *

"This stinks," Eustus muttered as he stared at the unbroken whiteness that was all either he or the pilots of the ship's cutter could see. He'd never seen or heard of anything like it in space. It wasn't a nebula, which was a lot denser than normal space, but nothing remotely like this. It was like flying through a cloud in atmosphere, with noticeable resistance against the vessel's screens and hull.

"Tell me about it, Top," the pilot in command, an ensign on his first tour, replied. "Talk about flying by the seat of your pants." None of the instruments that were normally keyed to the universe beyond the small hull were showing anything, the mist effectively isolating them from any points of reference except what the ship carried on board. The pilot knew only his relative velocity, distance, and bearing from *Furious* since the time they had launched. And if there were a gravity well in here – a planet or dwarf star, for instance – even the ship's inertial readings would be rendered useless and they could find themselves completely lost. After they had entered the mist in pursuit of the Kreelan boat, they had quickly lost all contact with the *Furious* and the destroyers. He had no idea at all what was in the space around them except where they had just passed, which by definition was empty, relatively speaking. "There could be a frigging planet hiding in here and we wouldn't know until we hit it."

"Yeah, well, maybe that's the idea, ensign," Eustus replied. "And maybe there *is* a planet in here somewhere."

"That makes me feel a whole lot better," the ensign answered nervously. He was a good pilot, but this was the first time in his short career that he had piloted a boat entirely on manual. For once, he was happy that the cutter had such a big forward viewport, for all the other times he had complained about it being too much of a distraction. "At least I don't have to do anything more than play taxi driver," he went on. "You jarheads are the ones who get to play touchy-feely if we find something. Providing, of course, that we don't smash ourselves into whatever it is first."

Eustus grunted agreement, thinking back over the turn of events that had landed him here. Three months after they had returned from Erlang, Eustus had been ordered back to fleet duty, never having seen Reza recover from his coma. Assigned to another of the Red Legion's battalions, his company had been parceled out to Marchand's "Roving Raiders" as they were sometimes known, and he had been sitting aboard the *Furious* with the rest of his troops for the last few months, waiting for action that never seemed to come.

Until now, he mused silently. And not only was this one of the most hare-brained and dangerous schemes he had ever been part of, but he had the dubious honor of having to take charge of it. Captain Dittmer, the company commander, had been seriously injured four days before when her pistol discharged while she was cleaning it. While Eustus had never had anything against Dittmer and had gotten along well with the woman, her level of tactical proficiency had never been demonstrated until then, and Eustus and the others who had seen combat had not exactly been impressed. While technically Eustus was outranked by the four platoon leaders (the company did not have an executive officer replacement yet), all of them were "ninety-day wonders" straight from Officer Candidate School, and none had any combat experience. In light of those facts, Commodore Marchand had made him a brevet captain and put him in charge of the company for this grand, suicidal tour.

Without thinking, he touched the locket that Enya had given him, that now hung around his neck. As wearing any kind of jewelry while in duty uniform was completely against regulations, he kept it hidden just below the neckline of his tunic, taped to his dog tags. *At least she's safe at home*, he thought. She had returned to Erlang to help her people rebuild, and had promised to wait for him, to have a home ready for the two of them. If Reza's word were true, as Eustus had always believed it would be, the Kreelans would never again bother Erlang.

He turned to look down the length of the cutter's passenger compartment, now in its modified configuration as a troopship. Since the commodore was only willing (thankfully, Eustus thought) to risk one cutter on this mission, Eustus had been forced to leave half his company behind. Worse, the two platoons now crammed into the cutter had hard vacuum gear but none of the powerful space armor like Eustus and Reza had trained with at Quantico so many years ago. He bit the inside of his lip as his eyes swept across the anxious faces of his people. If they ran into anything bigger than a bunch of rock-throwing, blue-skinned female neanderthals, he thought, they were in big, big trouble.

"Tai," said the copilot, a female petty officer, to the pilot, "check this out."

Not able to keep himself from butting in, Eustus said, "What is it?"

The pilot shook his head. "Don't know. Looks like a partial signal return from somewhere ahead."

"The lifeboat?"

"No," the copilot said decisively as she studied the signal. "The signal's too scattered. If it's hitting anything, it's got to be pretty big."

"Like how big?" Eustus asked, peering at the multicolored lines wiggling across her sensor display, unable to make sense of it.

"Like that big," the pilot said quietly.

As if they were emerging from an ocean fog bank, the clinging white tendrils that had surrounded the cutter for the last few hours suddenly dissipated: before them lay a planet, basking in the radiance of the surrounding globe of mist.

The pilot's eyebrows shot up at what the sensors were telling him. "This thing has an atmosphere that looks like it should be breathable," he said wonderingly. "One point two standard gees, oceans, cloud formations, the whole nine yards. All that, and no sun to warm the place. Maybe the mist does it somehow."

"Jesus," Eustus whispered, wondering if somehow the Kreelans had engineered this. "How could this be?"

"Beats me," the copilot said shortly, "but there's our friend." The lifeboat was clearly visible on the sensor display, which now was functioning normally within the confines of the hollowed out sphere within the mist. "Looks like they suffered some damage clearing their ship," she went on as she worked the instruments. "Scorch marks and some dents along her hull. Stabilizers look like they've been smashed up pretty good."

"Can we catch them?"

The pilot shook his head as he took in the information that was now flooding onto the viewscreen, which was really a massive head-up display showing flight and combat information provided by the ship's computer. "They'll make the surface first, but we'll be right behind them. From the size of the boat, there can't be more than a few blues aboard."

That was the least of Eustus's worries. "What about on the planet? Can you read anything?"

The copilot shook her head, frowning. "Nothing in orbit, no ships or satellites at all, anywhere in here. On the surface, I can make out what looks like non-natural structures. But there aren't any indications of habitation: no hot spots, no movement. Nothing. Looks like a damned ghost planet."

"Then why the hell were they so intent on getting here?" Eustus asked himself aloud. "What could they have hoped to gain?"

The pilot shrugged. "Maybe it wasn't always this way," he said, speculating. "Maybe they thought there would be some help here."

"And everybody just vanished?" the copilot snorted. "Come on, this is the Kreelans we're talking about here."

"True," Eustus said, "but something really weird's going on, been going on. Think about it: first, three heavy cruisers act like destroyer bait. Then they launch a lifeboat under fire – something I've never heard of, even in the tall tales you hear in the bars. And then they – whoever *they* are – head for what looks like a completely abandoned planet in the middle of whatever the hell this white stuff is." He shook his head. "As much as I hate being in here, I think the commodore may be right. There's something, or someone, in that boat that we need to know about."

"Well," the pilot said, "in about four and a half minutes you're going to get a chance to do exactly that." He glanced up at Eustus. "Better strap in, Top."

"Roger," Eustus said, quickly taking his seat – a flimsy affair compared to what the Marines' regular dropships had – and buckling in. A minute later, he and his troops all had their helmets on, weapons checked, and were ready to go.

"Stand by," the pilot announced over the intercom channel. "One minute."

Eustus could feel the slight perturbations in the ship's gravity controls as they balanced the internal artificial gravity against the rapidly increasing natural gravity of the planet. The scientists said that it was impossible to feel anything like that, because the equipment was so sensitive and sophisticated that it damped out the tiniest flutter. But Eustus could feel it, no matter what the scientists said.

"The enemy boat's down," the copilot reported. "I've got two targets moving away from it toward one of the structures, looks like an opening to a subterranean tunnel... Damn, lost them. Looks like you get to play hide and seek."

"Gee, thanks," Eustus replied sarcastically over their private channel. He did not need his troops to hear the very real fear in his voice. Following Kreelans into a tunnel on what looked like the only indigenous Kreelan world humans had ever discovered, knowing nothing about this place or whom they were chasing, was not Eustus's idea of fun, even without the creepy mist they'd flown through.

"Ten seconds," announced the pilot tensely as he guided the cutter as close as he dared to the yawning archway through which the escaping Kreelans had disappeared. "Ready... we're down! Disembark!"

The cargo doors on each side of the cutter hissed open, and Marines poured from the ship to take up a security perimeter. Eustus leaped from the forward passenger door, a tight squeeze with his armor and weapons, but landed lightly for someone so heavily loaded with gear.

As the last Marine jumped from the hold, the doors slid shut and the ship pulled away from the ground with a bone-tingling thrum. A few seconds later it was circling overhead, its two twin pulse guns snuffling the air and ground for targets.

Eustus quickly surveyed his surroundings. They had landed in what looked like a huge, open plaza. It was not earth under his feet, but intricately sculpted tiles that seemed soft and pliant, not at all like the stone they appeared to be. All around them was what looked like a great terrace, climbing in massive steps to reach dozens of meters into the sky. Each level was decorated with runes and symbols that meant nothing to him, but that – had he had the time to marvel – he could not but help find intrinsically beautiful. Above them, strangely, the sky had a slight magenta hue, and well hid the featureless white of the strange mist that surrounded the planet and mysteriously gave it light and warmth.

In front of them was a great stone arch that Eustus instinctively knew must have been built before humans had discovered fire. *How tiny we are in the scheme of things,* he thought suddenly, momentarily overwhelmed by these constructs of a people who had been plying the stars long before a human hand had ever put down the first words on a clay tablet. *How insignificant, how mortal we are, and yet we are here, perhaps at the mouth of a temple built to alien gods.* Perhaps this was where the throne of the Empress stood, or maybe this was where the pulsating crystal heart had been taken. Perhaps...

"The Kreelan boat's empty, Top," Grierson, the First Platoon leader, reported.

With a twinge of regret, Eustus called his attention back to the here and now. There was work to do. "Okay," he said. "Schoemann, leave a squad back here to cover our ass. The rest of us get to check out the tunnel of love here. First Platoon's got point."

The two platoon leaders, while inexperienced, were not hesitant or incompetent. With a minimum of orders and in short order the two platoons were moving into the mouth of the tunnel, with a small but potent force left behind to guard their avenue of escape.

"I hate underground work," someone grumbled on the common channel.

"Stop bitching," Eustus snapped, his skin prickling as they worked their way in. "Keep your links clear unless you've got something to report."

The floor, the rounded walls and ceiling, were covered with runes like the great terrace outside. While he could not say exactly how, he was sure there was some kind of purpose to them; they were not random or just for aesthetics. In the illumination, which itself seemed to come from within the walls, as if the surface of the stone gave off its own light, the lines of runes twisted and turned elegantly, precisely, reminding Eustus of a sculpted tree he had seen once. A bonsai, it was called, he remembered.

Trees, he thought. *Trees...*

"Of course," he said aloud as the realization struck him. "Trees. Family trees." Raising a closed fist as a signal for his troops to halt, he knelt down to the floor. His suit light gave him a better look at the writing in the stone that seemed never to have worn, despite the sense of ages having passed since this place was built. He could not read the runes, but he could see how some of the characters repeated in the entries of a branch, much like names or parts of names of predecessors given to the newborn to carry on a tradition that had begun thousands of generations before. He noted where some branches ended, the last of the line having died, perhaps in some battle along a distant frontier, or against humans.

But there was one thing that struck him as terribly odd. All the entries in a branch seemed to have only a single root name, not two, as there would have been in any human genealogy for the mother and father of a child. All the names here, if that is really what they were, were of females, he realized, the mothers and daughters. All the countless sons that had been born in the time of these engraved scrolls must have lived and died only to preserve their race, for no record had been kept of their passing.

"Top?" Grierson asked tightly. "You okay?"

"Yeah," Eustus said slowly. "Yeah. Let's move out."

They moved cautiously up the great tunnel in time that was measured in the harsh breathing and rapidly beating hearts of forty-six humans in a decidedly alien place.

"I've got something!" the Marine on point called. She was carrying a tracking device that was occasionally known to work, and now it was telling her that someone – or something – had passed this way not long before. "Heat trace on the wall." She examined it carefully, not sure what she was seeing. "Looks like a hand print."

"Well," Eustus said, "we seem to be going in the right direction. Let's step it up a bit. We can't afford to let them get away now."

Moving now at a trot, the Marines hastened through the great tunnel as it burrowed deeper into the earth and then leveled out. Eustus was struck by a sense of déjà vu, remembering the tunnel that had led him and Enya to the crystal heart.

"Hold up!" the point Marine reported softly.

"What is it?" Grierson demanded.

"We've got an intersection," she reported from her position, well forward of the others. She was the sacrificial lamb on this outing. Two other Marines followed behind her at an interval of a few dozen meters to report if anything untoward happened to her, hopefully in time for the main group behind them to react to the threat. "Another tunnel, same size as this one, crossing at a ninety-degree angle. Looks like more of the same in both directions. I don't have a read on anything from the tracker. Cold scent."

Eustus had been afraid of that. "Grierson, I'll take your third squad ahead. You take the left tunnel with the rest of your platoon," he ordered. "Schoemann, you take the right tunnel. Try to keep from splitting up any more than you have to, and let's just hope that our communications don't get screwed up any more than they are already." They could just barely read the squad that had been left outside. "Hurry people, we've got to catch these ladies."

Quickly the Marines split into three groups and started down the tunnels. Eustus hoped for a break soon, or they were sure to lose their quarry.

He did not have long to wait.

"Top!" the new Marine on point called excitedly. "I've got a trail! There's blood on the floor up here!"

"Keep your eyes open!" Eustus ordered sharply as he and the others moved at a run toward the corporal who was standing in the corridor ahead of them, barely visible at this distance. "Grierson! Schoemann! Get back here on the double!" he ordered over the company net.

Eustus, who now led the squad of charging Marines, could see the corporal kneeling on the floor, his weapon trained ahead of him. Hearing the approach of the reinforcements, he turned his head toward them.

That was when Eustus saw the shadow detach itself from the wall where the tunnel bent to the right. Even at this distance he could see it for what it was: a Kreelan warrior.

"Down!" he screamed into his helmet even as he raised his rifle, his finger already pulling the trigger. "Get down!"

The young Marine reacted instantly, diving for the floor as he rolled and fired down the tunnel, but it was an instant too late. Even as the Marines began to pour a volley of blue and red energy bolts toward their enemy, the shrekka that howled from the dark warrior cut across the corporal's chest, opening his heart and lungs to the cool air.

Eustus dived for the stricken Marine just as a second shrekka swept in from the chaos a split second after the first, slicing deeply into his upper thigh. The shrekka's blades were so sharp that, at first, he felt no pain. He hit the ground hard, one hand pressing against his leg, the other vainly trying to aim his rifle.

But what caught his attention was the apparition that clattered past him, right for the Marines who knelt and lay behind him, firing into the smoke and dust-filled tunnel to cover him and their fallen comrade. Freed and given the gift of motion by the cutting blades of the first shrekka, the dead corporal's munitions bandoleer and its six grenades skittered along the floor. As if looking at it through a microscope, Eustus could see that one of the grenades had somehow been armed.

"Grenade!" he screamed, throwing himself to the far side of the corporal's body in the forlorn hope that his still warm flesh might provide some protection to his own body.

The other Marines gaped at the deadly bundle that came to a jarring halt in their midst.

The armed grenade exploded, setting off the other five. Fire and thunder filled the tunnel just before it collapsed, burying the shattered corpses the blast had left behind.

* * *

The first thing Eustus noticed was the smell of blood. He wrinkled his nose and was rewarded with the rupture of the brittle crust of coagulated blood on his cheek that released a fresh flow down the side of his numbed face. He opened his eyes, unsure what he would see, and not sure if he wanted to see it. He knew there would be a lot more blood pouring out of his body than the little trickle from his cheek. There must be.

But, while he ached like hell and was completely deaf, he had suffered no major injuries except for the gash in his leg left by the second shrekka, and blood oozed slowly from the wound as it throbbed with pain. With trembling arms he pushed himself up onto his elbows, shedding dust and rocks like a sand crab emerging from a windswept beach. He looked from side to side, but the faceplate of his helmet, while more or less intact, was opaque with dust and a spider web of cracks. Reluctantly, with fingers like lifeless sausages, he undid the bindings, letting it fall from his head to the rock-strewn floor with a clatter that he felt more than heard.

The light that had glowed from the walls did so now with only a fraction of its former power, which, when he saw what he had been lying in, was probably for the best. Willing himself to hold back the nausea that fought to overcome him, he rolled out of what was left of the corporal who had been the first among them to die. But even in death, he had managed to help save another Marine's life, miraculously absorbing much of the explosive force of the grenades.

Of the others, there was no sign. The tunnel had collapsed completely behind him, burying anyone else who might possibly have survived the explosion. Worse, there was no way for him to contact the platoon leaders: his comm link, as with everything else except the blaster at his hip and the knife strapped to his leg, had been smashed into useless junk.

Pulling himself unsteadily to the support of the tunnel wall, Eustus sat down, legs straight out, and took a look at the gash in his thigh. If he could keep it from bleeding too much more, he might be all right. Although it was deep, it was still only a flesh wound, having severed no major veins or arteries. He opened his first aid kit and rummaged around for the only thing left that was not bent or crushed: a tube of liquid bandage. Ripping the cloth of his uniform from around the wound, he brushed the dirt from it as best he could before squirting some of the gray paste into and around the gash, noting how lucky he was that the shrekka had not simply taken off his entire leg. The patch job was not going to win any medical awards, he admitted, but it should keep him together until he could get out of here.

And that, he thought dejectedly, was not going to be an easy feat. Knowing that he would probably need it again, he put the bandage tube into one of his cargo pockets.

"Well," he said to himself, his own voice barely audible through a persistent ringing in his ears, "I guess I'd better get moving." He had no illusions about digging his way through the tons of rock and debris behind him, and he had serious doubts about any survivors out there being able to dig through to him. They had no heavy equipment, no blasting charges (*I think we've had enough of that*, he thought darkly), and – most importantly – no time. While Commodore Marchand had been keen on catching the survivors from the Kreelan cruiser, she was loath to have her squadron stay here for too long. The Marines had been given exactly twenty-four hours to conduct their business and return before the Roving Raiders roved on without them. He also had to hope that the other Marines and the Navy boat crew would wait until the last minute in the hope that someone from in here would make it back out. But they could not wait forever, and Eustus had no idea how long he had been unconscious. If he was going to get out of here, he was going to have to find another way to the surface. And quickly.

Shedding the burden of his horribly abused armor and other now-useless gear, Eustus gathered himself up and began shuffling deeper into the corridor, toward where the Kreelan had launched her attack. He held his blaster at the ready, but felt vaguely ridiculous in doing so. His aim was so unsteady that he would be lucky not to shoot himself if he had to fire, and there was no way to tell if the weapon would still work without testing it. And that would give away his position for sure if his enemy were still about.

Slowly, painfully, he worked his way through the shambles of the once-beautiful tunnel, peering through the gloom toward its fateful bend.

As he got closer, he lowered his pistol. The Kreelan's shrekka was not the only weapon to wreak havoc in the passageway. The fusillade from the doomed Marines' guns had collapsed this section of the tunnel, as well. While not completely blocked, it was choked with huge sections of ancient stone that had been blown from their long-held positions in the walls and ceiling, and littered with countless other fragments of black obsidian and cobalt blue inlay.

But he saw no bodies. While it was true that any one of the huge stones could conceal several crushed warriors, he felt uneasy. He raised his pistol again, holding its wavering muzzle before him as he stepped into the maze of fallen slabs. He struggled from rock to rock, clambering up on top of a massive stone, scrabbling across it, and dropping down to the debris-strewn floor before starting the process over again.

After letting himself down from a crazily canted slab, he was sizing up the next climb when he caught movement out of the corner of his eye. Forgetting about his ripped leg as he reached for his holstered blaster, he turned toward the movement and dropped into a crouch. At least, it would have been a crouch had his leg not collapsed under him. Cursing in pain, anger, and fear, he fell into a heap among the sharp shards of stone, cutting himself in a dozen different places. His pistol fell from his grip, clattering to the ground in a puff of dust.

Sitting motionless, helpless, he stared uncomprehendingly at what had startled him: a hand. A huge Kreelan hand, with the biggest set of talons he had ever seen, protruded from the gap formed by the huge slab as it rested on another, smaller chunk of rock. The hand moved, clawing at the rock, as the owner sought to escape from her prison.

"Holy shit," Eustus breathed, able now to hear his own curses beyond the slowly fading ring in his ears. Ignoring the pain in his leg, where blood again seeped from the partially stripped bandage, he moved closer to the hand and the dark aperture leading to the tiny prison of stone. He saw a pair of eyes glowering malevolently at him from a face that was shadowy, indistinct in the dim light. With an angry grunt the Kreelan assaulted the slab, pushing against it with all the leverage she could muster in her cramped position. He watched in awe as the enormous slab lifted as the warrior strained within, rising a few centimeters, then a few centimeters more.

But it was not enough. With a cry of anguish, the warrior gave up and the stone slammed home again, dust shaking from it like tiny flakes of snow. He could hear her harsh and ragged breathing through the persistent buzz in his ears.

He was tempted to just turn and leave her there, to die of thirst and starvation, or perhaps bleed to death if she was injured. But he knew Reza would not have approved. The Kreelan had done no more than her duty, he supposed, whatever that might have been. No, he told himself, it would not cost anything to put her out of her misery quickly. The Kreelans had killed many of his people, for whatever reason, but they had never sought simply to inflict pain on humans, as through torture; that seemed to be reserved for humans to do to themselves.

Turning away from her, he looked for his blaster in the rubble, cursing the fact that all of it appeared black and angularly shaped. He shuffled through the mess, kicking and prodding for his weapon. At last, he saw the stubby pistol, resting next to a smaller slab that had fallen from the wall. As he reached down into the odd bits of chipped stone to retrieve it, his thigh screaming at the effort, his fingers brushed against something soft, something definitely not stone. Curious, he took up the pistol with his other hand and began to brush away at whatever lay beneath the black gravel.

It was the face of a Kreelan child.

"This can't be," he murmured, shaking his head. In all the years that humans had fought the Empire, no one had ever encountered a Kreelan child. They were as mysterious as were the males of the species, of which Eustus had also been one of two humans to ever see, at least in mummified form. He wondered if the light might be playing tricks on him, but as he continued to brush away the dust and chunks of rock, it was clear that it was a child. But the face and shoulders were all he could uncover, for the rest of her body was covered by a fallen slab. It was smaller than the one entombing the adult behind him, but it had been large enough to crush the life from the child. Or had it?

Knowing that he was just wasting his own very limited time and strength, he carefully let himself down beside the child, leaning over her to see if he could see her breathing. He saw a bit of fine dust on her upper lip stir. Again. And again. She was still alive. He put a hand on her forehead and peeled back one of her eyelids. He was not sure what he might see, but he thought it might give him some clue as to how badly she was injured; there was a lot of blood on her face and head. Aside from the irises looking oddly dark and round in this light, he noted nothing that he could make heads or tails of.

"Kar'e nach Shera-Khan?"

He was startled by the plaintive voice that issued from the hole beneath the slab where the warrior was trapped. He had never heard the Kreelan language spoken, even by Reza, and certainly never by an enemy. "What did you say?" he asked, not knowing what else to do.

"*Shera-Khan*," the warrior said, her hand pointing in the girl's direction. "*Kar'e nach ii'la?*"

"She's alive," Eustus said quietly. *My God*, he thought, *what the hell is going on here?* Eustus had learned during his time in the service that you sometimes had to act on instinct. But there were other times when, regardless of how quickly you had to act, even one moment of concentrated thought was crucial. And this was one of those times.

Eustus sat for a moment, pondering this new situation. It did not take him long to come to a conclusion and decide upon a course of action. Commodore Marchand's hunch had been right: there had been something important on that ship – this girl. Eustus did not know why she was important, but the Kreelans, especially the warrior whom he now took to be her protector, had gone to the greatest lengths to keep her alive, despite their present condition of general confusion, which itself remained a mystery.

He had to take her back with him. The only question was how.

"Well," he said, struggling to his feet, "there's only one way to find out." Shuffling to the side of the slab that pinned the girl to the floor, he leaned over and grasped the exposed edge with his battered hands, doing his best not to rip open the wound on his leg.

He pulled. Nothing.

Grimacing, he pulled harder, feeling his muscles and tendons pop and crack with the strain, until the stone just barely moved under his grip.

But that was all. He tried one final time, but it was just too heavy, and he let it settle back into place with a sandy grinding noise. The girl did not cry out, and he thought that perhaps the stone merely pinned her, and had not crushed any of her limbs. But until the stone was removed, there was no way to know for sure.

Panting like a dog, he sat on the slab that had just thumbed its nose at him. "I'm sorry," he apologized to no one in particular, "but that's just a bit... too heavy."

The trapped warrior pointed at him. "*Sh'iamar tan lehtukh*," she said, hammering her hand against the stone that pinned her. She pointed at him again, then gestured with her hand for him to come, then pounded against the rock.

Then she pointed at the girl. "*Shera-Khan*."

"Yeah," he said. "Sure. If I helped you get out of there, even if we both could move that rock, the first thing you'd do is gut me like a pig." He shook his head. "I don't think so."

The warrior was adamant. "*Shera-Khan!*" she cried. While Eustus knew nothing of their ways and language, he had no doubt that a deep and frightful anguish lay behind the warrior's voice. He knew that her job must have been to protect the girl, to see her safely to wherever they were going, and that she was failing. Had failed. And if he let her out of her confinement, he had no doubt that she would kill him without a second thought and carry on with the girl.

On the other hand, he had come to realize that she might be his only hope of making it home. By his own admittedly unreliable estimate, it had taken over half an hour just for him to hobble down to this part of the tunnel, a distance of less than fifty or so meters, and clamber over a few slabs of rock. At that rate, how long might it be before he finally found his way out of here? Hours? Days? And how long had he been unconscious? Most likely, it would take him more time than the hours the boat would wait for him to return. And the warm stickiness he felt down his right leg told him he was still bleeding, a process that was already exhausting him and, if not stopped, could leave him dead. The bandage helped, but it was just that, a bandage, and not designed to hold up to what he was trying to do. Unfortunately, the more sophisticated medical tools in his first aid kit that could have sealed the wound permanently had been destroyed.

That settles it, then, he thought. "All right," he said, knowing that he was going to regret this. "I'll help you get out of there so you can help the girl." He pointed at himself, then the rock, and nodded, hoping she would understand. "In exchange," he went on, "you help me out of here and back to my ship." He pointed into the darkness and her glowing eyes, then at himself, then upward, toward the surface. He saw her blink, but that was the only acknowledgment he received.

Gritting his teeth at the pain in his thigh, he struggled up from the smaller slab pinning the girl and took the few steps back to where its larger cousin held the warrior trapped. Taking a deep breath, trying to still his mounting apprehension, he stepped within range of her hand. She did nothing. Accepting that as a positive sign, he planted his injured leg on the ground, hoping it would support him long enough to get this over with, and set his other foot against the wall. He gripped the edge of the rock with both hands and said, "Now!"

He pulled against the stone with all his might, his face contorted in a rictus of effort. Nothing was happening.

He was about to give up when he heard a savage cry from beneath him and the stone shuddered, rising upward.

"Push, damn you!" he spat through clenched teeth, pulling with his arms and upper body as his leg pushed against the wall with all the strength he had left. The slab continued to rise up and away from the wall, gaining speed as its center of gravity shifted to their advantage. Suddenly, it was standing on edge, and with a final shove the Kreelan warrior sent it crashing over and onto the floor. Eustus flung himself out of the way to avoid being crushed by its ponderous bulk. He lay on the floor, his lungs burning from the exertion, his leg a mass of pain as he waited for her to come and kill him.

But he waited in vain. Behind him, he heard her groan again, a sound that was followed by the crash of another slab falling to the floor. Rolling over, he saw her kneeling by the child's side, her great hands gently touching the child's face. Beside her lay the stone that she had pulled off of the girl.

He pulled his hand away from where it had been holding his thigh. It was slick with blood. "Damn," he whispered to himself as he was struck with lightheadedness. He waited a moment longer for the Kreelan to do something, and when she did not, he half crawled, half dragged himself to where the girl lay deathly still.

Looking at her small body, he saw that her injuries probably were severe. Her armor was creased and pierced by the shards of rock that had been blasted from the wall and then fell on top of her when the tunnel collapsed, and there was a lot of blood from a number of wounds in her head, chest, and legs. As he had guessed, while the slab that had fallen on her had undoubtedly produced its own injuries, at least it had not crushed her arms or legs, or anything else he could see. She might still live, but she would have to get medical attention fast.

He reached for the tube of liquid bandage in his pocket, eliciting a fierce glare from the warrior, whose muscles visibly tensed. "I'm going to try and help her," he said softly, holding his hands up, one empty, the other with the partially used tube. "This won't do much, but it might help stop some of the bleeding." The Kreelan watched suspiciously as he put some of the gray paste on the girl's head where the skin had been broken. Then he managed to get the woman to help him unfasten the girl's armor, letting him squeeze the bandage into some of the more serious wounds.

"Oh, man," Eustus breathed as he peeled away the tattered black undergarment that he had been accustomed to since basic training when he first saw Reza in one. "She's got some broken ribs," he said softly, being careful with the bandage. "Probably some internal injuries, too. We've got to get her to a doctor." The warrior only stared at him uncomprehendingly. "Isn't there a doctor here? Anybody?" He gestured around them, then at the bandage, then at the girl.

The Kreelan pointed at herself, the girl, then Eustus, then swept her arm around them, then pointed to the three of them again.

"So," Eustus said miserably, "it's just us chickens, I guess." He bit his lip, thinking. "Then we've got to get her to the ship. You've got to help me get her to the ship or she's going to die." He tried to convey the thought through a series of gestures, but the warrior only stared at him. He tried a different set of gesticulations. Nothing. No reaction.

He was about to try something else when she drew out a wicked looking knife that she held over the child's heart. Eustus knew what was about to happen. Unable to save her, she was going to kill the child, and then herself.

"Wait!" he said, grasping her hand and trying to move the knife away. But her hands were huge and powerful, and he might as well have been wrestling with a two hundred-kilo silverback mountain gorilla for all the effect he was having. "Dammit," he hissed angrily at her stubbornness, "I wish Reza was here."

"Reza?" the warrior whispered. "*Reza tu'umeh sameh ka'ash?*"

"You know him?" Eustus asked, shocked. "Reza Gard?"

The woman's eyes closed as she put a hand on her armored breast as if to keep her heart from stopping. The knife fell away from the girl's chest. Eustus watched in shock as she knelt there, her body trembling as if she were crying. She spoke softly, as if saying a prayer, mentioning Reza's name several times.

Suddenly, he understood. "He's not dead," he told her, cursing their inability to communicate. "He... listen." Her eyes remained closed. He grabbed her shoulders and shook her. "Listen! Reza didn't die. Look." He gestured to himself "Reza, right?" Then he took her knife from where it had fallen on the ground, pretending to thrust it into his chest. She turned away as if she had been struck. "Dammit, pay attention to me!" Eustus shouted angrily, shaking her again. She whirled around, ready to strike him, but he ignored her, repeating his enactment of the sword spearing through Reza's armor. He fell over like he was dead and closed his eyes.

Then he opened them again. "He didn't die," he told her again. He pulled himself painfully back up to a sitting position. "He was hurt really bad," he told her. "Look, this is Reza," he set a rock between them. "Reza. Doctors worked on him for a long time." He took the bandage tube and squeezed some of it on the rock. "It took a long time for him to get better, but he recovered." Eustus took the rock and stood it up like a doll, marching it around between them. "He's alive," he told her again. He pointed to her, to himself, then swept his arms around them.

"He's alive right now. Right now."

The light of understanding finally dawned on her. "Reza," she said through trembling lips. Then she pointed to the girl. "Reza."

"No," Eustus said, waving his hands. "She's not Reza. Reza's out there," he pointed upward, "on Earth still."

The warrior's eyes brightened. She pointed upward as Eustus had. "Reza?" she asked hopefully.

Eustus nodded. "Yes. He's on Earth, though, not here, not on the ships up there." He pointed at the girl again. "That's not Reza." He took a guess. "That's Shera-Khan."

The warrior nodded, as if copying his gesture. He did not know that she had learned it many years before from a very young human boy. "Shera-Khan," she repeated. "Reza. *E'la tanocht im.*" She gestured at her loins, and then at Eustus's, and then at the girl. "Esah-Zhurah. Reza. Shera-khan."

Eustus sat back, feeling like someone had slammed him over the head with a club. "She's his daughter," he said numbly. "Esah-Zhurah is her mother and Reza is her father. And Esah-Zhurah almost killed him. Jesus." He looked at the girl, shaking his head in sad wonder. "And he never even knew about her, did he?" On impulse, he reached out and pulled up one of the girl's eyelids again. There had been something strange about the iris, and now, taking a closer look in the dim light, he saw what it was: the child's eyes were green like Reza's, and the pupils were round, totally unlike the cat's eyes of the Kreelans. The "normal" Kreelans, that is. He had not noticed it before, mostly because he had not expected to find anything like that. But now...

"Listen," he said, wishing that she could understand what he was saying, "I can get you to Reza, and to some doctors who might be able to help Shera-Khan, but we've got to hurry. We've got to get to the surface and the ship that's waiting there – I hope – before it leaves." He gestured at the three of them, then upward. "Reza," he said again, pointing up.

He did not need a translator this time. The warrior understood perfectly. With infinite care, she gathered the child in her arms and stood waiting while Eustus staggered to his feet.

"This is really going to suck," he said, mimicking one of his older – and deceased – brothers as he tried his best to follow the warrior down the tunnel. He stumbled after the first few steps. His vision was turning gray as his leg beat at him with lancing pain. He only made half a dozen steps more before he collapsed, exhausted and bleeding.

He could only watch as she returned for him, and he felt himself plucked from the floor as if he were a mere paperweight before she draped him over her shoulder. The floor began to pass by in a blur with the woman's powerful strides, and her rhythm felt to him like waves rolling on the ocean. Eustus closed his eyes.

Darkness.

Forty-One

Vice Admiral Yolanda Laskowski sat back in her padded armchair, infinitely pleased with herself. It had taken her three times longer than she had originally estimated, but she had found a solution.

No, she corrected herself. She had found *the* solution. Working alone with the battle computer that was her only true friend, the only one she had ever felt she could really trust, she had finally found an answer to Evgeni Zhukovski's "hypothetical" scenario (which she knew quite well was more than hypothetical). The projected outcome, while not exactly a landslide in humanity's favor, nonetheless predicted victory. She had found a way, in theory – and with the help of some very special weapons – that a human fleet might be able to win.

While she had been forced to use a number of unverifiable assumptions in the decision matrix that the computer used to generate the result probabilities, she felt her assumptions were close enough to fit the available data. The Kreelans were in headlong retreat, and were ripe for a full, devastating pursuit.

She stood up and took her place behind the podium at the front of the briefing room.

"First," she began in her briefing to L'Houillier and the senior members of the General Staff, "this scenario is only valid as long as the Kreelan forces do not demonstrate their historical fighting potential. If at any point in the first phase of the operation they regain their will to fight, for lack of a better description, our odds drop to near zero." Heads nodded around the table. No one needed the battle computers to tell them that.

"Second, we must have complete surprise. Even in their present state, their fleet potentially could mass enough firepower to beat back the most determined attack we make. Just in measure of known numbers – and the STARNET figures are almost certainly conservative by a factor of at least fifty percent – the engagement will leave us outnumbered by one point seven to one. Only strategic and tactical surprise can balance out that inequality.

"Third, our commitment has to be total. I input every armed ship either currently afloat or ready to put out of drydock into the attack, giving us a total of two-thousand, eight-hundred, and forty-seven vessels. That includes Navy combat vessels and every armed coast guard and auxiliary ship with hyperlight drive that could be assembled in a forty-eight hour period, using midnight Zulu time tomorrow as H-hour."

She called up the holo image of space that extended from the human-explored Inner Arm sector, inward toward the galactic core. "This," she pointed to a red spheroid that appeared among the star clusters like a malignant tumor in a mass of neurons, "is the zone where the Kreelan fleet is gathering, which the scenario assumes to be the approximate location of their homeworld. As you can see, it has diminished somewhat in size since it was first identified, but we still do not know the precise location of their massing point." She paused, looking at L'Houillier, then Zhukovski. "That is the last, and most crucial, assumption I have had to make: that somehow we will discover that information before our fleet sails."

"I accept your assumptions, admiral," L'Houillier told her, but he was looking at Zhukovski. "As for the last one, we will see what can be done."

The Russian admiral said nothing, but stared impassively at the red corpuscle in the holo display as if he had not heard his superior.

"Please go on," L'Houillier said quietly.

"Sir," Laskowski said, nodding. Their exchange had not gone unnoticed. Zhukovski, her chief rival, was coming under some kind of pressure. Good. "The operation itself is fairly straightforward, with two simultaneous attacks, one in support of the other. The objective of the first attack is to engage and tie down the Kreelan fleet. It is not to destroy the enemy in a decisive manner, but to prevent it from engaging the ships taking part in the second attack. The objective of that effort will be the physical destruction of the Kreelan homeworld or worlds."

Faces among the staff suddenly became deadly serious. "Planet-busting," as it was often called, had always been more of a theoretical issue than a practical one. For one thing, humans had never encountered a Kreelan world. For another, many believed that it could not be done without involving a tremendous number of ships in an extended bombardment.

"A task force of seven ships," Laskowski went on, "will approach the Kreelan system from a different vector than the main body. They will be armed with kryolon and thermium torpedoes."

Laskowski felt an electric thrill run through her body at the mention of the device and the effect it had – stunned silence – on her audience. The kryolon torpedo was nearly a legend, a weapon that had been theoretically perfected years before, but that had never actually been used in anger. It was a star killer that caused a star to go nova, obliterating any orbiting planets. Their existence never confirmed to the populace or the military at large, the few weapons that had actually been constructed had remained in carefully protected secret bunkers on faraway asteroids, a suitable target for them never having been identified.

Until now.

"Three ships will launch their kryolon weapons at the system's primary star," Laskowski went on before anyone could interrupt, "while the others will seek out and attack any inhabited planets or moons in the system with improved thermium torpedoes." Thermium torpedoes had been developed with the help of research done on what was left of Hallmark. While not nearly as cataclysmic as the kryolon weapons, they would destroy the atmosphere of any Kreelan-held worlds. And these weapons had been tested against a real planet, an already-destroyed human colony. In a way, Laskowski thought, the Kreelans had sown the seeds of their own destruction.

She looked around the room. "Any planet attacked with one of these weapons will suffer the loss of its atmosphere, at a minimum. And the kryolon weapons launched into the star will trigger a massive flare that will destroy any units of the Kreelan fleet remaining in-system, as well as any planetary bodies that may have survived or escaped the thermium attacks." She paused dramatically, savoring her moment of triumph. "If all goes well and the intelligence estimates of the Kreelan population in-system are within expected parameters," she glanced significantly at Zhukovski, who pointedly ignored her, "we should be able to destroy most, if not all, of the entire Kreelan race."

Everyone in the room was quiet, considering the significance of her last words. To destroy an entire species was certainly nothing new to Mankind. Humans had eradicated thousands of unique forms of life on Earth and on colony worlds, and had even attempted over the centuries to eliminate some varieties of their own species. But to openly pursue the goal of annihilating an entire sentient race, regardless of the damage and loss of life it had incurred upon humanity, made some people uncomfortable. It hearkened back to the times of "racial purification" and "ethnic cleansing" that had been carried out by despotic powers against other humans in the darker times of Earth's history.

L'Houillier frowned. He wanted the war stopped and human lives saved, but the potential risk of what Laskowski presented was unfathomable. It was not an issue of hypothetical morality regarding the intentional annihilation of another sentient species. That, to L'Houillier, was not a concern in this case: the war must be brought to an end, and if the Kreelan race had to be exterminated, so be it.

But there was the question of repercussions. Who was to say that the ships gathering beyond the Inner Arm were but a token showing of the entire Kreelan fleet? How many colonies did they have beyond their homeworld from which another vengeful campaign of large-scale destruction could be waged against human worlds? The Kreelans, for reasons fully understood only by Reza Gard, did not engage in campaigns of wanton destruction, obliterating entire colonies without at least giving them the chance to fight back; they came looking for a fight for fighting's sake, and the humans had been forced to oblige them. But could they take the chance that the Kreelans would not retaliate in kind if the thermium weapons – let alone the kryolon star killers – were used? They had demonstrated with Hallmark that they could obliterate an entire world, and if those means continued to exist after the Kreelan homeworld was destroyed, Laskowski's plan could open the door to an interstellar Armageddon that would leave every human colony nothing more than a mass of molten rock.

He suddenly remembered Zhukovski's recounting of his conversation with Reza, recalling how long-lived had been the Kreelan civilization. *Over one hundred thousand years since the current Empire's founding*, he thought. And how many of those thousands had they been in space? Or developing weapons, a worthwhile pursuit for a race that thrived on warfare? How many planet-killers might the Kreelans have? And what other hideous weapons of mass destruction might they possess? The thought sent a chill up his spine. Glancing at Zhukovski, L'Houillier could see that his intelligence officer had come to similar conclusions. His perpetual scowl was deeper than usual. He was practically grimacing.

Laskowski was waiting with barely contained excitement for what L'Houillier would say about her plan. She had taken certain defeat and turned it into victory, coming up with a plan that dealt a massive and mortal blow to their enemy. While it was really more a consequence of the weapons she wished to employ than some kind of grand master strategy, the thought that humans could pay the Kreelans back in blood for human lives lost in the century-old war was one that she relished. *Vengeance*, she thought, *would surely be sweet*.

"Admiral?" she asked finally, becoming annoyed at L'Houillier's extended silence.

"It is impressive, Yolanda," he said finally, "and I wish you to pursue detailed planning along this line as a contingency–"

"As a contingency?" she blurted, unable to restrain herself. "Sir, with all due respect, this can give us victory! We have the opportunity here to destroy the Empire! We–"

"And that," L'Houillier said firmly, forcing himself to forgive – this once – her near insubordination, "is why you are to prepare contingency plans for an offensive. However, I think I see potential risks here that you may not have taken into account. For example, what happens to the scenario if there is a significant influx of Kreelan ships into the fray? Or if the target system is protected by automated defenses that do not rely on this 'psychic link,' as Admiral Zhukovski has related to us from Reza Gard, and is therefore not subject to whatever has caused their state of confusion?"

"But sir," she said, shaking her head, "the Kreelans could not possibly have more ships than I calculated into the probability matrix. And as for automated defenses, we've never seen any evidence of–"

"You are not answering my questions, admiral, unless you know for certain the size of the entire Kreelan fleet, which I doubt anyone does," L'Houillier said coldly. "The question, admiral, was, *what if?* That is the purpose for a scenario in the first place, is it not?" Laskowski, belatedly realizing her error in trying to tap-dance around L'Houillier, nodded sheepishly. "I ask you again: what if?"

"The operation would fail, sir," she said quietly.

"Casualties?"

"Depending on when the balance of forces shifted against our fleet, up to ninety-nine percent of the attacking force that had been committed to battle would be lost."

Which would be the entire human fleet, Zhukovski thought bitterly. Every armed vessel that could be gathered together in a forty-eight hour period, as Laskowski had put it.

"Repercussion extrapolation?" L'Houillier asked.

"Based on what little we know of their psychology and motivations, anywhere from fifty to one-hundred percent." Laskowski took a deep breath. She had not expected this... inquisition. "Using the Hallmark case as a benchmark, the matrix yields a minimum of twenty colonies destroyed in toto within six months."

"And what is maximum?" Zhukovski growled.

Laskowski looked at her feet. "All human inhabited domains: planets, moons, asteroids, orbital and deep space stations, and any surviving ships." In other words, the Kreelans were expected to destroy humans anywhere they lived, breathed, and used technology that could be identified and tracked. Any survivors would have to live at not just a pre-atomic level of civilization, but pre-electricity.

"Lord of All," someone whispered.

L'Houillier looked up at her. "I know you were given this task on the side, Yolanda, unofficially," he told her, "and you did an excellent job. But we must have another option. That is your task from me now. Find me that option, one that does not leave the fleet open to destruction and our homeworlds utterly defenseless if something goes wrong, as it inevitably does in such matters."

Making one last try, Laskowski said, "But the negative angles are all at the extremes of the matrix, admiral. I admit that the probabilities are not negligible, but the potential gain is more than worth the risks involved."

"That is not for us to decide," L'Houillier said. "That is for the Council and the president."

"Yes, sir," Laskowski responded tightly. You fool, she thought sullenly. Your only viable option is right in front of you. And if you won't listen to me, I know someone who will.

Forty-Two

Jodi smelled a rat, and it smelled suspiciously like Markus Thorella.

ACCESS DENIED.

The study cubicle's main screen displayed the words in blood red letters. Those two words had become her constant companions during the last half-hour of her informal – and strictly unauthorized – research.

"Eat me," she murmured, glaring angrily at the terminal. Had she bothered to look at the local time display in the lower right margin of the screen, she would have noticed that almost nine hours had passed since she left the hospital after Thorella's intrusion and Reza's mysterious fainting episode. And that was why she was here. It was just too convenient, she had told herself as she stalked out of the hospital, almost unconsciously heading for the General Staff HQ research center where she had spent most of her waking hours the last few months, studying for her doctorate in applied military theory. Reza was probably the most superb physical specimen the human race had ever known as far as endurance, strength for mass, and sheer toughness. He had only very recently awakened from a coma, true, but that did not seem enough to her to explain the spell that had visited him the moment he demonstrated aggression toward Thorella. And Thorella's own behavior: it was if he had been taunting Reza, deliberately trying to provoke him, to see... what?

"To see if something would work," she had thought aloud to herself as she strode into the building, startling the guard at the entrance. Working on the theory that Thorella was somehow exerting an unnatural influence over Reza, Jodi had begun to dig.

And, hours later, the gems she had found. She glanced down at the tiny storage card that now held all the information she had retrieved in the course of her travels through the center's vast databases. She had not hit the mother lode yet, had not found the answer to her underlying question, but she had discovered a cornucopia of "nice to know" items.

"Know your enemy" was the route she had initially taken in her quest, and Jodi had begun prowling for any information she could find on one Thorella, Markus Gustav.

At first, she had been disappointed. Born into a wealthy Terran industrialist family, Markus Thorella had been an excellent student in his primary and secondary schools, and quickly demonstrated his prowess at team and individual sports, as well.

He was never in trouble with the law, attended church regularly with his parents, and even worked frequently as a volunteer, donating his time to a local hospital as an orderly. On the face of it, he looked like every parent's dream: bright, almost brilliant, physically superb, and selflessly dedicated to those around him.

That person, Jodi told herself, was definitely not the same Markus Thorella that they all knew and loved.

Then she found out about the crash. For Markus's fourteenth birthday, his parents took him on a cruise to the Outer Rim, to a group of worlds that had been – for the most part – free of Kreelan attacks over the years, a place where tourism was still a thriving industry. In a freak accident while departing Earth orbit, the starliner had somehow collided with another ship that had been inbound. While such collisions were extremely rare, they did sometimes happen, and when they did, they were disastrous. Over fifteen thousand people lost their lives that day. Only eighty were finally rescued from residual air pockets in the shattered hulls; the collision had occurred so suddenly and unexpectedly that none of the passengers or crew of either vessel had been able to reach a single lifeboat.

One of the survivors had been Markus Thorella, who had been terribly injured. According to a subsequent press account of the incident, the body that bore the clothes of Markus Thorella had been reduced to little more than a pulsating lump of flesh.

And that is where Jodi began to run into dead ends. Curious as to what happened afterward, during his physical reconstruction and therapy, she could get no closer than a hospital record certifying his release more than a year later. Everything in between, everything, was either barred from her or listed as "information unavailable." That is when her unofficial research methods began to pay off. Using an unlocking program she had acquired from a young graduate student eager to impress her (too bad it had to be a guy, she lamented sourly), she began to worm her way through the passages that blocked access to Thorella's past.

The program finally turned the key to the information she wanted, and she was literally deluged with data ranging from Thorella's daily urine tests to the books the nurses read to him during the early phases of his recovery when his eyes were still regenerating in their sockets. While a medical student might have found interest in such things, the only thing she cared about was the DNA fingerprint.

The results, when she found them, did not surprise her as much as she would have liked. According to the official records, the DNA sample could not be firmly identified as belonging to Markus Thorella. The reason, she found out after doing some backtracking through press and a few restricted government files, was because all of Markus Thorella's previous medical records – from his schools, the two hospitals he had visited since he was born, and the Thorella family physician – had mysteriously disappeared. However, since the boy had been in possession of Markus Thorella's identity card and other personal effects when he was found in the starliner's wreckage, everyone assumed he was Markus Thorella. On top of that, no one could positively identify him physically because his entire body – including fingertips and teeth – had been damaged beyond recognition. When the surgeons rebuilt him, they used some old holos that the schools were able to provide. When they were finished, he again looked like Markus Thorella.

But was he? Jodi asked herself. Had the physical and emotional trauma of the crash altered his personality? Or had he always had a sadistic streak that never showed up in any of his early psychological profiles? Or was there something else?

As she followed the history of the "new" Markus Thorella, she discovered that he had become incredibly rich after the death of his parents. Since they had died and he had no surviving family members to contest the estate, he was awarded the entire Thorella inheritance. He was instantly worth hundreds of millions of credits. But in Earth's jurisdiction, he still had to have a legal guardian at that age.

The guardian's name turned out to be Strom Borge. The name rang a bell with her, but she could not quite place it. She knew she had seen or heard that name before, but where?

Running a search, it did not take long to find out. Strom Borge was a Terran Senator to the Confederation, member of the Confederation Council, and chairman of a dozen major committees within the government. The hairs at the back of her neck tingled.

"Now I remember you," she murmured to herself. He had been the leader of the group opposing the confirmation of Reza's citizenship after returning from the Empire, and had been in favor of the radical psychotherapy procedures demanded by Dr. Deliha Rabat, another of Jodi's personal favorites.

But there was something else. She had seen that name earlier this evening, during her research. Running another search on Borge, Strom Anaguay, she excluded all references after the crash and before Markus Thorella was born, limiting the search to the first fourteen or so years of Thorella's life. In but a few seconds, she had her answer.

"Jesus Horatio Christ," she breathed as the information scrolled up on her screen. Borge had been on the starliner with the Thorellas. He had been a friend of the family for some years, or so the records indicated, and he was frequently to be found in their company. Along with his son, Anton Borge.

Twenty minutes more of digging through increasingly compartmented files in the research center's data network for Anton Borge's DNA fingerprint confirmed what she suspected: "Markus Thorella" was Strom Borge's biological son.

She sat back, imagining to herself what must have happened. Borge, an aggressive and ruthless politician, had received the support and friendship of the Thorella family, who themselves had much to gain from Borge's rapidly growing political influence in the defense sector, since the Thorellas owned one of the largest shipbuilding firms on Terra.

But the genial relationship between the parents was not shared by the two boys, who apparently loathed each other. Not surprising, since psychologically Anton Borge was the complete antithesis of the Thorella boy: while they were in fact similar physically, Anton was arrogant and hateful, never failing to make those around him miserable. Arrested on a dozen charges ranging from petty theft to sexual assault against a seven year old boy, he always managed to avoid punishment because of his father's influence.

When the collision occurred, Strom Borge probably acted with his noted ruthlessness to take advantage of the situation. As evidenced by the hospital records, Borge's son must have been hideously injured in the crash. The question then, was what really happened to the Thorellas? Did Emilio and Augusta Thorella die outright, or did Borge murder them? Their bodies were never recovered. And what happened to the real Markus Thorella? If Strom Borge was able to somehow put the Thorella boy's clothes (what was left of them) and his identity card on his own mutilated son, Markus Thorella's body must still have been on the ship and more or less intact. Again, was he already dead, or did Borge kill him, perhaps tossing the body into a blazing compartment on the ship to hide the evidence of his crime?

Another thought nagged at her: how had Borge and his son managed to keep their true relationship a secret? Borge had obviously gone to great lengths to conceal the true identity of "Markus Thorella" by somehow destroying or confiscating all of the Thorella boy's medical records (and, she found out, the records of his parents, too, to prevent any DNA tracing). Not surprisingly, the official investigation into the disappearance of those records ended rapidly and prematurely, no doubt under the shadow of Senator Borge's influence.

But aside from all the possible paper trails that he had deftly covered up, how had his son reacted to suddenly becoming someone else? The boy was certainly old enough to know that he was not Markus Thorella, and all it would have taken was for him to call Borge "Dad" in the wrong company and someone might have become suspicious.

The answer was in a name that Jodi knew all too well: Dr. Deliha Rabat. Jodi reviewed the medical records again. She was looking for some clue as to why no one had suspected that Strom Borge and Markus Thorella were really father and son. Borge's wife wasn't part of the equation, since she had been killed in a Kreelan attack on a colony world not long after Anton was born. But then Jodi discovered that "Markus Thorella" had undergone psychotherapy at the hands of the young and ambitious Dr. Rabat, who treated him for emotional trauma. The reports showed that the newly reconstructed Thorella boy was having delusions that he was actually the son of Strom Borge.

Imagine that, Jodi thought acidly.

While she did not understand all the technobabble in the reports, she did see the effects of Rabat's treatment: the "delusions" rapidly disappeared. In the end, the boy retained all the awful traits of his true self, but came to believe that he was the sole survivor of the Thorella family and heir to all its wealth, and whose best friend in the galaxy was Strom Borge.

Not surprisingly, the young Dr. Rabat soon left the hospital for her own research lab, funded entirely by the Thorella estate and endorsed by Senator Borge, the estate's executor until Markus Thorella's coming of age.

"How very, very convenient," Jodi muttered. She hated Thorella, despised him, but she saw now that whatever evil had been in him before had been twisted even more by his scheming father and his sycophants. With the unwitting help of the hospital and the conniving of Dr. Rabat, Borge had transformed his own son into an incidental fortune that had financed his own interests. By the time Markus Thorella was handed the papers for the estate, he was already two years in the Marine Corps and safely out of Borge's hair. The good senator was left to oversee matters while the "son of his dear, departed friends" went off to war.

"Fucking bastard," Jodi hissed as she continued her scanning.

She discovered that their relationship did not end there, by any means. Reading over the official military records that mentioned Markus Thorella – she had not been able to gain access to his actual Marine Corps personnel files – she soon came to see that he had acquired a reputation as a hatchet man, as ruthless or more so than his secret father. And the enemies he was sent to fight did not have blue skin: not one single time in his career was the unit in which he was serving sent into the line against the Kreelans. Instead, he spent his service time engaged in police actions on various worlds, bashing in human heads in places like Erlang that had somehow earned Borge's ire.

That information, in turn, led her to discover the connection Borge had with those places. Millennium Industries – which originally had belonged to the Thorellas, but had long since come under Borge's control – had holdings or interests on every one of the planets where Thorella and his goons had been deployed: Erlang for precious and strategic minerals; Kauchin in the Outer Rim for cheap, undisturbed, labor; Wilhelmstadt for high tech items; the shipyards around Manifest. And a dozen more. From what Jodi could tell, every ship, weapon, or defense system built in half the Confederation contributed to the senator's coffers. If he wanted, Jodi did not doubt that he could build his own battle fleet; he already owned a sizable portion of the merchant marine. But all of it fell under the ownership of Millennium Industries, and any investigation short of the outright data penetrations that Jodi was conducting (which were completely illegal) would show Borge only as a minor shareholder and acting chairman of the umbrella company.

Jodi shook her head in wonder. Borge was using both his political position and his influence with the military – she hoped unwittingly – to boost his own power, employing his biological son as an agent any time he needed a dirty job done. And he was getting away with it at an untold cost in terms of human lives and suffering.

And in the case of Erlang, she discovered, President Belisle had not only been a tyrant, but he had also received kickbacks from Millennium Industries, presumably as a payoff to keep the Mallorys in line and ensure that Millennium got its cut of Erlang's mineral production. But, according to the figures she saw here, Belisle had not only failed to keep production at an acceptable level, he had lately been demanding more and more money from Millennium for his cooperation and silence. But when Reza appeared, soon assisted by Melissa Savitch, the role of Millennium – and Borge – in the rape of Erlang and the Mallorys could have become public. Borge had not sent Thorella there just to bring the Mallorys to heel and take care of Reza; he had been sent to kill Belisle, and had murdered Savitch because she happened to be in the way.

"They set you up, Reza," she murmured. That was the only way Thorella could have gotten any valid imagery of Reza killing Belisle, because Reza would have killed the good colonel, too, had he had the chance. Thorella had known what Reza would do, and he had set a very good trap for him, using Belisle as bait. In one stroke, Borge and Thorella were able to both get rid of Belisle and frame Reza for murder. And now, even though the Mallorys, who were now legally in charge of Erlang, insisted that the Confederation government not only drop the charges against Reza but give him a medal for what he had done, Borge somehow had bought enough influence to make the charges stick.

But they could not try him until he had recovered from his coma. And that was where she began to run into real problems. While the worm program she had been running was more than a match for the basic security codes that had been put on the older files, the more recent ones having to do with the Erlang incident and its aftermath were much better protected. In her last half hour at the research center, she had only been able to gain access to one document: the list of medical personnel who had participated in Reza's care over the last six months. And she was not terribly surprised to learn that one of the most frequent visitors had been Dr. Deliha Rabat.

She glowered at the screen, willing the current ACCESS DENIED warning to go away.

Trying again with the last bypass algorithm the worm program had been written to attempt, the words disappeared.

"All right," she said eagerly. "Maybe we're getting somewhere."

But what echoed on the screen was not at all reassuring:

VIOLATION OF SECURITY LOCK
128904-34-23341
USER 527-903-482-71 ACCESS SUSPENDED
SECURITY MANAGER ALERTED
REMOTE STATION DISCONNECT

The screen suddenly went blank and the terminal refused to respond to her frantic hammering on the keyboard.

"Oh, shit," she muttered. She quickly tossed everything but the data card with all the information she had downloaded into her shoulder bag. The card she put in her boot. It would not escape anything more than a cursory search, but it might make the difference.

Opening the door just a crack to see if anything unusual was going on, she saw that the center, crowded as always, remained quiet. She made her way toward the main lobby at a brisk walk, her eyes alert for any sign of trouble.

Because she was in trouble. She just did not realize yet how much.

Forty-Three

L'Houillier's eyes opened unwillingly at the urgent beep coming from the General Staff comm link beside his bed. Beside him, his wife rolled over, burying her head in her pillow in a reflex she had developed over many years of being married to a Navy officer constantly on call.

He rolled over and slapped the machine, nearly knocking it from the nightstand. "L'Houillier," he said groggily. Unlike many of his contemporaries, the ability to become alert immediately upon awakening had always eluded him.

"Forgive intrusion, admiral, but something most urgent has come up."

Zhukovski, L'Houillier thought. *Of course. Did the man never sleep?* "I'll be there in thirty minutes, Evgeni."

"Pardon, admiral, but matter cannot wait thirty minutes," Zhukovski's voice shot back. "I am on my way to you. Five minutes."

Before L'Houillier had a chance to protest, Zhukovski had terminated the transmission. "*Merde*," he muttered.

"Evgeni again?" his wife asked, fully awake.

"Who else?" L'Houillier said grumpily. She could fall asleep in five minutes, be awake instantly, and fall asleep again without missing a beat. The same cycle took him hours, if he could manage it at all. He was terribly jealous.

"I'll start the coffee and tea," she said crisply as she got up, donned a robe, and disappeared out of the room.

Forcing himself out of bed, he had just managed to go to the bathroom and put on his own robe when he heard Zhukovski hammering on the front door, pointedly ignoring the more pleasant doorbell.

A few minutes later, L'Houillier was indeed awake, and not because of his wife's special version of Navy coffee.

"Evgeni, this is fantastic," he said as he reviewed again the message from Commodore Marchand aboard *Furious*. "A willing Kreelan prisoner and a child they think belongs to Reza Gard?"

"So Commodore Marchand reports, sir," Evgeni said as he took another sip of the excellent tea proffered by L'Houillier's wife. For Zhukovski, that was enough incentive to rouse his commander from sleep for an impromptu visit. "We have great opportunity here, admiral. But we can do nothing without translator."

"Gard, you mean?"

Zhukovski nodded. "Correct, sir. This is our chance to find out more. We must bring all of them together."

"What if the Kreelans – or Reza – do not wish to help?"

Zhukovski shrugged. "Then we have lost nothing but time courier ship needs to bring prisoners to Earth."

L'Houillier did not hesitate. "Make it so, Evgeni."

* * *

The situation in the sick bay on board *Furious* was tense, Eustus thought, but it was under control. For the moment. The huge warrior stood a silent vigil over the Kreelan child, watching with the greatest trepidation every move made by the ship's surgeon as she began to work on the girl.

Eustus remembered little between passing out in the tunnel after the warrior started carrying him and waking up here on the *Furious*. But he had apparently managed to keep the Navy boat and the surviving Marines from shooting the Kreelan woman and the child, and Commodore Marchand had been ecstatic about their capture.

But no one on the ship who'd seen the warrior was under any delusions that she was truly a prisoner. Wisely, no one had tried to take her weapons. Even if someone had, her physical strength and her rapier claws would have wrought havoc in the close quarters of the ship before she could have been brought down. But there were no human weapons here, no Marines or armed sailors. The sickbay had been sealed off, the surgeon and two assistants tending to the girl as the warrior looked on, while Eustus was left to the accurate but less-than-tender ministrations of one of the automated aid stations that could easily repair the damage to his leg. But a platoon of fully armed Marines in battle armor waited tensely outside the door.

The surgeon was busy pulling away the lower part of the black undergarment to check on the girl's legs.

"Lord of All," she whispered. The two nurses gawked in astonishment.

"What is it?" Eustus asked just as Marchand's voice cut in over the intercom with the same question. The commodore, along with half the ship's officers, was glued to a screen in her ready room, watching the video feed from the operating theater.

"This isn't any girl," the surgeon pronounced. "We've got ourselves a male child here, people."

"Jesus," Eustus breathed. It was certainly a day of firsts.

The warrior looked at Eustus uncertainly, her great hands flexing in a gesture Eustus knew well from Reza. She was nervous, anxious.

"It's all right," he said quietly, hoping that a reassuring tone would suffice for words he did not know. "We just expected a girl, is all."

She frowned, but seemed to relax slightly. If a figure as imposing as she could be said to relax.

The surgeon worked on the boy for nearly two hours, doing the best she could to repair the damage to a kind of body she had never worked on before. She spliced bone and muscle, fused blood vessels closed. Thankfully there did not appear to be any injuries to the child's internal organs, the functions of some of which the surgeon wasn't sure.

"All right," she said finally, wiping her arm across a brow that had been sweating profusely the entire time, despite the nurse's best efforts to blot it away, "that's it. I think he'll make it."

There was a burst of applause from the comms terminal as the officers and crew gathered around similar sets throughout the ship offered their congratulations. At first, the warrior was terrified that something had gone wrong. Eustus quickly reassured her that the boy would live, reaching out a hand to hold hers. That, and the smile on his face, was enough to reassure her that the child was safe.

It was perhaps the first victory in the war in which a life from the opposing side had been saved, and Eustus could only hope that what they had accomplished here today would set a precedent for the days yet to come.

FORTY-FOUR

President Nathan slept fitfully, alone in the president's quarters in the Council Building. His wife slept without him, as she often did, in their home in the country. He missed her and she him, but the affairs of state, as it had so many times in the many years of their marriage, took precedence over their personal lives. It was a sacrifice that very few of his countrymen truly appreciated.

The previous few days had been an unending political nightmare as he sought to fend off repeated attacks by Borge and his growing retinue of virulent supporters. While Nathan agreed that the current situation presented a historic opportunity, the military had not yet given him a plan with which he felt comfortable, a plan that did not expose every single colony – even Earth itself – to possible counterattack and destruction. For probably the first time in his life, Nathan was truly afraid, not for himself, but for his people. The decision he made had to be right. The consequences were simply too awful to contemplate if he was wrong.

But that was not good enough. The Council was rapidly swaying toward Borge's arguments that the time to strike was now, and that they should strike with everything. Borge was quietly branding anyone who opposed the idea as a traitor, and had come within a word of calling Nathan a coward in the middle of the heated debate. Actually, he had done better than to state it explicitly. He had painted a picture with related words, leaving it to the listener to see the final portrait, false though it might be. Nathan was determined that Borge would not have his way, and so far he had managed to maintain enough support for his administration to thwart the ambitious senator's machinations.

Imagine, Nathan had thought, mutely horrified, *what would become of the democracy that had ruled the Confederation for the last century if this man came to power*. Borge had made no secret of his reactionary attitude toward the military and scientific communities, not to mention what he thought – and claimed he would do – with regard to his political rivals. The man was nothing short of a megalomaniac, the kind who is spawned only in times of intense political crisis and in places resonating with corrupting power. In his mind, he had so much to gain by stepping up to Nathan's position; and in Nathan's mind, humanity everywhere had so much to lose. He would have arrested Borge if he could, just to shut him away from the power he so craved and would do anything to gain more of. But Nathan could not do that. He had lived his life by the constitution he had sworn to uphold, and he did not feel himself above the laws that guided the common man and woman in this time of perpetual crisis.

And that was the source of Nathan's frustration: his inability to effectively combat Borge, for the senator was an enemy every bit as tenacious and far more inhuman even than the Kreelans. Nathan vowed to fight him tooth and nail in the Council chambers and wherever else he could claim as a battleground, but he knew that unless something drastic happened very soon, he would lose. It was inevitable. In his dreams, the president of the Confederation hoped for a miracle.

He did not hear the stealthy footsteps of the man who entered his room. The electronic guardian, the eyes and ears located throughout the large apartment, lay dormant, deactivated. The guards downstairs were alert, at their posts, but saw nothing. In the president's bedroom it was dark, but the intruder had no difficulty seeing. This was what night vision lenses were made for.

The dark form paused for a moment at the president's bedside. A smile passed across the intruder's face under the black mask as he considered his next move, one that he had rehearsed numerous times. He silently extracted a wicked looking dagger that had been fashioned by Kreelan hands, but whose most recent owner had been human. It was Reza's dagger, his most prized possession.

He moved close to the bed. He wanted to see Nathan's eyes. The intruder nudged the slumbering president. The older man's eyes snapped open wide.

The blade flashed down in a lethal arc as Nathan's mouth made an "O" of surprise. He raised his arms in a defensive gesture that was too slow, too late. The knife, which was made of the sharpest and most durable metal known, speared Nathan's chest directly over the heart, slipping through his ribs to rupture the vital muscle that pulsated beneath. A small ring of blood appeared on the sheet, but that was all.

With a gasp and shudder, the president of the Confederation, and democracy itself, died.

The intruder stood and watched the dead man for a few moments, savoring the feeling of the kill. He was sorely tempted to massage the massive erection in his pants to fruition, but he knew from experience that it would have to wait. This time. There had been others when waiting had been unnecessary. And he was sure there would be still more.

His erection grew harder. It was time to leave.

With the barest sigh of his rubber-soled boots on the plush carpet, the man made his exit. After he left the building through an exit that the guards thought was secure, the electronic guardian reactivated, its internal memory already adjusted to account for the moments it had been fooled: the horrified guards watched as Reza Gard appeared out of thin air, plunged a knife into their president's heart, and then just as quickly disappeared as the alarms began to sound.

* * *

While she did not realize it at the time, walking home very likely saved Jodi's life. She normally took the transit shuttle from the government complex to the rural hub four kilometers away that, in its turn, served the outlying areas where Nicole and Tony had their house. But after what she had discovered at the research center, she needed some time to think about what she had learned and had decided to take one of the many nature trails that wound their way through the countryside. It was dark, of course, but the sky was clear, the stars and waning moon lighting the way. Besides, she was not afraid. Even had she not been competent in Aikido and the street-style fighting Tony Braddock had taught her, she still could do more than her share of damage with the pocket blaster she carried under her tunic.

She was actually enjoying the cool smell of the night, the sounds of the crickets chirping and the high chittering of the bats that flew from the trees in search of their evening meal.

Fear did not take hold until she was within sight of the house and saw the three security skimmers pulled up in front.

"Not very subtle, are you?" she murmured to herself as she moved behind a fortuitously positioned hedge to conceal herself from the half dozen Internal Security troops wandering around the front yard. "Shit," she whispered.

In the doorway, she could see Tony gesticulating angrily at what must have been the head IS man, who gestured back. She could hear their voices, but they were still too far away to make out. But she did not doubt the reason for the IS presence here: her "research" had set off some big alarm bells.

Then she saw the gun. Silence suddenly descended on the house.

"Jesus," Jodi gasped. The IS man had pulled a gun on Tony, a junior senator and member of the Council, no less! "What the fuck is going on?" she murmured as she forced herself even lower behind the hedge.

The rest of the security troops wasted no time, pushing roughly past Tony on their way in to search the house, no doubt for Jodi. Tony had been trying to fend them off, she thought, because they probably did not have a warrant to search the house. But a gun against an unarmed man was quite persuasive, if not exactly legal.

"Don't do anything stupid, Tony," Jodi pleaded under her breath.

Braddock just stood there quietly, his arms raised, his face twisted in a mask of fiery anger as the IS man held his gun leveled at Tony's chest.

Suddenly, Jodi heard a female voice from within the house, screaming angrily at the intruders in what could only be French. *Nicole.* They had probably been in bed when the storm troops came knocking, Jodi thought, and Tony had gotten up to answer the door. Surprise.

But the biggest surprise was the sight of four IS men herding Nicole out the door, dressed only in her robe, then stuffing her into one of the skimmers. The leader nudged Tony along with the gun, pushing him roughly into the vehicle beside Nicole.

Then the IS people got into the skimmers and left, except for two men they left behind. After their comrades departed, they went into the house, closed the door, and turned off the lights. To wait for Jodi.

She felt her stomach drop away into infinity. Had she arrived a few minutes earlier, they would have caught her. Had she arrived a few minutes later, they would have caught her. Someone, presumably the God she had never really believed in, had been looking out for her. She could only hope that Nicole and Tony would be all right.

For now, she had to look out for herself, because she knew that if the security forces captured her, Borge's secret would never see the light of day. She would silently, tragically, disappear. She looked at her watch. Twenty-three hundred. She had about six more hours of darkness.

Six hours to find help.

* * *

"What in the hell is going on, senator?" Tony Braddock demanded angrily. He and Nicole sat on the opposite side of a security shield, guarded by four IS agents with drawn weapons. Senator Borge sat on the other side, his face a mask of sorrow.

"Please, Councilman, captain," he said solemnly, "this situation is not as I would like, but events have taken place that demand the most extreme action." He looked at them gravely.

"And what is this 'situation?'" Nicole asked coldly.

Borge nodded. "Earlier this evening, less than an hour ago, to be more precise, Reza Gard escaped from the detention facility at the hospital. Shortly thereafter, he murdered President Nathan."

"That is not possible!" Nicole said incredulously, jumping to her feet. "Reza would never do such a thing!"

"I wish that were the case, but there is evidence to the contrary." He nodded to his aid, who activated a holo recording showing Reza materializing in Nathan's bedroom. Moving close to the bed, he withdrew a knife and, after only a moment's hesitation, plunged it into the president's chest. The alarm went off a few seconds later, and Reza disappeared from the room as mysteriously as he had come.

"I don't believe it," Tony said firmly. "This is some kind of a hoax or a frame-up. Reza gave his word to Nicole that he would not try to escape, and he would never have broken it. You've got the wrong man, senator. I don't know how, but you've got the wrong man."

"Besides," Nicole asked, grudgingly retaking her seat, "what does this have to do with us? Are you implicating us as accomplices?"

Borge shook his head as if he were mortified at the thought. "You two? Heavens no. But Commander Mackenzie is another matter. She attempted to see Reza again tonight, even after her earlier little... tiff... with Colonel Thorella." He looked at them significantly. "I would like to know why. Internal Security knew, of course, that she was staying with you, and that naturally was the first place to look."

"This is ridiculous–" Nicole growled.

"Even if this is all true," Tony interrupted hotly, "does that give you the right to hold us at gunpoint in our own home, without so much as a search warrant?"

"I don't think you understand the gravity of the situation, Councilman Braddock," Borge said slowly. "In accordance with constitutional law, I legally inherited the powers of the president just as Nathan took his last breath. I will not allow his death – his murder – to go unpunished. I apologize for the zealotry shown by the IS agents at your home, but I am taking no chances, and I will spare no effort to get to the bottom of this. You two are friends of both Captain Gard and Commander Mackenzie, and are our only leads to them. I hope that you are able to put aside your personal feelings in this matter – and I realize that will be terribly difficult – and help Internal Security find Reza Gard and Commander Mackenzie."

"And if we do not?" Nicole asked.

Borge looked at them with eyes glowing with barely concealed ferocity. "I will have you both cited with contempt and thrown in prison until you decide to cooperate." He leaned forward, his hands spread before him. "Please," he begged, "please do not make this any more difficult than it already is. The president was a good friend of mine for many years, and to me his loss is a very personal one. Captain Gard is implicated in his murder, and Commander Mackenzie was in the wrong place at the wrong time. If he is innocent, and she is not involved, fine. We will find who is. But I want answers, my friends. Quickly. And I will have them, one way or another."

Nicole and Tony looked at each other helplessly. There was little they could do. And the image of Reza driving the knife into Nathan's heart was more than convincing, at least to anyone who did not know him. He had powers that were arguably supernatural, and both of them knew that Reza could easily do what the video had shown.

Until Tony remembered what Reza had said about what had happened on Erlang with Thorella's little holo act. Who was to say that they weren't witnessing a repeat performance? But he kept that to himself. Right now, Borge held all the cards in this particular deadly game.

"What do you want us to do?" he asked quietly.

* * *

Jodi was running out of time. She had made her way as quickly as she could back into the subterranean complex that made up the city's core. She realized that it would be more dangerous for her there, but she needed information, and that was the only place she could think of to get it.

The news, when she saw it broadcast on the holo banners in the main mall, stunned her. President Nathan was dead, murdered. Reza Gard, having escaped from the hospital, was the prime suspect, and Commander Jodi Mackenzie was believed to be involved. There was her picture, for all to see, on at least a dozen banners that were in her direct view.

The only thing that saved her was that the mall was so crowded with people seeking out the capitol's nightlife. Most of the wanderers ignored the holo banners. They ignored the broadcast. They ignored her. For the moment, at least, it appeared as if she could still move about. But that was not going to last for long.

She moved quickly to a vid terminal, putting her back to the crowd and the gruesome images of the president's death that were finally getting some attention: more and more people were stopping and staring.

"God," she whispered, "what in the fuck's going on? What am I going to do?" Her hands were shaking. *Come on*, she shouted at herself. *Think*. She needed shelter and information, maybe a new identity. Transportation. Money. More than all that, she needed to find Reza. She knew the escape story was garbage, but where did that leave him? And how could she possibly find him? She could not make it more than a few kilometers by herself. She needed help. But with Nicole and Tony out of the picture, whom could she turn to who was close by? She couldn't use any inter-city transportation or she'd be picked up for sure.

Something nagged at her memory. A name. Someone she knew, someone close by. For a while, it refused to come to her, instead fluttering just beyond her recollection, taunting her.

Tanya. Tanya Buchet.

The name sent a shiver up her spine. She closed her eyes and slumped against the wall of the booth. Of all the people in the world she would have to turn to, why did Tanya have to be the one? It just had to be someone who probably still hated her guts after all the years since they had last seen each other. Maybe even as much as Jodi hated her. They had not parted on the best of terms. But Tanya had everything that Jodi needed.

"Oh, Lord," she moaned. "Why her? Why that fucking bitch?"

After a moment, her mind was made up. She had no other choice. Calling up the directory, she quickly found Tanya's address. It was the same as it had been all those years ago. Glancing at the flow of people behind her, she darted to the rear of a boisterous group of Marines making their way back to one of the local barracks, using them to mask her escape through the nearest exit to the surface level.

* * *

The tiny suburb called Hamilton had changed little over the years. Jodi had last seen it while in her late teens, when she was still in school. She had befriended the daughter of a wealthy family that normally lived in Europe, but that had given their young daughter a cottage here, only a few kilometers from the capitol, where she could live during the school year. It probably would have come as no surprise to her parents to learn that she was seldom alone there. She was brilliant, beautiful, and cloaked by a touch of darkness that Jodi and many others had found irresistible. She was Jodi's first lover, and without doubt the cruelest.

Sensing Jodi's need for her affection, her approval, Tanya Buchet had kept her almost as an emotional slave, alternately tormenting her and pleasing her as she might an animal in an experiment. Jodi finally realized the extent of her plight when she found herself holding a blaster to her own skull, having discovered that her first love had been cheating on her. With the cold muzzle of the gun pressing into her temple, Jodi suddenly thought how much better it would be to kill Tanya instead, but she had let it go as only an unpleasant – if gratifying – thought. She had moved out that day, and it was not long after that the Navy whisked her away for what Jodi had hoped would be forever.

But forever hadn't been as long as she'd hoped. Walking up the steps to the cottage, she saw how well it had been kept up. In fact, except for the growth of the trees and new paint, it had hardly changed at all.

Her spine crawling with dreadful anticipation, she rapped on the door of what had once been an emotional Hell. *If there is a God*, she thought, *please let Him be with me now.*

There was no answer, no indication of anything or anyone stirring within. She hesitated, then knocked again, louder this time.

The old wooden door suddenly opened without a sound, swinging back on well-oiled hinges. Startled, Jodi took two steps backward, nearly falling down the steps in surprise.

The woman who stood in the doorway was stunning, clothed in a black dress that was as elegant and beautiful as it was plain. Her long brunette hair framed a flawless ivory face, the hazel eyes appraising, predatory. The smile, when it finally came, exposed perfect teeth behind full, sensuous lips.

"Jodi," those ruby lips said, exposing the husky voice that had come with womanhood, "how very nice to see you."

* * *

Now, sitting on the sofa in the small parlor and holding the cup of tea she had been given, spilling half of it in the saucer from her shaking hands, Jodi faced the witch of her adolescent years.

"Believe me, Tanya," she told the woman, who sat quietly in the chair opposite, her unblinking eyes focused on Jodi's, "I'm not here because I want to be."

"Jodi, dear, you didn't come all this way just to hurt my feelings, did you?" Tanya replied evenly, shifting herself to reveal a little more leg from under her dress.

"No, of course not," Jodi replied hastily, consciously looking away from Tanya. She would not, could not, let herself be drawn into that spider's web again. "I didn't even know you'd still be here. Even now, I can't believe you are."

"And why shouldn't I be? This has been my home. I go to the family estate in Europe sometimes, when I feel like it. But Hamilton and New York serve my purposes adequately. I sometimes board students here who attend our old school."

Jodi suppressed a shudder at what must happen to the students here.

"Didn't you ever do your civil or military service time?"

Tanya laughed. "Of course not, dear! Who do you think is going to make the only daughter and surviving member of the Buchet family play soldier in this silly little war? I'm one of the five richest people on this entire planet, probably in the entire Confederation, and have been since just after you ran away. I'm quite content to let you little generals run about and play war games with the Kreelans. My interests lie elsewhere."

Jodi gritted her teeth, forcing back the response that fought its way to the surface. "That's obvious enough," she muttered instead. "What about your parents?" she asked. "What happened to them?"

Tanya waved her hand, dismissing the issue as if her parents had never been of any consequence. "They got themselves killed on a transatlantic flight. I don't remember the details, really. It's not important now." Like a wraith, she uncoiled herself from her chair and came to sit beside Jodi on the sofa, putting her arm across the sofa back behind Jodi's neck. Jodi could feel her own body reacting instinctively to Tanya's nearness, sensing her warmth, smelling the alluring scent of her perfume. "What is important," Tanya whispered, "is you. Tell me, why are you here?"

Downing the last of the bitter tea that she suddenly hoped was not drugged, Jodi set the cup and saucer down on the coffee table and turned to face her nemesis-benefactor. Tanya's gaze held hers. Her lips were so close...

"I need your help, Tanya," Jodi told her, forcing out the words while looking Tanya in the eye. She had conjured up the sight of Nicole and Tony being held at gunpoint by the IS, and the anger that uncoiled in her chest gave her the strength she needed to resist Tanya's magnetic gaze.

"I thought as much," Tanya said, a smile touching her scarlet lips. "I suppose it's not every day that I have a chance to speak with someone who conspired to kill the president."

"That's total bullshit," Jodi spat. "Reza Gard did not kill the president and I didn't help him get out of the hospital. We were both set up: Reza because the real murderer needs a scapegoat and me because I found out something I'm not supposed to know."

One of Tanya's eyebrows arched. "Really? And just what might that be?"

"It's a long story," Jodi said uncomfortably, suddenly wondering why she had come here. More and more, she felt as if she were in a trap. The words suddenly came to her: *Come into my parlor, said the spider to the fly...*

"Well, dear," Tanya said, casually examining one of her perfectly manicured blood-red nails, "I have plenty of time."

Jodi bit her lip. "Please, Tanya. I have nowhere else to turn, no one else to go to. There's a lot riding on this, a lot more than just my life. There's something terribly wrong in the Confederation government. I think I know who murdered the president, but it wasn't Reza Gard."

"Well," Tanya said, looking up from her nails to pin Jodi with her gaze, "I'm sure President Borge would be happy to hear about it."

Jodi felt her black skin go pale as the blood drained from it. "*President* Borge," she whispered. She closed her eyes. She was too late. "Dear, sweet Jesus."

She felt a cool hand against her face. "Jodi," Tanya asked with what almost sounded like genuine concern in her voice, "are you all right?"

"No," Jodi choked. "The Confederation's fucked. We're all fucked, now that that bastard has gotten what he wanted."

"Tell me," Tanya said softly, "why do you say that? Borge has been a friend of our family for many years. I know him quite well."

Somehow, that did not surprise Jodi. Their personalities seemed to go hand in hand. *God*, she thought, *what do I do?* She had no choice but to tell her. "I think

Borge had President Nathan murdered, and I think I know who he used as an assassin." And then she began to tell Tanya about her time at the research center, about Borge and Thorella, and all that she had learned there.

When she finished, Tanya was quiet for a long time, looking out the window at the dawn sky. She was a night person, Jodi remembered, forsaking the light of the sun for the moon and stars. Like a vampire.

When she finally spoke, Jodi almost didn't recognize her voice: it was wooden, dead.

"I knew Markus Thorella," Tanya said. "Our parents were very good friends, actually. I had always liked Markus." She smiled bitterly. "He was everything a young girl could have wanted in a boy. I remember the accident, too, how horrible it was. I used to visit him in the hospital every Tuesday, when my parents would let me fly over to visit him. But when he finally woke up, he had... changed. He was quiet, sullen. Arrogant. But I didn't let that stop me. He had been through a lot. I would not abandon him. We were friends."

She stopped talking, her words drifting into the silent void that the room had become. Jodi felt her skin crawling at Tanya's revelation. The picture of Borge's evil, horrible as it was, was becoming ever clearer.

A single tear slid down Tanya's cheek, glistening in the morning light. "I kept seeing him even after he left the hospital," she went on, more softly now. "That's when I first met Senator Borge. He seemed like such a nice man. Much like Markus's father had been. I spent a great deal of time with them. That's why Mama and Papa bought me this cottage. Just so I could be closer to them. To him. My friend, Markus." Her voice dropped to a whisper. "The friend who raped me when I was fifteen." She smiled then, an evil, hateful smile that floated on a sea of anguish and pain. "But who could I tell? Who would believe me? That Markus Thorella had raped his best friend? No one would have believed it. I was no saint, even as a child, but Markus was. Had been." She shook her head. "I said nothing, because I still thought he might... love me. But my body was all he wanted, and he took it whenever and however it pleased him. He made me do things, terrible things. And when he was old enough to enroll in the academy, he left without a word. He tossed me aside like rubbish. And now you're telling me... that it was not even him."

Jodi was now beginning to understand her own past. In her anger and self-loathing, Tanya had taken out on everyone else the love/hate she had felt for Markus Thorella. He had warped her, had emotionally and physically raped her, and she was trying to purge herself of the demons he had left inside her. And there had been no one for her to confide in, no one who would believe her accusations because of the legacy of the real Markus Thorella, whose word had once been honorable and true. She had never told anyone what had happened until this day. Jodi had been one of her victims, and doubtless there had been many more, some probably not as lucky as Jodi had been. But the greatest victim of all had been Tanya herself.

"I will help you," Tanya said quietly after the tears had passed. "Tell me what you need."

* * *

"Pray to your God that I never rise from this table, doctor." For the hundredth time, Reza tried to free himself from the restraints that held him firmly to the cold stainless steel operating table. But as his determination crossed a magic threshold, he lost his strength, his will. He sagged back before the power of the restraints, exhausted. The electrodes pressed into his skull tingled as his head thumped gently against the table. He felt like Samson after losing his hair to Delilah's hand; he could call upon neither his psychic nor his physical powers to extricate himself from his bonds.

"This is my god," she replied as she worked the set of consoles that encircled him like hungry, flesh-craving electronic gargoyles. She shook her head in wonder at the data pouring from her instruments. "What a magnificent specimen you are." She turned to him and smiled. "We're going to become very close, you and I. Closer than you can possibly imagine."

Reza closed his eyes and tried to concentrate, but he could not channel his power. Normally, he could have simply willed himself to be somewhere else, and he would be gone. But she had done something to him, something that interfered with his most basic neural processes. He was helpless before her, and the only thing greater than his anger was his shame. He could not even commit suicide.

"I was going to do to you what I had originally suggested when you returned from the Empire," she explained, "to give you a deep-core probe. But I'm glad that things turned out differently. That would have been such a waste.

"You see, I've always hoped for an opportunity like this, and I've planned for it all these years. A deep-core, of course, depends on the external analysts being able to interpret the data that comes from the target brain. That means you need people who know the language, the culture, and who can understand the imagery that the target brain is projecting. We never recover everything, of course, but under ideal circumstances, we can successfully interpret up to thirty or even forty percent of the core data."

"And this is all you get for the price of the victim's sanity?"

"It's a small enough price," she said confidently. He felt her hands adjusting something on his head, almost as if she were checking the ripeness of a melon. A throb filled his skull, like a noise so low in pitch that it could not really be heard, but only felt. "But I've done better since then. Much better.

"Now," she explained, "instead of a gaggle of analysts struggling to understand the massive output of even the most diseased and atrophied brain, I can actually link my own cortex into the data stream as an on-line interpreter, drastically improving the recovery rate, bringing it up to nearly one-hundred percent. In effect, I will know everything you know, will feel everything that you feel. And these computers will record it all for later study in a format any qualified analyst can understand." He saw her face above his, looking down at him with eyes bright with anticipation. She wore a tiara of cerebral implants. "You're looking at the one person in the Universe who in a few minutes will know more about you than any other."

"You are a fool, Rabat," Reza warned. "You do not comprehend what you are about to trifle with. My brain, as my body, is alien. You shall not find there what you expect."

She smiled condescendingly. "Don't flatter yourself so much, Reza," she told him as she made some final adjustments on the small console in front of her. "I am the one who will be in control, not you. And I will also be the only one of us who will walk out of this room when we are finished." She ran a hand over his forehead as she looked down at him, an expression of consideration on her face. "It's a shame, really, to use you up like this. When we're done here, you'll be nothing but a drooling vegetable for Thorella to dispose of." She shrugged. "But they were going to kill you anyway. At least I convinced the senator – the *president* – that we could still get very valuable information from you."

"How generous of you," Reza hissed.

"We're going to start now. Just close your eyes and try to relax." Suddenly he felt a dizzying sensation, as if a thousand tiny jolts of electricity were coursing through his body. "What I'm doing right now," she said in a very clinical voice, as if she were speaking to a patient rather than a victim, "is scrambling your voluntary nervous system. You won't be able to twitch a muscle unless the computer commands it. A security precaution on my part, obviously. You see," he saw her smiling above him again, "you've been carrying a tiny implant around inside your head since just after you came back from Erlang. I took the liberty of implanting it while you were in your coma. A rather ingenious device, if I do say so myself." Reza felt a curious tingling behind his right ear, a scraping sound that seemed to come from inside his skull. She held up a tiny white capsule that was stained with blood. "This is what's been keeping you under control. Any time your brain waves reached a certain threshold, this acted like a jammer, influencing the key areas of your brain to reduce your adrenaline levels and critical neural signals. It has also been busy transmitting data on your brain activity all this time, allowing me to make much better calibrations for this experiment than otherwise would have been possible." She paused as she ran a skin sealer across the small wound, dropping the tiny device into a waiting bowl. "This is also why you were in a coma for so long. I wasn't ready for you until now, and it gave Borge the time he needed for his own plans."

Completely paralyzed and unable to speak, Reza silently wondered if she really believed that Borge would let her live; long enough to boil the essence of Reza's thoughts down to data understandable by her computers – and in turn by Borge's people – but no longer. If she did not know everything, she knew enough. She was a liability. And Borge did not tolerate liabilities.

"But when Thorella comes for you," she went on casually, ignorant of his silent monologue, "the capsule might make things look a little odd when you're... discovered. Not to mention that it interferes with the cerebral interaction we're about to induce."

Reza had no difficulty imagining a scenario. It would be much the same as when they brought him here. He suddenly had collapsed, unconscious, in his hospital room, and the next thing he knew he was here. In the near-vegetable state he would be in after Rabat finished with him, Thorella could hand him a weapon – Reza might have enough gray matter left to understand how to hold one – and put him in any setting he thought fitting. And then he could simply gun Reza down at the end of some concocted hunt, walking away with the laurels of a hero. Easy. Clean. Simple.

"There!" she said. "That's all done. Now we can get to work." She looked deeply into his eyes. "I've waited for this for a long, long time." On impulse, she leaned down and kissed him full on the mouth. Then her hand touched a control on one of the computers surrounding him, and suddenly the cold metal and machine world around him disappeared.

* * *

Deliha Rabat stood at the edge of a great plain, upon which stood a city that only one human had ever visited.

"Where are we, Reza?" she asked in wonder.

"This is the Homeworld of the Kreela," he answered from behind her. "That is the city where the First Empress was born, and where I first fought for the woman who would become my love."

She noted with pleasure that he was not speaking Standard; he was speaking Kreelan – the Old Tongue she knew now – and she understood it. She suddenly forgot about the city as her mind began to receive the first trickle of Reza's thoughts, his knowledge. She looked around her, at the mountains, the magenta sky, at the Empress moon above. The trickle soon turned into a torrent, filling her with all the images and memories of an alien lifetime. She felt the knowledge pouring into her, a fountain that seemed endless. She drank all that he had to offer her, and still demanded more. All that he knew was hers. *Everything.*

"No," she heard his voice say. "Not everything."

"What do you mean?" she demanded in a tongue she had never before spoken. "Give it to me! I want it all!"

"I warned you, doctor, but you would not listen. And now you shall pay the price for your vanity. Behold!"

She whirled around. Behind her should have been the mountains surrounding the valley that was the birthplace of the Empire so many eons ago. But as she watched, the great peaks disappeared behind a veil of fire, a wall of boiling scarlet flame that looked like bloody lava. "What is it? Tell me!"

"It is the Bloodsong of my people, human," Reza answered contemptuously, "the song of Her will. You and your machines can only comprehend the barest essence of the Way, of our lives. You can catalog the sights, sounds, smells, even the language of Her Children. But you do not understand our soul, or the power of the Empress, the power of Her spirit that dwells within us all. The Bloodsong is what unites us, all who have ever lived since the death of the First Empress. You wish to understand us? Then you must face the fire!"

"No!" she screamed as the wall of flame roared closer, devouring all that lay before it in a symphony of exploding trees and scorching rock. "I'm turning this off!" she screamed as she tried to flee back to her reality.

"Too late," Reza bellowed, and she felt his hands pinning her arms. She saw the silvery talons of his armored gauntlets pierce her flesh, felt the warm trickle of blood running down her arms. She struggled in vain. His breath was hot on her neck. "I warned you, you fool!" he shouted in her ear. "And now shall you know the truth! You wanted everything, and now you shall have it!"

As the wall of flame grew nearer, towering in the sky to blot out the glimmering Empress moon, Rabat could hear another sound above the din of the advancing apparition: voices. Thousands of them. Millions. All calling to her. They were angry, enraged. She looked into the flames and saw their terrible claws reaching for her, their mouths opened wide to reveal the fangs waiting to tear out her throat. Her skin began to blister in the heat, and she could smell the stench of her hair as it smoldered and then suddenly burst into flame.

She screamed, and kept on screaming as her skin and flesh began to boil away. Her eyes bulged and then exploded from her skull as the flames roared over her, the ethereal claws of the ancient warriors tearing at her flesh, at her soul, devouring her spirit as the world around her turned the color of blood.

* * *

"Reza! Jesus, are you all right?"

He felt hands moving along his body, tearing away the monitors and probes.

"Where is she?" he rasped. "Rabat."

"Looks like the good doctor's had it," Jodi said quietly. She had to look away from the body. The woman's face was frozen in a nightmarish grimace of agony, her hands clutching her breast as if her heart had exploded in her chest. In fact, as a coroner would ascertain some time later, it had.

Shaking her head, she turned her attention back to Reza. "Come on," she told him, helping him up from the table. She had managed to figure out how to turn off the suppressor field holding him to the table. The rest of the machines had apparently malfunctioned when Rabat died. She kissed him, then held him tightly. "I'm so glad I found you," she whispered, trying not to cry.

He smiled as he wrapped his arms around her, holding her shaking body gently as he kissed her hair. "I am, too, my friend."

After a moment, she unwillingly pushed him away. "We've got to get our asses out of here right now," she told him. "We're both in really deep shit."

"What has happened?"

"You're up on a rap for murdering the president, I'm your accomplice – helping you to get out of the hospital, no less – and Markus Thorella isn't really Markus Thorella at all. He's Senator – now President – Borge's son and an impostor. That's the scoop in a nutshell. Aren't you glad to hear it?" Jodi helped him to his feet and handed him some clothes. "Internal Security is crawling everywhere like a bunch of ants, and they picked up Nicole and Tony for questioning."

"What?" Reza asked incredulously as he pulled on the blue sweater and black pants that Jodi had brought for him, then some boots. Obviously, his uniformed days were over. Jodi was not wearing hers, either. "How could they?"

Jodi snorted. "Easy. Borge's the president now. I don't think he plans on doing anything with them except to try and lure us in, but I don't think they'll go for it. Anyway, he's declared martial law across the entire continent, which makes things that much more difficult for us."

When Reza was dressed, Jodi handed him a blaster. "Here," she said, "you're going to need this later. I already had to use it on the way in." She led him out and down a corridor that was deserted except for three bodies and the stink of burned flesh.

"How did you get in?" Reza asked. "How did you even find where they had taken me?"

Jodi shrugged. "An old friend of mine is helping us. She has... connections."

"Can you trust her?" Reza asked as they moved through a portal and into a tiny lobby. The research center where they had taken him was in a distant rural settlement that Rabat had thought would be sufficiently isolated to avoid any unwanted scrutiny. And, with Reza under her control, she had convinced Thorella and Borge that a lot of guards would just raise the visibility of the facility and the risk of exposure. And so, there had been only three guards. Had been.

"I don't know for sure," Jodi replied. She hopped into the pilot's seat of the waiting skimmer, closing the hatches after Reza had climbed in after her. "She certainly has a score to settle with our friend Thorella, though." She looked at Reza as the skimmer responded to her deft touch, quickly becoming airborne and heading east. "It doesn't really matter, anyway," she told him. "I had no one else to turn to."

Reza frowned. He was missing something. "But why would Borge be after you?" he asked.

Jodi smiled. And then she told him the entire tale of the man who would be president and his misbegotten son.

Forty-Five

President Borge did not rage. He appeared calm and cool, despite the massive confusion that swirled around him as the entire security network of planet Earth worked to find and kill – Borge had decided to dispense with any remaining pleasantries – Reza Gard and Jodi Mackenzie.

But there was a slight problem: they both had disappeared. Mackenzie had not been seen since the afternoon before, and Reza had broken out of Rabat's little torture chamber earlier this afternoon. Fortunately, her death and the deaths of the Internal Security agents there only sealed the lid tighter on the two fugitives' coffins. He would have had to kill all of them eventually to ensure that no one even peripherally involved in his designs could ever reveal what they knew. While he had no evidence in hand, Borge instinctively knew that Mackenzie must have been responsible for rescuing Reza from Rabat. Captain Carré and Councilman Braddock had been under constant surveillance since their release and had not been caught helping either of the two fugitives. Borge had decided that there was no point in keeping them in custody, especially since there was always the chance that they might prove incidentally useful.

The problem of Mackenzie, however, remained. How had she escaped the dragnet that had been thrown over the city since his security people had been alerted by her delving into his past and that of his son?

She must have had help, he decided. But from whom? And why would anyone help her when every form of public media carried the story of her aiding and abetting Reza Gard in his bloody escape from the hospital before "killing" Nathan (Thorella had arranged to have a particular Marine lieutenant and a few of his troops die in Reza's "breakout")? He knew Carré and Braddock would have helped the fugitives, but they had been effectively neutralized. Who else was there? His intelligence people and researchers had combed the files for anyone who had been associated with Gard and Mackenzie, but those relative few had all been ruled out. Reza did not have any other known associations on Earth, as most of the officers and enlisted members of the Red Legion only returned from their regiment as corpses sealed in boxes.

The search for people who had known Mackenzie, however, yielded a surprise: Tanya Buchet.

Borge shook his head. *Tanya, of all people.* He had known her since she was a child, and had often looked upon her as an adopted daughter. He had never known or suspected that she and Mackenzie had known each other. Borge had called her about the matter personally, and had been reassured that she had not seen Mackenzie in nearly twenty years, and if she had, she would have shot her herself.

He had eliminated Tanya Buchet from his list, leaving him a blank screen. Not a single lead presented itself. Borge silently fumed.

Colonel Markus Thorella entered the confusion of the Internal Security Command Post. Ignoring everyone around him, he made his way straight to the new president.

"It had better be important, Markus," Borge warned ominously. Despite his outward appearance of calm, his mood was homicidally ugly.

"It is," his secret son said quietly. "We need to talk. Privately."

Borge scowled. He looked at the anthill-like activity swirling about him. He could do nothing but wait. And it would not really matter if he waited here, alone but for his thoughts, or talking to the Marine standing before him. His son. "Very well," he said.

After the door to Borge's makeshift ready room closed behind them, he said, "All right. What is so important that you had to interrupt the hunt?"

Thorella snorted derisively, but he was not about to tell the president what he really thought of the incompetent IS troops and their "hunt." No, if Gard and Mackenzie were going to be found, he would have to do it. And he thought he had a good idea where to start. But that was not why he had come here.

"I was just talking to the fleet operations officer," he said, leaving out the slight detail that they had been talking while in bed. "She said she came up with a plan on the staff battle computers for beating the Kreelans. Decisively. She explained it to me, and it sounds like it could be done. But L'Houillier and Zhukovski didn't buy off on it. Neither did Nathan." He smiled. Slightly. "I think you ought to hear it from her yourself. Very soon. The Navy has a lot of information – a lot more now than they even had a few days ago – and she thinks she can pinpoint the location of the Kreelan homeworld. And, if her plan looks like it would work, we could take out the Kreelan fleet and homeworld in a single, massive attack."

Borge nodded, his eyes narrowed as he thought. If what Thorella said was true, the potential for making history could not be underestimated. The man who won this war would have power beyond measure, and everlasting glory in the pages of history. Indeed, this was worth his attention, even over and above what was going on in the room next door. "And those bastards have not bothered to bring this to my attention?" He did not mention that he had put off both officers while he conducted his witch-hunt for Gard and Mackenzie. "I want a briefing as soon as possible from this operations officer of yours," he ordered briskly. "After that I want to see the two admirals. I won't stand for this kind of behavior."

"There's something else you should know," Thorella said quietly. "A fleet squadron patrolling out beyond the Rim is bringing home some interesting cargo." He smiled again. Chillingly. "Two Kreelans, one of which they say is Gard's son."

Borge's face twitched into a smile. *Surely, this was a joke*, he thought. But he could tell from the younger man's face that it was not. "Incredible," he breathed. The opportunities were immediately obvious. "How do you suggest we proceed?"

That is what Markus Thorella had always loved about this man. He asked for his opinion, and even listened to him. A better father one could not have, adopted or otherwise. "Gard is going to find his way off-world somehow," he told the president, "despite the best efforts of the Internal Security Service." Borge frowned at his son's disdain, but he did not say anything. The ISS was not known for its brilliance in the field. "Once he does," Thorella went on, "it's going to be almost impossible to track him down."

"Unless we give him a destination he can hardly refuse?" Borge prompted.

Thorella nodded, handing Borge a stylus pad on which he had already outlined the operation. "If we want this to work," he told Borge, "we have to get on it right away..."

* * *

Several thousand kilometers away, on an estate fifty kilometers south of what had once been the city of Paris, was a private subterranean spaceport large enough to house the single vessel that had belonged to the Buchet family for over one hundred years: the *Golden Pearl*. She had not been moved from her berth in fifteen years, not since Tanya's parents had died. Tanya herself had only infrequently visited the old estate, and things there were not quite as pristine as they once had been. Things had been cared for, of course, from the massive bounty of wealth left by her parents, but the place lacked the look and feel of habitation, of an owner's love and pride.

Fortunately for Reza and Jodi, the *Pearl* had also been cared for, the ship having been tended and kept in perfect running order by the technicians who periodically were paid to visit from Le Havre and Brest. The two of them did not have the time nor the inclination to tour the estate itself, but if it was anything like the ship on which they now found themselves, Jodi could not believe that Tanya did not spend more time here. The ship was a work of art both in terms of engineering and creature comforts. Having quickly studied the most important of the operations tutorials, she quickly realized that this ship, despite her age, must still be one of the fastest ships in human space. It was a badly needed bit of luck.

But she found herself lamenting the fact that they could not take a more leisurely cruise. The ship was a traveling wonderland of luxury, a relic of the pre-war age when grace and refinement were more important than batteries of guns and torpedoes. Of course, at some point during the war she had been fitted with a complement of those, as well, along with a series of increasingly sophisticated upgrades to her electronics.

But the weapons were irrelevant in the ship's history and her mission of pleasure. A presidential yacht could not have offered as many graceful appointments as the *Pearl*. The ship could accommodate fifty guests in luxurious suites. *No hot-bunking on this tub*, Jodi thought. Guests ate their meals in a lavish dining room, with the food served on real silver and china. They could find entertainment ranging from casual conversation in the sitting room to plays on stage. According to the ship's log, the *Pearl* had even once hosted a performance of the Bolshoi Ballet Company.

Jodi had never realized just how rich the Buchet family was until she had come aboard this ship with the entrance codes Tanya had provided. She smiled to herself. It was too bad things hadn't worked out with Tanya, she thought. It would have been nice to marry rich.

Tanya had said she would join them as soon as she could, but that there was some unfinished business she had to take care of. Jodi was not entirely comfortable taking her along, but she was obligated to, for a lot of reasons. She just hoped they were the right ones. She also hoped that Tanya was not intending to do anything foolish. If she did, she would be on her own. Jodi would not be able to help her.

When she finished the pre-flight preparations, Jodi headed aft to find Reza asleep on a leather sofa in the library. She covered him with an immaculately decorated afghan. She could tell that even it had received its share of care over the years, for it smelled clean and fresh, without a trace of the stale reek of age. When his eyes fluttered open, she said, "Go back to sleep. We've got a while longer before we go."

Reza mumbled something unintelligible and did as he was told. Leaning down, she kissed him softly on the lips, then left him to rest.

Back in the cockpit, she went through the ship's abbreviated checklist again. The weapons, above all, were ready. While the yacht's armament made it no more formidable than a Coast Guard cutter, it could still deliver a sharp sting to anyone not being very careful. In addition to the four twin laser barbettes arrayed around the hull, she had two torpedoes in a ventral launcher for more serious situations.

She just hoped she would not have to use them at all. Compared to what was probably arrayed against them, it was little more than a last great act of defiance.

Sitting at the pilot's station, she switched on the data scanner. She had programmed it earlier to sweep any channels it could access for information pertaining to herself or Reza, as well as Tanya, Nicole, and Tony. She hoped the latter two were all right, but all she could do now was pray to a God that she was starting to believe in. She had been having too much luck to believe otherwise.

The computer had graciously prioritized the tidbits it had come across in the last hour or so. And after viewing the first one, Jodi did not need to see any more.

"Ladies and gentleman," announced some talking head news anchor Jodi did not recognize, "we have just received a startling announcement from General Staff Headquarters." The screen cut to the face of someone Jodi knew only from thin gossip: Admiral Laskowski.

"Commodore Marchand," the fleet operations officer said, "in command of the Seventy-Third Reconnaissance Squadron, with her flag aboard the cruiser *Furious*, has reported the capture of two Kreelans, a warrior and a child." The view cut to the two faces, then scenes of the two aliens in an isolation cell. While Jodi was no expert in things Kreelan, there was no mistaking the sheer exhaustion in both of them, notably in the older one, who was incredibly haggard. Worse, their faces were black, just as Reza's wife's face had been the day of the battle for Erlang.

"More significant than the capture itself, however, is that the child is a male, the first living Kreelan male to ever be discovered." There was an animated murmuring in the briefing room a few thousand miles away as the reporters and other attendees assimilated this bit of information. A few people raised their hands for questions, but the admiral ignored them.

"Even more startling," she went on after a suitable pause, "is that we believe the child is the product of the union–" she made it sound like a dirty word, "–between Reza Gard and a high-ranking Kreelan warrior."

The conference room went as silent as a grave. "This is not a joke or a publicity stunt, ladies and gentlemen," the admiral cautioned darkly. "Some of Commodore Marchand's people have been able to establish rudimentary communication with the adult warrior that led to this conclusion." Jodi was suddenly treated to the image of Eustus Camden gesturing to the warrior, and evidently receiving some kind of – to Eustus, anyway – intelligible response. "And the child's overt physiology bears out the claim." Another shot of the child's face.

"My God," Jodi whispered as she leaned closer to the display. "His eyes..." There could be no doubt they were Reza's eyes, the same penetrating green as the boy's mother had when Jodi saw her on Erlang.

Except for one detail near the very end, the rest of the press conference went by in a blur to Jodi, whose mind was still captivated by the face of the child born to parents of two races. The only other thing that she heard and understood was the destination of *Furious* and her living cargo: Erlang.

* * *

Markus Thorella was tired, his body and mind spent in what he considered a good day's work. He opened the door to his apartment and switched on the lights. The furnishings and other adornments, exactly opposite Borge's tastes, were spartan and plain. He spent little time here or in any of the five other dwellings that he held the keys to on as many planets, using it only as a place to rest and recover for the next day's work.

He carefully hung his cap on the hook that silently slid from the wall to accept it, then made his way to the living room – it might have been comfortable had it been furnished – and the waiting bar for a well-earned drink.

He stopped when he saw the glass of scotch sitting in the bar's outlet port.

"Scotch, straight," a female voice purred from the direction of the darkened bedroom. "Just the way you like it. Plain and boring, like you. Turn around, Markus. Slowly."

The back of Thorella's scalp crawled. "I know that voice," he murmured to himself. Turning around, he saw the woman emerge from the shadows. She held a blaster trained on his stomach. "Tanya," he said, a wry smile touching his lips. "It's been a long time."

"I'm so flattered that you recognized me... Anton Borge," she said quietly.

Thorella's smile cracked. "What's that supposed to mean?" he asked innocently. Tried to. He felt the weight of the knife in his uniform sleeve. "The senator has been a good friend of mine since my parents died," he said, "but he's hardly my father."

Tanya shook her head, the anger glowing in her eyes as she stepped further into the light. "Don't play games Anton. I hated your guts when we were children, and I can't say I shed any tears when I found out you'd died in the crash. And then what your father managed to pull off. And what you did to me..."

"Anton Borge is dead, Tanya," he said decisively. "Whatever Jodi Mackenzie told you – it was her, wasn't it? – was garbage. Lies." His voice softened. "I'm sorry that you felt hurt when we... broke up. But that was a long time ago–"

"And I've been living with it ever since," she snapped viciously. "I loved Markus, and you were jealous. I know you were. And after the crash, when I helped him – you – recover, what was my reward? To be raped like an animal until you grew tired of using me and left. It was the perfect crime, Anton. I was so blinded by my feelings for Markus that I never knew that I had been destroyed until you walked away. You took my soul, you bastard. You stole it. And what did your father do to Markus?" She stepped closer, the barrel of the gun unwavering. "Was Markus already dead, or did the good senator murder him?"

"I don't know what you're talking about." The knife slid unseen into his palm. "I am Markus Thorella. If you want to believe otherwise, that's up to you. But I suggest you leave now, or I'll have to call security." He moved toward the comm panel over the bar.

"He killed him, didn't he?" Tanya said almost to herself, her eyes boring into Thorella as he reached for the controls on the wall. "He murdered Markus and stuffed your beaten body into his clothes. And with his power, he bought silence and secrecy, even from his own accursed son." Her finger tensed on the trigger. "Goodbye, Anton."

As Tanya squeezed the trigger, the illegal Kreelan knife that Thorella always carried flew from his hand as he dodged away from the blast of her weapon. He rolled to the floor as the wall behind him exploded in a flash of sparks and the stench of molten plastic, and watched with satisfaction as Tanya slumped to the floor, the knife buried to the hilt just above her right collarbone. The gun fell from her lifeless arm and clattered onto the floor.

"You silly fool," Thorella said as he regained his feet. "You should have just killed me when you had the advantage. But you had to act out your ridiculous little passion play." He smiled. "And now it's going to cost you."

Tanya was already pulling herself toward the gun, the knife a searing pain in her chest as the handle dragged along the floor. A thin trickle of blood seeped from her lips; her right lung had been deeply punctured. She moaned, but did not cry out.

Thorella casually kicked the gun aside. "I'm afraid you already had your chance, Tanya," he said quietly. "Now it's my turn." He knelt down and roughly turned her over. His hands squeezed her breasts, then ran down her stomach to linger between her legs as she struggled weakly against him. "I'd very much like to relive old times," he glanced up at the SECURITY ALERT light, activated by Tanya's blaster firing, "but I'm afraid I just don't have the time."

He knew he would have to work fast. Gripping the knife's protruding handle in one hand, he clamped his other around her throat. "You see, I need to know where Reza and Jodi are, and you're going to tell me."

"Go fuck yourself, you murdering bastard," she hissed through bloody spittle. Working behind the cover of her injured body, one of her hands groped for the tiny transmitter hidden in her belt. A trembling finger pressed the single button on the device's face.

"That's not a very nice thing to say, Tanya," Thorella said with a blazing smile. His hand constricted around her throat to silence her. Then he began to saw the knife back and forth through her bleeding flesh, slowly.

Her mouth opened in a soundless scream.

* * *

"Where the fuck is she?" Jodi whispered to herself. The ship was powered up and ready to go at thirty seconds notice, the clamshell doors to the *Pearl's* docking bay open to the cloud-flecked skies of what was once central France.

"We cannot wait much longer, Jodi," Reza said from the cockpit ramp, startling her.

"How do you feel?" she asked, recovering quickly. She felt like her bare ass was sitting on a cushion of needles.

"I am alive... thanks to you." He sat down next to her, his gaze seeing through her.

"What's that look for?" she asked uncomfortably.

"You care for her, don't you?" he said. "Even after all that has happened, after all this time."

Jodi was silent for a moment. "I was in love with her once, Reza," she said. "And that's something that never really leaves you, I guess, no matter what happens." She frowned. "I think that at one time she was a good person, before Borge and his son corrupted her, suppressed or destroyed what was good in her. I wish I could have known her then."

"Perhaps," Reza said thoughtfully, "you gave her the chance to restore her honor."

Jodi was about to tell him of the news she saw when a voice interrupted them. It was Tanya.

"Jodi," the voice said as a holographic image of Tanya's face appeared on the screen, "if you're hearing this now, then you'll know I can't be with you. I had an old score to settle with a mutual friend of ours, but things haven't gone right and I won't be able to make our rendezvous. You and your friend will have to go on alone in the old *Pearl* to wherever your final destination might be. She's always been a good ship. She's yours, now, and everything else that belongs to me: you're the sole beneficiary in my will now." The recorded image of Tanya's face looked reflective for a moment before it went on. Tanya's real face lay a few thousand kilometers away, contorted in mortal agony. "There are so many things I'd like to say, Jodi, but... the only thing that might matter now – for what little it's worth – is that I'm sorry for what happened between us, for what I did to you. I can't make the past right again, and I won't have a chance to explain everything the way you deserve, but I wanted you to know." A bittersweet smile. "Good luck, Jodi. And goodbye."

The image vanished.

Jodi was silent, staring at the space where her one-time lover had spoken what she knew were Tanya's last words. "She's dead, isn't she?"

Reza nodded solemnly. "I grieve with you," he said quietly, his hand on her shoulder. Her hand covered his.

"Well," Jodi said in a raspy voice, taking her hand away to the more familiar territory of the control console, "I guess we'd better get this tub moving before more trouble shows up."

"Have you decided where we are going?"

"Yes," she said decisively. "Erlang."

As the *Golden Pearl* powered up for its first flight in years, Jodi told Reza of the son he never knew he had.

Forty-Six

She's dying, Eustus thought as he looked through the force field screen and into the brig where the two Kreelan prisoners were being held. The warrior lay on one of the cell's two beds that protruded from the wall, her massive frame overwhelming it. While her eyes were closed, Eustus was sure that she knew he was here, watching them. The boy-child, Shera-Khan, knelt next to her, gently stroking her hair with his red talons.

Eustus took in a deep breath. "All right, private," he said to the Marine at the brig controls, "open the door."

"Are you sure, gunny?" the commodore asked from behind him. "You don't have to do this." Eustus turned to the small knot of officers behind him. Without uttering a word, he only nodded his head.

Commodore Marchand nodded to the private at the door controls, who in turn exchanged a glance with the four other Marines who guarded the entrance. Their weapons snapped to the ready. The hum of the force field dropped away, and the force field warning light surrounding the portal went off. Inside, Shera-Khan stood up and turned to watch. The great warrior did not move.

"Okay, gunny," the private said in a hushed voice.

Eustus stepped into the cell, the force field snapping up behind him just as his feet cleared the doorway. For a long moment, he and Shera-Khan regarded one another in silence. The fact that they had managed to get this far was nothing short of miraculous, Eustus thought. He would have given anything to have seen the look on the faces of the cutter's crew and surviving Marines back on the planet in the mist when they opened the door, only to be faced with a giant of a Kreelan warrior holding a child in one arm and Eustus slung over her shoulder. According to the crew's report (Eustus having been unconscious at the time), the warrior had simply leaped into the passenger bay like she belonged there, pushing people out of the way to make a place for herself and the injured child after she carefully set Eustus down on the deck. Everyone had been too shocked to even think of shooting, and the flight back to the *Furious* was spent in silent awe.

Once aboard the cruiser, little had changed. Commodore Marchand perceived the situation correctly and realized that the warrior wanted them to help save the young one's life, just as she had saved Eustus. The two prisoners and the injured gunnery sergeant had been spirited to sickbay, where they had saved Shera-Khan. The boy's recovery, Eustus had noted with little surprise, had taken astonishingly little time. He was on his feet just four hours after surgery, and then he and the warrior were escorted by a platoon of Marines to the brig.

Now, looking at the boy, Eustus could not shake the tingle of excitement that came from the realization that this was the son, the flesh and blood, of Eustus's best friend. Looking into the boy's fierce green eyes, Eustus could see the fire that he had known to be in his father's, and an intellect that Eustus could not even guess at.

"I thought you might like some food," he said awkwardly. The boy had eaten nothing since his recovery, despite the best efforts of the intel officers and the cooks. Eustus finally convinced the commodore herself to allow him to try. After all, he had explained, he was the only one aboard who had ever known the one real Kreelan expert: Reza. He slowly set a tray of food down on the shelf that protruded from the wall near the head of the warrior's bed.

The boy's eyes flicked to the food – two slabs of raw meat (syntho, of course) and two mugs of the alcoholic concoction Reza had taught him to make – then back to Eustus. Then back to the food. Eustus could tell that he was starving, and not just from the last two days. Something told him the boy had probably not eaten for a lot longer than that.

"Go ahead," he urged as he stepped away. "Try it."

Shera-Khan made no move to sample what Eustus had brought him until a single whispered word escaped the lips of the warrior lying nearby.

"*N'yadeh*," she said. *Eat.*

The boy turned and bowed his head to her, and Eustus saw that her eyes, sparkling with silver, were open and fixed on Shera-Khan to ensure he obeyed. He saluted her with his left fist over his chest, uttering something that Eustus could not make out. The warrior said nothing, but closed her eyes as the boy turned away to regard the food more closely. Then, his decision made, he reached for one of the chunks of meat.

Eustus watched as he carefully carved it with the claws of his shaking hands, slicing the meat into finger-wide strips. Only when it was completely cut did he begin to eat, his eyes all the while fixed on Eustus.

Slowly, with his hands at his sides, Eustus backed up to the far wall and took a seat on the floor, watching as Shera-Khan inhaled his food. The boy sniffed at one of the mugs. Glancing at Eustus, he hefted it to his lips and swallowed some of the warm, bitter ale that had been Reza's favorite drink. He made a quiet humph of evident satisfaction before drinking down the rest.

In but a few minutes, both pieces of meat were gone, consumed by the boy's hunger and the whispered order of the warrior. That done, he turned to her with the other mug, offering her a drink. Drawn to the heady scent of the ale, the warrior tried to lever herself upright, but only managed a few centimeters before her strength gave out. Shera-Khan tried to lift her head, but she was too heavy for him to move.

"Let me help," Eustus offered, coming slowly over to them, his arms before him, palms up. *See*, he thought, *no weapons*.

Shera-Khan narrowed his eyes, but did not try to hinder Eustus as he knelt down beside him. With trembling hands, Eustus cradled the great warrior's head, lifting her enough that she could swallow some of the ale the boy held to her lips.

As Eustus gently lowered her back onto the bed, the Kreelan warrior's eyes met his. Her lips seemed to struggle, and then formed two words that Eustus would remember for the rest of his life.

"Thank... you," she said softly. He stared blankly at her for a moment, too shocked to speak.

"You're... you're welcome," he breathed finally. She motioned almost imperceptibly with her head in acknowledgment before her eyes closed again, a grimace of pain flickering over her blackened face.

"I wish I knew what was wrong with her," Eustus muttered to himself.

"She mourns," the boy beside him said softly.

Concealing his shock at the boy's knowledge of Standard, Eustus asked in a carefully controlled voice, "What do you mean, 'she mourns?' Who is she mourning for?" An explanation for how – and why – the boy had learned humanity's primary language would have to wait.

The boy turned his blazing green eyes to him. "She mourns for the Empress," he said with a voice far, far older than his years, with a sadness that gripped Eustus's heart, "who now sleeps in Darkness, Her heart and spirit broken by Her Own hand." The boy shivered, as if sobbing. "The hour that should have been the greatest in our history, the crowning glory of our people, cast us instead into chaos and ruin. Her voice no longer sings in our blood, Her spirit is silent. Behind a barrier of fire, She lays dying of guilt and grief. And so, too, shall we die."

"What do you mean?" Eustus asked. "Who's going to die?"

The boy looked up at him, a stricken expression on his face. "All that has ever been, all that is, all that will ever be, shall be no more the moment Her heart ceases to beat, Her last breath taken. With the First Empress was our Way destined. With Her heart stilled shall it end, and Her Children shall perish from the world."

Eustus glanced up just in time to see Commodore Marchand disappearing, no doubt for the comms center and a patch through to sector command. She had no more idea of what the boy was talking about than Eustus did, but the significance of those words was apparent enough. Something was seriously wrong in the Empire, and if it could be exploited to the Confederation's advantage, they might have a hope of winning this war.

Eustus was about to ask more questions, to press the boy for what he meant, when Shera-Khan curled onto the floor, trembling. Without thinking, Eustus reached out to him, taking him into his arms as he might have any bereaved human child. And then, when what he had just done struck home, he realized that this was not an alien enemy, implacable and unstoppable, but the son of his best friend.

"Shera-Khan," he said, "would you like to meet your father?"

The boy stiffened against him. "The priestess told me of this," he replied hesitantly, "that you had made signs to her while on the nursery world that my father was alive. But how can it be so? The Empress's blade cut through his heart."

"No, no," Eustus said, holding Shera-Khan so that their eyes met. "He didn't die in that battle. He was terribly wounded, yes, but he survived. He's still alive, on Earth." He paused. "He doesn't even know he has a son, that he has you."

Shera-Khan did not know what to believe. He desperately wished his father to be alive, but he could not understand how it could be so. His mother would never have let the humans take him had there been a breath remaining in his body.

The great priestess suddenly spoke, her voice little more than a murmur.

"The priestess bids you to take us to him," Shera-Khan translated for her. "To Reza. My father."

* * *

As he looked out over the apron of the New York flight terminal, Tony Braddock silently wondered how many times he had been at places like this. Dozens, hundreds, perhaps? But he had always been the one about to step onto a waiting shuttle, impatient loadmasters herding their human cargo aboard as if they were ignorant cattle, which perhaps they sometimes were.

But today, as he had on several previous occasions, he was bidding farewell to the woman he loved. They would see one another again as the Armada sailed into enemy space, but he couldn't shake the feeling that she was leaving him.

Nicole stood beside him, her mind focused on the anthill of humans and machines that had been working around the clock for the past two days. They were moving millions of tons of materiel and hundreds of thousands of people in support of the great armada that at this very moment was assembling in the skies above the Earth and a hundred other worlds that were home to Humanity. Her fighter, one of dozens that still crowded the ramps at this late hour, was fueled and ready. The crew chief, a man she had never met before, stood impatiently by.

He looked at her, and wondered if he were not a fool for not knocking her to the ground and carrying her away from this madness. She was hardly in shape for a fight, he told himself. The business with Reza – Braddock still refused to believe it – had eaten at her like a cancer since Reza's escape several days ago. Her bond to him was yet unbroken, he was sure, but where it would lead her, God alone only knew.

And then the new president had announced the formation of the great fleet to carry out Operation Millennium. The call for "every able-bodied flight officer and rating" to serve on the horde of warships and auxiliaries that was about to sail into Kreelan space had drawn her inexorably, like a bee to an intoxicating nectar. They had argued about it, but only once: Tony had learned early on that after Nicole had decided something, there was no appeal. She was a fighter pilot, she had told him firmly, and would not be denied the chance to participate in the Confederation's finest hour. Tony knew it was more than that: it was an opportunity, no matter how slight, of somehow finding Reza. She stood a better chance of finding him somewhere among the stars than anywhere on Earth.

Braddock, too, would be setting sail with The Armada, as it was now being called. Borge had insisted on going aboard the flagship, and had told the Council in not-so-subtle terms that anyone who did not accompany him was a coward and a traitor. The sycophants, of course, ever ready to seize any opportunity to implant themselves further in Borge's rectum, had hailed the action as a stroke of patriotic genius. Braddock and his few remaining compatriots were compelled to join the parade, regardless of their own opinions of the foolhardiness of the expedition. While Braddock had not had a chance to speak with Zhukovski directly, he had seen the resigned look on his face when Borge announced in a joint civil-military meeting that he and his entourage were going along. L'Houillier had hung his head. There was little doubt in Braddock's mind as to who would really be in charge of the operation. Braddock's greatest surprise was that Borge hadn't sacked both L'Houillier and Zhukovski, until he realized that the megalomaniac was keeping them as scapegoats in case of failure.

Like a dark cloud temporarily obscuring the sun, Tony found himself hoping the flagship would not return home.

"It is time," Nicole said quietly, washing away the dark thoughts in Braddock's mind. Across the apron, the crew chief was holding up his wrist and pointing. *Time to go.*

Tony kissed her, and they held one another for a brief moment. "Take care of yourself, Nicole. Please. I'll see you as soon as I can."

She nodded, squeezing him tighter. "I love you," she said before letting go.

"Je t'aime aussi," he replied.

She smiled, then turned to go.

He watched as she climbed into her ship. The crew chief made sure she was strapped in before he climbed down the crew ladder, saluted her, then headed off to the next waiting fighter.

Nicole waved one final time to Braddock, then her Corsair lifted off, soaring skyward. It grew smaller, dwindling with distance. Then it was gone.

"*Merde*," he whispered after her. *Good luck.*

Forty-Seven

"Gunnery Sergeant Camden reporting as ordered, ma'am."

Commodore Marchand acknowledged his crisp salute with a nod. "Please, gunny, sit down and be at ease."

Eustus glanced uncomfortably at the single empty chair at the end of the conference table. The other chairs were filled with the squadron's senior officers and the commander of *Furious's* Marine detachment.

"Uh... yes, ma'am." Stiffly, he took his seat, sitting bolt upright as he faced Marchand at the opposite end of the table. He had never been in the flag conference room before, and, under the circumstances, this was not a good time for a first visit. Some hours before, he had been a brevet captain. He had subsequently been reduced to his real rank in the aftermath of the day's news.

There was a moment of awkward silence as Eustus watched the officers mentally adjust themselves to his presence in the room. After the report of President Nathan's murder at the hands of Reza Gard, Eustus – guilty by association as a friend of the renegade – had quickly found himself ostracized from the ship's company. Since then, he had spent nearly all his time with the two Kreelans, for – ironically – they were the only ones aboard who didn't seem openly hostile to him.

"Gunny," Marchand began, "no doubt you've heard the rumors running through the ship regarding a possible fleet assault into Kreelan space."

"Yes, ma'am," Eustus replied uncertainly. There had been a lot of rumors through the ship since the Kreelan prisoners had been brought aboard, rumors that had become more fanciful and fierce with every turn of the watch since the news of the president's death.

Marchand nodded. "Well, as it turns out," she went on, "such an operation is in progress, and it's codenamed Operation Millennium. Even as we speak, ships are assembling throughout the Confederation for a sortie into the Empire for what Fleet HQ hopes will be the decisive blow against the enemy's fleet and their homeworld." She paused. "We have been given the opportunity to play a leading role in that operation, and that is where I need your help."

Eustus fought to suppress the trepidation he felt at what he knew must be coming. His fellow Marines, not to mention the squids, had branded him a traitor because he refused to believe the reports of Reza's involvement with the president's death and the other murders that had been committed in its wake. The morale on the ship had taken a nosedive after Marchand announced the news. Nathan had been a very popular president, and his death was not taken lightly. And now, Eustus knew with an instinctive certainty, he was going to be offered some way of "redeeming" himself before God, Corps, and Country. "Uh... sure, ma'am," he said. "What can I do?"

"The plans for Millennium have been underway since shortly before President Nathan's death," she told him gravely. "And Reza Gard's actions and his escape have endangered that operation. If he reaches Kreelan space to warn them, everything we have been preparing for could be lost. We have received orders to stop Reza Gard, by, as quoted in the orders, 'any and all means necessary, without limitation or exception.'" Marchand fixed Eustus with a calculated glare. "A plan was devised at Fleet HQ for getting the information we need, gunnery sergeant, but the success of this plan depends entirely upon your loyalty and devotion to the Confederation cause, regardless of the consequences to you personally."

Marchand's words were more than shocking. Eustus felt violated, raped. The very foundation of his existence had been loyalty to the Confederation, to humanity, and not least of all to the Corps whose uniform he wore. They were asking – no, telling – him that to be considered worthy, risking death for all these years was not enough. His mere association with Reza and his alleged crimes were enough to strip Eustus of all dignity, reducing his past sufferings and accomplishments to nothing. Offering his life to his nation was not enough. No, he had to do something more.

Ignoring the hot sting of tears that he felt boiling in his eyes, he said through clenched teeth, "What are my orders, ma'am?"

Marchand nodded. "High Command allowed extracts of your initial report on the prisoners, specifically that the boy appears to be Reza Gard's offspring," Marchand's mouth wrapped itself around the word with difficulty, as if it were an enormous, rotten apple, "to be released to the press after President Nathan's murder. Internal Security apparently was unable to capture Gard and Commander Jodi Mackenzie, who as you know is believed to have aided him. Security believes they escaped together off-world, and the information was broadcast in hopes of luring them to a chosen location: Erlang."

Enya, Eustus thought instantly. Lord of All, he thought helplessly, what is happening? And what do they want me to do, kill Reza and Jodi? He waited, dreading her next words.

Marchand understood what he was thinking. "You're the only one who can get close to him, Camden, close enough to either stun him or kill him. Either result will satisfy your orders. The same applies to Commander Mackenzie."

Eustus blinked. "But they haven't even been tried," he whispered hoarsely. "How can I be ordered to kill – *assassinate* – someone who hasn't even had a trial to determine their guilt or innocence?"

"Their guilt or innocence is not your concern, gunnery sergeant," Marchand warned stonily. "The president and the Council decided his fate and that of Mackenzie based on overwhelming evidence that no court could ignore. Now, I don't particularly care for your opinion on the matter. You have received your orders. The only question is, will you carry them out?"

Eustus sat quietly for a moment. *What if I'm wrong?* he thought. What if Reza *had* killed the president? Didn't they used to say that the best spies were the ones you never suspected?

No, he decided, at least not in this case. But even that did not matter. Reza was a Marine, trained to fight and kill his nation's enemies. But he was not a murderer, an assassin. Reza was a brother to him, and had offered his own life to protect Eustus countless times, and Eustus had returned the honor. On top of that, Reza was his best friend. Reza had never betrayed him. And Eustus simply couldn't accept that either he or Jodi had betrayed the Confederation.

The people around this table, he thought, throughout this ship, had belittled his sacrifices, his honor as a Marine and as a human being. Considering Marchand's offer, it was easy to make up his mind. Reza, even more than the Corps, had taught him the meaning of honor, and of being true to one's self regardless of the consequences. Eustus had offered his blood over the years to show his loyalty to the Confederation; he would not offer up his soul.

Straightening up in his chair, his eyes boring into Marchand's, he said, "Commodore Marchand, I respectfully submit that I cannot obey the orders you have given me. Ma'am."

The faces in the room turned to chilled stone.

"You know what this means, don't you?" she said in the hush of the room.

"Yes, ma'am."

Marchand leaned back in her chair, eyeing Eustus like some kind of offending insect. "You've got one chance to reconsider, Camden," she said icily.

"Negative, commodore," Eustus said firmly. "I cannot–" he hesitated, "– *will not* – help you in this. It's illegal and it's wrong."

She looked down at the table in disappointment. "Very well," she said quietly. Turning to the commander of the Marine contingent, she said, "Captain, please place Gunnery Sergeant Camden under arrest and throw him in the brig. Charges..." She paused, looking up at Eustus. "Charge him with high treason, as ordered by Confederation High Command."

"Aye, aye, commodore," the Marine officer said stiffly. With a signal from her console, two Marines appeared at the door to the conference room. This situation had been anticipated. "Marines," the captain ordered, "escort Gunnery Sergeant Camden to the brig." She glanced toward Marchand, who nodded. "Throw him in with the Kreelans."

"Yes, ma'am," the corporal in charge of the detail replied sharply.

Eustus stood up, saluted the commodore, and left with the guard detail.

Marchand turned her attention to the comms display facing her chair and hidden from everyone else's view. "I don't like this, General," she said sternly. "Camden is a good Marine."

"No one asked you to like it, commodore," replied the newly frocked Brigadier General Markus Thorella, Special Assistant to the President. "Just carry out your orders and be as predictable as Camden was." The smile disappeared behind a mask of vengeful conceit. "We have gone to great lengths to ensure that Reza Gard and his accomplice will head to Erlang and into your waiting arms, and you are to let nothing – I repeat, nothing – interfere with the execution," he smiled at the word, "of that mission. After that, you only have to hold him until the fleet rendezvous at Erlang and then transfer him to the flagship for his execution. And Mackenzie's." He stared at her. "Have I made myself clear, commodore?"

"Perfectly," she grunted, furious with this lackey's arrogance toward someone whose date of rank and command experience vastly outweighed his own.

Thorella nodded. "You will receive further instructions as necessary," he said tersely. "Thorella, out."

END TRANSMISSION blazed across the screen beneath the Confederation insignia.

Infuriated, Marchand slammed her hand on the control console, shutting down her end of the link.

"Bastard," she hissed.

* * *

Aboard the starliner *Helena*, Thorella leaned back in his ready room chair and smiled. Looking out the floor-to-ceiling viewport of his personal command ship, he saw over five hundred starships spread over thousands of cubic kilometers of space, all preparing for their final jump to Erlang where they would rendezvous with nearly three thousand more Confederation ships. It was the greatest armada in human history. And *he* was a key part of it. The thought exhilarated him and gave him a burning erection in his trousers.

But the part of the plan that he liked best was that he would finally get to see Reza Gard die. He had no doubt that Gard would try to escape; in fact, Thorella was counting on it. He knew Gard could do it on his own, but Thorella had decided to improve the odds, putting Camden on the inside and Carré on the outside, after convincing the president to order her put back on flight status. Between those two and Mackenzie, not to mention the two Kreelans, Thorella was perfectly confident that Gard would escape. And then he would joyfully hunt them down – Gard, Mackenzie, Camden, and Carré – and see them to the gallows. At last, after all these years, he would have them. He would have them all.

As he watched the ships of the armada wheel across space, his mind seduced by power, his right hand freed his throbbing member from the confines of its fabric keep. Alone in his ready room, his heart hammering in time with his hand, Thorella saluted the fleet that he knew would someday be his.

Forty-Eight

As the *Golden Pearl* slid through the whirling bands of light that were the only perceptible reality of hyperspace, Jodi contemplated the future, both for herself and for the few real friends she had in the Universe. For all of them, it looked unalterably bleak. Reza an accused murderer, with Jodi named as his accomplice; Nicole's career irreparably damaged by her association with both of them; and poor Tony, who might have someday gained enough political clout to really do the Confederation some good, politically devastated by the whole trumped-up scandal. *Things are looking pretty shitty for the home team*, she thought.

Checking on the *Pearl's* instruments to see how long they had before dropping back into reality, Jodi wondered if coming to Erlang was such a good idea. There was nothing, really, left on Erlang except the survivors who, like so many humans on so many worlds, were trying to pull themselves up from the rubble left in the wake of war. She thought they might have some friends there, but would they welcome the two fugitives with open arms or with the muzzles of pulse guns?

But those were better odds than they might face anywhere else. The news of Nathan's death had been broadcast on every human communication channel, and it was unlikely that, with the possible exception of the Erlangers, anyone who had been exposed to the propaganda – and that would be nearly everyone in the Confederation – would be willing to help them.

Besides, she thought, now that Reza knows that his son might be on his way to Erlang, there was no stopping him. While he spoke little, his few words conveyed to her the overpowering love he felt for his wife, and for the son he had never known. That alone, she thought, was something to really make one believe in God or the Devil, depending on how you looked at it.

What was the boy like? she wondered. She, along with the rest of humanity, had never seen anything other than an adult Kreelan female. She had heard Eustus and Enya describe the mummified remains of the adult males they had seen in the burial chamber on Erlang before the Kreelan attack there, but it was not the same. This was a living child, the blood of the man who had become a part of her life years ago, and who had shared his body and his soul with an alien, an enemy of Jodi's people. She remembered the woman's face, reliving her agony. From what Reza had said, it now appeared that Esah-Zhurah, too, was in mortal danger, as was her entire race. She wondered at the magnitude of an entire civilization suddenly dying out, with no survivors or descendants, and felt a sudden tremor of empathy for them.

"Christ in a chariot-driven sidecar," she muttered to herself, shaking her head in wonder. "What the hell am I thinking?" She glanced at one of the instruments on the copilot's side, noticing that Reza had slipped into the chair beside her without a sound. Anyone else might have been startled or surprised; Jodi had long since become accustomed to it.

"Five minutes to normal space and Erlang," she told him, noting that his face barely looked human, his features oddly contorted into a human mimicry of Kreelan expressions. He was reverting, she thought to herself, becoming a Kreelan again for what would probably be the last days – or hours – of his life. And of hers. "You feel okay?"

"Yes," he answered, then was silent as he stared out the viewscreen at the glowing starfield. "Jodi," he said after a moment, "I have decided to take a boat down to the surface, leaving you free to escape back into hyperspace. I can think of no way of getting a chance to see my son except by surrendering." He looked at her, his alien eyes sad now. "I would spare you the fate that will surely befall me."

"And where the hell am I supposed to go, Reza?" she asked, more hurt than angry. She needed him to need her right now. "I know Borge's dirty little secrets, remember? I don't think he's going to just let me walk away once he has you. I know the *Pearl's* a nice ship and all, but I really don't want to spend the rest of my life flitting around the galaxy in her, alone." She shook her head vigorously. "Look, brother, we're in this together, we stay in this together. If nothing else, we can hold hands as we swing on the gallows."

Reza nodded, knowing what she would say. He reached over and gently squeezed her hand.

The warning klaxon suddenly blared, announcing that the *Pearl* was about to drop back into real space. Beyond the wraparound viewport, the streaks of light suddenly quivered, then quickly began to contract and weave, soon becoming discrete points of light. Then they saw the glimmering bulk of Erlang.

But the planet's beauty was suddenly eclipsed by a Confederation destroyer that was sailing close enough to see the seams in her armor. The sight sent a chill up Jodi's spine. She instinctively reached for the weapons controls, but Reza stayed her hand.

"No," he said firmly. "They have been waiting for us."

"You knew?" she asked incredulously.

Reza nodded. "We have been led here," he said as he turned his attention to the destroyer.

There was nothing to do but go forward. With a deft movement of her fingers across the console, Jodi brought the *Pearl* away from her near-collision course with the warship. On the scanner, she noticed that there were three more Confederation ships, a cruiser and two destroyers, orbiting the planet.

"Well," Jodi muttered as an indicator winked in the display, "it looks like you're right about them expecting us." She opened a channel.

"Inbound vessel," a voice announced from an unfamiliar face that immediately appeared on the console, "identify yourself immediately!"

Jodi felt another tingle as she saw the lock-on indicators on the *Pearl's* defense display. The destroyer was tracking them with its main guns, at point blank range.

"This is Commander Jodi Mackenzie, piloting the *Golden Pearl*," she replied coolly, "serial B78-4C97101K, bound for Erlang."

The officer on the destroyer answered immediately. "Commander, you are hereby ordered to rendezvous with the cruiser *Furious*, where you and Captain Gard will be placed under arrest." He paused. "Any attempt to escape or reach the planet's surface will be met with the instant destruction of you and your vessel. Do you understand?"

"Yes," Jodi replied coolly. "We understand and will comply."

Beside her, Reza's green eyes were fixed on the gray-hulled cruiser that was even now drawing toward them. The ship that held his son.

* * *

Their reception aboard the *Furious* was little short of openly hostile. Fitted in the airlock with wrist and ankle binders that would explode if tampered with or opened without the proper electronic key, Jodi and Reza were marched separately, each inside a box of Marines armed with stunners, to the brig. Aside from the rhythmic stomping of their footsteps, the corridors were devoid of activity, the crew having been evacuated from the corridors the escort would use to get the prisoners to their destination.

A sense of uneasy anticipation had taken hold of Reza, not out of concern for his own welfare, but for his son, if he truly existed. For all the years Reza had been in the Empire and all the years since, he had never dreamed that such an honor – a child – could ever be his. But the Change that he and Esah-Zhurah had undergone those long years ago must have made it possible. And it was the fate of that legacy that most concerned him now, even more than his burning fear of what had befallen Esah-Zhurah, for he knew in his heart that in his son lay the key to the survival of both civilizations.

His only hope now was that the humans – he thought of himself as Kreelan again – would allow him at least to see the boy, if not speak to him. His hands clenched with nervous tension as they approached the slate gray armored doors to the brig.

The shielded doors opened as they approached, sliding back into the walls like the shifting jaws of a snake. Reza was led first through the security baffles and into the inner chamber. Along the rear wall were three cells, one of which was occupied.

"Reza!" Eustus called through the force field barrier.

But Reza did not hear him. His eyes and his mind were fixed on the Kreelan child who stood at Eustus's side, staring with equal fascination at Reza, his father. As if he were adrift in a river, Reza sensed himself being pushed and prodded into the cell. Standing within arm's reach of one another, father and son looked into each other's eyes, gauging their similarities, their differences, the miracle of their own unique existence.

Behind them, Jodi pulled Eustus to the side. Their time to speak would come, but not just now.

Slowly, Shera-Khan knelt before his father. Bowing his head, he saluted Reza. "Greetings, priest of the Desh-Ka," he said in the New Tongue, "my father."

"Greetings, my son," Reza choked, tears streaming down his cheeks. "What is thy name?"

"Shera-Khan, my father," the boy replied solemnly.

"Rise, Shera-Khan, my son," Reza said. "Let me look upon you." The boy stood and looked up at Reza, who offered his arms in the traditional greeting of warriors. Shera-Khan accepted, and the two touched one another for the first time, both afraid that the other was an illusion, a cruel hoax played by Fate. But the blood that trickled from the tiny punctures made by Shera-Khan's claws and the strength of Reza's grip on his son's arms convinced them both that each was very real. "Blessed be Her name," Reza whispered. "How much of thy mother do I see in thy face."

Shera-Khan trembled in mourning at his mention of his mother.

"The Empress now is she," he told Reza, sending a burning flare of apprehension through Reza's heart. "Oh, Father, She lays dying. Broken is Her heart, silent is Her spirit. We are lost!"

Instinctively, Reza pulled Shera-Khan close, wrapping his arms around him as his mind grappled with the boy's words.

It was then that he heard another voice, old and familiar, speak to him in the language of the Old Tongue. "Come to me, my son."

Turning to the left, toward the far wall of the cell, he saw the great warrior who had been so much a part of his life, who had given him her legacy of knowledge and power, who had given him her love.

"Tesh-Dar," he whispered, rocked by her state of mourning and her weak condition. Holding Shera-Khan close at his side, he swiftly knelt beside her, taking her great hands in his, her skin cold to his touch. "My mother."

Her wise eyes took in his face, and she smiled in the Kreelan way, an expression of joy in such an hour of sorrow. "Reza," she whispered, "my son, you are alive. The animal..." She stopped herself. "No. Your *friend's* words were true." She pulled him close to her, his head to her breast, and smelled his skin, his hair. Running her hands across his braids, pausing at the seventh that had been severed and where the hair had ceased to grow, she said, "Great was my fear, my child, that the human's words that you yet lived were false, that the sword of your love did take your life. I would have killed him, had I not sensed that he spoke truly." In but a few words, she described to him how Eustus had saved her and Shera-Khan, and how she had discovered that Reza was still alive, or at least had been given the hope that he was.

"And that has been my only hope, my son," she told him painfully, "for Shera-Khan, for the Empire. For without you, we are doomed."

"What has happened?" Reza asked quietly, watching with alarm as Tesh-Dar struggled for breath. Beside him, Shera-Khan pressed close, his body shivering with a grief no human could ever imagine. Reza would have felt it, too, except that his connection to the living Empress had been severed. He had lived the years since then in acute spiritual loneliness, but he had also been spared the horrible fate of the peers.

Tesh-Dar closed her eyes, and Reza feared that she had lost consciousness, perhaps for the last time.

But then she began to speak of the legend of Keel-Tath.

* * *

Long ago, so the legends say, after Keel-Tath cursed Her people for their treachery and what She believed to be the murder of Her lover, the First Empress was filled with anger and grief, sorrow and melancholy. The breath of life no longer appealed to Her, and so it was that She decided to hasten Her soul unto the Dark Place, where She could lament Her fate in solitude, forever. With a trembling hand, she raised a dagger over Her heart to steal away Her life, and that of Her people.

But a young priestess, Dara-Kol of the Desh-Ka, beseeched the heartbroken Empress for a chance for Her Children, now fallen from grace, to redeem themselves in Her eyes. So passionate was the young priestess's plea that Keel-Tath, Her wisdom overpowering Her distress, granted the young one's wish.

Gathering around Her a host of the now stricken males, the Imperial Guard, Keel-Tath returned them to their former grace and glory. "My guardians, My companions, shall you be, throughout Eternity," She proclaimed. The warriors fell to their knees in devotion to Her, their voices as one pledging their eternal honor to Her name, in life and in death.

Turning to Dara-Kol, who alone had had the courage to venture into the Empress's presence after the Fall, She produced a crystal heart. It was a work glorious to the eye, which was the greatest and last gift from Her lover. "When I rest," She told the young priestess, "this shall be the key to My awakening. For the one who holds the good fortune to find it, and has the courage to brave the host of guardians, the one who lays a living hand upon My heart shall awaken My spirit and My call to thee.

"But the Curse shall not be broken," She warned, "until My heart again feels the warmth of love. If I rise in spirit without such love, damned shall we all be to everlasting Darkness."

Dara-Kol fell at the Empress's feet in thanks, even then mourning the passing of the First Empress from the Spirit that bound their people together, the loss of Her power, Her magic. Her love.

Keel-Tath looked upon Dara-Kol and told her, "Rise, My child. For you shall be the First of the Last. In your blood shall flow My blood, that you may lead your people in their quest for redemption." Keel-Tath took the young woman's hand, and with the knife she carried at Her side caused their palms to bleed, then bound them together. "Your spirit shall bind with those who may follow in your footsteps, so that the wisdom of the living Empress shall be ever greater, as shall Her power. One female shall be born each great cycle, born with white hair and strong spirit, one who may ascend to the throne. I vow that this succession shall not be broken before the day the Last Empress receives Me into Her heart. This shall be My Promise to you, to My Children."

Dara-Kol closed her eyes, feeling the power of Keel-Tath as Her blood mingled with her own. She trembled with fear and anticipation, of longing to lead her people to their redemption. "And how, Empress, are we to find you?" she asked.

Keel-Tath answered softly, as if from afar, "That, daughter, shall be thy quest."

When Dara-Kol opened her eyes, Keel-Tath, along with the males who had pledged to guard Her forever, was gone. All that remained was a single braid of Her hair upon the floor, the Seventh Braid that joined Her to the spirit of the Empire. And as Dara-Kol watched, the braid fell into dust, to be carried away by a sudden tempest that swept through the great chamber and away into the great forests beyond.

Alone now, no longer a high priestess but the living Empress, Dara-Kol heard the anguished cries of Her people in Her blood, and She wept in Her heart for their loss.

* * *

Tesh-Dar shuddered under Reza's hands. "And so it happened, my son," she went on, "that Esah-Zhurah was fated to be the Last Empress before Keel-Tath's return." The pain in her voice deepened. "But Esah-Zhurah's soul was dead, for she lived in the belief that she had slain the keeper of her heart, that she had killed you, Reza. Black with mourning has been her body since the day you left us, and blacker still was her spirit after the day her sword pierced your breast. And when the Ascension took place, the old Empress passing Her flame to Esah-Zhurah, the new Empress took the glowing crystal heart in Her hands, for it was time for the last part of the Prophecy to be fulfilled, for Keel-Tath's return to the Blood." She moaned at the memory, her great hand constricting painfully around Reza's. "Never have I known such pain, my son, as when She cried out, as if Her heart had been torn from her breast. Then she fell to the dais of the throne and lay still.

"The Empire shuddered, my son," she went on quietly, her eyes fixed on a place that Reza knew contained only agony, a Kreelan incarnation of spiritual Hell. "Billions of voices cried out in fear and pain as Her voice suddenly was stilled in their blood. And in the palace on the Empress Moon, the crystal heart, lying dark beside Her, began again to glow. But this time it was not as a summons, but as a warning. For all who attempted to approach the wall of blue light that it cast around Her body died, vanishing in a shower of sparks and the stench of scorched flesh." She closed her eyes. "By the thousands did they perish, all the peers who witnessed the ceremony, all who tried to reach her. All of them. Gone."

"And you, my priestess?" Reza asked quietly.

Tesh-Dar grimaced, turning her mournful gaze toward him. "I would have joined them, so stricken with grief was I, save that I was entrusted with the life of your son. Since the day of his birth, Shera-Khan's welfare has been my honor and responsibility. Had I allowed either of us to be drawn into the fire, all my life would have counted for nothing but disgrace in Her eyes. Shera-Khan and I alone survived.

Of the high priestesses and warriors, they are no more, their spirits having fallen into darkness as their bodies burned to ashes in the light. I left with Shera-Khan, closing the doors to the throne room and forbidding anyone to enter, hoping to spare any more the fate of those already dead and gone. It was then that I left the Homeworld for the Nursery where Shera-Khan was born, where your human... friend... found me, for in my bereavement I knew not where else to go, for I believed you long dead." She shook her head sadly. "But even the nursery was empty, the Wardress having evacuated all of her charges when Her voice was silenced, her fleet returning the children – even the males – home. All that remained there were the Books of Time, dead stone recounting the lineage of a dying race."

Reza felt the meaning of her words settle upon his heart, oppressive and undeniable. He could not imagine the strength of will it must have taken for her to resist the urge to reach for the Empress. And the deaths of the high priestesses, the greatest of the Empire's warriors, meant that...

"I shall be the last," he said slowly, the full weight of the responsibility he bore settling upon his shoulders. When Tesh-Dar died, he would be the last of the warrior high priests and priestesses.

"True are your words, my son," Tesh-Dar said, gently stroking his face. "For when death takes me, you alone shall be the last of the warriors to bear the mark of the ancient orders. You alone have the gifts that have been passed down from generation to generation. You alone have the honor to lead the peers in this darkest of hours. You and your love are the last hope of the Empire, for all that we are and have ever been shall be lost if the breath of life is allowed to pass from Her body. Breathes does She still, but millions die each moment She sleeps in Darkness, in mourning, their crying souls lost in eternal Darkness. And in the moment Her heart stops and Her spirit passes into the Beyond, the Empire shall be lost forever – and all of us with it."

Reza watched as her eyes closed and her breathing slowed. Her hand loosened from his as she fell into sleep, exhaustion finally claiming its due. Leaning forward, he kissed her tenderly on the forehead.

"Sleep, my mother," he whispered. Beside him, Shera-Khan had fallen into a troubled slumber. The pain of reliving those horrible hours as thousands had cast themselves into the wall of blue fire in the desperate hope of reaching the Empress had drained what few reserves of strength the boy had. Reza laid him gently on the other bed, his blood burning with a cold fire at the Way that had been laid before him, the final steps of a great journey that had begun millennia ago.

Beside him, Jodi placed her tunic over the boy. Reza felt her hand on his arm.

"Will they be all right?" she asked quietly. Eustus had told her what he knew and what had happened to bring them to this strange crossroads, and Jodi had found herself filled with empathy not only for the boy, but for the dying warrior, as well.

Reza looked at her, and she was shocked by the stricken, almost desperate look in his eyes. "No," he said, his voice hoarse with emotion, "they are dying. All of them."

Eustus looked confused. "What do you mean?"

"Unless I can find a way back to the Empire," Reza told him, "the Empress... my wife, shall soon die. And with Her shall die our entire race. The Empire of Kreela shall be no more."

Jodi and Eustus exchanged a glance.

"Reza," Jodi said tentatively, not sure just how he might react to what she was going to say, "I'm not sure that would be... such a bad thing, at least for humanity. I mean, we've been at war with the Empire for nearly a hundred years. They killed your parents, remember? There aren't many people who would shed any tears if they all... died."

"It doesn't really matter," Eustus added quietly. "Marchand told me that a fleet's assembling for an assault into Kreelan space. While she didn't say as much, I imagine that some genius at Fleet HQ finally figured out where the Homeworld is, and now they're going after it. And whatever trouble the Kreelans are in is just icing on the cake."

"When is this attack to take place?" Reza asked sharply.

Surprised by his friend's intensity, Eustus took an involuntary step back. "It must be soon," he answered cautiously, looking at Jodi, whose face bore an expression of concern, "but she didn't bother to fill me in on the details, Reza. I'm only a grunt, remember, and a 'traitor,' at that."

"After all these years," Jodi murmured to herself, "we've finally got a chance to beat them." Looking at the warrior who lay dying, and the stricken child beside her, she said, "I'm sorry Reza, I really am. But if we've got the chance to put it to them once and for all, I'm all for it. We must be pulling every ship that can hold air for this battle, and when our fleet gets to the Homeworld and finds the warriors like this, they're going to kick their asses. I just wish I could be there to see it."

"You do not understand the dangers," Reza said ominously. "Every ship in the Empire is converging on the Homeworld by now, all the warships of a race that has visited more stars than are visible in the night skies of Earth. And while they are disheartened and disorganized, all will fight to the death to protect the Empress. The human fleet will die along with the Empire, and all those human worlds that depend on starships for their survival will be cast into a dark age that may last for centuries. It will be a disaster the likes of which humanity has never known." He shook his head. "The only hope is for me to reach the Empress in time."

"And then what?" Eustus asked. "Are all the warriors going to spring back to their feet just in time to blow our ships out of space? No," he said. "No, I don't think I want that, Reza. I'm sorry."

Reza looked at him as if Eustus had slapped him. "You doubt me," Reza whispered incredulously. "Have I ever led you astray, lied to you, in all these years? I tell you truly, my friends: if the fleet attacks the Homeworld as you have said, it shall meet its end. But if I can reach Her, save Her, there may be hope for us all. You see, as Empress, She cannot destroy the heritage of Her only son, the child of Her very blood: Shera-Khan is half-human, and *She will end the war*. But only if I reach Her in time." He looked at them pleadingly. "You must believe me. I cannot do this alone. Please."

"Reza..." Jodi began, feeling helpless and fated to lose the best friend she had ever had, even over and above Nicole. "I... I don't doubt you," she said, "but I can't help you, even if everything you say is true. I'm a Confederation officer, Reza, and the Kreelans are my enemy. I know I'm here because I'm accused of crimes that I didn't commit, but that doesn't mean that I'm ready to do the real thing. What you're talking about is treason, and... I just can't. I'm sorry."

"Me, too," Eustus said hoarsely, feeling like he wanted to die. "I'm sorry, Reza." Eustus turned his eyes to the floor in shame.

* * *

In Erlang's skies, the human fleet gathered. Enya watched the tiny lights as they flicked into normal space, sometimes individually, sometimes by the dozen. The Council of Erlang had been informed by the commodore aboard the *Furious* of what was happening, and had also been told that the new president and the entire Confederation Council would be aboard the flagship that would lead the great armada into enemy space. And President Borge had invited – decreed was more like it, Enya thought darkly – Erlang to send a representative along on this "most glorious of occasions." Under the circumstances, with thousands of Confederation warships soon to be orbiting their home, the still-struggling inhabitants of Erlang were hardly in a position to refuse.

Enya had immediately volunteered. She was intelligent and strong-willed, and was more aware than most of the risks their people were taking in carrying the war to the Empire. It also gave her a chance, no matter how slight, of seeing Eustus before fate would have a chance to steal him away from her forever. Little did she know that he was under arrest on charges of high treason.

The shuttle from *Warspite* screamed in the night air, its engines howling like a hurricane as its three sturdy landing struts made gentle contact with the ground. The hatch hummed open and a helmeted crew chief poked his head out the door.

"Good luck, lass," Ian Mallory said over the continued roar of the shuttle's engines. He took Enya in his arms and hugged her tightly. "Godspeed."

"Thank you, Ian," she replied, returning his affection. He had been her father since she had lost her own. "I'll not be away for long." Kissing him on the cheek, she gathered up her single bag, a worn but respectable leather traveler, and darted into the shuttle.

With a final look around to make sure the hatch and ship were clear, the crew chief pulled himself back inside and the door slid shut behind him. As the people around it waved farewell, the shuttle's engines roared with power and it began to lift from the ground. It was barely above the trees when the landing gear retracted and the ship accelerated rapidly out of sight, leaving nothing behind it but a glowing contrail that quickly faded.

High above, The Armada continued to assemble.

FORTY-NINE

"*Merde*, but this will not work!" L'Houillier sputtered angrily, slamming his fist down on the table. "This insanity has cost us fourteen ships already from collisions around Erlang, and there will be three times as many ships appearing in the target zone. And those blasted politicians strutting around this ship like a bunch of cheap whores, pandering to that... that..." L'Houillier's vocabulary failed to provide him an acceptable descriptor for the new Commander-in-Chief.

Sitting across from him, Zhukovski added to the fleet commander's gloom. "And that is without interference from Kreelans," he muttered. In all the years that the two had been friends, this was the first time that Zhukovski had seen L'Houillier lose his temper. Fortunately, it had been in private, in Zhukovski's stateroom. Had such words been uttered beyond the Russian admiral's electronically screened quarters, or within earshot of the wrong people, Borge would have acted quickly to see that L'Houillier – or anyone else, for that matter – quickly found his way into retirement. Or worse.

There seem to have been a lot of 'retirements' recently, Zhukovski noted bitterly of the virtual purge that had taken place among upper and middle grade Navy and Marine officers. He was amazed that he and L'Houillier had avoided the axe this long. *Perhaps*, he mused, *Borge has something special planned for us*.

"There is little we can do, admiral," Zhukovski went on, pouring another vodka for the two of them, "at least without exploring less pleasant... alternatives."

L'Houillier looked hard at his intelligence officer. "I would be lying to you if I said I had not experienced similar thoughts, Evgeni," he said quietly, "but to say more – let alone to do more – is treason of the worst sort. The Confederation does not need a military dictatorship, or for the military to decide on a civilian leader."

"Even now?"

L'Houillier nodded. "Even now. You know how I feel about this man and his minions, but I swore an oath, as did you, as did every member of the Confederation Defense Forces, to uphold its constitution and its legally established leaders. Borge succeeded Nathan legally, and that is that."

"I wonder," Zhukovski said aloud.

"What is that supposed to mean?" L'Houillier asked sharply.

"Being curious as cat – which is prerequisite for intelligence officer – I have taken liberty of conducting some... historical research into fearless leader's background."

"Evgeni!" L'Houillier hissed. "You had no right or authorization to do that! Using your position to gain access to classified–"

"Admiral misunderstands," Zhukovski gently interrupted him, putting up a hand to silence his friend and superior. "Public domain information only. No access to classified materials made," his eyes darkened. "None necessary."

The Grand Admiral frowned, still not liking it. The thought of what would happen to them should any of the current civilian leaders discover that a military officer had been digging into the background of the president...

But, as Zhukovski had known it would, curiosity got the better of him. "Well?" L'Houillier asked finally. "What did you find out?"

Zhukovski smiled. He knew his admiral well. "What I did not find out was probably more important," he said. "But of uncovered information, I found of great interest fact that Fearless Leader at one time was friend of Thorella family."

"The industrialist?" L'Houillier interjected. "Thorella's shipyards built half the ships I have served on."

Zhukovski nodded. "*Da*. Same family. Rich, powerful. Died in collision over Earth over thirty years ago. Terrible tragedy." He looked significantly at L'Houillier. "I found press report that says son of Borge died in accident, also."

"I did not know he ever had a son," L'Houillier said quietly.

"Is not widely advertised fact, it seems." Zhukovski took a sip of the cold vodka, feeling it warm his insides against the cold wind that blew in his heart. "And that is where tale becomes strange. You see, public records about Borge and Thorella families are almost blank for roughly year after accident. Very odd to say for one of Earth's richest families and popular young politician, especially when such tragedy is involved."

L'Houillier's brow creased. "Wait just a moment, Evgeni," he said. "I remember that there were many reports on that accident, and on the Thorellas, especially. I do not recall reading about Borge, specifically, but it was so long ago I probably would not remember, anyway. But I am sure the press was full of things."

With the smile of the angler who had hooked his prize, Evgeni began to reel L'Houillier in. "And that is my point, admiral," he said. "I remember much being in press, too, even as young weapons officer on destroyer patrolling Rim. It was 'Big News' at time. But now, most information is gone from available records. Disappeared. For example, article about Borge's son was text only, and last name was spelled wrong."

"Are you suggesting," L'Houillier asked incredulously, "that someone has somehow tampered with the information in the Central Library?" The Central Library had been created nearly two centuries before as a storehouse of human knowledge and information. Over the years, the various client states and colonies had come to rely on it almost exclusively for their information needs, and most smaller information libraries were not in themselves unique, but were abridged versions of the Central Library that carried a smaller quantity and narrower scope of data. The funding of the library was ostensibly from multi-source government appropriations to keep it "bias-free," but there were many significant individual contributions, as well. The Librarians had become a quasi-religious sect, guarding the integrity of the information under their care, and were expected to operate the Library with standards of intellectual and moral purity that would have astonished the most conservative of religious monks.

Zhukovski nodded grimly. "Library has been tampered with, admiral," he said. "I cannot tell how much or when, but things are not as they should be, and common factor seems to be Fearless Leader."

"Evgeni, if this is true, our... our entire history, the core of our knowledge... everything could be corrupted." L'Houillier was horrified at the thought.

"I believe that few records I found were missed for some reason: typo in text, bad picture that did not register on scan, and so forth," Zhukovski said. "I discovered other holes in information regarding past of close associates of president, information which is routinely reported by press or government register, but that is either gone entirely or selectively edited. There is no doubt. Originals are perhaps behind locked files, but in open domain where they should be? *Nyet.*"

L'Houillier sat back in his chair, looking out the port of his friend's room at the starfield of ships that were gathered, a third of the fleet that was about to strike at the Kreelan homeworld. But who, he wondered silently, was the enemy now? And what was he to do about it?

"There is also matter of Reza Gard to consider," Zhukovski said quietly, interleaving his own thoughts with L'Houillier's.

"What do you expect me to do, Evgeni?" L'Houillier asked tiredly. "We have gone through this before. I know you are convinced that he is not guilty, but that is out of our hands. We cannot override the Council's decision. Reza and Mackenzie will face a civilian tribunal and no doubt will be executed." He shrugged. "I do not like that kind of justice any more than you, my friend, but we are faced with less and less authority these days."

"Vote was not unanimous," Zhukovski said. "Perhaps we should speak to opposition–"

"One vote hardly qualifies as 'opposition,' Evgeni, and you know it. I admire what Councilman Braddock has done as much as you, but his days are numbered, as well. Borge will not tolerate him for long, and he will no doubt join our other redoubtable colleagues in 'retirement.'"

"Even more reason to consider other alternatives."

L'Houillier rolled his eyes. "You never give up, do–"

The comm panel beeped, accompanied by a blinking red light. L'Houillier slapped it with his hand. "*Oui?*" he barked.

Admiral Laskowski's face appeared on the panel. Out of sight from the comm panel's view, Zhukovski made an expression of exquisite disgust.

"The prisoners are about to arrive from *Furious*, sir," she said. "The president ordered–"

"I am aware of the president's orders, admiral," he snapped. It must be an effort for her, L'Houillier thought, to conceal her sentiment that the old Grand Admiral was long past retirement, holding a position that she was rightfully entitled to. *Well,* he thought sourly, *she would just have to wait a bit longer, now wouldn't she?* "I shall be down at once." He snapped the circuit closed.

Zhukovski was already on his feet, straightening his uniform, setting his face into its accustomed stony expression. "Since I was little boy, I always like to see parade," he said. "But not this time. Not today."

"Nor I," the Grand Admiral said quietly as he stood up to follow Zhukovski from the room. Pausing at the door, he looked back at the partially emptied bottle of vodka and suddenly wished that he could sit here and finish the rest of it, rather than participate in the spectacle that Borge had prepared.

Sighing, he relinquished the thought. Maybe when I retire with a bullet in the brain, he told himself bitterly.

* * *

Admiral Laskowski fumed at L'Houillier's brush-off. *Your day of reckoning is coming, old man*, she thought angrily. She knew he had been President Nathan's military pet, but it was a new administration, a new leader, and she was already on the inside track. For now, she would have to bide her time and be patient.

She was just about to head out of the Combat Information Center, or CIC, for the president's ceremony when she saw the sailor manning the STARNET terminal suddenly stiffen. He was obviously reading an incoming message, probably from one of the scoutships that were probing ever deeper into Kreelan space.

While she technically wasn't in charge of the watch – the officer of the deck was a full commander who was otherwise occupied on the far side of the dark, sprawling compartment – she was the senior officer present and had the privilege to poke her nose into whatever might be going on.

Curiosity drawing her onward, she walked over to the rating who was now staring in wonder at the STARNET display. "What's going on, sailor?" she asked.

The man turned to her, a look of awe on his face. "They found it," he said in little more than a whisper. "One of the scoutships – SV1287, commanded by Lieutenant Weigand – found the Kreelan homeworld!"

A tingle of excitement ran up Laskowski's spine. "Are they sure? Have you gotten confirmation?"

"There's none needed, ma'am," the sailor told her, his voice now laced with excitement. "Look at the plot: there are thousands of ships in the system they found. *Thousands!*"

Laskowski's eyes grew wide as she looked at the display sent in by the aptly – if informally – named *Obstinate*. She knew Lieutenant Weigand only by reputation, but in about ten minutes she would make sure that he was Lieutenant *Commander* Weigand. She quickly scanned the report: he had taken some incredible chances, doing a series of jumps along the vector of one of the Kreelan battle groups he had picked up. Hoping to emerge from one of the jumps close enough to pick up readings from any inhabited systems along that vector, he finally struck not just gold, but platinum. There were nearly three thousand combat vessels – the same number she had predicted, she thought smugly – in that system, and spectral analyses and neutrino readings indicated an incredibly advanced civilization was present. Most of it was concentrated on a planet and major moon in the system at a distance from the sun where water could exist as a liquid, and thus support carbon-based life. There were other targets in the system, including the asteroids, but the fourth planet from the star was obviously the primary target, along with its orbiting moon.

There was no mistake, no room for doubt. *They had found it.*

"My God," she whispered. Turning to the officer of the deck, who was heading her way to see what was going on, she said, "Commander, I want this information to be held closely until I say otherwise. No one – *no one* – else is to see or hear of this report until I have a chance to discuss it with Admiral L'Houillier. Is that clear?"

"Aye, ma'am," the commander replied crisply.

Satisfied, Laskowski turned on her heel and hurried out of CIC. But she had no plans of telling L'Houillier, at least not until *after* she had told the president himself.

* * *

"Tony?" Enya called above the murmur of the crowd. "Tony Braddock?" Her shuttle had arrived scant moments ago. After being led away from the landing zone by the courteous crew chief, she found herself among the crowd of dignitaries and other military and civilian personnel who had assembled in the *Warspite's* starboard landing bay.

"Enya!" Tony shouted, waving his arm for her to join him. He stood off by himself, his glum face brightening at her appearance. "What are you doing here?"

"I was chosen to represent Erlang on the Council," she told him, her eyes wide at the sight around her, the hundreds – thousands? – of people filling the great ship's landing bay.

But the sight of Tony Braddock and the look on his face diverted her attention to the here and now, as well as reaffirming her suspicions about the dark nature of the gathering of people around her. Looking around quickly, deciding that it was safe amid the background noise, she quietly told him, "We were told to supply a representative for the expedition or be cut off from all Confederation aid. Borge's hands around our throat are as tight as ever."

Braddock nodded grimly. "You aren't the only ones. He made the same speech to the entire Council, telling us all that anyone who doesn't toe the line is going to be cut off. Or worse."

Enya shook her head incredulously. The Kreelans had done damage enough. Now, humanity had inherited a maniacal leader, as well. "Where is Nicole?" she asked, hoping to brighten the conversation.

Tony frowned. "I don't know. They have me billeted with the rest of the politicos, and I haven't been able to spend much time with her since we left Earth." He craned his neck around, his eyes searching. "I haven't spotted her in the crowd, but I'm sure she's here somewhere."

"What is going on?" Enya asked. "Why is everyone gathering together like this? Is Borge going to address everyone, or what?"

Braddock was incredulous. "You didn't know?"

"Know what?" From the look on his face, she was sure she was going to regret finding out.

"They're transferring some Kreelan prisoners from the *Furious*," he paused, "along with Reza and Jodi Mackenzie. They were captured on their way to Erlang."

"I had heard a rumor, but didn't believe it. You don't believe it, do you?" she asked him. "I know that Reza is different from anyone I've ever known, but he would not have killed Nathan. I just can't accept–"

A glance and a frown from a nearby councilwoman caught Braddock's eye.

"Yes, I know," he said, raising his voice to make sure the eavesdropping councilwoman heard, "it amazes me that President Borge is even going to bother with a tribunal."

"Tony?" Enya said, confused at his turn of his speech, but stopped when his hand gripped her arm tightly, almost painfully.

Braddock watched out of the corner of his eye as the councilwoman turned back to her conversation, apparently satisfied. Then he guided Enya to the open space beneath a nearby Corsair's wing. "Enya," he whispered after they'd moved out of earshot of their neighbors, "you've got to be very careful about what you say and who hears you. Since Nathan died, the changes on the Council have been nothing short of terrifying." He glanced around quickly, and she recognized the look from her time in the resistance: he was making sure the area was secure.

"Almost all the old members of the Council – everyone who supported Nathan and his policies – are gone," he whispered. "Since he declared martial law after Nathan's death, Borge has dismissed most of the Senate and Council. He's installed sympathetic supporters or simply eliminated representation for some worlds in the legislature. Some of them, the most vocal opponents, have died suddenly and inexplicably." He looked around again. The crowd had grown larger, closer. "The checks and balances system is gone. Even the judiciary has been subverted since Savitch was killed. We've got a dictatorship with a rubber-stamp body masquerading as a democracy."

"And what about you?"

A look of shame crossed his face. "I've tried to make a stand for the things I've felt are really important, but it's no use," he said wearily. "My only hope is to try and gain enough support in an underground movement to restore some kind of order to the government. In public, I have to appear as just another lackey, or I face the same fate as the others. Then none of us will have any hope."

Enya took his arm. "Don't be ashamed," she told him. "Sometimes there is no alternative but to dress like the enemy so you can defeat him." She, of all people, knew the truth of that. She had worked against Belisle's corrupt government on Erlang by masquerading many times as a Ranier. Some of the things she had to do...

He managed a grim smile. "That's what worries me," he told her. "I don't want to become the thing I'm trying to destroy."

"May I have your attention, please!" a voice suddenly boomed over the PA system. Braddock recognized it immediately: Voronin Hack, the Council's Master-at-Arms and ceremonial mouthpiece. The crowd quieted down immediately. "Ladies and gentlemen," his smooth baritone voice continued, "honored guests and dignitaries... the President of the Confederated Alliance of Humanity!"

A massive cheer went up as Borge took his place at the podium, the white presidential robe billowing about his ample stomach, his face flushed with supreme confidence. He raised his hands to the crowd, basking in their adulation.

The applause, Braddock noted sadly, was enthusiastic and sincere. There were no guns at people's backs, no cue cards or faked admiration. With the exception of those on the Council or in the upper circles of the military, few people here knew or understood the implications of the transformation that had occurred in the Confederation government at Borge's hand. Most of them saw him as the inheritor of Nathan's tragic legacy, as the man who had pursued a humble life in the unglamorous world of creating and guiding the law, but who now was determined to end the war and bring peace to the galaxy.

After what was to Braddock an interminable interlude of applause, Borge finally gestured for the crowd to be silent. Slowly, unwillingly, they began to comply.

"Fellow citizens of the great Confederation!" he declared as the crowd at last was still. "Fellow humans, hear me:

"For many long years we have suffered and died at the hands of the alien enemy, losing our loved ones, our children to the claws of this insidious infestation that has swept across our galaxy like a plague. Campaign after campaign have we fought, not for glory or bounty, but for our very survival." His voice deepened, his tempo slowed as he went on, "For nearly a century have we lost world after world, colony after colony invaded, burned, destroyed. Neither man, nor woman, nor child has been spared this agony, this devastation."

He looked down at the podium, as if in communion with the now-thoughtful members of the audience, as if offering a silent prayer to those who had died in the century-long invasion. "But, my friends, the tide has turned," he said, looking up, casting his gaze upon the crowd before him. "The aliens have lost their strength, their will to fight," he told them. "They have run in full retreat from our worlds, fleeing to the sector of space from which they were spawned. We may never know the nature of the divine intervention that has driven them from our homelands, but know you this..." He paused, his brow wrinkling in righteous fury. "They cannot run far enough to escape our vengeance!"

The assemblage broke into a roar of cheering and whistling, voices taking up the challenge that Borge had laid before them.

Borge patiently waited for the tremendous reaction to subside, the shower of voices finally falling into silence within the great cavern of the landing bay.

"And seek vengeance we will, my friends," he promised them. "That is why we are gathered here this day, why tens of thousands of sailors and Marines, Coastguardsmen, and so many others have gathered in these three great fleets that shall sail as one toward the enemy's shores, the greatest armed force the galaxy has ever known." He was interrupted by more cheers and applause.

"As many of you know," he continued, "the Armada set out without us knowing the exact location of the Kreelan homeworld, only a comparatively vast area of space where we knew the enemy must be hiding." There were low murmurs in the audience, particularly among the naval personnel: many of them had thought it was insane to start the operation without knowing exactly where to strike. "My friends, just before taking the podium," he went on quietly, the thousands before him now utterly silent, "I was informed that one of our brave scoutships has pinpointed the location of the Kreelan homeworld, and has confirmed that their own battle fleet is assembling for a knockout blow against the Confederation." His fist suddenly hammered on the podium. "But *we* shall strike first! *We* shall strike at the enemy's heart with all our might, and for the first time in a century carry the battle into the enemy's territory. *We* shall end this terrible war with a single crushing blow, and *we* shall lead humanity to victory!"

Despite how much he hated Borge, Braddock found himself swept up in the religious fervor that washed over the audience in the landing bay like a tidal wave, carrying away all doubt, all reservations, all fears of what the immediate future held. Borge's words were irresistible to men and women who had fought and lost again and again in a war that had begun when their great-great-grandparents were children. Nearly everyone in the bay had lost a friend or relative, a spouse or a child, to the Kreelans. Their thirst for blood ran deep, and they were willing to sacrifice everything for a moment of that soon-to-be finest hour promised by Borge's words.

Beside him, Enya watched with wide eyes as the normally professional and disciplined Navy and Marine people around her applauded the president's speech with maniacal intensity.

They have no idea what might be in store, she thought suddenly, realizing that whatever intelligence information the human fleet had come up with, it could not have told them very much more than where to go looking for trouble. *And they don't care*, she thought. Coming from a planet and class of people that had been ravaged by humans for far longer and with much greater thoroughness than the Kreelans in their single attack, Enya had difficulty relating to the near-riot boiling around her. Even Braddock appeared to have been seduced by the president's passionate speech.

"Yes, my friends," Borge went on after the crowd regained its composure, "we shall seek out the enemy, wherever *he* is." The stress on the pronoun was unmistakable, and with a sudden chill, Enya realized whom he meant. "Years ago there came among us a man, who had once been a boy of human blood, but who was no longer entirely human. Raised by the alien horde, he was used and corrupted, molded into a weapon more insidious than any we have ever known. This man fought his former hosts well and with courage, earning our trust and respect, getting us to open our hearts to him, making us vulnerable." His eyes swept across the audience. "And then he betrayed us, all of us, by murdering in cold blood the one who had led humanity for so long and so well, a man most of you knew as the commander-in-chief, the president of the Confederation: Job Nathan." He wiped an imaginary tear from his eye. "He murdered the man who was my close friend for most of my adult life.

"But this alien prodigy was not alone in his treachery," Borge went on, his voice tight with barely suppressed rage, a performance that would have been the envy of a Broadway star. "For he was aided and abetted by another of our own kind, a woman who betrayed her uniform and her race to help this murderer escape from justice." He looked toward a group of Marines in dress uniforms carrying weapons that were anything but ceremonial. They were formed up next to the embarkation ramp of a newly arrived shuttle. "Bring out the prisoners," he ordered.

The Marine officer-in-charge rendered a sharp salute before turning toward the shuttle. "Bring out the prisoners!" he repeated sharply.

The hangar deck was so quiet that Enya could hear her heart beating. Even the deep thrum from the ship's drives seemed to have gone silent.

From the shuttle could be heard the sound of the chains that had been cuffed to the prisoners' hands and feet. Each prisoner also wore a thin band of metal around the neck with a small electronic control box: high explosive collars.

There was a collective gasp as Jodi, Shera-Khan, and Reza appeared in the light of the bay. Tesh-Dar, too weak to walk by herself, leaned heavily upon her adopted son, all the while casting a baleful eye on the human animals all around her, trying to force their stench from her nostrils. She felt the cold metal of the human device around her son's neck and her own, and instantly regretted consenting to having it put on; but the humans would have harmed Shera-Khan, and she knew that neither Reza nor herself could have kept the child from harm.

"There is no other way," Reza had told her grimly as he accepted the lethal necklace himself. It had seemed to her for a moment that he was surrendering, but the flame in his eyes burned brightly still, she had seen. The Power was yet within him.

Shera-Khan also had his arm wrapped around Tesh-Dar's waist to lend his slender body for her support. He was not afraid of the animals that peered at him with their strange pale faces, for he walked in the presence of a great warrior priest, his father, and Tesh-Dar, who was a living legend of the sword. He could not understand his father's command that they obey the animals and submit to this spectacle, but he did not question it; Reza's word was the word of the consort of the Empress, the only one among Her race permitted to kneel upon the pedestal of the throne. He was the most high of Her Children, the single warrior who had no peers.

Jodi, while cast in the same light as the other three, walked alone. The humiliation she felt at being paraded before these people and those who watched from all over the Confederation through the vid paled in comparison to the sadness in her heart at having had to deny Reza her help in his greatest hour of need. She had loved him dearly as a friend, and loved him still; but she could not help him. She knew that she would go to her death convicted of crimes she had never committed. But she could not betray her people.

She walked ahead of the others, her head upright, with her eyes fixed on the evil man who wore the robes of an angel. Borge.

Reza felt the crushing weight of the emotions of those around him. It was a burden so great it threatened to smother his spirit but for the cold flames that burned for vengeance against those who had betrayed not only him, but all of humanity. Tesh-Dar was an easy and welcome weight about his shoulders. Her musky scent, pleasant from memory, was reassuring, as was that of his newfound son. He tuned out the burning hatred of the thousands of souls around him and focused on the small comforts his physical senses provided him of his Kreelan family, wishing he could sense them in his spirit, as well. But he could not, even this close to them, any more than he had been able since the day he left the Empire.

It is strange, he had thought after speaking with Tesh-Dar, *that their blood is cold and silent as the Empress sleeps, but my blood still sings its mournful solo as it had since that day long ago*. His powers had not waned since the tragedy of the Ascension, and he was left to wonder at whatever miracle sustained him. He remembered the dream of the First Empress, as he lay dying from Esah-Zhurah's sword, remembered the fire in his veins as he imagined Her blood mingling with his. Others might have thought it a dream, but he knew that it was not.

The prisoners slowly shuffled their way toward the dais, past the rows of sailors and Marines, legislators and judges, the men and women whom they had served and had served with for years. But now the prisoners weren't friends or comrades, only criminals who had committed the gravest crime against humanity in all of history.

"In the name of God," Enya whispered. It sounded like a shriek in the silence of the bay, and she said nothing more. Beside her, Braddock's only reaction was a twitching muscle in his jaw.

Finally, there were no more steps for the prisoners to take; they had reached their destination. Standing before the dais, all of them glared upward at the leader of the Confederation.

Borge wasted no time. "It would take too much time to read all the crimes with which you have been charged, so the court has waived reading all but the most vital: murder and conspiracy to commit murder." He turned his attention toward Reza. "Captain Gard, you are charged with the murders of Job Kahane Nathan, President of the Confederation, and Dr. Deliha Rabat. How do you plead?"

Reza said nothing. He knew he could kill Borge at this instant, but his son's life likely would be forfeit, and any chances he might have of saving the Empire – and the Confederation – would be lost forever.

Borge frowned. "Silence is entered as a plea of guilty." He turned to Jodi. "Commander Jodi Mackenzie, you are charged with conspiring with Captain Gard to murder Doctor Rabat and President Nathan; further, you are charged with the despicable murder of Tanya Buchet. How do you plead?"

"Go fuck yourself," she spat.

Borge snorted in disgust, then turned to the new Chief Justice, another of his latest appointees, Anton Simoniak. "Your Honor, if you please."

Simoniak stepped up to the podium. "Due to the barbaric nature of these crimes and the subsequent bloody escape of the accused, the court was compelled to conduct their trial *in absentia*," the Chief Justice stated flatly, as if bored by the supposition that they could possibly be anything but guilty. "The call for justice was unanimous." He looked down upon the condemned. "You have both been found guilty, as charged, on all counts." Turning to Borge, he said, "The recommended sentence is death, Mr. President, to be carried out immediately."

Enya opened her mouth to speak, but found Braddock's hand over her lips.

"Don't," he whispered urgently, "or you'll find yourself condemned along with them." He looked around urgently, afraid that someone might have noticed their exchange. No one was paying them any attention. Good. "There's nothing you can do for them now."

She angrily pulled his hand away, ashamed that he was afraid to speak out against this madness. And she was even more ashamed that she herself remained silent. Braddock was right, she thought as she watched the tragedy unfold before her. There was nothing to be done for them.

Borge nodded gravely as the justice stepped back to his position among the rest of the luminaries on the dais. "I concur with the verdict," he said, "and with the sentence. However, with the power vested in me as president, I hereby commute the sentence until Operation Millennium has been completed and our fleets return home." His eyes bored into Reza. "I want these traitors to witness the destruction of the evil that has washed our galaxy in human blood for the last hundred years, to see the power of God's vengeance before they see the gates of Hell!"

Like a surging tide, the assembly roared its venomous approval.

* * *

From where she stood on a catwalk, high above the fateful ceremony, Nicole did not hear the thousands of voices shouting from below. The only sounds perceptible to her mind were the strange whisperings, the chill in her body, that had been her frequent companions since the day Reza had pressed a bloody hand against hers, showing her things that no other human – save him – had ever seen.

She had watched him from her catwalk perch like a peregrine in a cage, wanting to help, but unable. She felt his heart, his soul, and the pain and rage that spilled from him now threatened to bring tears to her eyes, harsh action from her clenched hands.

Below her, the verdict having been pronounced and the crowd's lust for vengeance temporarily sated, Reza and the others were led off to the ship's brig, enduring the humiliation of being spat upon and cursed like molesters of children.

Just before they passed through the blast door that led to the ship's internal transport system, the huge female warrior looked back, and up. For just a moment, an incalculable instant, her eyes locked with Nicole's.

Help him, Nicole read in the woman's eyes as plainly as if she had spoken the words aloud. *Help my son*.

And then she was gone.

Clutching the railing so hard that her knuckles were bled white, Nicole waited for the trembling to stop before she made her way unsteadily back to her cabin. She knew what must be done, almost as if by instinct. Guided by powers that she did not understand, she began her preparations as soon as her cabin door closed behind her.

The fact that what she was about to do would be considered high treason never even occurred to her.

FIFTY

As she stood at the podium of the conference room, Admiral Laskowski took smug satisfaction in the looks of grim submission on the faces of L'Houillier and Zhukovski. There was no longer any question of who was really in charge now. The man who sat at the head of the conference table had decided that issue when he had personally approved of Laskowski's plan, and reinforced it with the fourth star he had given her, promoting her on the spot to full admiral for her role in discovering the Kreelan homeworld. Technically she was still junior to L'Houillier, but that was a mere technicality. He and Zhukovski had only pushed forward their retirement dates by arguing against her strategy. And now, here they were, mere spectators to the operation that she had devised, that she was now in charge of in all but name, reviewing it for her president's pleasure.

It was all her dreams come true.

"Mr. President," she began, "the attack plan is fairly simple, necessarily so because of the huge number of vessels involved."

This brought a barely audible grunt from L'Houillier. They had lost another ten ships to collision at the last navigation checkpoint. Zhukovski's great eyebrows knotted as a frown chiseled itself from his glowering face.

Laskowski cast L'Houillier a disparaging look, but said nothing. *You are finished, old man*, she told herself. "As I was about to say, sir, the three battle groups – Lysander, Ulysses, and Heraklion – will jump into the system simultaneously from three different vectors.

"Lysander, the main battle group of which *Warspite* is the flagship, will engage the Kreelan main body that now orbits the homeworld. Our job will be to pin down the Kreelan fleet, and if possible destroy it en masse. Once that has been accomplished, we will proceed to neutralize the homeworld itself through orbital bombardment and, if and when appropriate, Marine landings."

Borge nodded magnanimously. His ignorance of military strategy and tactics allowed him to be properly impressed.

"Ulysses," she went on, "smaller than Lysander, will execute a similar operation against the moon that has been identified in orbit around the primary target.

"We don't have detailed information on the defenses for either target, but we don't believe at this time that planetary defense will be a major factor in the engagement: our primary threat is the enemy fleet."

This brought a raised eyebrow from Zhukovski to L'Houillier. The latter only shook his head in tiny, hopefully unnoticed movements. Merde, Zhukovski could imagine him saying. To himself, he thought: We know nothing of this system other than the fact of its existence and that many Kreelan warships are already there. And already we have made potentially fatal assumptions about it.

"The third group, Heraklion," Laskowski continued, her voice slowing as she sought to impress the president with the third group's real significance, "is the smallest of the three, but carries the greatest destructive power of all our forces. Should it be necessary and you authorize it, Mr. President, this group will employ thermium weapons against the planets in the system, and the kryolon devices we have brought along can help ensure... a final solution to the Kreelan problem."

"I've heard of the thermium devices," Borge said, intrigued, "but not of the kryolons. What are those?" He had not been briefed on the full array of military hardware prior to the fleet's sailing, but such details he found utterly fascinating.

"Kryolon bombs are proverbial 'ultimate weapon,' *Gospodin Prezident*," Zhukovski rumbled, interrupting Laskowski's monopoly on the man's attention. "They were designed many years ago, to destroy star of enemy system, and thus planets in orbit. They have been in carefully guarded storage for these years, until very recently." He paused. "None ever has been used, even operationally tested, and so true power of weapon is not known." He did not add that he thought with all his heart and soul that those weapons should have been destroyed long ago, rather than fall into the hands of a madman like Borge.

"Really?" Borge asked, his mind already contemplating the ramifications for his reign after he had defeated the Kreelans. *No system would dare oppose me while I have control of such weapons*, he thought. *And, perhaps*, he thought hopefully, *more could be built*. That was an option worth pursuing, but now was not the time.

Turning his attention back to Laskowski, who stood simmering at the head of the table after Zhukovski's interruption, he asked, "And how do you plan to employ these weapons, admiral?"

"Sir," she said, shooting Zhukovski a frigid glare, "we have brought them as an insurance policy. If you do not feel that the issue of the Kreelan problem has been resolved with the use of the fleet in conventional operations or with the thermium devices, the kryolons are a way for you to resolve the situation... utterly and permanently." She was careful to phrase her words in such a way as not to imply the possibility that the fleet could fail. She was sure that her plan would work.

"Very good, admiral," Borge said contemplatively. "Very good. Thank you." Then, looking at each of the faces clustered around the table, he said, "Well, if there is nothing else, ladies and gentlemen...? No? Then this meeting is concluded. Please inform me when we are within thirty minutes of jumping into enemy territory. Thank you all, and carry on."

The attendees stood and filed out, eager to get back to their stations and away from the cloying political atmosphere that shrouded Borge and those closest to him.

As they left, a huge Marine officer entered the room, shouldering aside the departing officers with little regard to their rank or stature. Thorella.

"And what good news do you have for me, general?" Borge asked as the last of the attendees had departed and the doors hissed shut.

"I split up the prisoners as you requested, sir," Thorella said, smiling. "I had Mackenzie transferred to the *Golden Pearl* where we've had Camden locked up." Eustus had not been on the shuttle that brought Reza and the others to *Warspite's* hate-filled landing bay. He was a gift from Borge to Thorella, a political pawn that had been lost through the administrative cracks in the fleet's preparations to attack the Empire. It was a gift that the younger man planned to enjoy immensely. "I'll have to give her credit," he said, shaking his head in wonder, "she certainly took her last flight in class. What a ship! No wonder you took it over for your personal quarters."

Borge chuckled. "Rank hath its privileges, my friend," he said, thinking of what was going to happen to Mackenzie at young Markus's hands. All of the prisoners would be set aside for Thorella's pleasure. He had certainly earned it.

As if reading his mind, Thorella asked, "What about Reza and the two blues?" He wanted them most of all.

"In time, Markus, in time. I shall not deprive you of your rewards. But his public visibility makes him a very valuable political commodity, much more so than Mackenzie or that cretin Camden. So you shall have to have your fun with them until Reza's *raison d'être* is no more."

Thorella nodded. It was what he expected, and it would do. For now. "Is there anything else you want me to work on in the meantime?"

Borge shook his head. "No, my friend. The wheels have been set in motion, and now we must simply wait." He smiled. "I suggest that you retire to our new ship and... enjoy the wait."

His pitch black eyes twinkling, Thorella thanked his master and left.

Behind him, Borge quietly laughed to himself.

* * *

"Are you sure this is the right place?" Enya asked quietly, her eyes darting up and down the corridor to see if they had been followed.

"This is where he said–" Braddock did not get the chance to finish as the stark gray metal door to one of two dozen container storage rooms lining the corridor suddenly hissed open.

"Quickly," a heavily accented voice said from the darkness beyond, a dimly seen hand gesturing for them to come in. "*Voiditye*. Enter."

Exchanging a worried glance, Enya and Braddock did as they had been ordered. The door closed behind them, the lock bars automatically sliding into place to hold the door closed.

"Admiral?" Braddock asked the shadowy figure looming in front of them.

"*Da*," Zhukovski's voice replied. The darkness was suddenly peeled back a meter or so as he turned on a small electric lamp that stood on a hexagonal container squatting between the three of them. Beside it was a device with shifting numbers and tiny waveforms on its display: an anti-surveillance unit. "Forgive choice of place for meeting," the admiral said, gesturing about them at the shadowy stacks of containers and pallets, "but circumstances dictate... radical approach to most basic problems."

"Why are we here, admiral?" Enya asked cautiously. "Surely, this is not some crude joke?"

Zhukovski allowed himself a humorless smile. "I most sincerely wish that it was joke, young lady," he told her, leaning against the container with his good arm, "but things are most serious, and – I fear – out of control. You see, Admiral L'Houillier and I believe that fleet is on course for rendezvous with disaster. Admiral Laskowski, fleet operations officer, has illustrious president's ear, and has convinced him that our fleet can destroy Kreelans." The smile flickered away. "And, for insurance, we have kryolon bombs to finish job."

"Lord of All," Braddock whispered. "I thought those were only a... a myth. I'd heard about them – everyone in the fleet has – but I never thought they were real. My God, I thought the thermium bombs were horrible enough..."

"They are real, young Councilman," Zhukovski said ominously. "All too real."

Enya suddenly interrupted. "What are these things?" she demanded, not sure that she really wanted to know.

Braddock turned to her. Even in this light, she could tell that he was pale, and she began to feel afraid. "They're doomsday weapons, Enya," he told her. "If rumor holds true, any one of those bombs can destroy a star, setting an entire system aflame, destroying every planet in its orbit." He looked at Zhukovski, who nodded.

"But why would anyone build such weapons?" Enya asked, horrified at the magnitude of it.

"Simple," Zhukovski said. "They were designed for time such as this, when only apparent solution to conflict is stellar genocide. And that might not be bad idea if only one weapon existed. But there are over a dozen, exact count even I do not know because of stringent security." He eyed the other two. "Slight overkill even for Kreelan homeworld, *da?*"

Braddock's insides turned to ice. "A dozen of those things controlled by Borge..." He let the thought drift off into the darkness of the abyss it promised.

Enya finished the thought for him. "No planet in the Confederation would be safe, ever again, from the threat of total destruction," she whispered. "Borge would hold absolute power over everyone. And if they have some now, they could build even more."

"There is worse." The old admiral looked at the floor, then at Enya. "Your young Camden is under arrest," he said softly. "He was charged with treason, and is being held in location that I have not yet discovered." He looked into Enya's eyes. "Sentence was by presidential order: he is to be put to death, along with Gard and Mackenzie."

"No," Enya breathed. "No! I don't believe it! Borge cannot get away with such a thing! I'll–"

"He can, *dorogaya*," Zhukovski interrupted gently but forcefully, "and he will, unless he is stopped. Borge's insanity knows no bounds, and all those around him have begun to fear him. That is why we must meet like this, because nowhere else is safe. People fearing for their own welfare will gladly point finger at someone else to escape suspicion. This fear has become fire, fanned by winds of Reza's alleged treason and proclaimed chance by president for victory over Kreelan enemy. And if what I believe is true, Reza and others – including Camden – will not survive coming encounter. Borge will have no more use for them; having won his great victory and returning home like Caesar, they will disappear, no doubt in unfortunate accident."

"And the Council is just as bad," Braddock said. "They're all terrified of him... including myself." He clenched his fists. "But, what can we do?"

"Kill him," Enya said quietly. She had lived her entire life under oppressive human rule, and knew that any cruelty visited upon humanity by the Kreelans had been inflicted a thousand-fold by Mankind upon itself in times past and present. *And future*, she thought bleakly, a vivid image playing in her mind of Erlang's sun exploding, obliterating her home and everything they had lived, suffered, and died for all these years.

"Enya," Braddock said uneasily, "I don't like Borge any more than you do, but he's the legal successor to Nathan, and–"

"I wonder," Zhukovski grumbled. At Braddock's questioning glance, he continued, "I have uncovered... discrepancies... in Borge's past, and in past of others who now are closely associated with him. Questionable things have been – how do you say? – tidied up. And I do not believe that Reza Gard killed Nathan. Assuming assumption is correct," he smiled at that particular turn of phrase, "hypothesis leaves obvious question of who did?"

"Thorella," Braddock murmured to himself, thinking of how he and Borge seemed to work together a bit too closely, and how so much of what the younger man did was concealed in shadows, out of sight. From what he himself had seen, and from what he had heard from Reza and Nicole over the years, the man certainly had what Braddock considered an antisocial personality, to say the least. "Borge had the motive," he went on, thinking aloud. "He never made any secret about his ambition to become president, although he had hardly advocated assassination to get there. He and Nathan had been friends for years."

"Reza and Thorella gave him both the opportunity and the instrument he needed," Enya joined in. "Reza was the perfect scapegoat, the one person no one would believe because he had been raised in the Empire, and it would be easy to label him a turncoat and a traitor. And enough people in key positions knew that if Reza had really wanted to, he could easily have killed Nathan. No security system could stop him."

"But Thorella was the actual killer," Braddock continued. "With Borge's backing, he could have gained access to the security system and somehow reprogrammed the sentinel monitors to show Reza killing Nathan." He shook his head. He knew that what they were thinking was pure speculation, but there did not seem to be any other explanation, and too many of the known facts fit the theory all too well. "Lord of All," he whispered.

"Almost perfect crime," Zhukovski said quietly. "If we allow him to succeed, he will have begun with murder of President Nathan what could be murder of millions of people, whether we win or lose in coming battle."

"Are you planning a coup, admiral?" Braddock asked. In his heart he knew the answer, and from the grim set of Enya's jaw he saw that she had already thrown her lot in with whatever Zhukovski had in mind, but he had to ask the question. For the sake of posterity, if nothing else.

Zhukovski suddenly looked uncomfortable. "Councilman, I have served Confederation for many years," he said slowly, "and always have I served civilian leaders. That is not only tradition and written law; I believe with all my heart that it is best way, best for all people in Confederation. So do many other officers who are not content with present leadership. They are not fools, they can see darkness in future, but they are bound to laws that have kept Confederation and its predecessors free." He looked squarely at Braddock. "There will be no military coup," he said firmly. "But... senior officers in Navy and Marine Corps will support new civilian leader." He paused. "They will support you."

"*Me?*" Braddock almost laughed. "Why me?" he said.

"Because there is no one else they would trust, Tony," Enya told him. "You know that as well as I."

Zhukovski nodded. "You are only survivor of purge that has swept vestiges of previous government away, Councilman. You have done well in your time in office, and fact that you are well-decorated Marine does not hurt either. You hold respect of officers and enlisted alike." He shrugged. "If you will not accept, then we must face destiny with Borge at the helm."

"That doesn't leave me much choice, does it?" Braddock asked quietly.

The old admiral shook his head. "None, councilman," he said. "None, if you wish to save Confederation from tyranny."

"Erlang is with you," Enya said, giving Braddock a reassuring squeeze with her hand. Turning to Zhukovski, she asked, "What must we do?"

Fifty-One

"Ma'am," the Internal Security guard said uneasily, "I can't just let you in there!"

"Then you can explain to President Borge why his instructions were not carried out, sergeant," Nicole said icily. "I'm sure he would be most sympathetic to your concerns." When the man hesitated, she shook her head as if pitying the poor sod, knowing what was in store for him, and turned on her heel to leave.

She had taken all of two steps back toward the main door to the brig when she heard him call from behind her, "Captain, wait!"

She didn't stop.

"Ma'am, wait, please!"

This time, she did turn around. "What is it, sergeant?" She could see a small film of perspiration on the man's forehead, and she could swear that she could feel his fear. But that was impossible, of course. Wasn't it? "You've already wasted enough of my time."

"I've reconsidered your orders, captain," he said nervously. "I mean, there's no need for... That is, if the president himself sent you down, I don't see any reason why there should be anything wrong."

Nicole frowned, but said nothing.

Gesturing toward the mantrap that sealed the brig cell in which Reza and the two Kreelans were being kept from the rest of the brig, the sergeant told her, "Step into the chamber there, and I'll tell you when it's safe to move into the cell. If they give you any trouble, just give a yell and we'll zap the bastards."

"Very well," she said, moving through the narrow doorway and into the gleaming half cylinder that protruded from the wall. The force field grid hissed on behind her, barring the only exit.

"Stand by," the guard said. A moment later, the cylinder began to rotate, and the opening she had come through sealed. For a long moment she was in a completely enclosed tube that she knew was armed with all sorts of devices to disable and – if need be – to kill a potential escapee. It was not a normal accessory on warships, of course; the regular brig was more than enough to handle the average sailor who was sent down here after captain's mast, or even a Kreelan prisoner, had there ever been any before now. No, this was something that had been specially installed in a rush before *Warspite* had sailed for Erlang. Borge had known there would be use for it.

Suddenly, the force field that guarded the cell side of the contraption came into view, and beyond the blue-green electronic haze of the force field stood Reza.

The cylinder stopped rotating around her, having fully unmasked the opposite door. "Okay, captain," the sergeant said through the man trap's intercom, "the grid's going down... now."

The field suddenly dissipated, leaving behind it only a slight scent of ozone. Without hesitation, she stepped across the threshold to the far side, the oddly misshapen reflections she cast on the polished walls of the chamber following her like silent alter egos.

As she stepped into the cell, the force field snapped on again behind her, and she could hear the cylinder rotate again, sealing her in.

"Nicole," Reza said softly, his swirling green eyes both mournful and pleased. He had known she was coming.

"I... I had to see you," she said unnecessarily, wanting to reach out and embrace him. But that would have condemned her in the ever-present eyes of the security cameras, and then she would be of no help to him at all.

"I knew you must come," Reza whispered.

A young but proud voice suddenly asked in the New Tongue, "Who is this animal, Father?"

Reza smiled at his son. "She is my friend of many, many cycles, Shera-Khan," he told him. "Do you understand what *friendship* is?"

The boy nodded. The priestess had taught him what she knew of the concept, what she had learned from Reza as he was growing up; among the Kreela, such relationships did not exist, for they were all bound by their very blood and spirit to the Empress. "I am honored to meet you, friend-of-my-father's," Shera-Khan told Nicole in Standard.

"Thank... thank you," Nicole replied, flabbergasted. She turned to Reza. "This is your son?" she asked incredulously.

"Yes," Reza told her, his own sense of awe undiminished at the miracle that stood in their midst. "His name is Shera-Khan."

"Is she of the Blood, my son?" Tesh-Dar suddenly asked, speaking in the Old Tongue as she lay in her bed, her eyes closed. Her voice was soft, but still carried the power of command that Reza had known since the first time that he had heard her speak.

"She is, my priestess," he admitted. He suspected that Tesh-Dar was greatly disappointed that he had shared the fire that flowed in his veins with another who was totally alien to the Way. "She and I have known each other since before I came to the Way. When I returned to them, I needed someone who could... understand who and what I was. I chose her."

"Bring her to me."

Reza turned to Nicole, who was utterly confused at the rapid exchange, not a word of which she could understand, except something that sounded like "friendship."

"What is wrong?" Nicole asked. "What are you talking about?"

"Do not fear, Nicole," he told her. "There is nothing wrong. The priestess – her name is Tesh-Dar – wishes to... become acquainted with you." He took her hand and guided her past Shera-Khan to the great warrior who lay on the hard bed that protruded from the cell's wall.

The two of them knelt down next to Tesh-Dar, who continued to lie still.

"Is she dying?" Nicole asked.

"Yes," Reza responded sadly. "The warriors – the clawed ones among our race – do not atrophy before death as humans do. Their bodies remain strong until very near the end. But when the time comes to die, everything fails at once, and quickly – usually a matter of days or a week – is it over."

"I am so sorry, Reza," Nicole told him. "I–"

Tesh-Dar's eyes opened, startling Nicole with their intensity, and before she could react both of the warrior's huge hands were cupped gently around Nicole's face. The Kreelan's flesh felt warm, hot, against her skin, and Nicole began to feel faint, as if the blood to her brain had been cut off. She felt herself floating, drifting above a world that she knew she had seen before. Looking down at her arms, she saw that they were sheathed in black armor, and at the ends of her fingertips were silver claws. The flimsy uniform that she was accustomed to wearing was gone.

And in her heart, in her blood, burned the fire of the Bloodsong. She had sensed it before, as a deaf person might sense the vibration of music, but now she felt it as it was meant to be and was overcome by it, became a part of it. Every cell in her body burst into a roaring flame, joining the symphony of infinite harmonies that intoxicated her senses, that overwhelmed her brain.

The tide of the song crested, then slowly began to ebb. At last it began to fade away, and she felt the warmth of the mourning marks spreading down her face, blackening her blue skin like the falling of night over the plains of Wra'akath. She felt around her neck, her fingers touching the collar that she had worn since her youth, an oath of her own honor toward the Empress and Her Children, and of the Empress's love for her.

"Nicole," a voice spoke softly from a distance, from somewhere beyond the horizon and the rising Empress Moon. It was a voice she knew. It was the voice of someone she loved.

"Reza?"

"Come away now, Nicole," he told her in the Old Tongue. He stood beside her now. "Take my hand."

She reached out for him, taking his hand as he had asked. "Do we have to leave, Reza?" she asked, looking over her shoulder, back at the mystical world that had been like home to her in her dreams for so many years.

"Yes, Nicole," he told her gently. "This world belongs to others," he said. "You must return to yours, where you belong."

Sadly, Nicole turned away from the golden light that reflected from the spires of the Great City, and suddenly found herself falling... falling...

"Nicole."

Her eyes flew open and she sucked in her breath in a gasp as if she had been thrown into freezing water. The Homeworld – if that is what it had been – was gone, replaced by surroundings and sensations that should have felt more familiar than they did.

"Rest easy," Reza said, his hand gripping her shoulder gently.

"You have chosen your companions wisely, my son," Tesh-Dar told him as she released Nicole. Her own eyes blazed with the heat of the fire that had burned in her heart her entire life, save the last few agonizing days since the Empress's heart had closed itself away from Her Children. The feeling was at once invigorating and monumentally depressing, for she realized that she might never again feel it before she passed into the unknown darkness where once the Ancient Ones had sung Her glory, but now lay silent as a timeless tomb. "As were you, she, too, is worthy of the Way."

"Captain!" an alien voice suddenly intruded. "Are you all right in there? Do you require assistance?"

"No," Nicole managed, shaking off the last of the vision, or whatever it was. "No, I am fine."

"I think it's time you came out, ma'am," the voice of the ISS sergeant said. His tone told her that her made-up orders and threats were wearing thin. Behind her, the mantrap began to cycle open.

"We shall speak again," Reza told her. "Soon."

Nicole nodded. "*Oui, mon ami.* Soon." Without another word, she stepped into the cylinder, her eyes fixed on Reza as the force field snapped on and the door swiftly closed.

Fifty-Two

Eustus regained consciousness face down, his cheek pressing numbly into what had once been a priceless original Persian rug that was now soaked and stained with blood from the half dozen cuts in his face.

"Camden," he heard someone saying urgently, "can you hear me?"

He tried to say "Yes," but it came out through his battered lips and swollen jaw like "Memph." He tasted blood and spat out the glassy remains of what had once been an upper incisor.

He felt himself being rolled over, and he groaned involuntarily from the pain. Mostly bruises, he thought automatically, his mind long accustomed to categorizing the type of pain his body felt. No spearing pain or grating bones; nothing was broken. But the pain of the bruises and contusions were enough to bring tears to his swollen eyes.

"Jesus, Eustus, you look like hell." Forcing his swollen eyes just a little wider while trying to blink away the tears, Eustus could barely make out the dark-faced form hovering above him.

"Commander... Mackenzie?" The face nodded. "Where are we?"

"We're aboard the *Golden Pearl*," she said as she tore a strip of her undershirt off and began to blot away some of the blood from Eustus's face. "It's the ship that Reza and I took from Earth. But that's a story for another time. What the devil happened to you, Marine? Who did this to you?"

"Don't know for sure," he slurred. "Looked like ISS types, but that couldn't be."

Jodi looked at him strangely. "Yes, I'm afraid it could, Eustus," she told him. "You were arrested, I take it. Do you have any idea why?"

"They wanted me to kill Reza," he told her.

"Who? Who did?"

"Don't know." He winced as she accidentally blotted over a particularly nasty gash, where one of his assailants had landed a blow with a set of brass knuckles. "The commodore ordered me to do it, but I don't know where exactly the orders came from. All I know is that she didn't seem to care for them any more than I did." He had known that Marchand was putting on an act. She was too good an officer to have done otherwise.

"I guess you refused, didn't you?" she asked.

He nodded, feeling his neck muscles spasm with the effort. "Yeah, I gave them the 'hell no' routine, and found myself charged with treason for refusing to commit murder. Imagine that." He shook his head, careful not to interrupt the rhythm of the blacksmith's hammer banging in his skull. "After you and Reza were taken off a while ago," he went on as Jodi slowly helped him into a sitting position, "they brought me here and half a dozen goons in ISS uniforms paralyzed me and then took turns remapping my face."

Jodi smiled. "It's a definite improvement, Camden."

Eustus managed a weak smile. "Thanks loads, commander." He suddenly turned serious. "Commander, I'm not one normally prone to foul language, but just what the fuck is going on?"

"Maybe I can fill you in," came a voice from the doorway. Silhouetted was a huge man in a Marine uniform, with four other, darker, forms behind him.

"Thorella," Eustus hissed.

"That's General Thorella to you, Marine," he shot back icily as he and four ISS guards entered the room, sealing the door behind them. Just before it closed, Eustus glimpsed two more figures outside. "It seems you still have a lot to learn about basic military etiquette."

"That's a pretty big word for a Neanderthal like you, general," Jodi said. She came to her feet, standing between Thorella and his men, and Eustus, who was still unable to stand. "Or should I call you by your real name... Anton Borge?"

Thorella laughed. "Don't be an idiot, commander," he told her casually as he took another step closer. "Anton Borge died a long, long time ago, the victim of a tragic accident." The smile. "As you know, of course."

Jodi felt chilled under his black, lifeless stare. Except that it wasn't lifeless. Not this time. There was a ripple, a crawling twinkle, like light reflecting from oozing crude oil, or a parasite boring its way just below dark and dank soil, that she saw there now. "You'll never get away with what you've done, Anton," she told him, standing her ground. "You're going to hang."

"I don't think so," he said quietly, eerily, as he stepped closer. "And you should not be so concerned with the past as with the present... and the immediate future."

"You bastard," Eustus growled. He recognized the men with Thorella as the ones who had beaten him. "You're behind all this, aren't you?"

"I see you need another lesson," Thorella said pleasantly. Before either Jodi or Eustus could react, Thorella landed a sharp kick with his rough-soled boots on the left side of Eustus's head, sending him sprawling across the floor.

"Jesus!" Jodi exclaimed. "Thorella, for the love of God–"

"You still don't understand what's happening, do you?" Thorella said, turning his attention from Eustus and back to her. "This isn't some petty boot camp game, Mackenzie. This is life and death, and I get to play God."

The dark form that she had seen wriggling in his eyes had transformed itself from a burrowing maggot to a glistening hydra, filled with hate and lust.

"You're insane," she said, her voice faltering as she took a step back, away from him. "Bug-fuck crazy."

"Funny you should mention that word," Thorella said, his smile gleaming dully. "*Fuck*, I mean. I've heard that you've never had a man. Well, my dear, this is your lucky day. You're going to have a bunch of men, all at once." He nodded his head at the four men with him who now seemed a lot closer than they had been only a moment before, and they all wore the kind of smile that the lowlifes she had encountered saved only for particularly attractive women.

"No!" Eustus shouted from behind them, weakly propelling himself at the knot of men that was closing around Jodi.

"Hold him," Thorella said contemptuously as two of the ISS men easily deflected Eustus's attack and pinned his arms painfully behind his back. "Make him watch. You never know, Camden," he said congenially, "you might learn something." He turned back to Jodi. "Now, bitch, you can have this easy, or–"

Jodi chose that moment to strike, aiming a kick at Thorella's left knee, her bellow of fury mixed with stark fear filling the room.

Thorella dodged it without noticeable effort. While Jodi was good, having learned her skills the hard way, in combat, Thorella had had years of close combat training and field experience, and was one of the most physically fit human beings in existence.

"–or the hard way," he concluded. A huge fist arced out like a steel piston, striking her right collarbone, which snapped with a nauseating crunch.

Jodi screamed, her left hand reflexively reaching for the source of the electrifying pain that flashed through her body. Thorella casually reached out and grabbed her hand, spun her around, then brutally yanked it up and backward, forcing her hand almost to her neck and nearly dislocating her shoulder. Slamming her face-first into the wall, he took a handful of her hair in his other hand and began to rhythmically smash her face against the unyielding plastisteel, leaving smears of blood from her torn lips and battered nose on the antique white finish.

As she began to slide down the wall, battered senseless, her legs losing their strength, he took the opportunity to land a fist over each kidney, smiling to himself as he heard the satisfying snapping of some of her ribs.

"Stop it!" Eustus was screaming. "Stop it! You're killing her!"

He let go of Jodi, who slid to the floor in a groaning heap, and turned to Eustus. "That's the idea," he said happily before landing a fist in Eustus's solar plexus. Eustus collapsed in a gasping heap.

"Oh, look at that," he said, mocking Jodi as she tried to crawl away from him. "What's wrong, commander? Did I upset you? Here, let me help you." He reached out and took another handful of Jodi's hair, yanking her to her feet. "How do you feel, commander?"

"Fuck... you... asshole," she sputtered, blood trickling down her chin.

"A woman with spirit, gentlemen," he said to the others, who nodded approvingly. "But I'm afraid, my dear, that it's you who are going to get fucked in the asshole." With an easy movement, he slammed Jodi up against a polished oak table.

"No," she whispered. "Please, don't..."

"What's the matter, Mackenzie?" he cooed as he removed his illegal Kreelan knife from an ankle sheath. "You want this, I know you do. A good fucking from a man will do wonders for a dyke bitch like you." He inserted the knife blade at the back of her pants and started to cut. The sharp edge whispered down the cleft of her buttocks, parting the heavy material of her uniform and underwear like they were paper. When the blade reached the inseam, he stopped. Jodi felt the cold steel disappear.

"Goddamn you, Thorella," she whispered, tears welling in her eyes as her body quivered with helpless rage and fear. "God damn you to hell."

Thorella said nothing. Instead, he pulled her back a ways from the table and reinserted the blade, this time in the front of her pants, the blade cutting toward her crotch. He was leaning heavily against her now, and she could feel his throbbing erection against her exposed buttocks.

"Help, me, Father," she whispered to herself. "Please." She tried to struggle away, but Thorella was too strong. "Please..."

The blade left a thin trace of blood as it just barely cut the skin on its way down her quivering belly to her pubic mound, and then down, down. With a tiny hiss, the material parted. Thorella roughly pulled the halves of her pants down each leg with his knife hand while his other held her head pinned to the table.

"Thorella," Eustus rasped, "please don't do this. I'll do anything you want..."

"You'll do anything that I want anyway, Camden," Thorella said harshly, his breathing now labored. "And after I fuck her, I might just do the same to you."

Too rushed by his raging lust to use the knife, Thorella dropped it to the floor and used his bare hands to rip open the back of Jodi's blouse and its built in bra. He tore away the fabric, ripping it from her body to let it fall to the floor like trash. His free hand groped for her breasts, squeezing them hard, bruising the tender flesh, pinching the nipples until they bled.

Jodi bit her tongue to keep from crying out. She tasted a fresh surge of copper as blood flooded her mouth. *Think of something*, she ordered herself desperately. *Do something...*

But there was nothing to be done. She felt Thorella's hand working at his pants, freeing the pulsating serpent within. She grunted in agony as he forced himself into her with a brutal thrust, crushing her thighs against the table's edge.

The last thing she heard was Eustus, screaming for Thorella to stop, his voice oddly muffled by Thorella's frenzied panting.

But then her mind shut down, locking itself away in a tiny place where light and love ruled over the darkness of men's hearts, and the world was still kind.

FIFTY-THREE

From the end of the flag bridge where the main view screen was located, Borge began his speech to the ships that had reached their final rendezvous point before making the hyperspace jump that would take them to the Kreelan homeworld.

"Men and women of the Fleet," he began, his face beaming with what was both genuine sincerity and a maniacal belief in his vision of his own empire-to-be, "this day shall be one not long forgotten in the history of the Confederation. For a century have we found ourselves locked in mortal combat with an alien enemy, an enemy who attacked us for no reason, and who attempted to exterminate our people, an attempt that has been in vain. We have paid our way in blood to the threshold where we now stand, and it is time now to make the enemy pay in kind a thousand-fold." He turned to L'Houillier. "Admiral, you may give the word."

L'Houillier did not hesitate. "Prepare to jump," he ordered. He exchanged a glance with Zhukovski, who stood unobtrusively near one of the bridge's three exits.

A moment later, Zhukovski quietly disappeared.

Amid the cheering throughout the three thousand ships of the great fleet, klaxons blared to announce the imminent jump into hyperspace. The pilots of the hundreds of fighters and attack craft that had been launched at this last rendezvous point snuggled up close to their mother ships, trying to make sure they were captured in the surrounding hyperdrive field and not left behind when the bigger ships jumped. It was a terribly dangerous maneuver, but Laskowski's plan had called for it, and the president had ordered it done.

L'Houillier turned to Laskowski. "Admiral, execute the jump," he ordered.

"Aye, aye, sir," she said sharply, turning to the battery of fleet controllers who were clustered around a myriad of consoles in a darkened alcove at the rear of the flag bridge. "Execute!" she snapped.

A moment later, under control of the *Warspite's* straining navigational computers, thousands of human warships disappeared from their dark and lonely rendezvous point, leaving behind nothing but ripples in the fabric of empty space.

* * *

The jump was a short one, Reza noted silently. He felt the first tremor in his flesh that had always announced to him that they had bridged the gap between normal space and what was beyond, followed a few short minutes later by the second tremor indicating their return to normal space.

"We have arrived," he told Tesh-Dar and Shera-Khan. "We are home. It will soon be time for us to depart this place."

"The animals will not allow us to leave, my son," Tesh-Dar noted. For some reason she could not explain, her health had markedly improved since her joining with Reza's human friend. Perhaps it was the breath of purity that flowed from the woman's vision, a legacy that Reza had left her when his blood had mingled with hers; perhaps it was only the final gasp of her body as it sought to stave off Death for but a while longer. *No matter*, she counseled herself. *I shall do all in my power to return Reza to Her, and to see that I die with honor, in battle.* "We shall have to fight them. The oath you swore to not spill the blood of your birth must be broken by deed as much as word."

"And so shall it be," Reza answered. "My honor do I forfeit for Her sake." He looked away. "No sacrifice may be too great."

He felt Tesh-Dar's hand on his arm. "Your honor is your love for Her, Reza," she told him gently. "Your debt to your forebears have you paid, ever since the very first day that you returned to them from the Empire."

"I am with you, Father," Shera-Khan told him quietly, but with a solemnity in his voice that Reza would always remember. His son would be a great warrior someday. If only he survived.

"You honor your mother well, my son," he said.

The lights suddenly dimmed, and the entire hull reverberated with artificial thunder.

"The battle is joined," Reza said, coming to his feet. "Soon, now. We must be prepared."

* * *

"*Merde*, admiral," L'Houillier shouted, "I ordered you to disperse the fleet! We are packed in here like sardines!"

"But–"

"Another word and you are relieved," he snarled. "You can go and have your beloved president relieve me of duty, but until then you are under my command and by God you will follow my orders!"

Such an exchange normally might have wrought complete, dumbfounded silence on the flag bridge. But even the curses of the Grand Admiral were lost in the frantic hubbub of the flag and ship's bridge staffs as they sought to make order out of the chaos that had erupted when the Armada dropped back into normal space after the last jump.

In the background was the main flag bridge viewscreen, and what it showed no human eyes had ever before witnessed, nor would they again. An assemblage of Confederation warships that swarmed through the skies of the alien homeworld, clashing with an equal, if not superior, armada that bore the runes of the enemy that Humanity had been fighting for nearly a century. Dozens of ships, most of them Kreelan, had already died, their death throes marked by flaring explosions that left nothing behind but slagged hulks and clouds of iridescent gas. Tens of thousands of energy bolts, crimson and green, joined hundreds of ships in the blink of an eye, bringing death to some, victory to others. And amid the great warships darted clouds of fighters.

But the human ships were at a great tactical disadvantage. In the initial deployment formation that Laskowski had chosen, the conical groups of human ships could only bring their forward batteries to bear, while many of the Kreelan ships, disorganized as they were, could bring their entire broadsides into action against the invaders. On the oceans of ancient Earth, this had been known as "crossing the T." It was a disastrous disadvantage that L'Houillier was desperately trying to redress.

"Aye, aye, sir," Laskowski responded woodenly, for the first time sensing that all might not go as she had planned. Without another word from L'Houillier, she turned to the operations section and began barking out the Grand Admiral's orders, feeling not so much resentment as a growing sense of fear as they fought to reorganize the fleet.

Slowly, ever so slowly, the three huge task forces began to change their shape, from the roughly conical formations in which they had arrived to a series of great staggered wedges, their courses altered to bring as many batteries to bear on the enemy as possible.

L'Houillier watched the tactical display with his fists knotted at his sides. He had agreed to Zhukovski's plan, but he was determined to fight his fleet as long as there was some possibility of victory. Even the crippling of the Kreelan fleet would suffice, if it were not at the cost of his own.

On the great screen, the number of engagements doubled, then trebled. The Kreelans were fighting back, but weakly. L'Houillier allowed himself a faint ray of hope. There was every chance that his fleet would inflict far more damage on the enemy than they themselves would sustain.

Perhaps, he thought, we might even win.

* * *

Zhukovski was beginning to feel the chill of panic rising in his throat. The corridor that ran through the outer hull and separated two banks of massive storage rooms was empty. *Where the devil was Braddock?* he wondered. "You can think of nowhere he might be found?" he asked Enya again.

"No, admiral," she said, equally worried. "He said he would meet us here, as agreed. He only wanted to speak with Nicole, to wish her luck on her mission, before he met with us."

Zhukovski's head whipped around. "Mission?" he snapped. "What mission? Carré was not to fly. Personal orders of Grand Admiral himself after she ferried a fighter aboard. *Chyort voz'mi*," he cursed. "Come! We check her cabin."

"But that's all the way across the ship!"

"You have better idea?" he asked over his shoulder. "Come! We waste precious time."

Unable to think of any alternative, Enya rushed after him. Her footsteps were lost in the cascade of godlike hammer blows that was *Warspite's* batteries engaging the enemy.

* * *

"Sarge," one of the guards whispered, "look."

Sergeant Ricardo Estefan, ISS, looked up to see Nicole Carré step through the blast doors and into the brig. She brought with her a large flight bag, obviously full, and she was wearing a strange expression.

Standing up, he said, "I'm sorry, ma'am, but the president ordered that no one – especially you – be allowed to see the pris–"

His sentence was interrupted by the bark of the blaster that suddenly appeared in Nicole's free hand. Set on stun, it was still powerful enough to send the one hundred-kilo sergeant reeling against the wall, unconscious.

The four others on the guard detail were already reaching for their weapons, but Nicole was faster, much faster. In the blink of an eye, all four had been blasted to the floor, unconscious.

Working quickly, Nicole shut down the monitoring devices and entered the security override code she had coaxed from an ISS officer who had wanted a physical reward for the information. She had not disappointed him, although it had not been what he had been expecting. He still lay unconscious and bleeding in his cabin.

With a hum, the mantrap began to cycle open. The force field within had been shut down completely.

Shera-Khan and Tesh-Dar emerged from the opening, Nicole wondering how the two had squeezed themselves into the tiny chamber.

"Sergeant Estefan," a belligerent voice suddenly spat from the control panel. "I'm not getting a reading from your monitors, and I show that the mantrap's been opened. What's going on?"

"Where is Reza?" she asked Shera-Khan urgently, as she took an electronic key from one of the unconscious guards and removed their explosive collars. The door to the mantrap slowly began to cycle back into the cell. *Too slow, too slow!* she thought frantically. She could see in her mind the two Kreelan warriors and herself exposed and vulnerable out here, with Reza trapped in the revolving cylinder as a dozen ISS guards burst in, shooting.

"He remains within," the boy replied.

Nicole saw that Tesh-Dar seemed to have regained something close to what must be her awesome natural strength, as she moved immediately toward the door to the corridor to watch for intruders, her muscles rippling beneath the leatherite armor. Without a word, she jammed a sliver of metal she had taken from somewhere in her armor into the door slot. It would not be closing on them unless they wanted it to.

"Estefan!" the voice shouted. "Respond!"

"Come on, come on!" Nicole urged the maddeningly slow cylinder. She could just see the edge of the opening when the mantrap suddenly stopped turning.

"Security alert, Brig Four!" the voice bleated over the ship's intercom. "ISS detachments to the brig, on the double! Intruder alert! Intruder alert!"

"*Merde!*" Nicole hissed. She tried the code again, but the controls had been overridden, probably somewhere in engineering, and she did not know enough about the systems to try a manual override. Behind her, the motors driving the door to the brig whined in futility against the metal Tesh-Dar had wedged in the doorway, trying to prevent their escape. "He is trapped! We have to–"

Her jaw went slack as she watched Reza walk through the ten centimeter-thick chromalloy of the mantrap, his body passing through the metal as if it were not there at all. The explosive collar was already gone from around his neck. She had no idea how he could have removed the otherwise foolproof device.

Before she could say anything, Reza said something to Shera-Khan, who immediately rushed to Tesh-Dar's side, a shrekka clutched in his claws.

"We must go," Reza told Nicole, taking her by the arm.

"Reza... wait," she managed, gesturing toward the flight bag. In a way, what she had seen did not surprise her; she knew from her dreams that – in his world, anyway – such miracles were possible. But here, now...

Without waiting for her to explain, Reza opened the flight bag. He knew instinctively that she would not have brought it without good reason, and sensed her confusion at what she had just witnessed. But explanations would have to wait. For all the infinite age of the Universe, they were running out of time.

Inside he saw the deep black of his Kreelan armor and, beneath that, the glittering of his weapons. His sword.

"In Her name," he whispered. Looking up, he said, "Thank you, Nicole."

"You are... welcome, *mon ami*," she said as he hastily stripped out of his uniform and donned what long ago had been his second skin. He had made crude adjustments to it over the years, and while it did not fit as it should, as the clawless ones would have made it, it was still comfortable. It felt right.

In less time than Nicole could believe, Reza was ready. With but a proud glance at her adopted son, Tesh-Dar moved quickly into the corridor, one of the guards' weapons clutched in her huge hand, her own weapons locked away in a security vault somewhere else in the ship.

When she signaled it was clear, Reza asked Nicole, "Where are we to go?"

"The only place we can get transportation off the ship," Nicole said, leading Reza into the corridor, her own weapon held before her. "Hangar deck."

* * *

After ringing at Nicole's cabin and receiving no answer, Zhukovski opened the door with his command override.

The door slid open to reveal Tony Braddock sprawled in Nicole's bunk.

"Tony!" Enya gasped as the two of them rushed into the room, the admiral closing the door behind him after casting a wary eye about the corridor to make sure no one had noticed them.

To be discovered now would be disaster, he muttered to himself. Around them, *Warspite* shuddered and boomed as the battle raged. *Good luck, my friend,* he silently wished L'Houillier.

"What happened?" Enya demanded as she shook Braddock back to consciousness.

"Nicole..." he rasped, "stunned me."

"Why, councilman?" Zhukovski demanded. "Why would she do this? What does she plan to do?"

"Reza," Enya knew the answer instantly. "She's gone to free him, hasn't she?"

Braddock nodded stiffly. He felt like someone was pricking him with a million needles. The feeling was not exactly painful, but it was hardly pleasant, either. "That must be it," he managed, shaking his head to clear it. His vision gradually began to clear. He took a breath of air through his nose, trying to clean out the sharp smell of ozone that was a peculiar side effect of being stunned.

"We must stop her," Zhukovski said. "They will know–"

"Security alert, Brig Four!" the ship's intercom announced. "ISS detachments to the brig, on the double! Intruder alert! Intruder alert!"

"That tears it," Braddock said, getting to his feet. He went over to a cabinet boasting a cipher lock, punched in some numbers, and opened it.

"What are you doing?" Enya asked.

Braddock withdrew two blasters. "Jodi was always paranoid that Nicole should have something to protect herself with," he told them. "She gave these to her on her birthday a few years ago, and Nicole promised Jodi she would keep them with her." He shook his head. "Nutcases, both of them. Thank God."

After checking to make sure the weapons were loaded and carried a full charge, he handed one to Enya, keeping the other for himself. Zhukovski wore his own sidearm.

Zhukovski opened the door, leading the other two out into the corridor. "Where do you think she will go?" he asked Braddock.

"Where else would a pilot go?" he replied. "Hangar deck."

* * *

Nicole had led Reza and the others through a maze of passageways and service tunnels to avoid being spotted by the alerted security teams and the damage repair crewmen whose duties required them to move through the ship while at battle stations. They were only a few yards from the last set of blast doors separating them from the hangar deck when *Warspite* shuddered and her metal body screamed in agony. The four of them were hurled against the bulkhead as the battleship recoiled under a direct hit, the already dim corridor lights flickering, dying.

Even as the echoes of the hit died away, Nicole could hear the sound of thunder beyond the blast door. The red tell-tales on the control panel told her all she needed to know.

"Hangar deck has been hit! It's venting air to space!" she shouted above the howling of hangar deck's air supply whirling away into vacuum on the other side of the bulkhead, just as the dim red emergency lights flickered on.

"Behind us!" Shera-Khan warned as several dim shapes appeared from the crimson murk of the corridor.

In the blink of an eye, a shrekka appeared in Tesh-Dar's hand, its lethal blades already tearing into their target in the elder warrior's mind. The muscles of her arm tensed in a pattern no less precise, yet infinitely more elegant, than any machine could have calculated.

Evgeni Zhukovski would have died had Reza not been an arrow's breath faster than his priestess.

"He is a friend," he told her as his hand gently touched her arm. He did not have to grab her or restrain her. She reacted instantly. Her arm relaxed. Slightly.

"Tony!" Nicole exclaimed, her face a mask of anguish as her husband embraced her. It had nearly killed her to stun him, but there was no way she could have explained what she had to do, and she did not want him to be associated with her crime. Then she noticed Zhukovski. "Admiral! What are you doing–"

"We have no time for unnecessary words, commander," he cut her off. Nodding to Reza, then to the two Kreelans, he said, "After forty years in Navy was I ready to commit mutiny, commander. This day even that has gone awry. Now we are all fugitives, with no way to escape." He gestured to the blast doors.

Warspite took another hit, worse this time. They found themselves curled up on the floor against the starboard bulkhead, a cloud of dust in the air from the shock.

Zhukovski noted with alarm that *Warspite's* return fire was starting to lose its cadence, becoming more random, sporadic. Fire control was breaking down. "Flagship is hurt," he told them. "Badly, I think."

Reza felt a minute fluctuation in the artificial gravity. It was a very, very bad sign. "Engineering has sustained damage," he told them. "Our warships" – Kreelan warships – "must be concentrating on *Warspite*. We must get away, and soon." He turned to Nicole. "What is left on this ship that could get to the moon orbiting the Homeworld?"

"The captain's gig, but that is all the way forward."

"Then that is where we must go."

"But Reza," Nicole said, "we will have to go through the main corridors! There will be no way to avoid the security patrols."

He glanced at Tesh-Dar, then turned to Nicole, his face a grim, alien mask. "They shall not stop us."

"There may be another way," Zhukovski growled. He stood at the wall, scrutinizing a miniature data display he held in his hand. Reza could see the trace of a smile, well hidden in the older man's beard, shining in the crimson light of the battle lanterns. He looked like Satan himself. "Borge has sent for *Golden Pearl*, as I thought he would," he told them. "He is abandoning ship."

"If we could get to it first..." Enya mused. The thought sent a chill up her spine. They were actually trying to make their way to the enemy's capital. But to do... what?

She shook her head. Whatever it was they were about to attempt, it was the only thing left that they could do.

"They are going to attempt docking at main gangway airlock," Zhukovski repeated from the interface. "We have less than eight minutes to get there."

"Let's move it, then," Braddock said gruffly.

Had Jodi been there, she would have recognized the voice of the hard-bitten gunnery sergeant who had looked after her on a backwater world, seemingly so long ago.

* * *

The battle was not going well, President Borge lamented angrily. He was furious at the failure of Grand Admiral L'Houillier and *Warspite's* captain to keep the ship – and himself – safe from peril while annihilating the enemy. He would have had them both shot, but the second Kreelan salvo to penetrate *Warspite's* failing shields had speared through the hull and destroyed the bridge. It was only a stroke of divine intervention that Borge had been in his private quarters, watching the battle develop with the Confederation's chief leaders: his own subordinates.

"I'm sorry, Mr. President," Laskowski reported over the comm unit that Borge held in his hand. "The reports are true. Ships throughout the fleet are picking up gravity spikes: more Kreelan ships are inbound." Her face was blackened and bloodstained. She happened to have been on her way back from the intel section to the flag bridge when the latter was blasted into wreckage. Had she passed through one more blast door on her short journey, she would have been dead. Like L'Houillier and the others. This was the worst moment in her life, the most difficult thing she had ever done. "I suggest we withdraw, sir. Immediately."

Borge's face flushed red on its way to purple. "We will do no such thing, admiral!" he snapped viciously. "We are winning! Your own estimates," he shook a handful of flimsies at the comm unit, "say so! We will return to Confederation space victorious or not at all," he went on softly against the background of firing and periodic hits absorbed by *Warspite's* thousands of tons of armor. "And if you or anyone else suggests such a traitorous idea again, I will have you shot. Do you understand, admiral?"

Laskowski choked back her fear. The honeymoon, it seemed, was over. "Yes, sir," she replied carefully. "In that case, I request permission to transfer my flag to *Southampton*. Sir. *Warspite* will be untenable soon, and the flag bridge is gone."

Borge grunted. Furious as he was, he could hardly deny that request as he made his own way to another vessel to carry on his crusade, forging humanity's future upon the ruins of the Empire. "Very well, admiral. Carry on." With that, he snapped off the comm link. "Bloody incompetents," he cursed to his aide, absently handing her the comm unit.

"Don't be concerned, sir," the woman said soothingly as she retrieved the device and stowed it carefully in the black case that also contained the control codes for the kryolon weapons that were stowed aboard another ship. Curiously, no one knew – except for the president himself – which ship that was. "We knew there would be some losses on our side. This is simply a minor inconvenience."

The two of them followed a squad of ISS guards, and behind them was a trail of senators and council members – his trusted lieutenants – that made up the bulk of the Confederation's government, corrupt though it now was.

"It is sloppy work, Elena," Borge said as they followed the guards around yet another bend in the long march to the gangway, "and there is no excuse for sloppiness. Not in my–"

"Look out!" someone shouted as a hail of crimson bolts came blasting down the corridor, followed by several shadowy blurs that Borge did not realize were Kreelan shrekkas.

Without hesitation, he pushed his aid and latest lover into the line of fire, her body absorbing three energy bolts that would otherwise have found him. Rolling to the floor with the agility of one well accomplished at escaping from tight situations, he snatched the black case from her still-twitching hand and began to crawl through the sudden panic that now filled the corridor, heading for the airlock.

More and more weapons fired as two more squads of ISS guards who had pushed their way through the mewling politicians joined the fray. The deck filled with smoke and the smell of charred flesh and freshly spilled blood, the muzzle flashes surreal in the dim red glare of the emergency lighting.

"Where's the president?" Borge could hear someone screaming hysterically. "Where's the pres–" The voice was cut off in the crackle of a blaster firing from somewhere down the corridor that ran perpendicular to the main gangway.

On the floor, like a man caught in a burning building, Borge could see clearly, unhindered by the cloying smoke of burning flesh, cloth, and plastic that now blinded anyone standing upright. Smoke from the *Warspite's* mortal wounds now filled the decks of the dying ship. The flashing red and yellow coaming lights around the main gangway airlock drew him like a moth to a flame, and he smiled grimly as he low-crawled his way toward it, dragging the all-important case along with him. He had no idea who had started the shooting, perhaps some disgruntled crewman who was jealous that they could leave this doomed hulk while he could not, but it did not matter: Borge would make it. He would reach the airlock where the *Golden Pearl* was even now docking. He would survive.

But Borge was not a patient man. As the airlock loomed closer, he rose from his crawl and into a crouch, using his legs to propel him faster than could his knees and elbows crabbing along the floor.

Again *Warspite* rocked from a hit, sending Borge sprawling to the deck, the precious case falling from his grip to bang and slide a few meters back the way he had come as the thunder of the great ship's armor being penetrated crashed through her hull.

"Dammit!" he cursed as he regained his bearings in the smoke-clogged gangway, his right knee ringing with pain from where it had smashed against the bulkhead when he fell. He started back for the case, lost in the haze–

–and stumbled over something. Looking down, he saw the body of a child at his feet. A Kreelan child.

His blood suddenly ran cold. *Reza's son*, a tiny voice in his mind informed him, quite unnecessarily. And where his son was, Reza was no doubt close by. Borge reacted quickly, doing what any politician of his caliber would have done. Seizing the dazed child by the hair with one hand, he drew his personal blaster with the other, pressing the muzzle against the boy's head. Then Borge put his back up against the wall to prevent any surprises from behind.

It was only then that he noticed the unnatural stillness in the corridor. The fighting had stopped. Only the subaudible thrum of the ship's engines and a periodic salvo of her guns now and then broke the silence.

"Gard!" he shouted into the swirling smoke. "I've got your boy, half-breed! Do you hear me?"

"I hear you." Reza's cool voice came from somewhere in the choking smoke roiling through the corridor. "Which is surprising, to hear the voice of a dead man."

Borge's brittle laugh cut through the air. "If I'm dead, so is your boy, Reza. Don't believe I won't kill him if you make me."

"Just like you killed Markus Thorella?" Zhukovski's voice accused from the fog. "Only this time, there will be no body to substitute, no fortune to collect for personal benefit."

"But there is a fortune, you short-sighted fool, a fortune in victory, a fortune in power that you could not possibly comprehend." Borge began to back cautiously toward the airlock, dragging Shera-Khan with him. Not quite so dazed now, the boy began to struggle, and Borge did not want to harm his insurance too soon. "Make him stop trying to break free, Reza, or I'll kill him right now," he warned.

A few words spoken in Kreelan from the darkness seemed to calm the boy. Perhaps too much.

"That's better," Borge said. "Now, there's a case sitting in the corridor somewhere near you. I want it. Now."

"What is in it?" Reza asked quietly. Borge could swear that his nemesis was speaking right into his ear, but there was no one to be seen.

"None of your business," Borge snapped. "Just hand it over."

The case suddenly skittered along the floor, coming to rest at Borge's feet. "Pick it up," he told Shera-Khan.

The boy did not move.

"Pick it up, damn you," Borge hissed as he pushed the muzzle harder against Shera-Khan's temple.

As Shera-Khan leaned down to do as he had been told, a hollow thump, followed by the airlock coaming flashing green, announced the arrival of the *Golden Pearl*.

"I'm going to see your planet burn, Reza," Borge shouted into the smoke, although his eyes were still riveted to the inboard airlock hatch and the telltales on the control panel. The outer lock was cycling open. Only a minute left before he was free from this floating coffin. "If you manage to make it to a lifeboat, you might have a chance to see it for your–"

Shera-Khan bolted from his grasp, slashing at his arms with his claws as he leaped into the smoke-shrouded darkness.

"Little bastard!" Borge cursed, raising his weapon to shoot the boy in the back.

As his finger convulsed on the trigger, a huge shadow suddenly materialized from the mist between the gun and the retreating boy. The blaster's energy bolt caught Tesh-Dar squarely in the middle of the chest, flaring her armor white with heat as it penetrated to the aged and dying flesh beneath.

But Borge was not to receive a second chance. One shot was all he would get. As if taking candy from a comatose child, Tesh-Dar slashed out with one hand, her claws severing Borge's arm at the wrist.

Borge opened his mouth to scream, not in pain, for he felt none yet, but in fear. He saw Tesh-Dar as the incarnate devil of his nightmares, the bogeyman come to horrid life. Her mouth opened to reveal fangs that could rip his throat open, but that was not Tesh-Dar's way. She did not care for the foul taste of human blood. Instead, she plunged the talons of her other hand into his ribcage. As she lifted him from the floor, his jaw hanging open in a scream of terrified agony, she let out her own roar of anguish and pain, and righteous vengeance upon an evil that fed upon its own kind. Slowly did her fingers close, drawing her talons together around his furiously pumping heart. He clawed at her hand, his throat now making hollow gagging sounds as his lungs filled with blood and collapsed. With one final, titanic heave, Tesh-Dar tore his heart, still beating, from his chest. She threw her head back and roared in triumph, crushing the disembodied organ in her Herculean grip.

And then, like a great stone pillar with a tiny but mortal flaw, she collapsed to the floor, her bloodied hands covering the still-smoking hole in her own chest.

Reza was there to catch her, and he gently, lovingly, lay her down to rest. "My priestess," he said softly. "My mother–"

She signed him to silence before putting a hand against his face. He held it in one of his own to ease the trembling he felt in hers. "My son," she said softly, "the Race is in your hands, now; our salvation is in your love for Her. Go to Her now... quickly. You must save Her... or we all shall face eternity... in darkness." A tiny tremor ran through her, and her hand clamped painfully around his. "May thy Way be long and glorious... my beloved son."

The strength passed from her hand as her eyes closed, her spirit fleeing her body for what should have been paradise, but without the Empress's light could only be a cold and terrifyingly lonely Hell. A Hell he had seen for himself.

"Reza," Enya whispered behind him, "why... why did she do this? Why didn't you stop her? You could have killed Borge without... without this."

Reza gently unclasped the band and its honors from around Tesh-Dar's neck. Now that her life had passed from her body, the ancient living metal clasp surrendered to his trembling fingers. "She did it because it was her Way," he told her softly.

"I do not mean to intrude on emotional discussion," Zhukovski interjected, "but time becomes short. Security will be here any mom–"

The airlock at the end of the gangway suddenly cycled open to reveal four ISS guards in battle dress.

"Where's the pres–" one of them began before seeing Borge's mangled body and the three humanoids in Kreelan armor.

The ISS sergeant's observation of the gory scene was cut short long before he or his men could raise their weapons. His eyes had just shifted from Borge's body to Reza when Shera-Khan's shrekka sheared his head cleanly from his torso. The head toppled to the deck like a bowling ball, the armored helmet clattering to a stop near one of the other guards' feet. The now headless torso spasmed as if in surprise, and a fountain of blood from the severed carotid artery sprayed the lock's ceiling before the corpse toppled backward into the airlock.

Nicole shot two of the others, while Braddock finished off the last.

"Let's go," Braddock said tightly, gesturing toward the waiting gangway into the smaller ship as he watched the blast doors down one of the other corridors start to cycle open. "More bad guys are on the way."

His last sentence was punctuated by a sudden burst of rifle fire that filled the corridor with crimson and emerald beams of lethal energy as a score of ISS guards rushed through the doors.

"I will cover you!" Zhukovski shouted into Reza's ear, and with his good hand he snatched up a pulse rifle from one of the fallen guards, training it with evident skill on the men advancing upon them. Zhukovski shot one, then another before he was forced back against the wall under a hail of return fire.

"Admiral, we can't leave you!" Nicole shouted above the riot of gunfire that was becoming uncomfortably accurate, as she loosed her own barrage on their attackers.

"Get on that ship, Carré!" Zhukovski shouted furiously. "That is direct order!"

After a moment's hesitation, everyone started toward the airlock, stumbling backward through the smoke and stench of ozone and scorched flesh as they sought the safety of the *Pearl's* main airlock, all the while firing back at the approaching guards.

"You, too, Reza," the old admiral said. "My work is done in this life. You have much yet to do. Good luck, my friend." With a devilish grin, without fear or remorse, he turned his attention back to his chosen enemy.

Reza wanted to thank him in some way, but there were no words. He said a silent prayer to the Empress for this man whose courage would have been the envy of the peers, then turned to make his way to the *Pearl*.

As he passed Borge's body, he noticed the black case that had been the focus of the dead usurper's final moments. Wondering what the man could have considered so important, he picked it up by the bloodied handle before dashing up the textured metal ramp and into the airlock.

The armored door slid closed behind him as Zhukovski's final battle raged toward its inevitable conclusion.

Fifty-Four

Reza immediately sensed that something was wrong; the aura of his surroundings had changed, darkened, as soon as he set foot inside the *Golden Pearl* and the airlock had cycled closed behind him.

Nicole, Tony, and Enya had already dashed for the cockpit, a muffled scuffle announcing that the *Golden Pearl* had just had a change in flight crew. Reza felt the *Pearl* lurch as she separated from the dying *Warspite*. In seconds, the sleek ship was accelerating toward the Empress moon as Reza had instructed, dodging through the web of energy fire and torpedoes from the massive battle raging around them.

"What is it, Father?" Shera-Khan asked in a whisper as Reza drew his sword. His own hand reached instinctively for one of the remaining shrekkas. He did not have his father's special senses, but he could sense the change in him, even without hearing his Bloodsong, as he could sense that hot had turned to cold.

"I know not, my son," he replied quietly as he set down the black case on a nearby table to leave his hands free for fighting. "Something is amiss; beware."

Together, the two warriors warily advanced down the chandelier-bedecked hallway that led toward the library.

* * *

The first thing Jodi became aware of was an unfamiliar taste in her mouth. There was blood, to be sure. But there was also something different, something she had never tasted before, but from descriptions she had heard from other women, she had no doubt as to what it was. Semen.

Forcing back the nausea that rose in her throat, she feebly spat the sticky substance from her mouth, along with some blood and the debris from a broken tooth. The effort resulted in a red-hot lance of pain from her stomach and ribs, and it was all she could do to keep from moaning aloud. The mixture of blood, semen, and enamel bubbled from between her lips to ooze down the side of her face in a warm, coppery stream.

With what seemed a titanic effort, she managed to pry one eye open, the other resisting her will with the force of the swelling that had deformed the right side of her face. Beyond the panorama of the carpet, stained with her own blood, she saw the blurred image of a combat boot, then its mate as it slowly swam into focus. For now, the vision of the two boots on the bloody rug was the extent of her world.

"Shouldn't Cerda have checked in with us?" a voice from somewhere above asked in a high, nasal voice. "Maybe we should go check on the president, or something."

"Shut up," said another, deeper voice, one familiar with being in charge of any situation. "If you want to brown nose, just butt snorkel with Cerda and keep away from Borge. Treak," he called to a third, "go forward and see what the hell's going on. Find out what we're supposed to do with this trash." A boot prodded Jodi's buttocks, but she only felt a vague pressure, nothing more. She was numb below the waist, and a tentative command to curl one of her toes disappeared into darkness, unheeded. Her lower body was paralyzed.

"Sure, sarge," someone answered casually, and she heard heavy soles clump toward an exit, a door slid open–

–and then all hell broke loose.

"Look out!" someone cried as a lion's roar ripped through the room, followed by her captors screaming and shouting. A few shots thundered out, and Jodi could see a rush of booted feet running toward the door.

And there was another sound, one she recognized instantly as the lethal whisper of a shrekka whirling through the air. One man's scream was cut off in mid-sentence, and Jodi heard two distinct thumps as his severed head and then his body hit the deck. She also heard the distinct rhythm of a blade scything through the air, armor, and flesh with equal ease.

The Kreelans have boarded, she thought, her hopes for rescue dying, replaced now by the hope that her torment would soon be ended.

Suddenly, the sounds of fighting were gone, and the only sign visible to Jodi that a battle had raged was the curling smoke that stung her single good eye.

A sandaled foot stepped into her view, and she closed her swelling eye, waiting for the final blow to come. If nothing else, she thought, the Kreelans had never sought to make humans suffer, as other humans did. Whatever their motives for war, it was to fight and die. To kill the enemy or be killed oneself. The desire for torture and suffering that Man inflicted upon others of his own kind was absent in the hearts and minds of the Kreelans. Death would come quickly, now, painlessly.

"Jodi?" she heard a hoarse whisper from lips she had once kissed.

"Reza?" she said, not willing to believe that her luck, perhaps, was finally turning, and for the better. "Is it you?" She tried to lift her head enough to see his face. The pain that was her reward left a moaning cry in her throat and a savage, flaming agony shooting up and down her spine.

She felt his hands tenderly grip her shoulders, but for a long time she could say nothing, a scream of raw pain issuing from her throat like a wall of water exploding from a breached dam as he tried to turn her over. After a time, it subsided into a dull throb that pulsed with every beat of her heart, and her mind was finally able to command her tongue to form words that Reza might hear, might understand.

"I... I think my back's broken, Reza," she whimpered. She hated the way she sounded, helpless, terrified, but she could not deny, even to herself, that it was true. "Thorella..." She cringed at the sound of the man's name, even from her own lips, "Thorella beat me... he..." She could not say what else he had done to her.

"Hush," Reza said, biting back the wave of black rage that rose in his soul. "Be still. I will–"

"Father," Shera-Khan called from the next room, his voice conveying concern, apprehension, but no fear; there was no threat to him in there. "There is another like her in here."

"What..." Jodi rasped, "what did he say?"

"Nothing," Reza lied. "Be still."

Uncoiling like a snake about to strike, Reza covered the distance to where his son stood in three paces.

"Eustus," he whispered, his heart catching in his throat. His friend hung in the air, suspended from the heavy chandelier above. His tormentors had tied his elbows together behind his back with a thin metal cable, pulled so tight that it had cut into the flesh of his arms, and then hoisted him from the ground. Then they had beaten him with what could only be a Kreelan grakh'ta, the whip with seven barbed tails like the one that had once scourged Esah-Zhurah's back.

Handing his sword to his son, he said, "Cut him down." Then he held onto Eustus's motionless body while Shera-Khan sliced the cruel metal wire that bound his father's friend. Ever so gently, Reza carried him into the other room, laying him next to Jodi so he could tend to them both. With a claw of his right hand, he severed the wire that bound Eustus's elbows, letting his shoulders and back spring back into something like their normal position.

Eustus let out a groan.

"Reza," Jodi asked, "what's going on? What is it?" Lying as she was, she could not see any of the three other living people in the room, only two of the mangled bodies of the ISS men who had raped her. Somehow, it was not as comforting a sight as she had at first thought it would be.

"It is Eustus," he told her as he pointed out to Shera-Khan a medikit that hung on one of the bulkheads. The boy immediately scrambled to retrieve it.

"How... how is he?"

"Alive," Reza said softly, fighting to keep his hands from trembling with the anger coursing through his veins. Thoughts of dark vengeance intermingled with compassion for his injured and beaten friends, friends who had become his family in this strange world that called itself humanity.

Taking the medikit from Shera-Khan, he told the boy in the New Tongue, "Go to the flight deck and get help. Tell them that Jodi and Eustus are aboard, and are hurt badly."

Shera-Khan nodded in acknowledgment, then bolted for the flight deck at a dead run.

In the meantime, Reza tore open the medikit and began to do what little he could until the others could help him get their friends into the ship's sickbay.

Fifty-Five

Above the Kreelan Homeworld, ships danced and died. But the one-sided slaughter of Kreelan ships that had been the hope of the now-deceased President Borge had become far fiercer than anyone, except Reza, could have predicted. The Kreelans did not fight with their usual expert skill, but they fought with the tenacity of cornered tigresses, and the tide of slaughter was beginning to turn against the invaders.

And yet, despite the carnage that was gutting both of the great fleets, the humans had managed to secure a tenuous perimeter around the solitary moon. Since the heavy ships and their big guns were still engaged with their Kreelan counterparts, and so could not be brought to bear for an orbital bombardment, the task force that had been assigned the moon had begun to disgorge hundreds of dropships. Thousands of Marines were deploying to attack the single built-up area on the moon's surface, a mountainous city that dwarfed the greatest such construct ever conceived by Man.

Leading them was recently promoted Major General Markus Thorella.

"Sir," reported one of the comms technicians, "the Third Fusiliers have landed at–" he read off coordinates that corresponded to a flashing blip on Thorella's tactical display "–and report no enemy present, no resistance. Colonel Roentgen reports 'proceeding toward primary objective.'"

Thorella frowned. He should have been elated that his troops were making such swift progress, but the lack of all resistance – of even sighting any Kreelans at all – thus far on the moon fundamentally disturbed him, especially since this was the fifth regiment on the ground, and the previous four had made nearly identical reports. "Advise all assault elements," he said, "to proceed with caution."

He turned to his deputy division commander for maneuver, the woman who was directly responsible for coordinating the activities of the units disembarking from the ships and moving on the ground. "This is too bloody strange," Thorella told her. "That place should be crawling with Kreelans, confused ones or otherwise. Where could they all have gotten to?"

"Withdrawn to ambush sites?" she suggested.

Thorella shook his head. "No, that's something we would do. The Kreelans prefer head-to-head fighting, whatever the terms."

"But this must be an extraordinary situation for them," she pointed out, simultaneously directing another regiment toward its destination on the moon below, the stylus in her hand marking the destination, which was then sent over the data link. "If Reza Gard can be believed, they've never faced an invasion before."

Thorella considered the thought. "No," he concluded, more to himself than for the other officer's benefit. "Something else is going on, but what?" He had to know, he thought to himself.

Turning to the command ship's captain, he snapped, "Get us down there, now."

* * *

"There is nothing more we can do for her now," Reza said quietly as he finished programming the ship's autodoc to do what it could for Jodi. "We can ease her pain, but that is all." With the help of the automated ship's surgeon, Reza had managed to numb Jodi's spine above the point where it had been severed, confusing her brain into believing that the great nerve pathway merely slept, and was not utterly destroyed halfway down her back, just below her heart. A more general painkiller shielded her from the many other points of damage that would have brought overwhelming pain as the shock slowly wore off.

"Will I be all right?" Jodi asked softly, unexpectedly regaining consciousness, if just for a moment.

"Yes, my friend," Reza replied as he watched the monitor, but he did not – could not – turn to face her. "You will be as good as new." He looked at her then and tried to smile. Failed.

Jodi smiled up at him. She knew he had just told the first lie of his adult life, and she felt honored somehow that he had done it for her, to make her feel better.

"I tried to stop them," Eustus said bitterly. His injuries, less severe than Reza had at first feared, had been dealt with quickly by the ship's electronic surgeon. He still carried terrible bruises, but that affected his looks more than his health. His greatest injury was guilt at not having been able to help Jodi, at having to helplessly watch the things they did to her. His own pain was nothing. Even without his second sight, Reza could feel the guilt feeding on his friend's soul. "But–"

"Eustus," Jodi said, opening the one eye that was not swollen shut. Sleep was not far away, a drug induced coma that would save her from the pain, but she would not let that stop her from comforting her friend. "Eustus," she said again, reaching out with a hand which held only broken fingers, now dead to any further sensation, "it's not your fault. It's Thorella's. If you want to blame someone, blame that bastard, not yourself."

Eustus took her hand in his as if it were an intricate, delicate sculpture of blown glass. "Jodi..." he closed his eyes, fighting the tears.

"I will find him," Reza told her quietly. "I swear in Her name that he shall not escape me again."

Slowly, she shook her head. "No, Reza," she whispered. "We've come too far... given up too much, for you to throw it away in an act of revenge. You have to save your Empress, and give your own people – and ours – a chance to survive. Ships and people are dying out there, and you're the only one who can stop it." Her mangled lips managed a smile that tore at Reza's heart. "Besides, you have a son to look out for now. What will happen to him if you throw your life away after Thorella?"

That thought had not occurred to him; he had not yet really begun to think like a father, to realize that until Shera-Khan well understood the Way and how to follow it, he, Reza, must guide him. And it would take both of them to save the Empress.

"The truth do you speak," Reza admitted grudgingly.

"Reza," Nicole called through the ship's intercom, "we are hitting the atmosphere. I need you to guide me."

"Coming," he answered immediately. He felt most sorry for Nicole: the only one among them qualified and able to pilot the ship, with Braddock keeping her company, she had to remain at the helm as her best friend lay grievously injured, dying. But there was nothing to be done. The ship's autopilot was not good enough to bring them unscathed through the maze of ships blasting at one another. Only Nicole's skill had made that possible, and even so, the *Pearl's* hull now sported a score of burn marks where salvoes from human and Kreelan ships alike had grazed her hull through the weakening shields.

"Good... luck," Jodi said, as the ship's computerized surgeon boosted the level of painkillers in her system. She closed her eyes, and her mangled hand, still clutched carefully in Eustus's own, released its tiny, childlike grip.

Reza's sandaled feet were silent as Death upon the deck as he made his way forward, Shera-Khan close behind him, leaving Eustus and Enya to tend to Jodi. He did not look back.

The view from the *Pearl's* flight deck brought tears to Reza's eyes. The Imperial City, Her home for thousands of generations, lay burning. Dim, almost forgotten memories from his youth of another shattered world, of a young boy orphaned by strangers from the sky, clouded his mind's eye. Streamers of flame reached as high as mountains, as hundreds of assault boats and fighters swarmed over the great buildings and spires. They fired their weapons randomly, and dropped bombs and cluster munitions into any portal or avenue that could have harbored any Kreelan defenders. Pillars of smoke blocked out many parts of the city, but Reza's imagination easily filled in the blanks. *Over one hundred thousand years,* he thought bitterly, *tomorrow shall be nothing more than smoldering ash.*

"Father," Shera-Khan said from behind him, the boy's hand gingerly touching Reza's shoulder. His voice was brittle with fear. Never before, even during the Great Chaos before Keel-Tath's ascension, had harm come to the Empress Moon. But now Shera-Khan and Reza were witness to its systematic destruction.

Reza put a hand over his son's, to reassure the boy as well as himself, although he said nothing; he did not trust his voice not to display the fear he himself felt.

Can Esah-Zhurah still be alive? he wondered. And what if she is? What is even the Empress to do against... this?

"How is Jodi?" Nicole asked from beside him, her voice carefully controlled. She had stopped worrying about either Kreelan defensive fire or being attacked by the scores of human ships prowling about. From the chatter she had been monitoring from the landing force, the Kreelans on the surface were offering no resistance at all, and the other human ships had not been alerted to the *Pearl's* escape. But she had not stopped worrying about Jodi.

"She..." Reza paused, not sure how to tell her. Death and suffering had been his constant companions since childhood, but this was different. Simply blurting the wounding truth was somehow impossibly difficult. "If we do not get her to a healer soon, she will surely die," he finally said. "The ship can only ease her pain, no more."

"And if we take her in time to someone who can help her," Nicole finished for him, "the Empress will die, and we will all be finished."

Reza only nodded.

Nicole stared through the viewscreen at the glowing hell below that was rushing up to meet them. "We have no choices left, Reza," she said grimly. "If there is a chance of you stopping this battle, this war, we must take it, no matter what the cost to ourselves." She looked at him hard, and he thought he saw a glimmer of Esah-Zhurah's strength in her eyes, and he wanted desperately simply to reach out and touch her, that he might touch a tiny part of the woman he loved. But he could not, dared not. "The tide of the battle is changing," she told him. She had been keeping watch on the tactical display as a staggering increase in the number of human ships was added to the casualty list, while fewer and fewer Imperial ships were being destroyed. "More Kreelan warships are arriving all the time, just as you predicted. The main battle group, most of our ships, is scattered, cut off from its jump point. They are being torn apart. Our only hope now is through you. Just show me the way."

Just as they emerged from another pillar of smoke, Reza saw their destination. "There," he said, pointing to a crystalline pyramid that rose over five kilometers in the sky. "The Throne Room is at the top of the Great Tower. That is our destination. We must find a landing bay as high up as possible."

"Reza, this is not a fighter, remember," Nicole reminded him as the computer scanned and rejected most of the bays as being too small. "We cannot land in a shoe box."

"Could we not use the Empress's portal?" Shera-Khan asked, pointing to a large bay complex that also happened to be the highest on the tower. "It will lead us directly to the Throne Room."

"It is closed, Shera-Khan," Nicole said, looking at the information the computer was showing from the scanners.

"No longer," the boy announced, touching his collar in a peculiar fashion. "Behold."

Less than two kilometers away now, the iris door of the great portal suddenly began to open, exposing a warmly lit bay that could have held a dozen ships the size of the *Pearl*, but that now lay empty and barren.

"All who are taught to fly as I have been are given a special device to open the portal," he explained proudly, "that any may serve Her when She calls."

"Well do you serve Her this day, my son," Reza said. He did not know until that moment that Shera-Khan had been trained as a pilot, no doubt under Tesh-Dar's tutelage. He only mourned that he had never known him until these last few desperate hours. *How much I have missed.*

With a precision that matched the grace of the big yacht, Nicole brought the *Pearl* inside the bay. She moved the ship in as far as she could to avoid damage from the raiding ships outside, and to put them closer to the many doorways that lay within. From her last glance at the tactical display of the fleet's desperate plight, every second would count against them from now on.

"Shall I close the portal?" Shera-Khan asked, his hand at his collar.

"No," Nicole advised, just as Reza was about to say the opposite. "We may need to leave quickly."

If we fail, Reza thought silently, *we will have nowhere to go*. "Let it be, then," he said. "We must go."

The others were waiting for them at the main hatch.

"Reza..." Nicole said, her gaze straying down the main hall toward the sickbay.

Reza nodded. "We shall wait for you," he told her as he slammed his fist down on the button to open the hatch and drop the ramp to the deck below. He did not offer to go with her; their farewells to one another would be a private matter.

"I will not be long," she told him.

Nicole entered the sickbay knowing what she would find, but not really prepared for it. To do that would have been to do the impossible. She bit back a small cry as she looked at what had become of Jodi's beautiful face, now little more than a hideous mask of torn flesh, glued loosely to a bruised and battered skull.

"Oh, Jodi," she whispered. "What have they done to you..."

Her friend opened her eyes in the way someone might when returning to the world from a vacant but pleasant dream. "Nikki," she said, "you shouldn't be here... you don't have time..."

"I have always had time for you," Nicole told her, tears flowing freely down her cheeks. She gently touched what looked like an unbruised spot on Jodi's cheek. "And I always will."

"I love you," Jodi said simply. They were words she had said to Nicole a thousand and more times in her dreams and daydreams, but never once in the flesh. She loved her too much to drive her away.

Nicole had no words to answer her. Instead, she leaned forward and kissed Jodi gently on her tattered lips. "I will be back for you, Jodi," she whispered. "I promise. Then... then we will have time together, to talk about things."

Jodi tried hard to smile, but her beaten face made it look more like a grimace. "I'm not going anywhere, babe," she said. "But you'd better. You've wasted enough time on me. Good luck, Nikki."

With bitter tears burning her eyes, Nicole quickly left to join the others at the ramp.

Time was running out.

Fifty-Six

"Where is everyone?" Enya whispered. They had been moving through the halls of the Great Tower toward the Throne Room for what seemed like half an hour, and they had not seen a single Kreelan – alive or dead – anywhere. Rooms and alcoves that were obviously meant to be occupied stood open and empty, and the halls through which they crept were eerily silent, devoid of any sound at all except the occasional boom of a bomb exploding somewhere outside, or perhaps a stray energy bolt from an attacking fighter. The invading Marines had apparently assumed the tower would be the most heavily defended position, and so had not attacked it directly. But, if the rest of the city were like this, they would make their way here very quickly, indeed.

"I am not sure," Reza answered uneasily as he saw the bluish glow from the Throne Room grow stronger with each step. His second sight told him that the entire Imperial City was dead. Or, more exactly, he thought with a tingling in his spine, the city was completely lifeless: none of the millions of Her Children who had once lived and toiled here in Her service remained. Except in the Throne Room. From there, and there alone, did he sense the faintest tremor of life.

"The Empress," he whispered to himself. "Let it be She."

"Could the Marines have already gotten here?" Enya asked.

"No bodies, no sign of firing," Braddock answered. He felt vulnerable in the business suit he usually wore under his councilman's robe, no Marine combat dress having been handy. But the blaster in his hand reassured him, and his political self had easily stepped aside to let the old Marine inside take charge. "It seems as if they just vanished into thin air, walked off a cliff or something."

Eustus, walking backward most of the time to keep an eye on whatever might be behind them, took the opportunity to turn around and add his two bits to the whispered conversation. "Then what happened?"

He almost blundered into Enya, who stood with the others at the massive doors to the Throne Room. None of them, except for Shera-Khan and Reza, who had both been inside before, had any idea of what to expect, other than something ornate, something alien. They had been awed by the halls through which they had come, the walls rising tens of meters to crystalline domes overhead, any one of which human architects could only dream of. But the Throne Room, hundreds of meters across and as many high, its hectares of sloping and curving walls graced with the work of artisans who had lived and died millennia before Michelangelo, overwhelmed them into stunned silence, immobility.

And in the great room's center, at the literal heart of the Empire, stood the Throne itself, poised upon a pyramid of steps that formed the watermark of the Empire's social ranking, the guiding weave of its cultural fabric. But She was not there. Instead, an unholy wall of cyan light, a kaleidoscope of turbulent lightning, encircled the great dais that stood above the highest steps, blocking the Throne itself from view. And only then did Reza understand why there was no one left in the city.

"It is as Tesh-Dar feared," he said quietly. "They are gone, all of them. Dead."

"Who... who is dead?" Nicole managed. She was not quite as stunned as the others, for she carried Reza's blood in her veins, and had seen this place before in her dreams. But to actually be here...

"The inhabitants of the city, of this moon," he explained bleakly. "All of them are dead."

"How can that be?" Eustus whispered, still unable to tear his eyes away from the incredible wonders that lay before him. "How did they die? Our Marines didn't kill them. Where did the bodies go? There must have been... well, millions living here. They couldn't have just disappeared!"

"Yes," he said, "they could have." Reza nodded toward the light that swirled as if something alive dwelt within. "They tried to reach Her, the Empress, through that," he explained quietly, "to save Her, to save the Empire itself. But the light..." He paused, a chill creeping up his spine. "The light is the essence of the guardians of the First Empress's spirit. It is a barrier, a fire that burns hot as the sun."

"Like in the cave, on Erlang..." Enya said slowly.

"You're right," Eustus murmured, a chill running down his spine at the eerie glow. "The light – it looks the same."

"But why here?" Nicole demanded. "Why now?"

"Because this was to be the time the circle closed," Reza told her, "the time when the First Empress's spirit rejoined with us, and fused Her Own power with that of the living Empress."

"That's what was in the crystal heart," Enya said quietly, "the spirit of this First Empress." She had no idea how such a thing was possible, but she had once read that the technology of an advanced civilization would seem like magic to more primitive people. And the Empire had been around for a very, very long time. Humans had been plying the stars for hundreds of years. The Kreelans had been a spacefaring race for *thousands*.

"Yes, the crystal heart," Reza said, "the vessel containing the spirit of the First Empress, whose power – and spirit – Esah-Zhurah also inherited, making Her the most powerful Empress, the most powerful Kreela, ever born. But with her heart and spirit broken, all the Empire was cast into darkness." He looked again at the swirling wall of light that blazed defiantly above them. "And that is the power of the Imperial Guard," he told them. "You saw their physical remains in the chamber on Erlang. Now do you witness the power of their spirit."

"Then what are we supposed to do?" Braddock asked. "Won't it kill you, too?"

"My blood is Her blood," he said cryptically. "My heart is Her heart, my spirit Her spirit. And my love shall be Her love, Her life." He turned to Nicole. "I must challenge them, to fight them as is our Way. If I do not survive," he told her, "I would ask that you and Tony... care for Shera-Khan."

"I will fight beside you," Shera-Khan proclaimed fiercely, his talons tightly gripping his sword in want of battle.

Reza held the young warrior's shoulders, his own talons digging into the hardened metal of Shera-Khan's armor as he met his son's gaze with his own. "I am your father," he told him softly in the rapid lilt of the New Tongue, "and you are my son, blood of my blood, flesh of my flesh. Proud am I of you, of what you are, and of the great warrior you will become as you follow the Way. Many battles have you yet to fight, and great victories shall you win for Her honor. But not this day. Not here, not now. This battle was preordained upon the deathbed of Keel-Tath in a prophecy that has passed from mothers to their daughters for thousands of generations, and this is the day of reckoning." He smiled at Shera-Khan, the Kreelan way, wishing he could wipe away the black stripes of the mourning marks on his son's face as he might the salty streaks of his own tears. "To fight are we born, I know," he told him, softer still, "and so it is difficult not to seek out the Challenge that to your heart calls. But patience is a skill well-suited to the warrior, Shera-Khan, and patience this day must be yours."

Shera-Khan nodded as Kreelans do, and said, "What shall become of me should you... not return?"

Reza nodded toward Nicole and Braddock. "They are my peers, fellow warriors of my old race; they are my friends, my family. The woman carries my blood in her veins, the blood of the Empress; our ways are not alien to her. Should I fail you, should the Empress die, you must go with them, for they will care for you with the love I would show you, that your mother held for you since the day of your birth. They shall guide you to the Way."

Shera-Khan lowered his head. "It shall be as you wish, Father," he said quietly, knowing that, if his father failed in his mission, his life would be meaningless, his spirit without hope of redemption in the Afterlife. But this weakness he would not show the warrior priest who called him Son.

"I love you, my son," Reza said, suddenly finding the boy in his arms, embracing him fiercely. "May thy Way be long and glorious."

With a final hug, the two separated. "Follow me," Reza said to the others as he began to climb the steps he had not seen since he was a young man.

Like tiny but determined ants climbing a great mountain, the six of them ascended the ancient stone stairway toward Hell.

* * *

"Have you been able to hail them?" Thorella snapped at the assault command ship's captain.

"No, sir," he answered. "I only get the IFF beacon, nothing else."

Thorella chewed his lip nervously. They had picked up the *Golden Pearl's* signature heading down to the surface. *Why is it here?* he wondered. He could understand the president's desire to bring the ship down to witness their victory, although he considered such a vain action to be nothing short of stupid. But why would it wind up inside a landing bay right at the top of what the Navy had considered an impregnable tower? Why had the president not contacted him to tell him what he was doing? And why had they left no one in the ship to monitor communications?

"It doesn't make any sense," he said. Turning to the comms officer, he said, "Contact *Warspite*. I want confirmation that the president got on board the yacht."

There was a beat of silence in the little ship's combat center.

"Well?" Thorella demanded angrily.

"*Warspite's* gone, sir," the captain said quietly. How many thousands of sailors had died in these last hours, he thought, and this fool was not even aware of the destruction of the fleet's flagship. "We won't be getting any confirmation – or anything else, for that matter – from her. *Southampton's* flying Admiral Laskowski's flag, now. She's in overall command."

"Contact *Southampton*, then!" Thorella ordered, angered by the man's impertinence. The significance of what he had just said, that the Confederation fleet had lost its flagship, was lost in the immediacy of finding out what had happened to the president.

A few moments passed, in which the necessary inquiries were made. "*Southampton* cannot confirm the president's safe transfer to the *Golden Pearl*," the comms officer announced. "They only know he was supposed to board her."

That clinched it. "Take us into that landing bay," he ordered the ship's captain, "and set us down beside the yacht. Lieutenant Riggs," he said to the leader of the command ship's platoon of Marines, "I want your platoon standing by to secure this ship from attack, but no one is to enter the *Golden Pearl* without my express permission." There were things in the yacht that he would rather not have the Marines see, lest they start asking awkward questions. "Is that understood?"

The ship captain nodded unenthusiastically, convinced the Marine general had just lost the last of his marbles, while the Marine second lieutenant, fresh from training and eager to please, barked a hearty, "Yes, sir!"

It took only a few minutes for the command ship to reach its destination. Thorella had already gone over the status of his units with the ops officer. He had hoped that there would be at least a single regiment free to leapfrog up to what looked like undefended high ground. But they were all heading to their primary and secondary objectives, already a long way from their dropships.

Thorella would be on his own.

FIFTY-SEVEN

The climb up the steps had left the humans out of breath by the time they reached the top. When Enya had asked the question of the practicality of an elevator, Shera-Khan shook his head in a practiced human gesture.

"The Empress ascends to the throne each day step by step," he told her in Standard, "a symbol that She favors none, that She loves all of Her Children. Great warrior or simple porter of water, the highest among the peers or the lowest, She considers the needs of each on Her way to the throne."

"I wish our own leaders cared as much for their people," Braddock murmured.

But any thoughts of the climb vanished when they reached the great dais. The view, like being atop a mountain peak overlooking a forest of priceless art, would have been stunning were it not for the malevolent wall of cyan light that swirled in front of them. The thunder of bombs exploding outside, in the city, reverberated throughout the great dome just as the first hint of smoke reached them, here at the pinnacle of the Empire's heart.

"I can feel them," Nicole murmured as she looked into the swirling blue wall before them. She wrapped her arms around herself to ward off the sensation of unseen eyes watching her, unblinking, hostile.

"You must wait here," Reza told them as he drew his sword. He, too, could feel them, the Guardians. He felt a surge of heat through his body and heard the faint strains of the lonely solo that had been his Bloodsong for longer than he cared to remember. *This shall be my final Challenge*, he knew. "No matter what happens," he told them, "do not go into the light. Do not so much as touch it. If I fail..." he paused, "If I fail, return to the ship as fast as you can and try to return to human space. There will be nothing left for you here but death."

"Reza," Nicole said softly beside him. He turned to her, and was met by warm lips pressing against his. "Good luck, Reza," she said, then stepped back with the others.

It was time. Without hesitation, he stepped forward into the eerie wall of light.

* * *

The place, he knew well: the temple of the Desh-Ka, high upon the mountain of Kular-Arash. But it was not the ancient ruin where in his youth he had been transformed into something more than a man, where he had bound himself to a woman not of his race. No, the temple in which he now stood was new, immaculate, filled with the power of the great warriors who dwelled there. This was the prize of their warrior civilization in its youth, its full glory.

Standing in the sand of the great arena, the glare of the sun was shaded by the dome that would last for another hundred thousand years. Reza saw that he was not alone. Before him, standing like a pillar at the far side of the arena, was a lone male warrior.

"Tara-Khan," Reza breathed. He did not need to see the symbols inscribed on the other warrior's collar to know his name or who he was. He was known to all Kreela who had come after him, for he was the greatest of the warriors ever to have fought for Her honor, in all the days of the Empire. He had been Keel-Tath's love, Her life. And here, in this place that was a dream that could yet draw blood, he was Her guardian, the last of the host She had taken with Her.

The warrior nodded. "Indeed," he said in a voice of ages-long sadness, "it is so."

Beyond Tara-Khan, Reza could see the dais at the head of the arena, where the world of the real and that of the spirit converged. And on it lay a figure in white. "The Empress," he whispered, his heart falling away at the sight of Esah-Zhurah's still body. She lay upon the dark marble altar at the center of the dais, draped in Her white robes, the thin gold collar gleaming from around Her neck. Reza could see the black mourning marks that ran from her eyes like rivers of sorrow against the snow white hair that lay in carefully coiled braids around her shoulders. Her breast rose and fell slowly, slowly, as her lungs labored on, and Her broken heart forced life through unwilling veins.

Turning back to Tara-Khan, he challenged, "And by what right do you stand before me?"

Tara-Khan's eyes followed Reza's to the still form of the vessel of Keel-Tath's spirit. "I stand here as Her last guardian and protector, an instrument of Her will," he said quietly. "This is my honor, Reza, to defend Her. The others are gone now. Only I remain." He turned his eyes back to Reza. "Long have I slept beside Her spirit in the Darkness until this, the day of redemption, of the final combat. It is my honor to see that you are worthy."

"And if you slay me this day," Reza asked, "what is to become of Her?"

"The Empress shall perish," Tara-Khan rasped miserably, "and with Her the Empire, our very souls cast into the pit of emptiness from which there shall be no escape for all eternity." He smiled. "But do not fear, young one," he said. "I have listened to your heart, your spirit; your love is true. But this, your final covenant with Her, must be made afresh in blood. This is as She long ago willed, and so shall it be."

"Let me pass, Tara-Khan," Reza implored him. "There has been enough death this day. Let me reach Her, that the lost may be saved, that the Empire shall not perish."

Setting his hand upon the grip of his great sword, whose blade had slain countless foes in ages past, Tara-Khan replied, "Fated by Her own hand were you to be here this day, to fulfill the Prophecy. But beware: there are no guarantees. I can pass none until they are proven worthy, until they can best my sword."

As the fire spread through his veins, his eyes taking in his dying Empress, his love, one last time, Reza hissed, "Then let it be done."

And the thunder of clashing swords filled the arena.

* * *

Thorella cautiously made his way up the ramp into the *Golden Pearl*, his sidearm held at the ready, his finger tensed on the trigger. Behind him, Lieutenant Riggs's Marines waited uncertainly in their defensive perimeter around the yacht, the roar of the command ship still loud in their ears as it reversed course, abandoning them in the huge hangar as it sought to avoid a possible ambush. None of them were thrilled with the idea of being stranded up here, still so far from even the closest regiment should they need help.

On his solitary reconnaissance, Thorella was completely uninterested in what his men thought. He was concerned only with what he found – or did not find – on the *Golden Pearl*. It did not take him long to find the bodies of the flight deck crew, holes drilled neatly through their chests by hand blasters. Even more cautious now, he went on to find the butchered remains of the ISS guards that he had left to take care of Mackenzie and Camden. Still, there was no sign of anyone who was still alive. Could Mackenzie and Camden have somehow taken over the ship and brought it here? *Impossible*, he thought to himself. *But, still...*

Slowly, sweat beading on his brow, he reentered the main corridor and began to make his way aft, toward sickbay and engineering.

"Sir," Riggs reported excitedly from outside, "the patrol we sent up the main hall has detected a small group of the enemy not far from here." To Riggs, the enemy was anyone who was not specifically designated as friendly.

"Details?" Thorella growled, annoyed that his concentration was being diverted from his search of the ship, but somehow relieved that someone had finally seen some activity from the Kreelans.

Riggs patched through the patrol leader. "It appears to be some kind of, I don't know, a royal hall or something, sir," reported the staff sergeant who was leading the patrol. "It's huge, like nothing I've ever–"

"The enemy, sergeant," Thorella snapped. "Tell me about the enemy!"

"Uh, yes, sir," the woman replied. "Five individuals, sir. At the very top of a big, I don't know, a pyramid, like." Pause. "But I could swear that four of them look like our people."

"What do you mean, 'our people?'" Thorella demanded. Any thoughts of exploring the *Golden Pearl* further were rapidly fading.

"Humans, sir," said the staff sergeant, reporting what she could make out through her image enhancers. "Two males and two females. One of the males is in Marine combat dress, one of the females in Navy uniform. The two others are in civvies of some kind. But the fifth one is definitely Kreelan, but she looks kind of small."

"About the size of a human teenager?" Thorella asked, his face contorting into a rictus of ice-cold rage.

Pause. "Now that you mention it, yes, sir, that's what she looks like. A young Kreelan–"

"Get them!" he choked.

"Sir?" Riggs cut in over the confused staff sergeant.

"You heard me!" Thorella raged as he whirled, running back down the corridor toward the hatchway. Now he knew what had happened to Borge: he had never made it off the doomed *Warspite*. "Get them! They're renegades, they killed the president!" Thorella did not need a body for evidence. He knew for sure that Borge was dead. Precisely how he had gotten that way was of no further concern. All that mattered now was that his own ascension to power was finally cleared of the last obstacle, his despicable father. He just needed to be sure that Reza Gard and his accomplices were noted in the history books as President Borge's murderers, and himself, the avenger. "And I want them alive!" He would not be denied the fulfillment of his long-lived vendetta.

Outside, Riggs felt his blood turn to ice. Such an outrage could not go unpunished. Two presidents, murdered? It was unthinkable. "Yes, sir! Sergeant Khosa," he ordered, "open fire! Pin them down, but do not – repeat, *do not* – shoot to kill. We're on our way."

* * *

Nicole stood close behind Shera-Khan. Lightly, she put a hand on his shoulder. He did not flinch away. "Do you... feel anything, Shera-Khan?" she asked as they all stared into the light that swirled and writhed like a living thing.

He shook his head. "I am empty," he said bleakly. "I cannot hear my father's song; I cannot touch his soul."

"How will we know if he's successful," Eustus asked, "or... if he fails?"

"If the Empress dies," Shera-Khan said, "this–" he gestured toward the light, "–will be no more, and Darkness shall fall upon the sun. All shall end; there shall be no more."

"Shera-Khan," Braddock said quietly, "I've known your father for a long time, and I know how much he loves her, and I know how much you must love her. But, even if she dies, the universe will still go on. You'll still be alive and well, and–"

"You do not understand," Shera-Khan interrupted. "She is not an individual. She is all of us. Our souls and spirits are bound to Her. Even now, now that I cannot feel Her or any others of my kind, should She perish, I shall surely die also. With Her last breath, so shall the Empire perish from the Universe. My father bade me come with you should he fail; he did this out of kindness and hope. But should the Empress perish, so shall I; so shall all my kind."

Braddock and Enya still did not understand, but Nicole did, and she drew Shera-Khan closer to her. "He will win the Challenge," she said, a tingling sensation running through her chest at the words. "He must."

"Hey," Eustus said from behind them. Unable to watch the eye-searing light anymore, he had turned to study the rest of the throne room. Now, as he watched Riggs's Marines darting in through the entrance they themselves had used, advancing on the great stairway, he almost wished he hadn't. "I think we've got company."

"Who–"

"Down!" Eustus cried, throwing the others to the floor of the dais just as a hail of energy bolts blasted chunks from the stairway below and ricocheted from the crystalline dome above.

* * *

Reza hissed as Tara-Khan's sword slashed through his armor, drawing blood from his shoulder.

"Well do you fight, young one," Tara-Khan told him through gritted teeth, for Reza's sword had found its mark on occasion also, "but still do you have much to learn."

For what seemed like hours the two had fought, caught in a cycle of desperate attrition, one to save the future, the other to slaughter imperfection, unworthiness. Both were perfect in their craft, unable to inflict a decisive blow, only able to harm. To hurt, to bleed.

"I have learned much already," Reza hissed. His sword swung through space with a power and speed that left thunder in the air as the great blade sought Tara-Khan's neck. It was perfectly timed, the razor's edge keening as it sought the older warrior's flesh.

Instead, it found only falling water.

"What?" Reza stammered in confusion. Tara-Khan had disappeared. Only a pool of water, rapidly sinking into the sand, was left where he had been standing. Warily, he stepped closer, prodding the wet sand with his foot.

A flutter caught his eye. *The Empress,* he thought. *She moved!* But as he studied Her, he knew it must have been an illusion. She was still as the stone upon which She lay. If he did not save Her soon, that was how She would forever remain. Pushing Tara-Khan from his mind, he took a step toward Her. Every second he waited was a grain of sand slipping through the waist of a cosmic hourglass. And so few grains were left, he thought. So very few.

Another step.

Where was Tara-Khan? He whirled about suddenly, his sword cutting a protective arc, but Tara-Khan was nowhere to be seen. There was only the cryptic stain upon the sand, quickly fading. Surely, he thought, Tara-Khan had not conceded, not in silence, without a word?

He took another step toward Esah-Zhurah, the Empress. And another. Closer to Her now, he could hear the slow, shallow rustle of Her breathing, could smell Her hair, and his insides began to tremble. The trickle of warm blood that ran down his side from his shoulder felt like a caress, as when her hand had touched him lovingly, when he had held her close. So long ago, he thought. So very, very long ago.

He was close to Her now, his sword ready at his side, but his eyes were filled with the image of Her face. She had become his world, the very Universe. The song that had turned his blood to fire sang still, not for battle, but for love, for Her.

At the dais, now. Climbing the steps. The sound of his feet through water. Her face, turned toward him–

Water?

– as if watching him, Her eyes closed...

He did not see the water stir as he passed, heard nothing as it rose and took shape and form, silent as a still pool as metal, flesh, and bone emerged.

His inner alarms clamored and his body reacted with the strength of a tiger and the speed of lightning, but it was too little, too late. With a triumphant roar, Tara-Khan attacked. The great blade speared through the side of Reza's armor, embedding itself deep within him in a searing flash of pain.

In agonized rage, Reza swung his own weapon at Tara-Khan's unprotected head, but again it found nothing but water.

I have failed, he thought miserably, as Tara-Khan rose again, his sword ready to strike.

"You fought well young one," the elder warrior said, "but you are not The One. You are not worthy of Her love, and thus shall you perish." The sword fell.

Water, the thought flashed through Reza's mind as the blade hissed through the air. *Water... and ice...*

At the last instant, Reza threw himself forward, sinking his claws into Tara-Khan's armor as the sword whistled past above his head. Laughing at Reza's desperate attempt to save himself, Tara-Khan did as Reza had hoped. His body melted into water, his essence slipping through Reza's fingers.

But they were no longer in the arena.

* * *

"Look out!" Enya cried, as an energy bolt sheared an elephant-sized chunk of the great glassine dome from the slender frame above.

With a jerk of his head, Braddock saw the huge glass fragment falling toward him. Twisting desperately to the side, he tried to get out of its way, but he was too late. With a crash that shook the dais itself, Braddock disappeared beneath the mass of crystal as it exploded into a million tiny shards.

"Tony!" Nicole screamed as she crawled through the debris toward him, the crystal fragments lacerating her hands and knees. She reached out to take hold of the glass shell that covered Braddock's body like the transparent lid of a coffin.

"No!" Shera-Khan cried, batting her unprotected hands away from the razor sharp edges. "Let me." Sensing a lull in the firing from below and using his armored hands and diamond-hard talons, he struggled to lift a fragment of the crystal that covered Braddock's body, but was unable to move it. It was far too large, too heavy.

Nicole slid up next to him, keeping her head down and out of the line of fire. Above them, the dome began to disintegrate, huge chunks falling into the throne room as the structure began to lose the last of its integrity.

"Tony," she whispered, peering at his smashed body through the clear crystal. His face, his coat, his hands were covered with blood. Blood was everywhere. "No," she moaned. "Please, Tony," she whispered, "You cannot die!" But she had seen death enough times to recognize it. And Tony Braddock was dead.

As Shera-Khan watched helplessly, Nicole laid her head on the crystal that covered her husband and began to silently weep.

On the other side of the dais, separated by the circle of blue light from the others, Enya and Eustus continued to fire at their attackers, trying to keep them pinned down.

"There are too many of them!" Enya shouted above the thunder of the guns.

"You have a talent for understatement, my love," he replied as he sent a round into a careless Marine's leg. He was trying desperately not to kill any of them, only to injure them or keep their heads down. The ISS guards were one thing; they were as much an enemy as the Kreelans had ever been. But the Marines were his people, his family. "Nicole," he bellowed, "how are you doing?"

Only the guns below answered him.

"Nicole?" he called again. They had been able to hear each other before. "What the hell are they doing over there?" he asked Enya as he turned, ready to skirt around toward the other side, where the other three of their little band had posted themselves.

The ugly snout of a blaster suddenly thrust itself into his face.

"Drop it," a voice growled from behind a combat helmet. Eustus saw that where the nameplate had been on the man's armor, there was nothing now but a still-hot scorch mark. "Both of you. Now."

Hesitating for just a moment, Eustus did as he was told. They had lost.

Behind him, Enya asked quietly, "Eustus?" She still held her weapon, clenched in her left hand.

"Drop it," Eustus told her. He heard the weapon clatter onto the cold stone floor.

"Where are the others?" Eustus asked.

"Shut up," the Marine snarled as three more armored figures appeared from the other side to surround them. The Marine motioned with his blaster toward where he had left Nicole, Braddock, and Shera-Khan. "Move it. Now."

Eustus led Enya around the cylindrical wall of light, ignoring the vicious shove the Marine gave him as he passed. As he walked, he heard something crunching under his feet, like glass. And then he saw Nicole slumped over a huge mass of crystal, Shera-Khan on his knees beside her, a Marine covering them with his rifle. A pool of blood seeped from beneath the crystal.

"Sweet Jesus," he whispered. "Nicole, what hap–"

A huge Marine slammed an elbow into Eustus's jaw, sending him sprawling dangerously close to the light. Through the stars dancing through his brain, he smelled hair burning, and a prickling sensation told him that it was the hair on his arm, being burned into plasma by whatever energy governed the barrier.

"Eustus!" Enya cried as she grabbed at his ankles, pulling him away from the shimmering wall. "You could have killed him!" she snarled at the figure looming behind her.

"He's a traitor," Lieutenant Riggs sneered over the suit's PA system, "just like you. I don't know why General Thorella wants you alive, but he does." He grimaced at all of them, a look of utter disgust diluted only with hatred, not caring that they could not see his expression behind his helmet. "And I follow orders." A booted foot kicked at Braddock's crystal sarcophagus.

"You bastard!" Nicole shrieked, leaping to her feet, her blood suddenly blazing with a fiery alien rage.

Shera-Khan watched in amazement as this human woman, this friend-warrior of his father, struck out at the animal in armor. She moved as if she had talons, with the deadly grace and speed of a warrior priestess.

Riggs was caught off-guard, and his head rang against the inside of his helmet as her hands slammed against his armor with a strength he never would have guessed at by looking at her. But sheer mass, if nothing else, was on his side, and he recovered quickly. As one armored fist fastened itself around one of Nicole's wrists, the other rose to smash her in the face.

In that instant, Shera-Khan sensed a tremor pulse through his body, and he knew that if he did not act, Nicole would be dead.

Like a tiger he leaped, his arms outstretched, his claws reaching not for Riggs, but for Nicole.

* * *

Reza fell to his knees upon the ice, his face already a cherry red from the freezing wind that howled over the great glacier at the south pole of the Homeworld, a place so cold that spit froze solid before it hit the ground.

Forcing his eyes open against the frigid wind, he saw Tara-Khan's face, frozen in a nightmare state that was half flesh, half ice. One eye was still fully formed, staring at him in astonishment, while the other was stretched, elongated like a broken yolk as it had begun to flow toward the ground. The mouth, misshapen, skewed, was open, but what emotion might have been conveyed there was unimaginable, horrible. His arms and sword had liquefied, falling to fuse with what was left of his legs, now mannequin-like sculptures in ice that had become one with the glacier.

And Reza's hands, which had been holding onto his opponent's armored chest, were now locked in an icy grip, fused inside Tara-Khan's partly-solidified torso, water and ice, flesh and blood.

With a cry of desperation, Reza broke his hands free, falling backward onto the ice, Tara-Khan's cooling blood-water on his hands. Struggling against the gale and his own rapidly ebbing strength, he stood up, facing what remained of Tara-Khan.

"May you find peace in Her name," he said to the nightmare face. Then, with his hands clasped together, he smashed the frozen warrior's head from his shoulders, sending frozen bits of ice and flesh across the plain of white.

He turned toward the sky, toward the Empress moon, which hung low on the horizon. *Running out of time*, he thought, his vision starting to turn gray from the blood that poured from the gaping wound in his side, his limbs numb from the cold. As his breath froze into crystals around his mouth, disturbed only by the small trickle of blood he had coughed up from his punctured lung, he closed his eyes, picturing the dying Empress in his mind.

After a time that was not time, he opened his eyes. The arena was dark around him, the walls hidden in shadow. Even the sky through the dome above was darkened, invisible to his failing vision. Only around the Empress was there a halo, an aura, of gently pulsating cyan light that faded as he watched, its power failing with Her will to survive.

Willing his dying body to move, he struggled toward her, his sandals dragging his frostbitten feet through the sand. He stumbled, fell against the stone of the dais, then dragged himself forward, up the steps on his hands and elbows, fighting pain, fighting time, fighting a cursed fate.

He made it to the top, facing the stone slab on which She lay. Around him now was darkness, as if the world itself was shrinking down upon Her, and even She was falling into shadow as the light around Her pulsed, faded.

"No," he moaned, forcing himself to his knees, crawling to Her side, leaving a trail of blood in his wake. Shaking off his gauntlets, he reached forward with trembling hands to touch Her, felt the coolness of Her skin, the silence of the spirit that cried for release from its pain. "I am here," he told her as he willed her to wake, to rise. "Please, my Empress, you must not die."

Then it was that he saw something clutched in her left hand, something about the size of his fist, and now black as coal. The crystal heart.

Not really knowing why, following an instinct that had been planted long ago in a race that was not his own by birth, he pried the scorched crystal from her hand, noting the scar on her palm that matched his own.

Drawing the dagger of the Empress, the one that Esah-Zhurah had given him so long ago, he joined his hand to hers, the cold metal between them. Once before had he done this with the woman who owned his heart; now he would do it with the woman who owned his spirit, and the spirit of his adopted people.

"With my last breath," he whispered to her, "do I give thee life, my Empress." He pulled the knife between them, feeling the pitiable trickle of warmth that welled from his numbed hand, then closed his bleeding palm over hers.

As the world faded toward darkness, he gently kissed her lips. The tingle of memory, of what once had been, surged through his mind as he touched her. Closing his eyes, he laid his head upon her breast. He rested next to her on the cold stone slab, his life rapidly draining away into the empty shadows where once the dais had been, where now the Darkness of Forever reigned.

"I love you," he whispered. The last of his strength did he give that his hand could hold hers. He hoped that the tiny spark of life that remained in his body would be enough to rekindle Her own.

His heart beat slower, ever slower. And then it was still.

He did not feel the quickening of Her breath, or the sudden warmth of Her breast beneath his gray, frozen cheek. He did not see as once again the crystal heart began to glow beneath the blood, his own, that coated it and had penetrated it as had Keel-Tath's millennia ago.

Beside him, the Empress awoke.

* * *

The Marine who had been guarding Shera-Khan spun around as the boy lunged toward Riggs, the projected sight reticle in the Marine's helmet tracking the boy with smooth precision. The Marine's finger tensed on the big weapon's trigger just as a jagged bolt of lightning streaked from the maelstrom that was the center of the dais, incinerating him with more heat than could be found on the surface of a star.

Shera-Khan slammed into Nicole, knocking her from Riggs's grasp just as the world exploded around them. The big Marine, caught off guard by the boy's attack and the blinding bolt of lightning, stumbled backward and fell off the dais just as another bolt crackled through the air where he had just been standing.

"What the hell?" Riggs cried as he went over the edge, landing hard on his back and then scrabbling madly to keep from rolling down the hundreds of steps that lay below. He saw as in a nightmare that the barrier had dissolved into a hydra of lightning that snapped and bit at the air over the great dais, its energy prickling his skin. He watched, dumbfounded, as the seething monster struck again, a blinding tentacle lashing out at another of his Marines. A flash and a roar crashed through Riggs's brain, loud enough to deafen him even with the suit's passive aural dampers. Blinking away the spots that peppered his vision, he saw nothing left of the Marine but a scorch mark on the stone.

"What's going on in there?" Riggs heard Thorella's voice through the pandemonium around him, his voice barely audible over the boosted voice link.

"I don't know, sir," the young lieutenant shouted back in a panic, rolling down another step as the deadly storm that turned and wheeled above him struck down yet another of his people, and then another. "We're getting killed up here!"

"Goddammit!" Thorella screamed into the radio from where he stood far below, at the entrance to the throne room. Looking up, he saw what looked like a lightning-whipped tornado whirling around the apex of the enormous pyramid of stairs, blinding flashes of light reflecting from the surrounding dome like a gigantic strobe. "Give me a proper report, lieutenant!" he shouted again. "What is happening? What do you see?"

Hauling himself up on his elbows, Riggs peered over the last step, his eyes coming just above the stone floor of the dais. "Jesus," he whispered to himself as he saw what awaited him. There, at the very center of the dais, stood a Kreelan woman clothed only in simple white robes. Her hands were lifted above her, and Riggs's eyes widened as he saw the lightning dancing from her palms, enveloping her in a swirling aura that was so bright that it hurt his eyes to look directly at her.

She looks like an angel, he thought to himself before the woman turned her burning eyes upon him. *An angel*, a hysterical voice in his mind echoed as he lost control of his bladder, a blade of fear cutting through his stomach. *An angel of death.*

He tried to push himself back down the stairs, away from her, but it was far too late. One of the dancing bolts of lightning arced from her hands, vaporizing Riggs in the blink of an eye.

* * *

Feeling Shera-Khan motionless close beside her, Nicole shivered on the floor as a roaring tide of energy coursed through her body, as if she had suddenly become a human conduit for raw, pure power. And then she heard the voice that was not a voice, but was more like a blast of sound through her brain, a single thought exploding inside her skull. A curtain of fire swept through her veins, scorching her flesh. Agony. Ecstasy.

"My Children..."

* * *

Even from his distant vantage point, Thorella was nearly blinded and deafened by the forces that gripped the throne room. He watched as Riggs's entire platoon was wiped out by what looked like nothing more complex, nothing less devastating, than lightning. He had no doubts that had he chosen to make the trek up those ancient stone steps, he, too, would now be dead.

But Thorella was a survivor, and always had been. "Marine One," he called the command ship that was orbiting somewhere overhead, "we need an emergency evac down here now!"

"On our way, sir," came the tinny reply.

"Move it," Thorella snapped as he turned to head down the hall toward the landing bay.

But, as he did so, he saw out of the corner of his eye the ship as it passed over the dome, low, too low. Thorella was about to shout a warning when a bolt of lightning shot upward through the dome, reaching a blazing claw toward the ship. In a blinding flash the ship exploded, leaving nothing but burning fragments whirling away from an expanding cloud of gas as its remains streaked out of sight, leaving behind a trail of sooty smoke.

Then the lightning surged into the structure of the dome itself, the blinding veins of cyan working their way through the stone and crystal like water through a plant thirsting for water, leaving in their wake a shimmering fluorescence.

Thorella ran alone from the carnage behind him. He ran for the *Golden Pearl.*

* * *

Enya was deafened by the sudden silence. The thunder and lightning that had exploded all around her were gone. The gale force winds that had swept over the dais were still. The great dome was silent, as was the city beyond. The bombs had stopped falling. Her whole body was shivering with fear, her eyes tightly closed. Eustus lay unconscious in her arms. His breathing was ragged. Against her better judgment, she opened her eyes.

The Marines were gone. There was nothing left of them but a faint trace of burned plastic and the stench of scorched flesh. While the blue fire was also gone, the throne room still glowed with eerie light that highlighted the scene of devastation that was the once pristine dais.

Nearby, Braddock's lifeless body lay entombed by the slab of crystal that had fallen from above. Next to him Nicole and Shera-Khan lay equally still. Enya was suddenly afraid, afraid that she was alone with whatever power now haunted this place.

It was then that a phantom stepped from the smoke that still clung to the dais. Enya's skin prickled as she saw the white braids that framed the blue skin of the Kreelan woman's face, proud and unblemished now by the black marks that she had worn for so many years. Her eyes blazed with wisdom and the power of her unfathomable spirit, just as the sleek muscles beneath the white robes belied her physical strength. Upon her head was a tiara, glittering with gemstone fire. With a liquid grace that seemed unlikely, unnatural, perhaps, as if her feet did not quite touch the floor, the woman made her way to where Nicole lay, and knelt beside her.

Enya stared as the woman delicately extended a hand to touch Nicole's face, and saw the scar across the Kreelan woman's palm, the blood-red talons.

She is Esah-Zhurah... The Empress, she thought silently, her eyes wide with awe.

Nicole stirred at the woman's touch, and the Kreelan spoke, but not in any language that Enya would ever understand.

* * *

Nicole's mind struggled against the rising sea of voices that threatened to drive her insane. The fire that had filled her blood had left her heart racing without cease, her body filled with adrenaline, but with no way to dissipate it. She lay helpless, her spirit dissolving in the maelstrom that roared within her.

And then she felt a touch, the sensation that someone had placed a hand on her face. But it was more than that. Amid the infinite mass of clamoring souls into which she was falling, the touch offered a rallying point, a focus. Then she heard a voice, felt a powerful mind lead her own back to order and purpose.

"Be not afraid," the Empress whispered soothingly in the Old Tongue. "All shall be well, my child. All shall be well."

"And what of my love?" Nicole heard herself ask in the same language, as the great choir burning in her veins began to subside and her mind began to reassert itself. "Death has taken all I have ever held dear. It has ruled my past, and now has it claimed my future."

"I know of the fondness your kind has for miracles, child," the Empress said gently. "*Behold.*"

* * *

Enya watched as the Empress rose and went to stand beside Braddock's body. With a gesture of her hand, as if she were lifting an invisible feather, the massive block of crystal that pinned him to the dark stone began to tremble, then rose from the floor. A flick of the Empress's hand sent it spinning away across the throne room to shatter against a distant wall.

She then cupped her hands together as if she were holding water, and Enya watched in open-mouthed wonder as the pulse of the Kreelan monarch's life force took shape between her palms, bathing all of them in an eerie cyan glow. She opened her hands to reveal a ball of light just smaller than one of her fists that, as if it possessed a will of its own, floated down toward Braddock's lifeless chest. It hung over his heart, growing larger, diffusing as it sent innumerable tendrils all over his body to envelop him in a shroud of blue fire that swirled and shimmered. In a moment, the glow began to fade, then disappeared.

Braddock's chest rose. With a groan, he rolled partway over, rubbing his eyes with the heels of his hands.

"Tony!" Enya cried.

"Enya?" he asked, perplexed. "What the hell? Nicole? Nicole!" Nicole knelt beside him, motionless, as if in a trance. He had no time to say any more as the Empress took careful hold of his hands and gracefully pulled him to his feet.

The shock of realizing whom he was facing hit Braddock like a hammer in the face. His mouth opened, but no sound came out.

"You have little time," the Empress told him in Standard. "You are now the supreme ruler of your people," She said as if She had known him all his life, "and if you are to save the remains of your great fleet, you must withdraw them with all haste. I will also allow you to retrieve your warriors here, in this place. Your ships will not be menaced so long as they do not attack My Own. But you must hurry."

"What about Nicole?" he blurted, his mind struggling to catch up with the whirlwind of events, many of which he suddenly realized he had missed completely. "I won't leave her."

"No harm to her shall come, I promise you. But I have need of her yet, and shall send her on to you when all is made right again."

"What do you mean?" Braddock demanded, concerned now, uncertain.

"Remember my words," the Empress said with finality, "and preserve your people." Before Braddock had a chance to breathe another word, he was gone. Vanished.

The Empress turned to Enya, but her eyes focused on Eustus's unconscious form. Without warning, his head still cradled against Enya's breast, Eustus seemed warm, far too warm, as if he had instantly developed a raging fever.

He suddenly opened his eyes. "Lord of all," he whispered, as the heat dissipated as quickly as it had come. "It's her."

"Are you all right?" Enya asked, relief flooding through her, overcoming the strange mixture of fear and elation at what the Empress could do, had done.

"Yeah, I think so," he replied, his attention riveted upon the Empress. Enya saw that the bruises that had covered his face were gone: the Empress had healed him completely. "I feel a little shaky, but I'll be okay."

"Yes," the Empress said, "indeed you shall. But your talents are required elsewhere. You must go to the place where your warriors shall gather, and help see them safely away from here upon the ships that even now are approaching. Several of your strange devices used to aid in this task are there, awaiting you."

"Beacons?" Eustus thought aloud. "Where did you get–"

"Eustus," Enya hushed him gently, "later." She did not understand much about the alien woman who stood facing her, but she had seen enough to grasp the incredible power she wielded, as well as her sincerity. But one question could not be set aside. "Does the war end here? Or tomorrow will we once again be enemies?"

Emulating the human gesture she had learned from Reza in their childhood, the Empress shook her head. "Never again after this day shall our two races meet," she replied solemnly. "The ancient prophecies this day shall be fulfilled, and so shall end the Way of the First Empire. And just as the coming dawn shall bring the first day of the Second Empire, so, too, shall the Way of your own people take a new, brighter course."

"And what of you?" Enya asked. "What of your people? And Reza, what of him?"

The Empress turned to where Shera-Khan now stood, content, his face no longer streaked with black. "We are something much more than we have ever been," she replied gently. "And Reza... awaits me." She bowed her head. "We shall remember you. Always."

And in the Empress's eyes, Enya fully understood those words. Gazing upon a face whose soul was thousands of generations old, Enya realized that "always" to these people truly meant forever.

"Farewell, and thank you..." was all Enya had time to utter before the throne room suddenly disappeared, to be replaced by a huge landing bay somewhere else in the city and an odd assemblage of human equipment, the beacons, that Eustus was feverishly working on. Moments later, as she stood watching, the first Marines arrived.

* * *

The Empress turned Her attention to the remaining human figure that still knelt upon the dais. "That which was shared with you, child," She said gently in the Old Tongue, "must now be returned."

Seemingly weightless, Nicole rose to her feet, her eyes fixed on the Empress. Her heart raced not with fear, but with joy at Her voice, Her command.

The Empress's hand closed gently around hers, and the Kreelan monarch led her to a point on the dais where there stood a crystal spire that Nicole dimly recognized as not having been there before, and saw at its apex the crystal heart aglow with blue flame. She did not feel the claw that gently drew against the skin of her palm, did not feel the warmth of her own blood as it welled up from her flesh. She watched as the Empress's hand placed her own against the pulsing crystal heart.

"Reza," Nicole gasped as she touched it, as her blood melded with something that was not merely a structure of inert mineral carved by artisans whose bodies had turned to dust countless centuries before, but was alive and had a spirit, a soul. A soul she had known for most of her life. Like a river swollen by monsoon rains, Nicole felt the alien spirit that Reza had shared with her so long ago rush across the living bridge that had been made between her hand and the crystal vessel. The fire in her blood, numbed by the Empress's empathic touch, flickered and died just as the last of the alien voices fell silent. And then all was still. All was as it should have been, as it had been before Reza had shared his blood with her. In a way that would take her many years to understand, she was terribly saddened at the silence that suddenly filled her, the same silence and isolation that Reza had faced all of his adult life.

Exhausted, drained, she staggered back from where the crystal was now rippling with blue fire, the details of the heart's surface lost in a cyan glare. She collapsed to the floor, her eyes fixed on the blinding radiance that began to grow, expand. She knew that her eyes must be blinded by such brilliance, but she felt no pain, and dared not turn away from what was now unfolding. There was no heat, no sound. There was only the light, and the figure of the Empress standing close by, staring into the center of the tiny star that burned beside the throne. The Empress lifted her arms, hands outstretched, as if beckoning to someone.

And then Reza stepped from the light, traversing a passage that linked the here and now with some other realm that Nicole felt she had once known, but that was now a universe beyond her mortal understanding. The palms of the two lovers touched, their fingers entwined, and the Empress drew him into an embrace that left no doubt of their love for each other, the queen and her knight, man and woman, husband and wife. Behind him, the pathway closed, the light fading away until the only trace left was the afterimage that flickered in Nicole's eyes.

The crystal heart was gone.

"Nicole," Reza said quietly, suddenly kneeling next to her.

"Reza..." she shook her head, not knowing what to say, or how. His armor gleamed as if new, the Kreelan steel black and infinitely deep as the great rune – she tried in vain to remember what it signified – glowed at its center. His eyes were alight with a fire that she had never seen, with the power of life, of fulfillment.

"Father Hernandez once told me that he believed in divine miracles," she said. "I was never sure I could believe in such things... until now."

Reza smiled and took her in his arms. Holding her close to him as a brother might a beloved sister, he said, "My life, my happiness, do I owe to you. And whatever the future may bring for you and your people, Nicole, remember that I shall always love you. Always."

He kissed her, lightly, on the lips, and she put a hand to his face, her fingers tingling at the warmth of his skin.

"*Adieu*, Reza," Nicole said quietly.

"Farewell, my friend," Reza said, and then in the Old Tongue, "and may thy Way be long and glorious."

And suddenly, he was gone. Nicole felt a cold chill blow over her, and a mist clouded her vision for a split second, as if the world had suddenly gone out of focus and then come back. In the blink of an eye, she found herself staring at the dumbstruck bridge crew of the battlecruiser *Sandhurst*.

"Captain Carré!" someone exclaimed. Turning numbly toward the speaker, she saw old Admiral Sinclaire rushing toward her, his ruddy face reflecting wonder, confusion, and concern. "What in blazes...?"

But Nicole's first thought was not about where she was or how she had gotten there. It was about someone she had left behind. "Jodi..."

Fifty-Eight

Being rich, regardless of how it had come about, had had its advantages for Markus Thorella. Among the many other pleasures he had experienced as a young man, he had learned how to pilot a starship. He was not as competent or as experienced as the Navy crews who flew as part of their careers, but he could fly.

The flight controls of the *Golden Pearl*, in fact, were much the same as the yacht his father had once bought for him so many years ago. Thus, his escape from the strange disaster that had befallen Lieutenant Riggs's platoon was all but assured, even without the ill-fated command ship to extract him. The *Pearl* was waiting in the landing bay, almost as if it had been meant for his use.

Unfortunately, escape was all he could manage for the moment. He could not get back into the battle yet, for he was unable to raise any of the nearby human ships on the *Pearl's* data link, with the net result that he was cut off from the rest of the fleet. It seemed that he could receive information, but could not transmit anything. He had to assume that the onboard comms package was malfunctioning, and that the IFF system probably would not work. Without that, the *Pearl* would be singled out by any nearby human warship as an approaching enemy and blasted out of space. All he could do was curse and wonder what was wrong with the ship.

For lack of any better ideas, Thorella steered to sunward, toward the volume of space that was nearly empty of ships while he pondered what he should do. From what he saw on the tactical display, it did not take a tactical genius to understand that the human fleet was now being slowly reduced to a scattering of flaming hulks, cut off from escape by an incoming tide of Kreelan warships. Hundreds of human ships already had been destroyed, and many more were damaged or dying as Kreelan warships surrounded them and pounded them into plasma.

It was then that a familiar voice came over the comm link, accompanied by a determined face in the holo display.

"Ships of the Fleet," the voice declared, "this is Councilman Braddock of the Confederation Council. As the senior surviving member of the council, and by law the president for this emergency, I hereby order all combat units to withdraw immediately, repeat, immediately. All Marine elements now on the Kreelan moon are ordered to rendezvous at your primary pickup zones. Follow the beacons that have been set up for you. You will meet no resistance, so move as quickly as possible. All troop transports are to retrieve their landing contingents from the Kreelan moon; you have been guaranteed safe passage as long as you do not fire on any Kreelan vessels. I repeat: you are safe as long as you hold your fire. Once you recover your troops, you are ordered to immediately withdraw to Confederation space at the best possible speed." The face paused for a moment, as if listening to something off-screen. "Detailed orders are now being forwarded over the fleet command links. Follow them to the letter. Good luck and Godspeed. That is all."

The display went blank.

Before Thorella's widened eyes, the terrible ballet of ships underwent an immediate and profound change. Suddenly, the Kreelans were ferociously attacking some ships while blatantly ignoring others. The pattern made no sense to him until he realized that the ships that were mysteriously immune to attack were lightly armed Marine transports – empty – headed back down to the moon from which he had just escaped. Kreelan ships maintained weapons lock on the human ships, but made no move to attack. The only ships being attacked were those that continued to return fire. Soon, even they were left alone as their commanders realized that the councilman's words were, on the surface, at least, true.

"This is impossible," Thorella hissed angrily as he saw human battleships winking off the tactical display as they jumped into hyperspace. In but minutes, the only capital ship that remained was *Sandhurst*, Sinclaire's flagship, and the carriers that were busy recovering the Marines under the watchful eyes of the Kreelan fleet. It was a sight no human could ever have foretold, and one that many would never be able to accept as being anything other than legend or fantasy.

To Thorella, it was nothing less than cowardice. Treason.

After the initial wave of anger caused by those thoughts, he realized the full implications – for himself – of what had happened. Camden and Mackenzie had obviously survived to tell their stories, and with Braddock as the senior councilman and acting president (unless someone else more senior happened to show up, which Thorella thought was unlikely, at best), Thorella's future back in Confederation space would be exceedingly grim. His ambitions, his destiny, were blown away as if by a battleship's guns.

In a daze, he left the cockpit, not even bothering to put the ship on autopilot. *It doesn't matter*, he thought. *Nothing matters now*. He wandered aft, toward the parlor and the liquor cabinet. The *Pearl* carried only the finest, he noted bitterly as he hefted a bottle of eighty year old scotch. None of that syntho crap for her passengers! He did not even bother with a glass, but removed the cap and lifted the bottle in a mock toast to his own failure and impending demise. Then he took a long swallow, his body nearly numb to the burning liquid's passage. Like a child with a favorite teddy bear, he carried the bottle to the overstuffed chair next to the artificial fireplace and collapsed into it, drained. Finished.

It was only after he had polished off a third of the bottle that he noticed the black case perched on a table on the far side of the room, near the door. Something about it was vaguely familiar, but through the fog of alcohol and depression, he could not quite place where he had seen it before. Intrigued as he could be in his present state, he mustered enough energy to get up. Not quite walking, but not staggering, either, he made his way to the table and the mysterious case. He ran a finger over the top, noting the perfectly smooth surface and the material's excessive strength.

Could it be? a tiny voice somewhere inside his skull cried. He picked it up, feeling the weight in his hand.

"I can't believe it," he whispered to himself as his heart began to race with excitement. Dropping the bottle of expensive scotch, he set the case back down on the table – carefully, oh, so carefully – and examined its latching system. "Ohmygod," he breathed, his body quivering as if in the throes of orgasm.

There was no mistake. It was the kryolon weapon command console. The fools, he thought, had somehow gotten hold of it, and then left it behind! That was the only reason he had not recognized it sooner: his mind could not accept the possibility that it had simply been left here, unattended.

Suddenly, his fortunes had changed yet again. He thought of *Sandhurst* standing by, watching over the recovery of the Marines, and Braddock and the others on board her.

"Thank you, God," he said aloud, a blasphemy coming from such lips.

Despite what Laskowski had briefed to the General Staff about the weapons being distributed among several ships, the entire arsenal had secretly been put aboard the ill-fated *Warspite*, with two of them being transferred to the *Golden Pearl* during Gard and Mackenzie's short-lived incarceration aboard the flagship.

Only three people had known the launch codes: Borge, who was now dead; Admiral Laskowski, who had recently gone down with the *Southampton*; and Thorella. He was now the only living human being who could launch the two remaining weapons.

And launch them he would.

* * *

Jodi forced her eyes open against the pain and drugs that were gradually working their way out of her system after her forced separation from the autodoc. She had to see what Thorella was doing, had to know what scheme he had come up with that had changed his somber mood to one of disquieting elation.

Wedged into a chair at the main engineering console in the *Pearl's* engine room, Jodi was managing to hold out, minute by minute. She had been asleep in the sickbay when Thorella came aboard, and the transition to flight had awakened her. She had called out for Nicole, for the others, but no one had come. Thank the Lord of All, she thought, that she had not used the ship's intercom. That would have brought Thorella right to her.

No, she had sensed that something was wrong, and had managed to pull herself out of her bunk and crawl to a monitor. From there, she could view the cockpit. It took her a long time to be sure that she would not scream at the sight of the thing that sat at the controls. Not long after that, she decided to act.

The first thing she had to do was to get out of sick bay and find a place that would be relatively safe if Thorella decided to prowl around. The second was to find a way to neutralize whatever threat he might pose to both her and the others, wherever they might be. After a moment's consideration, her knowledge of the *Golden Pearl* led her to the engineering section all the way aft as the best place to fulfill both requirements. After that, she only had to figure out a way to get there.

It did not take her long to realize that she would never make it on her own. Now separated from the autodoc, the pain that poured into her brain was agonizing, and it was only sheer willpower and a badly bitten tongue that kept her from crying out, perhaps letting Thorella know that he was not alone on this ship.

As she lay panting, trying to rally some strength, she remembered the ship's complement of service drones. Carried by many starships, such drones were the ship's handymen, performing many of the more monotonous maintenance tasks. They were neither aesthetically attractive nor particularly intelligent, but they more than made up for it in brute strength and reliability.

Pulling herself back up to the ship's comm console, Jodi waited for the pain to subside again before she began entering the commands that she hoped would bring one of the machines to her without attracting unwanted attention. A sailor would pay no attention to a passing drone, subconsciously knowing that the machine was merely setting off to check on some subsystem or other. A psychotic Marine, however, might take more notice.

Minutes passed as Jodi fought to keep from passing out, waiting for the drone to arrive. She had no way from this panel to monitor its progress; besides, she was more interested in keeping an eye on what Thorella was doing, which was, mercifully, nothing. For the moment.

Finally, after what seemed like hours, she was rewarded with the smooth humming of a drone entering sick bay, obediently coming to a stop in front of the chair where she had been sitting, waiting.

With another burst of effort, Jodi managed to drape herself over the boxy machine's back, its impellers instantly compensating for her weight.

"Engineering," she gasped, ignoring the flecks of blood that flew from her lips.

With nothing in the form of acknowledgment, the drone retraced its path out of the room and silently headed aft, hauling her along with it.

Once in engineering, the first thing Jodi had done after locking the door behind her was to make sure that Thorella could not communicate with the outside world. She had no idea what he was up to, why he was on this ship, but she had no intention of letting him get into more trouble – or causing any. Then she disabled his maneuvering controls. That took a while, during which she heard Tony Braddock's fleet broadcast.

His voice and his words told him that Nicole must be all right, too. The thought made her feel better, but it did nothing to improve her health. She was bleeding again, inside. And there was no autodoc here to help her.

Jodi watched with grim amusement as Thorella lost himself in depression at Braddock's words. To see him crushed, defeated, was a small victory, enough to bring a smile to her battered face, and with that accomplished, her body demanded rest, and she passed out into dark oblivion.

She woke up some time later to see him tinkering with a strange black case that he had found, and she was instantly worried by the change in his demeanor. She should not have been afraid, she told herself, because he could not access any of the ship's systems from outside this compartment, and there was no way he could get in here without blowing through the hardened bulkhead.

"What are you doing, you bastard?" she whispered as she watched his fingers fly over the console that was revealed to be inside the case. "What is that thing?"

A pair of flashing lights on the control panel suddenly caught her attention: TORPEDOES ARMED, the display said.

"Wait just a minute," she hissed. "Computer," she barked, "weapons status?"

"All weapons under local control are in standby mode," the synthesized female voice answered smugly. "No targets designated, no–"

"Then why are the torpedo status lights showing that they're armed?"

"Torpedo tubes one and two are not under local control," the computer answered as if Jodi were an idiot.

"Then who controls them?" Jodi felt a bead of sweat slip down her back.

"That information is classified."

"Do tubes one and two have targets?" she asked, frantic now as she watched the status display changed from simply armed to ready.

"Affirmative."

"What are the targets?" Jodi yelled at the console.

"That information is classified."

"Goddammit," Jodi shouted helplessly, "what the fuck isn't classified?"

"Tubes one and two were reloaded with unserialized weapons while we were docked with *Warspite*," the machine answered suddenly.

"What weapons?" Jodi asked. "Special weapons? What kind?"

"That information is–"

"Shut up!" Jodi shouted angrily. "Show me a theoretical torpedo trajectory based on current ship's vector and torpedo launcher alignment." She could not get the computer to tell her what the real target was, but maybe she could dupe it into giving it to her anyway.

"One moment." And then the holo screen showed the sector of space near the sun. A red line arced out from the icon that was the yacht, following a trajectory right into the sun.

"What the hell..." Jodi whispered to herself. Suddenly, she understood. She had heard the tales, but had never believed them until now. *Kryolon warheads*. And Thorella controlled them. Her blood turned to ice in her veins.

"Computer," she ordered, "shut down all power to weapons–"

The ship shuddered. Again.

"Torpedoes one and two away," the computer announced cheerfully. "Power-down to weapons systems commencing... Completed. Weapons successfully powered down."

Too late! Jodi cursed herself. On the holo display, the two weapons followed the computer's projected course with unsurprising precision.

There was only one thing left for her to do now, she thought. It would no doubt cost her life, but there was no choice. She reactivated the datalink, hoping that Thorella would not catch on until it was too late.

"All ships, all ships, this is the *Golden Pearl*..."

* * *

"Weapons launch!" *Sandhurst's* tactical officer cried, his eyes following the trajectories of two torpedoes launched from the small ship trailing behind the rest of the retreating fleet. For the last hectic forty minutes – it had seemed like hours – his primary job had been to keep human ships from firing on Kreelan ones, and for the most part he had been successful.

"Who?" Admiral Sinclaire demanded.

"It looks like that yacht, sir, the *Golden Pearl*," the tactical officer replied quickly as his fingers stabbed angrily at his console, "but I'm not getting an IFF response, no datalink, and no voice, either. She's not responding at all."

"What's she targeting?"

"Don't know, sir. There aren't any Kreelan ships in that quadrant." Pause. "The torpedoes are headed right into the sun."

What the Devil? Sinclaire thought. He had just gotten the fleet back into some kind of order, strange as it was, and he was not about to let things fall back into chaos, especially with the Marine transports still en route back from the Kreelan moon.

He was about to ask something else when the comms officer suddenly shouted, "Fleet emergency broadcast, admiral!"

"On screen!" Sinclaire demanded immediately. He was shocked by what he saw.

"All ships, all ships, this is the *Golden Pearl*."

"Jodi," Nicole whispered, fighting to keep the tears of rage held in check at the sight of her friend's mutilated face, guilt surging through her for abandoning Jodi in her hour of need.

"This is Admiral Sinclaire aboard *Sandhurst*. Go ahead, commander."

"Sir," Jodi said thickly, obviously in excruciating pain, "you've got to get the fleet away from here as fast as you can. You're all in great danger."

"Commander, the Kreelans have given us time–"

"It's not the Kreelans, sir," she interrupted him, "it's the weapons General Thorella, who's aboard this ship, just launched. You should be tracking two torpedoes, heading into the sun." A nod to Sinclaire from the tactical officer. Two maroon streaks were rapidly making their way across the holo image of this part of the system to the star at its center. "I think they're fitted with kryolon warheads." She paused in the sudden silence that enveloped *Sandhurst's* bridge.

"Thorella launched these things?" Sinclaire managed to say with what felt like someone else's tongue, so shocked was he to be hearing this. "On whose authority?"

She gave him a bitter smile through blood-caked lips. "His own, of course," she rasped. "He's never needed anyone else's."

"I am coming to get you, Jodi," Nicole said suddenly. She had made a quick mental calculation from the tactical display. "I'll be there in twenty minutes."

"Nicole," Tony said from behind her, putting a hand on her shoulder. She shrugged it off angrily.

Jodi shook her head slowly, wincing at the pain the movement caused. "You can't risk it, Nicole. There's no time. And... I don't think I'll last that long now, anyway." A bitter smile.

Sinclaire could feel the hair on the back of his neck stand on end. *Kryolons, of all things. Could it be true?* More to the point, could he discount the possibility? And what could he do about it? *Run like hell*, he told himself, a shudder rippling up his spine. "Mister Zhirinovski!" he bellowed to the acting fleet operations officer.

"Sir?"

"How much longer to jump?"

"We should be ready in seventeen minutes, sir." Five assault transports were still coming in; their carriers would jump as soon as they were aboard, and *Sandhurst* would follow them out, the last human ship to leave. The only ones now being left behind would never be coming home, anyway, their drives dead, their life support failing. There were simply not enough able ships left to rescue all the stragglers.

Sinclaire turned on his tactical officer. "How long before the torpedoes reach the corona?"

"Just under two minutes, sir," he replied, noting that the torpedoes had now run out of fuel and were coasting on toward their target. "If what I've heard about the kryolons is right, we'll have about fifteen minutes from initiation of the kryolon reaction – that'll be upon detonation in the corona – to the first stellar debris reaching us here." He looked helpless for a moment. "But that's just a guess."

"Better than nothing, lad," Sinclaire said quickly. "Zhirinovski, you've got ten minutes to get the other ships out of here. Tell the transports to push it past the limit. If they're not back aboard by then, they get left behind." Five minutes was not much of a safety margin, but it was all he could give them.

"Aye, sir!"

"Captain Jorgensen," Sinclaire spoke into the comm link to the ship's bridge, "we've got a problem."

"Sir?" the captain answered immediately, her attention riveted on the old sailor's face in the screen.

"Have *Sandhurst* ready for her jump in ten minutes, captain. The Kreelan sun may be... unstable. We're pushing up the timetable."

"Aye, admiral," Jorgensen answered. "We're ready any time, sir."

Sinclaire nodded.

"What about her?" Nicole demanded quietly, nodding toward Jodi's image. Her eyes were closed, head down.

"She's right, lass," Sinclaire said as gently as he could. "You couldn't get there in time to help her. You'd only die, too. Perhaps... keeping her company might be best. No one likes to go out of this world alone, and Lord knows she's earned what little comfort any of us can provide."

Nicole nodded in resignation, now welcoming Braddock's arm around her shoulder. But she looked up suddenly at Jodi's voice.

"Nicole," she said in a whisper, "It's Thorella. I think he's coming..."

FIFTY-NINE

Reza did not have to see what was taking place throughout the Empire; he could sense it. He was spiritually reconnected with Her Children, with the Bloodsong again echoing in his veins. He could again sense Her will, and knew that a great Change was about to take place, something that would alter his people forever and take them to the next step in their evolution as a species. Wherever they were, warriors and clawless ones waited for the rapture that they knew was about to come, only moments away now. Even the hapless males that had been evacuated from the nurseries knew that something was happening, for while they were witless creatures with but a single function in life, they, too, were bound to Her will. And in their own way, they felt the tremor in the life force that bound them all to one another, that was the endless thread of life that the Kreela called the Way. While they did not realize it in their blissful ignorance, they had been redeemed, and the glory and honor that had once been theirs was about to be again in the new form that was soon to come.

But Reza's mind was yet troubled, for there remained one task for him to complete. He did not have to ask his Empress for what he desired, for in Her great wisdom, She already knew.

"I know of the one you seek," She told him. "Do this thing and return to Me, my love. For our time here grows short; the new dawn is soon upon us."

"I shall not be long, my Empress," he replied, his hand fastened about the handle of the ancient sword Tesh-Dar had once given him.

"Let it be done."

And Reza vanished.

* * *

Jodi's plan would have worked completely had she only remembered to turn off the display monitors on the drones like the one that had brought her to engineering. She had finally cut Thorella off from accessing any of the other systems on the ship. But she had forgotten that one little thing.

Thorella was laying on his back, his head and shoulders buried in the ship's central computer core in a vain attempt to figure out what was ailing the *Pearl* when one of the idiot machines came up to him, intent on dislodging this odd parasite from its electronic parent. Thorella kicked at it in fury, not understanding or caring what the machine was trying to do, and accidentally turned up the volume control on the machine's internal voice relay.

"Thorella launched these things?" he heard someone say. "On whose authority?"

"His own, of course," came a choked reply. "He's never needed anyone else's."

Thorella did not need to hear any more.

"Mackenzie," he hissed, withdrawing himself from the computer's innards and pushing past the single-minded drone. His blaster in hand, he quickly made his way aft, to the one section of the ship he had not taken the time to check.

Engineering.

* * *

Jodi saw him on the monitor outside the door.

"He's here," she sighed, trembling inwardly. "Oh, shit." She tried to hold the blaster she had taken from the small weapons vault near the door, but her broken fingers could not hold it right. Even with both hands.

"Jodi," Nicole said from very, very far away, "can he get to you?"

He stood in front of the door, looking straight into the video pickup. Smiling.

"I don't think so," she said. But then he held up what could only be a coded magnetic key, and she watched in horror as he swiped it across the door's access panel. She had no way of knowing, but Borge had made sure Thorella was provided with a proper commander's key for the ship that could open any door. "Oh, shit," she moaned. "Yes, he can get in..."

"Jodi, try to–"

The door slid open.

"Game's over, bitch," Thorella said quietly as he leveled his blaster at her stomach. He would make sure she died, but he did not want to hurry her along too much.

"Fuck you, you bastard son of a who–"

Something unexpected happened just as Thorella squeezed the trigger. There was a blast of frigid air, a moving shadow, a high keening sound that Jodi thought she had heard before. But only the gun that was pointed at her mattered, the gun with a bore that seemed as big around as an irrigation pipe.

In a slow motion dream she saw Reza appear out of thin air to her left, his mouth open in a snarl of rage that she could not hear, his arm held out before him as if... as if he had... thrown something? In front of her, only a few paces away, she watched Thorella's face glow in the backlight of the blast his weapon made as it fired. But there was something odd about it, she thought, odd about his hand, the weapon. It took her an eternal moment to realize that they were no longer attached to his arm. Thorella's hand, still clutching the gun, was falling – so slowly falling – toward the deck, the stump of his arm now shooting blood at her instead of searing energy. Curious, she followed the crimson stream, noting with some small surprise that it intersected a gaping hole where her abdomen had once been. She touched the ragged edge with a numbed hand. Warm. Wet. *Oh, God.*

Reza stood still a moment, stunned by the horrible misfortune of his timing. *A second sooner*, he raged to himself, *and I could have saved her*. He turned his attention to Thorella. "I should have killed you a long time ago," Reza said softly through the smoke that rose around them from the shot that had smashed Jodi's body.

"You have to take me back for trial," Thorella cried as he tried to hold the stump of his arm with his good hand, Reza's shrekka having severed it just below the elbow. He nodded toward the screen where Nicole's horrified face still looked on. "You can't kill me," he gloated, "not with the whole fleet watching. It'd be murder."

"Enough." Reza had long debated how he would kill Thorella: slowly, the way he deserved to die for all the evil he had done, or quickly, mercifully. Reza decided on the latter, not to show Thorella mercy, but because he could simply stand this horrible pestilence no more.

But just as he was about to take Thorella's head with his sword, he heard a voice that tore open his heart.

"Reza..."

He turned to look at Jodi's pleading face. He hesitated, only a fraction of a second, but it was enough for Thorella to bolt through the still open door and disappear down the corridor.

"Reza," Jodi whispered. "How...?"

"Do not speak," he quieted her as he momentarily pushed Thorella from his mind. He cradled her gently as he fought not to look at what was left of her once beautiful body. For the first and only time in his adult life, he sincerely hoped there somewhere was a Hell like old Father Hernandez had believed existed, and that Thorella would fall there to burn forever. If nothing else, Reza would make sure that he would get to find out. "There is yet time. I can take you to the Empress. She can heal you–"

"No," Jodi shook her head weakly. "It's better this way, Reza. I think... my number's come up... I ought to take it like a lady." She looked up at him. "Tell me... Nicole will be... safe?"

He nodded. "She will. For always. The Empress will let no harm come to her. Ever."

Jodi smiled. *Nicole would be safe.* That was all that mattered.

"Reza?" Nicole's brittle voice called from the display beside him, yet from hundreds of thousands of leagues away. "You've got to get out of there."

"I cannot leave Jodi–"

"Reza," Nicole interrupted him, "your sun is going to explode any minute now. You've got to get out! We did not know how to tell you, we only found out for ourselves from Jodi before... before..."

"The Empress knows of this," he told her. "It is part of our future. We await it. But it is time for you and the others to leave here, Nicole." Reza felt a ripple in his bones. It was about to happen. "Quickly." He looked at her one last time. "May thy Way be long and glorious, my friend."

"Detonation!" someone cried on *Sandhurst's* bridge. On the main viewscreen, the Kreelan sun flared with crimson brilliance as its corona began to blow outward and the deeper layers of the stricken star began to expand behind it.

"Jodi..." Nicole said, but Jodi was no longer there to talk to. The image had suddenly filled with static. Both of her best friends were gone.

* * *

Aboard the *Golden Pearl*, Reza watched Nicole's image fade as the dying star's energy was released, destroying the data link to *Sandhurst*.

"Reza, you've got to leave me," Jodi implored him quietly. "Please."

Still holding her gently, he could feel the life running from her body like the last grains of sand from an hourglass. "Do not fear for me," he said softly as he kissed her hair. "I promised that I would always be there for you, remember?" He closed his eyes, his heart aching for her. "I won't leave you now," he whispered.

"Thank you, Reza," she sighed, cradled against his shoulder. "I... love you."

"I love you, too, Jodi," he told her softly, fighting back his tears as he felt her spirit slip away, leaving her body an empty shell. After kissing her tenderly on the lips, he gently laid her body down on the deck.

With a fleeting glance at the display on the engineering console that showed Thorella on the flight deck, Reza smiled grimly at his enemy's fate, trapped alone on a ship that was doomed by his own hand.

Then he conjured in his mind a vision of his waiting Empress, his love, and vanished from the *Golden Pearl* to join Her.

All alone now, Markus Thorella hammered at the *Pearl's* useless command console as the wall of fire from the exploding star rushed forward to claim him. He was still howling in fear and rage as the ship was torn to atoms.

* * *

"Jodi," she heard a voice call in the darkness. It was a voice Jodi recognized, one that she had once loved.

"Tanya?" she called, not sure where she was, growing afraid.

"Yes, darling," Tanya answered from beside her, taking Jodi's hand. "Don't be afraid. Everything's all right now." Jodi felt the warmth of Tanya's lips on hers, and suddenly saw her face, young and beautiful as it had once been, but without the shadow over her soul. "Come on," Tanya told her, smiling as she led Jodi by the hand toward a golden glow the color of a sunrise. "Everyone's waiting for you."

And together they stepped into the light, leaving the darkness behind forever.

* * *

"The *Golden Pearl's* gone." On the tactical display, Nicole watched as the sphere of superheated matter blotted out the tiny icon that had once been a ship and her friends, but that also meant the end of Thorella's reign of terror. The shock wave reached out ever further, consuming everything in its path.

"Zhirinovski, how many ships are left behind us?"

"None, sir. We're the last."

"Captain Jorgensen," Sinclaire called to the ship's captain, "are your boats all aboard?"

"Yes, sir."

"Very well. Stand by for jump."

"Radiation is in the yellow, admiral," the ops officer warned.

"A moment," Sinclaire replied, his attention riveted to the chaotic scene on the tactical display. He wondered at the Kreelan fleet now clustered around the homeworld and its strange moon. There were tens of thousands of ships now, some of them unbelievably huge, and more were still jumping in. *Lord of All*, he thought, *why don't they jump out? The Kreelans on the planet are doomed, but at least the ships could save themselves...*

"Jesus," someone whispered as the stellar matter's first tendrils brushed the homeworld. The main viewer and tactical display suddenly went dark.

"Overloaded," someone said somberly.

"Captain Jorgensen," Sinclaire ordered, his last act before he would allow exhaustion to overtake him, "take us home."

* * *

The star that had warmed and given life to their world was dying, but even in its death it served the needs of the Empress. Having blinded the primitive electronic eyes of the humans, who were not yet prepared to understand, She made ready to take Her Children on the next part of the journey that was their eternal Way.

The vast fleet of ships was arrayed to capture the necessary energy from the exploding sun and focus it like a great lens upon the Empress moon and the Empress Herself. Reaching out with Her mind and spirit, bending the massive influx of energy to Her will, She opened a gateway in space-time that would not even be theorized by humankind for another fifty-thousand years. As one, Her people – every soul spread across the ten thousand suns of the Empire – passed through it on their first step toward the next phase of their evolution. Had humans witnessed it, they would have thought it nothing more and nothing less than magic.

Beside Her, Reza looked back through the closing portal, wondering at what had been, what could have been. He mourned Jodi's death, and wondered about Nicole, feeling a sense of emptiness that he would never again be able to see her or speak to her.

"Fear not, my love," his Empress told him, her voice warming his soul as She embraced him, Her green eyes glittering with love. "You will see her yet once more..."

Epilogue

Nicole rose at eight-thirty, three hours later than was her custom on a workday. But today was special, a day that had become something of a ritual over the years. Today was the tenth anniversary of the Great Expedition, ten years since the Armada had returned home from battle with the Empire. Ten years since Jodi had died. And Reza. And so many others. It was a Confederation holiday, but Nicole would not be participating in any of the official functions with her husband, the president. In other times, perhaps, it would have been expected for a spouse – especially a woman – to participate in such affairs, to look dutifully somber before the media, but Nicole had paid her dues. She was a patriot, and had the scars and dead friends and family to prove it. Hers was a time of private contemplation. Shockingly, the people of the Confederation had respected this melancholy quirk without the heartless scrutiny that was usually turned upon public figures that did not quite fit the mold, and Nicole respected her people all the more for it.

She rose and showered, welcoming the soothing warmth of the hot water on her face, thankful for such a luxury, and content in the knowledge that the many throughout the Confederation who did not have such a simple thing as this someday would. For nearly a century, humanity had labored for simple survival. But now, with the war over, men and women were again free to look ahead, to plan and build for the future. They would not have to wonder if incoming ships bore Marines who promised salvation, or an alien horde that promised death. No longer would every resource have to be devoted to the making of war; while war and the chance of it would always be with them, for a while at least the young could grow old without the constant threat of death in combat. They could again take up art and philosophy, learn to love again, and do all the many things that made humanity something special in the Universe, something worth saving. There would always be wars, she knew, but there would also be sailors, Marines, and soldiers of the Territorial Army to protect the Confederation, for humankind had learned its lesson well. But now there was room for more, for humanity to again be human.

Sitting before a mirror now, she applied Navy regulation makeup, a process that was at once simple and difficult. Simple, because there was very little that regulations allowed; difficult, because she had become used to putting on more as the years had gone by, a token surrender, perhaps, to the inexorable advance of age. There were definite wrinkles now, but not too many, she decided. Some gray in her hair, but not too much. *Natural highlighting*, she thought with a smile. Time had treated her well these last years, and if anything she had become more beautiful with each birthday, at least if she was to go by Tony's compliments. She smiled into the mirror. A much younger woman's face smiled back.

That part of her ritual complete, she went to the bedroom that had been dubbed the house's official "junk" room. It was where all the flotsam and jetsam of life that was too valuable to throw away, yet not immediately significant enough to display from day to day, found a permanent resting place. In the closet she found her Navy dress black uniform in its environmentally controlled bag. Carrying it back to their bedroom, she laid it out carefully on the bed, running her hands over the smooth synthetic fabric, her fingers tracing the gold braid that proclaimed her a commodore, her last promotion before retirement. The rows of medals, including the Confederation Medal of Honor that would have made an old Marine colonel she had once known very proud, indeed, were bright against the dark fabric. The genuine leather boots that Tony had given her one year for Christmas gleamed like Kreelan armor.

She put the uniform on carefully, religiously, savoring the feel of the silk lining against her skin, the authoritarian firmness of the boots on her feet. She thought of how Reza used to dress when he had returned from the Empire, of the ritual it was for him each morning as he donned his armor and waited to meet the rising sun. Her heart became heavy at the thought, but she did not push it away. Today was reserved for him, for all of them, and she welcomed the pain of the memories as best she could, in their honor.

Standing before the full-length mirror, she appraised herself critically, glaring at herself as she might a subordinate in a formal inspection. She nodded to herself in approval. All was well, indeed perfect. She had never had it re-tailored, and it still fit as it had ten years ago, despite having had two children since then.

The children, she thought, a smile clearing her face of the fierce commodore's glare: Jodi Marie and Reza Georges Braddock, whose first names honored Jodi and Reza. Neither Nicole nor Tony could think of a more fitting way to honor their fallen friends.

She thought of the children now, no doubt standing beside their father as he read the ceremonial speech for today, which was different from those he had written for this day over the last ten years, and each of those different from the others. There had been enough pain, enough courage all those years ago to fill such eulogies anew for centuries to come.

Placing her cap just so upon her head, Nicole said good-bye to the servants and the Secret Service agents – none would accompany her this day – and stepped into the aircar that awaited her.

The pilot said nothing to her during the flight. One of Reza's troops from the Red Legion, Warren Zevon had finished his tour with the Marines and, on the recommendation of Sergeant Major of the Marine Corps Eustus Camden, had been accepted as Nicole's personal secretary and bodyguard. He took care of the administrative part of her public life and gave her the one precious gift that was so hard to find: extra time. Time for her family, time for herself. Zevon was not normally so quiet, but he knew that her thoughts were on the past, and he gave her privacy through his silence. He, in turn, nurtured his own remembrances of his friends now lost, of his old commander, of good times and bad.

Their destination was the small village of Hamilton, where a woman Nicole had never known had left a legacy beyond her own death in what had come to be known as the Fleet Shrine. A simple obelisk of black granite, polished smooth, in the center of a great and peaceful garden, the Fleet Shrine was not the most elaborate of the many war memorials on Earth and the rest of the Confederation, nor was it the most popularly known. But the words etched into the granite made it very special to Nicole, and it had become part of her ritual.

As she walked toward the obelisk through the garden of blooming flowers, she again read the words inscribed in the polished black granite:

To Those of the Armada Who Never Returned Home:
Your Sacrifice Shall Not Be Forgotten

Then, in smaller letters:

Dedicated to Commander Jodi Ellen Mackenzie,
Whose Hour of Need Led to My Salvation

The name of the woman who had arranged for the monument to be constructed and who had left millions of credits to the Service Relief Fund was not inscribed in the granite, although Nicole knew her name: Tanya Buchet. It had been a strange thing, she recalled: the Buchet woman had died mysteriously just before the Armada had left for Kreelan space, yet the instructions for the shrine had been part of her will. What her relationship was with Jodi, Nicole did not and would never know, but it was obvious that Jodi had been close to her heart.

In another strange coincidence, Jodi had been Tanya Buchet's sole beneficiary, and, in turn, Jodi had left her entire estate to Nicole. So, in the end, Fate had left Nicole rich beyond her wildest dreams. But she and Tony had decided that the money that Nicole had inherited would be put back into reconstruction programs on Erlang. She and Tony had each other and the children, in a galaxy that was, for the moment, safe to live in. She could ask God – or the Empress – for nothing more.

Sitting on the bench that faced the inscription, Nicole let her mind wander, just as Zevon wandered through the garden, lost in his own thoughts, but with one eye glued to Nicole in case she needed his protection. She sat that way for a long time, looking into the blackness of the granite, thinking of the past, and sometimes just not thinking at all.

She thought perhaps that she might have fallen asleep for a moment. For when she next opened her eyes something told her that her surroundings had somehow changed. Zevon still strolled through the gardens, more or less where she last remembered him; the sun had not moved appreciably, so not too much time had passed; the birds still sang. Everything seemed to be as it had been. And yet...

She suddenly looked up at the obelisk, into the shimmering blackness of the granite, and there he was, with the Empress and Shera-Khan – an adult warrior now – standing beside him.

"Reza," she breathed.

His image nodded, as if he was not accustomed to the gesture, but the warmth of the smile on his face was more than human.

"All is well, my friend," she heard him say, but his mouth did not form the words; he spoke directly to her mind. "On this day we celebrate the Last Ascension, Keel-Tath's return to us and our greatest journey upon the Way. And we wished to share this moment with you, to leave you something in remembrance of me, of us. For after this day, we shall never be able to return; we shall forever be... beyond this place, this time."

Nicole fought for words as she stood up and carefully approached the obelisk, unwilling to believe but unable to deny what she was seeing. "Reza, your planet was destroyed! How... where... where are you?"

"That is not important, child," the Empress, who had once been Esah-Zhurah, told her gently. "This, however, is." She held Her hand forth, Her fingers curled around something nestled in Her palm.

Nicole, eyes wide with disbelief, reached out toward the image in the obelisk, and drew back as she felt something placed in her cupped hands by the alien fingers that shimmered from the face of the stone.

It was the eyestone from the collar that Esah-Zhurah had once worn before becoming Empress. It was a deep, gleaming blue, engraved with the rune of what Nicole suddenly remembered was the order of the Desh-Ka, the oldest of all those that had ever served Her.

"To your name shall we always sing our praise," the Empress said. "Fare thee well, daughter."

Nicole looked up just in time to see the images fading, dissolving like a reflection in a pool into which a rock has been thrown.

"*Adieu*, Nicole," Reza said, as if from far away.

And then their images were gone. Nicole put a hand against the obelisk, but it was solid, unyielding as it should be. *I must have been hallucinating*, she told herself.

But then she felt something in her hand: it was the eyestone with the rune of the Desh-Ka carved in its center. It was real.

"Nicole?" Zevon asked from beside her. He had become worried when she had approached the obelisk and acted as if she were talking to it. "Is anything wrong?"

"No," she replied with a smile at his concerned expression. She closed her hands over the eyestone, glad in her heart at the knowledge that Reza and his people had somehow survived. It seemed to her that things this day were right in the world, and that tomorrow would dawn yet brighter than today. "Everything is fine, dear

Warren," she told him, taking his arm and leading him from the obelisk and out into the flowering gardens. "Come, it is time for us to go home."

If You've Enjoyed The Tale Thus Far...

The *In Her Name* saga continues with *First Contact*, the lead novel in a hard-hitting trilogy about how the human-kreelan war began. You can also get *First Contact* as part of *The Last War*, a trilogy collection that also includes *Legend Of The Sword* and *Dead Soul.*

To give you a taste of what's to come, here's the first chapter from *First Contact* - enjoy!

* * *

Captain Owen McClaren was extremely tense, although a casual observer would never have thought so. Commanding the survey vessel *TNS Aurora*, he was one of the best officers in the fleet, and to his crew he had never appeared as anything but calm and in control. Even when one of the ship's newly refitted reactors had suffered a breach during their last run into dry dock, McClaren's deep voice had never wavered, his fatherly face had never betrayed a hint of fear or apprehension as he personally directed the engineering watch to contain the breach. A man of unusual physical and moral courage, he was the perfect captain for the exploratory missions the *Aurora* and her sister ships mounted into distant space, seeking new homes for humanity.

McClaren had made thousands of jumps in his twenty-year career, but every one was like the very first: an adrenaline joyride. As the transpace sequence wound down to zero, his heart would begin to pound and his muscles tensed like spring steel. It wasn't fear that made him react that way, although there were enough things that could go wrong with a jump to make fear a natural enough reaction.

No, what made the forty-three-year-old former middleweight boxing champion of the Terran Naval Academy hold the arms of his command chair in a white-knuckle grip wasn't fear. It was anticipation. To *Aurora's* captain, every jump, particularly out here in uncharted space, was a potential winning lottery ticket, the discovery of a lifetime. No matter where the *Aurora* wound up, as long as she arrived safely, there was bound to be a wealth of astrogational information to help human starships travel ever farther from Man's birthplace: Earth.

On rare occasions, precious habitable planets were to be found. Finding such systems was the primary goal of the survey ships. McClaren was currently the fleet's leading "ace," with twelve habitable planets to his credit in return for nearly fifteen years of ship-time, sailing through uncharted space.

"Stand by for transpace sequence," the pilot announced, her words echoing through every passageway and compartment in the *Aurora's* five hundred meter length.

McClaren tensed even more, his strong arm and back muscles flexing instinctively as if he were back in the ring, preparing to land a solid upper cut to the chin of an imaginary opponent. But his calm expression never wavered. "Very well," he answered, his dark brown eyes drinking in the growing torrent of information on the navigation display.

"Computer auto-lock engaged," interjected a faux female voice reassuringly. McClaren always had to suppress a grimace: the one thing he had never liked about *Aurora* was the computer's voice. It reminded him too much of his first wife.

For the next few seconds, the crew was little more than excess baggage as the ship's computer guided the transition from hyperspace back into the Einsteinian universe with a precision measured in quadrillionths of a second. While the bridge, which was buried deep in the *Aurora's* core habitation section, had no direct observation windows, the wraparound display depicted the eerie streams of light that swirled around the ship in complete detail. But what the human eye saw in the maelstrom of quantum physics beyond the ship's hyperdrive field was an illusion. It was real in one sense, but in another it wasn't. Space and time as humans commonly understood it did not exist in this realm. As the captain of a starship, McClaren had to understand both the theory and the practical application of hyperspace and the means to travel through it. But he was content in the knowledge that he never could have come up with the breakthroughs that allowed this miracle to happen: he stood on the shoulders of the scientific giants who had made the first test jump into hyperspace long before he was born.

While in hyperspace, the display would normally show the computer's assessment of the relative location of stars and other known celestial waypoints as the ship moved along its straight-line (relatively speaking) course. But McClaren always cleared the display to show what was really outside the ship just before they dropped back into normal space. It was a sight he never tired of.

"Ten seconds..." the computer's voice began counting down to the transition. "Five...four...three...two...one....sequence initiated. Hyperspace Engines disengaged."

The display suddenly shifted, the swirling light streams condensing into a bright yellow sun against a background of stars. McClaren knew that the system had several planets; gravitational perturbations observed from their last jump point had confirmed that much. The question was whether there were any orbiting at a distance from the star where water could exist as a liquid. For where there was liquid water, there was the possibility of carbon-based life. The trick now was to find them. Planets were huge close up, but in the vast expanse of a star system they seemed incredibly small.

"Engineering confirms hyperspace engines are secure, sir," the executive officer, Lieutenant Commander Rajesh Kumar, reported. "Engineering is ready to answer all bells, and the ship is secured for normal space."

Nodding his thanks to his exec, McClaren turned to the most important person currently on the bridge: the navigator. "Raisa, what's the word?"

The navigator looked like she would have given McClaren a run for his money in the boxing ring. Big-boned and heavily muscled, Lieutenant Raisa Marisova had in fact been a champion wrestler in her college years. But it was her genius at stellar astrogation that had won her a place on the *Aurora's* all-volunteer crew.

"Well..." she murmured as she rechecked her readings for what McClaren knew was probably the fifth time in the few moments the ship had dropped back into normal space. Raisa was always able to confirm the ship's emergence point so quickly because her calculations for pointing the various telescopes and other sensors at known stars to make a positional fix were always so precise. "It seems we are...right where we are supposed to be," she said as she turned and smiled at her captain, "give or take a few meters. We're above the ecliptic plane based on our pre-jump survey information. Now it's up to the survey team to find your next habitable planet, captain."

McClaren grinned, then opened a channel to the entire ship. "Well, crew, it looks like we've made another successful jump, and emerged right on target. The bad news is that we're even farther out in the Middle of Nowhere. But that's what they pay us for. Great job, everyone." The last few words were more than just a token verbal pat on the back: he truly meant it. Unlike most transits that took regular ships into hyperspace for a few days or even a week or two, the *Aurora* routinely made jumps that lasted for weeks or months. While McClaren's crew made it look easy, he knew quite well that an amazing amount of planning and preparation went into every jump, and his crew followed it up with painstaking diligence every moment they were in hyperspace. It wasn't just that they didn't want to wind up somewhere other than where they had planned, or because their captain expected perfection. It was because they had no intention of settling for second best. Period. "Everybody gets an extra round on me when we get back to the barn. Carry on."

The bridge crew grinned at one another: the captain ran up a huge bar tab on every mission, but he never failed to deliver when the ship made port.

They had no way of knowing that all but one of them would be dead in a few short hours.

* * *

The stranger's arrival was no surprise to the Imperial warships that orbited the Settlements on the third and fourth planets from the star. While even the greatly advanced technology of the Empire could not track ships while in hyperspace, they could easily detect the gravity spikes of vessels about to emerge in normal space. The stranger had been detected many hours before, as measured in the time of humans.

While this system was at the distant edge of the Empire, far from the Homeworld and the Empress, its defenses were not lacking: of the dozens of starships in orbit around the two settled worlds and the hundreds plying the asteroid belt, four were battlecruisers built within the last century. Humans might have considered them old, until they understood that the warriors of the Empire had sailed among the stars for over one hundred thousand of Earth's years. Even the most ancient of Her warships still plying the void between the stars was tens of thousands of years more advanced than the arriving stranger. Humans would barely have recognized them as starships.

But the warriors charged with protecting this far-flung system had no way of knowing the primitive nature of the incoming stranger. Nor would they have cared. The Empire had encountered other sentient races over the millennia, and the first contact protocol was no different now than it had been in ages past: the stranger would be greeted with overwhelming force.

In unison, the four enormous battlecruisers left orbit for the gravity anomaly at maximum velocity, safe behind shields that could protect them from titanic energy discharges and made them all but invisible to anything but direct visual observation.

Behind them, smaller warships and the planetary defense systems prepared to welcome the new arrival should it prove more than a match for the great warships sent to greet it.

* * *

"Bridge, this is Survey..."

Captain McClaren frowned despite himself. He knew that Lieutenant Amundsen's survey team worked fast, but they had been in-system less than fifteen minutes. It often took days for them to identify the orbits of any planets in the temperate zone unless they had extensive perturbation data on the star or stars in the system. And that they rarely had: humanity's rapid expansion to the stars didn't allow for years-long observations of any given star. His frown deepened as he took in the expression on Amundsen's face in the comms display. The normally very reserved man was uncharacteristically excited. And just as frightened. "What is it, Jens?"

"Sir..." Amundsen began, his pale blue eyes darting away momentarily to another display. "Captain...we've confirmed not just one, but *two* planets in the temperate zone..."

"Hot damn!" McClaren couldn't help himself. One planet that might have liquid water was miracle enough. Their pre-jump analysis had suggested there was one, but two had been too much to hope for. "That's fantastic!"

"Sir...they're both inhabited," Amundsen said in hoarse whisper. Normally a quiet man, often more at home with the stars and planets than his fellow human beings, the volume of his voice dropped with every word. "We didn't have to find their orbits. We found them from their neutrino and infrared readings." He paused. "I've...I've never seen anything like this. Even Sol system doesn't have this level of activity. The two planets in the temperate zone are highly industrialized. There are other points of activity throughout the asteroid belt, and on several moons orbiting a solitary gas giant. We have also observed ships through the primary telescope. Hundreds of them. They are...nothing like ours."

The captain sat back, stunned. *First contact*, he thought. Humans had explored thousands of star systems and endless volumes of space, but had never once encountered another sentient species. They had found life aplenty on the hundred-odd discovered worlds that would support human life or could be terraformed. From humble bacteria to massive predators that would have been at home with Earth's dinosaurs, life in the Universe was as expansive as it was diverse if you looked long and far enough. But no one had discovered a single sign of sentient life beyond the mark *homo sapiens* had left behind in his celestial travels.

Until now.

"Jesus," the captain breathed, conscious now of the entire bridge crew staring at him. They hadn't heard Amundsen's words, but they immediately picked up on the captain's reaction. "XO," he ordered, pulling his mind back to the here and now, "let's have the first contact protocols." He looked pointedly at Kumar. "I want to make damn sure these folks understand we're harmless."

"Aye, sir," Kumar replied crisply as his fingers flew over his terminal. "Coming up on display one." A segment of the bridge wraparound screen darkened as the standing orders for first contact appeared.

"Lieutenant Amundsen," McClaren ordered, "let's see some of these ships of yours on display two."

"Sir." Amundsen's face bobbed about slightly in the captain's comms terminal as he patched the telescope feed to another segment of the main bridge display.

"Lord of All," someone whispered. The *Aurora's* primary telescope was nearly ten meters across, and dominated the phalanx of survey instruments mounted in the massive spherical section that made up the ship's bow. Normally used to search for and map stellar and planetary bodies, it could also be pressed into service to provide high magnification visuals of virtually anything, even moving objects that were relatively close, such as nearby (in terms of a stellar system) ships.

But what it showed now was as unlike the *Aurora* as she herself was unlike a wooden sailing ship. While the *Aurora* was largely a collection of cylindrical sections attached to a sturdy keel that ran from the engineering section at the stern to the instrumentation cluster at the bow, the alien ship displayed on the bridge display was insectile in appearance, her hull made up of sleek curves that gave McClaren the impression of a gigantic wasp.

"Why does the focus keep shifting?" Marisova asked into the sudden silence that had descended on the bridge. The alien vessel shimmered in the display as if a child were twisting an imaginary focus knob for the primary telescope back and forth, taking the image in and out of focus.

"That's what I was about to say," Amundsen answered, McClaren now having shifted the survey team leader's image onto yet a third segment of the bridge display. Before he had seemed both excited and frightened. Now it was clear that fear was crowding out his excitement. "That is one of at least four ships that is heading directly toward us from the outer habitable planet. The reason you are seeing the focusing anomaly is because the ships are moving at an incredible velocity, and the telescope cannot hold the image in alignment. Even what you see here has been enhanced with post-processing." He visibly gulped. "Captain, they knew we were coming, hours, possibly even a few days, before we arrived. They knew right where we were going to be, and they must have left orbit before we arrived. They *must* have. It's theoretically possible to predict a hyperspace emergence, but...we now know that it's not just a theory." He looked again at one of his off-screen displays, then back to the monitor. "I don't know exactly what their initial acceleration rate was, but they're now moving so fast that the light we're seeing reflected from their hulls is noticeably blue-shifted. I estimate their current velocity is roughly five percent of C."

Five percent of the speed of light, McClaren thought, incredulous. Nearly fifteen thousand kilometers per second. And they didn't take much time to reach it.

"I'm trying to estimate their acceleration rate, but it must be-"

"A lot higher than we could ever achieve," McClaren cut him off, looking closely at the wavering image of the alien vessel. "Any idea how big she is?"

"I have no data to estimate her length," Amundsen replied, "but I estimate the beam of this ship to be roughly five hundred meters. I can only assume that her length is considerably more, but we won't know until we get a more oblique view."

"That ship is five hundred meters *wide*?" Kumar asked, incredulous. *Aurora* herself was barely that long from stem to stern. While she was by no means the largest starship built by human hands, she was usually the largest vessel in whatever port she put into.

"Yes," Amundsen told him. "And the other three ships are roughly the same size."

"Christ," someone whispered.

"Raj," McClaren said, turning to his exec. "Thoughts?"

"Communications is running the initial first contact sequence now." He turned to face the captain. "Our signals will take roughly thirty minutes to reach the inner planets, but those ships..." He shook his head. "They're close enough now that they should have already received our transmissions. If they're listening." He looked distinctly uncomfortable. "If I were a betting man, I would say those were warships."

McClaren nodded grimly. "Comms," he looked over at Ensign John Waverly, "keep stepping through the first contact communications sequence. Just make sure that we're listening, too."

"I'm on it, sir," the young man replied. Waverly seemed incredibly young, but like the rest of *Aurora's* crew, he did his job exceptionally well. "I'm well versed in the FCP procedures, sir. So far, though, I haven't come across any emissions anywhere in the standard spectrum, other than what Lieutenant Amundsen's team have already reported. If they use anything anywhere in the radio frequency band, we're sure not seeing it. And I haven't identified any coherent light sources, either."

So, no radio and no communications lasers, McClaren thought uneasily. Even though the aliens knew that company was coming, they had remained silent. Or if they were talking, they were using some form of transmission that was beyond what *Aurora* was capable of seeing or hearing. Maybe the aliens were beyond such mundane things as radio- and light-based communications?

"How long until those ships get here?" McClaren asked Amundsen, whose worried face still stared out from the bridge display screen. *Aurora* herself was motionless relative to her emergence point: McClaren never moved in-system on a survey until they knew much more about their environment than they did now. And it made for a much more convenient reference point for a rapid jump-out.

"At their current velocity, they would overshoot us in just under three hours. But, of course, they will need to decelerate to meet us..."

"That depends on their intentions," Kumar interjected. "They could attack as they pass by..."

"Or they could simply stop," Marisova observed quietly. Everyone turned to gape at her. "We know nothing about their drive systems," she explained. "Nothing about those ships registers on our sensors other than direct visuals. What if they achieved their current velocity nearly instantaneously when they decided to head out to meet us?"

"Preposterous," Amundsen exclaimed. "That's simply not possible!"

"But-"

"Enough, people," McClaren said quietly. "Beyond the obviously impressive capabilities of the aliens, it all boils down to this: do we stay or do we go?" He looked around at his bridge crew, then opened a channel to the entire ship. "Crew, this is the captain. As I'm sure most of you are now aware, the system we've entered is inhabited. We're in a first contact situation. The *only* first contact situation anyone has ever faced. So what we do now is going to become part of The Book that will tell others either how to do it right, or how not to do it if we royally screw things up. I'll be completely honest with you: I'm not happy with the situation. We've got four big ships heading toward us in an awful hurry. They could be warships. I don't blame whoever these folks are for sending out an armed welcoming committee. If it were my home, I'd send some warships out to take a look, too.

"But I'd also make sure to send some diplomats along: people who want to talk with their new neighbors. What bothers me is that we haven't seen anything, from the ships or the two inhabited planets, that looks like any sort of communication. Maybe they're just using something we can't pick up. Maybe the ships coming our way are packed with scientists and ambassadors and they want to make it a big surprise. I just don't know.

"What I do know is that we've got about three hours to make a decision and take action. My inclination is to stay. Not to try and score the first handshake with an alien, but because...it's our first opportunity to say hello to another sentient race. We've been preparing for this moment since before the very first starship left Earth. It's a risk, but it's also the greatest opportunity humanity has ever had.

"So here's what we're going to do. We've got a little bit of time to discuss our options before our new friends reach us. Department heads, talk to your people. Get a feel for what they're thinking. Then all department heads and the senior chiefs are to meet in my ready room in exactly one hour. I'll make the final decision on whether we stay or go, but I want to hear what you all have to say. That is all." He punched the button on the touchpad, closing the circuit.

"In the meantime," he told Kumar and Marisova, "get an emergency jump sequence lined up. Pick a destination other than our inbound vector. If these ships come in with guns blazing, the last thing I want to do is point them back the way we came, toward home."

On the display screen, the alien ship and her sisters continued toward them.

* * *

The four battlecruisers sailed quickly to meet the alien vessel, but they hardly revealed their true capabilities. While it was now clear that the alien ship was extremely primitive, those who guarded the Empire took nothing for granted. They would reveal no more about themselves than absolutely necessary until they were sure the new arrival posed no threat. The Empire had not lasted through the ages by leaving anything to chance.

Aboard the lead ship, a group of warriors prepared for battle with the unknown, while healers and other castes made ready to learn all there was to know about the strangers.

They did not have much longer to wait.

* * *

There was standing room only in the captain's ready room an hour later. At the table sat the six department heads, responsible for the primary functional areas of the ship, the *Aurora's* senior chief, and the captain. Along the walls of the now-cramped compartment stood the senior enlisted member of each department and the ship's two midshipmen. The XO and the bridge crew remained at their stations, although they were tied in through a video feed on the bridge wraparound display.

The emotional tension ran high among the people in the room, McClaren could easily see. But from the body language and the expressions on their faces it wasn't from fear, but excited anticipation. It was an emotion he fully shared.

"I'm not going to waste any time on preliminaries," he began. "You all know what's going on and what's at stake. According to the Survey Department," he nodded at Amundsen, who was the only one around the table who looked distinctly unhappy, "the ships haven't changed course or velocity. So it looks like they're either going to blow by us, which I think would probably be bad news, or their technology is so radically advanced that they can stop on a proverbial dime."

At that, the survey leader's frown grew more pronounced, turning his normally pale face into a grimace.

"Amundsen?" McClaren asked. "You've got something to say. Spit it out."

"I think Lieutenant Marisova was right," he said grudgingly, nodding toward the video pickup that showed the meeting to the bridge crew. But McClaren knew that it wasn't because Marisova had said it. It was because he was afraid to believe that what she said could possibly be true, or even close to the truth. "I don't believe they could accelerate to their current velocity instantaneously, but even assuming several days' warning - even weeks! - the acceleration they must have achieved would have to have been...unbelievable." He shook his head. "No. I believe those ships will not simply pass by us. They will slow down and rendezvous with us sometime in the next two hours, decelerating at a minimum of two hundred gees. Probably much more."

A chill ran down McClaren's spine. *Aurora* had the most efficient reactionless drives in service by any of the many worlds colonized by Mankind, and was one of the few to be fitted with artificial gravity, a recent innovation, and acceleration dampers. She wasn't nearly as fast as a courier ship, certainly, but for a military survey vessel she was no slouch. But two hundred gees? Not even close.

"Robotic ships?" Aubrey Hannan, the chief of the Engineering Section suggested. "They could certainly handle that sort of acceleration."

"It doesn't matter," McClaren interjected, gently but firmly steering the conversation from interesting, but essentially useless, speculation back to the issue at hand. "From my perspective, it doesn't matter how fast the aliens can maneuver. We're not a warship, and I have no intention of masquerading as one. It's clear they have radically advanced technology. That's not necessarily a surprise; we could have just as easily stumbled upon a world in the pre-atomic era, and we would be the high-tech aliens. Our options remain the same: stay and say hello, or jump out with what I hope is a fat safety margin before they get here." He glanced around and his gaze landed on the junior midshipman. "Midshipman Sato, what's your call?"

Ichiro Sato, already standing ramrod straight against the bulkhead, stiffened even further. All of nineteen years old, he was the youngest member of the crew. Extremely courteous, conscientious, and intelligent, he was well respected by the other members of the crew, although his rigid outer shell was a magnet for good-natured ribbing. Exceptionally competent and a fast learner, he kept quietly to himself. He was one of a select few from the Terran Naval Academy who were chosen to spend one or more of their academy years aboard ship as advanced training as junior officers. It was a great opportunity, but came with a hefty commitment: deployed midshipmen had to continue their academy studies while also performing their duties aboard ship.

"Sir..." Sato momentarily gulped for air, McClaren's question having caught him completely off-guard.

The captain felt momentarily guilty for putting Sato on the spot first, but he had a reason. "Relax, Ichiro," McClaren told him. "I called this meeting for ideas. The senior officers, including myself, and the chiefs have years of preconceived notions drilled into our heads. We've got years of experience, yes, but this situation calls for a fresh perspective. If you were in my shoes, what would your decision be? There's no right or wrong answer to this one."

While Ichiro's features didn't betray it, the captain's last comment caused him even more consternation. He had been brought up in a traditional Japanese family on Nagano, where, according to his father, everything was either *right* or it was *wrong*; there was no in-between. And more often than not, anything Ichiro did was *wrong*. That was the main reason Ichiro had decided to apply for service in the Terran Navy when he was sixteen: to spite his father and escape the tyranny of his house, and to avoid the stifling life of a salaryman trapped in the web of a hegemonic corporate world. Earth's global military services accepted applicants from all but a few rogue worlds, and Ichiro's test scores and academic record had opened the door for him to enter the Terran Naval Academy. There, too, most everything was either right or wrong. The difference between the academy and his home was that in the academy, Ichiro was nearly always *right*. His unfailing determination to succeed had given him a sense of confidence he had never known before, putting him at the head of his class and earning him a position aboard the *Aurora*.

That realization, and his desperate desire not to lose face in front of the captain and ship's officers, gave him back his voice. "Sir. I believe we should stay and greet the ships."

McClaren nodded, wondering what had just been going on in the young man's mind. "Okay, you picked door number one. The question now is why?"

"Because, sir, that is why we are here, isn't it?" Loosening up slightly from his steel-rod pose, he turned to look at the other faces around the room, his voice suddenly filled with a passion that none of his fellow crew members would have ever thought possible. "While our primary mission is to find new habitable worlds, we really are explorers, discoverers, of whatever deep space may hold. With every jump we search for the unknown, things that no one else has ever seen. Maybe we will not find what we hope. Perhaps these aliens are friendly, perhaps not. There is great risk in everything we do. But, having found the first sentient race other than humankind, can we in good conscience simply leave without doing all we can to establish contact, even at the risk of our own destruction?"

The captain nodded, impressed more by the young man's unexpected burst of emotion than his words. But his words held their own merit: they precisely echoed McClaren's own feelings. That was exactly why he had spent so much of his career in survey.

"Well said, Ichiro," he told the young man. The two midshipmen on either side of Sato grinned and nudged him as if to say, *Good job*. Most of those seated at the table nodded or murmured their agreement. "So, there's an argument, and I believe a good one, for staying. Who's got one for bailing out right now?"

"I'll take that one, sir," Raj Kumar spoke up from the bridge, his image appearing on the primary screen in the ready room. "I myself agree with Midshipman Sato that we should stay. But one compelling argument for leaving now is to make sure that the news of this discovery gets back home. If the aliens should turn out to be hostile and this ship is taken, or even if we should suffer some unexpected mishap, Earth and the rest of human space may never know until they're attacked. And we have no way to let anyone know of our discovery without jumping back to the nearest communications relay."

That produced a lot of frowns on the faces around the table. Most of them had thought of this already, of course, but having it voiced directly gave it more substance.

Kumar went on, "That's also a specification in the first contact protocols, that one of the top priorities is to get word back home. But the bottom line is that any actions taken are at the captain's discretion based on the situation as he or she sees it."

"Right," McClaren told everyone. "Getting word back home is the only real reason I've been able to come up with myself for leaving now that isn't tied to fear of the unknown. And since all of us signed up to get paid to go find the unknown, as the good midshipman pointed out, those reasons don't count." He turned to the woman sitting to his left. "Chief, what's your take?"

Master Chief Brenda Harkness was the senior enlisted member of the crew, and her word carried a great deal of weight with McClaren. Completely at odds with the stereotype of someone of her rank, she was a tall, slim, and extremely attractive woman in her late thirties. But no one who had ever worked with her for more than five minutes ever took her for granted: she was a hard-core Navy lifer who never dished out bullshit and refused to tolerate it from anyone else. She would move mountains to help anyone who needed it, but her beautiful deep hazel eyes could just as easily burn holes in the skin of anyone foolish enough to cross her.

"I think we should stay, captain," she said, a light Texas drawl flavoring her smooth voice. "I completely agree with the XO's concerns about getting word of this back home, but with the alien ships so close now..." She shook her head. "I can't imagine that they'd be anything but insulted if we just up and disappeared on them."

"And the crew?" McClaren asked.

"Everyone I had a chance to talk to, and that was most of them, wanted to stay. A lot of them are uneasy about those ships, but as you said, we just happen to be the 'primitives' in this situation. We'd be stupid to not be afraid, sir. But I think we'd be even more stupid to just pack up and go home."

All of the other department heads nodded their agreement. Each had talked to their people, too, and almost without exception the crew had wanted to stay and meet with the aliens.

It was what McClaren expected. He would have been shocked had they come to any other conclusion. "Okay, that settles it. We stay." That brought a round of bright, excited smiles to everyone but Amundsen, whose face was locked in an unhappy grimace. "But here's the deal: the XO and navigator have worked out an emergency jump sequence, just in case. We'll spool up the jump engines to the pre-interlock stage and hold them there until we feel more confident of the aliens' intentions. We can keep the engines spooled like that for several hours without running any risks in engineering. If those ships are friendly, we get to play galactic tourist and buy them the first round at the bar.

"But if they're not," he looked pointedly at Amundsen, "we engage the jump interlock and the navigation computer will have us out of here in two minutes." That made the survey leader slightly less unhappy, but only slightly. "Okay, does anybody have anything else they want to add before we set up the reception line?"

"Sir..." Sato said formally, again at a position of attention.

"Go ahead, son."

"Captain, I know this may sound foolish," he glanced at Amundsen, who was at the table with his back to Sato, "but should we not also take steps to secure the navigation computer in case the ships prove hostile? If they took the ship, there is probably little they would learn of our technology that would be of value to them. But the navigation charts..."

"It's already taken care of, midshipman," Kumar reassured him from the bridge with an approving smile. Second year midshipmen like Sato weren't expected to know anything about the first contact protocols, but the boy was clearly thinking on his feet. Kumar's already high respect for him rose yet another notch. "That's on the very short list of 'non-discretionary' actions on first contact. We've already prepared a soft wipe of the data, and a team from engineering is setting charges around the primary core." He held up both hands, then simulated pushing buttons down with his thumbs. "If we get into trouble, *Aurora's* hull is all they'll walk away with."

And us, Amundsen thought worriedly.

* * *

The alien ship had activated its jump drive. While primitive, it was clearly based on the same principles used by Imperial starships. Such technology was an impressive accomplishment for any species, and gave the warriors hope that once again they had found worthy adversaries among the stars.

But the aliens would not - could not - be allowed to leave. Together, the battlecruisers moved in...

* * *

"Jump engines are spooled up, captain," Kumar reported from his console. The jump coordinates were locked in. All they had to do was engage the computer interlock and *Aurora* would disappear into hyperspace inside of two minutes.

"Very well, XO," McClaren replied, his eyes fixed intently on the four titanic ships, all of which were now shown clearly in the main bridge display.

Suddenly the ships leaped forward, closing the remaining ten million kilometers in an instant.

"What the devil..." McClaren exclaimed in surprise, watching as the alien vessels just as suddenly slowed down to take up positions around his ship.

"Sir," Kumar exclaimed, "they must've picked up the jump engines activating! I recommend we jump-"

"Execute!" McClaren barked, a cold sliver of ice sliding into his gut. Then he jabbed the button on his command console to open a channel to the crew. "General quarters! Man your battle stations and prepare for emergency jump!"

"Interlock engaged," came the unhurried and unconcerned voice of *Aurora's* navigation computer. "Transpace countdown commencing. Primary energy buffer building. Two minutes remaining."

McClaren looked at his command console, willing the countdown to run faster. But it was a hard-coded safety lock. There was no way to override it.

"Navigation lock confirmed-"

"*Captain!*" someone shouted.

McClaren looked up at the screen as a stream of interwoven lightning arced from the bow of the alien ship that had taken up position in front of them, hitting *Aurora's* spherical sensor section. Its effect was instantaneous.

"*Jesus!*" someone screamed as what looked like St. Elmo's fire suddenly exploded from every control console and electrical system on the ship. The dancing display of electric fury went on to cover everything, even the clothing of the crew. The entire ship was suddenly awash in electrical discharges.

But it clearly wasn't simple electricity. There was no smoke or heat from overloaded circuits, and no one was injured by whatever energy washed through the ship and their own bodies. Surprised and frightened, yes. But hurt, no.

Then every single electrical system on the ship died, plunging *Aurora's* crew into silent, terrifying darkness.

* * *

Having subdued the alien ship's simple electronic systems, the lead warship made ready the boarding party that had been awaiting this moment. While the great warship's crew now knew the layout of the alien ship and all it contained, including the aliens themselves, down to the last atom, the boarding party would be sent without this knowledge. They would give themselves no advantage over the aliens other than the surprise they had already achieved; even that, they would have given up if they could. They wished as even a field as possible, to prove their own mettle and to test that of the strangers. In this way, as through ages past, they sought to honor their Empress.

As one, the thirty warriors who had bested their peers in fierce ritual combat for the right to "greet" the strangers leaped into space toward the alien vessel. Thirty warriors pitted against seven times as many aliens. They hoped the odds would challenge their skills.

* * *

"*Calm down!*" Chief Harkness's voice cut through the sudden panic like a razor. At her assigned jump station in the survey module inside the spherical bow section, Harkness had immediately clamped down on her own fear in the aftermath of the terrifying electrical surge that apparently had killed her ship. She had people to take care of, and she was too much of a professional to panic. "Listen to me," she told the seven others in the cramped compartment. There were still a couple of them moaning in fear. "Listen, goddammit!" she snarled. That finally got their attention. Of all the things in the ship they might be afraid of, she would be the first and foremost if that helped them hold it together. "Get your heads screwed on straight. The ship's hull hasn't been ruptured. We've still got air. That's priority number one. All the electrical systems must've been knocked out, which is why the artificial gravity is gone, along with the lights." The darkness was disorienting enough, but being weightless on top of it was a cast iron bitch. She was actually more worried that the emergency lighting hadn't come on. Those weren't powered by the main electrical system, and their failure meant that something far worse had happened to her ship than a simple, if major, electrical blowout. "You've all experienced this before in training. So relax and start acting like the best sailors in the Navy. That's why you were picked to serve on this ship." She paused to listen, relieved to hear that the sniveling had stopped, and everyone's breathing had slowed down a bit.

"Now, feel around for the emergency lockers," she told them. "There should be three in here. Grab the flashlights and see if the damn things work." While they could survive for some time on the available oxygen, the total darkness was going to give way to fear again if they didn't get some light.

"Found one, chief," someone said off to her left. There was a moment of scrabbling around, the sound of a panel opening, then a bit of rummaging.

Click.

Nothing.

"Fuck," someone else whispered.

"Try another one," Harkness grated.

"Okay-"

Suddenly she could see something. But it wasn't the ship's lighting or one of the emergency flashlights. It was like the walls themselves had begun to glow, throwing a subdued dark blue radiance into the compartment.

"Chief, what is this stuff?" one of the ratings asked quietly, her eyes, visible now in the ghostly light, bulging wide as she looked at the glowing bulkheads around her.

"I don't know," Harkness admitted. "But whatever it is, we can see now." The compartment was now clearly, if softly lit. "So let's use it and find out what the hell's happened to the ship."

Then something else unexpected happened: the gravity returned. Instantly. All eight of them slammed down on the deck in a mass of flailing limbs and passionate curses. Fortunately, they all had been oriented more or less upright, and no one was hurt.

"Shit," Harkness gasped as she levered herself back onto her feet. "What the *hell* is going on..."

That's when she heard the screaming.

* * *

The warriors plunged toward the alien ship. They wore their ceremonial armor for this ritual battle, eschewing any more powerful protection. They soared across the distance between the ships with arms and legs outstretched, enjoying the sight of the universe afforded by the energy shields that invisibly surrounded them and protected them from hard vacuum. They needed no devices to assist in maneuvering toward their target: theirs was a race that had been plying the stars for ages, and their space-borne heritage led them to a fearless precision that humans could only dream of.

They were not concerned about any pathogenic organisms the aliens carried, as the healers who would be sent once the ship had been subdued would take care of such matters. The scan of the alien vessel had revealed an atmosphere that, while not optimal, was certainly breathable.

There was no warrior priestess in this system to bear the honor of leading them in this first encounter, but no matter. The senior warriors were well experienced and had the blessing of the Empress: they could sense Her will in their very blood, as She could sense what they felt. It was more a form of empathic bonding than telepathy, but its true essence was beyond intellectual understanding.

As they neared the ship, the warriors curled into a fetal position, preparing to make contact with the alien hull. The energy shields altered their configuration, warping into a spherical shape to both absorb the force of the impact and force an entry point through the simple metal rushing up to meet them.

The first warrior reached the hull, and the energy shield seared through the primitive alien metal, instantly opening a portal to the interior. The warrior smoothly rolled through to land on her feet inside, quickly readjusting to the gravity that the crew of the warship had restored for benefit of the aliens. The energy shield remained in place behind the warrior, sealing the hole it had created in the hull plating and containing the ship's atmosphere.

In only a few seconds more, all the other warriors had forced themselves aboard the hapless vessel.

* * *

The screaming Chief Harkness heard was from Ensign Mary Withgott. Her battle station was at a damage control point where the spherical bow section connected to the main keel and the passageway that led to the rest of the ship. The damage control point was on the sphere's side of a blast proof door that was now locked shut. She could open it manually, but wouldn't consider it unless she got direct orders from the captain.

"Ensign!" one of the two ratings with her shouted as a shower of burning sparks exploded from the bulkhead above them. The two crewmen stared, dumbstruck, as someone, some alien *thing*, somersaulted through a huge hole that had been burned through the hull and into the damage control compartment.

A blue-skinned nightmare clad in gleaming black armor, the alien smoothly pirouetted toward the two crewmen, exposing fangs between dark red lips. Its eyes were like those of a cat, flecked with silver, below a ridge of bone or horn. The creature's black hair was long and tightly braided, the coils wrapped around its upper shoulders. The armored breastplate had two smoothly contoured projections over what must be the alien equivalent of breasts. While Withgott had no idea what the alien's true gender (if any) might be, the creature's appearance was such that Withgott had the inescapable impression that it was female, a *she*.

The alien stood there for a moment, meeting Withgott's frightened gaze with her own inscrutable expression. Then the sword the alien held in her right hand hissed through the air, cleanly severing the head from the nearest crewman. His body spasmed as his head rolled from his neck, a gout of crimson spurting across the bulkhead behind him.

Withgott screamed, and kept on screaming as the alien turned to the second crewman with the ferocious grace of a hunting tigress and thrust the sword through the man's chest.

Then the fanged nightmare came for Withgott.

Season Of The Harvest

What if the genetically engineered crops that we increasingly depend on for food weren't really created by man? What if they brought a new, terrifying meaning to the old saying that "you are what you eat"?

In the bestselling thriller *Season Of The Harvest*, FBI Special Agent Jack Dawson investigates the gruesome murder of his best friend and fellow agent who had been pursuing a group of eco-terrorists. The group's leader, Naomi Perrault, is a beautiful geneticist who Jack believes conspired to kill his friend, and is claiming that a major international conglomerate developing genetically engineered crops is plotting a sinister transformation of our world that will lead humanity to extinction.

As Jack is drawn into a quietly raging war that suddenly explodes onto the front pages of the news, he discovers that her claims may not be so outrageous after all. Together, the two of them must face a horror Jack could never have imagined, with the fate of all life on Earth hanging in the balance...

Interested? Then read on and enjoy the prologue and first chapter of *Season Of The Harvest*. And always remember: *you are what you eat!*

* * *

Prologue

Sheldon Crane ran for his life. Panting from exhaustion and the agony of the deep stab wound in his side, he darted into the deep shadows of an alcove in the underground service tunnel. Holding his pistol in unsteady hands, he peered around the corner, past the condensation-covered pipes, looking back in the direction from which he'd come.

Nothing. All he could hear was the deep hum of the electric service box that filled most of the alcove, punctuated by the *drip-drip-drip* of water from a small leak in one of the water pipes a few yards down the tunnel. Only a third of the ceiling-mounted fluorescent lights were lit, a cost-saving measure by the university that left long stretches of paralyzing darkness between the islands of greenish-tinged light. He could smell wet concrete and the tang of ozone, along with a faint trace of lubricating oil. And over it all was the scent of blood. In the pools of light stretching back down the tunnel, all the way back to the intersection where he had turned into this part of the underground labyrinth, he could see the glint of blood on the floor, a trail his pursuer could easily follow.

He knew that no one could save him: he had come here tonight precisely because he expected the building to be empty. It had been. Almost. But there was no one to hear his shouts for help, and he had dropped his cell phone during the unexpected confrontation in the lab upstairs.

He was totally on his own.

Satisfied that his pursuer was not right on his heels, he slid deeper into the alcove, into the dark recess between the warm metal of the electric service box and the cold concrete wall. He gently probed the wound in his side, gasping as his fingertips brushed against the blood-wet, swollen flesh just above his left hip. It was a long moment before he was sure he wouldn't scream from the pain. It wasn't merely a stab wound. He had been stabbed and cut before. That had been incredibly painful. This, however, was far worse. His insides were on fire, the pain having spread quickly from his belly to upper chest. And the pain was accompanied by paralysis. He had lost control of his abdominal muscles, and the sensation was spreading. There was a sudden gush of warmth down his legs as his bladder suddenly let go, and he groaned in agony as his internal organs began to burn.

Poison, he knew.

He leaned over, fighting against the light-headedness that threatened to bear him mercifully into unconsciousness.

"No," he panted to himself. "No." He knew he didn't have much time left. He had to act.

Wiping the blood from his left hand on his shirt, cleaning it as best he could, he reached under his right arm and withdrew both of the extra magazines he carried for his weapon, a 10mm Glock 22 that was standard issue for FBI special agents. He ejected the empty magazine from the gun, cursing himself as his shaking hands lost their grip and it clattered to the floor.

It won't matter soon, he thought giddily as he slumped against the wall, sliding down the rough concrete to the floor as his upper thighs succumbed to the spreading paralysis, then began to burn.

Desperately racing against the poison in his system, he withdrew a small plastic bag from a pocket inside his jacket and set it carefully next to him. He patted it with his fingertips several times to reassure himself that he knew exactly where it was in the dark. His fingers felt the shapes of a dozen lumps inside the bag: kernels of corn.

Then he picked up one of the spare magazines and shucked out all the bullets with his thumb into a pocket in his jacket so he wouldn't lose them. Setting down the now-empty magazine, he picked up the tiny bag and carefully opened the seal, praying he wouldn't accidentally send the precious lumps flying into the darkness. For the first time that night, Fate favored him, and the bag opened easily.

Picking up the empty magazine from his lap, he tapped a few of the kernels onto the magazine's follower, the piece of metal that the bottom bullet rested on. He managed to squeeze a bullet into the magazine on top of the corn kernels. Once that was done, he slid the other bullets into place, then clumsily slammed the magazine into the weapon and chambered a round.

He took the bag and its remaining tiny, precious cargo and resealed it. Then he stuffed it into his mouth. The knowledge of the nature of the corn made him want to gag, but he managed to force it down, swallowing the bag. Crane suspected his body would be searched thoroughly, inside and out, for what he had stolen, and his mind shied away from how that search would probably be conducted. His only hope now was that his pursuer would be content to find the bag, and not think to check Crane's weapon. He prayed that his body and the priceless contents of his gun's magazine would be found by the right people. It was a terrible long-shot, but he was out of options.

His nose was suddenly assaulted by the smell of Death coming for him, a nauseating mix of pungent ammonia laced with the reek of burning hemp.

Barely able to lift his arms, his torso nearly paralyzed and aflame with agonizing pain, Crane brought up his pistol just as his pursuer whirled around the corner. He fired at the hideous abomination that was revealed in the flashes from the muzzle of his gun, and managed to get off three shots before the weapon was batted from his faltering grip. He screamed in terror as his pursuer closed in, blocking out the light.

The screams didn't stop for a long time.

* * *

One

Jack Dawson stood in his supervisor's office and stared out the window, his bright gray eyes watching the rain fall from the brooding summer sky over Washington, D.C. The wind was blowing just hard enough for the rain to strike the glass, leaving behind wet streaks that ran down the panes like tears. The face he saw reflected there was cast in shadow by the overhead fluorescent lights. The square jaw and high cheekbones gave him a predatory look, while his full lips promised a smile, but were drawn downward now into a frown. The deeply tanned skin, framed by lush black hair that was neatly combed back and held with just the right amount of styling gel, looked sickly and pale in the glass, as if it belonged on the face of a ghost. He knew that it was the same face he saw every morning. But it was different now. An important part of his world had been killed, murdered, the night before.

He watched the people on the street a few floors below, hustling through the downpour with their umbrellas fluttering as they poured out of the surrounding buildings, heading home for the evening. Cars clogged Pennsylvania Avenue, with the taxis darting to the curb to pick up fares, causing other drivers to jam on their brakes, the bright red tail lights flickering on and off down the street like a sputtering neon sign. It was Friday, and everyone was eager to get home to their loved ones, or go out to dinner, or head to the local bar. Anywhere that would let them escape the rat race for the weekend.

He didn't have to see this building's entrance to know that very few of the people who worked here would be heading home on time tonight. The address was 935 Pennsylvania Avenue Northwest. It was the J. Edgar Hoover Building, headquarters of the Federal Bureau of Investigation, the FBI. Other than the teams of special agents who had departed an hour earlier for Lincoln, Nebraska, many of the Bureau's personnel here at headquarters wouldn't leave until sometime tomorrow. Some would be sleeping in their offices and cubicles after exhaustion finally overtook them, and wouldn't go home for more than a few hours over the next several days.

A special agent had been brutally murdered, and with the addition of another name to the list of the FBI's Service Martyrs, every resource the Bureau could bring to bear was being focused on bringing his killer to justice. Special agents from headquarters and field offices around the country were headed to Nebraska, along with an army of analysts and support staff that was already sifting through electronic data looking for leads.

Everyone had a part in the investigation, it seemed, except for Dawson. In his hand, he held a plain manila folder that included the information that had been forwarded by the Lincoln field office. It was a preliminary report sent in by the Special Agent in Charge (SAC), summarizing the few known facts of the case. In terse prose, the SAC's report described the crime scene, the victim, and what had been done by the local authorities before the SAC's office had been alerted. And there were photos. Lots of photos. If a picture was worth a thousand words, then the ones Dawson held in his shaking hands spoke volumes about the agony suffered by the victim before he died. Because it was clear from the rictus of agony and terror frozen on Sheldon Crane's face that he had still been alive when–

"I'm sorry, Jack," came a gruff voice from behind him, interrupting Dawson's morbid train of thought as Ray Clement, Assistant Director of the Criminal Investigative Division, came in and closed the door. It was his office, and he had ordered Dawson to wait there until he had a chance to speak with him.

Ray Clement was a bear of a man with a personality to match. A star football player from the University of Alabama's Crimson Tide, Clement had actually turned down a chance to go pro, and had instead joined the FBI as a special agent. That had been his dream since the age of ten, as he had once told Jack, and the proudest moment of his life had been when he'd earned his badge. Jack knew that a lot of people might have thought Clement was crazy. "I loved football," Clement would say, "and I still do. But I played it because I enjoyed it. I never planned to do it for a living."

Over the years, Clement had worked his way up through the Bureau. He was savvy enough to survive the internal politics, smart and tough enough to excel in the field, and conformed to the system because he believed in it. He could be a real bastard when someone did something stupid, but otherwise worked tirelessly to support his people so they could do their jobs. He wasn't a boss that any of his special agents would say they loved, but under his tenure, the Criminal Investigative Division, or CID, had successfully closed more cases than under any other assistant director in the previous fifteen years. People could say what they wanted, but Clement got results.

When he had first taken over the division, Clement had taken the time to talk to each and every one of his special agents. He had been up front about why: he wanted to know at least a little bit, more than just the names, about the men and women who risked their lives every day for the American Taxpayer. They were special agents, he'd said, but they were also special human beings.

Jack had dreaded the interview. Whereas Clement could have been the FBI's poster child, Jack didn't quite fit the mold. He was like a nail head sticking up from the perfectly polished surface of a hardwood floor, not enough to snag on anything, just enough to notice. Outwardly, he was no different than most of his peers. He dressed the same as most special agents, eschewing a suit for more practical and casual attire for all but the most formal occasions. His well-muscled six foot, one inch tall body was far more comfortable in jeans and a pullover shirt, with a light jacket to conceal his primary weapon, a standard service-issue Glock 22. While he had no problems voicing his opinions, which had sometimes led to respectful but intense discussions with his superiors, he had never been a discipline problem. He was highly competent in the field, and was a whiz at data analysis. At first glance, he seemed like what he should be: an outstanding special agent who worked hard and had great career prospects.

But under the shiny veneer ran a deep vein of dark emptiness. Jack smiled, but it never seemed to reach his eyes, and he rarely laughed. He was not cold-hearted, for he had often displayed uncommon compassion toward others, especially the victims, and their families, of the crimes he was sent to investigate. But he had no social life to speak of, no significant other in his life, and there were very few people who understood the extent of the pain that lay at Jack's core.

That pain had its roots in events that took place seven years earlier, when Jack was serving in the Army in Afghanistan. His patrol had been ambushed by the Taliban and had taken heavy casualties before reinforcements arrived. Jack had been badly wounded, having taken two rounds from an AK-47 in the chest, along with shrapnel from a grenade. The latter had left its mark on his otherwise handsome face, a jagged scar marring his left cheek. That had been rough, but he was young, only twenty-six, and strong, and would make a full recovery from his wounds.

What had torn him apart was what happened back in the States. While he lay unconscious in the SSG Heath N. Craig Joint Theater Hospital in Bagram, his wife Emily was kidnapped while leaving a shopping mall not far from their home outside Fort Drum, New York. Emily had her own home business, and they had no children, so no one immediately noticed that she'd gone missing. Four days passed before a persistent Red Cross worker who had been trying to get in touch with Emily about

Jack's injuries contacted the provost marshal at Fort Drum. Two military policemen went to the house, and when they found it empty, they contacted the local police.

The police located her car that same day: the mall's security center had ordered it towed away after it had sat in the parking lot overnight, reporting it to the police as abandoned. The next day, the fifth since she had disappeared, police investigators found footage on one of the mall security cameras that vividly showed what had happened to her. A man stepped around the back of a nondescript van as she had walked by, laden with shopping bags. With a casual glance around to see if there were any witnesses, he turned as she passed and jabbed her in the back with a stun gun. Scooping her up in one smooth motion, he dumped her into the van through the already open side door, and then collected up the bags that had fallen to the ground. He didn't rush, didn't hurry as he threw the bags into the van. Then he climbed into the back and slammed the door closed. After a few minutes the van backed out of the space and drove away.

It had all happened in broad daylight.

Because it was clearly a kidnapping and so much time had passed since the crime had been committed, the local authorities contacted the FBI.

That was when Jack learned of his wife's disappearance. Immobilized in the hospital bed, still in a great deal of pain, he was paid a visit by his grim-faced commander and a civilian woman who introduced herself as an FBI special agent. His commander told him what had happened, and over the next three hours the FBI agent gathered every detail that Jack could remember about his wife's activities, associations, family and friends. Everything about her life that he could think of that might help track down her kidnapper. It had been the three most agonizing hours of his life. The special agent had assured him that everything was being done to find his wife and bring her back safely. Jack prayed that they would find her alive, but in his heart he knew she was gone.

His intuition proved brutally prophetic. Her body was found a week later, buried under bags of trash in a dumpster behind a strip mall in Cleveland, Ohio. She had been repeatedly raped and beaten before she'd finally been strangled to death. The FBI and law enforcement authorities in Ohio did everything they could to find her killer, but he had covered his tracks well and was never found.

When Jack was well enough to travel, the Army arranged for him to be flown home, where one of his first duties had been to formally identify Emily's battered, broken body. He had seen his share of horrors in Afghanistan, and some might think it would have made the trauma of viewing her body somewhat easier. It hadn't. Thankfully, the family lawyer, an old friend of his parents, who themselves had died in a car wreck a year before Jack had gone to Afghanistan, had made all the necessary arrangements for her burial. Jack simply had to endure the agony of laying her to rest.

After the funeral, Jack had found himself at a loss. His time in the Army was nearly up, and he was tempted to simply lapse into an emotional coma to shut off the pain and the nightmares of Emily's tortured face.

But a cold flame of rage burned in his core at what had happened to her, and the bastard who had done it. He found himself sitting in the kitchen one morning, holding the business card of the female special agent who had interviewed him in Bagram. As if his body was acting of its own accord, he found himself picking up the phone and dialing the woman's number. The conversation that followed was the first step on the path that eventually led him to become a special agent in the FBI.

She had tried to dissuade him, warning him that he wasn't going to find answers, or vengeance, to Emily's death. In truth, while the thought of finding her killer was more than appealing, he realized from the beginning that avenging Emily wasn't what was pulling him toward the Bureau: it was the thought that he might be able to help prevent what had happened to her from happening to others.

When he got to the FBI Academy, one of his fellow agents was Sheldon Crane. Sheldon had an irrepressible sense of humor, and immediately glued himself to Jack. At first, Jack had resented the unwanted attention, but Sheldon had gradually worn through Jack's emotional armor, eventually becoming the Yin to Jack's Yang. Sheldon was a self-proclaimed computer genius, recruited to work in the Bureau's Cyber Division, while Jack's skills in intelligence analysis and experience in combat made him a good candidate for the Criminal Investigative Division.

Jack had done well in CID, but remained an outsider, something of a mystery to his fellow agents. Most of his supervisors knew his background and were content to let it be, but when Clement took over and began his interviews, Jack had heard that he could be very pointed in his questions. Jack didn't want to be interrogated again about his experience in Afghanistan or Emily's murder. He didn't want anyone's sympathy. He just wanted to move on.

Clement had completely surprised him. He didn't talk or want to know about anything related to Jack's past or his work. Instead, he asked questions about Jack as a person outside of the Bureau, what he liked to do in his free time, his personal likes and dislikes. At first, Jack had been extremely uncomfortable, but after a while he found himself opening up. Clement talked to him for a full hour and a half. When they were through, Jack actually found himself laughing at one of Clement's notoriously bad jokes.

After that, while Jack couldn't quite call Clement a friend, he had certainly become a confidant and someone he felt he could really talk to when the need arose.

Now was certainly one of those times.

Clement walked across the office toward Jack, but stopped when his eyes fell on the folder Jack clutched in one hand. "Dammit, don't you know any better than to grab files off my desk, Special Agent Dawson?"

"Yes, sir," Dawson told him. "I took it from your secretary's desk."

"Lord," Clement muttered as he moved up to Dawson. Putting a hand on the younger man's shoulder, he said again, "I'm sorry, Jack. I'd hoped to have a chance to talk to you before you saw anything in that file." With a gentle squeeze of his massive hand, he let go, then sat down behind his desk. "Sit."

Reluctantly, still clutching the folder containing the professional analysis of Sheldon Crane's last moments alive, Jack did as he was told, dropping into one of the chairs arrayed around a small conference table before turning to face his boss.

"Why aren't you letting me go out with the teams to Lincoln?" he asked before Clement could say anything else.

"Do you really have to ask that?" his boss said pointedly. "Look at yourself, Jack. You're an emotional wreck. I'm not going to endanger an investigation by having someone who isn't operating at full capacity on the case." He raised a hand as Jack began to protest. "Don't start arguing," he said. "Look, Jack, I've lost close friends, too. I know how much it can tear you up inside. But you're not going to do Sheldon any favors now by screwing things up in the field because you're emotionally involved. I promise you, *we will not rest* until we've found his killer."

"My God, Ray," Jack said hoarsely, looking again at the folder in his hand, "they didn't just kill him. They fucking tore him apart!"

He forced himself to open the folder again. The top photo was a shot that showed Sheldon's entire body at the scene. It looked like someone had performed an autopsy on him. A deep cut had been made in his torso from throat to groin. The ribs had been cracked open to expose the heart and lungs, and the organs from his abdomen had been pulled out and dissected, the grisly contents dumped onto the floor. Then something had been used to carve open his skull just above the line of his eyebrows, and the brain had been removed and set aside. Another shot that he dared not look at again showed what was done inside the skull: his killer had torn his nasal cavities open.

Another photo showed Sheldon's clothing. He had been stripped from head to toe, and his clothes had been systematically torn apart, with every seam ripped open. In the background, on the floor next to the wall, was his gun.

Jack had seen death enough times and in enough awful ways that it no longer made him want to gag. But he had never, even in the hateful fighting in Afghanistan, seen such measured brutality as this.

The last photo he had looked at had been a close-up of Sheldon's face and his terrified expression. "He was still alive when they started...cutting him up."

"I know," Clement said, his own voice breaking. "I know he was."

"What was he doing out there?" Jack asked, sliding the photos back into the folder with numb fingers. "This couldn't have just been some random attack. What the hell was he working on that could have driven someone to do this to him?"

Pursing his lips, Clement looked down at his desk, his face a study in consideration. "This is classified, Jack," he said finally, looking up and fixing Jack with a hard stare, "as in Top Secret. The kind of information you have to read after you sign your life away and go into a little room with thick walls and special locks on the door. Even the SAC in Lincoln doesn't know the real reason Sheldon was there, and the only reason I'm telling you is because you held high-level clearances in the Army and you can appreciate how sensitive this is and keep your mouth shut about it."

Jack nodded. He had been an intelligence officer in the Army, and knew exactly what Clement was talking about. He also appreciated the fact that Clement could lose his job for what he was about to say. That was the level of trust that had built up between them.

Satisfied that Jack had gotten the message, Clement told him, "Sheldon was investigating a series of cyber attacks against several research laboratories doing work on genetically modified organisms, mainly food crops like corn. The FDA was also hacked: someone took a keen interest in what the Center for Food Safety and Applied Nutrition was doing along the same lines. And before you say, 'So what's the big super-secret deal,' there was also a series of attacks against computers, both at home and work, used by specific individuals across the government, including senior officials in the Department of Defense and the military services. Sheldon was convinced the perpetrators were from a group known as the Earth Defense Society, and that they're somewhere here in the U.S. He's been out in the field for the last three weeks, tracking down leads." He frowned. "Apparently he found something in Lincoln."

"What the hell are they after?" Jack asked, perplexed. It seemed an odd potpourri of targets for hackers to be going after. He could understand someone going after one group of targets or another, but what common thread could run through such a mixed bag, from labs working on how to improve crops to the military?

"That's the sixty-four thousand dollar question, isn't it?" Clement said. "So, now you know what Sheldon was doing. Just keep your mouth shut about it and pretend this conversation never happened."

Standing up and coming around his desk, Clement continued as Jack rose from his chair, "I want you to take some leave. Get out of here for a few days until you've pulled yourself together. Then come back in and we can talk. And I promise you, I'll keep you informed of what we find."

"Yes, sir," was all Jack said as he shook Clement's hand. He turned and walked out of the office, closing the door quietly behind him.

As Jack left, Clement saw that he still had the copy of Sheldon's case file in his hand. With a satisfied nod, he returned to his desk and checked his phone, which was blinking urgently. It hadn't been ringing because he had ordered his secretary to hold all of his calls. Quickly scanning the recent caller list on the phone's display, he saw that the director had called him. Twice.

He grimaced, then pulled out the two smart phones that he carried. He used one of them for everyday personal communication. That one the Bureau knew about. He had turned it off before talking to Dawson to avoid any interruptions, and now he turned it back on.

The other smart phone, the one he flipped open now, was used for an entirely different purpose, and something of which his bosses at the Bureau would not approve. Calling up the web application, he quickly logged into an anonymizer service and sent a brief, innocuous-sounding email to a particular address. Then he activated an application that would wipe the phone's memory and reset it to the factory default, effectively erasing any evidence of how he had used it.

Putting it back in his pocket, he picked up his desk phone and called the director.

A Small Favor

For any book you read, and particularly for those you enjoy, please do the author and other readers a very important service and leave a review. It doesn't matter how many (or how few) reviews a book may already have, your voice is important!

Many folks don't leave reviews because they think it has to be a well-crafted synopsis and analysis of the plot. While those are great, it's not necessary at all. Just put down in as many or few words as you like, just a blurb, that you enjoyed the book and recommend it to others. Your comments *do* matter!

And thank you again so much for reading this book!

Discover Other Books By Michael R. Hicks

The *In Her Name* Series

First Contact
Legend Of The Sword
Dead Soul
Empire
Confederation
Final Battle
From Chaos Born

"Boxed Set" Collections

In Her Name (Omnibus)
In Her Name: The Last War

Thrillers

Season Of The Harvest

Visit *AuthorMichaelHicks.com* for the latest updates!

About The Author

Born in 1963, Michael Hicks grew up in the age of the Apollo program and spent his youth glued to the television watching the original Star Trek series and other science fiction movies, which continues to be a source of entertainment and inspiration. Having spent the majority of his life as a voracious reader, he has been heavily influenced by writers ranging from Robert Heinlein to Jerry Pournelle and Larry Niven, and David Weber to S.M. Stirling. Living in Maryland with his beautiful wife, two wonderful stepsons and two mischievous Siberian cats, he's now living his dream of writing novels full-time.